EX LIBRIS

Also by Robert Harris

FICTION

Fatherland

Enigma

Archangel

Pompeii

Imperium

The Ghost

Lustrum

The Fear Index

An Officer and a Spy

NON-FICTION

Good and Faithful Servant: The Unauthorized Biography of Bernard Ingham

Selling Hitler

The Making of Neil Kinnock

Gotcha: Media, the Government and the Falklands Crisis

A Higher Form of Killing (with Jeremy Paxman)

ROBERT HARRIS

DICTATOR

HUTCHINSON
LONDON

3 5 7 9 10 8 6 4 2

Hutchinson
20 Vauxhall Bridge Road
London SW1V 2SA

Hutchinson is part of the Penguin Random House group
of companies whose addresses can be found at
global.penguinrandomhouse.com

First published in Great Britain in 2015 by Hutchinson

www.randomhouse.co.uk

A CIP catalogue record for this book is available from the British Library.

ISBN 9780091752101 (hardback)
ISBN 9780091799502 (trade paperback)

Typeset by Palimpsest Book Production Limited,
Falkirk, Stirlingshire

Printed and bound by Clays Ltd, St Ives plc

Penguin Random House is committed to a sustainable future
for our business, our readers and our planet. This book is made
from Forest Stewardship Council® certified paper.

To Holly

CONTENTS

NORTH SEA
FURTHER GAUL
NEARER GAUL
ITALY
1.
FURTHER SPAIN
NEARER SPAIN
2.
SARDINIA
MEDITERRA
SICILY
MAURETANIA
NUMIDIA
3.
NG

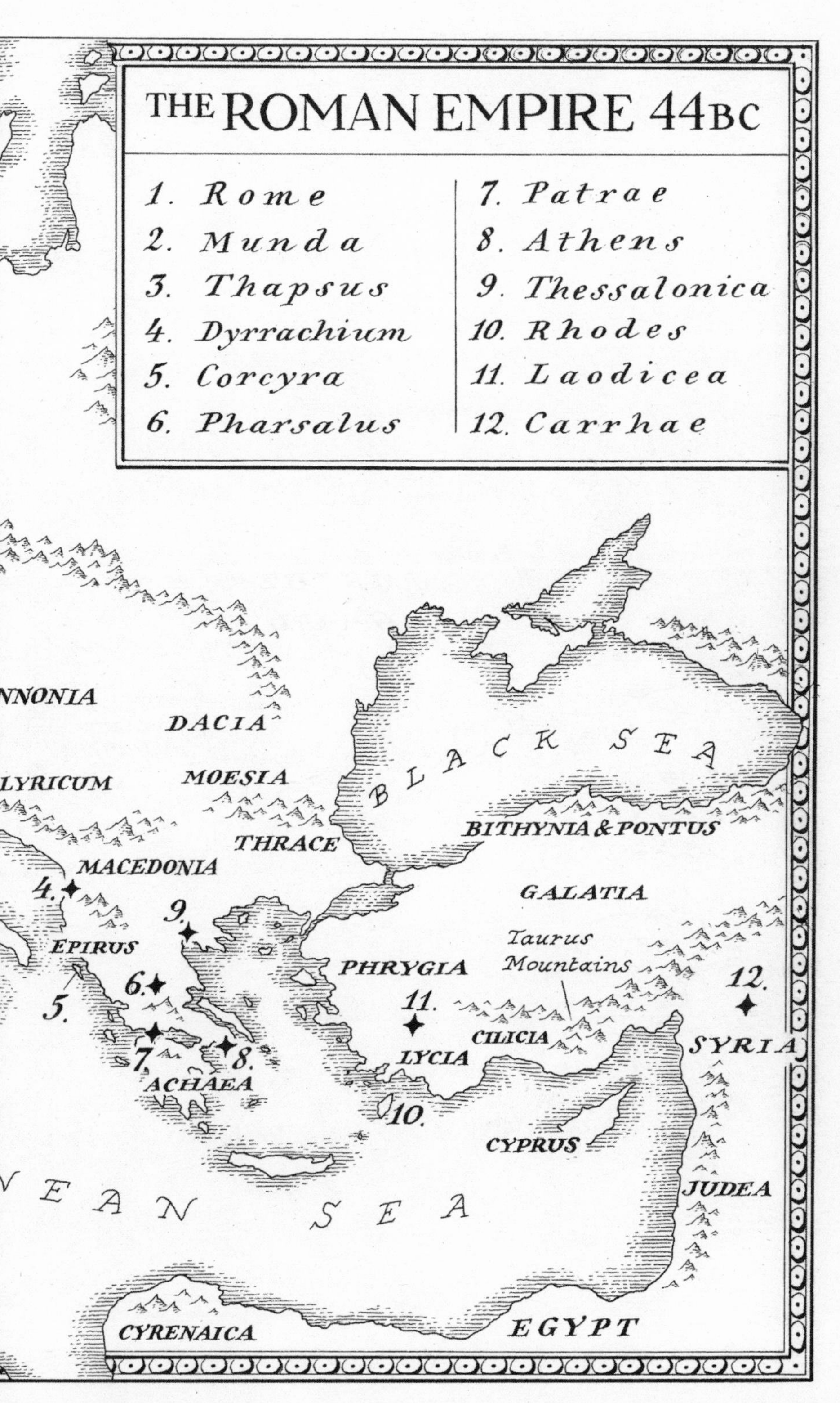
THE ROMAN EMPIRE 44 BC
1. Rome
2. Munda
3. Thapsus
4. Dyrrachium
5. Corcyra
6. Pharsalus
7. Patrae
8. Athens
9. Thessalonica
10. Rhodes
11. Laodicea
12. Carrhae
NNONIA
DACIA
BLACK SEA
LYRICUM
MOESIA
BITHYNIA & PONTUS
THRACE
MACEDONIA
GALATIA
4.
9.
EPIRUS
Taurus Mountains
PHRYGIA
12.
6.
11.
5.
CILICIA
SYRIA
7.
8.
LYCIA
ACHAEA
10.
CYPRUS
JUDEA
NEAN SEA
CYRENAICA
EGYPT

CICERO'S ITALY
Mutina
R. Rubicon
ADRIATIC SEA
Ancona
Rome
Tusculum
Arpinum
Astura
Formiae
Cumae
Puteoli
Bay of Naples
Pompeii
Brundisium
Tarentum
TYRRHENIAN SEA
Messina
Regium
Lilybaeum
Syracuse
IONIAN SEA
NG

AUTHOR'S NOTE

Dictator tells the story of the final fifteen years in the life of the Roman statesman Cicero, imagined in the form of a biography written by his secretary, Tiro.

That there was such a man as Tiro and that he wrote such a book are well-attested historical facts. Born a slave on the family estate, he was three years younger than his master but long outlived him, surviving, according to Saint Jerome, until he reached his hundredth year.

'Your services to me are beyond count,' Cicero wrote to him in 50 BC, 'in my home and out of it, in Rome and abroad, in private affairs and public, in my studies and literary work. . .' Tiro was the first man to record a speech in the senate verbatim, and his shorthand system, known as *Notae Tironianae*, was still in use in the Church in the sixth century; indeed some traces of it (the symbol '&', the abbreviations etc, NB, i.e., e.g.) survive to this day. He also wrote several treatises on the development of Latin. His multi-volume life of Cicero is referred to as a source by the first-century historian Asconius Pedianus; Plutarch cites it twice. But, like the rest of Tiro's literary output, the book disappeared amid the collapse of the Roman Empire.

What must it have been like, one wonders? Cicero's life was extraordinary, even by the hectic standards of the age. From relatively lowly origins compared to his aristocratic rivals, and despite his lack of interest in military matters, deploying his skill as an orator and the brilliance of his intellect he rose at meteoric speed through the Roman political system, until, against all the odds, he finally was elected consul at the youngest-permitted age of forty-two.

There followed a crisis-stricken year in office – 63 BC – during which he was obliged to deal with a conspiracy to overthrow the republic led by Sergius Catilina. To suppress the revolt, the Senate, under Cicero's presidency, ordered the execution of five prominent citizens – an episode that haunted his career ever afterwards.

When subsequently the three most powerful men in Rome – Julius Caesar, Pompey the Great and Marcus Crassus – joined forces in a so-called triumvirate to dominate the state, Cicero decided to oppose them. Caesar in retaliation, using his powers as chief priest, unleashed the ambitious aristocratic demagogue, Clodius – an old enemy of Cicero's – to destroy him. By allowing Clodius to renounce his patrician status and become a plebeian, Caesar opened the way for his election as tribune. Tribunes had the power to haul citizens before the people, to harass and persecute them. Cicero swiftly decided he had no choice but to flee Rome. It is at this desperate point in his fortunes that *Dictator* begins.

My aim has been to describe, as accurately as I can within the conventions of fiction, the end of the Roman Republic as it might have been experienced by Cicero and Tiro. Wherever possible, the letters and speeches and descriptions of events have been drawn from the original sources.

As *Dictator* encompasses what was arguably – at least until the convulsions of 1933–45 – the most tumultuous era in human history, a glossary and a cast of characters have been provided at the back of the book to assist the reader in navigating Cicero's sprawling and collapsing world.

Robert Harris

Kintbury, 8 June 2015

'The melancholy of the antique world seems to me more profound than that of the moderns, all of whom more or less imply that beyond the dark void lies immortality. But for the ancients that "black hole" was infinity itself; their dreams loom and vanish against a background of immutable ebony. No crying out, no convulsions – nothing but the fixity of a pensive gaze. Just when the gods had ceased to be and the Christ had not yet come, there was a unique moment in history, between Cicero and Marcus Aurelius, when man stood alone. Nowhere else do I find that particular grandeur.'

Gustave Flaubert, letter to Mme Roger des Genettes, 1861

'Alive, Cicero enhanced life. So can his letters do, if only for a student here and there, taking time away from belittling despairs to live among Virgil's Togaed People, desperate masters of a larger world.'

D. R. Shackleton Bailey, *Cicero*, 1971

PART ONE

EXILE

58 BC–47 BC

Nescire autem quid ante quam natus sis acciderit, id est semper esse puerum. Quid enim est aetas hominis, nisi ea memoria rerum veterum cum superiorum aetate contexitur?

To be ignorant of what occurred before you were born is to remain always a child. For what is the worth of human life, unless it is woven into the life of our ancestors by the records of history?

Cicero, *Orator*, 46 BC

I

I remember the cries of Caesar's war-horns chasing us over the darkened fields of Latium – their yearning, keening howls, like animals on heat – and how when they stopped there was only the slither of our shoes on the icy road and the urgent panting of our breath.

It was not enough for the immortal gods that Cicero should be spat at and reviled by his fellow citizens; not enough that in the middle of the night he be driven from the hearths and altars of his family and ancestors; not enough even that as we fled from Rome on foot he should look back and see his house in flames. To all these torments they deemed it necessary to add one further refinement: that he should be forced to hear his enemy's army striking camp on the Field of Mars.

Even though he was the oldest of our party Cicero kept up the same fast pace as the rest of us. Not long ago he had held Caesar's life in the palm of his hand. He could have crushed it as easily as an egg. Now their fortunes led them in entirely opposite directions. While Cicero hurried south to escape his enemies, the architect of his destruction marched north to take command of both provinces of Gaul.

He walked with his head down, not uttering a word and I imagined it was because he was too full of despair to speak.

Only at dawn, when we rendezvoused with our horses at Bovillae and were about to embark on the second stage of our escape, did he pause with his foot in the doorway of his carriage and say suddenly, 'Do you think we should turn back?'

The question caught me by surprise. 'I don't know,' I said. 'I hadn't considered it.'

'Well, consider it now. Tell me: why are we fleeing Rome?'

'Because of Clodius and his mob.'

'And why is Clodius so powerful?'

'Because he's a tribune and can pass laws against you.'

'And who made it possible for him to become a tribune?'

I hesitated. 'Caesar.'

'Exactly. Caesar. Do you imagine that man's departure for Gaul at that precise hour was a coincidence? Of course not! He waited till his spies had reported I'd left the city before ordering his army to move. Why? I'd always assumed his advancement of Clodius was to punish me for speaking out against him. But what if his real aim all along was to drive me out of Rome? What scheme requires him to be certain I've gone before he can leave too?'

I should have grasped the logic of what he was saying. I should have urged him to turn back. But I was too exhausted to reason clearly. And if I am honest there was more to it than that. I was too afraid of what Clodius's thugs might do to us if they caught us re-entering the city.

So instead I said, 'It's a good question, and I can't pretend I have the answer. But wouldn't it look indecisive, after bidding goodbye to everyone, suddenly to reappear? In any case, Clodius has burned your house down now – where would we return to? Who would take us in? I think you'd be wiser to stick to your original plan and get as far away from Rome as you can.'

He rested his head against the side of the carriage and closed his eyes. In the pale grey light I was shocked by how haggard he appeared after his night on the road. His hair and beard had not been cut for weeks. He was wearing a toga dyed black. Although he was only in his forty-ninth year, these public signs of mourning made him look much older – like some ancient, mendicant holy man. After a while he sighed. 'I don't know, Tiro. Perhaps you're right. It's so long since I slept I'm too tired to think any more.'

And so the fatal error was made – more through indecision than decision – and we continued to press on southwards for the remainder of that day and for the twelve days that followed, putting what we thought was a safe distance between ourselves and danger.

We travelled with a minimal entourage to avoid attracting attention – just the carriage driver and three armed slaves on horseback, one in front and two behind. A small chest of gold and silver coins that Atticus, Cicero's oldest and closest friend, had provided to pay for our journey was hidden under our seat. We stayed only in the houses of men we trusted, no more than a night in each, and steered clear of those places where Cicero might have been expected to stop – for example at his seaside villa at Formiae, the first place any pursuers would look for him, and along the Bay of Naples, already filling with the annual exodus from Rome in search of winter sun and warm springs. Instead we headed as fast as we could towards the toe of Italy.

Cicero's plan, conceived on the move, was to make for Sicily and stay there until the political agitation against him in Rome subsided. 'The mob will turn on Clodius eventually,' he predicted. 'Such is the unalterable nature of the mob. He will always be my mortal enemy but he won't always be tribune – we must never forget that. In nine months his term of office will expire and then we can go back.'

He was confident of a friendly reception from the Sicilians, if only because of his successful prosecution of the island's tyrannical governor, Verres – even though that brilliant victory, which launched his political career, was now twelve years in the past and Clodius had more recently been a magistrate in the province. I sent letters ahead giving notice of his intention to seek sanctuary, and when we reached the harbour at Regium we hired a little six-oared boat to row us across the straits to Messina.

We left the harbour on a clear cold winter morning of searing blues – the sea and the sky; one light, one dark; the line dividing them as sharp as a blade; the distance to Messina a mere three miles. It took us less than an hour. We drew so close we could see Cicero's supporters lined up on the rocks to welcome him. But stationed between us and the entrance to the port was a warship flying the red and green colours of the governor of Sicily, Gaius Vergilius, and as we approached the lighthouse it slipped its anchor and moved slowly forwards to intercept us. Vergilius stood at the rail surrounded by his lictors and, after visibly recoiling at Cicero's dishevelled appearance, shouted down a greeting, to which Cicero replied in friendly terms. They had known one another in the Senate for many years.

Vergilius asked him his intentions.

Cicero called back that naturally he intended to come ashore.

'That's what I'd heard,' replied Vergilius. 'Unhappily I can't allow it.'

'Why not?'

'Because of Clodius's new law.'

'And what new law would that be? There are so many, one loses count.'

Vergilius beckoned to a member of his staff who produced a document and leaned down to pass it to me and I then gave it to Cicero. To this day I can remember how it fluttered in his hands in the slight breeze as if it were a living thing; it was the only sound in the silence. He took his time and when he had finished reading it he handed it to me without comment.

Lex Clodia in Ciceronem

Whereas M. T. Cicero has put Roman citizens to death unheard and uncondemned; and to that end forged the authority and decree of the Senate; it is hereby ordained that he be interdicted from fire and water to a distance of four hundred miles from Rome; that nobody should presume to harbour or receive him, on pain of death; that all his property and possessions be forfeit; that his house in Rome be demolished and a shrine to Liberty consecrated in its place; and that whoever shall move, speak, vote or take any step towards recalling him shall be treated as a public enemy, unless those whom Cicero unlawfully put to death should first spring back to life.

It must have been the most terrible blow. But he found the composure to dismiss it with a flick of his hand. 'When,' he enquired, 'was this nonsense published?'

'I'm told it was posted in Rome eight days ago. It came into my hands yesterday.'

'Then it's not law yet, and can't be law until it's been read a third time. My secretary will confirm it. Tiro,' he said, turning to me, 'tell the governor the earliest date it can be passed.'

I tried to calculate. Before a bill could be put to a vote it had to be read aloud in the Forum on three successive market days.

But my reasoning was so shaken by what I had just read I couldn't remember what day of the week it was now, let alone when the market days fell. 'Twenty days from today,' I hazarded, 'perhaps twenty-five?'

'You see?' cried Cicero. 'I have three weeks' grace even if it passes, which I'm sure it won't.' He stood up in the prow of the boat, bracing his legs against the rocking of the hull, and spread his arms wide in appeal. 'Please, my dear Vergilius, for the sake of our past friendship, now that I have come so far, at least allow me to land and spend a night or two with my supporters.'

'No, as I say, I'm sorry, but I cannot take the risk. I've consulted my experts. They say even if you travelled to the very western tip of the island, to Lilybaeum, you'd still be within three hundred and fifty miles of Rome, and then Clodius would come after *me*.'

At that, Cicero ceased to be so friendly. He said coldly, 'You have no right under the law to impede the journey of a Roman citizen.'

'I have every right to safeguard the tranquillity of my province. And here, as you know, my word *is* the law. . .'

He was apologetic. I dare say he was even embarrassed. But he was immovable, and after a few more angry exchanges there was nothing for it but to turn round and row back to Regium. Our departure provoked a great cry of dismay from the shoreline and I could see that Cicero for the first time was seriously worried. Vergilius was a friend of his. If this was how a friend reacted then soon the whole of Italy would be closed against him. Returning to Rome to oppose the law was much too risky. He had left it too late. Apart from the physical danger such a journey would entail, the bill would almost certainly pass, and then we would be stranded four hundred miles from the legal limit it prescribed. To comply safely with the terms of his exile he would have to flee abroad immediately. Obviously Gaul was out of the question because of Caesar. So it would have to be somewhere in the East – Greece perhaps, or Asia. But unfortunately we were on the wrong side of the peninsula to make our escape in the treacherous winter seas. We needed to get over to the opposite coast, to Brundisium on the Adriatic, and find a big ship capable of making a lengthy voyage. Our predicament was exquisitely vile – as no doubt Caesar, the original sponsor and creator of Clodius, had intended.

It took us two weeks of arduous travel to cross the mountains, often in heavy rain and mostly along bad roads. Every mile seemed fraught with the hazard of ambush, although the primitive little towns we passed through were welcoming enough. At night we slept in smoky, freezing inns and dined on hard bread and fatty meat made scarcely more palatable by sour wine. Cicero's mood veered between fury and despair. He saw clearly now that he had made a terrible mistake by leaving Rome. It had been madness for him to quit the city and leave Clodius free to spread the calumny that he had put citizens to death 'unheard and uncondemned' when in fact each of the five Catiline conspirators had been allowed to speak in his own defence and their execution had been sanctioned by the entire Senate. But his flight was tantamount to an admission of guilt. He should have obeyed his instinct and turned back when he heard Caesar's departing trumpets and first began to realise his error. He wept at the disaster his folly and timidity had brought upon his wife and children.

And when he had finished lashing himself, he turned his scourge on Hortensius 'and the rest of the aristocratic gang', who had never forgiven him for rising from his humble origins to the consulship and saving the republic: they had deliberately urged him to flee in order to ruin him. He should have heeded the example of Socrates, who said that death was preferable to exile. Yes, he should have killed himself! He snatched up a knife from the dining table. He *would* kill himself! I said nothing. I didn't take the threat seriously. He couldn't stand the sight of others' blood, let alone his own. All his life he had tried to avoid military expeditions, the games, public executions, funerals – anything that might remind him of mortality. If pain frightened him, death terrified him – which, although I would never have been impertinent enough to point it out, was the principal reason we had fled Rome in the first place.

When finally we came within sight of the fortified walls of Brundisium, he decided not to venture inside. The port was so large and busy, so full of strangers, and so likely to be his destination, he was convinced it was the obvious spot for his assassination. Instead we sought sanctuary a little way up the coast, in the residence of his old friend Marcus Laenius Flaccus. That night we slept in decent beds for the first time in three weeks, and the next morning we went down to the beach. The waves were much rougher than on the Sicilian side. A strong wind was hurling the Adriatic relentlessly against the rocks and shingle. Cicero loathed sea voyages at the best of times; this one promised to be especially treacherous. Yet it was our only means of escape. One hundred and twenty miles beyond the horizon lay the shore of Illyricum.

Flaccus, noticing his expression, said, 'Fortify your spirits, Cicero – perhaps the bill won't pass, or one of the other tribunes will veto it. There must be *someone* left in Rome willing to stand up for you – Pompey, surely?'

But Cicero, his gaze still fixed out to sea, made no reply, and a few days later we heard that the bill had indeed become law and that Flaccus was therefore guilty of a capital offence simply by having a convicted exile on his premises. Even so he tried to persuade us to stay. He insisted that Clodius didn't frighten *him*. But Cicero wouldn't hear of it: 'Your loyalty moves me, old friend, but that monster will have dispatched a team of his hired fighters to hunt me down the moment his law passed. There is no time to lose.'

I had found a merchant ship in the harbour at Brundisium whose hard-pressed master was willing to risk a winter voyage across the Adriatic in return for a huge fee, and the next morning at first light, when no one was around, we went on board. She was a sturdy, broad-beamed vessel, with a crew of about twenty, used to ply the trade route between Italy and Dyrrachium. I was no judge of these things, but she looked safe enough to me. The master estimated the crossing would require a day and a half – but we needed to leave quickly, he said, and take advantage of the favourable wind. So while the sailors made her ready and Flaccus waited on the quayside, Cicero quickly dictated a final message to his wife and children: *It has been a fine life, a great career – the good in me, nothing bad, has brought me down. My dear Terentia, loyalest and best of wives, my darling daughter Tullia, and little Marcus, our one remaining hope – goodbye!* I copied it out and passed it up to Flaccus. He raised his hand in farewell. Then the sail was unfurled, the cables cast off, the oarsmen pushed us away from the harbour wall, and we set off into the pale grey light.

* * *

At first we made good speed. Cicero stood high above the deck on the steersmen's platform, leaning on the stern rail, watching the great lighthouse of Brundisium recede behind us. Apart from his visits to Sicily, it was the first time he had left Italy since his youth, when he went to Rhodes to learn oratory from Molon. Of all the men I ever knew, Cicero was the least equipped by temperament for exile. To thrive he needed the appurtenances of civilised society – friends, news, gossip, conversation, politics, dinners, plays, baths, books, fine buildings; to watch all these dwindle away must have been an agony for him.

Nevertheless, in little more than an hour they had gone, swallowed up in the void. The wind drove us forwards strongly, and as we cut through the whitecaps I thought of Homer's 'dark blue wave/foaming at the bow'. But then around the middle of the morning the ship seemed gradually to lose propulsion. The great brown sail became slack-bellied and the two steersmen standing at their levers on either side of us began exchanging anxious looks. Soon dense black clouds started to mass on the horizon, and within an hour they had closed over our heads like a trapdoor. The light became shadowy; the temperature dropped. The wind got up again, but this time the gusts were in our faces, driving the cold spray off the surface of the waves. Hailstones raked the heaving deck.

Cicero shuddered, leaned forwards and vomited. His face was as grey as a corpse. I put my arm around his shoulders and indicated that we should descend to the lower deck and seek shelter in the cabin. We were halfway down the ladder when a flash of lightning split the gloom, followed instantly by a deafening, sickening crack, like a bone snapping or a tree splintering, and I was sure we must have lost the mast, for suddenly we seemed to be tumbling over and over while all around us great glistening black mountains of jet towered and toppled in the lightning flashes. The shriek of the wind made it impossible to speak or hear. In the end I simply pushed Cicero into the cabin, fell in after him and closed the door.

We tried to stand, but the ship was listing. The deck was ankle-deep in water. Our feet slid from under us. The floor tilted first one way and then the other. We clutched at the walls as we were pitched back and forth in the darkness amid loose tools and jars of wine and sacks of barley, like dumb beasts in a crate on our way to slaughter. Eventually we wedged ourselves in a corner and lay there soaked and shivering as the boat shook and plunged. I was sure we were doomed and closed my eyes and prayed to Neptune and all the gods for deliverance.

A long time passed. How long I cannot say – certainly it was the remainder of that day, and the whole of the night, and part of the day that followed. Cicero seemed quite unconscious; on several occasions I had to touch his cold cheek to reassure myself he was still alive. Each time his eyes opened briefly and then closed again. Afterwards he said he had fully resigned himself to drowning but such was the misery of his seasickness he felt no fear: rather he saw how Nature in her mercy spares those *in extremis* from the terrors of oblivion and makes death seem a welcome release. Almost the greatest surprise of his life, he said, was when he awoke on the second day and realised the storm was over and his existence would continue after all: 'Unfortunately my situation is so wretched, I almost regret it.'

Once we were sure the storm had blown itself out, we went back on deck. The sailors were just at that moment tipping over the side the corpse of some poor wretch whose head had been smashed by a swinging boom. The Adriatic was oily-smooth and still, of the same grey shade as the sky, and the body slid into it with scarcely a splash. There was a smell on the cold wind I didn't recognise, of something rotten and decaying. About a mile away I noticed a wall of sheer black rock rising above the surf. I assumed we had been blown back home again and that it must be the coast of Italy. But the captain laughed at my ignorance and said it was Illyricum, and that those were the famous cliffs that guard the approaches to the ancient city of Dyrrachium.

Cicero had at first intended to make for Epirus, the mountainous country to the south, where Atticus owned a great estate that included a fortified village. It was a most desolate region, having never recovered from the terrible fate decreed it by the Senate a century earlier, when, as a punishment for siding against Rome, all seventy of its towns had been razed to the ground simultaneously and its entire population of one hundred and fifty thousand sold into slavery. Nevertheless, Cicero claimed he wouldn't have minded the solitude of such a haunted spot. But just before we left Italy Atticus had warned him – 'with regret' – that he could only stay for a month lest word of his presence become known: if it did, under clause two of Clodius's bill, Atticus himself would be liable to the death penalty for harbouring the exile.

Even as we stepped ashore at Dyrrachium Cicero remained in two minds about which direction to take – south to Epirus, temporary refuge though it would be, or east to Macedonia, where the governor, Apuleius Saturninus, was an old friend of his, and from Macedonia on to Greece and Athens. In the event, the decision was made for him. A messenger was waiting on the quayside – a young man, very anxious. Glancing around to make sure he was not observed, he drew us quickly into a deserted warehouse and produced a letter. It was from Saturninus, the governor. I do not have it in my archives because Cicero seized it and tore it to pieces the moment I had read it out loud to him. But I can still remember the gist of what it said: that 'with regret' (that phrase again!), despite their years of friendship, Saturninus would not be able to receive Cicero in his household as it would be 'incompatible with the dignity of a Roman governor to offer succour to a convicted exile'.

Hungry, damp and exhausted from our crossing, having hurled the fragments of the letter to the ground, Cicero sank on to a bale of cloth with his head in his hands. That was when the messenger said nervously, 'Your Excellency, there is another letter . . .'

It was from one of the governor's junior magistrates, the quaestor Gnaeus Plancius. His family were old neighbours of the Ciceros from their ancestral lands around Arpinum. Plancius said that he was writing secretly and sending his letter via the same courier, who was to be trusted; that he disagreed with his superior's decision; that it would be an honour for him to take the Father of the Nation under his protection; that secrecy was vital; that he had already set out on the road to meet him at the Macedonian border; and that in the meantime he had arranged for a carriage to transport Cicero out of Dyrrachium 'immediately, in the interests of your personal safety; I plead with you not to delay by so much as an hour; I shall explain more when I see you'.

'Do you trust him?' I asked.

Cicero stared at the floor and in a low voice replied, 'No. But what choice do I have?'

With the messenger's help I arranged for our luggage to be transferred from the boat to the quaestor's carriage – a gloomy contraption, little better than a cell on wheels, without suspension and with metal grilles nailed over the windows so that its fugitive occupant could look out but no one could see him. We clattered up from the harbour into the city and joined the traffic on the Via Egnatia, the great highway that runs all the way to Byzantium. It started to sleet. There had been an earthquake a few days earlier and the place was wretched in the downpour, with corpses of the native tribespeople unburied by the roadside and here and there little groups of survivors sheltering in makeshift tents among the ruins, huddled over smoking fires. It was this odour of destruction and despair that I had smelt out at sea.

We travelled across the plain towards the snow-covered mountains and spent the night in a small village hemmed in by the encroaching peaks. The inn was squalid, with goats and chickens in the downstairs rooms. Cicero ate little and said nothing. In this strange and barren land, with its savage-looking people, he had at last fallen into the full depths of despair, and it was only with difficulty that I roused him from his bed the next morning and persuaded him to continue our journey.

For two days the road climbed into the mountains, until we came to the edge of a wide lake, fringed with ice. On the far side was a town, Lychnidos, that marked the border with Macedonia, and it was here, in its forum, that Plancius awaited us. He was in his early thirties, strongly built, wearing military uniform, with half a dozen legionaries at his back, and there was a moment when they all began to stride towards us that I experienced a rush of panic and feared we had blundered into a trap. But the warmth with which Plancius embraced Cicero, and the tears in his eyes, convinced me immediately that he was genuine.

He could not disguise his shock at Cicero's appearance. 'You need to recover your strength,' he said, 'but unfortunately, we must leave here straight away.' And then he told us what he had not dared put into his letter: that he had received reliable intelligence that three of the traitors Cicero had sent into exile for their parts in Catilina's conspiracy – Autronius Paetas, Cassius Longinus and Marcus Laeca – were all out looking for him, and had sworn to kill him.

Cicero said, 'Then there is nowhere in the world where I am safe. How are we to live?'

'Under my protection, as I said. In fact come back with me to Thessalonica, and stay under my very roof. I was military tribune until last year and I'm still on active service, so there'll be soldiers to guard you as long as you stay within the frontiers of Macedonia. My house is no palace, but it's secure and it's yours for as long as you need it.'

Cicero stared at him. Apart from the hospitality of Flaccus, it was the first real offer of help he had received for weeks – for months, in fact – and that it should have come from a young man he barely knew, when old allies such as Pompey had turned their backs on him, moved him deeply. He tried to speak, but the words choked in his throat and he had to look away.

The Via Egnatia runs for one hundred and fifty miles across the mountains of Macedonia before descending to the plain of Amphaxis, where it enters the port of Thessalonica, and this was where our journey ended, two months after leaving Rome, in a secluded villa off a busy thoroughfare in the northern part of the town.

Five years earlier, Cicero had been the undisputed ruler of Rome, second only to Pompey the Great in the affections of the people. Now he had lost everything – reputation, position, family, possessions, country; even at times the balance of his mind. For reasons of security he was confined to the villa during the hours of daylight. His presence was kept secret. A guard was posted at the entrance. Plancius told his staff that his anonymous guest was an old friend suffering from acute grief and melancholia. Like all the best lies it had the merit of being partly true. Cicero barely ate, or spoke, or left his room; sometimes his fits of weeping could be heard from one end of the house to the other. He would not receive visitors, not even his brother Quintus, who was passing nearby on his way back to Rome after completing his term as governor of Asia: *You would not have seen your brother the man you knew*, he pleaded in mitigation, *not a trace or semblance of him but only the likeness of a breathing corpse.* I tried my best to console him, without success, for how could I, a slave, understand his sense of loss, having never possessed anything worth losing in the first place? Looking back, I can see that my attempts to offer solace through philosophy must only have added to his aggravation. Indeed on one occasion, when I tried to advance the Stoic argument that possessions and rank are unnecessary, given that virtue alone is sufficient for happiness, he threw a stool at my head.

We had arrived in Thessalonica at the beginning of spring, and I took it upon myself to send letters to Cicero's friends and family letting them know, in confidence, where he was hiding, and asking them to write in response using Plancius as a poste restante. It took three weeks for these messages to reach Rome, and a further three weeks before we started to receive replies, and the news they brought was anything but encouraging. Terentia described how the charred walls of the family house on the Palatine hill had been demolished so that Clodius's shrine to Liberty – the irony! – could be erected on the site. The villa at Formiae had been pillaged, the country estate in Tusculum also invaded, and even some of the trees in the garden carted off by the neighbours. Homeless, at first she had taken refuge with her sister in the House of the Vestal Virgins.

> *But that impious wretch Clodius, in defiance of all the sacred laws, broke into the temple, and dragged me to the Basilica Porcia, where in front of the mob he had the impertinence to question me about my own property! Of course I refused to answer. He then demanded that I hand over our little son as a hostage to my good behaviour. In answer I pointed to the painting that shows Valerius defeating the Carthaginians and reminded him that my ancestors fought in that very battle and that as my family had never feared Hannibal, we most certainly would not be intimidated by him.*

It was the plight of his son that most upset Cicero: 'The first duty of any man is to protect his children, and I am helpless to fulfil it.' Marcus and Terentia were now sheltering in the home of Cicero's brother, while his adored daughter, Tullia, was sharing a roof with her in-laws. But although Tullia, like her mother, tried to make light of her troubles, it was easy enough to read between the lines and recognise the truth: that she was nursing her sick husband, the gentle Frugi – whose health, never robust, seemed to have collapsed under the strain. *Ah, my beloved, my heart's longing!* Cicero wrote to his wife. *To think that you, dearest Terentia, once everybody's refuge in trouble, should now be so tormented! You are before my eyes night and day. Goodbye, my absent loves, goodbye.*

The political outlook was equally bleak. Clodius and his supporters were continuing their occcupation of the Temple of Castor in the southern corner of the Forum. Using this fortress as their headquarters, they could intimidate the voting assemblies and pass or block whatever bills they chose. One new law we heard about, for example, demanded the annexation of Cyprus and the taxation of its wealth, 'for the good of the Roman people' – that is, to pay for the free dole of corn Clodius had instituted for every citizen – and charged Marcus Porcius Cato with accomplishing this piece of theft. Needless to say, it passed, for what group of voters ever refused to levy a tax on someone else, especially if it benefited themselves? At first Cato refused to go. But Clodius threatened him with prosecution if he disobeyed the law. As Cato held the constitution to be sacred above all things, he felt he had no choice but to comply. He sailed off for Cyprus, along with his young nephew, Marcus Junius Brutus, and with his departure Cicero lost his most vocal supporter in Rome.

Against Clodius's intimidation, the Senate was powerless. Even Pompey the Great ('the Pharaoh', as Cicero and Atticus privately called him) was now becoming frightened of the over-mighty tribune he had helped Caesar create. He was rumoured to spend most of his time making love to his young wife Julia, the daughter of Caesar, while all the time his public standing declined. Atticus wrote gossipy letters about him to cheer Cicero up, one of which survives:

You remember that when the Pharaoh restored the King of Armenia to his throne a few years back, he brought his son to Rome as a hostage to ensure the old man behaved himself? Well, just after your departure, bored of having the young fellow under his own roof, Pompey decided to lodge him with Lucius Flavius, the new praetor. Naturally, our Little Miss Beauty [Cicero's nickname for Clodius] soon got to hear of it, whereupon he invited himself round to Flavius's for dinner, asked to see the prince, and then took him away with him at the end of the meal, as if he were a napkin! Why? I hear you ask. Because Clodius has decided to put the prince on the throne of Armenia in place of his father, and take all the revenues of Armenia away from Pompey and have them for himself! Unbelievable – but it gets better: the prince is duly sent back to Armenia on a ship. There is a storm. The ship returns to harbour. Pompey tells Flavius to get himself down to Antium straight away and recapture his prize hostage. But Clodius's men are waiting. There is a fight on the Via Appia. Many are killed – among them Pompey's dear friend Marcus Papirius.

Since then, things have gone from bad to worse for the Pharaoh. The other day, when he was in the Forum attending the trial of one of his supporters (Clodius is prosecuting them left, right and centre), Clodius called together a gang of his criminals and started a chant. 'What's the name of the lecherous imperator? What's the name of the man who is trying to find a man? Who is it who scratches his head with one finger?' After each question he made a sign by shaking the folds of his toga – in that way the Pharaoh does – and the mob, like a circus chorus, all roared out the answer: 'Pompey!'

No one in the Senate lifts a finger to help him, as they all think his harassment is eminently deserved for the way he abandoned you . . .

But if Atticus thought such news would bring comfort to Cicero, he was wrong. On the contrary, it served only to make him feel more isolated and helpless. With Cato gone, Pompey cowed, the Senate impotent, the voters bribed and Clodius's mob in control of all law-making, Cicero despaired of ever having his exile rescinded. He chafed against the conditions in which we were obliged to exist. Thessalonica may be nice enough for a short stay in the springtime. But as the months passed, summer came – and Thessalonica in the summer becomes a hell of humidity and mosquitoes. No breath of a breeze stirs the brittle vegetation. The air is suffocating. And because the walls of the town retain the heat, the nights can be even more sweltering than the days. I slept in the room next to Cicero's – or rather, I tried to sleep. Lying in my tiny cubicle, I felt as if I were a roasting pig in a brick oven, and that the sweat pooling beneath my back was my melted flesh. Often after midnight I would hear Cicero stumbling around in the dark, his door opening, his bare feet slapping across the mosaic tiles. Then I would slip out after him and watch from a distance to make sure he was all right. He would sit in the courtyard on the edge of the dried-up pool with its dust-clogged fountain, and stare up at the brilliant stars, as if he could read in their alignment some clue as to why his good fortune had so spectacularly deserted him.

The next morning he would often summon me to his room. 'Tiro,' he would whisper, his fingers gripping my arm tightly, 'I've got to get out of this shithole. I'm losing all sense of myself.' But where could we go? He dreamed of Athens, or possibly Rhodes. But Plancius would not hear of it: the danger of assassination, he insisted, was, if anything, even greater than before, as rumours of Cicero's presence in the region spread. After a while I began to suspect that he quite enjoyed having such a famous figure in his power and was reluctant to let us leave. I voiced my suspicions to Cicero, who said: 'He's young and ambitious. Perhaps he's calculating that the situation in Rome will change and he might eventually get some political credit for shielding me. If so, he deludes himself.'

And then late one afternoon, when the ferocity of the day's

heat had subsided a little, I happened to go into town with a packet of letters for dispatch to Rome. It was hard to persuade Cicero even to raise the energy to reply to his correspondence, and when he did so, it was mostly a list of complaints. *I am still stuck here with no one to talk to and nothing to think about. There could be no less suitable spot in which to bear calamity in such a state of grief as I am in.* But write he did, and to supplement the occasional trusted traveller who would carry our letters, I had arranged to hire couriers provided by a local Macedonian merchant named Epiphanes, who ran an import/export business with Rome.

He was an inveterate lazy crook, of course, as are most people in that part of the world. But I reckoned the bribes I paid him ought to have been enough to buy his discretion. He had a warehouse up the slope from the harbour, on the higher ground close to the Egnatian Gate, where a haze of red-grey dust hung permanently over the clustered roofs, thrown up by the traffic from Rome to Byzantium. To reach his office one had to cross a yard where his wagons were loaded and unloaded. And there, that afternoon – with its shafts resting on blocks and its horses unhitched and drinking noisily from a water trough – was a chariot. It was so unlike the usual ox carts that the sight of it brought me up short and I went over to give it a closer look. Obviously it had been ridden hard: it was so filthy from the road it was impossible to tell its original colour. But it was fast and strong and built for fighting – a war chariot – and when I found Epiphanes upstairs I asked him whose it was.

He gave me a crafty look. 'The driver did not say his name. He just asked me to look after it.'

'A Roman?'

'Undoubtedly.'

'Alone?'

'No, he had a companion – a gladiator, perhaps: both young men, strong.'

'When did they arrive?'

'An hour ago.'

'And where are they now?'

'Who can say?' He shrugged and bared his yellow teeth.

A terrible realisation gripped me. 'Have you been opening my letters? Have you had me followed?'

'Sir, I am shocked. Really . . .' He spread his hands to show his innocence and glanced around as if in silent appeal to some invisible jury. 'How could such a thing even be suggested?'

Epiphanes! For a man who made his living by lying, he was remarkably bad at it. I turned and ran out of that room and down those steps and didn't stop running until I was within sight of our villa, where a pair of rough-looking villains were loitering in the street. My footsteps slowed as the two strangers turned to look at me and I knew in my bones they had been sent to kill Cicero. One had a puckered scar that split the side of his face from his eyebrow to his jaw (Epiphanes was right: he was a fighter straight from the gladiator barracks), while the other could have been a blacksmith – given his swagger, he could have been Vulcan himself – with bulging sunburnt calves and forearms and a face as black as a Negro's. He called out to me, 'We're looking for the house where Cicero is living!' And when I started to plead ignorance, he cut me off and added, 'Tell him Titus Annius Milo has come to pay his compliments, all the way from Rome.'

Cicero's room was dark, his candle expiring for want of air. He lay on his side, facing the wall.

'Milo?' he repeated in a monotone. 'What sort of a name is that? Is he Greek, or what?' But then he rolled over on to his back and raised himself up on his elbows. 'Wait – hasn't a candidate of that name just been elected tribune?'

'It's the same man. He's here.'

'But if he's a tribune-elect, why isn't he in Rome? His term of office begins in three months.'

'He says he wants to talk to you.'

'It's a long way to come just for a chat. What do we know of him?'

'Nothing.'

'Maybe he's come to kill me?'

'Maybe – he has a gladiator with him.'

'That doesn't inspire confidence.' Cicero lay back and thought it over. 'Well, what does it matter? I might as well be dead in any case.'

He had skulked in his room so long that when I opened the door, the daylight blinded him and he had to put up his hand to protect his eyes. Stiff-limbed and waxen, half starved, with straggling grey hair and beard, he looked like a corpse freshly risen from its tomb. It was scarcely surprising that when he first came into the room, supported on my arm, Milo failed to recognise him. It was only when he heard that familiar voice bidding him good day that our visitor gasped, pressed his hand to his heart, bowed his head and declared this to be the greatest moment and the greatest honour of his life, that he had heard Cicero speak countless times in the law courts and from the rostra but had never thought to meet him, the Father of the Nation, in person, let alone be in a position (he dared to hope) to render him some service . . .

There was a lot more in this vein, and eventually it elicited from Cicero something I had not seen from him in months: laughter. 'Yes, very well, young man, that's enough. I understand: you're pleased to see me! Come.' And with that he stepped forward, arms open, and the two men embraced.

In later years, Cicero was to be much criticised for his friendship with Milo. And it is true that the young tribune-elect was headstrong, violent and reckless, but there are times when these traits are more to be prized than prudence, calmness and caution – and these were such times. Besides, Cicero was touched that Milo should have come so far to see him; it made him feel he was not entirely finished. He invited him to stay for dinner and to save whatever he had to say until then. He even tidied himself up a little for the occasion, combing his hair and changing into less funereal garb.

Plancius was away upcountry in Tauriana, judging the local assizes, so therefore only the three of us gathered to eat. (Milo's gladiator, a murmillo named Birria, took his meal in the kitchen; even a man as easy-going as Cicero, who had been known occasionally to tolerate the presence of an actor at his dinner table, drew the line at a gladiator.) We lay in the garden in a kind of fine-mesh tent designed to keep out the mosquitoes, and over the next few hours we learned something of Milo, and why he had made such an arduous journey of seven hundred miles. He came, he said, of a noble but hard-up family. He had been adopted by his maternal grandfather. Even so, there was little money and he had been obliged to earn a living as the owner of a gladiator school in Campania, supplying fighters for funeral games in Rome. ('No wonder we've never heard of him,' Cicero remarked to me afterwards.) His work brought him often to the city. He had been appalled, he claimed, by the violence and intimidation unleashed by Clodius. He had wept to see Cicero harried and pilloried and eventually driven from Rome. Given his occupation, he fancied himself to be in a unique position to help restore order, and through intermediaries he had approached Pompey with an offer.

'What I am about to disclose is in the strictest confidence,' he said, with a sideways glance at me. 'No word of it must go beyond us three.'

'Who am I to tell?' retorted Cicero. 'The slave who empties my chamber pot? The cook who brings my meals? I assure you I see no one else.'

'Very well,' said Milo, and then he told us what he had offered Pompey: to place at his disposal one hundred pairs of highly trained fighting men to recapture the centre of Rome and end Clodius's control of the legislative assembly. In return he had asked for a certain sum to cover expenses, and also Pompey's support in the elections for tribune: 'I couldn't just do this as a private citizen, you understand – I'd be prosecuted. I told him I needed the inviolability of the office.'

Cicero was studying him closely. He had barely touched his food. 'And what did Pompey say to that?'

'At first he brushed me off. He said he'd think about it. But then came the business with the Prince of Armenia, when Papirius was killed by Clodius's men. Did you hear about that?'

'We heard something of it.'

'Well, the killing of his friend seemed to make Pompey do that bit of extra thinking, because the day after Papirius was put on the pyre, he called me to his house. "That idea of your becoming tribune – you've got yourself a deal."'

'And how has Clodius reacted to your election? He must know what you have in mind.'

'Well that's why I'm here. And this you won't have heard

about, because I left Rome straight after it happened, and no messenger could have got here quicker than I.' He stopped and held out his cup for more wine. He had come a long way to tell his story; he was obviously a raconteur; he meant to do it in his own time. 'It was about two weeks ago, not long after the elections. Pompey was doing a little business in the Forum when he ran into a gang of Clodius's men. There was some pushing and shoving, and one of them dropped a dagger. A lot of people saw it, and a great shout went up that they were going to murder Pompey. His attendants hustled him out of there fast, and back to his house, and barricaded him in – and that's where he is still, as far as I know, with only the Lady Julia for company.'

Cicero said in astonishment, 'Pompey the Great is barricaded in his own house?'

'I don't blame you if you find it funny. Who wouldn't? There's rough justice in it, and Pompey knows it. In fact he said to me that the greatest mistake of his life was letting Clodius drive you out of the city.'

'Pompey said that?'

'That's why I've raced across three countries, barely stopping to eat or sleep – to give you the news that he's going to do everything he can to get your exile overturned. His blood is up. He wants you back in Rome, you and me and him, fighting side by side, to save the republic from Clodius and his gang! What do you say to that?'

He was like a dog that has just laid a kill at its master's feet; if he'd had a tail, it would have been thumping against the fabric of the couch. But if Milo had expected either delight or gratitude, he was to be disappointed. Depressed in spirit and ragged in appearance though he might be, Cicero had nevertheless seen straight through to the heart of the matter. He swilled his wine around in his cup, frowning before he spoke.

'And does Caesar agree to this?'

'Ah now,' said Milo, shifting slightly on his couch, 'that's for you to settle with him. Pompey will play his part, but you must play yours. It would be hard for him to campaign to bring you back if Caesar were to object very strongly.'

'So he wants me to reconcile with him?'

'His word was to *reassure* him.'

It had grown dark while we were talking. The household slaves had lit lamps around the perimeter of the garden; their gleams were clouded with moths. But no light was on the table, so I couldn't properly make out Cicero's expression. He was silent for a long while. It was terrifically hot as usual, and I was conscious of the night sounds of Macedonia – the cicadas and the mosquitoes, the occasional dog bark, the voices of local people in the street, speaking in their strange, harsh foreign tongue. I wondered if Cicero was thinking the same as I was – that another year in such a place as this would kill him. Perhaps he was, because eventually he let out a sigh of resignation and said, 'And in what terms am I supposed to "reassure" him?'

'That's up to you. If any man can find the right words, it's you. But Caesar has made it clear to Pompey that he needs something in writing before he'll even think of reconsidering his position.'

'Am I supposed to give you a document to take back to Rome?'

'No, this part of the arrangement has to be between you and Caesar. Pompey thinks it would be best if you sent your own private emissary to Gaul – someone you trust, who could deliver some form of written undertaking into Caesar's hands personally.'

Caesar – everything seemed to come back to him eventually. I thought again of the sound of his trumpets leaving the Field of Mars, and in the stifling gloom I sensed rather than saw that both men had turned to look at me.

II

How easy it is for those who play no part in public affairs to sneer at the compromises required of those who do. For two years Cicero had stuck to his principles and refused to join with Caesar, Pompey and Crassus in their 'triumvirate' to control the state. He had denounced their criminality in public; they had retaliated by making it possible for Clodius to become a tribune; and when Caesar had offered him a legateship in Gaul that would have given him legal immunity from Clodius's attacks, Cicero had refused it, because acceptance would have made him Caesar's creature.

But the price of upholding those principles had been banishment, poverty and heartbreak. 'I have made myself powerless,' he said to me, after Milo had gone off to bed, leaving us alone to discuss Pompey's offer, 'and where is the virtue in that? What use am I to my family or my principles stuck in this dump for the rest of my life? Oh, no doubt one day I could become some kind of shining example to be taught to bored pupils: the man who refused ever to compromise his conscience. Perhaps after I'm safely dead they might even put up a statue of me at the back of the rostra. But I don't want to be a monument. My skill is statecraft, and that requires me to be alive and in Rome.' He fell silent. 'Then again, the thought of having to bend the knee to Caesar is scarcely bearable. To have suffered all this, and then to have to go creeping back to him like some dog that's learnt its lesson . . .'

He was still undecided when he retired for the night, and the following morning, when Milo called to ask him what answer he should take back to Pompey, I could not have predicted what he would say. 'You can tell him this,' responded Cicero. 'That my whole life has been dedicated to the service of the state, and that if the state demands of me that I should reconcile with my enemy – then reconcile I shall.'

Milo embraced him and then immediately set off back to the coast in his war chariot with his gladiator standing beside him – such a pair of brutes longing for a fight that one could only tremble for Rome and all the blood that was bound to be spilt.

It was settled that I should leave Thessalonica on my mission to Caesar at the end of the summer, as soon as the military campaigning season was over. To have set off before then would have been pointless, as Caesar was with his legions deep inside Gaul, and his habit of rapid forced marches made it impossible to say with any certainty where he might be.

Cicero spent many hours working on his letter. Years later, after his death, our copy was seized by the authorities, along with all the other correspondence between Cicero and Caesar, presumably in case it contradicted the official history that the Dictator was a genius and that all who opposed him were stupid, greedy, ungrateful, short-sighted and reactionary. I assume it has been destroyed; at any rate, I have never heard of it since. However, I still possess my shorthand notes, covering most of the thirty-six years I worked for Cicero – such a vast mass of unintelligible hieroglyphics that the ignorant operatives who ransacked my archive doubtless assumed them to be harmless gibberish and left them untouched. It is from these that I have been able to reconstruct the many conversations, speeches and letters that make up this memoir of Cicero – including his humiliating appeal to Caesar that summer, which is not lost after all.

Thessalonica
From M. Cicero to G. Caesar, Proconsul, greetings.

I hope you and the army are well.

Many misunderstandings have unfortunately arisen between us in recent years but there is one in particular which, if it exists, I wish to dispel. I have never wavered in my admiration for your qualities of intelligence, resourcefulness, patriotism, energy and command. You have justly risen to a position of great eminence in our republic, and I wish only to see your efforts crowned with success both on the battlefield and in the counsels of state, as I am sure they will be.

Do you remember, Caesar, that day when I was consul, when we debated in the Senate the punishment of those five traitors who were plotting the destruction of the republic, including my own murder? Tempers were high. Violence was in the air. Each man distrusted his neighbour. Suspicion even unjustly fell upon you, astonishingly, and had I not intervened, the flower of your glory might have been cut off before it had a chance to bloom. You know this to be true; swear otherwise if you dare.

The wheel of fate has now reversed our positions, but with this difference: I am not a young man now, as you were then, with golden prospects. My career is over. If the Roman people were ever to vote for my return from exile, I should not seek any office. I should not put myself at the head of any party or faction, especially one injurious to your interests. I should not seek to overturn any of the legislation enacted during your consulship. In what little earthly time remains to me, my life will be devoted solely to restoring the fortunes of my poor family, supporting my friends in the law courts, and rendering such service as I can to the well-being of the commonwealth. On this you may rest assured.

I am sending you this letter via my confidential secretary M. Tiro, whom you may remember, and who can be relied upon to convey in confidence any reply you may wish to make.

'Well, there it is,' said Cicero, when it was finished, 'a shameful document, and yet if one day it were to be read aloud in court, I don't believe I would need to blush too deeply.' He copied it out carefully in his own hand, sealed it, and handed it to me. 'Keep your eyes open, Tiro. Observe how he seems and who is with him. I want an exact account. If he asks after my condition, hesitate, speak with reluctance, and then confide that I am utterly broken in body and spirit. The more certain he is I'm finished, the more likely he is to let me return.'

By the time the letter was done, our situation had in fact become much more precarious again. In Rome, the senior consul, Lucius Calpurnius Piso, who was Caesar's father-in-law and an enemy of Cicero's, had been awarded the governorship of Macedonia in a public vote rigged by Clodius. He would take office at the start of the new year: an advance guard from his staff was expected in the province shortly. If they caught Cicero they might kill him on the spot. Another door was starting to close on us. My departure could no longer be put off.

I dreaded the emotion of our parting, and so, I knew, did Cicero; therefore we colluded to avoid it. On the night before

I left, when we had dined together for the final time, he pretended to be tired and retired to bed early, while I assured him I would wake him in the morning to say a final goodbye. In fact I slipped away before dawn, while the house was still in darkness, without a fuss, as he would have wanted.

Plancius had arranged an escort to conduct me back over the mountains to Dyrrachium, and there I took ship and sailed to Italy – not straight across to Brundisium this time, but north-west, to Ancona. It was a much longer voyage than our original crossing and took almost a week. But it was still quicker than going overland, with the added advantage that I would not encounter any of Clodius's agents. I had never before travelled such a long distance on my own, let alone by ship. My terror of the sea was not the same as Cicero's – of shipwreck and of drowning. It was rather of the vast emptiness of the horizon during the day and the glittering, indifferent hugeness of the universe at night. I was at this time forty-six, and conscious of the void into which we all are voyaging; I thought of death often while sitting out on deck. I had witnessed so much; ageing in body though I was, in spirit I was even older. Little did I realise that actually I had lived less than half my life, and was destined to see things that would make all the wonders and dramas that had gone before seem quite pallid and insignificant.

The weather was favourable, and we landed at Ancona without incident. From there I took the road north, crossing the Rubicon two days later and formally entering the province of Nearer Gaul. This was territory familiar to me: I had toured it with Cicero six years earlier, when he was seeking election as consul and canvassing the towns along the Via Aemilia. The vineyards beside the road had all been harvested weeks before; now the vines were being cut back for winter, so that as far as one could see, columns of white smoke from the burning vegetation were rising over the flat terrain, as if some retreating army had scorched the earth behind it.

In the little town of Claterna, where I stayed the night, I learned that the governor had returned from beyond the Alps and had set up his winter headquarters in Placentia, but that with typical restless energy he was already touring the countryside holding assizes: he was due in the neighbouring town of Mutina the next day. I left early, reached it at noon, passed through the heavily fortified walls, and made for the basilica on the forum. The only clue to Caesar's presence was a troop of legionaries at the entrance. They made no attempt to ask my business, and I went straight inside. A cold grey light from the clerestory windows fell upon a hushed queue of citizens waiting to present their petitions. At the far end – too far away for me to make out his face – seated between pillars, dispensing judgement from his magistrate's chair, in a toga so white it stood out brightly amid the locals' drab winter plumage, was Caesar.

Uncertain how to approach him, I found myself joining the line of petitioners. Caesar was issuing his rulings at such a rate that we shuffled forwards almost continuously, and as I drew closer I saw that he was doing several things at once – listening to each supplicant, reading documents as they were handed to him by a secretary, and conferring with an army officer who had taken off his helmet and was bending down to whisper in his ear. I took out Cicero's letter so that I would have it ready. But then it struck me that this was not perhaps the proper place to hand over the appeal: that it was unconducive somehow to the dignity of a former consul for his request to be considered alongside the domestic complaints of all these farmers and tradespeople, worthy folk though they no doubt were. The officer finished his report, straightened, and was just walking past me towards the door, fastening his helmet, when his eyes met mine and he stopped in surprise. 'Tiro?'

I glimpsed his father in him before I could put a name to the young man himself. It was M. Crassus's son, Publius, now a cavalry commander on Caesar's staff. Unlike his father he was a cultured, gracious, noble man, and an admirer of Cicero, whose company he used to seek out. He greeted me with great affability – 'What brings you to Mutina?' – and when I told him, he volunteered at once to arrange a private interview with Caesar and insisted I accompany him to the villa where the governor and his entourage were staying.

'I'm doubly glad to see you,' he said as we walked, 'for I've often thought of Cicero, and the injustice done to him. I've talked to my father about it and persuaded him not to oppose his recall. And Pompey, as you know, supports it too – only last week he sent Sestius, one of the tribunes-elect, up here to plead his cause with Caesar.'

I could not help observing, 'It seems that everything these days depends upon Caesar.'

'Well, you have to understand his position. He feels no personal animosity towards your master – very much the opposite. But unlike my father and Pompey, he's not in Rome to defend himself. He's concerned about losing political support while his back is turned, and being recalled before his work here is complete. He sees Cicero as the greatest threat to his position. Come inside – let me show you something.'

We passed the sentry and went into the house, and Publius conducted me through the crowded public rooms to a small library where, from an ivory casket, he produced a series of dispatches, all beautifully edged in black and housed in purple slip-cases, with the word *Commentaries* picked out in vermilion in the title line.

'These are Caesar's own personal copies,' Publius explained, handling them carefully. 'He takes them with him wherever he goes. They are his record of the campaign in Gaul, which he has decided to send regularly to be posted up in Rome. One day he intends to collect them all together and publish them as a book. It's perfectly marvellous stuff. See for yourself.'

He plucked out a roll for me to read:

There is a river called the Saone, which flows through the territories of the Aedui and Sequani into the Rhone with such incredible slowness that it cannot be determined by the eye in which direction it flows. This the Helvetii were crossing by rafts and boats joined together. When Caesar was informed by spies that the Helvetii had already conveyed three parts of their forces across that river, but that the fourth part was left behind on this side of the Saone, he set out from the camp with three legions. Attacking them, encumbered with baggage, and not expecting him, he cut to pieces a great part of them . . .

I said, 'He writes of himself with wonderful detachment.'

'He does. That's because he doesn't want to sound boastful. It's important to strike the right note.'

I asked if I might be allowed to copy some of it, and show it to Cicero. 'He misses the regular news from Rome. What reaches us is sparse, and late.'

'Of course – it's all public information. And I'll make sure you get in to see Caesar. You'll find he's in a tremendously good mood.'

He left me alone and I settled to work.

Even allowing for a degree of exaggeration, it was plain from the *Commentaries* that Caesar had enjoyed an astonishing run of military successes. His original mission had been to halt the migration of the Helvetii and four other tribes who were trekking westwards across Gaul to the Atlantic in search of new territory. He had followed their immense column, which consisted both of fighting men and of the elderly and women and children, with a new army he had mostly raised himself of five legions. Finally he had lured them into battle at Bibracte. As a guarantee to his new legions that neither he nor his officers would abandon them if things went wrong, he had all their horses sent far away to the rear. They fought on foot with the infantry, and in the event Caesar, by his own account, did not merely halt the Helvetii – he slaughtered them. Afterwards a list giving the total strength of the migration had been discovered in the enemy's abandoned camp:

Helvetii	*263,000*
Tulingi	*36,000*
Latobrigi	*14,000*
Rauraci	*23,000*
Boii	*32,000*
	368,000

Of these, according to Caesar, the total number who returned alive to their former homeland was 110,000.

Then – and this was what no one else surely would have dreamed of attempting – he had force-marched his weary legions back across Gaul to confront 120,000 Germans who had taken advantage of the Helvetii's migration to cross into Roman-controlled territory. There had been another terrific battle, lasting seven hours, in which young Crassus had commanded the cavalry, and by the end of it the Germans had been entirely annihilated. Hardly any had been left alive to flee back across the Rhine, which for the first time became the natural frontier of the Roman Empire. Thus, if Caesar's account was to be believed, almost one third of a million people had either died or disappeared in the space of a single summer. To round off the year, he had left his legions in their new winter camp, a full one hundred miles north of the old border of Further Gaul.

By the time I had finished my copying it was beginning to get dark, but the villa was still noisy with activity – soldiers and civilians wanting an appointment with the governor, messengers rushing in and out. As I could no longer see to write, I put away my tablet and stylus and sat in the gloom. I wondered what Cicero would have made of it all had he been in Rome. To have condemned the victories would have seemed unpatriotic; at the same time, such sweeping cleansing of populations and adjustments to the frontier, without the authorisation of the Senate, were illegal. I also pondered what Publius Crassus had said: that Caesar feared Cicero's presence in Rome lest he be 'recalled before his work here is complete'. What did 'complete' mean in this context? The phrase seemed ominous.

My reverie was interrupted by the arrival of a young officer, barely more than thirty, with tight blond curls and an improbably immaculate uniform, who introduced himself as Caesar's aide-de-camp, Aulus Hirtius. He said that he understood I had a letter for the governor from Cicero, and that if I would be so kind as to give it to him, he would see that he received it. I replied that I was under firm instructions to give it to Caesar personally. He said that was impossible. I said that in that case I would follow the governor from town to town until such time as I got the chance to speak to him. Hirtius scowled at me and tapped his neatly shod foot, then went away again. An hour passed before he reappeared and curtly asked me to follow him.

The public part of the house was still thronged with callers, even though it was now night-time. We went down a passage, through a stout door and into a warm, heavily scented, thickly carpeted room, brilliantly lit by a hundred candles, in the centre of which on a table lay Caesar, flat on his back and entirely naked, having oil worked into his skin by a Negro masseur. He glanced at me briefly and held out his hand. I gave Cicero's letter to Hirtius, who broke the seal and handed it to Caesar. I directed my gaze to the floor as a mark of respect.

Caesar said, 'How was your journey?'

I replied, 'Good, Excellency, thank you.'

'And are you being looked after?'

'I am, thank you.'

I dared then to look at him properly for the first time. His body was glistening, well muscled, and plucked entirely hairless in every respect – a disconcerting affectation which had the effect of emphasising his numerous scars and bruises, presumably picked up on the battlefield. His face was undeniably striking – angular and lean, dominated by dark and penetrating eyes. The overall effect was one of great power, of both the intellect and the will. One could see why men and women alike fell easily under his spell. He was then in his forty-third year.

He turned on to his side towards me – there was no spare flesh, I noticed: his stomach was entirely hard – propped himself up on his elbow and gestured to Hirtius, who produced a portable inkstand and carried it over to him.

He said, 'And how is Cicero's health?'

'It's very poor, I'm afraid.'

He laughed. 'Oh no, I don't believe a word of *that*! He'll outlive us all – or me, at any rate.'

He dipped his pen in the inkpot, scrawled something on the letter, and gave it back to Hirtius, who sprinkled sand on the wet ink, blew away the residue, rolled the document up again, and returned it to me without expression.

Caesar said, 'If you need anything during your stay, be sure to ask.' He lay on his back once more and the masseur resumed his kneading.

I hesitated. I had come such a long way. I felt there should be something more, if only by way of an anecdote for me to take back to Cicero. But Hirtius touched my arm and nodded towards the door.

As I reached it, Caesar called after me, 'Do you still practise that shorthand of yours?'

'I do.'

He made no further comment. The door closed and I followed Hirtius back up the passage. My heart was pounding, as if I had survived a sudden fall. It wasn't until I had been shown to the room where I was to sleep overnight that I thought to check what he had written on the letter. Two words only – either elegantly brief or typically contemptuous, depending on how you chose to interpret them: *Approved. Caesar.*

When I rose the following morning, the house was silent; Caesar had already left with his entourage for the next town. My mission concluded, I too set off on my long return journey.

When I reached the harbour at Ancona, I found a letter from Cicero waiting for me: the first of Piso's soldiers had just arrived in Thessalonica and therefore as a precaution he was departing immediately for Dyrrachium – which, as it lies in the province of Illyricum, was beyond Piso's influence. He hoped to meet me there. Depending on Caesar's answer and on developments in Rome, we would then decide where to go next: *Like Callisto, it seems we are doomed to wander throughout eternity.*

I had to wait ten days for a favourable wind and did not reach Dyrrachium until the festival of Saturnalia. The City Fathers had placed at Cicero's disposal a well-defended house up in the hills with a view across the sea, and this was where I found him, gazing at the Adriatic. He turned at my approach. I had forgotten how much exile had aged him. My dismay must have shown in my expression, because his own face fell the moment he saw me, and he said bitterly, 'So I take it the answer was no?'

'On the contrary.'

I showed him his original letter with Caesar's scrawl in the margin. He held it in his hands and studied it for a long while.

'"Approved. Caesar",' he said. 'Will you look at that? "Approved. Caesar"! He's doing something he doesn't want to do and he's as sulky about it as a child.'

He sat on a bench under an umbrella pine and made me recount my visit in every detail, and then he read the extracts I had copied from Caesar's *Commentaries*. When he had finished, he said, 'He writes very well in his brutal way. Such artlessness requires some art – it will add to his reputation. But where will his campaigning take him next, I wonder? He could grow strong – very strong. If Pompey is not careful, he will wake up to find a monster on his back.'

There was nothing we could do now but wait, and whenever I think of Cicero at this time, I always picture him in the same way: on that terrace, leaning over the balustrade, a letter bearing the latest news from Rome clenched in his hand, staring grimly at the horizon, as if somehow by sheer willpower he could see all the way to Italy and impose himself on events.

First we heard from Atticus of the swearing-in of the new tribunes, eight of whom were Cicero's supporters and only two his declared enemies – but two was enough to impose a veto on any law repealing his exile. Then from Cicero's brother, Quintus we learned that Milo, as tribune, had brought a prosecution against Clodius for violence and intimidation, and that Clodius's response had been to order his bullies to attack Milo's house. On New Year's Day the new consuls took office. One, Lentulus Spinther, was already a firm supporter of Cicero. The other, Metellus Nepos, had long been considered his enemy. But someone must have got at him, because in the inaugural debate of the new Senate, Nepos declared that while he still did not care for Cicero personally, he would not oppose his recall. Two days later, a motion to repeal Cicero's exile, drawn up by Pompey, was laid by the Senate before the people.

At that moment it was possible to believe that Cicero's banishment would soon be over, and I began to make discreet preparations for our departure to Italy. But Clodius was a resourceful and vindictive enemy. On the night before the people were due to meet, he and his supporters occupied the Forum, the comitium, the rostra – in sum, the whole legislative heart of the republic – and when Cicero's friends and allies arrived to vote, they attacked them without mercy. Two tribunes, Fabricius and Cispius, were set upon and their attendants murdered and flung in the Tiber. When Quintus tried to get up on to the rostra, he was dragged off and beaten up so badly he only survived by pretending to be dead. Milo responded by unleashing his own squad of gladiators. Soon the centre of Rome was a battlefield, and the fighting went on for days. But although Clodius for the first time suffered severe punishment, he was not entirely driven out, and he still had the two tribunes with their vetoes. The law to bring Cicero home had to be abandoned.

When Cicero received Atticus's account of what had happened, he fell into a despair almost as great as that which had gripped him in Thessalonica. *From your letter,* he wrote back, *and from the facts themselves I see that I am utterly finished. In matters where my family needs your help I beg you not to fail us in our misery.*

However, there is always this to be said for politics: it is never static. If the good times do not last, neither do the bad. Like Nature, it follows a perpetual cycle of growth and decay, and no statesman, however cunning, is immune to this process. If Clodius had not been so arrogant, reckless and ambitious, he never would have achieved the heights he did. But being all those things, and subject to the laws of politics, he was bound to overreach and topple eventually.

In the spring, during the Festival of Flora, when Rome was crowded with visitors from all over Italy, Clodius's mob found itself for once outnumbered by ordinary citizens who despised their bullying tactics. Clodius himself was actually jeered at the theatre. Unused to anything other than adulation from the people, according to Atticus he looked around him in astonishment at the slow handclapping, taunts, whistles and obscene gestures, and realised – almost too late – that he was in danger of being lynched. He retreated hastily, and that was the beginning of the end of his domination, for the Senate now recognised how he could be beaten: by appealing over the heads of the urban plebs to the population at large.

Spinther duly laid a motion calling for the entire citizenry of the republic to be summoned together in its most sovereign body, the electoral college of one hundred and ninety-three centuries, and for them to determine the fate of Cicero once and for all. The motion passed in the Senate by four hundred and thirteen votes to one, the one being Clodius. It was further agreed that the vote on Cicero's recall should take place at the same time as the summer elections, when the centuries would already be assembled on the Field of Mars.

The moment he heard what had been decided, Cicero was so certain he was reprieved he arranged for a sacrifice to be made to the gods. Those tens of thousands of ordinary citizens from across Italy were the solid, sensible foundation on which he had built his career; he was sure they would not let him down. He sent word to his wife and family asking them to meet him in Brundisium, and rather than lingering in Illyricum to await the result, which would take two weeks to reach us, he decided to sail for home on the day the vote was held. 'If there is a tide flowing in one's direction, one must catch it early, and not allow it time to ebb. Besides, it will look good if I show confidence.'

'If the vote goes against you, you will be breaking the law by returning to Italy.'

'But it won't. The Roman people will never vote to keep me in exile – and if they do, well there's no point in going on, is there?'

And so, fifteen months to the day after we had landed in Dyrrachium, we went down to the harbour to begin the journey back to life. Cicero had shaved off his beard and cut his hair and had put on a white toga with the purple stripe of a senator. As chance would have it, our return crossing was on the same merchant ship that had brought us over. But the contrast between the two journeys could not have been more marked. This time we skimmed across a flat sea all day with a favourable wind, spent the night lying out on the open deck, and the following morning came in sight of Brundisium. The entrance to the greatest harbour in Italy opens like an immense pair of outstretched arms, and as we passed between the booms and approached the crowded quayside, it felt as if we were being clasped to the heart of a dear and long-lost friend. The whole town seemed to be at the harbour and *en fête*, with pipes and drums playing, young girls carrying flowers, and youths waving boughs decorated with coloured ribbons.

I thought they were for Cicero, and said so in great excitement, but he cut me off and told me not to be a fool. 'How would they have known we were coming? Besides, have you forgotten everything? Today is the anniversary of the founding of the colony of Brundisium, and therefore a local holiday. You would have known that once, when I was running for office.'

Nevertheless, some of the people had noticed his senatorial toga and quickly realised who he was. The word was passed. Soon a sizeable crowd was shouting his name and cheering. Cicero, standing on the upper deck as we glided towards our berth, raised his hand in acknowledgement and turned this way and that so all could see him. Among the multitude I spotted his daughter, Tullia. She was waving with the rest and calling out to him, even jumping up and down to attract his attention. But Cicero was sunning himself in the applause, his eyes half closed, like a prisoner released from a dungeon into the light, and in the noise and tumult of the crowd he did not see her.

III

That Cicero did not recognise his only daughter was less peculiar than it may seem. She had changed greatly in the time we had been away. Her face and arms, once plump and girlish, were thin and pale; her fair hair was covered by the dark headdress of mourning. The day of our arrival was her twentieth birthday, although I am ashamed to say that I had forgotten it and so had failed to remind Cicero.

His first act on stepping down from the gangplank was to kneel and kiss the soil. Only after this patriotic act had been loudly cheered did he look up and notice his daughter watching him in her widow's weeds. He stared at her and burst into tears, for he truly loved her, and he had loved her husband too, and now he saw by the colour and style of her dress that he was dead.

He enfolded her in his arms, to the crowd's delight, and after a long embrace took a step back to examine her. 'My dearest child, you cannot imagine how much I have yearned for this moment.' Still holding her hands, he switched his gaze to the faces behind her and scanned them eagerly. 'Is you mother here, and Marcus?'

'No, Papa, they're in Rome.'

This was hardly surprising – in those days it was an arduous journey, especially for a woman, of two or three weeks from

Rome to Brundisium, with a serious risk of robbery in the remoter stretches; if anything, the surprise was that Tullia *had* come, and come alone at that. But Cicero's disappointment was obvious although he tried to hide it.

'Well, it's no matter – no matter at all. I have you, and that's the main thing.'

'And I have you – and on my birthday.'

'It's your birthday?' He gave me a reproachful look. 'I almost forgot. Of course it is. We shall celebrate tonight!' And he took her by the arm and led her away from the harbour.

Because we did not yet know for certain that his exile had been repealed, it was decided that we should not set off for Rome until we had official confirmation, and once again Laenius Flaccus volunteered to put us up at his estate outside Brundisium. Armed men were stationed around the perimeter for Cicero's protection, and he spent much of the next few days with Tullia, strolling through the gardens and along the beach, learning at first hand how difficult her life had been during his exile – how, for example, her husband, Frugi, had been set upon by Clodius's henchmen when he was trying to speak on Cicero's behalf, stripped naked and pelted with filth and driven from the Forum, and how his heart had ceased to beat properly afterwards until, a few months later, he died in her arms; how, because she was childless, she had been left with nothing except a few pieces of jewellery and her returned dowry, which she had given to Terentia to help pay off the family's debts; how Terentia had been obliged to sell a large part of her own property, and had even steeled herself to plead with Clodius's sister to intercede with her brother to grant her and her children some mercy, and how Clodia had mocked her and boasted that Cicero had tried to have an affair with her; how families they had always thought of as friends had closed their doors on them in fear; and so on and so forth.

Cicero told me all this sadly one night after Tullia had gone to bed. 'Little wonder Terentia isn't here. It seems she avoids going out in public as much as she can and prefers to stay cooped up in my brother's house. As for Tullia, we need to find her a new husband as soon as possible, while she's still young enough to give a man some children safely.' He rubbed his temples, as he always did at times of stress. 'I'd thought that coming back to Italy would mark the end of my troubles. Now I see it is merely the beginning.'

It was on our sixth day as Flaccus's guests that a messenger arrived from Quintus with the news that despite a last-minute demonstration by Clodius and his mob, the centuries had voted unanimously to restore to Cicero his full rights of citizenship, and that he was accordingly a free man once more. Oddly, the news did not seem to give him much joy, and when I remarked on his indifference he replied: 'Why should I rejoice? I have merely had returned to me something that should never have been taken away in the first place. Otherwise, I am weaker than I was before.'

We began our journey to Rome the next day. By then the news of his rehabilitation had spread among the people of Brundisium, and a crowd of several hundred had gathered outside the gates of the villa to see him off. He got down from the carriage he was sharing with Tullia, greeted each well-wisher with a handshake, made a short speech, and then we resumed our journey. But we had not gone more than five miles when we encountered another large group at the next settlement, also clamouring for the opportunity to shake his hand. Once again he obliged. And so it went on throughout that day, and the days that followed, always the same, except that the crowds grew steadily larger as word preceded us that Cicero would be passing through. Soon people were coming from miles around, even walking down from the mountains to stand by the roadside. By the time we reached Beneventum, the numbers were in their thousands; in Capua, the streets were entirely blocked.

To begin with, Cicero was touched by these unfeigned demonstrations of affection, then delighted, then amazed, and finally thoughtful. Was there some means, he wondered, of turning this astonishing popularity among the ordinary citizens of Italy into political influence in Rome? But popularity and power, as he well knew, are separate entities. Often the most powerful men in a state can pass down a street unrecognised, while the most famous bask in feted impotence.

This was brought home to us soon after we left Campania, when Cicero decided we should call in at Formiae and inspect his villa on the seashore. He knew from Terentia and Atticus that it had been attacked, and was braced to find a ruin. In fact, when we turned off the Via Appia and entered the grounds, the shuttered property appeared perfectly intact, albeit the Greek statuary had gone. The garden was neatly tended. Peacocks still strutted between the trees and we could hear the distant motion of the sea. As the carriage halted and Cicero climbed out, members of the household began to materialise from various parts of the property, as if they had been in hiding. Seeing their master again, they flung themselves to the ground, crying with relief. But when he began to move towards the front door, several tried to block his path, pleading with him not to go inside. He gestured to them to move out of the way and ordered the door to be unlocked.

The first shock to confront us was the smell – of smoke and damp and human waste. And then there was the sound – empty and echoing, broken only by the crunch of plaster and pottery beneath our feet, and the cooing of the pigeons in rafters. As the shutters started to come down, the summer afternoon sunlight revealed a vista of room after room stripped bare. Tullia put her hand to her mouth in horror and Cicero gently told her to go and wait in the carriage. We moved on into the interior. All the furniture was gone, all the pictures, the fixtures. Here and there sections of the ceilings were hanging down; even the mosaic floors had been prised up and carted away; weeds grew out of bare earth amid the bird shit and human faeces. The walls were scorched where fires had been lit, and covered with the most obscene drawings and graffiti, all executed in dripping red paint.

In the dining room a rat scuttled along the side of the wall and squeezed itself down a hole. Cicero watched it disappear with a look of infinite disgust on his face. Then he marched out of the house, clambered back into his carriage, and ordered the driver to rejoin the Via Appia. He did not speak for at least an hour.

Two days later we reached Bovillae, on the outskirts of Rome.

We woke the next morning to find yet another crowd waiting to escort us into the city. As we stepped out into the heat of that summer morning, I was apprehensive: the state of the villa at Formiae had unnerved me. It was also the eve of the Roman Games, a public holiday. The streets would be packed, and reports had already reached of us of a shortage of bread that had led to rioting. I was sure Clodius would use the pretext of the disorder to attempt some kind of ambush. But Cicero was calm. He believed the people would protect him. He asked for the roof to be removed from the carriage, and with Tullia holding a parasol seated beside him, and me stationed up on the bench next to the driver, we set off.

I do not exaggerate when I say that every yard of the Via Appia was lined with citizens and that for nearly two hours we were borne northwards on a wave of continuous applause. Where the road passes over the River Almo, by the Temple of the Great Mother, the crowd was three or four deep. Further on, they occupied the steps of the Temple of Mars so densely it resembled a stand at the games. And just outside the city walls, along that stretch where the aqueduct runs beside the highway, young men were perched precariously on the tops of the arches, or clinging to the palm trees. They waved, and Cicero waved back. The din and the heat and the dust were terrific. Eventually we were forced to a halt just outside the Capena Gate, where the press of humanity was simply too great for us to go on.

I jumped down with the intention of opening the door, and tried to push my way round to the side of the carriage. But a surge of people, desperate to get closer to Cicero, pinned me against it so hard I could neither move nor breathe. The carriage shifted and threatened to topple, and I do believe that Cicero might have been killed by an excess of love just ten paces short of Rome, had not his brother Quintus appeared at that moment from the recesses of the gate along with a dozen attendants who pushed the crowd back and cleared a space for Cicero to descend.

It was four years since the two had last met, and Quintus no longer appeared the younger brother. His nose had been broken during the fighting in the Forum. He was obviously drinking too much. He looked like a beaten-down old boxer. He held out his arms to Cicero and they locked hold of one another, unable to speak for emotion, tears pouring down their cheeks, each silently pounding the back of the other.

When they separated, Quintus told him what he had arranged, and then we entered the city on foot, Cicero and Quintus walking hand in hand, with Tullia and me behind them, a file of attendants on either side. Quintus, who used to be Cicero's campaign manager, had devised the route in order to show off his brother to as many supporters as possible. We passed the Circus Maximus, its flags already flying in anticipation of the games, and as we progressed slowly along the crowded valley between the Palatine and the Caelian hills, it seemed as if everyone Cicero had ever represented in the law courts, or helped out with a favour, or even just shaken hands with at election time had come out to bid him welcome. Even so, I noticed that not all were cheering, and that here and there small groups of sullen plebeians scowled at us or turned their backs, especially as we drew close to the Temple of Castor, where Clodius had his headquarters. Fresh slogans had been daubed across it, in the same angry red paint that had been used at Formiae: *M. CICERO STEALS THE PEOPLE'S BREAD; WHEN THE PEOPLE ARE HUNGRY THEY KNOW WHO TO BLAME.* One man spat at us. Another slyly drew back the folds of his tunic to show me his knife. Cicero affected not to notice.

A crowd of several thousand cheered us all the way across the Forum and up the Capitoline steps to the Temple of Jupiter, where a fine white bull was waiting to be sacrificed. At every moment I feared an assault, despite my reason telling me it would have been suicidal: any attacker would have been torn apart by Cicero's supporters, even assuming he could have got close enough to strike a blow. Nevertheless, I would have preferred it if we could have got into a place with walls and a door. But that was impossible: on this day Cicero belonged to Rome. First we had to listen to the priests recite their prayers, then Cicero had to cover his head and step forward to deliver his ritual thanks to the gods, and stand and watch while the beast was killed and its entrails examined until the auspices were pronounced propitious. Then he entered the temple and laid offerings at the feet of a small statue of Minerva he had placed there before his exile. Finally, when he emerged, he was surrounded by many of those senators who had campaigned hardest for his restoration – Sestius, Cestilius, Curtius, the Cispius brothers and the rest, led by the senior consul, Lentulus Spinther – each of whom had to be thanked individually. Many were the tears shed and the kisses exchanged, and it must have been well after noon before he was able to start walking home, and even then Spinther and the others insisted on accompanying him; Tullia, unnoticed by any of us, had already gone on ahead.

'Home' of course was no longer his own fine mansion on the slopes of the Palatine: looking up, I could see that it had been entirely demolished to make room for Clodius's shrine to Liberty. Instead we were to be lodged just below it, in the house of Quintus, where we would live until such time as Cicero could get the site restored to him and begin rebuilding. This street, too, was packed with well-wishers, and Cicero had to struggle to reach the threshold. Beyond it, in the shade of the courtyard, waited his wife and children.

I knew, because he had so often spoken of it, how much Cicero had looked forward to this moment. And yet there was an awkwardness to it that made me want to hide my face. Terentia, decked out in her finery, had plainly been waiting for him for several hours, and in the interim little Marcus had grown bored and fretful. 'So, husband,' she said, with a thin smile, tugging savagely at the boy to make him stand up properly, 'you are home at last! Go and greet your father,' she instructed Marcus, and pushed him forwards, but immediately he darted around her and hid behind her skirts. Cicero stopped some distance short, his arms outstretched to the boy, uncertain how to respond, and in the end the situation was only retrieved by Tullia, who ran to her father, kissed him, led him over to her mother and gently pressed her parents together, and in this way at last the family was reunited.

Quintus's villa was large, but not sufficiently spacious to accommodate two full households in any comfort, and from that first day there was friction. Out of respect for his brother's superior age and rank, Quintus, with typical generosity, had insisted that Cicero and Terentia should take over the master's quarters, which he usually shared with his wife, Pomponia, the sister of Atticus. It was clear she had objected bitterly to this, and could barely bring herself to give Cicero a civil greeting.

It is not my intention to dwell on personal gossip: such matters fall beneath the dignity of my subject. Nevertheless, I cannot give a proper account of Cicero's life without mentioning what happened, for this was when his domestic unhappiness really started, and it was to have an effect upon his political career.

He and Terentia had been married for more than twenty years. They had often argued. But underlying their disputes was a mutual respect. She was a woman of independent wealth: that was why he had married her; it was certainly not for her looks or the sweetness of her temper. It was Terentia's fortune that had enabled him to enter the Senate. In return, his success had increased her social standing. Now the disaster of his fall had exposed the inherent weaknesses of this partnership. Not only had she been obliged to sell a good part of her property in order to protect the family in his absence, she had been reviled and insulted and reduced to lodging with her in-laws – a family she snobbishly considered far beneath her own. Yes, Cicero was alive and he was back in Rome and I am sure she was glad for that. But she made no secret of her view that his days of political power were over, even if he – still floating on the clouds of popular adulation – had failed to grasp the fact.

I was not asked to dine with the family that first evening, and given the tensions between them, I cannot say I minded especially. I was, however, dismayed to find that I had been given a bed in the slaves' quarters in the cellar, sharing a cubicle with Terentia's steward, Philotimus. He was an oily, avaricious creature of middle age: we had never liked one another, and I should guess he was no happier to see me than I him. Still, his love of money at least made him a diligent manager of Terentia's business affairs, and it must have pained him to see her fortune depleted month after month. The bitterness with which he assailed Cicero for placing her in this situation infuriated me, and after a while I told him curtly to shut his mouth and show some respect, or I would make sure the master gave him a whipping. Later, as I lay awake listening to his snores, I wondered how many of the complaints I had just heard were his, and how many he was merely repeating from the lips of his mistress.

The next day, because of my restlessness, I overslept and woke in a panic. Cicero was due to attend the Senate that morning to express his formal thanks for their support. Normally he learnt his speeches by heart and delivered them without a note. But it was so long since he had spoken in public he feared he might stumble over his words, therefore this oration had had to be dictated and written out during the journey from Brundisium. I took it from my dispatch box, checked I had the full text, and hurried upstairs, at the same time as Quintus's secretary, Statius, was showing two visitors into the tablinum. One was Milo, the tribune who had visited us in Thessalonica; the other was Lucius Afranius, Pompey's principal lieutenant, who had been consul two years after Cicero.

Statius said to me, 'These gentlemen wish to see your master.'

'I'll see if he's available.'

At which Afranius remarked, in a tone I didn't much care for, 'He'd better be available!'

I went at once to the principal bedroom. The door was closed. Terentia's maid put her finger to her lips and told me Cicero wasn't there. Instead she directed me along the passage to the dressing room, where I found him being helped into his toga by his valet. As I was describing who had come to see him, I noticed over his shoulder a small makeshift bed. He caught my glance and muttered, 'Something's wrong but she won't tell me what it is,' and then, perhaps regretting his candour, brusquely ordered me to go and fetch Quintus so that he too could hear what his visitors had come to say.

At first the meeting was friendly. Afranius announced that he brought with him the warmest regards of Pompey the Great, who hoped soon to welcome Cicero back to Rome in person. Cicero thanked him for the message and thanked Milo for all that he had done to bring about his recall. He described the enthusiasm of his reception in the countryside and of the crowds that had turned out to see him in Rome the previous day: 'I feel it is a whole new life that I am beginning. I hope Pompey will be in the Senate to hear me praise him with such poor eloquence as I can muster.'

'Pompey won't be attending the Senate,' Afranius said bluntly.

'I'm sorry to hear it.'

'He doesn't feel it appropriate, in view of the new law that is to be proposed.' Whereupon he opened a small bag and handed over a draft bill, which Cicero read with evident surprise and then gave to Quintus, who eventually handed it to me.

Whereas the people of Rome are being denied access to a sufficient supply of grain; and to the extent that this constitutes a grave threat to the well-being and security of the state; and mindful of the principle that all Roman citizens are entitled to the equivalent of at least one free loaf of bread per day – it is hereby ordained that Pompey the Great shall be granted the power as Commissioner of Grain to purchase, seize or similarly obtain throughout the entire world enough grain to secure a plentiful supply for the city; that this power should be his for a term of five years; and that to assist him in this task he shall have the right to appoint fifteen lieutenant commissioners of grain to carry out such duties as he directs.

Afranius said, 'Naturally, Pompey would like you to have the honour of proposing the legislation when you address the Senate today.'

Milo said, 'It's a cunning stroke, you must agree. Having retaken the streets from Clodius, we shall now remove his ability to buy votes with bread.'

'Is the shortage really so serious it demands an emergency law?' asked Cicero. He turned to Quintus.

Quintus said, 'It's true, there's little bread to be had, and what there is has risen to an extortionate price.'

'Even so, these are astonishing, unprecedented powers over the nation's food supply to bestow upon one man. I'd really need to find out more about the situation before I offered an opinion, I'm afraid.'

He tried to hand the draft bill back to Afranius, who refused to take it. He folded his arms and glared at Cicero. 'I must say, we expected a little more gratitude than that – after all we've done for you.'

'It goes without saying,' added Milo, 'that you'd be one of the fifteen lieutenant commissioners.' And he rubbed his finger and thumb together to indicate the lucrative nature of the appointment.

The ensuing silence became uncomfortable. Eventually Afranius said, 'Well, we'll leave the draft with you, and when you address the Senate we'll listen to your words with interest.'

After they had gone, it was Quintus who spoke first. 'At least now we know their price.'

'No,' said Cicero gloomily, 'this isn't their price. This is merely the first instalment of their price – a loan that in their eyes will never be repaid, however much I give them.'

'So what will you do?'

'Well, it's a devil's alternative, is it not? Propose the bill, and everyone will say I'm Pompey's creature; say nothing, and he'll turn against me. Whatever I do, I lose.'

As was often the case, he had not decided which course to take even when we set off to attend the Senate. He always liked to take the temperature of the chamber before he spoke – to listen to its heartbeat like a doctor with a patient. Birria, the scarred gladiator who had accompanied Milo when he visited us in Macedonia, acted as a bodyguard, along with three of his comrades. In addition, I suppose there must have been twenty or thirty of Cicero's clients, who served as a human shield; we felt quite safe. As we walked, Birria boasted to me of their strength: he said that Milo and Pompey had a hundred pairs of gladiators on standby in a barracks on the Field of Mars, ready to deploy at a moment's notice if Clodius tried any of his tricks.

When we reached the Senate building, I handed Cicero the text of his speech. On entering he touched the ancient doorpost and looked around him at what he called 'the greatest room in the world' in thankful amazement that he should have lived to see it again. As he approached his customary position on the front bench nearest to the consuls' dais, the neighbouring senators rose to shake his hand. It was an ill-attended house – not just Pompey was absent, I noticed, but also Clodius, and Marcus Crassus, whose pact with Pompey and Caesar was still the most powerful force in the republic. I wondered why they had stayed away.

The presiding consul that day was Metellus Nepos, the long-standing enemy of Cicero who was nevertheless now publicly reconciled with him – albeit only grudgingly and under pressure from the majority of the Senate. He made no acknowledgement of Cicero's presence but instead rose to announce that a new dispatch had just arrived from Caesar in Further Gaul. The chamber fell silent and the senators listened intently as he read out Caesar's account of yet more brutal encounters with savage and exotically named tribes – the Viromandui, the Atrebates and the Nervii – fought out amid those gloomy echoing forests and swollen impassable rivers. It was clear that Caesar had pushed much further north than any Roman commander before him, almost to the cold north sea, and again his victory was little short of an annihilation: of the sixty thousand men who had made up the army of the Nervii, he claimed to have left alive only five hundred. When Nepos had finished, the house seemed to let out its breath; only then did the consul call on Cicero to speak.

It was a difficult moment to make a speech, and in the event

Cicero mostly restricted himself to a list of thanks. He thanked the consuls. He thanked the Senate. He thanked the people. He thanked the gods. He thanked his brother. He thanked just about everybody except Caesar, whom he did not mention. He thanked especially Pompey ('whose courage, fame and achievements are unapproached in the records of any nation or any age') and Milo ('his whole tribunate was nothing but a firm, unceasing, brave and undaunted championship of my well-being'). But he did not raise either the grain shortage or the proposal to give Pompey extra powers, and as soon as he sat down, Afranius and Milo promptly got up from their places and left the building.

Afterwards, as we walked back to Quintus's house, I noticed that Birria and his gladiators were no longer with us, which I thought was odd, for the danger had hardly gone away. There were a great many beggars among the streams of spectators milling around, and perhaps I was mistaken, but it seemed to me that the number of hostile looks and gestures Cicero attracted was substantially greater than before.

Once we were safely indoors, Cicero said, 'I couldn't do it. How could I take the lead in a controversy I know nothing about? Besides, it wasn't the proper occasion to make a proposal of that sort. All anyone could talk about was Caesar, Caesar, Caesar. Perhaps now they'll leave me alone for a while.'

The day was long and sunny, and Cicero spent much of it in the garden reading or throwing a ball for the family dog, a terrier named Myia, whose antics greatly delighted young Marcus and his nine-year-old cousin, Quintus Junior, the only child of Quintus and Pomponia. Marcus was a sweet, straightforward lad whereas Quintus, spoilt by his mother, had a streak of something nasty in him. But they played together happily enough. Occasionally the roar of the crowd in the Circus Maximus carried up from the valley on the other side of the hill – a hundred thousand voices crying out or groaning in unison: a sound at once exhilarating and frightening, like the growl of a tiger; it made the hairs tingle on my neck and arms. In the middle of the afternoon Quintus suggested that perhaps Cicero should go down to the Circus and show himself to the audience and watch at least one of the races. But Cicero preferred to stay where he was: 'I am tired of exhibiting myself to strangers.'

Because the boys were reluctant to go to bed and Cicero, having been away so long, wished to indulge them, dinner was not served until late. This time, to Pomponia's obvious irritation, he invited me to join them. She did not approve of slaves eating with their masters, and doubtless felt it was her prerogative, not her brother-in-law's, to decide who should be present at her own table. In the event we were six: Cicero and Terentia on one couch, Quintus and Pomponia on another, Tullia and I on the third. Normally Pomponia's brother, Atticus, would have joined us. He was Cicero's closest friend. But a week before Cicero's return he had abruptly left Rome for his estates in Epirus. He pleaded urgent business but I suspect he foresaw the looming family arguments. He always preferred a quiet life.

It was dusk and the slaves were just bringing in tapers to light the lamps and candles when from somewhere in the distance arose a cacophony of whistles, drums, horn blasts and chanting. At first we dismissed it as a passing procession connected with the games. But the noise seemed to come from directly outside the house, where it remained.

Finally Terentia said, 'What on earth is that, do you suppose?'

'You know,' replied Cicero, in a tone of scholarly interest, 'I wonder if it might not be a *flagitatio*. Now there's a quaint custom! Tiro, would you take a look?'

I don't suppose such a thing exists any more, but back in the days of the republic, when people were free to express themselves, a *flagitatio* was the right of citizens who had a grievance, but were too poor to use the courts, to demonstrate outside the house of the person they held responsible. Tonight the target was Cicero. I could hear his name mingled among their chants, and when I opened the door I got the message clear enough:

Whoreson Cicero where's our bread?
Whoreson Cicero stole *our bread!*

A hundred people packed the narrow street, repeating the same phrases over and over, with occasional and saltier variations on the word 'whoreson'. When they noticed me looking at them, a terrific jeer went up. I closed the door, bolted it and went back to the dining room to report.

Pomponia sat up in alarm. 'But what shall we do?'

'Nothing,' said Cicero calmly. 'They're entitled to make their noise. Let them get it off their chests, and when they tire of it they'll go away.'

Terentia asked, 'But why are they accusing *you* of stealing their bread?'

Quintus said, 'Clodius blames the lack of bread on the size of the crowds coming into Rome to support your husband.'

'But the crowds aren't here to support my husband – they've come to watch the games.'

'Brutally honest, as always,' agreed Cicero, 'and even if they *were* here for me, the city has never to my knowledge run short of food on a festival day.'

'So why has it happened now?'

'I imagine someone has sabotaged the supply.'

'Who would do that?'

'Clodius, to blacken my name; or perhaps even Pompey, to give himself a pretext to take over distribution. In any case, there's nothing we can do about it. So I suggest we eat our meal and ignore them.'

But although we tried to carry on as if nothing was happening, and even made jokes and laughed about it, our conversation was strained, and every time there was a lull, it was filled by the angry voices outside:

Cocksucker Cicero stole our bread!
Cocksucker Cicero ate *our bread!*

Eventually Pomponia said, 'Will they go on like that all night?'

Cicero said, 'Possibly.'

'But this has always been a quiet and respectable street. Surely you can do something to stop them?'

'Not really. It's their right.'

'Their right!'

'I believe in the people's rights, if you remember.'

'Good for you. But how am I to sleep?'

Cicero's patience finally gave in. 'Why not put some wax in your ears, madam?' he suggested, then added under his breath, 'I'm sure I'd put some in mine if I were married to you.'

Quintus, who had drunk plenty, tried to stifle his laughter. Pomponia turned on him at once. 'You'll allow him to speak to me in that way?'

'It was only a joke, my dear.'

Pomponia put down her napkin, rose with dignity from her couch and announced that she would go and check on the boys.

Terentia, after a sharp look at Cicero, said that she would join her. She beckoned to Tullia to follow.

When the women had gone, Cicero said to Quintus, 'I'm sorry. I shouldn't have spoken in that way. I'll go and find her and apologise. Besides, she's right: I've brought trouble on your house. We'll move out in the morning.'

'No you won't. I'm master here, and my roof will be your roof for as long as I'm alive. Insults from that rabble are of no concern to me.'

We listened again.

Bumfucker Cicero where's our bread?
Bumfucker Cicero sold *our bread!*

Cicero said, 'It's a marvellously flexible metre, I'll give them that. I wonder how many more versions they can come up with.'

'You know we could always send word to Milo. Pompey's gladiators would clear the street in no time.'

'And put myself even further in their debt? I don't think so.'

We went our separate ways to bed, although I doubt any of us slept much. The demonstration did not cease as Cicero had predicted; if anything, by the following morning it had increased in volume, and certainly in violence, for the mob had started digging up the cobblestones and were hurling them against the walls, or lobbing them over the parapet so that they landed with a crash in the atrium or the garden. It was clear our situation was becoming parlous, and while the women and children sheltered indoors, I climbed up on to the roof with Cicero and Quintus to estimate the danger. Peering cautiously over the ridge tiles, it was possible to see down into the Forum. Clodius's mob was occupying it in force. The senators trying to get to the chamber for the day's session had to run a gauntlet of abuse and chanting. The words drifted up to us, accompanied by the banging of cooking utensils:

Where's our bread?
Where's our bread?
Where's our bread?

Suddenly there was a scream from the floor beneath us. We scrabbled down from the roof and descended to the atrium in time to see a slave fishing out a black-and-white object, like a pouch or a small bag, that had just dropped through the aperture in the roof and fallen into the impluvium. It was the mangled body of Myia, the family dog. The two boys crouched in the corner of the atrium, hands over their ears, crying. Heavy stones battered against the wooden door. And now Terentia turned on Cicero with a bitterness I had never before witnessed: 'Stubborn man! Stubborn, foolish man! Will you do something at last to protect your family? Or must I crawl out yet again on my hands and knees and plead with this scum not to hurt us?'

Cicero swayed backwards in the face of her fury. Just then there was a fresh bout of childish sobbing and he looked across to where Tullia was comforting her brother and cousin. That seemed to settle the issue. He said to Quintus, 'Do you think you can smuggle a slave out through a window at the back?'

'I'm sure we can.'

'In fact best send two, in case one doesn't get through. They should go to Milo's barracks on the Field of Mars and tell the gladiators we need help immediately.'

The messengers were dispatched, and in the meantime Cicero went over to the boys and distracted them by putting his hands around their shoulders and telling them stories of the bravery of the heroes of the republic. After what seemed a long interval, during which the assault on the door increased in fury, we heard a fresh wave of roars from the street, followed by screaming. The gladiators controlled by Milo and Pompey had arrived, and in this way Cicero saved himself and his family, for I do believe that Clodius's men, finding they were unopposed, were fully intending to break into the house and massacre us all. As it was, after only a short battle in the street, the besiegers, who were not nearly so well armed or trained, fled for their lives.

Once we were sure the street was clear, Cicero, Quintus and I went up on to the roof again and watched as the fighting spilled down into the Forum. Columns of gladiators ran in from either side and started laying about them with the flats of their swords. The mob scattered but did not break entirely. A barricade built of trestle tables, benches and shutters from the nearby stores was thrown up between the Temple of Castor and the Grove of Vesta. This line held, and at one point I saw saw the blond-headed figure of Clodius himself directing the fighting, wearing a cuirass over his toga and brandishing a long iron spike. I know it was him because he had his wife, Fulvia, beside him – a woman as fierce and cruel and fond of violence as any man. Here and there fires were lit, and the smoke drifting in the summer heat added to the confusion of the melee. I counted seven bodies, although whether they were dead or merely injured I could not tell.

After a while, Cicero could not bear to watch any longer. Leaving the roof, he said quietly, 'It is the end of the republic.'

We stayed in the house all day as the skirmishing continued in the Forum, and what is most striking to me now is that throughout all this time, less than a mile away, the Roman Games continued uninterrupted, as if nothing unusual were happening.

Violence had become a normal part of politics. By nightfall it was peaceful again, although Cicero prudently decided not to venture out of doors until the following morning, when he walked together with Quintus and an escort of Milo's gladiators to the Senate house. The Forum now was full of citizens who were supporters of Pompey. They called out to Cicero to make sure they had bread again by sending for Pompey to solve the crisis. Cicero, who carried with him the draft of the bill to make Pompey commissioner of grain, made no response.

It was another ill-attended house. Because of the unrest, more than half the senators had stayed away. The only former consuls on the front bench apart from Cicero were Afranius and M. Valerius Messalla. The presiding consul, Metellus Nepos, had been hit by a stone while crossing the Forum the previous day and was wearing a bandage. He brought up the grain riots as the first item on the order paper, and several of the magistrates actually suggested that Cicero himself should take control of the city's supply, at which Cicero made a modest gesture and shook his head.

Nepos said reluctantly, 'Marcus Cicero, do you wish to speak?'

Cicero nodded and rose. 'We none of us needs to be reminded,' he began, 'least of all the gallant Nepos, of the frightful violence that gripped the city yesterday – violence which has at its core a shortage of that most basic of human needs, bread. Some of us believe it was an ill day when our citizens were granted a free dole of corn in the first place, for it is human nature that what starts as gratitude quickly becomes dependency and ends as entitlement. This is the pass we have reached. I do not say we should rescind Clodius's law – it is too late for that: the public's morals are already corrupted, as no doubt he intended. But we must at least ensure that the supply of bread is continuous if we are to have civil order. And there is only one man in our state with the authority and genius of organisation to ensure such a thing, and that is Pompey the Great. Therefore I wish to propose the following resolution . . .'

And here he read out the draft bill I have already quoted, and that part of the chamber which was packed with Pompey's lieutenants rose in acclamation. The rest sat solemn-faced, or muttered angrily, for they had always feared Pompey's lust for power. The cheering was heard outside and taken up by the crowds waiting in the Forum. When they learned that it was Cicero who had proposed the new law, they started clamouring for him to come and address them from the rostra, and all the tribunes – save for two supporters of Clodius – duly sent an invitation to him to speak. When the request was read out in the Senate, Cicero protested that he was not prepared for such an honour. (In fact I had with me a speech he had already written out, and which I was able to give him just before he mounted the steps to the platform.)

He was met by a tremendous ovation, and it was some time before he could make himself heard. When the applause died away, he started to speak, and had just reached the passage in which he thanked the people for their support – *Had I experienced nothing but an unruffled tranquillity, I should have missed the incredible and well-nigh superhuman transports of delight which your kindness now permits me to enjoy* – when who should appear at the edge of the crowd but Pompey. He stood ostentatiously alone – not that he had any need of bodyguards when the Forum was full of his gladiators – and pretended that he had come merely as an ordinary citizen to listen to what Cicero had to say. But of course the people would not permit that, so he allowed himself to be thrust forward to the rostra, which he mounted, and where he embraced Cicero. I had forgotten what a massive physical presence he was: that majestic torso and manly bearing, the famous thick quiff of still-dark hair rising like the beak of a warship above his broad and handsome face.

The occasion demanded flattery, and Cicero rose to it. 'Here is a man,' he said, lifting Pompey's arm, 'who has had, has, and will have, no rival in virtue, sagacity and renown. He gave to me all that he had given to the republic, what no other has ever given to a private friend – safety, security, dignity. To him, fellow citizens, I owe a debt such as it is scarce lawful for one human being to owe to another.'

The applause was prolonged, and Pompey's beam of pleasure was as wide and warm as the sun.

Afterwards he consented to walk back with Cicero to Quintus's house and take a cup of wine. He made no reference to Cicero's exile, no enquiries after his health, no apology for his failure years before to help Cicero stand up to Clodius, which was what had opened the door to the whole disaster in the first place. He talked only of himself and of the future, childlike in his eager anticipation of his grain commissionership and the opportunities it would give him for travel and patronage. 'And you, of course, my dear Cicero, must be one of my fifteen legates – whichever one you like, wherever you want to go. Sardinia? Sicily? Egypt? Africa?'

'Thank you,' said Cicero. 'It is generous of you, but I must decline. My priority now has to be my family – restoring us to our property, comforting my wife and children, revenging us on our enemies and trying to recover our fortune.'

'You'll recover your fortune quicker in the grain business than any other, I assure you.'

'Even so, I must remain in Rome.'

The broad face fell. 'I'm disappointed, I can't pretend otherwise. I want the name of Cicero attached to this commission. It will add weight. What about you?' he said, turning to Quintus. 'You could do it, I suppose.'

Poor Quintus! The last thing he wanted, having returned from two tours of duty in Asia, was to go abroad again and deal with farmers and grain merchants and shipping agents. He squirmed. He protested his unfitness for the office. He looked to Cicero for support. But Cicero could hardly deny Pompey a second request, and this time he said nothing.

'All right: it's done.' Pompey clapped his hands on the armrests of his chair to signal that the matter was settled, and pushed himself up on to his feet. He grunted with the effort and I noticed he was getting rather stout. He was in his fiftieth year, the same age as Cicero. 'Our republic is passing through the most strenuous times,' he said, putting his arms around the brothers' shoulders. 'But we shall come through them, as we always have, and I know that you will both play your part.' He clasped the two men tightly, squeezed them, and held them there, pinned on either side of his commodious chest.

IV

Early the following morning, Cicero and I walked up the hill to inspect the ruins of his house. The palatial building in which he had invested so much of his wealth and prestige had been entirely pulled down; nine tenths of the huge plot was weeds and rubble; it was barely possible to discern the original layout of the walls through the tangled overgrowth. Cicero stooped to pick up one of the scorched bricks poking from the ground. 'Until this place is restored to me, we shall be entirely at their mercy – no money, no dignity, no independence . . . Every time I step outdoors I shall have to look up here and be reminded of my humiliation.' The edges of the brick crumbled in his hands and the red dust trickled through his fingers like dried blood.

At the far end of the plot a statue of a young woman had been set up on top of a high plinth. Fresh offerings of flowers were piled around the base. By consecrating the site as a shrine to Liberty, Clodius believed he had made it inviolable and thus impossible for Cicero to reclaim. The marble figure was shapely in the morning light, with long tresses and a diaphanous dress slipping down to expose a naked breast. Cicero regarded her with his hands on his hips. Eventually he said, 'Surely Liberty is always depicted as a matron with a cap?' I agreed. 'So who, pray, is this hussy? Why, she is no more the embodiment of a goddess than I am!'

Until that moment he had been sombre, but now he started to laugh, and when we returned to Quintus's house he set me the task of discovering where Clodius had acquired the statue. That same day he petitioned the College of Pontiffs to return his property to him on the grounds that the site had been improperly consecrated. A hearing was fixed for the end of the month, and Clodius was summoned to defend his actions.

When the day arrived, Cicero admitted he felt ill-prepared and out of practice. Because his library was still in storage, he had been unable to consult all the legal sources he needed. He was also, I am sure, nervous at the prospect of confronting Clodius face to face. To be beaten by his enemy in a street brawl was one thing; to lose to him in a legal dispute would be a calamity.

The headquarters of the pontifical college were then in the old Regia, said to be the most ancient building in the city. It stood like its modern successor at the point where the Via Sacra divides and enters the Forum, although the noise of that busy spot was entirely deadened by the thickness of its high and windowless walls. The candlelit gloom of the interior made one forget that outside it was bright and sunny. Even the chilly, tomblike air smelt sacred, as if it had been undisturbed for more than six hundred years.

Fourteen of the fifteen pontiffs were seated at the far end of the crowded chamber, waiting for us. The only absentee was their chief, Caesar: his chair, grander than the others, stood empty. Among the priests were several I knew well – Spinther, the consul; Marcus Lucullus, brother of the great general, Lucius, who was said to have lately lost his reason and to be confined to his palace outside Rome; and the two rising young aristocrats, Q. Scipio

Nasica and M. Aemilius Lepidus. And here at last I saw the third triumvir, Crassus. The curious conical hat of animal fur the pontiffs were required to wear robbed him of his most distinctive feature, his baldness. His crafty face was quite impassive.

Cicero took a seat facing them while I sat on a stool at his back, ready to pass any documents he required. Behind us was an audience of eminent citizens, including Pompey. Of Clodius there was no sign. Whispered conversations gradually ceased. The silence grew oppressive. Where was he? Perhaps he might not come. With Clodius one never knew. But then at last he swaggered in, and I felt myself turn cold at the sight of the man who had caused us so much anguish. 'Little Miss Beauty', Cicero used to call him, but in middle age he had outgrown the insult. His luxuriant blond curls were nowadays cut as tight to his skull as a golden helmet; his thick red lips had lost their pout. He appeared hard, lean, disdainful – a fallen Apollo. As is often the case with the bitterest of enemies, he had started out as a friend. But then he had outraged law and morality once too often, by disguising himself as a woman and defiling the sacred rite of the Good Goddess. Cicero had been obliged to give evidence against him, and from that day on Clodius had sworn vengeance. He sat on a chair barely three paces from Cicero, but Cicero continued to stare straight ahead, and the two men never once looked at one another.

The senior pontiff by age was Publius Albinovanus, who must have been eighty. In a quavering voice he read out the point at issue – 'Was the shrine to Liberty, lately erected on the property claimed by M. Tullius Cicero, consecrated in accordance with the rites of the official religion or not?' – and invited Clodius to speak first.

Clodius left it just long enough to indicate his contempt for the whole proceeding, and then slowly got to his feet. 'I am appalled, holy fathers,' he began in his slangy patrician drawl, 'and dismayed, but not surprised, that the exiled murderer Cicero, having brazenly slaughtered Liberty during the time of his consulship, should now seek to compound the offence by tearing down her image . . .'

He brought up every slander that had ever been made against Cicero – his illegal killing of the Catiline conspirators ('the sanction of the Senate is no excuse for executing five citizens without a trial'), his vanity ('if he objects to this shrine, it is mostly out of jealousy since he regards himself as the only god worth worshipping') and his political inconsistency ('this is the man whose return was supposed to mean the restoration of senatorial authority, and yet whose first act was to betray it by winning dictatorial powers for Pompey'). It was not without impact. It would have played well in the Forum. But it failed entirely to address the legal point at issue: was the shrine properly consecrated or not?

He argued for an hour, and then it was Cicero's turn, and it was a measure of how effective Clodius had been that he was obliged to speak extempore to begin with, defending his support for Pompey's grain commission. Only after he had answered that could he turn to making his main case: that the shrine could not be held to be consecrated because Clodius was not legally a tribune when he dedicated it. 'Your transfer from patrician to pleb was sanctioned by no decree of this college, was entered upon in defiance of all pontifical regulations, and must be held to be null and void; and if that is invalid your entire tribunate falls to the ground.' This was dangerous territory: everyone knew it was Caesar who had organised Clodius's adoption as a pleb. I saw Crassus lean forwards listening intently. Sensing the danger, and perhaps remembering his undertaking to Caesar, Cicero swerved away: 'Does this mean I am saying that all Caesar's laws were illegal? By no means; for none of them any longer affects my interests, apart from those aimed with hostile intent against my own person.'

He pressed on, switching to an attack on Clodius's methods, and now his oratory took flight – his arm outstretched, his finger pointing at his enemy, the words almost tumbling from his mouth in his passion: 'Oh, you abominable plague spot of the state, you public prostitute! What harm had you suffered at the hands of my unhappy wife that you harassed, plundered and tortured her so brutally? Or from my daughter, who lost her beloved husband? Or from my little son, who still lies awake weeping at night? But it was not just my family you attacked – you waged a bitter war against my very walls and doorposts!'

However his real coup was to reveal the origins of the statue Clodius had set up. I had tracked down the workmen who had erected it and learnt that the piece had been donated by Clodius's brother Appius, who had carried it off from Tanagra, in Boeotia, where it had graced the tomb of a well-known local courtesan.

The whole room roared with laughter when Cicero revealed this fact. 'So this is his idea of Liberty – a courtesan's likeness, erected over a foreign tomb, stolen by a thief and set up again by a sacrilegious hand! And *she* is the one who drives me from my house? Holy fathers, this property cannot be lost to me without inflicting disgrace upon the state. If you believe that my return to Rome has been a source of pleasure to the immortal gods, to the Senate, to the Roman people and to all of Italy, then let it be your hands that reinstall me in my home.'

Cicero sat to loud murmurs of approval from the distinguished audience. I stole a look at Clodius. He was scowling at the floor. The pontiffs leaned in to confer. Crassus seemed to be doing most of the talking. We had expected a decision at once. But Albinovanus straightened and announced that the college would need more time to consider their verdict: it would be relayed to the Senate the following day. This was a blow. Clodius stood, bent down to Cicero as he passed and hissed, through a false smile, just loud enough for me to hear, 'You will die before that place is rebuilt.' He left the chamber without another word. Cicero pretended nothing had happened. He lingered to chat with many old friends, with the result that we were among the last to leave the building.

Outside the chamber was a courtyard containing the famous white board on which the chief priest by tradition in those days published the state's official news. This was where Caesar's agents posted his *Commentaries*, and here was where we found Crassus standing – ostensibly reading the latest dispatch but in truth waiting to intercept Cicero. He had taken off his cap; here and there little wisps of brown fur still adhered to his high-domed skull.

'So, Cicero,' he said in his unsettlingly jovial manner, 'you were pleased with the effect of your speech?'

'Reasonably, thank you. But my opinion has no value. It's for you and your colleagues to decide.'

'Oh, I thought it effective enough. My only regret is that Caesar wasn't present to hear it.'

'I shall send him a copy.'

'Yes, be sure that you do. Mind you, reading is all very well. But how would he *vote* on the issue? That's what I have to decide.'

'And why do you have to decide that?'

'Because he wishes me to act as his proxy and cast his vote as I think fit. Many colleagues will follow my lead. It is important I get it right.'

He grinned, showing yellow teeth.

'I have no doubt you will. Good day to you, Crassus.'

'Good day, Cicero.'

We passed out of the gate, Cicero cursing under his breath, and had gone only a few paces when Crassus suddenly called out after him, and hurried to catch us up. 'One last thing,' he said. 'In view of these tremendous victories that Caesar has won in Gaul, I wondered if you would be good enough to support a proposal in the Senate for a period of public celebration in his honour.'

'Why does it matter if I support it?'

'Obviously it would add weight, given the history of your relations with Caesar. People would notice. And it would be a noble gesture on your part. I'm sure Caesar would appreciate it.'

'How long would this period of celebration last?'

'Oh . . . fifteen days should just about do it.'

'*Fifteen days*? That's nearly twice as long as Pompey was voted for conquering Spain.'

'Yes, well one could argue that Caesar's victories in Gaul are twice as important as Pompey's in Spain.'

'I'm not sure Pompey would agree.'

'Pompey,' retorted Crassus with emphasis, 'must learn that a triumvirate consists of three men, not one.'

Cicero gritted his teeth and bowed. 'It would be an honour.'

Crassus bowed in return. 'I knew you would do the patriotic thing.'

The following day, Spinther read out the pontiffs' judgement to the Senate: unless Clodius could provide written proof that he had consecrated the shrine on instructions from the Roman people, 'the site can be restored to Cicero without sacrilege'.

A normal man now would have given up. But Clodius wasn't normal. Though he might pretend to be a pleb, he was still a Claudian – a family who took pride in hounding their enemies to the grave. First he lied and told a meeting of the people that the judgement had actually gone in his favour and called on them to defend 'their' shrine. Then, when the consul-designate Marcellinus proposed a motion in the Senate to return to Cicero his three properties – in Rome, Tusculum and Formiae, 'with compensation to restore them to their former state' – Clodius tried to talk out the session, and would have succeeded had he not, after three hours on his feet, been howled down by an exasperated Senate. Nor were his tactics entirely without effect. Frightened of antagonising the plebs, and to Cicero's dismay, the Senate agreed to pay compensation of only two million sesterces to rebuild the house on the Palatine, and just half a million and a quarter of a million respectively for the repairs at Tusculum and Formiae – far below the actual costs.

For the past two years most of Rome's builders and craftsmen had been employed on Pompey's immense development of public buildings on the Field of Mars. Grudgingly – because anyone who has ever employed builders learns quickly never to let them out of one's sight – Pompey agreed to transfer a hundred of his men to Cicero. Work on restoring the Palatine house began at once, and on the first morning of construction Cicero had the great pleasure of swinging an axe at the head of Liberty and smashing it clean off, then crating up the remains and having them delivered to Clodius with his compliments.

I knew Clodius would retaliate, and one morning soon afterwards, when Cicero and I were working on some legal papers in Quintus's tablinum, we heard what sounded like heavy footsteps clumping across the roof. I went out into the street and was lucky not to be struck on the head by bricks dropping from the sky. Panicking workmen came running round the corner and shouted that a gang of Clodius's toughs had overrun the site and were demolishing the new walls and hurling the debris down on to Quintus's house. Just then Cicero and Quintus came out to see what the trouble was, and yet again they had to send a messenger to Milo to request the assistance of his gladiators. It was just as well, for no sooner had the runner gone than there was a series of flashes overhead, and burning brands and lumps of flaming pitch started landing all around us. Fires broke out on the roof. The terrified household had to be evacuated, and everyone, including Cicero and even Terentia, was pressed into service to pass buckets of water, drawn from the street fountains, from hand to hand to try to prevent the house from burning down.

Crassus had a monopoly of the city's fire services, and fortunately for us, he was at his home on the Palatine. He heard the commotion, came out into the street, saw what was going on, and turned up himself in a shabby tunic and slippers, with one of his teams of fire slaves dragging a water tender equipped with pumps and hoses. But for them the building would have been lost; as it was, the damage caused by the water and smoke rendered the place uninhabitable, and we had to move out while it was repaired. We loaded our luggage into carts and, with night coming on, made our way across the valley to the Quirinal hill, to seek temporary refuge in the house of Atticus, who was still away in Epirus. His narrow, ancient house was fine for an elderly bachelor of fixed and moderate habits; it was less ideal for two families with extensive households and warring spouses. Cicero and Terentia slept in separate parts of the building.

Eight days later, as we were walking along the Via Sacra, we heard an outburst of shouts and the sound of running feet behind us, and turned to see Clodius and a dozen of his henchmen flourishing cudgels and even swords, sprinting to attack us. We had the usual bodyguard of Milo's men and they hustled us into the doorway of the nearest house. In their panic, Cicero was pushed to the ground and gashed his head and twisted his ankle but otherwise was unharmed. The startled owner of the house in which we sought refuge, Tettius Damio, took us in and gave us a cup of wine, and Cicero talked calmly to him of poetry and philosophy until we were told that our attackers had been driven off and the coast was clear; then he said his thanks and we continued on our way home.

Cicero was in that state of elation that sometimes follows a close brush with death. His appearance, however, was a different matter – limping, with a bloodied forehead and torn and dirty clothes – and the instant Terentia saw him she cried out in shock. Useless for him to protest that it was nothing, that Clodius had been put to flight, and that his descent to such tactics showed how desperate he was becoming: Terentia would not listen. The siege, the fire and now this: she insisted that they all should leave Rome at once.

Cicero replied mildly, 'You forget, Terentia: I've tried that once, and see where it left us. Our only hope is to stay here and win back our position.'

'And how are you to do that when you can't even walk in safety down a busy street in broad daylight?'

'I shall find a way.'

'And in the meantime, what lives do the rest of us have?'

'Normal lives!' Cicero suddenly shouted back at her. 'We defeat them by leading normal lives! We sleep together as man and wife for a start.'

I glanced away in embarrassment.

Terentia said, 'You wish to know why I keep you from my room? Then look!'

And to Cicero's astonishment and certainly to mine, this most pious of Roman matrons began to unfasten the belt of her dress. She called to her maid to come and help. Turning her back to her husband, she opened her gown and her maid pulled it down all the way from the nape of her neck to the base of her spine, exposing the pale flesh between her thin shoulders, which was savagely criss-crossed by at least a dozen livid red welts.

Cicero stared at the scars, transfixed. 'Who did this to you?'

Terentia pulled the dress back up and her maid knelt to fasten her belt.

'Who did this?' repeated Cicero quietly. 'Clodius?'

She turned to face him. Her eyes were not wet but dry and full of fire. 'Six months ago I went to see his sister, as one woman to another, to plead on your behalf. But Clodia is not a woman: she is a Fury. She told me I was no better than a traitor myself – that my presence defiled her house. She summoned her steward and had him whip me off the premises. She had her louche friends with her. They laughed at my shame.'

'*Your* shame?' cried Cicero. 'The only shame is theirs! You should have told me!'

'Told *you*? You, who greeted the whole of Rome before he greeted his own wife?' She spat out the words. 'You may stay and die in the city if you wish. I shall take Tullia and Marcus to Tusculum and see what lives we can have there.'

The following morning, she and Pomponia left with the

children, and a few days later, amid much mutual shedding of tears, Quintus also departed to buy grain for Pompey in Sardinia. Prowling round the empty house, Cicero was keenly aware of their absence. He told me he felt every blow that Terentia had endured as if it were a lash upon his own back, and he tortured his brain to find some means of avenging her, but he could see no way through, until one day, quite unexpectedly, the glimmer of an opportunity presented itself.

It happened that around this time, the distinguished philosopher Dio of Alexandria was murdered in Rome while under the roof of his friend and host, Titus Coponius. The assassination caused a great scandal. Dio had come to Italy supposedly with diplomatic protection, as the head of a delegation of one hundred prominent Egyptians to petition the Senate against the restoration of their exiled pharaoh, Ptolemy XII, nicknamed 'the Flute Player'.

Suspicion naturally fell on Ptolemy himself, who was staying with Pompey at his country estate in the Alban hills. The Pharaoh, detested by his people for the taxes he levied, was offering the stupendous reward of six thousand gold talents if Rome would secure his restoration, and the effect of this bribe upon the Senate was as dignified as if a rich man had thrown a few coins into a crowd of starving beggars. In the scramble for the honour of overseeing Ptolemy's return, three main candidates had emerged: Lentulus Spinther, the outgoing consul, who was due to become governor of Cilicia and therefore would legally command an army on the borders of Egypt; Marcus Crassus, who yearned to possess the same wealth and glory as Pompey and Caesar; and Pompey himself, who feigned disinterest in the commission but behind the scenes was the most active of the three in trying to secure it.

Cicero had no desire to become embroiled in the affair. There was nothing in it for him. He was obliged to support Spinther, in return for Spinther's efforts to end his exile, and lobbied discreetly behind the scenes on his behalf. But when Pompey asked him to come out and meet the Pharaoh to discuss the death of Dio, he felt unable to turn the summons down.

The last time we had visited the house was almost two years earlier, when Cicero had gone to plead for help in resisting Clodius's attacks. On that occasion Pompey had pretended to be out to avoid seeing him. The memory of his cowardice still rankled with me, but Cicero refused to dwell on it: 'If I do, I shall become bitter, and a man who is bitter hurts no one but himself. We must look to the future.' Now, as we rattled up the long drive to the villa, we passed several groups of olive-skinned men wearing exotic robes and exercising those sinister yellowish prick-eared greyhounds so beloved of the Egyptians.

Ptolemy awaited Cicero with Pompey in the atrium. He was a short, plump, smooth figure, dark-complexioned like his courtiers, and so quietly spoken that one found oneself bending forward to catch what he was saying. He was dressed Roman-style in a toga. Cicero bowed and kissed his hand, and I was invited to do the same. His perfumed fingers were fat and soft like a baby's, but the nails I noticed with disgust were broken and dirty. Coyly peering around him with her arms clasped across his stomach was his young daughter. She had huge charcoal-black eyes and a painted ruby mouth – an ageless slattern's mask even at the age of eleven, or so it seems to me now, but perhaps I am being unfair and allowing my memory to be distorted by what was to come, for this was the future Queen Cleopatra, later to cause such mischief.

Once the niceties were out of the way and Cleopatra had departed with her maids, Pompey came to the point: 'This killing of Dio is starting to become embarrassing, both to me and to His Majesty. And now to cap it all, a murder charge has been brought by Titus Coponius, Dio's host when he was killed, and by his brother Gaius. The whole thing is ridiculous, of course, but apparently they are not to be persuaded out of it.'

'Who is the accused?' enquired Cicero.

'Publius Asicius.'

Cicero paused to remember the name. 'Isn't he one of your estate managers?'

'He is. That's what makes it embarrassing.'

Cicero had the tact not to ask whether Asicius was guilty or not. He considered the matter purely as a lawyer. He said to Ptolemy, 'Until this matter blows over, I would strongly advise Your Majesty to remove yourself as far away from Rome as possible.'

'Why?'

'Because if I were the Coponius brothers, the first thing I should do is issue a subpoena summoning you to give evidence.'

'Can they do that?' asked Pompey.

'They can try. To save His Majesty the embarrassment, I would advise him to be miles away when the writ is served – out of Italy, if possible.'

'But what about Asicius?' said Pompey. 'If he's found guilty, that could look very bad for me.'

'I agree.'

'Then he must be acquitted. You'll take the case, I hope? I'd regard it as a favour.'

This was not what Cicero wanted. But Pompey was insistent,

and in the end, as usual, he had no option but to accede. Before we left, Ptolemy, as a token of his thanks, presented Cicero with a small and ancient jade statue of a baboon, which he explained was Hedj-Wer, the god of writing. I expect it was quite valuable, but Cicero couldn't abide it – 'What do I want with their primitive mud gods?' he complained to me afterwards, and he must have thrown it away; I never saw it again.

Asicius, the accused man, came to see us. He was a former legionary commander who had served with Pompey in Spain and the East. He looked eminently capable of murder. He showed Cicero his summons. The charge was that he had visited Coponius's house early in the morning with a forged letter of introduction. Dio was in the act of opening it when Asicius whipped out a small knife he had concealed in his sleeve and stabbed the elderly philosopher in the neck. The blow had not been immediately fatal. Dio's cries had brought the household running. According to the writ, Asicius had been recognised before he managed to slash his way out of the house.

Cicero did not enquire about the truth of the matter. He merely advised Asicius that his best chance of acquittal lay in a good alibi. Someone would need to vouch that he was with them at the time of the murder – and the more witnesses he could produce and the less connection they had with Pompey, or indeed Cicero, the better.

Asicius said, 'That's easy enough. I have just the fellow lined up: a man known to be on bad terms both with Pompey and yourself.'

'Who?'

'Your old protégé Caelius Rufus.'

'Rufus? What's he doing mixed up in this business?'

'Does it matter? He'll swear I was with him at the hour the

old man was killed. And he's a senator nowadays, don't forget – his word carries weight.'

I half expected Cicero to tell Asicius to find another advocate, such was his distaste for Rufus. But to my surprise he said, 'Very well, tell him to come and see me and we'll depose him.'

After Asicius had gone, Cicero said, 'Surely Rufus is a close friend of Clodius? Doesn't he live in one of his apartments? In fact, isn't Clodia his mistress?'

'She certainly used to be.'

'That was what I thought.' The mention of Clodia made him thoughtful. 'So what is Rufus doing offering an alibi to an agent of Pompey?'

Later that same day, Rufus came to the house. At twenty-five, he was the youngest member of the Senate, and very active in the law courts. It was odd to see him swaggering through the door wearing the purple-striped toga of a senator. Only nine years before, he had been Cicero's pupil. But then he had turned on his former mentor, and eventually beaten him in court by prosecuting Cicero's consular colleague, Hybrida. Cicero could have forgiven him that – he always liked to see a young man on the rise as an advocate – but his friendship with Clodius was a betrayal too far. So he greeted him very icily and pretended to read various documents while Rufus dictated his statement to me. Cicero must have been listening keenly, however, for when Rufus described how he was entertaining Asicius in his house at the time of the killing, and gave as his home address a property on the Esquiline, Cicero suddenly looked up and said, 'But don't you rent a property from Clodius on the Palatine?'

'I've moved,' replied Rufus casually, but there was something too offhand in his tone, and Cicero detected it at once.

He pointed his finger at him and said, 'You've quarrelled.'

'Not at all.'

'You've quarrelled with that devil and his sister from hell. That's why you're doing this favour for Pompey. You always were the most hopeless liar, Rufus. I see through you as clearly as if you were made of water.'

Rufus laughed. He had great charm: he was said to be the most handsome young man in Rome. 'You seem to forget, I don't live in your house any more, Marcus Tullius. I don't have to give an account of my friendships to you.' He swung himself easily on to his feet. He was also very tall. 'Now I've given your client his alibi, as was requested, and our business here is done.'

'Our business will be done when I say it is,' Cicero called after him cheerfully. He did not bother to rise. I showed Rufus out, and when I returned, he was still smiling. 'This is what I've been waiting for, Tiro. I can feel it. He's fallen out with those two monsters, and if that's the case, they won't rest until they've destroyed him. We need to ask around town. Discreetly. Spread some money around if we have to. But we must find out why he's left that house!'

The trial of Asicius ended the day it began. The case boiled down to the word of a few household slaves against that of a senator, and on hearing Rufus's affidavit, the praetor directed the jury to acquit. This was the first of many legal victories for Cicero following his return, and he was soon in high demand, appearing in the Forum most days, just as in his prime.

Throughout this time the violence in Rome worsened. On some days the courts could not sit because of the risks to public safety. A few days after setting upon Cicero in the Via Sacra,

Clodius and his followers attacked the house of Milo and attempted to burn it down. Milo's gladiators drove them off and retaliated by occupying the voting pens on the Field of Mars in a vain attempt to prevent Clodius's election as aedile.

Cicero sensed opportunity in the chaos. One of the new tribunes, Cannius Gallus, laid a bill before the people demanding that Pompey alone should be entrusted with restoring Ptolemy to the throne of Egypt. The bill so incensed Crassus that he actually paid Clodius to organise a popular campaign against Pompey. And when Clodius eventually won the aedileship, he used his powers as a magistrate to summon Pompey to give evidence in an action he brought against Milo.

The hearing took place in the Forum in front of many thousands. I watched it with Cicero. Pompey mounted the rostra, but had hardly uttered more than a few sentences when Clodius's supporters started to drown him out with catcalls and slow handclaps. There was a kind of heroism in the way that Pompey simply put his shoulders down and went on reading out his text, even though no one could hear him. This must have gone on for an hour or more, and then Clodius, who was standing a few feet along the rostra, started really working up the crowd against him.

'Who's starving the people to death?' he shouted.

'Pompey!' roared his followers.

'Who wants to go to Alexandria?'

'Pompey!'

'Whom do you want to go?'

'Crassus!'

Pompey looked as if he had been struck by lightning. Never had he been insulted in such a way. The crowd started heaving like a stormy sea, one side pushing against the other, with little eddies of scuffles breaking out here and there, and suddenly from the back, ladders appeared and were passed rapidly over our heads to the front, where they were thrown up against the rostra and a group of ruffians began scaling it – Milo's ruffians, it transpired, for the moment they reached the platform they charged at Clodius and hurled him off it, a good twelve feet down on to the spectators. There were cheers and screams. I didn't see what happened after that, as Cicero's attendants hustled us out of the Forum and away from danger, but we learned later that Clodius had escaped unharmed.

The following evening, Cicero went off to dine with Pompey and came home rubbing his hands with pleasure. 'Well, if I'm not mistaken, that's the beginning of the end of our so-called triumvirate, at least as far as Pompey's concerned. He swears Crassus is behind a plot to murder him, says he'll never trust him again, threatens that if necessary Caesar will have to return to Rome to answer for his mischief in creating Clodius in the first place and destroying the constitution. I've never seen him in such a rage. As for me, he couldn't have been friendlier, and assures me that whatever I do, I can rely on his support.

'But better even than that – when he was deep in his cups, he finally told me why Rufus has switched allegiance. I was right: there's been the most tremendous falling-out between him and Clodia – so much so that she's claiming he tried to poison her! Naturally, Clodius has taken his sister's side, thrown Rufus out of his house and called in his debts. So Rufus has had to turn to Pompey in the hope of some Egyptian gold to pay off what he owes. Isn't it all marvellous?'

I agreed it was all marvellous, though I couldn't see why it warranted quite such ecstasies of joy.

Cicero said, 'Bring me the praetors' lists, quick!'

I went and fetched the schedule of court cases that were due to be heard over the next seven days. Cicero told me to look up when Rufus was next due to appear. I ran my finger down the various courts and cases until I found his name. He was scheduled to begin a prosecution in the constitutional court for bribery in five days' time.

Cicero said, 'Who is he prosecuting?'

'Bestia.'

'Bestia! That villain!'

Cicero lay back on the couch in his familiar posture when cooking up a scheme, with his hands clasped behind his head, staring at the ceiling. L. Calpurnius Bestia was an old enemy of his, one of Catilina's tame tribunes, lucky not to have been executed for treason with his five fellow conspirators. Yet here he was, apparently still active in public life, being prosecuted for buying votes during the recent praetorian elections. I wondered what possible interest Bestia could hold for Cicero, and after a long period during which he said nothing, I ventured to ask him.

His voice seemed to come from a long way away, as if I had interrupted him in a dream. 'I was just thinking,' he said slowly, 'that I might offer to defend him.'

V

The next morning, Cicero went to call on Bestia, taking me with him. The old rogue had a house on the Palatine. His expression when Cicero was shown in was comical in its astonishment. He had with him his son Atratinus, a clever lad who had only just donned the toga of manhood and was eager to begin his career. When Cicero announced that he wished to discuss his impending prosecution, Bestia naturally assumed he was about to receive another writ and grew quite menacing. It was only thanks to the intervention of the boy, who was in awe of Cicero, that he was persuaded to sit down and listen to what his distinguished visitor had to say.

Cicero said, 'I have come here to offer my services in your defence.'

Bestia gaped at him. 'And why in the name of the gods would you do that?'

'I have undertaken later in the month to appear on behalf of Publius Sestius. Is it true that you saved his life during the fighting in the Forum when I was in exile?'

'I did.'

'Well then, Bestia, chance for once throws us on the same side. If I appear for you, I can describe the incident at great length and that will help me lay the ground for Sestius's defence, which will be heard by the same court. Who are your other advocates?'

'Herennius Balbus to open, and then my son here to follow.'

'Good. Then with your agreement I'll speak third and do the winding-up – my usual preference. I'll put on a good show, don't worry. We should have the whole thing wrapped up in a day or two.'

Bestia by this time had moved from an attitude of deep suspicion to one of hardly being able to believe his luck that the greatest advocate in Rome was willing to speak on his behalf. And when Cicero strolled into court a couple of days later, his appearance provoked gasps of surprise. Rufus in particular was stunned. The very fact that Cicero, of all people – whom Bestia had once plotted to murder – should now appear as his supporter more or less guaranteed his acquittal. And so it proved. Cicero made an eloquent speech, the jury voted, and Bestia was found not guilty.

As the court was rising, Rufus came over to Cicero. For once his normal charm was gone. He had been counting on an easy victory; instead his career had been checked. He said bitterly, 'Well I hope you're satisfied, although such a triumph brings you nothing but dishonour.'

'My dear Rufus,' replied Cicero, 'have you learnt nothing? There is no more honour in a legal dispute than there is in a wrestling match.'

'What I've *learnt*, Cicero, is that you still bear me a grudge and will stop at nothing to gain revenge on your enemies.'

'Oh my dear, poor boy, I don't regard *you* as my enemy. You're not important enough. I have bigger fish to catch.'

That really infuriated Rufus. He said, 'Well, you can tell your client that as he insists on continuing as a candidate, I shall bring a second charge against him tomorrow – and the next time you rise in his defence, if you dare, I give you fair warning: I shall be waiting for you!'

He was as good as his word: very soon afterwards, Bestia and his son brought the new writ round to show Cicero. Bestia said hopefully, 'You'll defend me again, I hope?'

'Oh no, that would be very foolish. One can't spring the same surprise twice. No, I'm afraid I can't be your advocate again.'

'So what's to be done?'

'Well, I can tell you what *I'd* do in your place.'

'And what's that?'

'I'd lay a counter-suit against him.'

'For what?'

'Political violence. That takes precedence over bribery cases. Therefore you'll have the advantage of putting him on trial first, before he can get you into court.'

Bestia conferred with his son. 'We like the sound of it,' he announced. 'But can we really make a case against him? Has he actually committed political violence?'

'Of course,' said Cicero. 'Didn't you hear? He was involved in the murder of several of those Egyptian envoys. Ask around town,' he continued. 'You'll find lots of people willing to tell tales. There's one man in particular you should go to see, although of course you never heard the name from me: you'll understand why the moment I say it. You should talk to Clodius, or better still to that sister of his. I hear Rufus used to be her lover, and when his ardour cooled, he tried to get rid of her with poison. You know what that family is like – they love their vengeance. You should offer to let them join your suit. With the Claudii beside you, you'll be unbeatable. But remember – you never got any of this from me.'

I had worked very closely with Cicero for many years. I had grown used to his clever tricks. I did not think him capable of surprising me any more. That day proved me wrong.

Bestia thanked him profusely, swore to be discreet and went off full of purpose. A few days later, a notice to prosecute was posted in the Forum: he and Clodius had combined forces to charge Rufus with both the attacks on the Alexandrian envoys and the attempted murder of Clodia. The news caused a sensation. Almost everyone believed that Rufus would be found guilty and sentenced to exile for life, and that the career of Rome's youngest senator was over.

When I showed him the list of charges, Cicero said, 'Oh dear. Poor Rufus. He must be feeling very wretched. I think we should visit him and cheer him up.'

And so we set off to find the house that Rufus was renting. Cicero, who at the age of fifty was starting to feel stiff in his limbs on cold winter mornings, rode in a litter, while I walked alongside him. Rufus turned out to be lodging on the second floor of an apartment block in the less fashionable part of the Esquiline, not far from the gate where the undertakers ply their trade. The place was gloomy even at midday, and Cicero had to ask the slaves to light candles. In the dim light we discovered their master in a drunken sleep, curled up beneath a pile of blankets on a couch. He groaned and rolled over and begged to be left alone, but Cicero dragged away his covers and told him to get up on his feet.

'What's the point? I'm finished!'

'You're not finished. Quite the contrary: we have that woman exactly where we want her.'

'We?' repeated Rufus, squinting up at Cicero through bloodshot eyes. 'When you say "we", does that imply you're on my side?'

'Not merely on your side, my dear Rufus. I am going to be your advocate!'

'Wait,' said Rufus. He touched his hand gently to his forehead, as if checking it was still intact. 'Wait a moment – did you *plan* all this?'

'Consider yourself to have been given a political education. And now let us agree that the slate is wiped clean between us, and concentrate on beating our common enemy.' Rufus began to swear. Cicero listened for a while, then interrupted him. 'Come, Rufus. This is a good bargain for us both. You'll get that harpy off your back once and for all, and I'll satisfy the honour of my wife.'

Cicero held out his hand. At first Rufus recoiled. He pouted and shook his head and muttered. But then he must have realised he had no choice. At any rate, eventually he extended his own hand, Cicero shook it warmly, and with that the trap he had laid for Clodia snapped shut.

The trial was scheduled to take place at the start of April, which meant it would coincide with the opening of the Festival of the Great Mother, with its famous parade of castrated holy men. Even so, there was no doubting which would be the greater attraction, especially when Cicero's name was announced as one of Rufus's advocates. The others were to be Rufus himself, and Crassus, in whose household Rufus had also served an internship as a young man. I am certain Crassus would have preferred not to have performed this service for his former protégé, especially given the presence of Cicero on the bench beside him, but the rules of patronage placed him under a heavy obligation. On the other side once again were young Atratinus and Herennius

Balbus – both furious at Cicero's duplicity, not that he cared a fig for their opinion – and Clodius, representing the interests of his sister. No doubt he too would have preferred to be at the Great Mother's festivities, which he, as aedile, was supposed to oversee, but he could hardly have backed out of the trial when his family's honour was at stake.

I cherish my memories of Cicero at this time, in the weeks before Rufus's trial. He seemed once again to hold all the threads of life in his hands, just as he had in his prime. He was active in the courts and in the Senate. He went out to dinner with his friends. He even moved back in to the house on the Palatine. True, it was not entirely finished. The place still reeked of lime and paint; workmen trailed mud in from the garden. But Cicero was so delighted to be back in his own home, he did not care. His furniture and books were fetched out of storage, the household gods were placed on the altar, and Terentia was summoned back from Tusculum with Tullia and Marcus.

Terentia entered the house cautiously and moved between the rooms with her nose wrinkled in distaste at the pungent smell of fresh plaster. She had never much cared for the place from the start, and was not about to change her opinion now. But Cicero persuaded her to stay: 'That woman who caused you so much pain will never harm you again. She may have laid a hand on you. But I promise you: I shall flay her alive.'

He also, to his great delight, after two years' separation, heard that Atticus had at last returned from Epirus. The moment he reached the city gates, he came straight round to inspect Cicero's rebuilt house. Unlike Quintus, Atticus had not changed at all. His smile was still as constant, his charm as thickly laid-on – 'Tiro, *my dear fellow*, thank you *so much* for taking care of my oldest friend *so devotedly*' – his figure as trim, his silvery hair as sleek and well cut. The only difference was that now he trailed a shy young woman at least thirty years his junior, whom he introduced to Cicero . . . as his fiancée! I thought Cicero might faint with shock. Her name was Pilia. She was of an obscure family, with no money and no particular beauty either – just a quiet, homely country girl. But Atticus was besotted. At first Cicero was greatly put out. 'It's ridiculous,' he grumbled to me when the couple had gone. 'He's three years older even than I am! Is it a wife he's after or a nurse?' I suspect he was mostly offended because Atticus had never mentioned her before, and worried that she might disrupt the easy intimacy of their friendship. But Atticus was so obviously happy, and Pilia so modest and cheerful, that Cicero soon came round to her, and sometimes I saw him glancing at her in an almost wistful way, especially when Terentia was being shrewish.

Pilia quickly became a close friend and confidante of Tullia. They were the same age and of similar temperaments, and I often saw them walking together, holding hands. Tullia had been a widow by this time for a year and encouraged by Pilia now declared herself ready to take a new husband. Cicero made enquiries about a suitable match and soon came up with Furius Crassipes – a young, rich, good-looking aristocrat, of an ancient but undistinguished family, eager for a career as a senator. He had also recently inherited a handsome house and a park just beyond the city walls. Tullia asked me for my opinion.

I said, 'What I think doesn't matter. The question is: do you like him?'

'I think I do.'

'Do you *think* you do or are you sure?'

'I'm sure.'

'Then that is enough.'

In truth I thought Crassipes was more in love with the idea of Cicero as a father-in-law than Tullia as a wife. But I kept this view to myself. A wedding date was fixed.

Who knows the secrets of another's marriage? Certainly not I. Cicero, for example, had long complained to me of Terentia's peevishness, of her obsession with money, of her superstition and her coldness and her rude tongue. And yet the whole of this elaborate legal spectacle he had contrived to be enacted in the centre of Rome was for her – his means of making amends for all the wrongs she had suffered because of the failure of his career. For the first time in their long marriage, he laid at her feet the greatest gift he had to offer her: his oratory.

Not that she wanted to listen to it, mind you. She had hardly ever heard him speak in public, and never in the law courts, and had no desire to start now. It took considerable amounts of Cicero's eloquence simply to persuade her to leave the house and come down to the Forum on the morning he was due to speak.

By this time the trial was in its second day. The prosecution had already laid out its case, Rufus and Crassus had responded, and only Cicero's address remained to be heard. He had sat through the other speeches with barely concealed impatience; the details of the case were irrelevant to him and the advocates bored him. Atratinus, in his disconcertingly piping voice, had portrayed Rufus as a libertine, addicted to pleasure, sunk in debt, 'a pretty-boy Jason in perpetual search of a golden fleece' who had been paid by Ptolemy to intimidate the Alexandrian envoys and arrange the murder of Dio. Clodius had spoken next and described how his sister, 'this chaste and distinguished widow', had been tricked by Rufus into giving him gold out of the goodness of her heart – money she had thought was to finance public entertainment but which he had used to bribe Dio's assassins – and how Rufus had then provided poison to her slaves to kill her and so cover his traces. Crassus, in his plodding way, and Rufus, with typical verve, had rebutted each of the charges. But the balance of opinion was that the prosecution had made its case and that the young reprobate was likely to be found guilty. This was the state of play when Cicero arrived in the Forum.

I conducted Terentia to her seat while he made his way through the thousands of spectators and went up the steps of the temple to the court. Seventy-five jurors had been empanelled. Beside them sat the praetor Domitius Calvinus with his lictors and scribes. To the left was the prosecution, with their witnesses arrayed behind them. And there in the front row, modestly attired but very much the centre of attention, was Clodia. She was almost forty but still beautiful, a grande dame with those famous huge dark eyes of hers that could invite intimacy one moment and threaten murder the next. She was known to be excessively close to Clodius – so much so that they had often been accused of incest. I saw her head turn very slightly to follow Cicero as he walked across to his place. Her expression was one of disdainful indifference. But she must have wondered what was coming.

Cicero adjusted the folds of his toga. He had no notes. A hush fell over the vast throng. He glanced across to where Terentia was sitting. Then he turned to the jury. 'Gentlemen, anyone who doesn't know our laws and customs might wonder why we are here, during a public festival, when all the other courts are suspended, to judge a young man of hard work and brilliant intellect – especially when it turns out he is being attacked by a person he once prosecuted, and by the wealth of a courtesan.'

At that, a great roar went rolling around the Forum, like the sound the crowd makes at the start of the games when a famous gladiator makes his first thrust. This was what they had come to see! Clodia stared straight ahead as if she had been turned to marble. I am sure that she and Clodius would never have brought their prosecution if they had thought there was a chance of Cicero being against them; but there was no escape now.

Having laid down a marker of what was to come, Cicero then proceeded to build his case. He conjured a picture of Rufus that was unrecognisable to those of us who knew him – of a sober, hard-working servant of the commonwealth whose main misfortune was to be 'born not unhandsome', and thus to have come to the attention of Clodia, 'the Medea of the Palatine', into whose neighbourhood he had moved. He stood behind the seated Rufus and clasped his hand on his shoulder. 'His change of residence has been for this young man the cause of all his misfortunes and of all the gossip, for Clodia is a woman not only of noble birth but of notoriety, of whom I will say no more than what is necessary to refute the charges.'

He paused to allow the sense of anticipation to build. 'Now, as many of you will know, I am on terms of great personal enmity with this woman's husband . . .' He stopped and snapped his fingers in exasperation. 'I meant to say brother: I always make that mistake.'

His timing was perfect, and to this day even people who otherwise know nothing of Cicero still quote that joke. Almost everyone in Rome had felt the arrogance of the Claudii at some point down the years; to see them ridiculed was irresistible. Its effect not just on the audience but on the jury and even the praetor was wonderful to behold.

Terentia turned to me in puzzlement. 'Why is everyone laughing?'

I did not know what to reply.

When order was restored, Cicero continued, with menacing friendliness: 'Well, I am truly sorry to have to make this woman an enemy, especially as she is every other man's friend. So let me first ask her whether she prefers me to deal with her severely, in the old-fashioned manner, or mildly, in the modern way?'

And then, to her evident horror, Cicero actually started walking across the court towards her. He was smiling, hand extended, inviting her to choose – the tiger playing with its prey. He halted barely a pace away from her.

'If she prefers the old method, then I must call up from the dead one of those full-bearded men of antiquity to rebuke her . . .'

I have often pondered what Clodia should have done at this point. On reflection I believe her best course would have been to laugh along with Cicero – to try to win over the sympathy of the crowd by some piece of pantomime that would have shown she was entering into the spirit of the joke. But she was a Claudian. Never before had anyone dared openly to laugh at her, let alone the common people in the Forum. She was outraged, probably panicking, and so she responded in the worst way possible: she turned her back on Cicero like a sulky child.

He shrugged. 'Very well, let me call up a member of her own family – to be specific, Appius Claudius the Blind. He will feel the least sorrow since he won't be able to see her. If he were to appear, this is what he would say . . .'

And now Cicero addressed her in a ghostly voice, his eyes closed, his arms raised straight out in front of him; even Clodius started laughing. 'Oh woman, what hast thou to do with Rufus, this stripling who is young enough to be thy son? Why hast thou been either so intimate with him as to give him gold, or caused such jealousy as to warrant the administering of poison? Why was Rufus so closely connected with thee? Is he a kinsman? A relative by marriage? A friend of thine late husband? None of these! What else could it have been then between you two except reckless passion? O woe! Was it for this that I brought water to Rome, that thou mightest use it after thy incestuous debauches? Was it for this that I built the Appian Way, that thou mightest frequent it with a train of other women's husbands?'

With that, the ghost of old Appius Claudius evaporated and Cicero addressed Clodia's turned back in his normal voice. 'But if you prefer a more congenial relative, let us speak to you in the voice of your youngest brother over there, who loves you *most* dearly – who, as a boy, in fact, being of a nervous disposition and prey to night terrors, always used to get into bed with his big sister. Imagine him saying to you' – and now Cicero perfectly imitated Clodius's fashionable slouching stance and plebeian drawl – 'what's there to worry about, sister? So what if you fancied some young fellow. He was handsome. He was tall. You couldn't get enough of him. You knew you were old enough to be his mother. But you were rich. So you bought him things to purchase his affection. It didn't last long. He called you a hag. Well, forget him – just find yourself another one, or two, or ten. After all, that's what you usually do.'

Clodius was no longer laughing. He looked at Cicero as if he would like to clamber over the benches of the court and strangle him. But the audience were laughing right enough. I glanced around and saw men and women with tears running down their cheeks. Empathy is the essence of the orator's art. Cicero had that immense crowd entirely on his side, and after he had made them laugh with him, it was easy for him to make them share his outrage as he moved in for the kill.

'I am now forgetting, Clodia, the wrongs you have done me; I am putting aside the memory of what I have suffered; I pass over your cruel actions towards my family during my absence; but I ask you this: if a woman without a husband opens her house to all men's desires, and publicly leads the life of a courtesan; if she is in the habit of attending dinner parties with men who are perfect strangers; if she does this in Rome, in her park outside the city walls, and amid all those crowds on the Bay of Naples; if her embraces and caresses, her beach parties, her water parties, her dinner parties, proclaim her to be not only a courtesan, but also a shameless and wanton courtesan – if she does all that and a young man should be discovered consorting with this woman, should he be considered the corrupter or the corrupted, the seducer or the seduced?

'This whole charge arises from a hostile, infamous, merciless, crime-stained, lust-stained house. An unstable and angry wanton of a woman has forged this accusation. Gentlemen of the jury: do not allow Marcus Caelius Rufus to be sacrificed to her lust. If you restore Rufus in safety to me, to his family, to the state, you will find in him one pledged, devoted and bound to you and to your children; and it is you above all, gentlemen, who will reap the rich and lasting fruits of all his exertions and labours.'

And with that it was over. For a moment Cicero stood there – one hand stretched towards the jury, the other towards Rufus – and there was silence. Then some great subterranean force seemed to rise from beneath the Forum, and an instant later the air began to tremble as several thousand pairs of feet stamped the ground and the crowd roared their approval. Someone started pointing repeatedly at Clodia and shouting, 'Whore! Whore! Whore!' and very quickly the chant was taken up all around us, the arms flashing out again and again: 'Whore! Whore! Whore!'

Clodia looked out blank-faced with incredulity across this sea of hatred. She didn't seem to notice that her brother had moved across the court and was standing beside her. But then he grasped her elbow and that seemed to jolt her out of her reverie. She glanced up at him, and finally, after some gentle coaxing, she allowed herself to be led off the platform and out of sight and into an obscurity from which it is fair to say she never again emerged as long as she lived.

Thus did Cicero exact his revenge on Clodia and reclaim his place as the dominant voice in Rome. It is hardly necessary to add that Rufus was acquitted and that Clodius's loathing of Cicero was redoubled. 'One day,' he hissed, 'you will hear a sound behind you, and when you turn, I shall be there, I promise you.' Cicero laughed at the crudeness of the threat, knowing he was too popular for Clodius to dare to attack him – at least for now. As for Terentia, although she deplored the vulgarity of Cicero's jokes and was appalled by the rudeness of the mob, nevertheless she was pleased by the utter social annihilation of her enemy, and as she and Cicero walked home, she took his arm – the first time I had witnessed such a public gesture of affection for years.

The following day, when Cicero went down the hill to attend a meeting of the Senate, he was mobbed both by the ordinary people and by the scores of senators waiting outside the chamber for the session to begin. As he received the congratulations of his peers, he looked exactly as he had done in his days of power, and I could see that he was quite intoxicated by his reception.

As it happened, this was the Senate's final meeting before it rose for its annual vacation, and there was a febrile mood in the air. After the haruspices had ruled the heavens propitious, and just as the senators started to file in for the start of the debate, Cicero beckoned me over and pointed on the order paper to the main subject to be discussed that day: the grant of forty million sesterces from the treasury to Pompey, to finance his grain purchases.

'This could be interesting.' He nodded to the figure of Crassus, just then stalking in to the chamber, wearing a grim expression. 'I had a word with him about it yesterday. First Egypt, now this – he's in a rage at Pompey's megalomania. The thieves are at one another's throats, Tiro: there could be an opportunity for mischief here.'

'Be careful,' I warned him.

'Oh dear, yes: "Be careful!"' he mocked, and tapped me on the head with the rolled-up order paper. 'Well, I have a little power after yesterday, and you know what I always say: power is for using.'

With that he went off cheerfully into the Senate building.

I had not been intending to stay for the session, having much work to do in preparing Cicero's speech of the previous day for publication. But now I changed my mind and went and stood at the doorway. The presiding consul was Cornelius Lentulus Marcellinus, a patriotic aristocrat of the old sort – hostile to Clodius, supportive of Cicero and suspicious of Pompey. He made sure to call a series of speakers who all denounced the granting of such a huge sum to Pompey. As one pointed out, there was no money available in any case, every spare copper being swallowed up implementing Caesar's law that gave the Campanian lands to Pompey's veterans and the urban poor. The house grew rowdy. Pompey's supporters heckled his opponents. His opponents shouted back. (Pompey himself was not allowed to be present, as the grain commission conveyed imperium – a power that barred its holders from entering the Senate.) Crassus looked gratified with the way things were going. Finally, Cicero indicated that he wished to speak, and the house became quiet as senators leaned forwards to hear what he had to say.

'Honourable members,' he said, 'will recall that it was on my proposal that Pompey was given this grain commission in the first place, so I am hardly going to oppose it now. We cannot order a man to do a job one day, and then deny him the means with which to accomplish it the next.' Pompey's supporters murmured loud assent. Cicero held up his hand. 'However, as has been eloquently pointed out, our resources are finite. The treasury cannot pay for everything. We cannot be expected to buy grain all over the world to feed our citizens for nothing and at the same time give free farms to soldiers and plebs. When Caesar passed his law, even he, with all his great powers of foresight, can hardly have imagined that a day was coming – and coming very soon – when veterans and the urban poor would have no need of farms to grow grain, because the grain would simply be given to them for nothing.'

'Oh!' shouted the benches of the aristocrats in delight. 'Oh! Oh!' And they pointed at Crassus, who, along with Pompey and Caesar, was one of the architects of the land laws. Crassus was staring hard at Cicero, although his face was impassive and it was impossible to tell what he was thinking.

'Would it not be prudent,' continued Cicero, 'in the light of changing circumstances, for this noble house to look again at the legislation passed during the consulship of Caesar? Now is obviously not the right occasion to discuss it fully, complex as the question is, and conscious as I am that the house is eager to rise for the recess. I would therefore propose that the issue be placed on the order paper at the first available opportunity when we reconvene.'

'I second that!' shouted Domitius Ahenobarbus, a patrician who was married to Cato's sister, and who hated Caesar so much he had recently called for him to be stripped of his command in Gaul.

Several dozen other aristocrats also jumped up clamouring to add their support. Pompey's men seemed too confused to react: after all, the main thrust of Cicero's speech had seemed to be in support of their chief. It was indeed a tidy piece of mischief that Cicero had wrought, and when he sat down and glanced along the aisle in my direction, I almost fancy he winked at me. The consul held a whispered conference with his scribes and then announced that in view of the obvious support for Cicero's motion, the issue would be debated on the Ides of May. With that the house was adjourned and the senators started moving towards the exit – none quicker than Crassus, who almost knocked me flying in his eagerness to get away.

Cicero, too, was determined to have a holiday, feeling he deserved one after seven months of non-stop strain and labour, and he had in mind the ideal destination. A wealthy tax farmer for whom he had done much legal work had lately died, leaving Cicero some property in his will – a small villa on the Bay of Naples, at Cumae, between the sea and the Lucrine Lake. (In those days, I should add, it was illegal to accept direct payment for one's services as an advocate, but permissible to receive legacies; the rule was not always strictly observed.) Cicero had never seen the place but had heard that it enjoyed one of the loveliest aspects in the region. He proposed to Terentia that they should travel to inspect it together, and she agreed, although when she discovered I was to be included in the party, she plunged into another of her sulks.

'I know how it will be,' I overheard her complaining to Cicero. 'I shall be left alone all day while you are closeted with your official wife!'

He made some soothing reply to the effect that no such thing would happen, and I was careful to keep out of her way.

On the eve of our departure, Cicero gave a dinner for his future son-in-law, Crassipes, who happened to mention that Crassus, to whom he was very close, had left Rome in a hurry the previous day, telling no one where he was going. Cicero said, 'No doubt he's heard of some elderly widow in a remote spot who is at death's door and who might be persuaded to part with her property cheaply.'

Everyone laughed apart from Crassipes, who looked very prim. 'I am sure he is simply taking a vacation, like everyone else.'

'Crassus doesn't take holidays – there's no profit in them.' Then Cicero raised his cup and proposed a toast to Crassipes and Tullia. 'May their union be long and happy and blessed with many children – for preference I should like three at least.'

'Father!' exclaimed Tullia. She laughed and blushed and looked away.

'What?' asked Cicero, with an air of innocence. 'I have the grey hairs and now I need the grandchildren to go with them.'

He rose from the table early. Before he left for the south he wanted to see Pompey. In particular he wanted to plead the case for Quintus to be allowed to relinquish his legateship and return home from Sardinia. He travelled to Pompey's in a litter but ordered the porters to go slowly so that I could walk alongside and we could have some conversation. It was getting dark. We had to travel a mile or so, beyond the city walls, to the Pincian hill, where Pompey had his new suburban villa – or palace would be a better word for it – looking down on his vast complex of temples and theatres then nearing completion on the Field of Mars.

The great man was dining alone with his wife, and we had to wait for them to finish. In the vestibule a team of slaves was busy transferring piles of luggage to half a dozen wagons drawn up in the courtyard – so many trunks of clothes and boxes of tableware and carpets and furniture and even statues that it looked as if Pompey were planning to set up a new home somewhere. Eventually the couple appeared and Pompey presented Julia to Cicero, who in turn presented me to her.

'I remember you,' she said to me, although I'm sure she didn't. She was only seventeen but very gracious. She possessed her father's exquisite manners, and also something of his piercing way of looking at one, so that I had a sudden, disconcerting memory of Caesar's naked hairless torso reclining on the massage table at his headquarters in Mutina: I had to shut my eyes to banish it.

She left almost at once, pleading the need to get a good night's sleep before her travels the next day. Pompey kissed her hand – he was famously devoted to her – and took us through into his study. This was a vast room the size of a house, crammed with trophies from his many campaigns, including what he insisted was the cloak of Alexander the Great. He sat on a couch made out of a stuffed crocodile, which he said Ptolemy had given him, and invited Cicero to take the seat opposite.

Cicero said, 'You look as though you are embarking on a military expedition.'

'That's what comes of travelling with one's wife.'

'Might I ask where you're going?'

'Sardinia.'

'Ah,' said Cicero, 'that's a coincidence. I wanted to ask you about Sardinia.' And he proceeded to make an eloquent case for his brother to be allowed home, citing three reasons in particular – the length of time he had been away, his need to spend time with his son (who was turning into a troubled boy) and his preference for military rather than civil command.

Pompey heard him out, stroking his chin, reclining on his Egyptian crocodile. 'If that's what you want,' he said. 'Yes, he can come back. You're right anyway – he isn't much good at administration.'

'Thank you. I'm obliged to you, as always.'

Pompey regarded Cicero with crafty eyes. 'So I hear you caused a stir in the Senate the other day.'

'Only on your behalf – I was simply trying to secure the funds for your commission.'

'Yes, but by challenging Caesar's laws.' He wagged his finger in reproach. 'That's naughty of you.'

'Caesar is not a god, infallible; his laws have not come down to us from Mount Olympus. Besides, if you'd been there and seen the pleasure Crassus was taking in all the attacks on you, I believe you would have wanted me to find some way to wipe the smile from his face. And by criticising Caesar, I certainly did that.'

Pompey brightened at once. 'Oh well, I'm with you there!'

'Believe me, Crassus's ambition and disloyalty to you have been far more destabilising to the commonwealth than anything *I* have done.'

'I agree entirely.'

'In fact I'd suggest that if your alliance with Caesar is threatened by anyone, it's him.'

'How is that?'

'Well, I don't understand how Caesar can stand back and allow him to plot against you in this way, especially letting him employ Clodius. Surely as your father-in-law he owes his first duty to you? If Crassus carries on like this, he will sow much discord, I predict it now.'

'He will.' Pompey nodded. He looked crafty again. 'You're right, of course.' He stood, and Cicero followed suit. He took Cicero's hand in both his immense paws. 'Thank you for coming to see me, my old friend. You have given me much food for thought during my voyage to Sardinia. We must write to one another often. Where exactly will you be?'

'Cumae.'

'Ah! I envy you. Cumae – the most beautiful spot in Italy.'

Cicero was well pleased with his night's work. On the way home he said to me, 'This triple alliance of theirs can't last. It defies nature. All I have to do is keep chipping away at it, and sooner or later the whole rotten edifice will come crashing down.'

We left Rome at first light – Terentia, Tullia and Marcus all in the same carriage, along with Cicero, who was in great good humour – and made quick progress, stopping first for a night at Tusculum, which Cicero was glad to find habitable again, and then at the family estate in Arpinium, where we remained for a week. Finally from those cold high peaks of the Apennines we descended south to Campania.

With every mile the clouds of winter seemed to lift, the sky became bluer, the temperature warmer, the air more fragrant with the scent of pines and herbs, and when we joined the coastal road, the breeze off the sea was balmy. Cumae was then a much smaller and quieter town than it is today. At the Acropolis I gave a description of our destination and was directed by a priest to the eastern side of the Lucrine Lake, to a spot low in the hills, looking out across the lagoon and the narrow spit of land to the variegated blueness of the Mediterranean. The villa itself was small and dilapidated, with half a dozen elderly slaves to look after it. The wind blew through open walls; a section of the roof was missing. But it was worth every discomfort simply for the panorama. Down on the lake, little rowing boats moved among the oyster beds, while from the garden at the back there rose a majestic view of the lush green pyramid of Vesuvius. Cicero was enchanted, and set to work at once with the local builders, commissioning a great programme of renovation and redecoration. Marcus played on the beach with his tutor. Terentia sat on the terrace and sewed. Tullia read her Greek. It was a family holiday of a sort they had not taken for many years.

There was one puzzle, however. That whole stretch of coast from Cumae to Puteoli, then as now, was dotted with villas belonging to members of the Senate. Naturally Cicero assumed that once word spread he was in residence, he would begin to receive callers. But nobody came. At night he stood on the terrace and looked up and down the seashore and peered up into the hills and complained he could see hardly any lights. Where were the parties, the dinners? He patrolled the beach, a mile in either direction, and not once did he spot a senatorial toga.

'Something must be happening,' he said to Terentia. 'Where are they all?'

'I don't know,' she replied, 'but speaking for myself, I am happy there is no one with whom you can discuss politics.'

The answer came on our fifth morning.

I was on the terrace answering Cicero's correspondence when

I noticed that a small group of horsemen had turned off the coastal road and were coming up the track towards the house. My immediate thought was *Clodius!* I stood to get a better view and saw to my dismay that the sun was glinting on helmets and breastplates. Five riders: soldiers.

Terentia and the children had gone off for the day to visit the sibyl who was said to live in a jar in a cave at Cumae. I ran inside to alert Cicero, and by the time I found him – he was choosing the colour scheme for the dining room – the horsemen were already clattering into the courtyard. Their leader dismounted and took off his helmet. He was a fearsome apparition: dust-rimed, like some harbinger of death. The whiteness of his nose and forehead was in contrast to the grime of the rest of his face. He looked as if he wore a mask. But I knew him. He was a senator, albeit not a very distinguished one – a member of that tame, dependable class of pederii who never spoke but merely voted with their feet. Lucius Vibullius Rufus was his name. He was one of Pompey's officers from Pompey's home region of Picenum naturally.

'Could I have a word?' he said gruffly.

'Of course,' said Cicero 'Come inside, all of you. Come and have something to eat and drink, I insist.'

Vibullius said, 'I'll come in. They'll wait out here and make sure we're not disturbed.' He moved very stiffly, a clay effigy come to life.

Cicero said, 'You look all in. How far have you ridden?'

'From Luca.'

'Luca?' repeated Cicero. 'That must be three hundred miles!'

'More like three hundred and fifty. We've been on the road a week.' As he lowered himself to a seat, he gave off a shower of dust. 'There's been a meeting concerning you, and I've been sent to inform you of its conclusions.' He glanced at me. 'I need to speak in confidence.'

Cicero, baffled and plainly wondering if he was dealing with a madman, said, 'He's my secretary. You can say all you have to say in front of him. What meeting?'

'As you wish.' Vibullius tugged off his gloves, unbuckled the side of his breastplate, reached under the metal and pulled out a document, which he carefully unwrapped. 'The reason I've come from Luca is because that's where Pompey, Caesar and Crassus have been meeting.'

Cicero frowned. 'No, that's impossible. Pompey is going to Sardinia – he told me so himself.'

'A man can do both, can he not?' replied Vibullius affably. 'He can go to Luca and then go to Sardinia. I can tell you in fact how it came about. After your little speech in the Senate, Crassus travelled up to see Caesar in Ravenna to tell him what you'd said. Then they both crossed Italy to intercept Pompey before he took ship at Pisa. The three of them spent several days together, discussing many matters – among them what's to be done about *you*.'

I felt suddenly queasy. Cicero was more robust: 'There's no need to be impertinent.'

'And the gist of it is this: *shut up, Marcus Tullius!* Shut up in the Senate about Caesar's laws. Shut up trying to cause trouble between the Three. Shut up about Crassus. Shut up generally, in fact.'

'Have you finished?' asked Cicero calmly. 'Do I need to remind you – you are a guest in my house?'

'Not quite finished, no.' Vibullius paused and consulted his notes. 'Also present for part of the conference was Sardinia's governor, Appius Claudius. He was there to make certain undertakings on behalf of his brother, the upshot of which is that Pompey and Clodius are to be publicly reconciled.'

'Reconciled?' repeated Cicero. Now he sounded uncertain.

'In future they will stand together in the best interests of the commonwealth. Pompey wishes me to tell you that he's very unhappy with you, Marcus Tullius: very unhappy. I am quoting his exact words now. He believes he demonstrated great loyalty to you in campaigning for your recall from exile, in the course of which he made certain personal undertakings about your future conduct to Caesar – undertakings, he reminds you, which you repeated to Caesar in writing, and have now broken. He feels let down. He feels embarrassed. He insists, as a test of friendship, that you withdraw your motion on Caesar's land laws from the Senate, and that you do not pronounce on the issue again until you have consulted him in person.'

'I only spoke as I did in Pompey's interest—'

'He would like you to write him a letter confirming that you will do as he asks.' Vibullius rolled up his document and tucked it away under his cuirass. 'That's the official part. What I am about to tell you next is strictly confidential. You understand what I'm saying?'

Cicero made a weary gesture. He understood.

'Pompey wishes you to appreciate the scale of the forces at work: that is why the others gave him permission to inform you. Later this year, both he and Crassus will put their names forward in the consular elections.'

'They'll lose.'

'If the elections were to be held as usual in the summer, you might be right. But the elections will be postponed.'

'Why?'

'Because of violence in Rome.'

'What violence?'

'Clodius will provide the violence. As a result, the elections won't take place until the winter, by which time the campaigning season in Gaul will be over and Caesar will be able to send thousands of his veterans to Rome to vote for his colleagues. *Then* they will be elected. At the end of their terms as consul, Pompey and Crassus will both take up proconsular commands – Pompey in Spain, Crassus in Syria. Instead of the usual one year, these commands will last for five years. Naturally, in the interests of fairness, Caesar's proconsular command in Gaul will also be extended for another five years.'

'This is quite unbelievable—'

'And at the end of his extended term, Caesar will come back to Rome and be elected consul in his turn – Pompey and Crassus making sure *their* veterans are on hand to vote for him. Those are the terms of the Luca Accord. It is designed to last for seven years. Pompey has promised Caesar you will abide by it.'

'And if I do not?'

'He will no longer guarantee your safety.'

VI

'Seven years,' said Cicero with great contempt after Vibullius and his men had gone. 'Nothing in politics can be planned in advance for *seven years*. Is Pompey entirely lacking in sense? Does he not see how this devils' pact works entirely in Caesar's favour? In effect, he promises to protect Caesar's back until such time as Caesar has finished pillaging Gaul, whereupon the conqueror will return to Rome and take control of the whole republic – Pompey included.'

He sat slumped on the terrace in despair. From the shore below came the lonely cries of seabirds as the oyster fishermen landed their catch. We knew now why the neighbourhood was so deserted. According to Vibullius, half the Senate had got wind of what was happening in Luca and more than a hundred had gone north to try to get their share of the spoils. They had forsaken the sun of Campania to bask in the warmest sun of all: power.

'I am a fool,' said Cicero, 'to be counting the waves down here while the future of the world is being decided at the other end of the country. Let's face it, Tiro. I am a spent force. Every man has his season, and I have had mine.'

Later in the day Terentia returned from her visit to the sibyl's cave in Cumae. She noticed the dust on the carpets and the furniture and asked who had been in the house. Reluctantly Cicero described what had happened.

Her eyes shone. She said excitedly, 'How strange that you should tell me this! The sibyl prophesied this very outcome. She said that first Rome would be ruled by three, and then by two, and then by one, and then by none.'

Even Cicero, who regarded the notion of a sibyl living in a jar and predicting the future as entirely fatuous, was impressed. 'Three, two, one, none . . . Well we know who the three are – that's obvious. And I can guess who the one will be. But who will be the two? And what does she mean by none? Is that her way of predicting chaos? If so, I agree – that's what will follow if we allow Caesar to tear up the constitution. But for the life of me I can't see how I am to stop him.'

'Why should *you* be the one to stop him?' demanded Terentia.

'I don't know. Who else is there?'

'But why does it always fall to *you* to block Caesar's ambitions when Pompey, the most powerful man in the state, will do nothing to assist you? Why is it your responsibility?'

Cicero fell silent. Eventually he responded, 'It's a good question. Perhaps it's just conceit on my part. But can I really, with honour, stand back and do nothing, when every instinct tells me the nation is heading for disaster?'

'Yes!' she cried with passion. 'Yes! Absolutely! Haven't you suffered enough for your opposition to Caesar? Is there another man in the world who has endured more? Why not let others take up the fight? Surely you've earned the right to some peace at last?' Then quietly she added, 'I am sure that I have.'

Cicero did not answer for a long time. The truth, I suspect, is that from the moment he learnt about the Luca agreement, he knew in his heart that he could not continue opposing

Caesar – not if he wanted to live. All he needed was for someone to put the issue to him bluntly, as Terentia had just done.

Finally he sighed with a weariness I had never before heard. 'You're right, my wife. At least no one will ever be able to reproach me for not having seen Caesar for what he is, and for not trying to stop him. But you are right – I'm too old and tired to fight him any longer. My friends will understand and my enemies will denounce me whatever I do, so why should I care what they think? Why shouldn't I enjoy some leisure at last down here in the sun with my family?'

And he reached over and took her hand.

Nevertheless, he was ashamed of his capitulation. I know that, because although he wrote a long letter to Pompey in Sardinia setting out his change of heart – his 'palinode', he called it – he never let me see it and kept no copy. Nor did he show it to Atticus. At the same time he wrote to the consul Marcellinus announcing that he wished to withdraw his motion calling on the Senate to re-examine Caesar's land laws. He offered no explanation; he did not need to; everyone recognised that the political firmament had shifted and the new alignment was against him.

We returned to a Rome full of rumours. Few knew for sure what Pompey and Crassus were planning, but gradually word got around that they were intending to run on a joint ticket for the consulship, just as they had in the past, even though everyone knew they had always loathed one another. Some senators, however, were determined to fight back against the cynicism and arrogance of the Three. A debate was scheduled on the allocation of consular provinces, and one motion called for

Caesar to be stripped of both Nearer and Further Gaul. Cicero knew that if he attended the chamber, he would be asked his views. He considered staying away. But then he reasoned that he would have to recant publicly sooner or later: he might as well get it over with. He began working on his speech.

And then, on the eve of the debate, after more than two years away in Cyprus, Marcus Porcius Cato returned to Rome. He arrived in fine style, in a flotilla of treasure ships, sailing up the Tiber from Ostia, accompanied by his nephew, Brutus, a young man of whom great things were expected. The whole of the Senate, and all of the magistrates and priests, as well as most of the population, turned out to welcome Cato home. There was a landing stage with painted poles and ribbons where he was supposed to disembark and meet the consuls, but he sailed on past them, standing in the prow of a royal galley that had six banks of oars, his bony profile fixed straight ahead, wearing a shabby black tunic. The crowds at first gasped and groaned with disappointment at his high-handedness, but then his treasure started to be unloaded – ox wagon after ox wagon of it, seven thousand silver talents' worth in all, that wound in procession from the Navalia all the way to the state treasury in the Temple of Saturn. With this one contribution, Cato transformed the finances of the nation – it was enough to provide free grain to the citizenry for five years – and the Senate went into immediate session to vote him an honorary praetorship, together with the right to wear a special purple-bordered toga.

Called upon by Marcellinus to respond, Cato scornfully denounced what he called 'these corrupt baubles': 'I have discharged the duty placed upon me by the Roman people – an assignment I never requested and would have preferred not to have undertaken. Now that it is done, I need no Eastern flattery or showy garments to puff myself up: the knowledge that I have performed my duty is reward enough for me, as it should be for any man.'

He was back in the chamber for the next day's debate on the provinces, as if he had never been away – sitting in his customary position, going through a set of the treasury's accounts as he always did to make sure there was no waste in public expenditure. Only when Cicero rose to speak did he put them aside.

It was quite late on in the session and most ex-consuls had already given their opinions. Even so, Cicero managed to spin out the suspense a little longer by devoting the first part of his speech to an attack on his old enemies Piso and Gabinius, governors of Macedonia and Syria respectively. Then the consul, Marcius Philippus, who was married to Caesar's niece, and who was growing restless like many others, interrupted him to ask why he spent all his time attacking those two puppets when the man who had really instigated the campaign that led to his exile was Caesar. This gave Cicero precisely the opening he wanted. 'Because,' he said, 'I am taking account of the public welfare rather than my own grievances. It is this old and unfailing loyalty of mine to the republic which restores, reconciles and reinstates me in friendship with Gaius Caesar.

'For me,' he went on, having to shout now to be heard above the jeers, 'it is impossible not to be the friend of one who renders good service to the state. Under Caesar's command we have fought a war in Gaul, whereas before we merely repelled attacks. Unlike his predecessors he believes the whole of Gaul should be brought under our rule. And so he has, with brilliant success, crushed in battle the fiercest and greatest tribes of Germania and Helvetia; the rest he has terrified, checked and subdued and taught to submit to the rule of the Roman people.

'But the war is not yet won. If Caesar is removed, the embers may yet burst out again into flame. Therefore, as a senator – even as the man's personal enemy, if you like – I must lay aside private grievances for the sake of the state, for how can I be the enemy of this man, whose dispatches, whose fame, whose envoys fill our ears every day with fresh names of races, peoples and places?'

It was not his most convincing performance, and towards the end he rather tripped himself up by trying to pretend that he and Caesar had never really been enemies at all, a piece of sophistry that was greeted with derision. Still, he got through it. The motion to replace Caesar was defeated and at the end of the session, even though the most passionate anti-Caesareans – men like Ahenobarbus and Bibulus – pointedly turned their backs on him in contempt, Cicero walked towards the exit with his head unbowed. That was when Cato intercepted him. I was waiting by the door and was able to overhear their whole exchange.

Cato: 'I am beyond disappointed in you, Marcus Tullius. Your desertion has just cost us what may have been our last chance to stop a dictator.'

Cicero: 'Why should I want to stop a man who is winning victory after victory?'

Cato: 'But who is he winning these victories for? Is it for the republic or is it for himself? And when did it become national policy to conquer Gaul in any case? Has the Senate or the people ever authorised this war of his?'

Cicero: 'Then why don't you put down a motion to end it?'

Cato: 'Perhaps I shall.'

Cicero: 'Yes – and see how far it gets you! Welcome home, incidentally.'

But Cato was in no mood for such pleasantries and stamped off to talk to Bibulus and Ahenobarbus. From this time on it was he who led the opposition to Caesar, while Cicero retreated to his house on the Palatine, and to a quieter life.

There was nothing heroic in what Cicero had done. He realised his loss of face. *Good night to principle, sincerity and honour!* was how he summed it up in a letter to Atticus.

Yet even after all these years, and even with the wisdom of hindsight, I do not see what else he could have done. It was easier for Cato to spit defiance at Caesar. He was from a rich and powerful family, and he did not have the constant threat of Clodius hanging over him.

Everything now proceeded exactly as the Three had planned, and Cicero could not have stopped it even if he had sacrificed his life. First, Clodius and his ruffians disrupted the canvassing for the consular elections so that the campaign came to a stop. Then they threatened and intimidated the other candidates until they withdrew. Finally the elections had to be postponed. Only Ahenobarbus, with the support of Cato, had the courage to continue to stand for the consulship against Pompey and Crassus. Most of the Senate put on mourning in protest.

That winter, for the first time, the city was filled with Caesar's veterans – drinking, whoring and threatening any who refused to salute the effigy of their leader when they set it up at cross-roads. On the eve of the postponed poll, Cato and Ahenobarbus went down by torchlight to the voting pens to try to stake out their canvassing position. But they were attacked en route, either by Clodius's men or Caesar's and their torchbearer was killed. Cato was stabbed in his right arm, and although he entreated

Ahenobarbus to stand firm, the candidate fled back to his house and barricaded the door and refused to come out. The next day Pompey and Crassus were elected consuls, and soon after that, as agreed at Luca, they made sure they were allotted the provinces they desired to govern at the end of their joint term of office: Spain for Pompey, Syria for Crassus, both commands awarded for five years instead of the normal one, with a further five-year extension for Caesar as proconsul in Gaul. Pompey never even left Rome, but governed Spain through his subordinates.

Throughout all this, Cicero kept clear of politics. On the days when he had no engagements in the law courts, he stayed at home and supervised the schooling of his son and nephew in grammar, Greek and rhetoric. He dined quietly most evenings with Terentia. He composed poetry. He began to write a book on the history and practice of oratory.

'I am still an exile,' he remarked to me, 'only now my exile is in Rome.'

Caesar quickly heard reports of Cicero's about-face in the Senate and immediately sent him a letter of thanks. I recall Cicero's surprise when it arrived, delivered by one of Caesar's superbly swift and reliable military couriers. As I have explained, nearly all their correspondence has since been seized. But I remember the opening, because it was always the same:

From: G. Caesar, Imperator, to M. Cicero, greetings.

I and the army are well . . .

And this particular letter had one other passage I have never forgotten: *It pleases me to know I have a place in your heart. There is not a man in Rome whose opinion I prize more than yours. You may rely on me in all things.* Cicero was torn between feelings of gratitude and shame, relief and despair. He showed the letter to his brother Quintus, who had just returned from Sardinia.

Quintus said, 'You have done the right thing. Pompey has proved a fickle friend. Caesar may be more loyal.' And then he added, 'To be honest, Pompey treated me with such contempt while I was away that I wondered if I might not do better to throw in my own lot with Caesar.'

'And how would you do that?'

'Well, I am a soldier, am I not? Perhaps I could ask for a position on his staff. Or perhaps you could ask for a commission on my behalf.'

At first Cicero was uncertain: he had no desire to beg for favours from Caesar. But then he saw how unhappy Quintus was to be back in Rome. There was his miserable marriage to Pomponia, of course, but it was more than that. He was not an advocate or orator like his elder brother. Neither the law courts nor the Senate held much appeal. He had already served as praetor and as a governor in Asia. The sole remaining step for him in politics was a consulship, and he would never gain that unless he enjoyed some spectacular stroke of good fortune or patronage. And then again, the only sphere in which such a transformation might come his way was on the battlefield . . .

The possibility seemed remote, but by such reasoning the brothers convinced themselves that they should further tie their fortunes to those of Caesar. Cicero wrote to him requesting a commission for Quintus, and Caesar replied at once that he would be delighted to oblige. Not only that: he asked Cicero in return if he would help supervise the great rebuilding programme he was planning in Rome to rival Pompey's. Some hundred million sesterces was to be spent on laying out a new forum in the centre of the city and creating a covered walkway a mile long on the Field of Mars. As recompense for his efforts Caesar gave Cicero a loan of eight hundred thousand sesterces at two and a quarter per cent interest, half the market rate.

That was how he was. He was like a whirlpool. He sucked men in by the sheer force of his energy and power until almost the whole of Rome was mesmerised by him. Whenever his *Commentaries* were posted up outside the Regia, crowds would gather and remain there all day reading of his exploits. That year his young protégé Decimus defeated the Celts in a great naval battle in the Atlantic, after which Caesar caused their entire nation to be sold into slavery and their leaders executed. Brittany was conquered, the Pyrenees pacified, Flanders suppressed. Every community in Gaul was required to pay a levy, even after he had sacked their towns and carted off all their ancient treasures. A vast but peaceful German migration of 430,000 members of the Usipetes and Tencteri tribes crossed the Rhine and was lulled by Caesar into a false sense of security when he pretended to agree a truce; then he annihilated them. His engineers erected a bridge across the Rhine and he and his legion rampaged about through Germany for eighteen days before withdrawing back into Gaul and dismantling the bridge behind them. Finally, as if this were not enough, he put to sea with two legions and landed on the barbarian shores of Britain – a place that many in Rome had refused to believe even existed, and which certainly lay beyond the limits of the known world – burned a few villages, captured some slaves, and then sailed home before the winter storms trapped him.

To celebrate his victories Pompey summoned a meeting of the Senate to vote his father-in-law a further twenty days of public supplication, whereupon a scene ensued that I have never forgotten. One after another the senators rose to praise Caesar, Cicero dutifully among them, until at last there was no one left for Pompey to call except Cato.

'Gentlemen,' said Cato, 'yet again you have all taken leave of your senses. By Caesar's own account he has slaughtered four hundred thousand men, women and children – people with whom we had no quarrel, with whom we were not at war, in a campaign not authorised by a vote either of this Senate or of the Roman people. I wish to lay two counter-proposals for you to consider: first, that far from holding celebrations, we should sacrifice to the gods that they do not turn their wrath for Caesar's folly and madness upon Rome and the army; and second, that Caesar, having shown himself a war criminal, should be handed over to the tribes of Germany for them to determine his fate.'

The shouts of rage that greeted this speech were like howls of pain: 'Traitor!' 'Gaul-lover!' 'German!' Several senators jumped up and started shoving Cato this way and that, causing him to stumble backwards. But he was a strong and wiry man. He regained his balance and stood his ground, glaring at them like an eagle. A motion was proposed that he be taken directly by the lictors to the Carcer and imprisoned until such time as he apologised. Pompey, however, was too shrewd to permit his martyrdom. 'Cato by his words has done himself more harm than any punishment we can inflict,' he declared. 'Let him go free. It does not matter. He will stand forever condemned in the eyes of the Roman people for such treacherous sentiments.'

I too felt that Cato had done himself great damage among all moderate and sensible opinion; I remarked as much to Cicero as we walked home. Given his new-found closeness to Caesar, I expected him to agree. But to my surprise he shook his head. 'No, you are quite wrong. Cato is a prophet. He blurts out the truth with the clarity of a child or a madman. Rome will rue the day it tied its destiny to Caesar's. And so shall I.'

I make no claim to be a philosopher, but this much I have observed: that whenever a thing seems at its zenith, you may be sure its destruction has already started.

So it was with the triumvirate. It towered above the landscape of politics like some granite monolith. Yet it had weaknesses that none could see and which were only to be revealed with time. Of these the most dangerous was the inordinate ambition of Crassus.

For years he had been feted as the richest man in Rome, with a fortune of some eight thousand talents, or nearly two hundred million sesterces. But latterly this had come to seem almost paltry compared to the wealth of Pompey and Caesar, who each had the resources of entire countries at their disposal. Therefore Crassus had set his heart on going out to Syria not to administer it but to use it as a base from which to mount a military expedition against the Parthian empire. Those who knew anything of the treacherous sands and cruel peoples of Arabia thought the plan was hugely risky – not least, I am sure, Pompey. But such was his detestation of Crassus that he did nothing to dissuade him. As for Caesar, he too encouraged him. He sent Crassus's son Publius – whom I had met in Mutina – back to Rome from Gaul with a detachment of one thousand highly trained cavalry so that he could join his father as deputy commander-in-chief.

Cicero despised Crassus more than he did any other man in Rome. Even for Clodius he could occasionally summon a certain reluctant respect. But Crassus he considered cynical, grasping and duplicitous, all traits that he covered over with a slippery and false bonhomie. The two had a furious argument in the Senate around this time, when Cicero denounced the retiring governor of Syria, Gabinius – his old enemy – for finally succumbing to Ptolemy's bribe and restoring the Pharaoh to the Egyptian throne. Crassus defended the man he was about to replace. Cicero accused Crassus of putting his personal interests above those of the republic. Crassus jeered that Cicero was an exile. 'Sooner an honourable exile,' retorted Cicero, 'than a pampered thief.' Crassus stalked over to him and thrust out his chest, and the two ageing statesmen had to be physically prevented from exchanging blows.

Pompey took Cicero aside and told him he would not tolerate such abuse of his consular colleague. Caesar wrote a stern letter from Gaul that he regarded any attack on Crassus as an insult to himself. What worried them, I believe, was that Crassus's expedition was proving so unpopular with the people, it was beginning to undermine the authority of the Three. Cato and his followers denounced it as illegal and immoral to make war on a country with which the republic had treaties of friendship; they produced auguries to show it was offensive to the gods and would bring ruin down on Rome.

Crassus was sufficiently concerned to seek a public reconciliation with Cicero. He approached him via Furius Crassipes, his friend who was also Cicero's son-in-law. Crassipes offered to host a dinner for them both on the eve of Crassus's departure. To have refused the invitation would have shown disrespect to Pompey and Caesar; Cicero had to go. 'But I want you to be on hand as a witness,' he said to me. 'This villain will put words in my mouth and invent endorsements I never gave.'

Naturally I was not present for the meal itself. Still, I remember some parts of the evening very clearly. Crassipes had a fine suburban house set in the middle of a park about a mile south of the city, on the banks of the Tiber. Cicero and Terentia were the first to arrive so that they could spend some time with Tullia, who had recently miscarried. She looked pale, poor child, and thin, and I noticed how coldly her husband treated her, criticising her for such domestic oversights as the wilting flower arrangements and the poor quality of the canapés. Crassus turned up an hour later in a veritable convoy of carriages that clattered to a halt in the courtyard. With him was his wife Tertulla – an elderly sour-faced lady, almost as bald as he was – together with their son Publius and Publius's new bride Cornelia, a very gracious seventeen-year-old, the daughter of Scipio Nasica and considered to be the most eligible heiress in Rome. Crassus also trailed a retinue of adjutants and secretaries who seemed to have no function except to hurry back and forth with messages and documents, conveying a general impression of importance. When the principals went in to dinner and the coast was clear, they lolled about on Crassipes's furniture and drank his wine, and I was struck by the contrast between these unmilitary amateurs and Caesar's efficient, battle-hardened staff.

After the meal, the men went into the tablinum to discuss military strategy – or rather Crassus held forth and the others listened. He was very deaf by this time – he was sixty – and talked too loudly. Publius was embarrassed – 'It's all right, Father, there's no need to shout, we're not in the other room' – and once or twice he glanced at Cicero and raised his eyebrows in silent apology. Crassus announced that he would head east through Macedonia, then Thrace, the Hellespont, Galatia, and the northern part of Syria, traverse the desert of Mesopotamia, cross the Euphrates and thrust deep into Parthia.

Cicero said, 'They must be well aware you're coming. Aren't you worried you will lack the element of surprise?'

Crassus scoffed, 'I have no need of the element of surprise. I prefer the element of certainty. Let them tremble as we approach.'

He had his eye on various rich pickings along the way – he cited the temples of the goddess Derceto at Hierapolis and of Jehovah at Jerusalem, the jewelled effigy of Apollo at Tigraocerta, the golden Zeus of Nicephorium and the treasure houses of Seleucia. Cicero joked that it sounded less a military campaign than a shopping expedition, but Crassus was too deaf to hear.

At the end of the evening the two old enemies shook hands warmly and expressed profound satisfaction that any slight misunderstandings that might have arisen between them had been put to rest at last. 'These are mere figments of the imagination,' declared Cicero, with a twirl of his fingers. 'Let them be utterly eradicated from our memories. Between two such men as you and I, whose lot has fallen on the same political ground, I would hope that alliance and friendship will continue to the credit of both. In all matters affecting you during your absence, my devoted and indefatigable service and any influence I command are absolutely and unreservedly at your disposal.'

'What an utter villain that fellow is,' said Cicero as we settled into the carriage to drive home.

A day or so later – and a full two months before the expiry of his term as consul, so eager was he to be off – Crassus left Rome wearing the red cloak and full uniform of a general on active service. Pompey, his fellow consul, came out of the Senate house to see him off. The tribune Ateius Capito attempted to arrest him in the Forum for his illegal war-making, and when he was knocked aside by Crassus's lieutenants he ran ahead to the city gate and set up a brazier. As Crassus passed by he threw incense and libations on to the flames and called down curses on him and upon his expedition, mingling his incantations with the names of strange and terrible deities. The superstitious people of Rome were appalled and cried out to Crassus not to go. But he laughed at them, and with a final jaunty wave turned his back on the city and spurred his horse.

Such was Cicero's life at this period, walking on tiptoe between the three great men in the state, endeavouring to keep on good terms with all of them, doing their bidding, privately despairing of the future of the republic, but waiting and hoping for better times.

He sought refuge in his books, especially philosophy and history, and one day, soon after Quintus had gone off to join Caesar in Gaul, he announced to me that he had decided to produce a work of his own. It was too dangerous, he said, to write an open attack on the current state of politics in Rome. But he could approach it in a different way, by updating Plato's *Republic* and setting out what an ideal state might look like: 'Who could object to that?' The answer, I thought, was a large number of people, but I kept my opinion to myself.

I look back on the writing of that work, which took us in the end almost three years, as one of the most satisfying periods of my life. Like most literary compositions, it entailed much heart-break and many false starts. Originally he planned to write it in nine rolls, but then reduced that to six. He decided to cast it in the form of an imagined conversation between a group of historical characters – chief among them one of his heroes, Scipio Aemilianus, the conqueror of Carthage – who gather in a villa on a religious holiday to discuss the nature of politics and how societies should be organised. He reasoned that no one would mind if dangerous notions were placed in the mouths of the legendary figures of Roman history.

He started dictating it in his new villa in Cumae during the senatorial recess. He consulted all the ancient texts, and on one particularly memorable day we rode over to the villa of Faustus Cornelius Sulla, the son of the former dictator, who lived a little way along the coast. Cicero's ally Milo, who was rising in politics, had just married Sulla's twin sister Fausta, and at the wedding breakfast, which Cicero attended, Sulla had invited him to use his library whenever he liked. It was one of the most valuable collections in Italy. The volumes had been carted back by Sulla the Dictator from Athens almost thirty years earlier, and amazingly included most of the original manuscripts of Aristotle, written in his own hand three centuries earlier. I shall never forget as long as I live the sensation of unrolling each of the eight books of Aristotle's *Politics*: tiny cylinders of minute Greek characters, the edges slightly damaged by damp from the caves in Asia Minor where they had been hidden for many years. It was like reaching back through time and touching the face of a god.

But I am wandering too far from my subject. The essential point was that Cicero for the first time laid out his political credo in black and white, and I can summarise it in a sentence: that politics is the most noble of all callings ('there is really no other occupation in which human virtue approaches more closely the august function of the gods'); that there is 'no nobler motive for entering public life than the resolution not to be ruled by wicked men'; that no individual, or combination of individuals, should be allowed to become too powerful; that politics is a profession, not a pastime for dilettantes (nothing is worse than rule by 'clever poets'); that a statesman should devote his life to studying 'the science of politics, in order to acquire in advance all the knowledge that it may be necessary for him to use at some future time'; that authority in a state must always be divided; and that of the three known forms of government – monarchy, aristocracy and people – the best is a mixture of all three, for each one taken on its own can lead to disaster: kings can be capricious, aristocrats self-interested, and 'an unbridled multitude enjoying unwonted power more terrifying than a conflagration or a raging sea'.

Often today I reread *On the Republic*, and always I am moved, especially by the passage at the end of book six, when Scipio describes how his grandfather appears to him in a dream and takes him up into the heavens to show him the smallness of the earth in comparison to the grandeur of the Milky Way, where the spirits of dead statesmen dwell as stars. The description was inspired by the vast, clear night skies above the Bay of Naples:

> *I gazed in every direction and all appeared wonderfully beautiful. There were stars which we never see from earth, and they were all larger than we have ever imagined. The starry spheres were much greater than the earth; indeed the earth itself seemed to me so small that I was scornful of our empire, which covers only a single point, as it were, upon its surface.*

'If only you will look on high,' the old man tells Scipio, 'and contemplate this eternal home and resting place, you will no longer bother with the gossip of the common herd or put your trust in human reward for your exploits. Nor will any man's reputation endure very long, for what men say dies with them and is blotted out with the forgetfulness of posterity.'

Composing such passages was Cicero's chief comfort in the

lonely days of his wilderness years. But the prospect that he might ever again have the chance to put his principles into effect seemed remote indeed.

Three months after Cicero began writing *On the Republic*, in the summer of Rome's seven hundredth year, Pompey's wife Julia gave birth to a baby boy. The moment he was brought the news at his morning levee, Cicero hastened round to see the happy couple bearing a gift, for the son of Pompey and the grandson of Caesar would be a mighty presence in the years to come, and he wanted to be among the first with his congratulations.

It was not long after dawn yet already hot. In the valley beneath Pompey's house loomed his newly opened theatre, with its temples and gardens and porticoes, its fresh white marble dazzling in the sun. Cicero had attended its dedication ceremony just a few months earlier – a spectacle that had included fights involving five hundred lions, four hundred panthers, eighteen elephants and the first rhinoceros ever seen in Rome. He had found it all revolting, especially the slaughter of the elephants: *What pleasure can a cultivated man get out of seeing a weak human being torn to pieces by a powerful animal or a noble creature transfixed by a hunting spear?* But naturally he had kept his feelings to himself.

From the moment we entered the immense house it was clear something terrible had occurred. Senators and clients of Pompey stood in worried, silent groups. Someone whispered to Cicero that no announcement had been made, but Pompey's failure to appear, and an earlier glimpse of several of Julia's maids fleeing, weeping, across an inner courtyard, suggested the worst. Suddenly from the interior there was a flutter of activity, a curtain parted and Pompey emerged in the midst of a retinue of slaves. He stopped, as if shocked by the number of people waiting for him, and searched for a familiar face. His eye fell on Cicero. He raised his hand and walked towards him. Everyone watched. At first he seemed entirely calm and clear-eyed. But then as he reached his old ally the effort at self-control abruptly became too much. His whole body and face seemed to sag and with a terrible choking sob he cried out, 'She's dead!'

A great groan went round the vast room – of genuine shock and grief, I have no doubt, but also of alarm, for these were politicians and this was a much bigger thing than the death of one young woman, tragic though it was. Cicero, in tears himself, put his arms round Pompey and tried to comfort him, and after a few moments Pompey asked him to come and see the body. Knowing how squeamish Cicero was about death, I thought he might try to refuse. But that would have been impossible. He was not being invited purely as a friend. He was to be an official witness on behalf of the Senate in what was a matter of state. He went off holding Pompey's hand, and when he returned shortly afterwards, the others gathered round.

'She started bleeding again soon after the birth,' reported Cicero, 'and the flow could not be stopped. The end was peaceful and she was brave, as befits her lineage.'

'And the child?'

'He will not last the day.'

More groans greeted this announcement and then everyone left to spread the news across the city. Cicero said to me, 'The poor girl was whiter than the sheet in which they'd wound her. And the boy was blind and limp. I am truly sorry for Caesar. She was his only child. It's as if Cato's prophecies of the gods' rage are starting to come true.'

We went back to the house and Cicero wrote Caesar a letter of consolation. As ill luck would have it, Caesar was in the most inaccessible place it was possible for him to be, having crossed over to Britain again, this time with an invasion force of twenty-seven thousand men, including Quintus. It was not until he returned to Gaul several months later that he found the packets of letters informing him of his daughter's death. He showed by all accounts not a tremor of emotion but retired to his quarters, never spoke of it, and after three days of official mourning went on with his normal duties. It was, I guess, the secret of his achievements that he was quite indifferent to the death of anyone – enemy or friend, his only child or even ultimately himself – a coldness of nature that he concealed beneath his famous layers of charm.

Pompey was at the opposite end of the human spectrum. All his depths were on the surface. He loved his various wives with great (some said excessive) tenderness, and Julia most of all. At her funeral – which was, despite Cato's objections, a state occasion held in the Forum – he found it hard to deliver the eulogy through his tears, and generally gave every appearance of being broken in spirit. The ashes were afterwards interred in a mausoleum in the precincts of one of his temples on the Field of Mars.

It must have been perhaps two months later that he asked Cicero to come and see him and showed him the letter he had just received from Caesar. After commiserating with him on the loss of Julia, and thanking him for his condolences, Caesar proposed a new marital alliance, but of double the strength: he would give his sister's granddaughter, Octavia, to Pompey, and Pompey in return would give him the hand of his daughter, Pompeia.

'What do you make of this?' demanded Pompey. 'I believe the

barbarian air of Britain must have affected his brain! For one thing, my daughter's already betrothed to Faustus Sulla – what am I supposed to tell him? "Very sorry, Sulla, someone more important has just come along"? And then Octavia of course is married – and not to just some nobody, either, but to Caius Marcellus: how's he going to feel about my stealing his wife? Damn it all, Caesar's married himself, come to that, to that poor little drab Calpurnia! All these lives to be turned upside down, and meanwhile dear little Julia's side of our bed is not yet cold! Do you know, I haven't even had the heart to clear out her hairbrushes?'

Cicero for once found himself speaking up for Caesar: 'I'm sure he's only thinking of the stability of the republic.'

But Pompey was not to be pacified. 'Well I shan't do it. If I marry for a fifth time, it will be to a woman of my choice; and as for Caesar, he will have to find himself a different bride.'

Cicero, who loved gossip, could not resist describing Caesar's letter to several friends, swearing each to secrecy. Naturally, after extracting a similar oath, each friend mentioned it to several others, and so it went on until the news of Caesar's proposal was the talk of Rome. Marcellus especially was outraged that his wife was being spoken of by Caesar as if she were his chattel. Caesar was embarrassed when he heard what was being said; he blamed Pompey for revealing his plans. Pompey was unapologetic; he in turn blamed Caesar for the clumsiness of his matchmaking. Another crack had appeared in the monolith.

VII

The following year during the Senate recess Cicero set off as usual with his family for Cumae in order to continue work on his political book; and I, as usual, went with him. It was not long before my fiftieth birthday.

For most of my life I had enjoyed good health. But when, to break the journey, we reached the cold mountain heights of Arpinum, I started to shiver, and the next morning I could barely move my limbs. When I tried to continue with the others I fainted and had to be carried to bed. Cicero could not have been kinder. He postponed his departure in the hope I would recover. But my fever worsened and I was told afterwards he spent long hours at my bedside. In the end he had to leave me behind, along with instructions to the household slaves that I should receive exactly the same care they would give to him. From Cumae two days later he wrote to say that he was sending me his Greek doctor, Andricus, and also a cook: *If you care for me, see that you get well and join us when you are thoroughly strong again. Goodbye.*

Andricus purged and bled me. The cook produced delicious meals that I was too ill to eat. Cicero wrote constantly.

> *You cannot imagine how anxious I feel about your health. If you relieve my mind on this score, I shall relieve yours of every worry.*

I should write more if I thought you could read with any pleasure. Put your clever brain, which I value so highly, to the job of preserving yourself for us both.

After about a week, the fever eased. By then it was too late to travel to Cumae. Cicero wrote telling me to join him instead at Formiae, on his way back to Rome.

Let me find you there, my dear Tiro, well and strong. My (our) literary brainchildren have been drooping their heads missing you. Atticus is staying with me, enjoying himself in cheerful mood. He wanted to hear my compositions but I told him that in your absence my tongue of authorship is tied completely. You must get ready to restore your services to my Muses. My promise will be performed on the appointed day. Now mind you get thoroughly well. I shall be with you soon. Goodbye.

I shall relieve your mind of every worry . . . My promise will be performed on the appointed day . . . I read the letters over and over, trying to make sense of those two phrases. I deduced that he must have said something to me when I was delirious, but I had no recollection of what it was.

As arranged, I arrived at the villa in Formiae on the afternoon of my fiftieth birthday, the twenty-eighth day of April. It was cold and blustery, not at all propitious, with rain gusting off the sea. I still felt frail. The effort of hurrying into the house so as not to be soaked left me dizzy. The place appeared deserted and I wondered if I had misunderstood my instructions. I went from room to room, calling out, until I heard a young boy's stifled laughter coming from the triclinium. I pulled back the curtain and discovered the whole dining room crammed full of people trying to stay silent: Cicero, Terentia, Tullia, Marcus, young Quintus Cicero, all the household staff, and (even more bizarrely) the praetor Caius Marcellus with his lictors – that same noble Marcellus whose wife Caesar had tried to bestow on Pompey, and who had a villa nearby. At the sight of my astonished face they all started laughing, then Cicero took me by the hand and led me into the centre of the room while the others made space for us. I felt my knees weaken.

Marcellus said, 'Who wishes this day to free this slave?'

Cicero replied, 'I do.'

'You are the legal owner?'

'I am.'

'Upon what grounds is he to be freed?'

'He has shown great loyalty and given exemplary service to our family ever since he was born into the condition of slavery, and to me in particular, and also to the Roman state. His character is sound and he is worthy of his freedom.'

Marcellus nodded. 'You may proceed.'

The lictor briefly touched his rod of office to my head. Cicero stepped in front of me, grasped my shoulders and recited the simple legal formula: 'This man is to be free.' He had tears in his eyes; so had I. Gently he turned me round until I had my back to him, and then he let me go, as a father might release a child to take its first steps.

It is difficult for me to describe the joy of becoming free. Quintus expressed it best when he wrote to me from Gaul: *I could not be more delighted, my dear Tiro, believe me. Before you were our slave but now you are our friend.* Outwardly, nothing much changed. I continued to live under Cicero's roof and to perform the same duties. But in my heart I was a different man. I exchanged my tunic for a toga – a cumbersome garment that I wore without ease or comfort, but with intense pride. And for the first time I began to make plans of my own. I started to compile a comprehensive dictionary of all the symbols and abbreviations used in my shorthand system, together with instructions on how to use it. I drew up a scheme for a book on Latin grammar. I also went back through my boxes of notes whenever I had a spare hour and copied down particularly amusing or clever quotations thrown out by Cicero over the years. He greatly approved of the idea of a book of his wit and wisdom. Often after a particularly fine remark he would stop and say, 'Note that down, Tiro – that's one for your compendium.' Gradually it became understood between us that if I outlived him, I would write his biography.

I asked him once why he had waited so long to set me free, and why he had decided to do it at that moment. He answered, 'Well, you know I can be a selfish man, and I rely on you entirely. I thought to myself, "If I free him, what's to stop him going off and transferring his allegiance to Caesar or Crassus or someone? They'd certainly pay him plenty for all he knows about me." Then when you fell ill in Arpinum I realised how unjust it would be if you died in servitude, and so I made my pledge to you, even though you were too feverish to understand it. If ever there was a man who deserved the nobility of freedom, it is you, dear Tiro. Besides,' he added with a wink, 'nowadays I have no secrets worth selling.'

Love him though I did, I nevertheless wanted to end my days under my own roof. I had some savings and now was paid a salary; I dreamed of buying a smallholding near Cumae where I could keep a few goats and chickens and grow my own vines and olives. But I feared loneliness. I suppose I could have gone down to the slave market and bought myself a companion, but the idea repulsed me. I knew with whom I wanted to share this dream of a future life: Agathe, the Greek slave girl whom I had met in the household of Lucullus and whose freedom I had asked Atticus to purchase on my behalf before I went into exile with Cicero. Atticus confirmed he had done as I asked and that she had been manumitted. But although I made enquiries as to what had happened to her, and always kept an eye out whenever I walked through Rome, she had vanished into the teeming multitudes of Italy.

I did not have long to enjoy my freedom in tranquillity. My modest plans, like everyone else's, were about to be mocked by the immensity of events. As Plautus has it:

Whatever the mind may hope for
The future is in the hands of the gods.

A few weeks after my liberation, in the month that was then named Quintilis but that we are now required to call July, I was hurrying along the Via Sacra, trying not to trip over my new toga, when I saw a crowd gathered ahead. They were deathly still – not at all animated as they usually were when news of one of Caesar's victories was posted on the white board. I thought immediately that he must have suffered a terrible defeat. I joined the back of the throng and asked the man in front of me what was happening. Irritated, he glanced over his shoulder and muttered in a distracted voice, 'Crassus has been killed.'

I stayed just long enough to pick up the few details that were available. Then I hastened back to tell Cicero. He was working in his study. I gasped out the news and he quickly stood up, as if such grave information should not be acknowledged sitting down.

'How did it happen?'

'In battle, it's reported – in the desert, near a town in Mesopotamia named Carrhae.'

'And his army?'

'Defeated – wiped out.'

Cicero stared at me for a few moments. Then he shouted to one slave to bring his shoes and another to arrange a litter. I asked him where he was going. 'To see Pompey, of course – come too.'

It was a sign of Pompey's pre-eminence that whenever there was a major crisis in the state, it was to his house that people always flocked – be it the ordinary citizens, who that day crowded the surrounding streets in silent, watchful multitudes; or the senior senators, who even now were arriving in their litters and being ushered by Pompey's attendants into his inner sanctum. As luck would have it, both the elected consuls, Calvinus and Messalla, were under indictment for bribery and had been unable to take up office. Present instead was the informal leadership of the Senate, including senior ex-consuls such as Cotta, Hortensius and the elder Curio, and prominent younger men like Ahenobarbus, Scipio Nasica and M. Aemilius Lepidus. Pompey took command of the meeting. No one knew the eastern empire better than he: after all, much of it he had conquered. He announced that a dispatch had just been received from Crassus's legate, G. Cassius Longinus, who had managed to escape from enemy territory and get back into Syria, and that if everyone was in agreement he would now read it out.

Cassius was a cold, austere man – 'pale and thin', as Caesar later complained – not given to boastfulness or lying, so his words were heard with all the greater respect. According to him, the Parthian king, Orodes II, had sent an envoy to Crassus on the eve of the invasion to say that he was willing to take pity on him as an old man and allow him to return in peace to Rome. But Crassus had boastfully replied that he would give his answer in the Parthian capital, Seleucia, at which the envoy had burst out laughing and pointed to the palm of his upturned hand, saying, 'Hair will grow here, Crassus, before you set eyes on Seleucia!'

The Roman force of seven legions, plus eight thousand cavalry and archers, had bridged the Euphrates at Zeugma in a thunderstorm – itself a bad omen – and at one point during the traditional offerings to placate the gods, Crassus had dropped the entrails of the sacrificial animal into the sand. Although he had tried to make a joke of it – 'That's what comes of being an old man, lads, but I can grip my sword tightly enough!' – the soldiers groaned, remembering the curses that had accompanied their departure from Rome. *Already*, wrote Cassius, *they sensed that they were doomed.*

> *From the Euphrates* [he continued] *we advanced ever deeper into the desert, with insufficient supplies of water and no clear sense of a route or objective. The land is trackless, flat, with no living tree to offer shade. After wading for fifty miles with full packs through soft sand in desert storms during which hundreds of our men succumbed to thirst and heat, we reached a river called the Balissus. Here for the first time our scouts sighted elements of the enemy's forces on the opposite bank. On the orders of M. Crassus we crossed the river at noon and set off in pursuit. But by now the enemy had entirely disappeared again. We marched for several more hours until we were in the midst of a wilderness.*

Suddenly from all around us we heard the beating of kettle drums. At that moment, as if springing out of the sand, arose in every direction an immense horde of mounted archers. The silken banners of the Parthian commander, Sillaces, were visible behind.

Against the advice of more experienced officers, M. Crassus ordered the army to be drawn up in a single large square, twelve cohorts across. Our archers were then sent forward to engage the enemy. However, they were soon obliged to retreat in the face of the Parthians' vastly superior forces and speed of manoeuvre. Their arrows spread much slaughter through our packed ranks. Nor did death come easily or quickly. In the convulsion and agony of their pain, our men would writhe as the arrows struck them; they would snap them off in their wounds and then lacerate their flesh by trying to tear out the barbed arrowheads that had pierced through their veins and muscles. Many died in this way, and even the survivors were in no state to fight. Their hands were pinioned to their shields and their feet nailed through to the ground so that they were incapable of either running away or defending themselves. Any hopes that this murderous rain would exhaust itself were dashed by the sight of fresh supplies of arrows appearing on the battlefield on heavily laden camel trains.

Apprehending the danger that the army would soon be entirely wiped out, P. Crassus applied to his father for permission to take his cavalry, together with some infantry and archers, and pierce the encircling line. M. Crassus endorsed the plan. This breakout force of some six thousand men moved forwards and the Parthians quickly withdrew. But although Publius had been expressly ordered not to pursue the enemy, he disobeyed these instructions. His men advanced out of sight of the main army, whereupon the Parthians reappeared behind them. Rapidly surrounded, Publius withdrew his men to a narrow ridge, where they presented an easy target.

Once again the enemy's archers did their murderous work. Perceiving the situation to be hopeless and fearing capture, Publius bade his men farewell and told them to look after their own safety. Then, since he was unable to use his hand, which had been pierced through with an arrow, he presented his side to his shield-bearer and ordered him to run him through with his sword. Most of his officers followed his example and put themselves to death.

Once they had overrun the Roman position, the Parthians cut off the head of Publius and mounted it on a spear. They then carried it back to the main Roman army and rode up and down our lines, taunting M. Crassus to come and look upon his son. Seeing what had happened, he addressed our men as follows: 'Romans, this grief is a private thing of my own. But in you, who are safe and sound, abide the great fortune and the glory of Rome. And now, if you feel any pity for me, who have lost the best son that any father has ever had, show it in the fury with which you face the enemy.'

Regrettably, they paid no heed. On the contrary, this sight more than all the other dreadful things that had happened broke the spirit and paralysed the energies of our forces. The airborne slaughter resumed, and it is a certainty that the entire army would have been annihilated had not night fallen and the Parthians withdrawn, shouting that they would give Crassus the night to grieve for his son and would return to finish us off in the morning.

This provided us with an opportunity. M. Crassus being prostrate with grief and despair, and no longer capable of issuing orders, I took over the direction of our forces, and in silence and under cover of darkness those who could walk made a forced march to the town of Carrhae, leaving behind, amidst the most piteous cries and pleadings, some four thousand wounded who were either massacred or enslaved by the Parthians the following day.

At Carrhae our forces divided. I led five hundred men in the direction of Syria while M. Crassus took the bulk of our surviving army towards the mountains of Armenia. Intelligence reports indicate that outside the fortress of Sinnaca he was confronted by an army led by a subordinate of the Parthian king, who offered a truce. M. Crassus was compelled by his mutinous legionaries to go forward and negotiate, even though he believed it to be a trap. As he went, he turned and spoke these words: 'I call upon all you Roman officers present to see that I am being forced to go this way. You are eyewitnesses of the shameful and violent treatment that I have received. But if you escape and get home safely, tell them all that Crassus died because he was deceived by the enemy, not because he was handed over to the Parthians by his own countrymen.'

These are his last known words. He was killed along with his legionary commanders. I am informed that afterwards his severed head was delivered personally to the king of the Parthians by Sillaces during a performance of The Bacchae *and that it was used as a prop on stage. Afterwards the king caused Crassus's mouth to be filled with molten gold, remarking: 'Gorge yourself now with that metal for which in life you were so greedy.'*

I await the Senate's orders.

When Pompey finished reading, there was silence.

Finally Cicero said, 'How many men have we lost, do we have any idea?'

'I estimate thirty thousand.'

There was a groan of dismay from the assembled senators. Someone said that if that were true, then it was the worst defeat since Hannibal had wiped out the Senate's army at Cannae, one hundred and fifty years before.

'This document,' said Pompey, waving Cassius's dispatch, 'must go no further than this room.'

Cicero said, 'I agree. Cassius's frankness is admirable in private, but a less alarming version must be prepared for the people, stressing the bravery of our legionaries and their commanders.'

Scipio, who was Publius's father-in-law, said, 'Yes, they all died heroes – that's what we must tell everyone. That's what I'm going to tell my daughter, certainly. The poor girl is a widow at nineteen.'

Pompey said, 'Please give her my condolences.'

Then Hortensius spoke up. The ex-consul was in his sixties and mostly retired, but still listened to with respect. 'What happens next? Presumably the Parthians won't leave it at that. Knowing our weakness, they'll invade Syria in retaliation. We can barely muster a legion in its defence and we have no governor.'

'I would propose we make Cassius acting governor,' said Pompey. 'He's a hard, unsparing man – exactly what this emergency demands. As for an army – well, he must raise and train a new one locally.'

Ahenobarbus, who never lost an opportunity to undermine Caesar, said, 'All our best fighting men are in Gaul. Caesar has ten legions – a huge number. Why don't we order him to send a couple to Syria to fill the breach?'

At the mention of Caesar's name there was a perceptible stirring of hostility in the room.

'He recruited those legions,' pointed out Pompey. 'I agree they would be more useful in the east. But he regards those men as his own.'

'Well he needs to be reminded they are not his own. They exist to serve the republic, not him.'

Looking round at the senators all nodding vigorously in agreement, Cicero said afterwards that it was only at that moment that he realised the true significance of Crassus's death. 'Because, dear Tiro, what have we learned while writing our *Republic*? Divide power three ways in a state and tension is balanced; divide it in two and sooner or later one side must seek to dominate the other – it is a natural law. Disgraceful as he was, Crassus at least preserved the equilibrium between Pompey and Caesar. But with him gone, who will do it now?'

And so we drifted towards calamity. At times, Cicero was shrewd enough to see it. 'Can a constitution devised centuries ago to replace a monarchy, and based upon a citizens' militia, possibly hope to run an empire whose scope is beyond anything ever dreamed of by its framers? Or must the existence of standing armies and the influx of inconceivable wealth inevitably destroy our democratic system?'

And then at other times he would dismiss such apocalyptic talk as excessively gloomy and argue that the republic had endured all manner of disasters in the past – invasions, revolutions, civil wars – and had always somehow survived them: why should this time be any different?

But it was.

The elections that year were dominated by two men. Clodius sought to be praetor. Milo ran for the consulship. The violence and the bribery of the campaign were beyond anything the city had ever seen, and yet again polling day had to be postponed repeatedly. It was now more than a year since the republic had elected legitimate consuls. The Senate was presided over by an interrex, often a nonentity, on a rolling five-day mandate; the fasces of the consuls were placed symbolically in the Temple of Libitina, goddess of the dead. *Hurry back to Rome,* Cicero wrote to Atticus, who was on another of his business trips. *Come and look at the empty husks of the real old Roman Republic we used to know.*

It was a measure of how desperate things were becoming that Cicero vested all his hopes in Milo, even though Milo was entirely his opposite: crude and brutal, lacking in eloquence or indeed any political skill apart from the staging of gladiatorial games to enthuse the voters, the costs of which had left him bankrupt. Milo had outlived his usefulness to Pompey, who would have nothing more to do with him, and who was supporting his opponents, Scipio Nasica and Plautius Hypsaeus. But Cicero still needed him. *I have firmly concentrated all my efforts, all my time, care, diligence and thought, my whole mind in short, on winning the consulship for Milo.* He saw him as the best bulwark against the eventuality he dreaded most: Clodius's election to the consulship.

Cicero often asked me to perform small services for Milo during that campaign. For example, I went back through our files and prepared lists of our old supporters for him to canvass. I also set up meetings between him and Cicero's clients in the various tribal headquarters. I even took him bags of money that Cicero had raised from wealthy donors.

One day in the new year, Cicero asked me, as a favour, if I would spend a short time observing Milo's campaign at first hand. 'To put the matter bluntly, I'm worried he's going to lose. You know elections as well as I do. Watch him with the voters. See if anything can be done to improve his prospects. If he loses and Clodius wins, I don't need to tell you it will be a disaster for me.'

I cannot pretend that I was delighted with the assignment, but

I did as I was asked, and on the eighteenth day of January I turned up at Milo's house, which was on the steepest part of the Palatine, behind the Temple of Saturn. A listless crowd was gathered outside, but of the would-be consul himself there was no sign. I knew then that Milo's candidacy was in trouble. If a man is standing for election and feels himself to have a chance of winning, he works every hour of the day. But Milo did not emerge until the middle of the morning, and when he did, he took me to one side to complain about Pompey, who he said was entertaining Clodius that very morning at his country house in the Alban Hills.

'The man's ingratitude is unbelievable! Do you remember how he used to be so frightened of Clodius and his gang that he daren't even set foot out of doors until I brought in my gladiators to clear the streets? And now he has taken that snake under his roof, yet he won't even bid me good morning!'

I sympathised – we all knew what Pompey was like: a great man, but entirely preoccupied with himself – and then tried tactfully to steer the conversation back to Milo's campaign. There was not long until polling day. Where did he plan to spend these precious final hours?

'Today,' he announced, 'I am going to Lanuvium, my adopted grandfather's ancestral home.'

I could scarcely believe it. 'You're leaving Rome, this close to the actual vote?'

'It's only twenty miles. A new priest is to be nominated for the Temple of Juno the Saviour. She is the municipal deity, which means that the ceremony will be huge – you'll see, hundreds of voters will be there.'

'Even so, surely these voters are already committed to you, given your family connection to the town? Wouldn't your time be better spent pursuing voters who are undecided?'

But Milo refused to discuss it further. Indeed his refusal was so absolute that now, when I look back on it, I wonder if he hadn't already given up hope of winning the election in the voting pens and decided to go looking for trouble instead. After all, Lanuvium is also in the Alban Hills, and the road to it would take us practically past Pompey's gates. He must have calculated there was a good chance we would meet Clodius on the way. It would have been just the sort of opportunity for a fight he relished.

By the time we set out that afternoon he had gathered together a considerable wagon train of luggage and servants, protected by his usual small private army of slaves and gladiators armed with swords and javelins. Milo rode in a carriage at the head of this menacing column together with his wife, Fausta. He invited me to join them but I preferred the discomfort of horseback to sharing a carriage with those two, whose tempestuous relationship was notorious. We clattered off down the Via Appia, arrogantly forcing all the other traffic out of our way – again, I noted, poor electoral tactics – and had been going for about two hours when of course, on the outskirts of Bovillae, we duly encountered Clodius heading in the opposite direction, back to Rome.

Clodius was on horseback with perhaps thirty attendants – less well armed than Milo's, and far less numerous. I was in the middle of our column. As he passed, he caught my eye. He knew me pretty well as Cicero's secretary. He certainly gave me a foul look.

The rest of his party followed him. I averted my gaze. I wanted no trouble. But moments later, from behind me, there was a shout and then the clash of steel hitting steel. I turned and saw that a fight had broken out between our gladiators, who were bringing up the rear, and some of Clodius's men. Clodius himself had already gone a little way further along the road. He drew up his horse and turned, and at that moment Birria, the gladiator who had sometimes acted as a bodyguard to Cicero, hurled a javelin at him. It did not hit him full on, but rather in his side as he was in the act of turning, and the force of it almost knocked him from his saddle. The barbed tip buried itself deep in his flesh. He looked at it in astonishment, and screamed and clutched at the shaft with both hands, his whitened toga turning crimson with blood.

His bodyguards spurred their horses and surrounded him. Our convoy halted. I noticed we were close to a tavern – the same place, by bizarre coincidence, where we had stopped to pick up our horses on the night Cicero fled Rome. Milo jumped out of his carriage with his sword drawn and walked down the side of the road to see what was going on. All along the column men were dismounting. By now Clodius's attendants had pulled the javelin from his ribs and were helping him towards the tavern. He was sufficiently conscious to be able to half walk supported on the arms of his companions. Meanwhile small groups of men were fighting hand-to-hand along the road and in the fields next to it – desperate, hacking struggles, some on horseback, some on foot – such a confused melee that I could not at first distinguish our men from theirs. But gradually I perceived that ours were winning, for we outnumbered them three to one. I saw several of Clodius's men, despairing of victory, fling up their arms in surrender or fall to their knees. Others simply threw aside their weapons, turned and ran, or galloped off. No one bothered to pursue them.

The struggle over, Milo, with his arms akimbo, surveyed the carnage, then gestured to Birria and a few others to go and fetch Clodius from the tavern.

I got down from my horse. I had no idea what would happen next. I walked towards Milo. Just then there was a shout, or rather a scream from the tavern, and Clodius was carried out by four gladiators, each holding an arm or a leg. Milo had a calculation to make: would he let Clodius live and take the consequences, or kill him and have done with it? They laid him on the road at his feet. Milo took a javelin from the man standing next to him, checked the tip with his thumb, placed it in the centre of Clodius's chest, grasped the shaft and plunged it in with all his force. Clodius's mouth fountained blood. After that, they all took turns in slashing at the corpse, but I could not bring myself to watch.

I was no horseman, yet I believe I galloped back to Rome at a speed a cavalryman would have been proud of. I urged my exhausted mount up to the Palatine, and for the second time in half a year I found myself blurting out to Cicero the news that one of his enemies – the greatest of them all – was dead.

He gave no sign of pleasure. He was ice-cold, calculating. He drummed his fingers and then said, 'Where is Milo now?'

'I believe he carried on to Lanuvium for the ceremony as planned.'

'And Clodius's body?'

'The last time I saw it, it was still by the roadside.'

'Milo made no attempt to conceal it?'

'No, he said there was no point – there were too many witnesses.'

'That's probably true – it's a busy spot. Were *you* seen by many people?'

'I don't think so. Clodius recognised me, but not the others.'

He gave a hard smile. 'Clodius at least we no longer have to worry about.' He thought it over and nodded. 'That's good – good that you weren't seen. I think it would be better if we agree you were here with me all afternoon.'

'Why?'

'It wouldn't be wise for me to be implicated in this business, even indirectly.'

'You anticipate this will cause you trouble?'

'Oh, I am quite certain of it. The question is: how much?'

We settled down to wait for word of what had happened to reach Rome. In the fading light of the afternoon I found it difficult to banish from my mind the image of Clodius dying like a stuck pig. I had witnessed death before, but that was the first time I had seen a man killed in front of me.

About an hour before darkness, a woman's piercing shriek arose from some place nearby. It went on and on – a frightening, other-worldly ululation.

Cicero walked over and opened the door to his terrace and listened. 'The Lady Fulvia,' he said judiciously, 'if I am not mistaken, has just learned she is a widow.'

He sent a servant up the hill to find out what was happening. The man came back and reported that Clodius's body had arrived in Rome on a litter belonging to the senator Sextus Tedius, who had discovered it beside the Via Appia. The corpse had been conveyed to Clodius's house and received by Fulvia. In her grief and fury she had stripped it naked, apart from its sandals, propped it up, and was now sitting beside it in the street beneath flaming torches, crying out that everyone should come and see what had been done to her husband.

Cicero said, 'She means to whip up the mob.' He ordered the guard on the house to be doubled overnight.

The following morning it was judged far too dangerous for Cicero or any other prominent senator to venture out. We watched from the terrace as a huge crowd led by Fulvia escorted the body on its bier down to the Forum and placed it on the rostra, and then we listened as Clodius's lieutenants worked the plebs up to a fury. At the end of the bitter eulogies the mourners broke into the Senate house and carried Clodius's corpse inside, then went back across the Forum to the Argiletum and started dragging out benches and tables and chests full of volumes from the booksellers' shops. To our horror we realised they were constructing a funeral pyre.

Around midday, smoke began to issue from the small windows set high up in the walls of the Senate chamber. Sheets of orange flame and scraps of burning books whirled against the sky, while from inside came a terrifying and uninterrupted roar, as if a vent had been opened to the underworld. An hour later the roof split from end to end; thousands of tiles and spars of fiery timber plunged soundlessly from view; there was a strange interval of silence; and then the noise of the crash passed over us like a hot wind.

The fountain of smoke and dust and ashes lingered above the centre of Rome in a pall for several days, until the rain washed it away; and in this manner the last mortal vestiges of Publius Clodius Pulcher and the ancient assembly building he had reviled all his life vanished together from the face of the earth.

VIII

The destruction of the Senate house had a powerful effect on Cicero. He went down the next day under heavy guard, grasping a stout stick, and clambered around the smouldering ruins. The blackened brickwork was still warm to the touch. The wind howled through the gaping holes, and from time to time from above our heads some piece of debris would dislodge and fall with a soft thump into the drifts of ash. Six hundred years that temple had stood there – a witness to the greatest moments in Rome's existence, and his own – and now it had gone in less than half an afternoon.

Everyone, including Cicero, assumed that Milo would now go into voluntary exile, or at any rate that he would keep well clear of Rome. But that was to underrate the bravado of the man. Far from lying low, he put himself at the head of an even larger force of gladiators and re-entered the city that same afternoon, barricading himself in his house. The grieving supporters of Clodius immediately laid siege to it. But they were easily driven off by arrows. They then went in search of a less formidable fortress on which to vent their anger, and found one in the home of the interrex, Marcus Aemilius Lepidus.

Although he was only thirty-six, and not yet even praetor, Lepidus was a member of the College of Pontiffs, and in the absence of any elected consuls that was enough to make him temporary chief magistrate. The damage inflicted on his property was slight – his wife's nuptial couch was broken up and her weaving destroyed – but the assault created a sense of outrage and panic in the Senate.

Lepidus, ever conscious of his dignity, played up the incident for all it was worth; indeed, this was the beginning of his rise to prominence. (Cicero used to say that Lepidus was the luckiest politician he knew: every time he made a mess of something he was showered with rewards – 'He is a sort of genius of mediocrity.') The young interrex summoned a meeting of the Senate to be held outside the city walls, on the Field of Mars, in Pompey's new theatre – a large chamber within the complex had to be specially consecrated for the occasion – and he invited Pompey to attend.

This was three days after the burning of the Senate house.

Pompey duly obliged, sweeping down the hill from his palace surrounded by two hundred legionaries in full battle array – an entirely legal display of force, as he held military imperium as governor of Spain. But still – nothing like it had been seen since the days of Sulla. He left them picketed in the portico of the theatre while he went inside and listened modestly as his supporters demanded that he be appointed dictator for six months so that he could take the steps necessary to restore order: call up all the military reservists in Italy, put Rome under curfew, suspend the imminent elections and bring the killers of Clodius to justice.

Cicero saw the danger at once and rose to speak. 'No one has greater respect for Pompey than I,' he began, 'but we must be careful not to do our enemies' work for them. To argue that to preserve our freedoms we must suspend our freedoms, that to safeguard elections we must cancel elections, that to defend ourselves from dictatorship we must appoint a dictator – what logic is this? We have elections scheduled. We have candidates on the ballot. The canvass is completed. The best way for us to show confidence in our institutions is to allow them to function normally and to elect our magistrates as our ancestors taught us in the olden time.'

Pompey nodded, as if he could not have put the issue better himself, and at the end of the session he made an elaborate show of congratulating Cicero on his staunch defence of the constitution. But Cicero was not fooled. He saw exactly what Pompey was up to.

That night, Milo came to visit him for a council of war. Also present was Caelius Rufus, now a tribune and a long-term supporter and close friend of Milo. From down in the valley came the sound of scuffling, of dogs barking and occasional shouts and cries. A group of men carrying flaming torches ran across the Forum. But most citizens were too afraid to venture out and stayed in their houses behind barred doors. Milo seemed to think he had the election in the bag. After all, he had rid the state of Clodius, for which most decent people were grateful, and the burning-down of the Senate house and the violence in the streets had appalled the majority of voters.

Cicero said, 'I agree that if there were a ballot tomorrow, Milo, you would probably win it. But there is not going to be a ballot. Pompey will see to that.'

'How can he?'

'He'll use the campaign as a cover to manufacture an atmosphere of hysteria so that the Senate and the people will be forced to turn to him to abort the elections.'

Rufus said, 'He's bluffing. He doesn't have the power.'

'Oh, he has the power, and he knows it. All he has to do is sit tight and wait for things to come to him.'

Milo and Rufus both dismissed Cicero's fears as the nervousness of an old man, and the next day resumed campaigning with fresh energy. But Cicero was right: the mood in Rome was too jittery for normal electioneering and Milo walked straight into Pompey's trap. One morning soon after their meeting Cicero received an urgent summons to see Pompey. He found the great man's house ringed with soldiers and Pompey himself in an elevated part of the garden with double his normal bodyguard. Seated in the portico with him was a man Pompey introduced as Licinius, the owner of an eating house near the Circus Maximus. Pompey ordered Licinius to repeat his tale to Cicero, and Licinius duly described how he had overheard a group of Milo's gladiators plotting at his counter to murder Pompey, and how, when they realised he was listening, they had tried to silence him by stabbing him: as proof he showed Cicero a minor flesh wound just beneath his ribs.

Of course, as Cicero said to me afterwards, the whole story was absurd. 'For a start, whoever heard of such feeble gladiators? If that kind of man wishes to silence you, you are silenced.' But it didn't matter. The eating-house plot, as it became known, joined all the other rumours now circulating about Milo – that he had turned his house into an arsenal filled with swords, shields and javelins; that he had stocks of brands hidden throughout the city in order to burn it down; that he had shipped arms along the Tiber to his villa at Ocriculum; that the assassins who had murdered Clodius would be turned loose on his opponents in the election . . .

The next time the Senate met, no less a figure than Marcus Bibulus, Caesar's former consular colleague and passionate life-long enemy, rose to propose that Pompey should hold office by emergency decree as sole consul. This was remarkable enough; what no one had anticipated was the reaction of Cato. A hush fell over the chamber as he got to his feet. 'I would not have proposed this motion myself,' he said, 'but seeing as it has been laid before us, I propose we accept it as a sensible compromise. Some government is better than no government; a sole consulship is better than a dictatorship; and Pompey is more likely to rule wisely than anyone else.'

Coming from Cato, this was almost unbelievable – he had used the word 'compromise' for the first time in his life – and no one looked more stunned than Pompey. Afterwards, so the story went, he invited Cato back to his house to thank him personally and to ask him in future to be his private adviser in all matters of state. 'You have no need to thank me,' replied Cato, 'for I only did what I believed to be in the best interests of the republic. If you wish to talk to me alone I shall certainly be at your disposal. But I shall say nothing to you in private that I wouldn't say anywhere else, and I shall never hold my tongue in public to please you.'

Cicero observed their new closeness with deep foreboding. 'Why do you think men like Cato and Bibulus have suddenly thrown in their lot with Pompey? Do you imagine they believe all this nonsense about a plot to murder him? Do you think they've suddenly changed their minds about him? Not at all! They've given him sole authority because they see him as their best hope of checking the ambitions of Caesar. I'm sure Pompey recognises this and believes he can control them. But he's wrong. Don't forget I know him. His vanity is his weakness. They will flatter him and load him down with powers and honours, and he won't even notice what they're doing, until one day it will be too late – they will have set him on a collision course with Caesar. And then we shall have war.'

Cicero went straight from the Senate meeting to find Milo, and told him in blunt terms that he must now abandon his campaign for the consulship. 'If you send a message to Pompey before nightfall and announce that you are withdrawing your candidacy in the interests of national unity, you might just head off a prosecution. If you don't, you're finished.'

'And if I *am* prosecuted,' responded Milo slyly, 'will you defend me?'

I had expected Cicero to say it was impossible. Instead he sighed and ran his hand through his hair. 'Listen to me, Milo – listen carefully. When I was at the lowest point of my life, six years ago in Thessalonica, you were the only one who offered me hope. Therefore you can rest assured, whatever happens I shan't turn my back on you now. But for pity's sake, don't let it come to that. Write to Pompey today.'

Milo promised to think about it, although naturally he did not withdraw. The vaulting ambition that had carried him, in a mere half-dozen years, from ownership of a gladiator school to the brink of the consulship, was hardly likely at this late stage to be bridled by caution and good sense. Besides, his campaign debts were so enormous (some said the amount he owed was seventy million sesterces) that he was facing exile whatever he did; he gained nothing by giving up now. So he continued with his canvass and Pompey moved ruthlessly to destroy him by setting up an inquiry into the events of the eighteenth and nineteenth of January – including the murder of Clodius, the burning of the Senate house and the attack on the home of Lepidus – under the chairmanship of Domitius Ahenobarbus. The slaves of Milo and Clodius were put to the torture to ascertain the facts, and I feared that some poor wretch, in his desperation, might remember my presence at the scene, which would have been embarrassing to Cicero. But I seem to have been blessed with the sort of personality that nobody notices – the reason perhaps why I have survived to write this account – and nobody mentioned me.

The inquiry led to Milo's trial for murder at the beginning of April and Cicero was required to honour his pledge to defend him. It was the only time I ever saw him prostrated by nerves. Pompey had filled the centre of the city with soldiers to guarantee order. But the effect was the opposite of reassuring. They blockaded every approach to the Forum and guarded the main public buildings. All the shops were closed. An atmosphere of tension and dread lay over the city. Pompey himself came to watch proceedings and took a seat high up on the steps of the Temple of Saturn, surrounded by troops. Yet despite the show of force, the vast pro-Clodian crowd was allowed to intimidate the court. They jeered both Milo and Cicero whenever they tried to speak and made it difficult for the defence to be heard. All outrage and emotion was on their side – the brutality of the crime, the spectacle of the weeping widow and her fatherless children, and above all perhaps that curious retrospective sanctity that settles over the reputation of any politician, however worthless, if his career is cut off in its prime.

As chief defence advocate, allowed under the special rules of the court only two hours to speak, Cicero had an almost impossible task. He could hardly pretend that Milo, who had openly boasted of what he had done, was innocent of the crime. Indeed some of Milo's supporters, such as Rufus, thought that Cicero should make a virtue of it and argue that the murder was not a crime at all but a public service. Cicero recoiled from that line of reasoning. 'What are you saying? That any man can be condemned to death without trial and summarily executed by his enemies if it suits enough people? That's mob rule, Rufus – exactly what Clodius believed in – and I refuse to stand up in a Roman court and make such a case.'

The only feasible alternative was to argue that the killing was justified on the grounds of self-defence – but that was difficult to reconcile with the evidence that Clodius had been dragged out of the tavern and finished off in cold blood. Still, it was not impossible. I had known Cicero win from weaker positions. And he wrote a good speech. However, on the morning he was due to deliver it, he woke gripped by a terrible anxiety. At first I took no notice. He was often nervous before a big oration, and suffered from loose bowels and vomiting. But this morning was different. He was not gripped by fear, which he sometimes called 'cold strength' and had learned how to harness; rather he was simply in a funk and could not remember a word of what he was supposed to say.

Milo suggested he should go down to the Forum in a closed litter and wait somewhere out of sight, calmly composing himself until it was time for him to speak; and this was what we tried. Cicero, at his request, had been provided with a bodyguard by Pompey for the duration of the trial, and they cordoned off a part of the Grove of Vesta and kept everyone away while the orator reclined beneath the thick embroidered canopy, trying to commit his speech to memory and occasionally leaning out to retch on the sacred earth. But although he could not see the crowd, he could hear it chanting and roaring nearby, and that was almost worse. When the praetor's clerk finally came to fetch us, Cicero's legs were so weak he could barely stand. As we walked into the Forum, the noise was terrific, and the sunlight glinting on the armour and weapons of the soldiers dazzled our eyes.

The Clodians jeered Cicero when he appeared and jeered him all the louder when he tried to speak. His nerves were so obvious he actually confessed them in his opening sentence – 'I am afraid, gentlemen of the jury: an unseemly condition in which to begin a speech in defence of the bravest of men, but there it is' – and blamed his fear squarely on the rigged nature of the hearing: 'Wherever I look, I look in vain for the familiar environment of the courts and the traditional procedure of the law.'

Unfortunately, complaining about the rules of a contest is always a sure sign of a man who knows he is about to lose it, and although Cicero made some effective points – 'Suppose, gentlemen, I could induce you to acquit Milo, but only on condition that Clodius comes back to life again: why all those terrified glances?' – a speech is only as good as its delivery. By thirty-eight votes to thirteen the jury found Milo guilty, and he was sent into exile for life. His property was hastily auctioned at knock-down prices to pay his creditors, and Cicero directed Terentia's steward, Philotimus, to buy a lot of it anonymously so that it could be disposed of later and the profits handed to Milo's wife, Fausta: she had made it clear she would not be accompanying her husband into exile. A day or two later Milo went off with remarkable cheerfulness to Massilia in southern Gaul. His departure was very much in the spirit of a gladiator who knew he would lose eventually and was simply grateful to have lived so long. Cicero tried to make amends by publishing the speech he would have given if his nerves hadn't got the better of him. He sent a copy to Milo, who replied charmingly a few months later that he was glad Cicero hadn't spoken it, *for otherwise I should not be eating such wonderful Massilian mullets*.

* * *

Soon after Milo left Rome, Pompey invited Cicero to dinner to show there were no hard feelings. Cicero went off grumbling and reeled home afterwards in such a state of amazement that he came and woke me up, for who should have been at the dinner table but the widow of Publius Crassus, the teenaged Cornelia – and Pompey had married her!

Cicero said, 'Well, naturally I congratulated him – she's a beautiful and accomplished girl, even if she is young enough to be his granddaughter – and then I asked him, by way of conversation, what Caesar had made of the match. He looked at me with great disdain and said that he hadn't even told Caesar: what business was it of Caesar's? He was fifty-three years old and he would marry whomever he pleased!

'I replied, as gently as I could, that perhaps Caesar might take a different view – after all, he had sought a marital alliance and been rebuffed, and the bride's father has not exactly shown himself a friend of Caesar's. To which Pompey replied, "Oh, don't worry about Scipio, he's entirely friendly. I'm appointing him my consular colleague for the remainder of my term!" Is the man mad, do you suppose? Caesar is going to look at Rome and think that the whole place has been taken over by the aristocratic party, with Pompey at their head.' Cicero groaned and closed his eyes; I guessed he had drunk rather a lot. 'I told you this would happen. I am Cassandra – doomed to see the future yet destined never to be believed.'

Cassandra or not, there was one consequence of Pompey's special consulship that Cicero had not foreseen. To help end electoral corruption, Pompey had decided to reform the laws relating to the fourteen provincial commands. Up to this point, consuls and praetors had always left Rome immediately upon the expiry of their term of office to take up their allotted province; and because of the huge sums that could be extorted from such commands, a practice had arisen of candidates borrowing against their expected earnings in order to fund their election campaigns. Pompey, with amazing hypocrisy considering his own abuse of the system, decided to put a stop to all that. Henceforth, a period of five years would have to elapse between holding office in Rome and taking up a governorship overseas. To fill such positions in the interim it was decreed that every senator of praetorian rank who had never done their turn as governor would have to draw lots for the vacant provinces.

To his horror, Cicero now realised he was in danger of having to do what he had always sworn to avoid: sweating it out in some corner of the empire, administering justice to the natives. He went to see Pompey to plead to be excused. His health was poor, he said. He was getting old. He even suggested that the time he had spent in exile might be counted as his term abroad.

Pompey wouldn't hear of it. Indeed he seemed to take a malicious pleasure in running through all the possible commands that might now fall to Cicero, with their various unique drawbacks – extreme distance from Rome, rebellious tribesmen, ferocious customs, hostile climates, savage wild beasts, impassable roads, incurable local diseases and so forth. Lots to determine who went where were drawn at a special session of the Senate, with Pompey in the chair. Cicero went up and plucked his token from the urn and handed it to Pompey, who read out the result with a smile: 'Marcus Tullius draws Cilicia.'

Cilicia! Cicero could barely conceal his dismay. This mountainous, primitive homeland of pirates at the extreme eastern edge of the Mediterranean – which included within its administration the island of Cyprus – was about as far away from

Rome as it was possible to get. It also shared a border with Syria, and so was within range of the Parthian army, if Cassius was unable to hold them in check. Finally, to cap Cicero's woes, the current governor was Clodius's brother, Appius Clodius Pulcher, who could be relied upon to make his successor's life as difficult as possible.

I knew he would expect me to go with him and I tried desperately to think of excuses why I should stay behind. He had just completed *On the Republic*. I told him that in my view I would be more use to him in Rome, overseeing its publication.

'Nonsense,' he said, 'Atticus will take care of copying and circulation.'

'There's also my health,' I continued, 'I've never really recovered from that fever I contracted at Arpinum.'

'In that case a sea voyage will do you good.'

And so it went on. My every objection was met by an answer. He started to become offended. But I had a bad feeling about this expedition. Although he swore we would only be gone a year, I sensed it would be longer. Rome felt strangely impermanent to me. Perhaps it was a consequence of having to pass the burnt-out shell of the Senate house every day, or maybe it was my knowledge of the widening split between Pompey and Caesar. Whatever the reason, I had a superstitious dread that if I left I might never come back, and that even if I did return it would be to a different city.

Eventually Cicero said, 'Well, I cannot force you to come – you're a free man now. But I feel you owe me this one last service, and I'll make a bargain with you. When we return, I'll give you the money to buy that farm you've always wanted, and I shan't press you to perform any more duties for me. The rest of your life will be your own.'

I could hardly refuse such an offer, and so I tried to ignore my forebodings and set about helping him plan his administration.

As governor of Cilicia, Cicero would have command of a standing army of about fourteen thousand men, with every prospect of having to fight a war. He decided therefore to appoint two legates with military experience. One was his old comrade Caius Pomptinus, the praetor who had helped him round up Catilina's co-conspirators. For the second he turned to his brother Quintus, who had expressed a strong desire to quit Gaul. At first his service under Caesar had been a great success. He had taken part in the invasion of Britain, and on his return Caesar had placed him in command of a legion that soon afterwards was attacked in its winter camp by a vastly superior force of Gauls. The fighting had been fierce: nine tenths of the Romans had been wounded. But Quintus, although ill and exhausted, had kept a cool head and the legion had survived the siege long enough for Caesar to arrive and relieve them; afterwards he had been singled out for praise by Caesar in his *Commentaries*.

The following summer he was promoted to command of the newly formed Fourteenth Legion. This time, however, he had disobeyed Caesar's orders. Instead of keeping all his men in camp, he had sent out several hundred raw recruits to forage for food. They had been cut off by an invading force of Germans. Caught in the open, they had stood gaping at their commanders, unsure of what to do, and half of them had been massacred when they tried to make a run for it. *All my previous good standing with Caesar has been destroyed*, Quintus wrote sadly to his brother. *He treats me to my face with civility but I detect a certain coldness, and I know he goes behind my back to consult with my junior officers; in short I fear I may never fully regain his trust.* Cicero wrote to

Caesar asking if his brother might be allowed to join him in Cilicia; Caesar readily agreed; and two months later Quintus arrived back in Rome.

As far as I am aware, Cicero never uttered a word of reproach to his brother. Nevertheless, something was altered in their relationship. I believe Quintus felt a keen sense of failure. He had hoped to find fame and fortune and independence in Gaul; instead he came back tarnished, out of pocket and more dependent than ever on his famous sibling. His marriage remained bitter. He was still drinking heavily. And his only son, young Quintus, who was now fifteen, had all the charms of that particular age, being sullen, secretive, insolent and duplicitous. Cicero believed the boy needed more of his father's attention and suggested he should accompany us to Cilicia, along with his own son, Marcus. My expectations of our trip, already low, receded further.

When we left Rome at the start of the senatorial recess, we were a huge party. Cicero had been invested with imperium and was obliged to travel with six lictors as well as a great retinue of slaves carrying all our baggage for the voyage abroad. Terentia came part of the way to see her husband off, and so did Tullia, who had just been divorced by Crassipes. She was closer to her father than ever and read him poetry on the journey. Privately he fretted to me about her future: twenty-five years old, no child, no husband . . . We stopped off at Tusculum to say goodbye to Atticus, and Cicero asked him as a favour to keep an eye on Tullia and try to find her a new match while he was away.

'Of course I shall,' Atticus replied, 'and would you in return do a favour for me? Will you try to make Quintus just a little kinder to my sister? I know Pomponia is a difficult woman, but he has returned from Gaul in a permanent foul temper, and their constant arguments are having a bad effect on their boy.'

Cicero agreed, and when we met up with Quintus and his family at Arpinum, he took his brother aside and repeated what Atticus had said. Quintus promised to do his best. But Pomponia, I'm afraid, was quite impossible, and it was not long before the couple were refusing to speak to one another, let alone share a bed, and they parted very coldly.

Relations between Terentia and Cicero were more civil, apart from the one vexed area that had been a source of antagonism between them all their married life – money. In contrast to her husband, Terentia had welcomed his appointment as governor, seeing in it a wonderful opportunity for enrichment. She had even brought her steward, Philotimus, along on the journey south so that he could give Cicero the benefit of his various ideas for skimming off a profit. Cicero kept postponing the conversation and Terentia kept nagging him to have it until at last on their final day together he lost his temper.

'This fixation of yours with making money is really most unseemly.'

'This fixation of yours with spending it gives me no choice!'

Cicero paused for a moment to control his irritation and then tried to explain the matter calmly. 'You don't seem to understand – a man in my position cannot risk the slightest impropriety. My enemies are just waiting for an opportunity to prosecute me for corruption.'

'So you intend to be the only provincial governor in history not to come home richer than he went out?'

'My dear wife, if you ever read a word I wrote, you would know I am just about to publish a treatise on good government. How will that sit with a reputation for thievery in office?'

'Books!' said Terentia with great contempt. 'Where is the money in *books*?'

They repaired their quarrel sufficiently to dine together that night, and to humour her Cicero agreed that at some stage in the coming year he would at least listen to Philotimus's business proposals – but only on condition they were legal.

The next morning the family parted, with many tears and much embracing – Cicero and Marcus, who was now fourteen, setting off on horseback together side by side, while Terentia and Tullia stood at the gate of the family farm, waving. I remember that just before the road carried us out of sight I took a final look over my shoulder. Terentia had gone in by then but Tullia was still there watching us, a fragile figure against the majesty of the mountains.

We were due to embark on the first leg of our voyage to Cilicia from Brundisium, and it was while we were on the road there, at Venusia, that Cicero received an invitation from Pompey. The great man was taking the winter sun at his villa in Tarentum and suggested that Cicero should come and stay for a couple of days 'to discuss the political situation'. As Tarentum was only forty miles from Brundisium, and as our route would take us practically past the door, and as Pompey was not a man to whom it was easy to say no, Cicero had little option but to accept.

Once again we found Pompey living in a state of great domestic happiness with a young bride: they seemed almost to be playing at being a married couple. The house was surprisingly modest; as governor of Spain Pompey had a mere fifty legionaries to protect him, and they were billeted on the neighbouring properties. Otherwise he was without executive authority, having given up his consulship amid universal praise for his wisdom. In fact I would say he was at the summit of his popularity. Crowds of locals stood around outside hoping to catch a glimpse of him; once or twice a day he would sally forth to shake hands and pat the heads of infants. He was quite corpulent now, breathless and rather an unhealthy purplish colour. Cornelia fussed over him like a little mother, trying to restrain his appetite at meals and encouraging him to take walks along the seashore, his guards following at a discreet distance. He was idle, somnolent, uxorious. Cicero presented him with a copy of *On the Republic*. He expressed great pleasure but immediately laid it aside and I never saw him open it.

Whenever I look back at this three-day interlude, it seems to stand out in my memory like some sunlit glade in the middle of a vast and darkening forest. Watching the two ageing statesmen throwing a ball for Marcus, or standing with their togas hitched up, skimming stones across the waves, it was impossible to believe that anything sinister was impending – or if it was, that it would amount to much. Pompey exuded absolute confidence.

I was not privy to all that passed between him and Cicero, although Cicero told me most of it afterwards. The political situation in essence was this: that Caesar had completed his conquest of Gaul; that the Gallic leader, Vercingetorix, had surrendered and was in custody; and that the enemy's army was wiped out (the final engagement had been the capture of the hilltop fortress of Uxellodunum along with its garrison of two thousand Gallic fighters, all of whom, on Caesar's orders, according to his *Commentaries*, had had both hands cut off before being sent home, *so that everyone might see what punishment was meted out to those who resisted Rome's rule*; there had been no trouble since).

Given all this, the question now arose of what to do with Caesar. His own preference was to be allowed to stand for a second consulship *in absentia* so that he could enter Rome with legal immunity for all the crimes and misdemeanours he had committed during his first; at the very least he wanted his command extended so that he could remain as ruler of Gaul. His opponents, led by Cato, believed that he should return to Rome and submit himself to the electorate just like any other citizen; and failing that, he should be forced to give up his army, it being intolerable to have a man in control of what was now eleven legions, sitting on the Italian border issuing diktats to the Senate.

'And what is Pompey's view?' I asked.

'Pompey's view varies according to the hour of the day you ask him. In the morning he thinks it entirely proper, as a reward for his achievements, that his good friend Caesar should be permitted to stand for the consulship without entering Rome. After lunch he sighs and wonders why Caesar can't simply come home and canvass face to face like anybody else: after all, that was what he did in Caesar's position, and what was so undignified about that? And then by evening, when – despite the best efforts of the good Lady Cornelia – he is flushed with wine, he starts shouting, "To hell with bloody Caesar! I'm sick of hearing about Caesar! Let him just try and set one toe in Italy with his bloody legions, and you'll see what I can do – I'll stamp my foot and a hundred thousand men will rise up at my command and come to the defence of the Senate!"'

'And what do you think will happen?'

'My guess is that if I were here I could probably just about persuade him to do the right thing and avoid civil war, which would be the ultimate calamity. My fear,' he added, 'is that when the vital decisions are being taken, I shall be a thousand miles from Rome.'

IX

I do not propose to describe in any detail Cicero's time as governor of Cilicia. I am sure history will judge it as of minor importance in the scale of things; Cicero judged it minor even at the time.

We reached Athens in the spring and stayed for ten days with Aristus, the principal professor of the Academy, who was at that time the greatest living exponent of the philosophy of Epicurus. Like Atticus, who was also a devoted Epicurean, Aristus took a practical, material view of what makes for a happy life: a healthy diet, moderate exercise, pleasant surroundings, congenial company and the avoidance of stressful situations. Cicero, whose god was Plato and whose life was full of stress, disputed this. He believed that Epicureanism amounted to a kind of anti-philosophy: 'You say happiness depends on bodily well-being. But continual physical well-being is beyond our control. If a man is suffering an agonising illness, say, or if he is being tortured, then in your philosophy he cannot be happy.'

'Perhaps he cannot be *supremely* happy,' conceded Aristus, 'but happiness will still be there in some form.'

'No, no, he cannot be happy *at all*,' insisted Cicero, 'because his happiness is entirely contingent on the physical. Whereas the most magnificent and fruitful promise in the entire history of philosophy is the simple maxim: *nothing is good except what is morally good*. From this we can prove that *moral goodness is sufficient by itself to create the happy life*. And from that derives a third maxim: *moral goodness is the only sort of good there is*.'

'Ah, but if I torture you,' objected Aristus, with a knowing laugh, 'you will be every bit as unhappy as I am.'

Cicero, however, was very serious. 'No, no, because if I remain morally good – which I am not claiming is easy, by the way, let alone that I have achieved it – then I must remain happy, however great my pain. Even as my torturer falls back in exhaustion there will be something beyond the physical that he cannot reach.'

Naturally I am simplifying a long and complicated discussion that lasted several days as we toured the buildings and antiquities of Athens. But this was what it boiled down to, and it was now that Cicero began to conceive of the idea of writing some work of philosophy that would not be a set of high-flown abstractions but rather a practical guide to achieving the good life.

From Athens we sailed down the coast and then hopped from island to island across the Aegean in a fleet of a dozen vessels. The Rhodian boats were large, cumbersome and slow; they pitched and rolled in even moderate seas and were open to the elements. I remember how I shivered in a rainstorm as we passed Delos, that melancholy rock where up to ten thousand slaves are said to be sold in a single day. Everywhere the crowds that turned out to see Cicero were immense; among Romans only Pompey and Caesar, and I suppose just possibly Cato, can have been more famous in the world. At Ephesus our teeming expedition of legates, quaestors, lictors and military tribunes, with all their slaves and baggage, was transferred to a convoy of ox carts and pack mules and we set off along the dusty mountain roads into the interior of Asia Minor.

It was a full fifty-two days after leaving Italy that we reached Laodicea, the first town in the province of Cilicia, where Cicero was immediately required to begin hearing cases. The poverty and exhaustion of the common people, the endless shuffling queues of petitioners in the gloomy basilica and the glaring white-stone forum, the constant moans and groans about customs officials and poll taxes, the petty corruption, the flies, the heat, the dysentery, the sharp stink of goat and sheep dung that seemed always in the air, the bitter-tasting wine and oily spicy food, the small scale of the town and the lack of anything beautiful to look at, or sophisticated to listen to, or savoury to eat – oh, how Cicero hated being stuck in such a place while the fate of the world was being decided back in Italy without him! I had barely unpacked my ink and stylus before he was dictating letters to everyone he could think of in Rome, pleading with them to make sure his term was restricted to a year.

We had not been there long when a dispatch arrived from Cassius reporting that the King of Parthia's son had invaded Syria at the head of such a massive force he had been obliged to withdraw his legions to the fortified city of Antioch. This meant Cicero had to set off immediately to join his own army at the foot of the Taurus mountains, the immense natural barrier separating Cilicia from Syria. Quintus was greatly excited, and for a month there seemed a real possibility that Cicero might have to command the defence of the entire eastern flank of the empire. But then a fresh report came from Cassius: the Parthians had retreated before the impregnable walls of Antioch; he had pursued and defeated them; the king's son was dead and the threat was over.

I am not sure whether Cicero was more relieved or disappointed. However, he still managed to have a war of sorts. Some of the local tribes had taken advantage of the Parthian crisis to rise in revolt against Roman rule. There was one fortress in particular, named Pindessium, where the rebel forces were concentrated, and Cicero laid siege to it.

We lived in an army camp in the mountains for two months, and Quintus was as happy as a schoolboy building ramps and towers, digging moats and bringing up artillery. I found the whole adventure distasteful, and so I think did Cicero, for the rebels stood no chance. Day after day we launched arrows and flaming projectiles into the town, until eventually it surrendered and our legionaries poured into the place to ransack it. Quintus had the leaders executed. The rest were put in chains and led off to the coast to be shipped to Delos and sold into slavery. Cicero watched them go with a gloomy expression. 'I suppose if I were a great military man like Caesar I would have all their hands amputated. Isn't that how one brings peace to these people? But I can't say I derive much satisfaction from using all the resources of civilisation to reduce a few barbarian huts to ashes.' Still, his men hailed him as imperator in the field, and afterwards he had me write six hundred letters – that is, one to every member of the Senate – requesting that he be awarded a triumph: a tremendous labour for me, working in the primitive conditions of an army camp, that left me prostrate with exhaustion.

Cicero placed Quintus in command of the army for the winter and returned to Laodicea. He was rather shocked by the relish with which his brother had crushed the rebellion, and also by his brusque manner with subordinates (*irritable, rude, careless*, as he described him to Atticus); he did not care much for his nephew, either – *a boy with a fine conceit for himself*. Quintus Junior liked to make sure everyone knew who he was – his name alone saw to that – and he treated the locals with great disdain. Still, Cicero tried to do his duty as an affectionate uncle, and at that spring's Festival of Liberalia, in the absence of the boy's father, he presided over the ceremony at which young Quintus became a man, personally helping him to shave his wispy beard and dress in his first toga.

As for his own son, young Marcus gave him cause for concern in a different way. The lad was affable, lazy, fond of sport and somewhat slow on the uptake when it came to his schoolwork. Rather than study Greek and Latin, he liked to hang around the army officers and practise swordplay and javelin throwing. 'I love him dearly,' Cicero said to me, 'and he is certainly a good-hearted fellow, but sometimes I wonder where on earth he comes from – I detect nothing in him of me at all.'

Nor was that the end of his family worries. He had left the choice of Tullia's new husband up to her and her mother, having made clear simply that his own preference was for a safe, worthy, respectable young aristocrat such as Tiberius Nero or the son of his old friend Servius Sulpicius. But the women had set their hearts instead on Publius Cornelius Dolabella, a most unsuitable match in Cicero's view. He was a notorious rake, only nineteen – about seven years younger than Tullia – yet remarkably he had already been married once, to a much older woman.

By the time the letter announcing their choice reached him, it was too late for Cicero to intervene: the wedding would have taken place before his answer arrived in Rome – a fact the women must have known. 'What is one to do?' he sighed to me. 'Well, such is life – let the gods bless what is done. I can understand why Tullia wants it – no doubt he's a handsome, charming type, and if anyone deserves a taste of life at last, it's she. But Terentia!

What is *she* thinking of? It sounds as though she's half in love with the fellow herself. I'm not sure I understand her any more.'

And here I come to the greatest of all Cicero's personal worries: that something clearly was amiss with Terentia. Recently he had received a reproachful letter from the exiled Milo demanding to know what had happened to all that property of his that Cicero had bought so cheaply at auction: his wife, Fausta, had never received a penny. As it happened, the agent who had acted on Cicero's behalf – Philotimus, Terentia's steward – was still hoping to persuade Cicero to adopt some dubious money-making scheme and was due to visit him in Laodicea.

Cicero received him in my presence and told him bluntly that there was no question of him or any member of his staff or family engaging in any shady business. 'So you can save your breath as far as that's concerned and tell me instead what's become of Milo's bankrupt estate. You remember the sale was fixed so you got it all for next to nothing, and then you were supposed to sell it at a profit and give the proceeds to Fausta?'

Philotimus, plumper than ever and already sweating in the summer heat, flushed even redder and started to stammer that he couldn't recall the details precisely: it was more than a year ago; he would have to consult his accounts and they were in Rome.

Cicero threw up his hands. 'Come now, man, you must remember. It's not that long ago. We're talking about tens of thousands. What has become of it all?'

But Philotimus would only repeat the same tale over and over: he was very sorry; he couldn't remember; he would need to check.

'I'm beginning to think you've pocketed the money yourself.'

Philotimus denied it.

Suddenly Cicero said, 'Does my wife know about this?'

At the mention of Terentia, a remarkable change came over Philotimus. He stopped squirming and became completely silent, and no matter how many times Cicero pressed him, he refused to say another word. Eventually Cicero told him to clear off out of his sight. After he had gone he said to me, 'Did you note that last piece of impertinence? Talk about defending a lady's honour – it was as if he thought I wasn't fit to utter my own wife's name.'

I agreed it was remarkable.

'*Remarkable* – that's one word for it. They were always very close, but ever since I went into exile . . .'

He shook his head and didn't finish the sentence. I made no reply. It did not seem proper to comment. To this day I have no idea whether his suspicions were correct. All I can say is that he was deeply perturbed by the whole affair and wrote at once to Atticus asking him to investigate discreetly: *I can't put all I fear into words.*

A month before the end of his official term as governor, Cicero, escorted by his lictors, set off back to Rome taking me and the two boys with him and leaving his quaestor in charge of the province.

He knew he could face censure for abandoning his post prematurely and for placing Cilicia in the hands of a first-year senator, but he calculated that with Caesar's governorship of Gaul about to come to an end, most men would have bigger issues on their minds. We travelled via Rhodes, which he wanted to show to Quintus and Marcus. He also desired to visit the tomb of Apollonius Molon, the great tutor of oratory whose lessons almost thirty years before had started him on his political ascent. We found it on a headland looking across the Carpathian Straits. A simple white marble stone bore the orator's name, and beneath it was carved in Greek one of his favourite precepts: *Nothing dries more quickly than a tear.* Cicero stood looking at it for a long time.

Unfortunately the diversion to Rhodes slowed our return considerably. The Etesian winds were unusually strong that summer, blowing in from the north day after day, and they trapped our open boats in harbour for three weeks. During that period the political situation in Rome worsened sharply, and by the time we reached Ephesus there was a sackful of alarming news waiting for Cicero. *The nearer the struggle approaches,* wrote Rufus, *the plainer the danger appears. Pompey is determined not to allow Caesar to be elected consul unless he surrenders his army and provinces; whereas Caesar is persuaded that he cannot survive if he leaves his army. So this is what their love affair, their scandalous union has come to – not covert backbiting, but outright war!*

In Athens, a week later, Cicero found more letters, including ones from both Pompey and Caesar, each complaining about the other and appealing to his loyalty. *As far as I am concerned, he may be consul or he may keep his legions,* wrote Pompey, *but I am certain that he cannot do both; I assume that you agree with my policy and will stand resolutely on my side and on the side of the Senate as you have always done.* And from Caesar: *I fear that Pompey's noble nature has blinded him to the true intentions of those individuals who have always wished me harm; I rely upon you, dear Cicero, to tell him that I cannot be, should not be, and will not be left defenceless.*

The two letters plunged Cicero into a state of acute anxiety. He sat in Aristus's library with both laid on the table before him and looked back and forth from one to the other. *I fancy I see the greatest struggle that history has ever known,* he wrote to Atticus. *There looms ahead a tremendous contest between them. Each counts me as his man. But what am I to do? They will try to draw a statement of my views. You will laugh when I say it, but I wish to heaven I was still back in my province.*

That night I lay shivering despite the Athens heat, my teeth chattering, hallucinating that Cicero was dictating a letter to me, a copy of which had to go to both Pompey and Caesar, assuring each of his support. But a phrase that would please one would infuriate the other, and I spent hour after hour in a panic trying to construct sentences that were utterly neutral. Whenever I thought I had managed it, the words would become disorganised in my head and I would have to start again. It was utter madness yet at the same time it seemed absolutely real, and when morning came I realised in a lucid interval that I had lapsed back into the fever that had afflicted me at Arpinum.

That day we were due to set off again by ship to Corinth. I tried hard to carry on as normal. But I guess I must have looked ghastly and hollow-eyed. Cicero tried to persuade me to eat but I was unable to keep food in my stomach. Although I managed to board the boat unaided, I spent the day's voyage almost comatose, and when we landed at Corinth that evening, apparently I had to be carried off the ship and put to bed.

The question now arose of what should be done with me. I was desperate not to be left behind, and Cicero did not want to abandon me. But he needed to get back to Rome, firstly to do what little was in his power to avert the impending civil war, and secondly to try to lobby for a triumph, of which, unrealistically, he still had slight hopes. He could not afford to waste days in Greece waiting for his secretary to recover. In retrospect I should have stayed in Corinth. Instead we gambled that I would be strong enough to withstand the two-day journey to Patrae, where a ship would be waiting to take us to Italy. It was a foolish decision. I was wrapped in blankets and placed in the back of a carriage and conveyed along the coastal road in great discomfort. When we reached Patrae, I begged them to go on without me. I was sure a long sea voyage would kill me. Cicero was still reluctant, but in the end he agreed. I was put to bed in a villa near the harbour belonging to Lyso, a Greek merchant. Cicero, Marcus and young Quintus gathered around my bed to say goodbye. They shook my hand. Cicero wept. I made some feeble joke about our parting scene resembling the deathbed of Socrates. And then they were gone.

Cicero wrote me a letter the following day and sent it back with Mario, one of his most trusted slaves.

> *I thought I could bear the want of you not too hard, but frankly I find it unendurable. I feel I did wrong to leave you. If after you are able to take nourishment you think you can overtake me, the decision is in your hands. Think it over in that clever head of yours. I miss you but I love you. Loving you I want to see you fit and well; missing you I want to see you as soon as possible. The former therefore must come first. So make it your chief concern to get well. Of your countless services to me this is the one I shall most appreciate.*

He wrote me many such letters during the time I was ill – once he sent three in a single day. Naturally I missed him as much as he missed me. But my health was broken. I could not travel. It was to be eight months before I saw him again, and by then his world, our world, was utterly transformed.

Lyso was an attentive host and brought in his own doctor, a fellow Greek named Asclapo, to treat me. I was purged and sweated and starved and hydrated: all the standard remedies for a tertian fever were attempted when what I really needed was rest. Cicero, however, fretted that Lyso was *a little casual: all Greeks are*, and arranged for me to be moved after a few days to a larger and more peaceful house up the hill, away from the noise of the harbour. It belonged to a childhood friend of his, Manius Curius: *All my hopes of your getting proper treatment and attention are pinned on Curius. He has the kindest of hearts and the truest affection for me. Put yourself entirely in his hands.*

Curius was indeed an amiable, cultured man, a widower, a banker by profession, and he looked after me well. I was given a room with a terrace looking westwards to the sea, and later, when I started to feel strong enough, I would sit outside for an hour in the afternoons watching the merchant ships going in and out of the harbour. Curius was in regular touch with all sorts of contacts in Rome – senators, equestrians, tax farmers, shipowners – and his letters, plus mine, together with the geographical situation of Patrae as the gateway to Greece, meant that we received the political news as quickly as anyone could in that part of the world.

One day around the end of January – this must have been about three months after Cicero's departure – Curius came into my room with a grim expression and asked me whether I was strong enough to take bad news. When I nodded, he said, 'Caesar has invaded Italy.'

Years afterwards, Cicero used to wonder whether the three weeks we had lost on Rhodes might have made the difference between war and peace. If only, he lamented, he could have reached Rome a month earlier! He was one of the few who was listened to by both sides, and in the short time he was on the outskirts of Rome before the conflict broke out – which was barely a week – he told me he had begun to broker the beginnings of a compromise: Caesar to give up Gaul and all his legions apart from one, and in return to be allowed to stand for the consulship *in absentia*. But by then it was far too late. Pompey was dubious about the deal; the Senate rejected it; and Caesar, he suspected, had already made up his mind to strike, having calculated that he would never be stronger than at that moment: 'In short, I was among madmen wild for war.'

The moment he heard that Caesar had invaded, he went straight to Pompey's house on the Pincian hill to pledge his support. It was packed with the leaders of the war party – Cato, Ahenobarbus, the consuls Marcellinus and Lentulus: fifteen or twenty men in all. Pompey was enraged, and he was panicking. He was under the misapprehension that Caesar was advancing at full strength, with perhaps fifty thousand troops. In fact, that inveterate gambler had crossed the Rubicon with only a tenth of that number and was relying on the shock effect of his aggression. But Pompey did not yet know that, and so he decreed that the city should be abandoned. He was ordering every senator to leave Rome. Any who remained behind would be regarded as traitors. When Cicero demurred, arguing that this was a mad policy, Pompey turned on him: 'And that includes you, Cicero!' This war would not be decided in Rome, he declared, or even in Italy – that was to play into Caesar's hands. Instead it would be a world war, fought in Spain, Africa, the eastern Mediterranean and especially at sea. He would blockade Italy. He would starve the enemy into submission. Caesar would rule over a charnel house.

I shuddered at the kind of war intended, wrote Cicero to Atticus, *savage and vast beyond what men yet envision.* Pompey's personal hostility towards him was also a shock. He left Rome as ordered and withdrew to Formiae and brooded on what course to take. Officially he was placed in charge of sea defences and recruitment in northern Campania; practically he did nothing. Pompey sent him a cold reminder of his duties: *I strongly urge you, in view of your outstanding and unswerving patriotism, to make your way over to us, so that in concert we may bring aid and comfort to our afflicted country.*

Around this time, Cicero wrote to me: I received the letter about three weeks after I learned of the outbreak of war.

From Cicero to his dear Tiro, greetings.

My existence and that of all honest men and the entire commonwealth hangs in the balance, as you may tell from the fact that we have left our homes and the mother city herself to plunder or burning. Swept along by some spirit of folly, forgetting the name he bears and the honours he has won, Caesar seized Ariminium, Pisaurum, Ancona and Arretium. So we abandoned Rome – how wisely or how courageously it is idle to argue. We have reached the point when we cannot survive unless some god or accident comes to our rescue. To add to my vexations, my son-in-law Dolabella is with Caesar.

I wanted you to be aware of these facts. Mind you don't let them upset you and hinder your recovery. Since you could not be with me when I most needed your services and loyalty, make sure you do not hurry or be so foolish as to undertake the voyage either as an invalid or in winter.

I obeyed his instruction and thus I found myself following the collapse of the Roman Republic from my sick room – and in my memory, my illness and the madness being played out in

Italy are forever merged in a single fevered nightmare. Pompey and his hastily assembled army headed to Brundisium to embark for Macedonia to begin their world war. Caesar chased after him to stop him. He tried to blockade the harbour. He failed. He watched the sails of Pompey's troopships dwindle into the distance, then turned round and marched back the way he had come, towards Rome. His route along the Via Appia took him past Cicero's door in Formiae.

Formiae, 29 March
From Cicero to his dear Tiro, greetings.

So I have seen the madman at last – for the first time in nine years, can one believe it? He appeared quite unchanged. A little harder, leaner, greyer, and more lined perhaps; but I fancy this life of brigandage suits him. Terentia, Tullia and Marcus are with me (they send their love, by the way).

What happened was this. All yesterday his legionaries were streaming past our door – a wild-looking lot, but they left us unmolested. We were just settling down to dinner when a commotion at the gate signalled the arrival of a column of mounted men. What an entourage, what an underworld! A grimmer group of desperadoes you have never seen! The man himself – if man he is: one starts to wonder – was alert and audacious and in a hurry. Is he a Roman general or is he Hannibal? 'I could not pass so close without stopping for a moment to see you.' As if he was a country neighbour! To Terentia and Tullia he was most civil. He refused all hospitality ('I must press on') and we went into my study to talk. We were quite alone. He came straight to the point. He was summoning a meeting of the Senate in four days' time.

'On what authority?'

'This,' he said, and touched his sword. 'Come along and work for peace.'

'At my own discretion?'

'Naturally. Who am I to lay down rules for you?'

'Well then, I shall say that the Senate should not give its approval if you plan to send your troops to Spain or Greece to fight the armies of the republic. And I shall have much to say in defence of Pompey.'

At this he protested that these were not the sort of things he wanted said.

'So I supposed,' I replied, 'and that is just why I don't want to be present. Either I must stay away or speak in that strain – and bring up much else besides which I could not possibly suppress if I was there.'

He became very cold. He said I was in effect passing judgement against him, and that if I was reluctant to come across to him, others would be too. He told me I should think the matter over and let him know. With that he got up to leave. 'One last thing,' he said. 'I should like your counsels, but if I cannot have them I shall take advice wherever I can, and I shall stop at nothing.'

On that note we parted. I don't doubt our meeting has put him out of humour with me. It is becoming ever clearer that I cannot remain here much longer. I see no end to the mischief.

I did not know how to reply, and besides, I was frightened that any letter I sent would be intercepted, for Cicero had discovered that he was surrounded by Caesar's spies. The boys' tutor, Dionysius, for example, who had accompanied us to Cilicia, turned out to be an informant. So too, much more shockingly to Cicero, was his own nephew, young Quintus, who sought an interview with Caesar directly after his visit to Formiae and told him that his uncle was planning to defect to Pompey.

Caesar was at that time in Rome. He had pressed ahead with the plan he had outlined to Cicero and had summoned a meeting of the Senate. Hardly anyone attended: senators were abandoning Italy on almost every tide to join Pompey in Macedonia. But by an unbelievable stroke of incompetence, in his eagerness to flee, Pompey had forgotten to empty the treasury in the Temple of Saturn. Caesar went to seize it at the head of a cohort of troops. The tribune L. Caecilius Metellus barred the door and made a speech about the sanctity of the law, to which Caesar replied, 'There is a time for laws and a time for arms. If you don't like what is being done, save me your speeches and get out of the way.' And when Metellus still refused to move, Caesar said, 'Get out of the way or I shall have you killed, and you know, young man, that I dislike saying this more than I would dislike doing it.' Metellus moved out of the way very swiftly after that.

Such was the man to whom Quintus betrayed his uncle. The first clue Cicero had about his treachery was a letter he received a few days later from Caesar, on his way now to fight Pompey's forces in Spain.

En route to Massilia, 16 April
Caesar Imperator to Cicero Imperator.

I am troubled by certain reports and therefore I feel I ought to write and appeal to you in the name of our mutual goodwill not to take any hasty or imprudent step. You will be committing a grave offence against friendship. To hold aloof from civil quarrels is surely the most fitting course for a good, peace-loving man and a good citizen. Some who favoured that course were prevented from following it by fears for their safety. But you have the witness of my career and the judgement implied in our friendship. Weigh them well, and you will find no safer and no more honourable course than to keep aloof from all conflict.

Cicero told me afterwards that it was only when he read this letter that he knew for certain that he would have to take ship and join Pompey – 'by rowing boat if necessary' – because to submit to such a crude and sinister threat would be intolerable to him. He summoned young Quintus to Formiae and gave him a furious dressing-down. But secretly he felt quite grateful to him, and persuaded his brother not to treat the young man too harshly. 'What did he do, after all, except tell the truth about what was in my heart – something I had not had the courage to do when I met Caesar? Then when Caesar offered me a funk hole where I could sit out the rest of the war in safety while other men died for the cause of the republic, my duty suddenly became clear to me.'

In strictest confidence he sent me a cryptic message via Atticus and Curius that he was travelling *to that place where you and I were first visited by Milo and his gladiator, and if, when your health permits, you would care to join me there again, nothing would give me greater joy.*

I knew at once that he was referring to Thessalonica, where Pompey's army was now assembling. I had no desire to become involved in the civil war. It sounded highly dangerous to me. On the other hand, I was devoted to Cicero and I supported his decision. For all Pompey's faults, he had shown himself in the end to be willing to obey the law: he had been given supreme power after the murder of Clodius and had then surrendered it; legality was on his side; it was Caesar, not he, who had invaded Italy and destroyed the republic.

My fever had passed. My health was restored. I, too, knew what I had to do. Accordingly, at the end of June, I said farewell to Curius, who had become a good friend, and set off to chance my fortunes in war.

X

I travelled by ship mostly – east across the Bay of Corinth and north along the Aegean coast. Curius had offered me one of his slaves as a manservant but I preferred to journey alone: having once been another man's property myself, I was uneasy in the role of master. Gazing at that ancient tranquil landscape with its olive groves and goatherds, its temples and fishermen, one would never have guessed at the stupendous events now in train across the world. Only when we rounded a headland and came within sight of the harbour of Thessalonica did everything appear different. The approaches to the port were crammed with hundreds of troopships and supply vessels. One could almost have walked dry-footed from one side of the bay to the other. Inside the port, wherever one looked there were signs of war – soldiers, cavalry horses, wagons full of weapons and armour and tents, siege engines – and all that vast concourse of hangers-on who attend a great army mustering to fight.

I had no idea amid this chaos of where to find Cicero, but I remembered a man who might. Epiphanes didn't recognise me at first, perhaps because I was wearing a toga and he had never thought of me as a Roman citizen. But when I reminded him of our past dealings, he cried out and seized my hand and pressed it to his heart. Judging by his jewelled rings and the hennaed slave girl pouting on his couch, he seemed to be prospering nicely from the war, although for my benefit he lamented it loudly. Cicero, he said, was back in the same villa he had occupied almost a decade before. 'May the gods bring you a swift victory,' he called after me, 'but not perhaps before we have done good business together.'

How odd it was to make that familiar walk again, to enter that unchanged house, and to find Cicero sitting in the courtyard on the same stone bench, staring into space with the same expression of utter dejection. He jumped up when he saw me, threw wide his arms and clasped me to him. 'But you're too thin!' he protested, feeling the boniness of my shoulders and ribs. 'You'll become ill again. We must fatten you up!'

He called to the others to come and see who was here, and from various directions came his son, Marcus, now a strapping, floppy-haired sixteen-year-old, wearing the toga of manhood; his nephew, Quintus, slightly sheepish as he must have known his uncle would have told me of his malicious blabbing; and finally Quintus senior, who smiled to see me but whose face quickly lapsed back into melancholy. Apart from young Marcus, who was training for the cavalry and loved spending his time around the soldiers, it was plainly an unhappy household.

'Everything about our strategy is wrong,' Cicero complained to me over dinner that evening. 'We sit here doing nothing while Caesar rampages across Spain. Far too much notice is being taken of auguries, in my opinion – no doubt birds and entrails have their place in civilian government, but they sit badly with commanding an army. Sometimes I wonder if Pompey is quite the military genius he's cracked up to be.'

Cicero being Cicero, he did not restrict such opinions to his own household but voiced them around Thessalonica to whoever would listen, and it was not long before I realised he was regarded as something of a defeatist. Not surprisingly Pompey hardly ever saw him, but then I suppose this may have been because he was away so much training his new legions. Close to two hundred senators with their staffs were crammed into the city by the time I arrived, many of them elderly. They hung around the Temple of Apollo with nothing to do, bickering among themselves. All wars are horrible, but civil wars especially so. Some of Cicero's closest friends, such as young Caelius Rufus, were fighting with Caesar, while his new son-in-law, Dolabella, actually had command of a squadron of Caesar's fleet in the Adriatic. Pompey's first words to Cicero when he arrived had been a curt 'Where's your new son-in-law?' To which Cicero had replied, 'With your old father-in-law.' Pompey had grunted and walked away.

I asked Cicero what Dolabella was like. He rolled his eyes. 'An adventurer like all of Caesar's crew; a rogue, a cynic, too full of animal spirits for his own good – I rather like him actually. But oh dear, poor Tullia! What kind of husband has she landed herself with this time? The darling girl gave birth at Cumae prematurely just before I left but the child didn't last out the day. I fear another attempt at motherhood will kill her. And of course the more Dolabella wearies of her and her illnesses – she's older than him – the more desperately she loves him. And still I haven't paid him the second part of her dowry. Six hundred thousand sesterces! But where am I to find such a vast sum when I'm trapped here?'

That summer was even hotter than the one when Cicero was exiled – and now half of Rome was exiled with him. We wilted in the humidity of the teeming city. Sometimes I found it hard not to take a certain grim satisfaction at the sight of so many men who had ignored Cicero's warnings about Caesar – who had been prepared indeed to see Cicero driven from Rome in the interests of a quiet life – and who now found themselves experiencing what it was like to be far from home and facing an uncertain future.

If only Caesar had been stopped earlier! That was the lament upon everyone's lips. But now it was too late and all the momentum of war was with him. At the height of the summer's heat, messengers reached Thessalonica with the news that the Senate's army in Spain had surrendered to Caesar after a campaign of just forty days. The news provoked intense dismay. Not long afterwards the commanders of that defeated army arrived in person: Lucius Afranius, the most loyal of all Pompey's lieutenants, and Marcus Petreius, who fourteen years earlier had defeated Catilina on the field of battle. The Senate-in-exile was flabbergasted at their appearance. Cato rose to ask the question on the minds of them all: 'Why are you not dead or prisoners?' Afranius had to explain somewhat shamefacedly that Caesar had pardoned them, and that all the soldiers who had fought for the Senate had been allowed to return to their homes.

'Pardoned you?' raged Cato. 'What do you mean, *pardoned* you? Is he now a king? You are the legitimate leaders of a lawful army. He is a renegade. You should have killed yourselves rather than accept a traitor's mercy! What's the use of living when you've lost your honour? Or is the point of your existence now just so that you can piss out of the front and shit out of the back?'

Afranius drew his sword and declared in a trembling voice that no man would ever call him a coward, not even Cato. There might have been serious bloodshed if the two had not been jostled away from one another.

Cicero said to me later that of all the clever strokes that Caesar pulled, perhaps the most brilliant was his policy of clemency. It was, in a curious way, akin to sending home the garrison of Uxellodunum with their hands cut off. These proud men were humbled, neutered; they crept back to their astonished comrades as living emblems of Caesar's power. And by their very presence they lowered morale across the entire army, for how could Pompey persuade his soldiers to fight to the death when they knew that if it came to it they could lay down their arms and return to their families?

Pompey called a council of war to discuss the crisis, consisting of the leaders of the army and of the Senate. Cicero, who was still officially the governor of Cilicia, naturally attended, and was accompanied to the temple by his lictors. He tried to take Quintus in with him but he was barred at the door by Pompey's aide-de-camp, and much to his fury and embarrassment Quintus had to stay outside with me. Among those I watched going in were Afranius, whose conduct in Spain Pompey staunchly defended; Domitius Ahenobarbus, who had managed to escape from Massilia when Caesar besieged it and now saw traitors wherever he looked; Titus Labienus, an old ally of Pompey's who had served as Caesar's second in command in Gaul but had refused to follow his chief across the Rubicon; Marcus Bibulus, Caesar's former consular colleague, now admiral of the Senate's huge fleet of five hundred warships; Cato, who had been promised command of the fleet until Pompey decided it would not be wise to give so fractious a colleague so much power; and Marcus Junius Brutus, who was only thirty-six and Cato's nephew, but whose arrival was said to have given more joy to Pompey than anyone else's, because Pompey had killed Brutus's father back in Sulla's time and there had been a blood feud ever since.

Pompey, according to Cicero, exuded confidence. He had lost weight, had put himself on an exercise regime, and looked a full decade younger than he had in Italy. He dismissed the loss of Spain as inconsequential, a sideshow. 'Listen to me, gentlemen; listen to what I have always said: *this war will be won at sea.*' According to Pompey's spies in Brundisium, Caesar had less than half the number of ships that the Senate possessed. It was purely a question of mathematics: Caesar did not have sufficient troop transports to break out of Italy in anything like the strength he would need to confront Pompey's legions; therefore he was trapped. 'We have him where we want him, and when we are ready we shall take him. From now on, this war will be fought on my terms and according to my timetable.'

It must have been about three months after this, in the middle of the night, that we were roused by a furious hammering on the door. We gathered bleary-eyed in the tablinum, where the lictors were waiting with an officer from Pompey's headquarters. Caesar's forces had landed four days earlier on the coast of Illyricum, near Dyrrachium; Pompey had ordered the entire army to begin moving out at dawn to confront them. It would be a march of three hundred miles.

Cicero said, 'Is Caesar with his army?'

'So we believe.'

Quintus said, 'But I thought he was in Spain.'

'Indeed he *was* in Spain,' replied Cicero drily, 'but apparently now he's here. How strange: I seem to remember being categorically assured that such a thing was impossible because he didn't have sufficient ships.'

At daybreak we went up to the Egnatian Gate to see if we

could discover any more. The ground was vibrating with the weight of the military traffic on the road – a vast column was passing through the town, forty thousand men in all. I was told it stretched for thirty miles, although of course we could only see a fraction of it – the legionaries on foot carrying their heavy packs, the cavalrymen with their javelins glinting, the forest of standards and eagles all bearing the thrilling legend 'SPQR' ('The Senate and People of Rome'), trumpeters and cornet players, archers, slingers, artillerymen, slaves, cooks, scribes, doctors, carts full of baggage, pack mules laden with tents and tools and food and weapons, horses and oxen dragging crossbows and ballistae.

We joined the column around the middle of the morning, and even I, the least military of men, found it exhilarating; even Cicero for that matter was filled with confidence for once. As for young Marcus, he was in heaven, moving back and forth between our section and the cavalry. We rode on horseback. The lictors marched in front of us with their laurelled rods. As we tramped across the plain towards the mountains, the road began to climb and I could see far ahead the reddish-brown dust raised by the endless column and the occasional glitter of steel as a helmet or a javelin caught the sun.

At nightfall we reached the first camp, with its ditch and earthen rampart and its spiked palisade. The tents were already pitched, the fires lit; a wonderful scent of cooking rose into the darkening sky. I remember especially the clink of the blacksmiths' hammers in the dusk, the whinnying and movement of the horses in their enclosure, and also the pervading smell of leather from the scores of tents, the largest of which had been set aside for Cicero. It stood at the crossroads in the centre of the camp, close to the standards and to the altar, where Cicero that evening presided over the traditional sacrifice to Mars. He bathed and was anointed, dined well, slept peacefully in the fresh air, and the following morning we set off again.

This pattern was repeated for the next fifteen days as we made our way across the mountains of Macedonia towards the border with Illyricum. Cicero constantly expected to receive a summons to confer with Pompey, but none came. We did not know even where the commander-in-chief was, although occasionally Cicero received dispatches, and from these we pieced together a clearer picture of what was happening. Caesar had landed on the fourth day of January with a force of several legions, perhaps fifteen thousand men in all, and had achieved complete surprise, seizing the port of Apollonia, about thirty miles south of Dyrrachium. But that was just one half of his army. While he stayed with the bridgehead, his troopships had set off back to Italy to bring over the second half. (Pompey had never factored into his calculations the audacity of his enemy making two trips.) At this point, however, Caesar's famous luck ran out. Our admiral, Bibulus, had managed to intercept thirty of his transports. These he set on fire and all their crews he burnt alive, and then he deployed his immense fleet to prevent Caesar's navy returning.

As matters stood, therefore, Caesar's position was precarious. He had his back to the sea and was blockaded, with no chance of resupply, with winter coming on, and was about to be confronted by a much larger force.

As we were nearing the end of our march, Cicero received a further dispatch from Pompey:

Pompey Imperator to Cicero Imperator.

I have received a proposal from Caesar that we should hold an immediate peace conference, disband both our armies within three days, renew our old friendship under oath, and return to Italy together. I regard this as proof not of his friendly intentions but of the weakness of his position and of his realisation that he cannot win this war. Accordingly, knowing that you would concur, I have rejected his offer, which I suspect was in any case a trick.

'Is he right?' I asked him. 'Would you have concurred?'

'No,' responded Cicero, 'and he knows perfectly well I wouldn't. I would do anything to stop this war – which of course is why he never asked for my opinion. I cannot see anything ahead of us except slaughter and ruin.'

At the time I thought that Cicero was being unduly defeatist even for him. Pompey deployed his vast army in and around Dyrrachium, and contrary to expectations, he once again settled down to wait. No one in the supreme war council could fault his reasoning: that with every passing day Caesar's position became weaker; that he might eventually be starved into submission without the need for fighting; and that in any case, the best time to attack would be in the spring when the weather was less treacherous.

The Ciceros were billeted in a villa just outside Dyrrachium, built up high on a headland. It was a wild spot, with commanding views of the sea, and I found it odd to think of Caesar encamped only thirty miles away. Sometimes I would lean out over the terrace and crane my neck to the south in the hope that I might see some evidence of his presence, but naturally I never did.

And then at the beginning of April a very remarkable spectacle presented itself. The weather had been calm for several days, but suddenly a storm blew up from the south that howled around our house in its exposed position, the rain whipping down on the roof. Cicero was in the middle of composing a letter to Atticus, who had written from Rome to inform him that Tullia was desperately short of money. Sixty thousand sesterces was missing from the first payment of her dowry, and once again Cicero suspected Philotimus of shady dealing. He had just dictated the words *You tell me she is in want of everything; I beg you not to let this continue* when Marcus came running in and said that a great number of ships were visible out at sea and that he thought a battle might be in progress.

We put on our cloaks and hurried into the garden. And there indeed was a vast fleet of several hundred vessels a mile or more offshore, being tossed up and down in the heavy swell and driven at speed by the wind. It reminded me of our own near-shipwreck when we were crossing to Dyrrachium at the start of Cicero's exile. We watched for an hour until they had all passed out of sight, and then gradually a second flotilla began to appear – making, as it seemed to me, much heavier weather of it, but obviously trying to catch up with the ships that had gone before. We had no idea what it was that we were watching. To whom did these ghostly grey ships belong? Was it actually a battle? If so, was it going well or badly?

The next morning Cicero sent Marcus to Pompey's headquarters, to see what he could discover. The young man returned at dusk in a state of eager anticipation. The army would be breaking camp at dawn. The situation was confused. However, it appeared that the missing half of Caesar's army had sailed over from Italy. They had been unable to make land at Caesar's camp at Apollonia, partly because of our blockade but also because of the storm, which had blown them more than sixty miles north along the coast. Our navy had tried to pursue them, without success. Reportedly, men and materiel were now coming ashore around the port of Lissus. Pompey's intention was to crush them before they could link up with Caesar.

The next morning we rejoined the army and headed north. It was rumoured that the newly arrived general we would be facing was Mark Antony, Caesar's deputy – a report Cicero hoped was true, for he knew Antony: a young man of only thirty-four with a reputation for wildness and indiscipline; Cicero said he was not nearly as formidable a tactician as Caesar. However, when we drew closer to Lissus, where Antony was supposed to be, we found only his abandoned camp, dotted with dozens of smouldering fires where he had burned all the equipment his men could not carry with them. It turned out that he had led them east into the mountains.

We performed an abrupt about-turn and marched back south again. I thought we would return to Dyrrachium. Instead we passed by it in the distance, pressed on further south and after a four-day march took up a new position in a vast camp around the little town of Apsos. And now one began to get a sense of just how brilliant a general Caesar was, for we learned that somehow he *had* linked up with Antony, who had brought his army through the mountain passes, and that although Caesar's combined force was smaller than ours, nevertheless he had retrieved a hopeless position and was now on the offensive. He captured a settlement to our rear and cut us off from Dyrrachium. This was not a fatal disaster – Pompey's navy still commanded the coast, and we could be resupplied by sea across the beaches as long as the weather was not too rough. But one began to experience the uneasy sensation of being hemmed in. Sometimes we could see Caesar's men moving on the distant slopes of the mountains: he had control of the heights above us. And then he began a vast programme of construction – felling trees, building wooden forts, digging trenches and ditches and using the excavated earth to erect ramparts.

Naturally, our commanders tried to interrupt these works, and there were many skirmishes – sometimes four or five in a day. But the labour went on more or less continuously for several months until Caesar had completed a fifteen-mile fortified line that ran all the way round our position in a great loop, from the beaches to the north of our camp to the cliffs to the south. Within this loop we built our own system of trenches facing theirs, with perhaps fifty or a hundred paces of no man's land between the two sides. Siege engines were brought up and the artillerymen would lob rocks and flaming missiles at one another. Raiding parties would creep across the lines at night and slit the throats of the men in the opposing trench. When the wind dropped, we could hear them talking. Often they shouted insults at us; our men yelled back. I remember a constant atmosphere of tension. It began to prey on one's nerves.

Cicero fell ill with dysentery and spent most of his time reading and writing letters in his tent. 'Tent' was something of a misnomer. He and the leading senators seemed to vie with one another to see who could make their accommodation the most luxurious. There were carpets, couches, tables, statues and silverware shipped over from Italy on the inside, and walls of turf and leafy bowers outside. They dined with one another and bathed together as if they were still on the Palatine. Cicero became particularly close to Cato's nephew Brutus, who had the tent next door, and who was seldom seen without a book of philosophy in his hand. They would spend hours sitting up talking late into the night. Cicero liked him for his noble nature and his learning but worried that his head was actually crammed too full of philosophy for him to make practical use of it: 'I sometimes fear he may have been educated out of his wits.'

One of the peculiarities of this style of trench warfare was that one could also have quite friendly contact with the enemy. The ordinary soldiers would periodically meet in the unoccupied middle ground to talk or gamble, although our officers inflicted severe penalties for fraternisation. Letters were lobbed over from one side to the other. Cicero received several messages by sea from Rufus, who was in Rome, and even one from Dolabella, who was with Caesar less than five miles away, and who sent a courier under a flag of truce:

If you are well I am glad. I myself am well and so is our Tullia. Terentia has been rather out of sorts, but I know for certain that she has now recovered. Otherwise all your domestic affairs are in excellent shape.

You see Pompey's situation. Driven out of Italy, Spain lost, he is now, to crown it all, blockaded in his camp – a humiliation which I fancy has never previously befallen a Roman general. One thing I do beg of you: if he does manage to escape from his present dangerous position and takes refuge with his fleet, consult your own best interests and at long last be your own friend rather than anybody else's.

My most delightful Cicero, if it turns out that Pompey is driven from this area too and forced to seek yet other regions of the earth, I hope you will retire to Athens or to any peaceful community you please. Any concessions that you need from the commander-in-chief to safeguard your dignity you will obtain with the greatest ease from so kindly a man as Caesar. I trust to your honour and kindness to see that the courier I am sending you is able to return to me and brings a letter from you.

Cicero's breast could barely contain all the conflicting emotions aroused by reading this extraordinary missive – delight that Tullia was well, outrage at his son-in-law's impudence, guilty relief that Caesar's policy of clemency still extended to him, fear that the letter could fall into the hands of a fanatic like Ahenobarbus who might use it to bring a charge of treason against him . . .

He scribbled a cautious line to say that he was well and would continue to support the Senate's cause, and then he had the courier escorted back across our lines.

As the weather began to turn hotter, life became more unpleasant. Caesar had a genius for damming springs and diverting water – it was how he had often won sieges in France and Spain, and now he used the same tactic against us. He controlled the rivers and streams coming down from the mountains and his engineers cut them off. The grass turned brown. Water had to be brought in by sea in thousands of amphorae and was rationed. The senators' daily baths were forbidden on Pompey's orders. More importantly, the horses began to fall sick from dehydration and lack of forage. We knew that Caesar's men were in an even worse state – unlike us, they could not be resupplied with food by sea, and both Greece and Macedonia were closed to them. They were reduced to making their daily bread out of roots they grubbed up. But Caesar's battle-hardened veterans were tougher than our men; they showed no sign of weakening.

I am not sure how much longer this could have gone on. But about four months after our arrival in Dyrrachium, there was a breakthrough. Cicero was summoned to one of Pompey's irregular war councils in his vast tent in the centre of the camp, and returned a few hours later looking almost cheerful for once. He told us that two Gallic auxiliaries serving in Caesar's army had been caught stealing from their legionary comrades and sentenced to be flogged to death. Somehow they had managed to escape and come over to our side. They offered information in return for their lives. There was, they said, a weakness in Caesar's fortifications some two hundred paces wide, close to the sea: the outer perimeter appeared sound but there was no secondary line behind it. Pompey warned them they would die the most horrible death if what they had said proved to be false. They swore it was true, but begged him to hurry before the hole was plugged. He saw no reason to disbelieve them, and an attack was fixed for dawn the following day.

All that night our troops moved stealthily into position. Young Marcus, now a cavalry officer, was among them. Cicero fretted sleeplessly about his safety, and at first light he and I, accompanied by his lictors and Quintus, went over to watch the battle. Pompey had brought up a huge force. We could not get close enough to see what was happening. Cicero dismounted and we walked along the beach, the waves lapping at our ankles. Our ships were anchored in a line about a quarter of a mile offshore. Up ahead we could hear the noise of fighting mingling with the roar of the sea. The air was dark with clouds of arrows, occasionally lit up by flaming missiles. There must have been five thousand men on the beach. We were asked by one of the military tribunes not to proceed any further because of the danger, so we sat down under a myrtle tree and had something to eat.

Around midday the legion moved off and we followed it cautiously. The wooden fort Caesar's men had built in the dunes was in our hands, and in the flat lands beyond it thousands of men were deploying. It was very hot. Bodies lay everywhere, pierced by arrows and javelins or with horrible gaping wounds. To our right we saw several squadrons of cavalry galloping towards the fighting. Cicero was sure he spotted Marcus among them and we all cheered them loudly, but then Quintus recognised their colours and announced that they were Caesar's. At that point Cicero's lictors hustled him away from the battlefield and we returned to camp.

The battle of Dyrrachium, as it became known, was a great victory. Caesar's line was irretrievably broken and his entire position thrown into danger. Indeed he would have been utterly defeated that very day had it not been for the network of trenches that slowed up our advance and meant we had to dig in for the night. Pompey was hailed as imperator by his men on the field, and when he got back to the camp in his war chariot, attended by his bodyguards, he raced around inside the perimeter and up and down the torchlit tented streets, cheered by his legionaries.

The next day, towards the end of the morning, far in the distance in the direction of Caesar's camp, columns of smoke began to rise over the plain. At the same time reports started coming in from all around our front lines that the trenches opposite were empty. Our men ventured out cautiously at first but were soon wandering over the enemy's fortifications, astonished that so many months of labour could be so readily abandoned. But there was no doubt about it: Caesar's legionaries were marching off to the east along the Via Egnatia. We could see the dust. Whatever equipment they could not take was burning behind them. The siege was over.

Pompey summoned a meeting of the Senate-in-exile late in the afternoon to decide what should be done next. Cicero asked me to accompany him and Quintus so that he could have a record of what was decided. The sentries guarding Pompey's tent nodded me through without question and I took up a discreet position, standing at the side, along with the other secretaries and aides-de-camp. There must have been almost a hundred senators present, seated on benches. Pompey, who had been out all day inspecting Caesar's positions, arrived after everyone else, and was given a standing ovation, which he acknowledged with a touch of his marshal's baton to the side of his famous quiff.

He reported on the situation of the two armies after the battle. The enemy had lost about a thousand men killed and three hundred taken prisoner. Immediately Labienus proposed that the prisoners should all be executed. 'I worry they will infect our own men who guard them with their treasonous thoughts. Besides, they have forfeited the right to life.'

Cicero, with a look of distaste, rose to object. 'We have achieved a mighty victory. The end of the war is in sight. Isn't now the time to be magnanimous?'

'No,' replied Labienus. 'An example must be made.'

'An example that can only cause Caesar's men to fight with even more determination once they learn the fate that awaits them if they surrender.'

'So be it. This tactic of Caesar's of offering clemency is a danger to our fighting spirit.' He glanced pointedly at Afranius, who lowered his head. 'If we take no prisoners, Caesar will be forced do the same.'

Pompey spoke with a firmness that was designed to settle the matter. 'I agree with Labienus. Besides, Caesar's soldiers are traitors who have taken up arms illegally against their own countrymen. That puts them in a different category to our troops. Let's move on.'

But Cicero wouldn't let the matter drop. 'Wait a moment. Are we fighting for civilised values or are we wild beasts? These men are Romans just like us. I would like it to be recorded that in my view this is a mistake.'

'And I would like it to be recorded,' said Ahenobarbus, 'that it isn't only those who have fought openly on Caesar's side who should be treated as traitors, but all those who have tried to be neutral, or have argued for peace, or had contact with the enemy.'

Ahenobarbus was warmly applauded. Cicero's face flushed and he fell silent.

Pompey said, 'Well then, that's settled. Now it is my proposal that the entire army, bar let's say fifteen cohorts which I'll leave behind to defend Dyrrachium, should set off in pursuit of Caesar with a view to offering him battle at the first opportunity.'

This fateful pronouncement met with loud grunts of approval.

Cicero hesitated, glanced around and then stood up again. 'I seem to find myself playing the role of perennial contrarian. Forgive me – but is there not a case for seizing this opportunity and instead of chasing Caesar eastwards, sailing west instead to Italy and regaining control of Rome? That is after all supposed to be the point of this war.'

Pompey shook his head. 'No, that would be a strategic error. If we return to Italy, there will be nothing to stop Caesar conquering Macedonia and Greece.'

'Let him – I'd trade Macedonia and Greece for Italy and Rome any day. Besides, we have an army there under Scipio.'

'Scipio can't beat Caesar,' retorted Pompey. 'Only I can beat Caesar. And this war won't end merely because we're back in Rome. This war will end only when Caesar is dead.'

At the end of the conference, Cicero approached Pompey and asked for permission to remain behind in Dyrrachium rather than join the army on the campaign. Pompey, plainly irritated by his criticism, looked him up and down with something like contempt, then nodded. 'I think that's a good idea.' He turned from Cicero as if dismissing him, and began discussing with one of his officers the order in which the legions should depart the next day. Cicero waited for their conversation to end, presumably intending to wish Pompey good fortune. But Pompey was too engrossed in the logistics of the march, or at any rate he pretended to be, and eventually Cicero gave up and left the tent.

As we walked away, Quintus asked him why he didn't want to go with the army.

Cicero said, 'This global strategy of Pompey's means we could be stuck out here for years. I can't support it any longer. Nor to be frank can I face another journey through those damned mountains.'

'People will say it's because you're afraid.'

'Brother, I *am* afraid. So should you be. If we win, there'll be a massacre of good Roman blood – you heard Labienus. And if we lose . . .' He left it at that.

When we got back to his tent, he made a half-hearted attempt to persuade his son not to go either, even though he knew it was hopeless: Marcus had shown much bravery at Dyrrachium and despite his youth had been rewarded with the command of his own cavalry squadron. He was eager for battle. Quintus's son was also determined to fight.

Cicero said, 'Well then, go if you must. I admire your spirit. However, I shall stay here.'

'But Father,' protested Marcus, 'men will speak of this great clash of arms for a thousand years.'

'I'm too old to fight and too squeamish to watch others doing it. You three are the soldiers in the family.' He stroked Marcus's hair and pinched his cheek. 'Bring me back Caesar's head on a stick, won't you, my darling boy?' And then he announced that he needed to rest and turned away so that no one could see that he was crying.

Reveille was scheduled for an hour before dawn. Plagued by insomnia it seemed to me that I had barely fallen asleep when the infernal caterwauling of the war horns started. The legion's slaves came in and began dismantling the tent around me. Everything was timed exactly. Outside the sun had yet to show over the ridge. The mountains were still in shadow. But above them loomed a cloudless blood-red sky.

The scouts moved off at dawn, followed half an hour later by a detachment of Bythinian cavalry, and then, a further half-hour after that, Pompey, yawning loudly, surrounded by his staff officers and bodyguards. Our legion had been chosen for the honour of serving as the vanguard on the march and therefore was the next to leave. Cicero stood by the gate, and as his brother and son and nephew passed, he raised his hand and called farewell to each in turn. This time he did not try to conceal his tears. Two hours later, all the tents were down, the refuse fires were burning and the last of the baggage mules was swaying out of the deserted camp.

With the army gone, we set off to ride the thirty miles to Dyrrachium escorted by Cicero's lictors. Our road took us past Caesar's old defensive line, and soon we came upon the spot where Labienus had massacred the prisoners. Their throats had been cut and a gang of slaves was burying the corpses in one of the old defensive ditches. The stench of ripening flesh in the summer heat and the sight of the vultures circling overhead are among the many memories of that campaign I would prefer to forget. We spurred our horses and pressed on to Dyrrachium, reaching it before dusk.

We were billeted away from the cliffs this time for safety, in a house within the walls of the city. Command of the garrison should, in principle, have been awarded to Cicero, who was the senior ex-consul and who still possessed imperium as governor of Cilicia. But it was a sign of the mistrust in which he had come to be held that Pompey gave the position instead to Cato, who had never risen higher than praetor. Cicero was not offended. On the contrary, he was glad to escape the responsibility: the troops Pompey had left behind were his least reliable, and Cicero had serious doubts about their loyalty if it came to fighting.

The days dragged by very slowly. Those senators who, like Cicero, had not gone with the army acted as if the war was already won. For example they drew up lists of those who had stayed behind in Rome, and who would be killed on our return, and whose property would be seized to pay for the war; one of the wealthy men they proscribed was Atticus. Then they squabbled over who would get which house. Other senators fought shamelessly over the jobs and titles that would fall vacant with the demise of Caesar and his lieutenants – Spinther I remember was adamant that he should be pontifex maximus. Cicero observed to me, 'The one outcome worse than losing this war will be winning it.'

As for him, his mind was full of cares and anxieties. Tullia continued to be short of money and the second instalment of her dowry remained unpaid, despite Cicero's instructions to Terentia to sell some of his property. All his old worries about her relationship with Philotimus and their fondness for questionable money-making schemes came crowding back into his mind. He chose to convey his anger and suspicion by writing her infrequent, short and chilly letters in which he did not even address her by name.

But his greatest fears were for Marcus and Quintus, still on the march somewhere with Pompey. Two months had passed since their departure. The Senate's army had pursued Caesar across the mountains to the plain of Thessalonica and had then struck south: that much was known. But where exactly they were now, no one knew, and the further Caesar drew them away from Dyrrachium and the longer the silence went on, the more uneasy the atmosphere in the garrison became.

The commander of the fleet, Caius Coponius, was a clever but highly strung senator who had a strong belief in signs and omens, especially portentous dreams, which he encouraged his men to share with their officers. One day, when there was still no news from Pompey, he came to dine with Cicero. Also at the table were Cato and M. Terentius Varro, the great scholar and poet, who had commanded a legion in Spain and who, like Afranius, had been pardoned by Caesar.

Coponius said, 'I had an unsettling encounter just before I set off to come here. You know that immense Rhodian quinquereme, the *Europa*, anchored offshore down there? One of the oarsmen was brought to see me to recount his dream. He claims to have had a vision of a terrible battle on some high Grecian plain, with the blood soaking into the dust and men limbless and groaning, and then this city besieged with all of us fleeing to the ships and looking back and seeing the place in flames.'

Normally this was just the sort of gloomy prophecy Cicero liked to laugh at, but not this time. Cato and Varro looked equally pensive. Cato said, 'And how did this dream end?'

'For him, very well – he and his comrades will enjoy a swift voyage back to Rhodes, apparently. So I suppose that's hopeful.'

Another silence fell over the table. Eventually Cicero said, 'Unfortunately, that merely suggests to me that our Rhodian allies will desert us.'

The first hints that some terrible disaster had occurred began to emanate from the docks. Several fishermen from the island of Corcyra,[1] about two days' voyage to the south, claimed to have passed a group of men encamped on a beach on the mainland, who had shouted out that they were survivors from Pompey's army. Another merchant vessel put in the same day with a similar tale – of desperate, starving men crowding the little fishing villages trying to find some means of escape from the soldiers they cried out were pursuing them.

Cicero attempted to console himself and others by saying that all wars consisted of rumours that frequently turned out to be false, and that perhaps these phantoms were merely deserters, or the survivors of some skirmish rather than a full-scale battle. But I think he knew in his heart that the gods of war were with Caesar: I believe he had foreseen it all along, which was why he did not go with Pompey.

Confirmation came the next evening, when he received an urgent summons to attend Cato's headquarters. I went with him. There was a terrible atmosphere of panic and despair. The secretaries were already burning correspondence and account books in the garden to prevent them falling into enemy hands. Inside, Cato, Varro, Coponius and some of the other leading senators were seated in a grim circle around a bearded, filthy man, badly cut about the face. This was the once-proud Titus Labienus, commander of Pompey's cavalry and the man who had slaughtered the prisoners. He was exhausted, having ridden non-stop

1 Corfu

for ten days with a few of his men across the mountains. Sometimes he would lose the thread of his story and forget himself, or nod off, or repeat things – occasionally he would break down entirely – so that my notes are incoherent and perhaps it is best if I simply say what we eventually discovered happened.

The battle, which at that time had no name but afterwards came to be called Pharsalus, should never have been lost, according to Labienus, and he spoke bitterly of Pompey's generalship, calling it vastly inferior to Caesar's. (Mind you, others, whose tales we heard later, blamed the defeat partly on Labienus himself.) Pompey occupied the best ground, he had the most troops – his cavalry outnumbered Caesar's by seven to one – and he could choose the timing of the battle. Even so, he had hesitated to engage the enemy. Only after some of the other commanders, notably Ahenobarbus, had openly accused him of cowardice had he drawn up his forces to fight. Labienus said, 'That was when I saw his heart wasn't in it. Despite what he said to us, he never felt confident of beating Caesar.' And so the two armies had faced one another across a wide plain; and the enemy, at last offered his chance, had attacked.

Caesar had obviously recognised from the start that his cavalry was his greatest weakness and therefore had cunningly stationed some two thousand of his best infantry out of sight behind them. So when Labienus's horsemen had broken the charge of their opponents and gone after them in an attempt to turn Caesar's flank, they suddenly found themselves confronted by a line of advancing legionaries. The cavalrymen's attack broke upon the shields and javelins of these fierce unyielding veterans and they galloped from the field, despite Labienus's attempts to rally them. (All the time he was speaking I was thinking of

Marcus: a reckless youth, he, I was sure, would not have been one of those who fled.) With their enemy's cavalry gone, Caesar's men had fallen upon Pompey's unprotected archers and wiped them out. After that, it was a slaughter as Pompey's panicking infantry had proved no match for Caesar's disciplined, hardened troops.

Cato said, 'How many men did we lose?'

'I cannot say – thousands.'

'And where was Pompey amid all this?'

'When he saw what was happening, he was like a man paralysed. He could barely speak, let alone issue coherent orders. He left the field with his bodyguard and returned to camp. I never saw him after that.' Labienus covered his face with his hands; we waited; when he had recovered, he went on: 'I'm told he lay down in his tent until Caesar's men broke through the defences and then he got away with a handful of others; he was last seen riding north towards Larissa.'

'And Caesar?'

'No one knows. Some say he's gone off with a small detachment in pursuit of Pompey, others that he's at the head of his army and coming this way.'

'Coming this way?'

Knowing Caesar's reputation for forced marches and the speed at which his troops could move, Cato proposed that they should evacuate Dyrrachium immediately. He was very cool. To Cicero's surprise, he revealed that he had already discussed precisely this contingency with Pompey, and that it had been decided that in the event of a defeat, all the surviving leadership of the senatorial cause should attempt to make for Corcyra – which, as an island, could be sealed off and defended by the fleet.

By now, rumours of Pompey's defeat were spreading

throughout the garrison, and the meeting was interrupted by reports of soldiers refusing to obey orders; there had already been some looting. It was agreed that we should embark the next day. Before we returned to our house, Cicero put his hand on Labienus's shoulder and asked him if he knew what had happened to Marcus or Quintus. Labienus raised his head and looked at him as if he were crazy even to ask the question – the slaughter of thousands seemed to swirl like smoke in those staring, bloodshot eyes. He muttered, 'What do I know? I can only tell you that at least I did not see them dead.' Then he added, as Cicero turned to go, 'You were right – we should have returned to Rome.'

XI

And so the prophecy of the Rhodian oarsman came true, and the following day we fled from Dyrrachium. The granaries had been ransacked and I remember how the precious corn was strewn across the streets and crunched beneath our shoes. The lictors had to clear a passage for Cicero, striking out with their rods to get him through the panicking crowds. But when we reached the dockside, we found it even more impassable than the streets. It seemed that every captain of a seaworthy craft was being besieged by offers of money to carry people to safety. I saw the most pitiful scenes – families with all the belongings they could carry, including their dogs and parrots, attempting to force their way on to ships; matrons wrenching the rings from their fingers and offering their most precious family heirlooms for a place in a humble rowing boat; the white doll-like corpse of a baby dropped from the gangplank by its mother in a fumble of terror and drowned.

The harbour was so clogged with vessels it took hours for the tender to pick us up and ferry us out to our warship. By then it was growing dark. The big Rhodian quinquereme had gone: Rhodes, as Cicero had predicted, had deserted the Senate's cause. Cato came aboard, followed by the other leaders, and immediately we slipped anchor – the captain preferring the dangers of a night-time voyage to the risks of remaining where we were. When we had gone a mile or two we looked back and saw an immense red glow in the sky; afterwards we learnt that the mutinying soldiers had set all the ships in the harbour on fire so that they could not be forced to sail to Corcyra and continue to fight.

We rowed on throughout the night. The smooth sea and the rocky coastline were silvered in the moonlight. The only sounds were the splash of the oars and the murmur of men's voices in the darkness. Cicero spent a long time talking alone with Cato. Later he told me that Cato was not merely calm, he was serene. 'This is what a lifetime's devotion to stoicism can do for you. As far as he's concerned, he has followed his conscience and is at peace; he is fully resigned to death. He is as dangerous in his way as Caesar and Pompey.'

I asked him what he meant. He took his time replying.

'Do you remember what I wrote in my little work on politics? How long ago that seems! "Just as the purpose of a pilot is to ensure a smooth passage for his ship, and of a doctor to make his patient healthy, so the statesman's objective must be the happiness of his country." Not once has either Caesar or Pompey conceived of their role in that way. For them, it is all a matter of their personal glory. And so it is with Cato. I tell you, the man is actually quite content simply to have been right, even though this is where his principles have led us – to this fragile vessel drifting alone in the moonlight along a foreign shore.'

He was utterly disillusioned with it all – recklessly so, in truth. When we reached Corcyra, we found that beautiful island crowded with refugees from the carnage of Pharsalus. The tales of chaos and incompetence were appalling. Of Pompey, there was no word. If he was alive, he sent no message; if he was dead, no one had seen his body: he had vanished from the earth. In the absence of the commander-in-chief, Cato called a meeting of the Senate in the Temple of Zeus, on its promontory overlooking the sea, to decide the future conduct of the war. That once-numerous assembly was now reduced to about fifty men. Cicero had hoped to be reunited with his son and brother, but they were nowhere to be found. Instead he saw other survivors – Metellus Scipio, Afranius and young Gnaeus, the son of Pompey, who had convinced himself that his father's ruin was entirely the result of treachery. I noticed how he kept glaring at Cicero; I feared he could be dangerous. Cassius was also present. But Ahenobarbus was not – it turned out that he was one of the many senators who had been killed in the battle. Outside, it was hot and dazzling; inside, cool and shadowy. A statue of Zeus, twice the size of a man, looked down with indifference upon the deliberations of these beaten mortals.

Cato began by stating that in Pompey's absence the Senate needed to appoint a new commander-in-chief. 'It should go, according to our ancient custom, to the most senior ex-consul among us, and therefore I propose it should be Cicero.'

Cicero burst out laughing. All heads turned to look at him.

'Seriously, gentlemen?' responded Cicero with incredulity. 'Seriously – after all that has occurred, you think that *I* should assume direction of this catastrophe? If it was my leadership you wanted, you should have listened to my counsel earlier, and then we would not be in our present desperate straits. I refuse this honour absolutely.'

It was unwise for him to have spoken so harshly. He was exhausted and overwrought, but then so were they all, and some were also wounded. The cries of protest and disgust were eventually stilled by Cato, who said, 'I take it from what Cicero says that he regards our position as hopeless, and that he would sue for peace.'

Cicero said, 'I would, most certainly. Haven't enough good men died to satisfy your philosophy?'

Scipio said, 'We have suffered a reverse but we are not defeated. There are still allies loyal to us all over the world, especially King Juba in Africa.'

'So that is what we have sunk to, is it? Fighting alongside Numidian barbarians against our fellow Romans?'

'Nevertheless, we still have seven eagles.'

'Seven eagles would be fine if we were fighting *jackdaws*.'

'What do you know of fighting,' demanded Gnaeus Pompey, 'you contemptible old coward?' And with that he drew his sword and lunged at Cicero. I was sure that Cicero was about to die, but with the skill of an expert swordsman Gnaeus checked his thrust at the last moment and left the tip of his blade touching Cicero's throat. 'I propose we kill this traitor, and I ask the Senate's permission to do the deed this instant.' And he pressed just a fraction harder so that Cicero had to tilt his head right back to avoid having his windpipe pierced.

'Stop, Gnaeus!' cried Cato. 'You will bring shame on your father! Cicero is a friend of his – he wouldn't want to see him insulted in this way. Remember where you are and put your sword down.'

I doubt whether anyone else could have stopped Gnaeus when his blood was up. For a moment or two the young brute hesitated, but then he withdrew his sword, and swore and stamped back to his place. Cicero straightened and stared directly ahead. A trickle of blood ran down his neck and stained the front of his toga.

Cato said, 'Listen to me, gentlemen. You know my views.

When our republic was under threat, I believed it was our right and duty to compel every citizen, the lukewarm and the bad included, to support our cause and protect the state. But now the republic is lost . . .' He paused and looked around; no one challenged his assertion. 'Now that our republic is lost,' he repeated quietly, 'even I believe it would be senseless and cruel to compel any individual to share in its ruin. Let those who wish to continue the fight remain here, and we shall discuss our future strategy. Let those who wish to retire from the struggle depart from this assembly now – and let no man do them harm.'

At first no one moved. And then very slowly Cicero rose to his feet. He nodded to Cato, whom he knew had saved his life, and then turned and walked out – out of the temple, out of the senatorial cause, out of the war and out of public life.

Cicero feared that if he stayed on the island he would be murdered – if not by Gnaeus then by one of his associates. Accordingly we left that same day. We could not sail back north again in case the coast had fallen into enemy hands. Instead we found ourselves drifting further south, until after several days we arrived in Patrae, the port where I had spent my illness. As soon as the ship docked, Cicero sent word by one of his lictors to his friend Curius to say that we were in the city, and without waiting for a reply, we hired litters and porters to transport us and our baggage to his house.

I believe the lictor must have lost his way, or perhaps he was tempted by the bars of Patrae, for all six lictors in their boredom since our departure from Cilicia had fallen into the habit of drinking heavily. At any rate, we arrived at the villa before our messenger did, only to be told that Curius was away for two days on business, at which point we heard male conversation emanating from the interior. The voices sounded familiar. We glanced at one another, neither of us quite believing what we were hearing, then hurried past the steward and into the tablinum to discover Quintus, Marcus and Quintus Junior seated in a huddle. They turned to stare at us in amazement, and I sensed at once a certain embarrassment. I am fairly certain they must have been speaking ill of us – or rather of Cicero. This awkwardness, I should add, was over in an instant – Cicero never even noticed it – and we fell upon one another and kissed and embraced with the sincerest affection. I was shocked by how haggard they looked. There was something haunted about them, as there had been with the other survivors of Pharsalus, although they tried not to show it.

Quintus said, 'This is the most wonderful good fortune! We'd engaged a ship and were planning to set off for Corcyra tomorrow, having heard that the Senate was assembling there. And to think we might have missed you! What happened? Did the conference end earlier than expected?'

Cicero said, 'No, the conference is still going on, as far as I know.'

'But you're not with them?'

'Let us discuss that later. First let us hear what happened to you.'

They took it in turns to tell their story, like runners in a relay race handing on the baton – first the month-long march in pursuit of Caesar's army and the occasional skirmishes along the way, and then at last the great confrontation at Pharsalus. On the eve of the battle Pompey had dreamed that he was in Rome entering the Temple of Venus the Victorious, and that the people were applauding him as he offered the goddess the spoils of war. He awoke content, thinking this a good omen, but then someone pointed out that Caesar claimed direct descent from Venus, and immediately he decided the meaning of the dream was the opposite of what he'd hoped. 'From that moment on,' said Quintus, 'he seemed resigned to losing and acted accordingly.' The Quinti had been in the second line and so had avoided the worst of the fighting. Marcus, though, had been in the middle of the struggle. He reckoned he had killed at least four of the enemy – one with his javelin, three with his sword – and had been confident of victory until the cohorts of Caesar's Tenth Legion had seemed to rise up out of the ground before them. 'Our units lost formation: it was massacre, Father.' It had taken them the best part of a month, much of it spent living rough and dodging Caesar's patrols, to escape to the western coast.

'And Pompey?' asked Cicero. 'Is there news of him?'

'None,' replied Quintus, 'but I believe I can guess where he went: east, to Lesbos. That's where he sent Cornelia to await news of his victory. In defeat I'm certain he would have gone to her for consolation – you know what he's like with his wives. Caesar must have guessed the same. He's after him like a bounty hunter in pursuit of a runaway slave. My money is on Caesar in that particular race. And if he catches him, or kills him, what do you think that will that mean for the war?'

Cicero said, 'Oh, the war will go on, it seems, whatever happens – but it will continue without me,' and then he told them what had happened at Corcyra. I am sure he did not mean to sound flippant. It was simply that he was happy to have found his family alive, and naturally that light-hearted mood coloured his remarks. But as he repeated, with some satisfaction, his quip about eagles and jackdaws, and mocked the very idea that he should take command of "this losing cause", and derided the bone-headedness of Gnaeus Pompey – 'He makes even his father look intelligent' – I could see Quintus's jaw beginning to work back and forth in irritation; even Marcus's expression was clenched with disapproval.

'So that's it, then?' said Quintus in a cold, flat voice. 'As far as this family is concerned, it's over?'

'Do you disagree?'

'I feel I should have been consulted.'

'How could I consult you? You weren't there.'

'No, I wasn't. How could I have been? I was fighting in the war you encouraged me to join, and then I was trying to save my life, along with those of your son and your nephew!'

Too late Cicero saw how casually he had spoken. 'My dear brother, I assure you, your welfare – the welfare of all of you – has ever been uppermost in my mind. '

'Spare me your casuistry, Marcus. Nothing is ever uppermost in your mind except yourself. *Your* honour, *your* career, *your* interests – so that while other men go off to die, you sit behind with the elderly and the womenfolk, polishing your speeches and your pointless witticisms!'

'Please, Quintus – you are in danger of saying things you will regret.'

'My only regret is that I didn't say them years ago. So let me say them now, and you will do me the courtesy of sitting there and listening to *me* for once! My whole life has been lived as nothing more than an appendix to yours – I am no more important to you than poor Tiro here, whose health has been broken in your service; less important, actually, as I don't have his skills as a note-taker. When I went out to Asia as governor, you tricked me into staying for two years rather than one, so that you could have access to my funds to pay off your debts. During your exile I almost died fighting Clodius in the streets of Rome, and my reward when you came home was to be packed off again, to

Sardinia, to appease Pompey. And now here I am, thanks largely to you, on the losing side in a civil war, when it would have been perfectly honourable for me to have stood side by side with Caesar, who gave me command of a legion in Gaul . . .'

There was more in this vein. Cicero endured it without comment or movement, apart from the occasional clenching and unclenching of his hands on the armrests of his chair. Marcus looked on, white with shock. Young Quintus smirked and nodded. As for me, I yearned to leave but couldn't: some force seemed to have pinned my feet to the spot.

Quintus worked himself up into such a pitch of fury that by the end he was breathless, his chest heaving as if he had shifted some heavy physical load. 'Your action in abandoning the Senate's cause without consulting me or considering my interests is the final selfish blow. Remember, my position wasn't exquisitely ambiguous like yours: I *fought* at Pharsalus – I am a marked man. So I have no choice: I shall have to try to find Caesar, wherever he is, and plead for his pardon, and believe me, when I see him, I shall have something to tell him about *you*.'

With that he stalked out of the room, followed by his son; and then, after a short hesitation, Marcus left too. In the shocking silence that ensued, Cicero continued to sit immobile. Eventually I asked if there was anything I could fetch him, and when still he made no response, I wondered if he might have suffered a seizure. Then I heard footsteps. It was Marcus returning. He knelt beside the chair.

'I have said goodbye to them, Father. I will stay with you.'

Wordless for once, Cicero grasped his hand, and I withdrew to let them talk.

* * *

Cicero took to his bed and remained in his room for the next few days. He refused to see a doctor – 'My heart is broken and no Greek quack can fix that' – and kept his door locked. I hoped that Quintus would return and the quarrel might be repaired, but he had meant what he said and had left the city. When Curius got back from his business trip, I explained what had happened as discreetly as I could, and he agreed with me and Marcus that the best course was for us to charter a ship and sail back to Italy while the weather was still fair. Such, then, was the grotesque paradox we had reached: that Cicero was likely to be safer in a country under Caesar's control than he would be in Greece, where armed bands belonging to the republican cause were only too eager to strike down men perceived as traitors.

As soon as his depression had lifted sufficiently for him to contemplate the future, Cicero approved this plan – 'I'd rather die in Italy than here' – and when there was a decent south-easterly wind we embarked. The voyage was good, and after four days at sea we saw on the horizon the great lighthouse at Brundisium. It was a blessed sight. Cicero had been away from the mother country for a year and a half, I for more than three years.

Fearful of his reception, Cicero remained in his cabin below decks while I went ashore with Marcus to find somewhere for us to stay. The best we could manage for that first night was a noisy inn near the waterfront, and we decided that the safest course would be for Cicero to come ashore at dusk wearing an ordinary toga belonging to Marcus rather than one of his own with the purple stripe of a senator. An additional complication was the presence, like the chorus in a tragedy, of his six lictors – for absurdly, although he was entirely powerless, he still technically possessed imperium as governor of Cilicia, and was reluctant even now to break the law by sending them away; nor would they leave him until they had been paid. So they too had to be disguised and their fasces wrapped in sacking and rooms hired for them.

Cicero found this procedure so humiliating that after a sleepless night he resolved the next day to announce his presence to whoever was the most senior representative of Caesar in the town and accept whatever fate was decreed for him. He had me search through his correspondence for Dolabella's letter guaranteeing his safety – *Any concessions that you need from the commander-in-chief to safeguard your dignity you will obtain with the greatest ease from so kindly a man as Caesar* – and I made sure I had it with me when I went to the military headquarters.

The new commander of the region turned out to be Publius Vatinius, widely known as the ugliest man in Rome, and an old opponent of Cicero's – indeed it was Vatinius, as tribune, who had first proposed the law awarding Caesar both the provinces of Gaul and an army for five years. He had fought with his old chief at the battle of Dyrrachium and returned to take control of the whole of southern Italy. But by a great stroke of good fortune Cicero had made up his quarrel with Vatinius at Caesar's request several years before and had defended him in a prosecution for bribery. As soon as he learned of my arrival, I was shown straight into his presence and he greeted me most affably.

Dear gods, he *was* ugly! His eyes were crossed, and his face and neck were covered in scrofulous growths the colour of birthmarks. But what did his looks matter? He barely even glanced at Dolabella's letter before assuring me that it was an honour to welcome Cicero back to Italy, that he would protect his dignity as he was sure Caesar would wish, and that he would arrange for suitable accommodation to be provided while he awaited instructions from Rome.

The latter phrase sounded ominous. 'May I ask who will issue these instructions?'

'Well indeed – that is a good question. We are still sorting out our administration. Caesar has been appointed dictator for a year by the Senate – *our* Senate, that is,' he added with a wink, 'but he is still away chasing your former commander-in-chief, and so in his absence, power is vested in the Master of Horse.'

'And who is that?'

'Mark Antony.'

My spirits sank further.

That same day Vatinius sent a platoon of legionaries to escort us with our baggage to a house in a quiet district of the town. Cicero was carried all the way in a closed litter so that his presence remained a secret.

It was a small villa, old, with thick walls and tiny windows. A sentry was posted outside. To begin with, Cicero was simply relieved to be back in Italy. Only gradually did he realise that he was in fact under house arrest. It was not so much that he was physically prevented from leaving the villa – he did not venture beyond the gate, so we never discovered what orders the guards had been given. Rather, Vatinius implied, when he came to check how Cicero was settling in, it would be dangerous for him to leave, and, worse, disrespectful towards Caesar's hospitality. For the first time we tasted life under a dictatorship: there were no freedoms any more; no magistrates, no courts; one existed at the whim of the ruler.

Cicero wrote to Mark Antony asking permission to return to Rome. But he did so without much hope. Although he and Antony had always been polite to one another, there was a long-standing enmity between them, born of the fact that Antony's stepfather, P. Lentulus Sura, had been one of the five co-conspirators of Catilina that Cicero had had executed. Therefore it was no surprise when Antony refused Cicero's request. Cicero's fate, he said, was a matter for Caesar, and until Caesar made a ruling, he must stay in Brundisium.

I would say that the months that followed were the worst of Cicero's life – worse even than his first exile in Thessalonica. At least then there had still been a republic to fight for, there was honour in his struggle, and his family was united; now these supports had gone, and all was death, dishonour and discord. And so much death! So many old friends gone! One could almost smell it in the air. We had only been in Brundisium a few days when we were visited by C. Matius Calvena, a wealthy member of the equestrian order and a close associate of Caesar, who told us that both Milo and Caelius Rufus had died trying to stir up trouble together in Campania – Milo, at the head of a ragamuffin army of his old gladiators, had been killed in battle by one of Caesar's lieutenants; Rufus had been put to death on the spot by some Spanish and Gallic horsemen he had been trying to bribe. The death of Rufus at the age of only thirty-four was a particular blow to Cicero, and he wept when he heard of it – which was more than he did when he learned of the fate of Pompey.

Vatinius brought us the news of that himself, his hideous features especially composed for the occasion into a simulacrum of grief.

Cicero said, 'Is there any doubt?'

'None whatever – I have a dispatch here from Caesar: he has seen his severed head.'

Cicero blanched and sat down, and I pictured that massive

head with its thick crest of hair and that bull neck: it must have taken some effort to hack it off, I thought, and been quite a sight for Caesar to behold.

'Caesar wept when he was shown it,' Vatinius added, as if he had seen into my mind.

Cicero said, 'When did this happen?'

'Two months ago.'

Vatinius read aloud from Caesar's account. It transpired that Pompey had done exactly as Quintus had predicted: he had fled from Pharsalus to Lesbos to seek solace with Cornelia; his youngest son, Sextus, was also with her. Together they had embarked in a trireme and sailed to Egypt, in the hope of persuading the Pharaoh to join his cause. He had anchored off the coast at Pelusium and sent word of his arrival. But the Egyptians had heard of the disaster at Pharsalus and preferred to side with the winner. Rather than merely send Pompey away, they saw an opportunity to gain credit with Caesar by taking care of his enemy for him. Pompey was invited ashore for talks. A tender was sent to fetch him, containing Achillas, general of the Egyptian army, and several senior Roman officers who had served under Pompey and now commanded the Roman forces protecting the Pharaoh.

Despite the entreaties of his wife and son, Pompey had boarded the tender. The assassins had waited until he was stepping ashore and then one of them, the military tribune Lucius Septimius, had run him through from behind with his sword. Achillas then drew his dagger and stabbed him, as did a second Roman officer, Salvius.

'Caesar wishes it to be known that Pompey met his death bravely. According to witnesses, he drew his toga over his face with both hands and fell down upon the sand. He did not beg or plead but only groaned

a little as they finished him off. The cries of Cornelia, who watched the murder, could be heard from the shore.

'Caesar was only three days behind Pompey. When he arrived in Alexandria he was shown the head and Pompey's signet ring on which is engraved a lion holding a sword in its paws; he encloses it with this letter as proof of the story. The body having already been burnt where it fell, Caesar has given orders for the ashes to be sent to Pompey's widow.'

Vatinius rolled up the letter and handed it to his aide.

'My condolences,' he said, and saluted. 'He was a fine soldier.'

'But not fine enough,' said Cicero, after Vatinius had gone.

Later he wrote to Atticus:

> *As to Pompey's end I never had any doubt, for all rulers and peoples had become so thoroughly persuaded of the hopelessness of his case that wherever he went I expected this to happen. I cannot but grieve for his fate. I knew him for a man of good character, clean life and serious principle.*

That was all he had to say. He never wept over the loss, and thereafter I barely heard him mention Pompey again.

Terentia did not offer to visit Cicero and he did not ask to see her; on the contrary: *There is no reason for you to leave home at present*, he wrote to her. *It is a long, unsafe journey, and I do not see what good you can do if you come.* He sat by the fire that winter and brooded on the state of his family. His brother and nephew were still in Greece and writing and speaking about him in the most poisonous terms: Vatinius and Atticus both showed him copies of their letters. His wife, whom he had no desire to meet, was refusing to send him any money to pay for his living expenses; when finally he arranged for Atticus to advance him some cash via a local banker, he discovered that she had deducted two thirds of it for her own use. His son was out all hours drinking with the local soldiers and refusing to attend to his studies: he yearned for war and often did not trouble to hide his contempt for his father's situation.

But mostly Cicero brooded on his daughter.

He learned from Atticus that Dolabella, who had returned to Rome as tribune of the plebs, now ignored Tullia entirely. He had left the marital home and was having affairs all over the city, most notoriously with Antonia, the wife of Mark Antony (an infidelity that enraged Antony, even though he lived quite openly with his own mistress, Volumnia Cytheris, a nude actress; later he divorced Antonia and married Fulvia, the widow of Clodius). Dolabella gave Tullia no money for her upkeep, and Terentia – despite Cicero's repeated pleas – was refusing to pay off her creditors, saying it was her husband's responsibility. Cicero blamed himself entirely for the wreckage of his public and private lives. *My ruin is my own work*, he wrote to Atticus. *Nothing in my adversity is due to chance. I am to blame for it all. Worse than the rest of my afflictions put together, however, is that I shall leave that poor girl despoiled of her father, of her inheritance, of all that was supposed to be hers . . .*

In the spring, with still no word from Caesar who was said to be in Egypt with his latest paramour, Queen Cleopatra, Cicero received a letter from Tullia announcing her intention of joining him in Brundisium. He was alarmed that she should undertake such an arduous expedition alone. But it was too late for him to stop her – she had made sure she was already on the road before he learned of her intentions – and I shall never forget his horror when at last she arrived, after a month of travelling, attended only by a maid and one elderly male slave.

'My darling girl, don't tell me this is the extent of your entourage . . . How could your mother have allowed it? You might have been robbed, or worse.'

'There's no point in worrying about it now, Father. I'm here safe and well, aren't I? And to see you again is worth any risk or discomfort.'

The journey showed the strength of the spirit that burned within that fragile frame, and soon her presence was brightening the entire household. Rooms shut up for the winter began to be cleaned and redecorated. Flowers appeared. The food improved. Even young Marcus tried to be civilised in her company. But more important than these domestic improvements was the revival in Cicero's spirits. Tullia was a clever young woman: if she had been born a man, she would have made a good advocate. She read poetry and philosophy and – what was harder – understood them well enough to hold her own in a discussion with her father. She did not complain, but made light of her troubles. *I believe her like on earth has never been seen*, Cicero wrote to Atticus.

The more he came to admire her, the less he could forgive Terentia for the way she had treated her. Occasionally he would mutter to me, 'What kind of mother allows her daughter to travel hundreds of miles without an escort, or stands by and allows her to be humiliated by tradesmen whose bills she cannot pay?' One night when we were having dinner he asked Tullia straight out what she thought could explain Terentia's behaviour.

Tullia answered simply, 'Money.'

'But that's ridiculous. Money – it's so demeaning.'

'She's got it into her head that Caesar will need to raise a huge sum to pay for the costs of the war, and the only way he'll get it is by confiscating the property of his opponents – you chief among them.'

'And for that reason she lets you live in penury? Where's the logic in that?'

Tullia hesitated before replying. 'Father, the last thing I want to do is to add to your anxieties. That's why until this moment I've said nothing. But now that you seem stronger, I think you ought to know why I wanted to come, and why Mother wanted to stop me. She and Philotimus have been plundering your estate for months – perhaps years. Not just the rent from your properties, but your houses themselves. You'd barely recognise some of them any more – they've been almost entirely stripped.'

Cicero's first reaction was disbelief. 'It can't be true. Why? How could she do such a thing?'

'I can only tell you what she said to me: "He may sink into ruin because of his own folly but I shan't let him take me with him."' Tullia paused and added quietly, 'If you want the truth, I believe she's been taking back her dowry.'

And now Cicero began to grasp the situation. 'You mean she's divorcing me?'

'I don't think she's fully decided yet. But I believe she's taking precautions in case it comes to that and you no longer have the means of repaying her yourself.' She leaned across the table and grasped his hand. 'Try not to be too angry with her, Father. Money is her only means of independence. She still has very strong feelings for you, I know it.'

Cicero, unable to control his emotions, left the table and went out into the garden.

Of all the disasters and betrayals that had struck him over recent years, this was the worst. It completed the collapse of his fortunes. He was numbed by it. What made it harder was that

Tullia begged him to say nothing about it until such time as he could confront Terentia face to face, otherwise her mother would know it was she who was his informant. The notion of a meeting seemed a remote prospect. And then, out of the blue, just as the heat of the summer was starting to become uncomfortable, a letter arrived from Caesar.

Caesar Dictator to Cicero Imperator.

I have received various messages from your brother complaining of dishonesty on your part towards me and insisting that but for your influence he would never have taken up arms against me. I have sent these letters to Balbus to pass on to you. You may do with them as you wish. I have pardoned him, and his son. They may live where they please. But I have no desire to renew relations with him. His behaviour towards you confirms a certain low opinion I had begun to form of him in Gaul.

I am travelling ahead of my army and will return to Italy earlier than expected next month, landing at Tarentum, when I hope it will be possible for us to meet to settle matters regarding your own future once and for all.

Tullia was greatly excited when she read this: she called it 'a handsome letter'. But Cicero was secretly thrown into confusion. He had hoped he would be allowed to make his way back quietly to Rome, without fuss. He viewed the prospect of actually meeting Caesar with dread. The Dictator would doubtless be friendly enough, even if the gang around him were rough and insolent. However, no amount of politeness could disguise the basic truth: that he would be begging for his life from a conqueror who had usurped the constitution. Meanwhile fresh reports were coming in almost every day from Africa, where

Cato was raising a huge new army to continue to uphold the republican cause.

He put on a cheerful face for Tullia's sake, only to collapse into agonies of conscience once she had gone to bed. 'You know that I have always tried to steer the right course by asking myself how history would judge my actions. Well, in this instance I can be certain of the verdict. History will say that Cicero wasn't with Cato and the good cause because in the end Cicero was a coward. Oh, I have made such a mess of it all, Tiro! I actually believe Terentia is quite right to salvage what she can from the wreckage and divorce me.'

Soon afterwards Vatinius brought the news that Caesar had landed at Tarentum and wished to see Cicero the day after tomorrow.

Cicero said, 'Where exactly are we to go?'

'He is staying in Pompey's old villa by the sea. Do you know it?'

Cicero nodded. No doubt he was recalling his last visit, when he and Pompey had skimmed stones across the waves. 'I know it.'

Vatinius insisted on providing a military escort, even though Cicero said that he would prefer to travel without ostentation: 'No, I'm afraid that's out of the question: the countryside is too dangerous. I hope we will meet again soon in happier circumstances. Good luck with Caesar. You will find him gracious, I'm sure.'

Afterwards, as I was showing him out, Vatinius said, 'He doesn't seem very happy.'

'He feels his humiliation keenly. The fact that he will have to bow the knee in his old chief's former home will only add to his discomfort.'

'I might let Caesar know that.'

We set off the next morning – ten cavalrymen in the vanguard, followed by the six lictors; Cicero, Tullia and me in a carriage; Marcus on horseback; a baggage train of pack mules and servants; and finally another ten cavalry bringing up the rear. The Calabrian plain was flat and dusty. We saw almost no one apart from the occasional shepherd or olive farmer, and I realised that of course our escort wasn't for our protection at all, but to make sure Cicero didn't escape. We stayed overnight at a house reserved for us in Uria and continued the following day until around the middle of the afternoon, when we were only two or three miles from Tarentum, and then we saw a long column of horsemen in the distance, coming towards us.

In the rising heat and dust they seemed mere watery apparitions. It wasn't until they were only a few hundred paces away that I recognised by the red crests on their helmets and the standards in their midst that they were soldiers. Our column halted, and the officer in charge dismounted and hurried back to tell Cicero that the oncoming cavalry was carrying Caesar's personal standard. They were his praetorian guard and the Dictator was with them.

Cicero said, 'Dear gods, is he planning to have me done in by the roadside, do you suppose?' Then, seeing Tullia's horrified expression, he added, 'That was a joke, child. If he'd wanted me dead it would have happened long ago. Well, let's get it over with. You'd better come, Tiro. It will make a scene in your book.'

He clambered out of the carriage and called to Marcus to join us.

Caesar's column had drawn up about a hundred paces away and deployed across the road as if for battle. It was huge: there must have been four or five hundred men. We walked towards them. Cicero was between Marcus and me. At first I couldn't make out which of them was Caesar. But then a tall man swung himself out of his saddle, took off his helmet and gave it to an aide, and began to advance towards us, stroking his thin hair flat across his head.

How unreal it felt to watch the approach of this titan who had so dominated everyone's thoughts for so many years – who had conquered countries and upended lives and sent thousands of soldiers marching hither and thither and had smashed the ancient republic to fragments as if it were nothing more substantial than a chipped antique vase that had gone out of fashion – to watch him, and to find him, in the end . . . just an ordinary breathing mortal! He walked in short strides with great rapidity – there was something curiously birdlike about him, I always thought: that narrow avian skull, those glittering watchful dark eyes. He stopped just in front of us. We stopped too. I was close enough to see the red indentations that his helmet had made in his surprisingly soft pale skin.

He looked Cicero up and down and said in his rasping voice, 'Entirely unscathed, I am glad to see – exactly as I would have expected! I have a bone to pick with you,' he said, jabbing a finger at me, and for a moment I felt my insides turn to liquid. 'You assured me ten years ago that your master was at death's door. I told you then he would outlive me.'

Cicero said, 'I'm glad to hear of your prediction, Caesar, if only because you are the one man in a position to make sure it comes true.'

Caesar threw back his head and laughed. 'Ah yes, I've missed you! Now look here – do you see how I've come out of the town to meet you, to show you my respect? Let's walk in the direction you're headed and talk a little.'

And so they strolled on together for perhaps half a mile towards Tarentum, Caesar's troops parting to allow them through. A few bodyguards walked behind them, one leading Caesar's horse. Marcus and I followed. I could not hear what was said, but observed that Caesar occasionally took Cicero's arm while gesturing with his other hand. Afterwards Cicero said that their conversation was friendly enough, and he roughly summarised it for me as follows:

Caesar: 'So what is it you would like to do?'

Cicero: 'To return to Rome, if you'll permit it.'

Caesar: 'And can you promise you will cause me no trouble?'

Cicero: 'I swear it.'

Caesar: 'What will you do there? I'm not sure I want you making speeches in the Senate, and the law courts are all closed.'

Cicero: 'Oh, I'm finished in politics, I know that. I shall retire from public life.'

Caesar: 'And do what?'

Cicero: 'I thought I might write philosophy.'

Caesar: 'Excellent. I approve of statesmen who write philosophy. It means they have given up all hope of power. You may go to Rome. Will you teach the subject as well as write it? If so, I might send you a couple of my more promising men for instruction.'

Cicero: 'Aren't you worried I might corrupt them?'

Caesar: 'Nothing worries me when it comes to you. Do you have any other favours to ask?'

Cicero: 'Well, I would like to be relieved of these lictors.'

Caesar: 'It's done.'

Cicero: 'Doesn't it require a vote of the Senate?'

Caesar: 'I am the vote of the Senate.'

Cicero: 'Ah! So I take it you have no intention of restoring the republic . . .?'

Caesar: 'One cannot rebuild using rotten timber.'

Cicero: 'Tell me – did you always aim at this outcome: a dictatorship?'

Caesar: 'Never! I sought only the respect due to my rank and achievements. For the rest, one merely adapts to circumstances as they arise.'

Cicero: 'I wonder sometimes, if I had come out to Gaul as your legate – as you were kind enough once to suggest – whether all of this might have been averted.'

Caesar: 'That, my dear Cicero, we shall never know.'

'He was perfectly amiable,' recalled Cicero. 'He allowed no glimpse of those monstrous depths. I saw only the calm and glittering surface.'

At the end of their talk, Caesar shook Cicero's hand. Then he mounted his horse and galloped away in the direction of Pompey's villa. His action took his praetorian guard by surprise. They set off quickly after him, and the rest of us, Cicero included, had to scramble into the ditch to avoid being trampled.

Their hooves threw up the most tremendous cloud of dust. We choked and coughed, and when they had thundered past, we climbed back up on to the road to clean ourselves off. For a while we stood watching until Caesar and his followers had dissolved into the haze of heat, and then we began our journey back to Rome.

PART TWO

REDUX

47 BC–43 BC

Defendi rem publicam adulescens; non deseram senex.

I defended the republic in my youth; I will not desert it in old age.

Cicero, Second Philippic, 44 BC

XII

This time no crowds turned out to cheer Cicero on his way home. With so many men away at war, the fields we passed looked untended, the towns dilapidated and half empty. People stared at us sullenly; either that or they turned away.

Venusia was our first stop. From there Cicero dictated a chilly message to Terentia:

> *I think I shall go to Tusculum. Kindly see that everything is ready. I may have a number of people with me and shall probably make a fairly long stay there. If there is no tub in the bathroom, get one put in; likewise whatever else is necessary for health and subsistence. Goodbye.*

There was no term of endearment, no expression of eager anticipation, not even an invitation to her to meet him. I knew then he had made up his mind to divorce her, whatever she might have decided.

We broke our journey for two nights at Cumae. The villa was shuttered; most of the slaves had been sold. Cicero moved through the stuffy, unventilated rooms and tried to remember what items were missing – a citrus-wood table from the dining room, a bust of Minerva that had been in the tablinum, an ivory stool from his library. He stood in Terentia's bedroom and contemplated the bare shelves and alcoves. It was to be the same story in Formiae; she had taken all her personal belongings – clothes, combs, perfumes, fans, parasols – and he said, 'I feel like a ghost revisiting the scenes of my life.'

At Tusculum she was waiting for us. We knew she was inside because one of her maids was looking out for us by the gate.

I recoiled at the prospect of another terrible scene, like the one between Cicero and his brother. In the event, she was gentler than I had ever known her. I suppose it was the effect of seeing her son again after such a long and anxious separation – he was certainly the person she ran to first and she clutched him to her tightly; it was the only time in thirty years I saw her cry. Next she embraced Tullia and finally she turned to her husband. Cicero told me later that he felt all his bitterness drain away the moment she came towards him, for he saw that she had aged. Her face was creased with worry; her hair flecked grey; her once proud back was slightly stooped. 'Only at that moment did I realise how much she must have suffered, living in Caesar's Rome and being married to me. I cannot say I felt love for her any more, but I did feel great pity and affection and sadness, and I resolved there and then to make no mention of money or property – it was all done with, as far as I was concerned.' They clung to one another like strangers who had survived a shipwreck, then parted, and as far as I know they never embraced again for the remainder of their lives.

Terentia returned to Rome the following morning, divorced. Some regard it as a threat to public morality that a marriage, however long its duration, may be broken so easily, without any form of ceremony or legal document. But such is the ancient freedom, and at least on this occasion the desire to end the partnership was mutual. Naturally I was not present for their private talk. Cicero said it was amicable: 'We had been apart too much; amid the vast upheaval of public events our old shared private interests were gone.' It was agreed that Terentia would live in the house in Rome until she moved into a property of her own. In the meantime, Cicero would remain in Tusculum. Marcus chose to go back to the city with his mother; Tullia – whose faithless husband Dolabella was about to sail to Africa with Caesar to fight Cato – stayed with her father.

If one of the miseries of being human is that happiness can be snatched away at any moment, one of the joys is that it may be restored equally unexpectedly. Cicero had long relished the tranquillity and clear air of his house in the Frascati hills; now he could enjoy it uninterrupted, and in the company of his beloved daughter. As it was to become his principal residence from now on, I shall describe the place in more detail. There was an upper gymnasium that led to his library and which he called the Lyceum in honour of Aristotle: this was where he walked in the mornings, composed his letters and talked with his visitors, and where in the old days he had practised his speeches. From here one could see the pale undulation of the seven hills of Rome, fifteen miles in the distance. But because what went on there was now entirely beyond his control, he no longer had to fret about it and was free to concentrate on his books – in that sense paradoxically dictatorship had liberated him. Below this terrace was a garden with shady walks like Plato's, in whose memory he called it his Academy. Both these areas, Lyceum and Academy, were adorned with beautiful Greek statues in marble and bronze, of which Cicero's favourite was the Hermathena, a Janus-like bust of Hermes and Athena staring in opposite directions, given to him by Atticus. From the various fountains came the soft music of trickling water, and that combined with the birdsong and the scent of the flowers created an atmosphere of Elysian tranquillity. Otherwise the hillside was quiet because most of the senatorial owners of the neighbouring villas were either fled or dead.

It was here that Cicero lived with Tullia for the whole of the next year, apart from occasional excursions to Rome. Afterwards he regarded this interlude as the most contented period of his life, as well as his most creative, for he made good on his undertaking to Caesar to confine his activity to writing. And such was the force of his energy, no longer dispersed into the law and politics but channelled solely into literary creation, that he produced in one year as many books on philosophy and rhetoric as most scholars might in a lifetime, turning them out one after another without pause. His objective was to put into Latin a summary of all the main arguments of Greek philosophy. His method of composition was extremely rapid. He would rise with the dawn and go straight to his library, where he would consult whatever texts he needed and scrawl notes – he had poor handwriting: I was one of the few who could decipher it – and then when I joined him an hour or two later he would stroll around the Lyceum dictating. Often he would leave me to look up quotations, or even to write whole passages according to the scheme he had laid out; usually he did not bother to correct them, as I had learned very well how to imitate his style.

The first work he completed that year was a history of oratory, which he named *Brutus* after Marcus Junius Brutus and dedicated to him. He had not seen his young friend since their tents stood side by side in the army camp at Dyrrachium. Even to choose such a subject as oratory was provocative, given that the art was no longer much valued in a country where the elections, the Senate and the law courts were under the control of the Dictator:

> *I have reason to grieve that I entered on the road of life so late that the night which has fallen upon the republic has overtaken me before my journey was ended. But I grieve more deeply when I look on you, Brutus, whose youthful career, faring in triumph amidst the general applause, has been thwarted by the onset of a malign fortune.*

A malign fortune . . . I was surprised at the risk Cicero was willing to run in publishing such passages, especially considering that Brutus was now an important member of Caesar's administration. Having pardoned him after Pharsalus, the Dictator had recently appointed him governor of Nearer Gaul, even though Brutus had never been praetor let alone consul. People said it was because he was the son of Caesar's old mistress Servilia, and that the promotion was meant as a favour to her, but Cicero dismissed such talk: 'Caesar never does anything out of sentiment. He has given him the job in part no doubt because he is talented, but mostly because he is Cato's nephew and this is a good way for Caesar to divide his enemies.'

Brutus, who along with a certain lofty idealism also had a good share of his uncle's perversity and stiffness, did not like the work named in his honour, nor a companion volume, *Orator*, which Cicero wrote not long afterwards and also dedicated to him. He sent a letter from Gaul to say that Cicero's speaking style had been fine in its day but was too high-flown both for good taste and for the modern age – too full of tricks and jokes and funny voices: what was needed was absolute flat, emotionless sincerity. I considered it typical of Brutus's conceit that he should presume to lecture the greatest orator of the age on how to speak in public, but Cicero always respected Brutus for his honesty and refused to take offence.

These were oddly happy, I would almost say carefree, days. The old Lucullus property next door, which had long stood empty, was sold, and the new occupant turned out to be Aulus Hirtius, the immaculate young aide to Caesar whom I had met in Gaul all those years ago. He was now praetor, though the law courts met so rarely he was mostly at home, where he lived with his elder sister. One morning he came round to invite Cicero to dinner. He was a noted gourmet and had grown quite plump on such delicacies as swan and peacock. He was still in his thirties, like nearly all Caesar's inner circle, with impeccable manners and exquisite literary taste. He was said to have written many of Caesar's *Commentaries*, which Cicero had gone out of his way to praise in *Brutus* (*they are like nude figures, upright and beautiful, stripped of all ornament of style as if they had removed a garment*, he dictated to me, before adding, not for publication, 'yes, and as characterless as stick figures drawn in the sand by an infant'). Cicero saw no reason not to accept Hirtius's hospitality. He went round that evening accompanied by Tullia, and so began an unlikely country friendship; often I was invited too.

One day Cicero asked if he could give Hirtius anything in return for all these splendid dinners he was enjoying, and Hirtius replied yes, as a matter of fact, he could: that Caesar had urged him, if he ever got the chance, to study philosophy and rhetoric 'at the feet of the Master' and that he would appreciate some instruction. Cicero agreed and started to give Hirtius lessons in declamation, similar to those he had received as a young man from Apollonius Molon. The lessons took place in the Academy beside the water clock, where Cicero taught him how to memorise a speech, to breathe, project his voice and use his hands and arms to make gestures that would better convey his meaning. Hirtius boasted about his new skills to his friend Gaius Vibius Pansa, another young officer from Caesar's Gallic staff, who was scheduled to replace Brutus as governor of Nearer Gaul at the end of the year. As a result, Pansa too became a regular visitor to Cicero's villa that year and he also learned how to speak better in public.

A third pupil in this informal school was Cassius Longinus, the battle-hardened survivor of Crassus's expedition to Parthia and the former ruler of Syria, whom Cicero had last seen at the war conference on the island of Corcyra. Like Brutus, to whose sister he was married, he had surrendered to Caesar and been pardoned; now he was impatiently awaiting a senior appointment. I always found him hard company, taciturn and ambitious, and Cicero didn't much care for his philosophy either, which was extreme Epicureanism: he picked at his food, never touched wine and exercised fanatically. He once confided to Cicero that the greatest regret of his life was accepting his pardon from Caesar: that it ate away at his soul from the start and that six months after his surrender he attempted to kill Caesar when the Dictator was returning from Egypt after the death of Pompey. He would have succeeded, too, if only Caesar had moored for the night on the same side of the Cydnus river as Cassius's triremes; instead he had unexpectedly chosen the opposite bank, and by then it was too late at night and he was too far away for Cassius to reach him. Even Cicero, who was not easily shocked, was alarmed by his indiscretion and advised him not to repeat it, and certainly not to do so under his roof in case Hirtius and Pansa got to hear of it.

Finally I must mention a fourth visitor, and he in many ways was the least likely of the lot, for this was Dolabella, Tullia's errant husband. She believed he was in Africa, campaigning with Caesar against Cato and Scipio, but at the beginning of spring Hirtius received a report that the campaign was finished and that Caesar had just won a great victory. Hirtius cut short his lesson and hastened back to Rome, and a few days later, first thing in the morning, a messenger brought Cicero a letter:

From Dolabella to his dear father-in-law, Cicero.
I have the honour to inform you that Caesar has beaten the enemy and that Cato is dead by his own hand. I arrived in Rome this morning to give a report to the Senate. I called at my house and was told that Tullia is with you. May I have your permission to come out to Tusculum and see the two people who are dearest to me in the world?

'Shock after shock after shock,' observed Cicero. 'The republic beaten, Cato dead and now my son-in-law asks to see his wife.' He stared bleakly over the countryside towards the distant hills of Rome, blue in the early spring light. 'The world will not be the same place without Cato in it.'

He sent a slave to fetch Tullia, and when she came, he showed her the letter. She had spoken so often of Dolabella's cruelty towards her that I assumed, as did Cicero, that she would insist she didn't want to see him. Instead she said it was up to her father and that she didn't much care either way.

Cicero said, 'Well, if that is really how you feel, then perhaps I shall let him come – if only so that I can tell him what I think of the way he's treated you.'

Tullia said quickly, 'No, Father, I beg you, please don't do that.

He's too proud to submit to a scolding, and besides, I have only myself to blame – everyone warned me what he was like before I married him.'

Cicero was uncertain what to do, but in the end, his desire to hear at first hand what had happened to Cato overcame his distaste at having such a scoundrel under his roof – a scoundrel not just as a husband, incidentally, but as a rabble-rousing politician in the mould of Catilina and Clodius, who favoured the cancellation of all debts. He asked me if I would go to Rome at once with an invitation for Dolabella. Just before I left, Tullia took me aside and asked if she could have her husband's letter. Naturally I gave it to her; only afterwards did I discover she had none of her own and wanted it as a keepsake.

By midday I was in Rome – a full five years after I had last set foot in the city. In the fervid dreams of my exile I had pictured wide streets, and fine temples and porticoes clothed in marble and gold, all filled with elegant, cultured citizens. I found instead filth, smoke, rutted muddy roads much narrower than I remembered them, unrepaired buildings and limbless, disfigured veterans begging in the Forum. The Senate building was still a blackened shell. The places in front of the temples where the law courts used to meet were deserted. I was amazed at the general emptiness. When a census was taken later that year, the population was found to be less than half what it had been before the civil war.

I thought I might find Dolabella attending the Senate, but no one seemed to know where it was or even if it was in session these days. In the end I went to the address on the Palatine that Tullia had given me, which was where she said she had last lived with her husband, and there I found Dolabella in the company of an elegant, expensively dressed woman who I later discovered was Metella, daughter of Clodia. She behaved as if she was the mistress of the house, ordering refreshment for me and a chair to be brought, and I saw at a glance the hopelessness of Tullia's situation.

As for Dolabella, he was striking for three attributes: the fierce handsomeness of his features, the obvious strength of his physique, and the shortness of his stature. (Cicero once joked, 'Who has tied my son-in-law to that sword?') This pocket Adonis, for whom I had long tended an intense dislike because of the way he treated Tullia, even though I had never met him, read Cicero's invitation and declared that he would return with me immediately. He said, 'My father-in-law writes here that this message is brought to me by his trusted friend Tiro. Would that be the Tiro who created the famous shorthand system? Then I am delighted to meet you! My wife has always talked of you most fondly, as a kind of second father to her. May I shake your hand?' And such was the charm of the rogue that I felt my hostility immediately begin to wilt.

He asked Metella to send his slaves after him with his luggage, and then joined me in the carriage for the journey to Tusculum. Most of the way he slept. By the time we reached the villa, the slaves were preparing to serve dinner, and Cicero ordered an extra place to be set. Dolabella made straight for Tullia's couch and reclined with his head in her lap. After a while I noticed she began to stroke his hair.

It was a fair spring evening with the nightingales calling to one another, and the incongruity between the charm of the setting and the horror of the story Dolabella unfolded made it all the more unsettling. First there was the battle itself, named Thapsus, at which Scipio had commanded the republican force of seventy thousand men in alliance with King Juba of the Numidians. They had used a shock force of elephant cavalry to try to break Caesar's line, but volleys of arrows and flaming missiles from the ballistae had caused the wretched beasts to panic, turn and trample their own infantry. Thereafter it was the same story as at Pharsalus: the republican formations had broken on the iron discipline of Caesar's legionaries, only this time Caesar had decreed there would be no prisoners taken: all ten thousand who surrendered were massacred.

'And Cato?' asked Cicero.

'Cato was not present at the battle but was three days' journey away, commanding the garrison at Utica. Caesar went there straight away. I rode with him at the head of the army. He wanted very much to capture Cato alive so that he could pardon him.'

'A wasted mission, I could have told you that: Cato would never have accepted a pardon from Caesar.'

'Caesar was sure he would. But you are right, as always: Cato killed himself the night before we arrived.'

'How did he do it?'

Dolabella pulled a face. 'I'll tell you if you really want to know, but it's not a fit subject for a woman's ears.'

Tullia said firmly, 'I'm quite strong enough, thank you.'

'Even so, I think it would be better if you withdrew.'

'I shall certainly do no such thing!'

'And what does your father say about that?'

'Tullia is stronger than she looks,' said Cicero, adding pointedly, 'She has had to be.'

'Well, you asked for it. According to Cato's slaves, when he learned that Caesar would arrive the next day, Cato bathed and dined, discussed Plato with his companions, and retired to his room. Then when he was alone he took his sword and slashed himself just here.' Dolabella reached up and drew a finger under Tullia's breastbone. 'All his guts spilled out.'

Cicero, squeamish as ever, winced, but Tullia said, 'That's not so bad.'

'Ah,' said Dolabella, 'but that's not the end of the story. He failed to make the wound fatal and the sword slipped out of his bloodied hand. His attendants heard his groans and rushed in. They summoned a doctor. The doctor arrived and pushed his intestines back in to the cavity and sewed up the wound. I might add that Cato was entirely conscious throughout. He promised he would not make another attempt, and his staff believed him, although as a precaution they took his sword away. As soon as they had gone, he tore the wound open with his fingers and dragged his intestines out again. That killed him.'

The death of Cato had a powerful effect on Cicero. As the lurid details became more widely known, there were those who said it was proof that Cato was insane; certainly this was Hirtius's view. Cicero disagreed. 'He could have had an easier death. He could have thrown himself from a building, or opened his veins in a warm bath, or taken poison. Instead he chose that particular method – exposing his entrails like a human sacrifice – to demonstrate the strength of his will and his contempt for Caesar. In philosophical terms it was a good death: the death of a man who feared nothing. Indeed I would go so far as to say he died happy. Neither Caesar, nor any man, nor anything in the world could touch him.'

The effect on Brutus and Cassius – both of whom were related to Cato, the one by blood and the other by marriage – was if anything even stronger. Brutus wrote from Gaul to ask if Cicero would compose a eulogy of his uncle. His letter arrived at the same time as Cicero learned that he had been named in Cato's will as one of the guardians of his son. Like the others who had accepted Caesar's pardon, Cicero found the suicide of Cato shaming. So he ignored the risk of offending the Dictator, complied with Brutus's request, and dictated a short work, *Cato*, in little more than a week.

> *Sinewy in thought and person; indifferent to what men said of him; scornful of glory, titles and decorations, and even more of those who sought them; defender of laws and freedoms; vigilant in the public interest; contemptuous of tyrants, their vulgarities and presumptions; stubborn, infuriating, harsh, dogmatic; a dreamer, a fanatic, a mystic, a soldier; willing at the last to tear the very organs from his stomach rather than submit to a conqueror – only the Roman Republic could have bred such a man as Cato, and only in the Roman Republic did such a man as Cato desire to live.*

Around this time Caesar returned from Africa, and soon afterwards, at the height of summer, he staged finally four separate triumphs on successive days to commemorate his victories in Gaul, the Black Sea, Africa and on the Nile – such an epic of self-glorification as even Rome had never seen. Cicero moved back into his house on the Palatine in order to attend – not that he wanted to: *In civil war*, as he wrote to his old friend Sulpicius, *victory is always insolent*. There were five wild-beast hunts, a mock battle in the Circus Maximus that included elephants, a naval battle in a lake dug out near the Tiber, stage plays in every quarter of the city, athletics on the Field of Mars, chariot races, games in honour of the memory of the Dictator's daughter Julia, a banquet for the entire city at which meat from the sacrifices was served, a distribution of money, a distribution of bread, endless parades of soldiers and treasure and prisoners coiling through the streets – that noble leader of the Gauls, Vercingetorix, after six years of imprisonment, was garrotted in the Carcer – and day after day we could hear the vulgar chanting of the legionaries even from the terrace:

Home we bring our bald whoremonger,
Romans, lock your wives away!
All the bags of gold you lent him
Went his Gallic tarts to pay!

Yet despite their bombast, or perhaps because of it, Cato's reproachful ghost seemed to haunt even these proceedings. When a float went by during the Africa triumph depicting him tearing out his entrails, the crowd let out a loud groan. It was said that Cato's death had a particular religious meaning: that he had done it to bring down the wrath of the gods on Caesar's head. When that same day the axle on the Dictator's triumphal chariot broke and he was pitched to the ground, it was held to be a sign of divine displeasure, and Caesar took the crowd's disquiet seriously enough to lay on the most extraordinary spectacle of all: at night, with forty elephants on either side of him ridden by men holding flaming torches, he mounted the slope of the Capitol on his knees to atone to Jupiter for his impiety.

Just as some particularly faithful dogs are said to lie by the graves of their masters, unable to accept that they are dead, so there were those in Rome who clung to the hope that the old republic might yet twitch back into life. Even Cicero fell briefly victim to this delusion. After the triumphs were over, he decided to attend a meeting of the Senate. He had no intention of speaking. He went partly for old times' sake and partly because he knew that Caesar had appointed several hundred new senators and he was curious to see what they looked like.

'It was a chamber full of strangers,' he said to me afterwards, 'a few of them actually foreign, many not elected – and yet somehow it was still a Senate for all that.' It met on the Field of Mars, in the same room within Pompey's theatre complex where it had assembled in emergency session after the old Senate house was burned down. Caesar had even allowed the large marble statue of Pompey to remain in its original position, and the image of the Dictator presiding from the dais with Pompey's statue behind him gave Cicero hope for the future. The issue for debate was whether the ex-consul, M. Marcellus, one of the most intransigent of Caesar's opponents, who had gone into exile after Pharsalus and was living on Lesbos, might be allowed to return to Rome. His brother Caius – the magistrate who had sanctioned my manumission – led the appeals for clemency, and he was just finishing his speech when a bird seemed to appear from nowhere, fluttered over the senators' heads and swooped out of the door. Caesar's father-in-law, L. Calpurnius Piso, immediately got up and declared it to be an omen: the gods were saying that Marcellus too should be given the freedom to fly home. Then the whole Senate, Cicero included, rose as one and approached Caesar to appeal for clemency; Caius Marcellus and Piso actually fell to their knees at his feet.

Caesar gestured at them to return to their seats. He said, 'The man for whom you all plead has heaped more deadly insults upon me than any other person living. And yet I am touched by your entreaties and the omen seems to me especially propitious. There is no need for me to place my dignity above the unanimous desire of this house: I have lived long enough for nature or for glory. Therefore let Marcellus come home and dwell in peace in the city of his distinguished ancestors.'

This was received with loud applause, and several of the senators sitting around Cicero urged him to rise and make some expression of gratitude on behalf of them all. The scene so affected Cicero that he forgot his vow never to speak in Caesar's illegitimate Senate and did as they asked, lauding the Dictator to his face in the most extravagant terms: 'You seem to have vanquished Victory herself, now that you have surrendered to the vanquished all that Victory had gained. Truly you are invincible!'

Suddenly it seemed possible to him that Caesar might rule as 'first among equals' rather than as a tyrant. *I thought I saw some semblance of reviving constitutional freedom*, he wrote to Sulpicius. The next month he pleaded for the pardon of another exile, Quintus Ligarius – a senator almost as detestable to Caesar as Marcellus – and again Caesar listened and gave judgement in favour of clemency.

But the notion that this amounted to a restoration of the republic was an illusion. A few days afterwards, the Dictator had to leave Rome in a hurry in order to return to Spain and deal with an uprising led by Pompey's sons, Gnaeus and Sextus. Hirtius told Cicero that the Dictator was in a rage. Many of the rebels were men he had pardoned on condition they did not take up arms again; now they had betrayed his forgiving nature. There would be no further acts of clemency, Hirtius warned: no more gracious gestures. For his own sake Cicero would be well advised to stay away from the Senate, keep his head down and stick to philosophy: 'This time it will be a fight to the death.'

* * *

Tullia was pregnant again by Dolabella – the result, she told me, of her husband's visit to Tusculum. At first she was delighted by the discovery, believing it would save her marriage. Dolabella seemed happy too. But when she returned to Rome with Cicero to attend Caesar's four triumphs, and when she went to the house she shared with Dolabella intending to surprise him, she discovered Metella asleep in her bed. It was a terrible shock and to this day I feel the most profound guilt that I failed to warn her of what I had seen when I went there earlier.

She asked my advice and I urged her to divorce Dolabella without delay. The baby was due in four months. If she was still married when she gave birth, he would be entitled under the law to take the child; however if she were divorced, the situation would be much more complicated. Dolabella would have to take her to court to prove paternity, and at the very least, thanks to her father, she would have the best legal counsel available. She talked to Cicero and he agreed: the baby would be his sole grandchild and he had no intention of seeing it taken away from his daughter and entrusted to the care of Dolabella and the daughter of Clodia.

Accordingly, on the morning that Dolabella was due to leave with Caesar for the war in Spain, Tullia went to his house, accompanied by Cicero, and informed him that the marriage was over but that she wished to look after the baby. Cicero told me Dolabella's reaction: 'The scoundrel merely shrugged, wished her well with the child, and said that of course it must remain with its mother. Then he drew me aside to say that there was no way at the moment that he could repay her dowry and he hoped this would not affect our relations! What could I say? I can hardly afford to make an enemy of one of Caesar's closest lieutenants, and besides, I still can't bring myself entirely to dislike him.'

He was anguished and blamed himself for allowing the mess to develop. 'I should have insisted that she divorce him the moment I heard of the way he was carrying on. Now what is she to do? An abandoned mother of thirty-one with a weak constitution and no dowry is hardly the most marriageable of prospects.'

If there was any marrying to be done, he realised grimly, the person who would have to do it would be him. Nothing could have suited him less. He liked his new bachelor existence, preferred living with his books to the prospect of living with a wife. He was now sixty, and although he still cut a handsome figure, sexual desire – never a strong part of his character even in his youth – was waning. It is true that he flirted more as he got older. He liked dinner parties where pretty young women were present – he even once attended the same table as Mark Antony's mistress, the nude actress Volumnia Cytheris, a thing he would never have countenanced in the past. But murmured compliments on a dining couch and the occasional love poem sent round by a messenger the next morning were as far as things went.

Unfortunately, he now needed to marry to raise some money. Terentia's clandestine recovery of her dowry had crippled his finances; he knew Dolabella would never repay him; and although he had plenty of properties – including two new ones, at Astura on the coast near Antium and at Puteoli on the Bay of Naples – he could barely afford to run them. You might ask, 'Well why did he not sell some of them?' But that was never Cicero's way. His motto was always 'Income adjusts to meet expenditure, not the other way round.' Now that his income could no longer be expanded by legal practice the only realistic alternative was once again to take a rich wife.

It is a sordid story. But I swore at the outset to tell the truth, and I shall do so. Three potential brides were available. One was Hirtia, the elder sister of Hirtius. Her brother was immensely rich from his time in Gaul, and to get this tiresome woman off his hands he was prepared to offer her to Cicero with a dowry of two million sesterces. But as Cicero put it in a letter to Atticus, she was *quite remarkably ugly*, and it struck him as absurd that the cost of keeping his beautiful houses should be to install in them a hideous wife.

Then there was Pompeia, the daughter of Pompey. She had been the wife of Faustus Sulla, the owner of Aristotle's manuscripts, recently killed fighting for the Senate's cause in Africa. But if he married her, that would make Gnaeus – the man who had threatened to kill him at Corcyra – his brother-in-law. It was unthinkable. Besides, she bore a strong facial resemblance to her father. 'Can you imagine,' he said to me with a shudder, 'waking up beside Pompey every morning?'

That left the least suitable match of all. Publilia was only fifteen years old. Her father, M. Publilius, a wealthy equestrian friend of Atticus, had died leaving his estate in trust for his daughter until she married. The principal trustee was Cicero. It was Atticus's idea – 'an elegant solution', he called it – that Cicero should marry Publilia and so gain access to her fortune. There was nothing illegal about this. The girl's mother and uncle were all for it, flattered by the prospect of forming a connection with such a distinguished man. And Publilia herself, when Cicero hesitantly broached the subject, declared that she would be honoured to be his wife.

'Are you sure?' he asked her. 'I am forty-five years older than you – old enough to be your grandfather. Do you not find that . . . unnatural?'

She stared at him quite frankly. 'No.'

After she had gone, Cicero said, 'Well, she seems to be telling the truth. I wouldn't dream of it if she was repulsed by the very thought of me.' He sighed heavily and shook his head. 'I suppose I had better go through with it. But people will be very disapproving.'

I could not help remarking, 'It isn't *people* you have to worry about.'

'What are you referring to?'

'Well, Tullia, of course,' I replied, amazed that he hadn't considered her. 'How do you think she is going to feel?'

He squinted at me in genuine puzzlement. 'Why would Tullia be opposed? I'm doing this for her benefit as much as mine.'

'Well,' I said mildly, 'I think you'll find she *will* mind.'

And she did. Cicero said that when he told her of his intention she fainted, and for an hour or two he feared for her health and that of the baby. When she recovered, she wanted to know how he could possibly think of such a thing. Was she really expected to call this child her stepmother? Were they to live under the same roof? He was dismayed by the strength of her reaction. However, it was too late for him to back out. He had already borrowed from the moneylenders on the expectation of his new wife's fortune. Neither of his children attended the wedding breakfast: Tullia moved to live with her mother for the final stages of her pregnancy, while Marcus asked his father for permission to go out and fight in Spain as part of Caesar's army. Cicero managed to persuade him that such an action would be dishonourable to his former comrades, and instead he went to Athens on a very generous allowance to try to have some philosophy dinned into his thick skull.

I did attend the wedding, which took place in the bride's house.

The only other guests from the groom's side were Atticus and his wife Pilia – who was herself, of course, thirty years her husband's junior but who seemed quite matronly beside the slender figure of Publilia. The bride, dressed all in white, with her hair pinned up and wearing the sacred belt, looked like an exquisite doll. Perhaps some men could have carried the whole thing off – Pompey I am sure would have been entirely at ease – but Cicero was so obviously uncomfortable that when he came to recite the simple vow ('Where you are Gaia, I am Gaius'), he got the names the wrong way round, an ill omen.

After a long celebratory banquet the wedding party walked to Cicero's house in the fading daylight. He had hoped to keep the marriage secret and almost scuttled through the streets, avoiding the gaze of passers-by, gripping his wife's hand firmly and seeming to drag her along. But a wedding procession always attracts attention, and his face was too famous for anonymity, so that by the time we reached the Palatine we must have been trailing a crowd of fifty or more. At least that number of applauding clients was waiting outside the house to throw flowers over the happy couple. I had worried that Cicero might injure his back if he tried to carry his bride over the threshold, but he hoisted her easily and swept her into the house, hissing at me over his shoulder to close the door behind us, quick. She went straight upstairs to Terentia's old suite of rooms, where her maids had already unpacked her belongings, to prepare for her wedding night. Cicero tried to persuade me to stay up a little longer and take some wine with him, but I pleaded exhaustion and left him to it.

The marriage was a disaster from the start. Cicero had no idea how to treat his young wife. It was as if a friend's child had come to stay. Sometimes he played the role of kindly uncle, delighting in her playing of the lyre or congratulating her on her embroidery. On other occasions he was her exasperated tutor, appalled at her ignorance of history and literature. But mostly he tried to keep out of her way. Once he confided to me that the only workable basis for such a relationship would have been lust, and that he simply did not feel. Poor Publilia – the more her famous husband ignored her, the more she clung to him, and the more irritated he became.

Finally Cicero went to see Tullia to plead with her to move back in with him. She could have the baby at his house, he said – the birth was imminent – and he would send Publilia away, or rather he would get Atticus to send her away for him, as he found the situation too upsetting to deal with. Tullia, who was distressed to see her father in such a state, agreed, and the long-suffering Atticus duly found himself having to visit Publilia's mother and uncle to explain why the young woman would have to return home after less than a month of married life. He held out the hope that once the baby was born the couple might be able to resume their relationship, but for now Tullia's wishes took priority. They had little option but to agree.

It was January when Tullia moved back into the house. She was brought to the door in a litter and had to be helped inside. I recall a cold winter's day, everything very clear and bright and sharp. She moved with difficulty. Cicero fussed around her, telling the porter to close the door, ordering more wood for the fire, worrying that she would catch a chill. She said that she would like to go to her room to lie down. Cicero sent for a doctor to examine her. He came out soon afterwards and reported that she was in labour. Terentia was fetched, along with a midwife and her attendants, and they all disappeared into Tullia's room.

The screams of pain that rang through the house did not sound like Tullia at all. They did not sound like any human being in fact. They were guttural, primordial – all trace of personality obliterated by pain. I wondered how they fitted in to Cicero's philosophical scheme. Could happiness remotely be associated with such agony? Presumably it could. But he was unable to bear the shrieks and howls and went out into the garden, walking around and around it, for hour after hour, oblivious to the cold. Eventually there was silence and he came back in again. He looked at me. We waited. A long time seemed to pass, and then there were footsteps and Terentia appeared. Her face was drawn and pale but her voice was triumphant.

'It's a boy,' she said, 'a healthy boy – and she is well.'

She was well. That was all that mattered to Cicero. The boy was robust and was named Publius Lentulus, after his father's adopted patronymic. But Tullia could not feed the infant and the task was assigned to a wet nurse, and as the days passed following the trauma of the birth, she did not seem to get any stronger. Because it was so cold in Rome that winter, there was a lot of smoke, and the racket from the Forum disturbed her sleep. It was decided that she and Cicero should go back to Tusculum, scene of their happy year together, where she could recuperate in the tranquillity of the Frascati hills while he and I pressed on with his philosophical writings. We took a doctor with us. The baby travelled with his nurse, plus a whole retinue of slaves to look after him.

Tullia found the journey difficult. She was breathless and flushed with fever, although her eyes were wide and calm and she said she felt contented: not ill, just tired. When we reached the villa, the doctor insisted she went straight to bed. Afterwards he took me to one side and said that he was fairly certain now that she was suffering from the final stages of consumption and she would not last the night: should he inform her father, or would it be better if I did it?

I said that I would do it. After I had composed myself, I found Cicero in his library. He had taken down some books but had made no attempt to unroll them. He was sitting, staring straight ahead at nothing. He didn't even turn to look at me. He said, 'She's dying, isn't she?'

'I'm afraid she is.'

'Does she know it?'

'The doctor hasn't told her, but I think she's too clever not to realise, don't you?'

He nodded. 'That was why she was so keen to come here, where her memories are happiest. This is where she wants to die.' He rubbed his eyes. 'I think I shall go and sit with her now.'

I waited in the Lyceum and watched the sun sink behind the hills of Rome. Some hours later, when it was entirely dark, one of her maids came to fetch me, and conducted me by candlelight to Tullia's room. She was unconscious, lying in bed with her hair unpinned and spread across her pillow. Cicero sat on one side, holding her hand. On her other side, her baby lay asleep. Her breathing was very shallow and rapid. There were people in the room – her maids, the baby's nurse, the doctor – but they were in the shadows and I have no memory of their faces.

Cicero saw me and beckoned me closer. I leaned over and kissed her damp forehead, then retreated to join the others in the semi-darkness. Soon afterwards her breathing began to slow. The intervals between each breath became longer, and I kept imagining she must have died, but then she would take another gasp of air. The end when it came was different and unmistakable – a long sigh, accompanied by a slight tremor along the length of her body, and then a profound stillness as she passed into eternity.

XIII

The funeral was in Rome. Only one good thing came out of it: Cicero's brother Quintus, from whom he had been estranged ever since that terrible scene in Patrae, came round to offer his condolences the moment we got back, and the two men sat beside the coffin, wordless, holding hands. As a mark of their reconciliation, Cicero asked Quintus to deliver the eulogy: he doubted he would be able to get through it himself.

That apart, it was one of the most melancholy occasions I have ever witnessed – the long procession out on to the Esquiline Field in the freezing winter dusk; the wail of the musicians' dirges mingled with the cawing of the crows in the sacred grove of Libitina; the small enshrouded figure lying on its bier; the racked face of Terentia, like Niobe's seemingly turned to stone by grief; Atticus supporting Cicero as he put the torch to the pyre; and finally the great sheet of flame that suddenly shot up, illuminating us all in its scorching red glow, our rigid expressions set like masks in a Greek tragedy.

The following day, Publilia turned up on the doorstep with her mother and uncle, sulky that she had not been invited to the funeral and determined to move back into the house. She made a little speech that had obviously been written out for her and that she had memorised: 'Husband, I know that your daughter found my presence difficult, but now that this impediment has been removed, I hope that we can resume our married life together and that I may help you to forget your grief.'

But Cicero didn't want to forget his grief. He wished to be enveloped by it, consumed by it. Without telling Publilia where he was going, he fled the house that same day, carrying the urn containing Tullia's ashes. He moved in to Atticus's place on the Quirinal, where he locked himself away in the library for days on end, seeing no one and compiling a great handbook of all that has ever been written by the philosophers and poets on how to cope with grief and dying. He called it his *Consolation*. He told me that while he worked, he could hear Atticus's five-year-old daughter playing in her nursery next door, exactly as Tullia had done when he was a young advocate: 'The sound was as sharp to my heart as a red-hot needle; that kept me at my task.'

When Publilia discovered where he was, she began to pester Atticus for admittance, so Cicero fled again, to the newest and most isolated of all his properties – a villa on the tiny island of Astura, at the mouth of a river, only a hundred yards or so from the shore of the Bay of Antium. The island was entirely deserted and covered with trees and groves, cut into shady walks. In this lonely place he shunned all human company. Early in the day he would hide himself away in the thick, thorny wood, with nothing to disturb his meditations but the cries of the birds, and would not emerge till evening. *What is the soul?* he asks in his *Consolation. It is not moist or airy or fiery or compounded of the earth. There is nothing in these elements that accounts for the power of memory, mind or thought, that recalls the past, foresees the future or comprehends the present. Rather the soul must be counted as a fifth element – divine and therefore eternal.*

I remained in Rome and handled all his affairs – financial, domestic, literary and even marital, as now it fell to me to fend off the hapless Publilia and her relatives by pretending I had no idea where he was. As the weeks passed, his absence became increasingly difficult to explain, not just to his wife but to his clients and friends, and I was aware that his reputation was suffering, it being considered unmanly to surrender to grief so completely. Many letters of condolence arrived, including a line from Caesar in Spain, and these I forwarded to Cicero.

Eventually Publilia discovered his hiding place and wrote to him announcing her intention of visiting him in the company of her mother. To escape such a fraught confrontation, he abandoned the island, ashes in hand, and finally nerved himself to write a letter to his wife setting out his desire for a divorce. No doubt it was cowardly of him not to do it face to face. But he felt that her lack of sympathy over Tullia's death had made their ill-conceived relationship entirely untenable. He left Atticus to sort out the financial details, which entailed selling one of his houses, and then he invited me to join him in Tusculum, saying he had a project he wished to discuss.

By the time I arrived, it was the middle of May. I had not seen him for more than three months. He was seated in his Academy reading when he heard my approach, and turned to look at me with a sad smile. His appearance shocked me. He was much gaunter, especially around the neck. His hair was greyer, longer and unkempt. But the real change was beneath the surface. There was a kind of resignation about him. It showed in the slowness of his movements and the gentleness of his manner – as if he had been broken and remade.

Over dinner I asked him if he had found it painful to return to a place where he had spent so much time with Tullia.

He replied: 'I dreaded the prospect of coming, naturally, but when I arrived it was not so bad. One deals with grief, I have come to believe, either by never thinking of it or by thinking of it all the time. I chose the latter path, and here at least I am surrounded by memories of her, and her ashes are interred in the garden. Friends have been very kind, especially those who have suffered similar losses. Did you see the letter Sulpicius wrote me?'

He passed it to me over the table:

> *I want to tell you of something which has brought me no slight comfort, in the hope that perhaps it may have some power to lighten your sorrow too. As I was on my way back from Asia, sailing from Aegina towards Megara, I began to gaze at the landscape around me. There behind me was Aegina, in front of me Megara, to the right Piraeus, to the left Corinth; once flourishing towns, now lying low in ruins before one's eyes. I began to think to myself: 'Ah! How can we manikins wax indignant if one of us dies or is killed, ephemeral creatures as we are, when the corpses of so many towns lie abandoned in a single spot? Check yourself, Servius, and remember that you were born a mortal man.' That thought, I do assure you, strengthened me not a little. Can you really be so greatly moved by the loss of one poor little woman's frail spirit? If her end had not come now, she must none the less have died in a few years' time, for she was mortal.*

'I never thought Sulpicius could be so eloquent,' I remarked.

'Nor I. You see how all of us poor creatures strive to make sense of death, even dry old jurists such as him? It's given me an idea. Suppose we were to compose a work of philosophy that helped relieve men of their fear of death.'

'That would be an achievement.'

'The *Consolation* seeks to reconcile us to the deaths of those we love. Now let us try to reconcile ourselves to our own deaths. If we were to succeed – well, tell me, what could bring humanity greater relief from terror than that?'

I had no answer. His proposition was irresistible. I was curious to see how he would manage it. And so was born what is now known as the *Tusculan Disputations*, upon which we started work the following day. From the outset, Cicero conceived it as five books:

1. *On the fear of death*
2. *On the endurance of pain*
3. *On the alleviation of distress*
4. *On the remaining disorders of the soul*
5. *On the sufficiency of virtue for a happy life*

Once again we assumed our old routine of composition. Like his hero Demosthenes, who hated to be beaten to the dawn by a diligent workman, Cicero would rise in the darkness and read in his library by lamplight until the day had broken; later in the morning he would describe to me what was in his mind and I would probe his logic with questions; in the afternoon while he napped I would write up my shorthand notes into a draft, which he would then correct; we would discuss and revise the day's work over dinner in the evening, and finally before retiring we would decide the topics for the following morning.

The summer days were long and our progress swift, mostly because Cicero decided to cast the work in the form of a dialogue between a philosopher and a student. Usually I played the student and he was the philosopher, but occasionally it was the other way round. These *Disputations* of ours are still widely available, so it is unnecessary, I hope, for me to describe them in detail. They are the summation of all that Cicero had come to believe after the battering of recent years: namely, that the soul possesses a divine animation different to the body's and therefore is eternal; that even if the soul is not eternal and ahead of us lies only oblivion, such a state is not to be feared as there will be no sensation and therefore no pain or misery (*the dead are not wretched, the living are wretched*); that we should think about death constantly and so acclimatise ourselves to its inevitable arrival (*the whole life of a philosopher, as Socrates said, is a preparation for death*); and that if we are determined enough, we can teach ourselves to scorn death and pain, just as professional fighters do:

> *What even average gladiator has ever uttered a groan or changed expression? Which has ever disgraced himself after a fall by drawing in his neck when ordered to suffer the fatal stroke? Such is the force of training, practice and habit. Shall a gladiator be capable of this while a man who is born to fame proves so weak in his soul that he cannot strengthen it by systematic preparation?*

In the fifth book, Cicero offered his practical prescriptions. A human being can only train for death by leading a life that is morally good; that is – to desire nothing too much; to be content with what one has; to be entirely self-sufficient within oneself, so that whatever one loses, one will still be able to carry on regardless; to do none harm; to realise that it is better to suffer an injury than to inflict one; to accept that life is a loan given by Nature without a due date and that repayment may be demanded at any time; that the most tragic character in the world is a tyrant who has broken all these precepts.

Such were the lessons Cicero had learned and desired to impart to the world in the sixty-second summer of his life.

About a month after we started work on the *Disputations*, in the middle of June, Dolabella came to visit. He was on his way back to Rome from Spain, where he had once again been fighting alongside Caesar. The Dictator had been victorious; the remnants of Pompey's forces were smashed. But Dolabella had been wounded in the battle of Munda. There was a slash from his ear to his collarbone and he walked with a limp: his horse had been killed beneath him by a javelin, throwing him to the ground and rolling on him. Still, he was as full of animal spirits as ever. He wanted particularly to see his son, who was living with Cicero at this time, and also to pay his respects at the place where Tullia's ashes were buried.

Baby Lentulus at four months old was a large and rosy specimen, as healthy-looking as his mother had been frail. It was almost as if he had sucked all the life out of her, and I am sure that was the reason why I never saw Cicero hold him or pay him much attention – he could not quite forgive him for being alive when she was dead. Dolabella took the baby from the nurse and turned him around and examined him as if he were a vase, before announcing that he would like to take him back to Rome. Cicero did not object. 'I have made provision for him in my will. If you wish to discuss his upbringing, come and see me any time.'

They strolled together to view the spot where Tullia's ashes were resting, beside her favourite fountain in a sunny spot in the Academy. Cicero told me later that Dolabella knelt and placed some flowers on the grave, and wept. 'When I saw his tears I ceased to feel angry with him. As she always said, she knew the type of man she was marrying. And if her first husband was more of a school friend to her than anything, and her second just a convenient way of escaping her mother, at least her third was someone she loved passionately, and I am glad she experienced that before she died.'

Over dinner Dolabella, who was unable to recline because of his wound but had to eat sitting up in a chair like a barbarian, described the campaign in Spain, and confided to us that it had been a near-disaster: that at one point the army's line had broken and Caesar himself had been obliged to dismount, seize a shield and rally his fleeing legionaries. 'He said to us when it was over, "Today for the first time I fought for my life." We killed thirty thousand of the enemy, no prisoners taken. Gnaeus Pompey's head was stuck on a pole and publicly displayed on Caesar's orders. It was grim work, I can tell you, and I fear you and your friends will not find him as amenable as before when he gets home.'

'As long as he leaves me alone to write my books, he'll get no trouble from me.'

'My dear Cicero, you of all men have no need to worry. Caesar loves you. He always says that you and he are the last two left.'

Late in the summer Caesar returned to Italy, and all the ambitious men in Rome flocked to welcome him. Cicero and I stayed in the country, working. We finished the *Disputations* and Cicero sent it to Atticus so that his team of slaves could copy it and distribute it – he particularly asked for one to be sent to Caesar – and then he began composing two new treatises, *On the Nature of the Gods* and *On Divination*. Occasionally the barbs of grief still pierced him and he would withdraw for hours into some remote part of the grounds. But increasingly he was contented:

'What a lot of trouble one avoids if one refuses to have anything to do with the common herd! To have no job, to devote one's time to literature, is the most wonderful thing in the world.'

Even in Tusculum, however, we were aware, as if it were a storm in the distance, of the Dictator's return. Dolabella had spoken correctly. The Caesar who came back from Spain was different to the Caesar who had gone out. It was not simply his intolerance of dissent; it was as if his grasp on reality, once so terrifyingly secure, had at last begun to loosen. First he circulated a riposte to Cicero's eulogy of Cato, which he called his *Anti-Cato*, full of vulgar gibes that Cato was a drunkard and a crank. As nearly every Roman had at least a grudging respect for Cato, and most revered him, the pettiness of the pamphlet did the Dictator's reputation far more harm than it did Cato's. ('What is this restless desire of his to dominate everyone?' Cicero wondered aloud when he read it. 'That requires him to trample even on the dust of the dead?') Then there was his decision to hold yet another triumph, this time to celebrate his victory in Spain: it seemed to most people that the annihilation of thousands of fellow Romans, including the son of Pompey, was not a thing to glory in. There was also his continuing infatuation with Cleopatra: it was bad enough that he installed her in a grand house with a park beside the Tiber, but when he had a golden statue of his foreign mistress erected in the Temple of Venus, he offended the pious and the patriotic alike. He even had himself declared a god – 'the Divine Julius' – with his own priesthood, temple and images, and like a god began to interfere in all aspects of daily life: restricting overseas travel for senators and banning elaborate meals and luxurious goods – to the extent of stationing spies in the marketplaces who would burst into citizens' homes in the middle of dinner to search, confiscate and arrest.

Finally, as if his ambition had not caused enough bloodshed in recent years, he announced that in the spring he would be off to war again at the head of an immense army of thirty-six legions, to eliminate Parthia first of all, in revenge for the death of Crassus, and then to wheel around the far side of the Black Sea in a vast swathe of conquest that would encompass Hyrcania, the Caspian Sea and the Caucasus, Scythia, all the countries bordering on Germany and finally Germany itself, before returning to Italy by way of Gaul. He would be away three years. Over none of this did the Senate have any say. Like the men who built the pyramids for the pharaohs, they were mere slaves to their master's grand design.

In December, Cicero proposed that we should transfer our labours to a warmer climate. A wealthy client of his on the Bay of Naples, M. Cluvius, had died recently, leaving him a substantial property at Puteoli, and it was to this that we headed, taking a week over the journey and arriving on the eve of Saturnalia. The villa was large and luxurious, built on the seashore, and even more beautiful than Cicero's nearby house at Cumae. The estate came with a substantial portfolio of commercial properties located inside the town and a farm just outside it. Cicero was as delighted as a child with his new possession, and the moment we arrived he took off his shoes, hoisted his toga, and walked down the beach to the sea to bathe his feet.

The following morning, after he had handed out Saturnalian gifts to all the slaves, he called me into his study and gave me a handsome sandalwood box. I assumed that the box was my present, but when I thanked him, he told me to open it. Inside I found the deeds to the farm near Puteoli. It had been transferred to my name. I was as stunned by the gesture as I had been on the day he granted me my freedom.

He said, 'My dear old friend, I wish it were more and I wish I could have given it to you sooner. But here it is at last, that farm you always wanted – and may it bring you as much joy and comfort as you have brought to me over the years.'

Even though it was a holiday, Cicero worked. He had no family anymore with whom to celebrate – dead, divorced and scattered as they were – and I suppose that writing eased his loneliness. Not that he was melancholy. He had started a new work, a philosophical investigation of old age, and he was enjoying it (*O wretched indeed is that old man who has not learned in the course of his long life that death should be held of no account*). But he insisted that I, at any rate, should have the day off, and so I went for a walk along the beach, turning over in my mind the extraordinary fact that I was now a man of property – a farmer indeed. It felt like the end of one part of my life and the start of another, a portent that my work with Cicero was almost done and that we would soon part.

All along that stretch of coast one encounters large villas looking west across the bay towards the promontory of Misenum. The property next door to Cicero's was owned by L. Marcius Philippus, a former consul a few years younger than Cicero, who had been awkwardly placed during the civil war, given that he was Cato's father-in-law and yet was also married to Caesar's closest living relative, his niece Atia. He had been granted permission by both sides to keep out of the conflict, and had sat it out down here – a cautious neutrality that perfectly suited his nervous temperament.

Now, as I drew closer to the boundary of his estate, I saw that the beach was blocked off by soldiers who were preventing people passing in front of the house. For a moment I wondered what was happening, and when at last I worked it out, I turned and hurried back to tell Cicero – only to find that he had already received a message:

Caesar Dictator to M. Cicero.

Greetings.

I am in Campania inspecting my veterans and shall be spending part of Saturnalia with my niece Atia at the villa of L. Philippus. If it is convenient, my party and I could visit you on the third day of the festival. Please let my officer know.

I asked, 'How did you reply?'

'How else does one reply to a god? I said yes, of course.'

He pretended to be put-upon, but I could tell that secretly he was flattered, although when he enquired as to the size of Caesar's entourage, which he would also have to feed, and was told it consisted of two thousand men, he had second thoughts. His entire household were obliged to postpone their holiday, and for the remainder of that day and the whole of the next made frantic preparations, emptying the food markets of Puteoli and borrowing couches and tables from neighbouring villas. A camp was pitched in the field behind the house and sentries were posted. We were given a list of twenty men who were to dine in the house itself, headed by Caesar and including Philippus, L. Cornelius Galba and C. Oppius – these last two Caesar's closest associates – and a dozen officers whose names I have forgotten. It was organised like a military manoeuvre, according to a strict timetable. Cicero was informed that Caesar would be working with his secretaries in Philippus's house until shortly after noon, that he would then take an hour's vigorous exercise along the seashore, and would appreciate it if a bath could be provided for his use before dinner. As to the menu, the Dictator was following a course of emetics and so would have an appetite equal to whatever was provided, but he would particularly appreciate oysters and quail if they were available.

By this time Cicero was heartily wishing he had never agreed to the visit: 'Where am I to find quail in December? Does he think I am Lucullus?' Nevertheless, he was determined, as he put it, 'to show Caesar that we know how to live', and took pains to provide the finest of everything, from scented oils for the bathroom to Falernian wine for the table. Then, just before the Dictator was due to walk through the door, the ever-anxious Philippus hurried round with the news that M. Mamurra, Caesar's chief engineer – the man who had built the bridge across the Rhine, among many other amazing feats – had died of apoplexy. For a moment it looked as if the occasion might be ruined. But when Caesar swept in, red-faced from the exertion of his walk, and Cicero broke the news to him, his expression did not even flicker.

'That's too bad for him. Which way is my bath?'

No further mention was made of Mamurra – and yet, as Cicero observed, he must have been one of Caesar's closest comrades for more than a decade. Oddly, that brief insight into the coldness of Caesar's character is the thing I remember most clearly of his visit, for I was soon distracted by the house being full of noisy men, spread between three dining rooms, and naturally I was not at the same table as the Dictator. In my room they were all soldiers – a rough crowd, polite enough to begin with but soon drunk, and there was a lot of trooping in and out between courses to vomit on the beach. All the talk was of Parthia and the forthcoming campaign. Afterwards I asked Cicero what had passed between him and Caesar.

He said, 'It was really surprisingly pleasant. We avoided politics and talked mostly of literature. He said that he had just read our *Disputations* and was full of compliments – "Except," he said, "I have to tell you that I am the living refutation of your principal proposition." "And what is that?" "You claim that one can only conquer one's fear of death by living a good life. Well, according to your definition I have hardly done that, and yet I have no fear of dying. What is your answer?" To which I replied that for a man with no fear of dying, he certainly travelled with a large bodyguard.'

'Did he laugh?'

'No he did not! He turned very serious, as if I had insulted him, and said that as the head of state he had a responsibility to take proper precautions, that if anything happened to him there would be chaos, but this didn't mean that he was afraid to die – far from it. So I probed a little further into the subject and asked why it was that he was so unafraid: did he believe the soul was eternal, or did he think we all die with our bodies?'

'And what was his reply?'

'He said that he didn't know about anyone else, but that obviously *he* wouldn't die along with his body because *he* was a god. I looked to see if he was joking but I'm not sure that he was. At that moment, I tell you honestly, I ceased to envy him all his power and glory. It has driven him mad.'

The only time I saw Caesar again that night was when he left. He emerged from the principal dining room, leaning on Cicero and laughing at some remark he had just made. He appeared slightly flushed with wine, which was rare for him as he usually drank in moderation, if at all. His soldiers formed into lines as an honour guard and he lurched off into the night supported by Philippus and followed by his officers.

The next morning Cicero wrote an account of the visit to Atticus: *Strange that so onerous a guest should leave a memory not disagreeable. But once is enough. He is not the kind of person to whom one says, 'Do drop round the next time you are in the neighbourhood.'*

As far as I know, that was the last time Cicero and Caesar ever spoke to one another.

On the eve of our return to Rome, I rode over to look at my farm. It was difficult to find, almost invisible from the coastal road, at the end of a long track leading up into the hills: an ancient, ivy-covered building commanding a wonderful panorama of the island of Capri. There was an olive grove and a small vineyard surrounded by low dry-stone walls. Goats and sheep grazed in the fields and on the nearby slopes; the tinkle of their neck bells rang soft as wind chimes; otherwise the place was entirely silent.

The farmstead was modest but fully appointed: a courtyard with portico, barns containing an olive press and stalls and feed racks, a fish pond, a vegetable and herb garden, a dovecote, chickens, a sundial. Beside the wooden gate a shaded terrace with fig trees faced out to sea. Inside, up a stone staircase, beneath the terracotta roof, was a large, dry, raftered room where I could keep my books and write: I asked the overseer to have some shelves built. Six slaves maintained the place and I was glad to see that all appeared healthy, unfettered and well fed. The overseer and his wife lived on the premises and had a child; they could read and write. Forget Rome and its empire: this was more than world enough for me. I should have stayed and told Cicero that he would have to return to the city on his own – I knew it even at the time. But that would have been poor thanks for his generosity, and besides, there were still books he wanted to finish and my assistance was needed. So I bade farewell to my little household, undertook to return to them as soon as I could, and rode back down the hill.

The Spartan statesman Lycurgus, seven hundred years ago, is said to have observed:

When falls on man the anger of the gods,
First from his mind they banish understanding.

Such was to be the fate of Caesar. I am sure Cicero was correct: he *had* gone mad. His success had made him vain, and his vanity had devoured his reason.

It was around this time – 'since the days of the week are all taken', as Cicero joked – that he had the seventh month of the year retitled 'July' in his honour. He had already declared himself a god and decreed that his statue should be carried in a special chariot during religious processions. Now his name was added to those of Jove and the Penates of Rome in every official oath. He was granted the title Dictator for Life. He styled himself Emperor and Father of the Nation. He presided over the Senate from a golden throne. He wore a special purple and gold toga. To the statues of the seven ancient kings of Rome that stood on the Capitol, he added an eighth – himself – and his image was introduced on the coinage – another prerogative of royalty.

Nobody spoke now of the revival of constitutional freedom – it was surely only a matter of time before he was declared monarch. At the Lupercalian festival in February, watched by a crowd in the Forum, Mark Antony actually placed a crown upon his head, whether mockingly or as a serious gesture none could say; but it was placed there, and the people resented it. On the statue of Brutus – the distant forefather of our contemporary Brutus – who had driven out the kings of Rome and established the consulship, graffito appeared: *If only you were alive now!* And on Caesar's statue someone scrawled:

Brutus was elected consul
When he sent the kings away;
Caesar sent the consuls packing,
Caesar is our king today.

He was scheduled to leave Rome at the start of his campaign of world conquest on the eighteenth day of March. Before he left, it was necessary for him to decree the results of all the elections for the next three years. A list was published. Mark Antony was to be consul for the remainder of the year alongside Dolabella; they would be succeeded by Hirtius and Pansa; Decimus Brutus (whom I shall henceforth call Decimus, to distinguish him from his kinsman) and L. Munatius Plancus would take over the year after that. Brutus himself was to be urban praetor and thereafter governor of Macedonia; Cassius was to be praetor and then governor of Syria; and so on. There were hundreds of names; it was drawn up like an order of battle.

The moment he saw it, Cicero shook his head in amazement at the sheer hubris of it: 'Julius the god seems to have forgotten what Julius the politician never would: that every time you fill an appointment, you make one man grateful and ten resentful.' On the eve of Caesar's departure, Rome was full of angry, disappointed senators. For example, Cassius, already insulted not to be chosen for the Parthian campaign, was offended that the less-experienced Brutus should be given a praetorship superior to his. But the greatest resentment was Mark Antony's at the prospect of sharing the consulship with Dolabella, a man whom he had never forgiven for committing adultery with his wife, and to whom he felt greatly superior; in fact such was his jealousy, he was actually using his powers as an augur to block the nomination on the grounds that it was ill-omened. A meeting of the Senate was summoned in Pompey's portico for the fifteenth, three days before Caesar's departure, to settle the issue once and for all. The rumour was that the Dictator would also demand to be granted the title of king at the same session.

Cicero had avoided the Senate as much as possible. He could not bear to look upon it. 'Do you know that some of these upstarts from Gaul and Spain that Caesar has put into the place can't even speak Latin?' He felt old and out of touch. His eyesight was poor. Nevertheless, he decided to attend on the Ides – and not merely to attend, but to speak for once, on behalf of Dolabella and against Mark Antony, whom he regarded as another tyrant in the making. He suggested that I should accompany him, as in the old days, 'if only to see what the Divine Julius has done to our republic of mere mortals'.

We set off two hours after dawn, in a pair of litters. It was a public holiday. A gladiator fight was scheduled for later in the day and the streets around Pompey's theatre, where the contest was to be held, were already packed with spectators. Lepidus, whom Caesar shrewdly judged weak enough to be a suitable deputy and therefore was the new Master of Horse, had a legion stationed on Tiber Island, ready to embark for Spain, of which he was to be governor; many of his men were heading for a final visit to the games.

Inside the portico, a troop of about a hundred gladiators belonging to Decimus, the governor of Nearer Gaul, practised their lunges and feints in the shadow of the bare plane trees, watched by their owner and a crowd of aficionados. Decimus had been one of the Dictator's most brilliant lieutenants in Gaul, and Caesar was said to treat him almost as a son. But he was not widely known in the city and I had hardly ever seen him. He was stocky and broad-shouldered: he could have been a gladiator himself. I remember wondering why he needed so many pairs of fighters for what were only minor games. Around the covered walkways several of the praetors, including Cassius and Brutus, had set up their tribunals, conveniently closer to the Senate than the Forum, and were hearing cases. Cicero leaned out of his litter and asked the porters to set us down in a sunny spot so that we could have some spring warmth. They did as ordered, and while he reclined on his cushions and read through his speech, I enjoyed the sensation of the sun upon my face.

Presently, through half-closed eyes, I saw Caesar's golden throne being carried through the portico and into the Senate chamber. I pointed it out to Cicero. He rolled up his speech. A couple of slaves helped him to his feet and we joined the throng of senators queuing to go in. There must have been three hundred men at least. Once I could have named almost every member of that noble order, and identified his tribe and family, and told you his particular interests. But the Senate that I knew had bled to death on the battlefields of Pharsalus, Thapsus and Munda.

We filed into the chamber. In contrast to the old Senate house it was light and airy, in the modern style, with a central aisle of black-and-white mosaic tiles. On either side rose three wide, shallow steps, along which the benches were arranged in tiers, facing one another. At the far end, on its dais, stood Caesar's throne beside the statue of Pompey, upon the head of which some subversive hand had placed a laurel wreath. One of

Caesar's slaves kept jumping up, trying to knock it off, but much to the amusement of the watching senators he couldn't quite reach it. Eventually he fetched a stool and climbed up to remove the offending symbol and was rewarded with mocking applause. Cicero shook his head and rolled his eyes at such levity and went off to find his place. I stayed by the door with the other spectators.

After that, a long time passed – I should say at least an hour. Eventually Caesar's four attendants came back in from the portico, walked up the aisle to the throne, hoisted it on to their shoulders with difficulty (for it was made of solid gold) and carried it out again. A groan of exasperation went round the chamber. Many senators stood to stretch their legs; some left. Nobody seemed to know what was happening. Cicero strolled down the aisle. He said to me, 'I don't much want to deliver this speech in any case. I think I'll go home. Will you find out if the session is definitely cancelled?'

I went out into the portico. The gladiators were still there, but Decimus had gone. Brutus and Cassius had given up listening to their petitioners and were talking together. I knew both men well enough to approach them – Brutus the noble philosopher, still youthful-looking at forty; Cassius the same age, but grizzled, harder. About a dozen other senators were hanging round them, listening – the Casca brothers, Tillius Cimber, Minucius Basilus and Gaius Trebonius, who had been designated by Caesar to be governor of Asia; I also remember Quintus Ligarius, the exile whom Cicero had persuaded the Dictator to allow home, and Marcus Rubrius Ruga, an old soldier who had also been pardoned and had never got over it. They fell silent and turned to look at me as I approached. I said, 'Forgive me for disturbing you, gentlemen, but Cicero would like to know what's happening.'

The senators looked sideways at one another. Cassius said suspiciously, 'What does he mean by "what's happening"?'

Puzzled, I replied, 'Why, he simply wants to know if there will there be a meeting.'

Brutus said, 'The omens are unpropitious, therefore Caesar is refusing to leave his house. Decimus has gone to try to persuade him to come. Tell Cicero to be patient.'

'I'll tell him, but I think he wants to go home.'

Cassius said firmly, 'Then persuade him to stay.'

It struck me as odd, but I went and relayed the remark to Cicero. He shrugged. 'Very well, let's give it a little longer.'

He returned to his seat and looked at his speech again. Senators came up and spoke to him and drifted away. He showed Dolabella what he was planning to say. Another long wait ensued. But eventually, after a further hour, Caesar's throne was carried back in and placed upon the dais. Clearly Decimus had persuaded him to come after all. Those senators who had been standing around talking resumed their places, and an air of expectation settled over the chamber.

I heard cheering outside. Turning, I saw through the open door that a crowd was streaming into the portico. In the middle of the throng, like battle standards, I could see the fasces of Caesar's twenty-four lictors, and swaying above their heads the golden canopy of the Dictator's litter. I was surprised there was no military bodyguard. Only later did I learn that Caesar had recently dismissed all those hundreds of soldiers he used to travel around with, saying, 'It is better to die once by treachery than live always in fear of it.' I have often wondered if his conversation with Cicero three months earlier had anything to do with this piece of bravado. At any rate, the litter was carried across the open space and set down outside the Senate, and when his lictors helped him out of it, the crowd was able to get very close to him. They thrust petitions into his hands, which he passed immediately to an aide. He was dressed in the special purple toga embroidered with gold that he alone was permitted by the Senate to wear. He certainly looked like a king; all that was missing was the crown. And yet I could see at once that he was uneasy. He had a habit, like a bird of prey, of cocking his head this way and that, and looking about him, as if searching for some slight stirring in the undergrowth. At the sight of the open door to the chamber, he seemed to draw back. But Decimus took him by the hand, and I suppose the momentum of the occasion must also have propelled him forwards: certainly he would have lost face if he had turned round and returned home; there were already rumours that he was ill.

His lictors cleared a path for him and in he came. He passed within three feet of me, so close I could smell the sweet and spicy scent of the oils and unguents with which he had been anointed after his bath. Decimus slipped in after him. Mark Antony was just behind Decimus, also on his way in, but Trebonius suddenly intercepted him and drew him aside.

The Senate stood. In the silence Caesar walked down the central aisle, frowning and pensive, twirling a stylus in his right hand. A couple of scribes followed him, carrying document boxes. Cicero was in the front row, reserved for ex-consuls. Caesar did not acknowledge him, or anyone else. He was glancing back and forth, up and down, flicking that stylus between his fingers. He mounted the dais, turned to face the senators, gestured to them to be seated, and lowered himself into his throne.

Immediately various figures rose and approached him offering petitions. This was normal practice now that the debates themselves no longer mattered: they had become instead rare opportunities to give the Dictator something in person. The first to reach him – from the left, both his hands stretched out in supplication – was Tillius Cimber. He was known to be seeking a pardon for his brother, who was in exile. But instead of lifting the hem of Caesar's toga to kiss it, he suddenly grabbed the folds of fabric around Caesar's neck and yanked so hard on the thick material that Caesar was pulled sideways, effectively pinioned and unable to move. He shouted angrily, but his voice was half strangled so I couldn't quite make it out. It sounded something like, 'But this is violence!' A moment later, one of the Casca brothers, Publius, strode towards him from the other side and jammed a dagger into Caesar's exposed neck. I couldn't believe what I was seeing: it was unreal – a play, a dream.

'Casca, you villain, what are you doing?' Despite his fifty-five years, the Dictator was still a strong man. Somehow he grabbed the blade of Casca's dagger with his left hand – he must have torn his fingers to shreds – squirmed free of Cimber's grasp, then swung round and stabbed Casca in the arm with his stylus. Casca cried in Greek, 'Help me, brother!' and an instant later his brother Gaius knifed Caesar in the ribs. The Dictator's gasp of shock echoed round the chamber. He dropped to his knees. More than twenty toga-clad figures were now stepping up on to the dais and surrounding him. Decimus ran past me to join in. There was a frenzy of stabbing. Senators rose in their places to see what was happening. People have often asked me why none of these hundreds of men, whose fortunes Caesar had made and whose careers he had advanced, attempted to go to his aid. I cannot answer except to say that it was all so fast, so violent and so unexpected, one's senses were stupefied.

I could no longer see Caesar through the ring of his assailants. I was told afterwards by Cicero, who was closer than I, that by some superhuman effort he briefly regained his feet and tried to break away. But such was the force, the desperate haste and the closeness of the attack that escape was impossible. His assailants even wounded one another. Cassius knifed Brutus in the hand. Minucius Basilus stabbed Rubrius in the thigh. It is said that the Dictator's last words were a bitter reproach to Decimus, who had tricked him into coming: 'Even you?' Perhaps it is true. I wonder, though, how much speech he was capable of by then. Afterwards the doctors counted twenty-three stab wounds on his body.

Their business done, the assassins drew back from what a moment before had been the beating heart of the empire and was now a punctured skein of flesh. Their hands were gloved in blood. Their gory daggers were held aloft. They shouted a few slogans: 'Liberty!' 'Peace!' 'The republic!' Brutus even called out 'Long live Cicero!' Then they ran down the aisle and out into the portico, their eyes staring wildly in their excitement, their togas spattered like butchers' aprons.

The moment they had gone, it was as if a spell had been broken. Pandemonium erupted. Senators clambered over the benches and even over one another in their panic to get away. I was almost trampled in the rush. But I was determined not to leave without Cicero. I ducked and twisted my way through the oncoming press of bodies until I reached him. He was still seated, staring at Caesar's body, which lay entirely unattended – his slaves having fled – sprawled on its back, its feet pointed towards the base of Pompey's statue, its head lolling over the edge of the dais, facing the door.

I told Cicero we needed to leave, but he did not seem to hear me. He was staring at the corpse, transfixed. He murmured, 'No one dares go near him, look.'

One of the Dictator's shoes had come off; his bare depilated legs were exposed where his toga had ridden up his thighs; his imperial purple was ragged and bloodied; there was a slash across his cheek that exposed the pale bone; his dark eyes seemed to stare, outraged, upside down, at the emptying chamber; blood ran from his wound diagonally across his forehead and dripped on to the white marble.

All those details I see today as clearly as I saw them forty years ago, and for an instant there flashed into my mind the prophecy of the sibyl: that Rome would be ruled by three, then two, then one, and finally by none. It took an effort for me to drag my gaze away, to seize Cicero by the arm and pull him to his feet. Finally, like a sleepwalker, he allowed himself to be led from the scene, and together we made our way out into the daylight.

XIV

The portico was in chaos. The assassins had gone, escorted by Decimus's gladiators. No one knew their destination. People were rushing to and fro trying to find out what had happened. The Dictator's lictors had thrown away their symbols of authority and made a run for it. The remaining senators were also leaving as fast as they could; a few had even stripped off their togas to disguise their rank and were trying to infiltrate themselves into the crowd. Meanwhile, at the far end of the portico, some of the audience from the gladiator fights in the adjacent theatre had heard the commotion and were pouring in to see what was going on.

I sensed that Cicero was in mortal danger. Even though he'd known nothing in advance of the conspiracy, Brutus had called out his name; everyone had heard it. He was an obvious target for vengeance. Caesar's loyalists might even assume he was the assassins' leader. Blood would demand blood.

I said, 'We have to get you away from here.'

To my relief, he nodded, still too stunned to argue. Our porters had fled, abandoning their litters. We had to hurry out of the portico on foot. Meanwhile the games continued oblivious. From Pompey's theatre welled the roar of applause as the gladiators fought. One would never have guessed what had just occurred, and the more distance we put between ourselves and the portico, the more normal things seemed, so that by the time we reached the Carmenta Gate and entered the city it appeared to be a perfectly ordinary holiday and the assassination felt as if it had been a lurid dream.

Nevertheless, invisible to us, along the back streets and through the markets, conveyed on running feet and in panicky whispers, the news was travelling faster than we could – so that somehow, by the time we reached the house on the Palatine, it had overtaken us, and Cicero's brother Quintus and Atticus were already arriving from separate directions with garbled versions of what had happened. They did not know much. There had been an attack in the Senate, was all they had heard: Caesar was hurt.

'Caesar is dead,' said Cicero, and described what we had just seen. It seemed even more fantastical in recollection than it had at the time. Both men were at first disbelieving and then overjoyed that the Dictator was slain. Atticus, normally so urbane, even performed a little skipping dance.

Quintus said, 'And you truly had no idea this was coming?'

'None,' replied Cicero. 'They must have kept it from me deliberately. I ought to be offended, but to be honest I'm relieved to have been spared the anxiety. It demanded far more nerve than I could ever have mustered. To have come to the Senate with a concealed blade, to have waited all that time, to have held one's nerve, to have risked massacre by Caesar's supporters, and finally to have looked the tyrant in the eye and plunged in the dagger – I don't mind confessing I could never have done it.'

Quintus said, 'I could!'

Cicero laughed. 'Well, you're more used to blood than I am.'

'And yet do none of you feel any sorrow for Caesar, simply

as a man?' I asked. 'After all,' I said to Cicero, 'it's only three months since you were laughing with him over dinner.'

Cicero looked at me with incredulity. 'I'm amazed that you should ask me that. I imagine I feel as you must have felt on the day you received your freedom. Whether Caesar was a kind master or a cruel one is neither here nor there – master he was, and slaves was what he made us. And now we have been liberated. So let's have no talk of sorrow.'

He sent out a secretary to see if he could discover the whereabouts of Brutus and the other conspirators. The man came back soon afterwards and reported that they were said to be occupying the upper ground of the Capitol.

Cicero said, 'I must go at once and offer my support.'

'Is that wise?' I asked. 'As things stand, you bear no responsibility for the killing. But if you go and show your solidarity with them in public, Caesar's supporters may not see much difference between you and Cassius and Brutus.'

'Let them. I intend to thank the men who've given me back my liberty.'

The others agreed and we set off at once, all four of us, with a few slaves for protection – along the slope of the Palatine, down the steps into the valley and across the road of Jugarius to the foot of the Tarpeian Rock. The air was eerily still and torpid with an approaching storm; the thoroughfare, normally busy with ox carts, was deserted apart from a few people wandering in the direction of the Forum. Their expressions were stunned, bewildered, fearful. And certainly if one sought for portents one had only to glance up at the sky. Massy dense black clouds seemed to be pressing down upon the roofs of the temples, and as we began to climb the steep flight of steps there was a flash and a crack of thunder. The rain was cold and heavy. The stones became slippery. We had to pause halfway to recover our breath. Beside us a stream ran over the green mossy rock and turned into a waterfall; below us I could see the curve of the Tiber, the city walls, the Field of Mars. I realised then how shrewd a piece of military planning it had been to retire straight from the scene of the assassination to the Capitol: its sheer cliffs made it a naturally impregnable fortress.

We pressed on until we came to the gate at the summit, which was guarded by gladiators, fearsome-looking characters from Nearer Gaul. With them was one of Decimus's officers. He recognised Cicero and ordered the men to admit us, then he conducted us himself into the walled compound, past the chained dogs that guarded the place at night, and into the Temple of Jupiter, where at least a hundred men were gathered, sheltering in the gloom from the rain.

As Cicero entered he was greeted with applause and he went round shaking hands with all of the assassins apart from Brutus, whose hand was bandaged because of the wound Cassius had accidentally inflicted on him. They had changed out of their bloodied clothes into freshly laundered togas, and their demeanour was sober, even grim, with nothing left of the euphoria that had immediately followed the killing. I was amazed to see how many of Caesar's closest followers had rushed to join them: L. Cornelius Cinna, for example, the brother of Caesar's first wife and uncle of Julia – Caesar had recently made him praetor, yet here he was with his ex-brother-in-law's murderers. And here too was Dolabella – the ever-faithless Dolabella – who had raised not a finger to defend Caesar in the Senate chamber, and who now had his arm round the shoulder of Decimus, the man who had lured their old chief to his doom. He came over to join in the conversation that Cicero was having with Brutus and Cassius.

Brutus said, 'So you approve of what we have done?'

'Approve? It's the greatest deed in the history of the republic! But tell me,' asked Cicero, with a glance around the sombre interior, 'why are you all cooped up here out of sight like criminals? Why aren't you down in the Forum rallying the people to your cause?'

'We are patriots, not demagogues. Our aim was to remove the tyrant, nothing more.'

Cicero stared at him in surprise. 'But then who is running the country?'

Brutus said, 'At the moment, no one. The next step is to establish a new government.'

'Shouldn't you simply declare yourselves to be the government?'

'That would be illegal. We didn't pull down a tyrant in order to set ourselves up as tyrants in his place.'

'Well then summon the Senate here now, to this temple – you have the power as praetors – and let the Senate declare a state of emergency until elections can be held. That would be entirely legal.'

'We think it would be more constitutional if Mark Antony, as consul, summoned the Senate.'

'Mark Antony?' Cicero's surprise was turning to alarm. 'You mustn't let him anywhere near this business. He has all of Caesar's worst qualities and none of his best.' He appealed to Cassius to back him up.

Cassius said, 'I agree with you. In my view we should have killed him at the same time as we killed Caesar. But Brutus wouldn't tolerate it. Therefore Trebonius delayed him on his way in to the chamber, so that he could get away.'

'And where is he now?'

'Presumably in his house.'

'That I would doubt, knowing him,' said Dolabella. 'He will be busy in the city.'

Throughout these exchanges I had noticed Decimus talking to a couple of his gladiators. Now he hurried across, his expression grim. He said, 'There's a report that Lepidus is moving his legion off Tiber Island.'

Cassius said, 'We'll be able to see for ourselves from here.'

We went outside and followed Cassius and Decimus around the side of the great temple to the raised paved area to the north that gives a view for miles over the Field of Mars and beyond. And there was no doubt of it: the legionaries were marching across the bridge and forming up on the riverbank nearest the city.

Brutus betrayed his anxiety by a constant tapping of his foot. He said, 'I sent a messenger to Lepidus hours ago but he hasn't returned an answer.'

Cassius pointed. 'That's his answer.'

Cicero said, 'Brutus, I implore you – I implore you all – go down to the Forum and tell the people what you've done and why you've done it. Fire them with the spirit of the old republic. Otherwise Lepidus will trap you up here and Antony will take control of the city.'

Even Brutus could now see the wisdom of this, and so a procession of the conspirators – or assassins, or freedom fighters, or liberators: no one ever could agree exactly what to call them – descended the twisting road that led from the summit of the Capitol around behind the Temple of Saturn and down into the Forum. At Cicero's suggestion they left their bodyguard of gladiators behind: 'It will make the best possible impression of our sincerity if we walk alone and unarmed; besides, if there is trouble, we can retreat quickly enough.'

It had stopped raining. Three or four hundred citizens had gathered in the Forum and were standing around listlessly among the puddles, apparently waiting for something to happen. They saw us coming when we were still quite a long way off, and moved towards us. I had no idea how they would react. Caesar had always been a great favourite of the mob, although latterly even they had come to weary of his kingly ways – to dread his looming wars and to pine for the old days of elections when they had to be courted by the dozens of candidates with flattery and bribes. Would they applaud us or try to tear us apart? In the event they did neither. The crowd watched in absolute silence as we entered the Forum and then parted to let us pass. The praetors – Brutus, Cassius and Cinna – went up on to the rostra to address them, while the rest of us, including Cicero, stood at the side to watch.

Brutus spoke first, and although I can remember his sombre opening line – 'As my noble ancestor Junius Brutus drove the tyrant-king Tarquin from the city, so today have I rid us of the tyrant-dictator Caesar' – the rest of it I have forgotten. That was the problem. He had obviously laboured hard over it for days, and no doubt as an essay on the wickedness of despotism it read well. But as Cicero had long tried to convince him, a speech is a performance, not a philosophical discourse: it must appeal to the emotions more than to the intellect. A fiery oration at that moment might have transformed the situation – might have inspired the crowd to defend the Forum and their liberty from the soldiers who even now were massing on the Field of Mars. But Brutus gave them a lecture that was three parts history to one part political theory. I could hear Cicero beside me muttering under his breath. It did not help that while he was speaking, Brutus's wound began to bleed beneath its bandage; one was distracted from what he was saying by that gory reminder of what he had done.

After what felt like a long time, Brutus ended to applause best described as thoughtful. Cassius spoke next, and not badly either, for he had taken lessons in oratory from Cicero in Tusculum. But he was a professional soldier who had spent little time in Rome: he was respected but he was not much known, let alone loved. He received less applause even than Brutus. The disaster, however, was Cinna. He was an orator of the old-fashioned, melodramatic school, and tried to inject some passion into proceedings by tearing off his praetorian robe and hurling it from the rostra, denouncing it as the gift of a despot that he was ashamed to be seen wearing. The hypocrisy was too much to bear. Someone yelled out, 'You didn't say that yesterday!' The remark was cheered, which emboldened another heckler to shout: 'You'd have been nothing without Caesar, you old has-been!' In the chorus of jeering, Cinna's voice was lost – and the meeting with it.

Cicero said, 'Now this is a fiasco.'

'You are the orator,' said Decimus. 'Will you say something to retrieve the situation?' and to my horror I saw that Cicero was tempted. But at that moment Decimus was handed a new report that Lepidus's legion appeared to be moving towards the city. He beckoned urgently to the praetors to come down off the rostra, and with as much confidence as we could muster, which was little, we all trooped back up to the Capitol.

It was typical of Brutus's other-worldliness that he should have believed right up until the last moment that Lepidus would never dare to break the law by bringing an army across the sacred boundary and into Rome. After all, he assured Cicero, he knew the Master of Horse extremely well: Lepidus was married to his sister Junia Secunda (just as Cassius was married to his half-sister Junia Tertia).

'Believe me, he's a patrician through and through. He won't do anything illegal. I have always found him an absolute stickler for dignity and protocol.'

And at first it seemed he might be right, as the legion, after crossing the bridge and moving towards the city walls, halted on the Field of Mars and pitched camp about half a mile away. Then soon after nightfall, we heard the plaintive notes of the war horns. They set the dogs barking in the walled compound of the temple and sent us hurrying out to see what was going on. Heavy cloud obscured the moon and stars but the distant lights of the legion's campfires shone clearly in the darkness. Even as we watched, the fires seemed to splinter and rearrange themselves into snakes of fire.

Cassius said, 'They are marching with torches.'

A line of light began wavering along the road towards the Carmenta Gate. Presently on the moist night air we heard the faint tramp of the legionaries' boots. The gate was almost directly beneath us, obscured from sight by outcrops of rock. Lepidus's vanguard found it locked and hammered for admittance and cried out to the porter. But I guess he must have run away. There was a long interval when nothing happened. Then a battering ram was brought up. A series of heavy thuds was followed by the noise of splintering wood. Men cheered. Leaning over the parapet, we watched the legionaries with their torches slip quickly through the ruptured gate, deploy around the base of the Capitol and fan out across the Forum to secure the main public buildings.

Cassius said, 'Will they attack us tonight, do you think?'

'Why should they,' replied Decimus bitterly, 'when they can take us at their leisure in the daylight?' The anger in his tone suggested he held the others responsible, that he regarded himself as having fallen in among fools. 'Your brother-in-law, Brutus, has proved more ambitious and more daring than you led me to believe.'

Brutus, his foot tapping ceaselessly, did not respond.

Dolabella said, 'I agree, a night attack would be too hazardous. Tomorrow is when they'll make their move.'

Now Cicero spoke up. 'The question is surely whether Lepidus is acting in alliance with Antony or not. If he is, then our position is frankly hopeless. If he isn't, then I doubt Antony will want him to have the sole glory of wiping out Caesar's assassins. That, gentlemen, I fear, is our best hope.'

Cicero was now obliged to take his chances with the rest: it would have been far too risky to attempt to leave – not in darkness, with the place surrounded by potentially hostile soldiers and with Antony at large in the city. So there was nothing for it except to settle down for the night. It was to our advantage that the summit of the Capitol can only be approached in four ways: by the Moneta Steps to the north-east, the Hundred Steps to the south-west (the route we had climbed that afternoon) and by the two routes that lead up from the Forum – one a flight of stairs, the other a steep road. Decimus strengthened the guard of gladiators at the top of each and then we all retreated to the Temple of Jupiter.

I cannot say we got much rest. The temple was damp and chilly, the benches hard, the memory of the day's events too vivid. The dim light from the lamps and candles played upon the stern faces of the gods; from the shadows of the roof the wooden eagles looked down with disdain. Cicero talked for a while with Quintus and Atticus – quietly, so as not to be overheard. He couldn't believe how ill-thought-out the assassination had been. 'Was ever a deed carried through with such manly resolution and yet such childish judgement? If only they *had* brought me into their confidence! I could at least have told them that if you are going to kill the devil, there's no point in leaving his apprentice alive. And how could they have neglected Lepidus and his legion? Or let an entire day go by with no attempt to seize control of the government?'

The edge of frustration in his voice, if not the words themselves, must have carried to Brutus and Cassius, who were sitting nearby, and I saw them look across at Cicero and frown. He noticed them too. He lapsed into silence and sat propped up against a pillar, huddled in his toga, doubtless brooding on what had been done, what hadn't, and what might be done yet.

With the dawn it became possible to see the main event that had occurred overnight. Lepidus had moved perhaps a thousand men into the city. The smoke from their cooking fires rose over the Forum. A further three thousand or so remained encamped on the Field of Mars.

Cassius, Brutus and Decimus convened a meeting to discuss what should be done. Cicero's proposal of the previous day, that they should summon the Senate to the Capitol, had plainly been overtaken by events. Instead it was decided that a delegation of ex-consuls, none of whom had been party to the assassination, should go to the house of Mark Antony and ask him formally, as consul, to convene the Senate. Servius Sulpicius, C. Marcellus and L. Aemilius Paullus, the brother of Lepidus, all volunteered to go, but Cicero refused to join them, arguing that the group would do better to approach Lepidus directly: 'I don't trust Antony. Besides, any agreement reached with him will only have to be approved by Lepidus, who at the moment is the man with the power, so why not deal with him and cut out Antony altogether?' But Brutus's argument that Antony had legal if not military authority carried the day, and in the middle of the morning the former consuls set off, preceded by an attendant carrying a white flag of truce.

We could do nothing now except wait and watch developments in the Forum – literally so, for if one was willing to scramble down to the roof of the public records office, one had a clear view of proceedings. The entire space was packed with soldiers and civilians listening to speeches from the rostra. They crammed the steps of the temples and clung to the pillars; more still were pressing to enter from the Via Sacra and the Argiletum, which were backed up as far as the eye could see. Unfortunately we were too far away to be able to hear what was being said. Around noon, a figure in full military uniform and the red cloak of a general began to address the crowd and spoke for well over an hour, receiving prolonged applause: that, I was told, was Lepidus. Not long afterwards, another soldier – his Herculean swagger and his thick black hair and beard identifying him unmistakably as Mark Antony – also appeared on the platform. Again, I could not hear his words, but it was significant simply that he was there at all, and I hastened back to tell Cicero that Lepidus and Antony were now apparently in alliance.

The tension on the Capitol by this time was acute. We had had little to eat all day. Nobody had slept much. Brutus and Cassius expected an attack at any time. Our fate was out of our hands. Yet Cicero was oddly serene. He felt himself to be on the right side, he told me, and would take the consequences.

Just as the sun was starting to go down over the Tiber, the

delegation of ex-consuls returned. Sulpicius spoke for them all: 'Antony has agreed to call a meeting of the Senate tomorrow at the first hour in the Temple of Tellus.'

Joy greeted the first part of his statement, groans the second, for the temple was right across town, on the Esquiline, very close to Antony's house. Cassius said at once, 'That's a trap, to lure us out of our strong position. They'll kill us for sure.'

Cicero said, 'You may be right. But you could all stay here and I could go. I doubt they'd kill me. And if they did – well, what does it matter? I'm old, and there could be no better death than in defence of freedom.'

His words lifted our hearts. They reminded us why we were here. It was agreed on the spot that while the actual assassins would remain on the Capitol, Cicero would lead a delegation to speak on their behalf in the Senate. It was also decided that rather than spend another night in the temple, he and all the others who were not actually part of the original conspiracy would return to their homes to rest before the debate. Accordingly, after an emotional farewell, and under the flag of truce, we set off down the Hundred Steps into the gathering twilight. At the foot of the stairs, Lepidus's soldiers had erected a checkpoint. They demanded Cicero go forward and show himself. Fortunately he was recognised, and after he had vouched for the rest of us, we were all allowed to go through.

Cicero worked on his speech late into the night. Before I went to bed he asked if I would accompany him to the Senate the next day and take it down in shorthand. He thought it might be his last oration and he wanted it recorded for posterity: a summation of all he had come to believe about liberty and the republic, the healing role of the statesman and the moral justification for murdering a tyrant. I cannot say I relished the assignment but of course I could not refuse.

Of all the hundreds of debates Cicero had attended over the past thirty years none promised to be tenser than this one. It was scheduled to begin at dawn, which meant that we had to leave the house in darkness and pass through the shuttered streets – a nerve-racking business in itself. It was held in a temple that had never before served as a meeting place for the Senate, surrounded by soldiers – and not just those of Lepidus but many of Caesar's roughest veterans, who on hearing the news of their old chief's murder had armed themselves and come to the city to protect their rights and take revenge on his killers. And finally when we had run the gauntlet of pleas and imprecations and entered the temple, it proved so cramped that men who hated and distrusted one another were nonetheless packed into close proximity so that one sensed that the slightest ill-judged remark might turn the thing into a bloodbath.

And yet from the moment Antony rose to speak it became clear that the debate would be different to Cicero's expectation. Antony was not yet forty – handsome, swarthy, his wrestler's physique fashioned by nature for armour rather than a toga. Yet his voice was rich and educated, his delivery compelling. 'Fathers of the nation,' he declared, 'what is done is done and I profoundly wish it were not so, because Caesar was my dearest friend. But I love my country more even than I loved Caesar, if such a thing is possible, and we must be guided by what is best for the commonwealth. Last night I was with Caesar's widow, and amid her tears and anguish that gracious lady Calpurnia spoke as follows: "Tell the Senate," she said, "that in the agony of my grief I wish for two things only: that my husband be given a funeral appropriate to the honours he won in life, and that there be no further bloodshed."'

This drew a loud, deep-throated growl of approval, and to my surprise I realised the mood was more for compromise than revenge.

'Brutus, Cassius and Decimus,' continued Antony, 'are patriots just as we are, men from the most distinguished families in the state. We can salute the nobility of their aim even as we may despise the brutality of their method. In my view enough blood has been shed over these past five years. Accordingly I propose that we show the same clemency towards his assassins that was the mark of Caesar's statecraft – that in the interests of civic peace we pardon them, guarantee their safety, and invite them to come down from the Capitol and join us in our deliberations.'

It was a commanding performance, but then of course Antony's grandfather was regarded by many, including Cicero, as one of Rome's greatest orators, so perhaps the gift was in his blood. At any rate he set a tone of high-minded moderation – so much so that Cicero, who spoke next, was entirely wrong-footed and could do little except praise him for his wisdom and magnanimity. The only point with which he took issue was Antony's use of the word 'clemency':

'Clemency in my view means a pardon, and a pardon implies a crime. The murder of the Dictator was many things but it was not a crime. I would prefer a different term. Do you remember the story of Thrasybulus, who more than three centuries ago overthrew the Thirty Despots of Athens? Afterwards he instituted what was called an amnesty for his opponents – a concept taken from their Greek word *amnesia*, meaning "forgetfulness". That is what is needed here – a great national act not of forgiveness but of forgetfulness, that we may begin our republic anew freed from the enmities of the past, in friendship and in peace.'

Cicero received the same applause as Antony and a motion was immediately proposed by Dolabella offering amnesty to all those who had taken part in the assassination and urging them to come to the Senate. Only Lepidus was opposed: not I am sure out of principle – Lepidus was never a man for principles – so much as because he saw his chance of glory slipping away. The motion passed and a messenger was dispatched to the Capitol. During the recess while this was being done, Cicero came to the door to talk to me. When I congratulated him on his speech, he said, 'I arrived expecting to be torn to pieces and instead I find myself drowning in honey. What is Antony's game, do you suppose?'

'Perhaps there isn't one. Perhaps he is sincere.'

Cicero shook his head. 'No, he has some plan, but he's keeping it well hidden. Certainly he's more cunning than I gave him credit for.'

When the session resumed, it soon became not so much a debate as a negotiation. First Antony warned that when the news of the assassination reached the provinces, particularly Gaul, it might lead to widespread rebellion against Roman rule: 'In the interests of maintaining strong government in a time of emergency, I propose that all the laws promulgated by Caesar, and all appointments of consuls, praetors and governors made before the Ides of March should be confirmed by the Senate.'

Then Cicero rose. 'Including your own appointment, of course?'

Antony replied, with a first hint of menace, 'Yes, obviously including my own – unless, that is, you object?'

'And including Dolabella's, as your fellow consul? That was Caesar's wish as well, as I recall, until you blocked it by your auguries.'

I glanced across the temple to Dolabella, suddenly leaning forward in his place.

This was obviously a bitter draught for Antony to swallow – but swallow it he did. 'Yes, in the interests of unity, if that is the will of the Senate – including Dolabella's.'

Cicero pressed on. 'And you confirm therefore that both Brutus and Cassius will continue as praetors, and afterwards will be the governors of Nearer Gaul and Syria, and that Decimus will in the meantime take control of Nearer Gaul, with the two legions already allotted to him?'

'Yes, yes and yes.' There were whistles of surprise, some groans and some applause. 'And now,' continued Antony, 'will your side agree: all acts and appointments issued before Caesar's death are to be confirmed by the Senate?'

Later Cicero said to me that before he rose to make his answer, he tried to imagine what Cato would have done. 'And of course he would have said that if Caesar's rule was illegal, it followed that his laws were illegal too and we should have new elections. But then I looked out of the door and saw the soldiers and asked myself how we could possibly have elections in these circumstances – there would be a bloodbath.'

Slowly Cicero got to his feet. 'I cannot speak for Brutus, Cassius and Decimus, but speaking for myself, since it is to the advantage of the state, and on condition that what goes for one goes for all – yes, I agree that the Dictator's appointments should be allowed to stand.'

'I cannot regret it,' he told me afterwards, 'because I could have done nothing else.'

The Senate continued its deliberations for the whole of that day. Antony and Lepidus also laid a motion calling for Caesar's grants to his soldiers to be ratified by the Senate, and in view of the hundreds of veterans waiting outside, Cicero could hardly dare to oppose that either. In return Antony proposed abolishing forever the title and functions of dictator; it passed without protest. About an hour before sunset, after issuing various edicts to the provincial governors, the Senate adjourned and walked through the smoke and squalor of the Subura to the Forum, where Antony and Lepidus gave an account to the waiting crowd of what had just been agreed. The news was greeted with relief and acclamation, and this sight of Senate and people in civic harmony was almost enough to make one imagine the old republic had been restored. Antony even invited Cicero up on to the rostra, the first time the ageing statesman had appeared there since he had addressed the people after his return from exile. For a moment he was too emotional to speak.

'People of Rome,' he said at last, gesturing to quiet the ovation, 'after the agony and violence not just of the last few days but of the last few years, let past grievances and bitterness be set aside.' Just at that moment a shaft of sunlight pierced the clouds, gilding the bronze roof of Jupiter's temple on the Capitol, where the white togas of the conspirators were plainly visible. 'Behold the sun of Liberty,' cried Cicero, seizing the moment, 'shining once again over the Roman Forum! Let it warm us – let it warm the whole of humanity – with the beneficence of its healing rays.'

Shortly afterwards Brutus and Cassius sent a message down to Antony that in view of what had been decided at the Senate, they were willing to leave their stronghold, but only on condition that he and Lepidus sent hostages to remain on the Capitol overnight as a guarantee of their safety. When Antony went up on to the rostra and read this aloud, there were cheers. He said, 'As a token of my good faith, I am willing to pledge to them my own son – a lad of barely three, who the gods know I love more than any living thing. Lepidus,' he said, holding out his hand to the Master of Horse who was standing next to him, 'will you do the same with your son?'

Lepidus had little choice but to agree, and so the two boys – one a toddler, the other in his teens – were collected from their homes and taken with their attendants up on to the Capitol. As dusk fell, Brutus and Cassius appeared, descending the steps without an escort. Yet again the crowd roared its pleasure, especially when they shook hands with Antony and Lepidus, and accepted a public invitation to dine with them as a symbol of reconciliation. Cicero was also invited but he declined. Utterly exhausted by his efforts over the past two days, he went home to sleep.

At dawn the following day the Senate met again in the Temple of Tellus; and once again I went with Cicero.

It was astonishing to enter and see Brutus and Cassius sitting a few feet away from Antony and Lepidus and even from Caesar's father-in-law, L. Calpurnius Piso. There were far fewer soldiers hanging around the door and the atmosphere was tolerant, indeed notable for a certain dark humour. For example when Antony rose to open the session he welcomed back Cassius in particular and said that he hoped this time he wasn't carrying a concealed dagger, to which Cassius replied that he wasn't, but would certainly bring a large one if ever Antony tried to set himself up as a tyrant. Everyone laughed.

Various items of business were transacted. Cicero proposed a motion thanking Antony for his statesmanship as consul, which had averted a civil war; it passed unanimously. Antony then proposed a complementary motion thanking Brutus and Cassius for their part in preserving the peace; that too was accepted without objection. Finally Piso rose to express his thanks to Antony for providing guards to protect his daughter Calpurnia and all Caesar's property on the night of the assassination.

He went on: 'It remains for us now to decide what to do with Caesar's body and with Caesar's will. As regards the body, it has been brought back from the Field of Mars to the residence of the chief priest, has been anointed and awaits cremation. As regards the will, I must tell the house that Caesar made a new one six months ago, on the Ides of September, at his villa near Lavicum, and sealed and deposited it with the Chief Vestal. No one knows its contents. In the spirit of openness and trust that has now been established, I move that both these things – the funeral and the reading of the will – should be conducted in public.'

Antony spoke strongly in favour of the proposal. The only senator who rose to object was Cassius. 'This seems to me a dangerous course. Remember what happened the last time there was a public funeral for a murdered leader – when Clodius's followers burned down the Senate house? Just as we've established a fragile peace, it would be insanity to put it at risk.'

Antony said, 'From what I've heard, Clodius's funeral was allowed to get out of hand by some who might have known better.' He paused for laughter: everyone knew he was now married to Clodius's widow, Fulvia. 'As consul, I shall preside over Caesar's funeral, and I can assure you order will be maintained.'

Cassius indicated by an angry gesture that he was still opposed. For a moment the truce threatened to break. Then Brutus rose. He said, 'Caesar's veterans who are in the city will not understand it if their commander-in-chief is denied a public funeral. Besides, what sort of message will it send to the Gauls, already said to be contemplating rebellion, if we dump the body of their conqueror in the Tiber? I share Cassius's unease, but in truth we have no alternative. Therefore in the interests of concord and amity I support the proposal.'

Cicero said nothing and the motion carried.

The reading of Caesar's will took place the following day, a little way up the hill in Antony's house. Cicero knew the place well. It had been Pompey's main residence before he moved out to his palace overlooking the Field of Mars. Antony, in charge of auctioning the confiscated assets of Caesar's opponents, had sold it to himself at a knockdown price. It was not much changed. The famous battering rams of the pirate triremes, trophies of Pompey's great naval victories, were still set into the outside walls. Inside, the elaborate decoration had scarcely been touched since the old man's day.

Cicero found it unsettling to be back – the more so when he was confronted by the scowling face of the villa's new mistress, Fulvia. She had hated him when she was married to Clodius, and now that she was married to Antony she hated him all over again – and made no attempt to hide it. The moment she saw him, she ostentatiously turned her back and began talking to someone else.

'What a shameless pair of grave-robbers,' Cicero whispered to me, 'and how typical of that harpy to be here. Why *is* she, in fact? Even the widow isn't here. What business of Fulvia's is the reading of Caesar's will?'

But that was Fulvia. More than any other woman in Rome – more even than Servilia, Caesar's old mistress, who at least had the grace to operate behind the scenes – Fulvia loved meddling in politics. And watching her move from visitor to visitor, ushering them towards the room where the will was to be read, I felt a sudden sense of unease: what if hers was the brain behind Antony's skilful policy of reconciliation? That would put it in a very different light.

Piso stood on a low table so that everyone could see him, and with Antony on one side and the Chief Vestal on the other, and with all the most prominent men of the republic listening in the audience, he first displayed the wax seal to show that it had not been tampered with, then broke it open and started to read.

To begin with, its meaning buried in legal jargon, the will seemed entirely innocuous. Caesar left his whole estate to any son that might be born to him after the drawing up of the document. However, in the absence of such a son, his wealth passed to the three male descendants of his late sister: that is to Lucius Pinarius, Quintus Pedius and Gaius Octavius, to be divided in the proportions one eighth each to Pinarius and Pedius and three quarters to Octavius, whom he now adopted as his son, henceforth to be known as Gaius Julius Caesar Octavianus . . .

Piso stopped reading and frowned, as if he was not sure what he had just announced. *An adopted son?* Cicero glanced at me, screwed up his eyes in an effort at memory and mouthed, 'Octavius?' Antony meanwhile looked as if he had been struck in the face. Unlike Cicero, he knew at once who Octavius was – the eighteen-year-old son of Caesar's niece Atia – and for him it must have been a bitter disappointment as well as a total surprise: I am sure he must have hoped to be named as the Dictator's main heir. Instead, he was merely mentioned as an heir in the second degree – that is, one who would inherit only if the first heirs died or turned down their legacy – an honour he shared with Decimus, one of the assassins! In addition, Caesar bequeathed every citizen of Rome the sum of three hundred sesterces in cash, and decreed that his estate beside the Tiber should become a public park.

The meeting broke up into puzzled groups, and afterwards, walking home, Cicero was full of foreboding. 'That will is a Pandora's box – a posthumous poisoned gift to the world that lets loose all manner of evils amongst us.' He was thinking not so much of the unknown Octavius, or Octavian as he was now restyled, who promised to be a short-lived irrelevance (he was not even in the country but was in Illyricum); it was the mention of Decimus combined with the gifts to the people that troubled him.

All through the remainder of that day and throughout the next, preparations went on in the Forum for Caesar's funeral. Cicero watched them from his terrace. A golden tabernacle, built to resemble the Temple of Venus the Victorious, was erected on the rostra for the body to lie in. Barriers were put up to control the crowds. Actors and musicians rehearsed. Hundreds more of Caesar's veterans began to appear on the streets, carrying their weapons: some had travelled a hundred miles to attend. Atticus came round and remonstrated with Cicero for having allowed such a spectacle to go ahead: 'You and Brutus and the others have all gone mad.'

'It's easy for you to say that,' replied Cicero, 'but how was it to be prevented? We control neither the city nor the Senate. The crucial mistakes were made not *after* the assassination but *before* it – a child should have foreseen the consequences of simply removing Caesar and leaving it at that. And now we have the Dictator's will to contend with.'

Brutus and Cassius sent messages to say that they intended to remain indoors throughout the day of the funeral: they had hired guards and advised Cicero to do the same. Decimus with his gladiators had barricaded his house and turned it into a fortress. Cicero, however, refused to take such precautions, although he prudently decided not to show himself in public. He suggested instead that I might attend the funeral and report back to him.

I did not mind going. No one would recognise me. Besides, I wanted to see it. I could not help feeling a certain secret regard for Caesar, who over the years had always been civil to me. Accordingly I went down into the Forum before dawn (this was now five days after the assassination – it was hard, amid the rush of events, to keep track of time). The centre of the city was already packed with thousands, women as well as men – not so much the polite citizenry but mostly old soldiers, the urban poor, many slaves, and a large contingent of Jews, who revered Caesar for allowing them to rebuild the walls of Jerusalem. I managed to work my way around the vast crowd to the corner of the Via Sacra, where the cortège would pass, and a few hours after daybreak I saw in the distance the procession start to leave the official residence of the chief priest.

It paraded right in front of me, and I was amazed by the planning that had gone into it: Antony and I am sure Fulvia had left out nothing that might be relied upon to inflame the emotions. First came the musicians, playing their haunting plangent dirges; then dancers dressed as spirits from the Underworld, who ran up shrieking to the front of the crowd striking poses of grief and horror; then came household slaves and freedmen carrying busts of Caesar; then not one but five actors went marching past representing each of Caesar's triumphs, wearing masks of the Dictator fashioned from beeswax that were so incredibly lifelike one felt he had risen from the dead five-fold in all his glory; then, carried on an open litter, came a life-size model of the corpse, naked except for a loincloth, with each of the stab wounds, including that to his face, depicted as deep red gashes in the white wax flesh – this caused the spectators to gasp and cry and some of the women to swoon; then came the body itself, lying on an ivory couch, carried on the shoulders of senators and soldiers and shrouded from view by covers of purple and gold, followed by Caesar's widow Calpurnia and niece Atia, veiled in black and holding on to one another, accompanied by their relatives; and finally came Antony and Piso, Dolabella, Hirtius, Pansa, Balbus, Oppius, and all the leading supporters of Caesar.

After the cortège had passed, there was a strange hiatus while the body was taken to the steps behind the rostra. Neither before nor afterwards did I ever hear such a profound silence in the centre of Rome in the middle of the day. During this ominous lull the leading mourners were filing on to the platform, and when at last the corpse appeared, Caesar's veterans began banging their swords against their shields as they must have done on the battlefield – a terrific, warlike, intimidating din. The body was placed carefully into the golden tabernacle; Antony stepped forward to deliver the eulogy, and held up his hand for silence.

'We come to bid farewell to no tyrant!' he declared, his

powerful voice ringing round the temples and statues. 'We come to bid farewell to a great man foully murdered in a consecrated place by those he had pardoned and promoted!'

He had assured the Senate he would speak with moderation. He broke that assurance with his opening words, and for the next hour he worked the vast assembly, already aroused by the spectacle of the procession, to a pitch of grief and fury. He flung out his arms. He sank almost to his knees. He beat his breast. He pointed to the heavens. He recited Caesar's achievements. He told them of Caesar's will – the gift to every citizen, the public park, the bitter irony of his honouring of Decimus. 'And yet this Decimus, who was like a son to him – and Brutus and Cassius and Cinna and the rest – these men swore an oath – they made a sacred promise – to serve Caesar faithfully and to protect him! The Senate has given them amnesty, but by Jupiter what revenge I should like to take if prudence did not restrain me!' In short he used every trick of oratory that the austere Brutus had rejected. And then came his – or was it Fulvia's? – masterstroke. He summoned up on to the platform one of the actors wearing Caesar's lifelike mask, who in a rasping voice declaimed to the crowd that famous speech from Pacuvius's tragedy *The Trial for Arms*:

That ever I, unhappy man, should save
Wretches, who thus have brought me to the grave!

The impersonation was uncannily good. It was like a message from the Underworld. And then, to groans of horror, the manikin of Caesar's corpse was raised by some mechanical contraption and rotated full circle so that all the wounds were shown.

From that point onwards Caesar's funeral followed the pattern of Clodius's. The body was supposed to be burned on a pyre already prepared on the Field of Mars. But as it was being borne down from the rostra, angry voices cried out that it should instead be cremated in Pompey's Senate chamber, where the crime was committed, or on the Capitol, where the conspirators had taken refuge. Then the crowd, with some collective impulse, changed its mind and decided that it should be burned on the spot. Antony did nothing to stop any of this but looked on indulgently as once again the bookshops of the Argiletum were ransacked and the benches of the law courts were dragged into the centre of the Forum and stacked in a pile. Caesar's bier was set upon the bonfire and torched. The actors and dancers and musicians pulled off their robes and masks and threw them into the flames. The crowd followed suit. They tore at their own clothes in their hysteria and these along with everything else flammable went flying on to the fire. When the mob started running through the streets carrying torches, looking for the houses of the assassins, I finally lost my nerve and headed back to the Palatine. On my way I passed poor Helvius Cinna, the poet and tribune, who had been mistaken by the mob for his namesake the praetor Cornelius Cinna, whom Antony had mentioned in his speech. He was being dragged away screaming with a noose around his neck, and afterwards his head was paraded around the Forum on a pole.

When I staggered back into the house and told Cicero what had happened, he put his face in his hands. All that night the sounds of destruction went on and the sky was lit up by the houses that had been set on fire. The following day Antony sent a message to Decimus warning that the lives of the assassins could no longer be protected and urging them to withdraw from Rome. Cicero advised them to do as Antony suggested: they would be more useful to the cause alive than dead. Decimus went to Nearer Gaul to try to take control of his allotted province. Trebonius travelled by a circuitous route to Asia to do the same. Brutus and Cassius retreated to the coast at Antium. Cicero headed south.

XV

He was finished with politics, he said. He was finished with Italy. He would go to Greece. He would stay with his son in Athens. He would write philosophy.

We packed up most of the books he needed from his libraries in Rome and Tusculum and set off with a large entourage, including two secretaries, a chef, a doctor and six bodyguards. The weather had been unseasonably cold and wet ever since the assassination, which of course was taken as yet another sign of the gods' displeasure at Caesar's murder. My strongest memory of those days spent travelling is of Cicero in his carriage composing philosophy with a blanket over his knees while the rain drummed continuously on the thin wooden roof. We stayed one night with Matius Calvena, the equestrian, who was in despair over the future of the nation: 'If a man of Caesar's genius could find no way out, who will find one now?' But apart from him, in contrast to the scenes in Rome, we found no one who was not glad to see the back of the Dictator. 'Unfortunately,' as Cicero observed, 'none of them has control of a legion.'

He sought refuge in his work, and by the time we reached Puteoli on the Ides of April, he had completed one entire book – *On Auguries* – half of another – *On Fate* – and had begun a third – *On Glory* – three examples of his genius that will live for as long as men are still capable of reading. And no sooner had he got out of his carriage and stretched his legs along the seashore than he began sketching the outline of a fourth, *On Friendship* (*With the single exception of wisdom, I am inclined to regard it as the greatest of all the gifts the gods have bestowed upon mankind*), which he planned to dedicate to Atticus. The physical world might have become a hostile and dangerous place for him, but in his mind he lived in freedom and tranquillity.

Antony had dismissed the Senate until the first day of June, and gradually the great villas around the Bay of Naples began to fill with the leading men of Rome. Most of the new arrivals, like Hirtius and Pansa, were still in a state of shock at Caesar's death. The pair were supposed to take over as consuls at the end of the year, and as part of their preparation they asked Cicero if he would give them further lessons in oratory. He didn't much want to – it was a distraction from his writing, and he found their doleful talk about Caesar irritating – but in the end he was too easy-going to refuse. He took them on to the beach to learn elocution as Demosthenes had done, by speaking clearly through a mouth full of pebbles, and to learn voice projection by delivering their speeches into the crashing waves. Over the dinner table they were full of stories of Antony's high-handedness: of how he had tricked Calpurnia on the night of the assassination into giving him custody of her late husband's private papers as well as his fortune; of how he now pretended these documents contained various edicts that had the force of law, whereas in fact he had forged them in return for enormous bribes.

Cicero said, 'So he has his hands on all the money? But I thought three quarters of Caesar's fortune was supposed to go to this boy Octavian?'

Hirtius rolled his eyes. 'He'll be lucky!'

Pansa added, 'He'll have to come and get it first, and I wouldn't give much for his chances.'

Two days after this exchange, I was sheltering from the rain in the portico, reading the elder Cato's treatise on agriculture, when the steward came up to me to announce that L. Cornelius Balbus had arrived to see Cicero.

'Then tell the master he's here.'

'But I'm not sure that I should – he gave me strict instructions that he was not to be disturbed, no matter who came to call.'

I sighed and laid aside my book: Balbus was one man who would have to be seen. He was the Spaniard who had handled Caesar's business affairs in Rome. He was well known to Cicero, who had once defended him in the courts against an attempt to strip him of his citizenship. He was now in his middle fifties and owned a huge villa nearby. I found him waiting in the tablinum with a toga-clad youth I took at first to be his son or grandson, except when I looked more closely I saw that he couldn't be, for Balbus was swarthy whereas this boy had damp blond hair badly cut in a basin style; he was also rather short and slender, pretty-faced but with a pasty complexion pitted by acne.

'Ah, Tiro,' cried Balbus, 'will you kindly drag Cicero away from his books? Just tell him I have brought Caesar's adopted son to see him – Gaius Julius Caesar Octavianus – that ought to do it.'

And the young man smiled shyly at me, showing gapped uneven teeth.

Naturally Cicero came at once, overwhelmed by curiosity to meet this exotic creature, seemingly dropped into the tumult of Roman politics from the sky. Balbus introduced the young man, who bowed and said, 'It is one of the greatest honours of my life to meet you. I have read all your speeches and works of philosophy. I have dreamed of this moment for years.' His voice was pleasant: soft and well educated.

Cicero fairly preened at the compliment. 'You are very kind to say it. Now please tell me, before we go further: what am I to call you?'

'In public I insist on Caesar. To my friends and family I am Octavian.'

'Well, since at my age I would find another Caesar hard to get used to, perhaps it could be Octavian for me as well, if I may?'

The young man bowed again. 'I would be honoured.'

And so began two days of unexpectedly friendly exchanges. It turned out that Octavian was staying next door with his mother Atia and his stepfather Philippus, and he wandered back and forth quite freely between the two houses. Often he appeared on his own, even though he had brought an entourage of friends and soldiers over with him from Illyricum, and more had joined him at Naples. He and Cicero would talk in the villa or walk along the seashore together in the intervals between showers. Watching them, I was reminded of a line in Cicero's treatise on old age: *just as I approve of the young man in whom there is a touch of age, so I approve of the old man in whom there is some flavour of youth . . .* Oddly enough, it was Octavian who sometimes seemed the older of the two: serious, polite, deferential, shrewd; it was Cicero who made the jokes and skimmed the stones across the sea. He told me that Octavian had no small talk. All he wanted was political advice. The fact that Cicero was publicly aligned with his adopted father's killers appeared to be neither here nor there as far as he was concerned. How soon should he go to Rome? How should he handle Antony? What should he say to

Caesar's veterans, many of whom were hanging around the house? How was civil war to be avoided?

Cicero was impressed: 'I can understand entirely what Caesar saw in him – he has a certain coolness rare in one of his years. He might make a great statesman one day, if only he can survive long enough.' The men around him were a different matter. These included a couple of Caesar's old army commanders, with the hard, dead eyes of professional killers; and some arrogant young companions, two in particular: Marcus Vipsanius Agrippa, not yet twenty but already bloodied by war, taciturn and faintly menacing even in repose; and Gaius Cilnius Maecenas, a little older, effeminate, giggling, cynical. '*Those*,' said Cicero, 'I do not care for *at all*.'

On only one occasion did I have an opportunity to observe Octavian closely for any length of time. That was on the final day of his stay, when he came to dinner with his mother and step-father, along with Agrippa and Maecenas; Cicero also invited Hirtius and Pansa; I made up the nine. I noticed how the young man never touched his wine, how quiet he was, how his pale grey eyes flicked from one speaker to another and how intently he listened, as if he was trying to commit everything they said to memory. Atia, who looked as if she might have been the model for a statue commemorating the ideal Roman matron, was far too proper to voice a political opinion in public. Philippus, however, who certainly did drink, became increasingly voluble, and towards the end of the evening announced, 'Well if anyone wants to know *my* opinion, I think Octavian should renounce this inheritance.'

Maecenas whispered to me, '*Does* anyone want to know his opinion?' and he bit on his napkin to stifle his laughter.

Octavian said mildly, 'And what leads you to that opinion, Father?'

'Well, if I may speak frankly, my boy, you can *call* yourself Caesar all you like but that doesn't *make* you Caesar, and the closer you get to Rome the greater the danger will be. Do you really think Antony is just going to hand over all these millions? And why would Caesar's veterans follow you rather than Antony, who commanded a wing at Pharsalus? Caesar's name is just a target on your back. You'll be killed before you've gone fifty miles.'

Hirtius and Pansa nodded in agreement.

Agrippa said quietly, 'No, we can get him to Rome safely enough.'

Octavian turned to Cicero. 'And what do you think?'

Cicero dabbed carefully at his mouth with his napkin before replying. 'Just four months ago your adopted father was dining precisely where you are now and assuring me he had no fear of death. The truth is, all our lives hang by a thread. There is no safety anywhere, and no one can predict what will happen. When I was your age, I dreamed only of glory. What I wouldn't have given to be in your place now!'

'So you would go to Rome?'

'I would.'

'And do what?'

'Stand for election.'

Philippus said, 'But he's only eighteen. He's not even old enough to vote.'

Cicero continued: 'As it happens, there's a vacancy for a tribune: Cinna was killed by the mob at Caesar's funeral – they got the wrong man, poor devil. You should propose yourself to fill his place.'

Octavian said, 'But surely Antony would never allow it?'

Cicero replied, 'That doesn't matter. Such a move would

show your determination to continue Caesar's policy of championing the people: the plebs will love it. And when Antony opposes you – as he must – he'll be seen as opposing them.'

Octavian nodded slowly. 'That's not a bad idea. Perhaps you should come with me?'

Cicero laughed. 'No, I'm retiring to Greece to study philosophy.'

'That's a pity.'

After the dinner, when the guests were preparing to leave, I overheard Octavian say to Cicero, 'I meant what I said. I would value your wisdom.'

Cicero shook his head. 'I fear my loyalties lie in the other direction, with those who struck down your adopted father. But if ever there was a possibility of your reconciling with them – well then, in such circumstances, in the interests of the state, I would do all I could to help you.'

'I'm not opposed to reconciliation. It's my legacy I want, not vengeance.'

'Can I tell them that?'

'Of course. That's why I said it. Goodbye. I shall write to you.'

They shook hands. Octavian stepped out into the road. It was a spring evening, not yet entirely dark, no longer raining either but with moisture still in the air. To my surprise, standing silently in the blue gloom across the street were more than a hundred soldiers. When they saw Octavian they set up the same din I had heard at Caesar's funeral, banging their swords against their shields in acclamation: it turned out these were some of the Dictator's veterans from the Gallic wars, settled nearby on Campanian land. Octavian went over with Agrippa to talk to them. Cicero watched for a moment, then ducked back inside to avoid being seen.

When the door was shut I asked, 'Why did you urge him to go to Rome? Surely the last thing you want is to encourage another Caesar?'

'If he goes to Rome he'll cause problems for Antony. He'll split their faction.'

'And if his adventure succeeds?'

'It won't. Philippus is right. He's a nice boy, and I hope he survives, but he's no Caesar – you only have to look at him.'

Nevertheless, he was sufficiently intrigued by Octavian's prospects to postpone his departure for Athens. Instead he conceived a vague idea of attending the Senate meeting Antony had summoned for the first of June. But when we arrived in Tusculum towards the end of May, everyone advised him not to go. Varro sent a letter warning that there would be murder. Hirtius agreed. He said, 'Even I'm not going, and no one's ever accused *me* of disloyalty to Caesar. But there are too many old soldiers in the streets too quick to draw their swords – look what happened to Cinna.'

Octavian, meanwhile, had arrived in the city unscathed and sent Cicero a letter:

From G. Julius Caesar Octavianus to M. Tullius Cicero, greetings.

I wanted you to know that yesterday Antony finally agreed to see me at his house: the one that used to be Pompey's. He kept me waiting for more than an hour – a silly tactic that I believe shows his weakness rather than mine. I began by thanking him for looking after my adopted father's property on my behalf, invited him to take from it whatever trinkets he desired as keepsakes, but asked him to hand over the rest to me at once. I told him I needed the money to make an immediate cash disbursement to three hundred thousand citizens in accordance with my father's will.

The rest of my expenses I asked to be met by a loan from the public treasury. I also told him of my intention to stand for the vacant tribunate and asked him for evidence of the various edicts he claims to have discovered in my father's papers.

He replied with great indignation that Caesar had not been king and had not bequeathed me control of the state; that accordingly he did not have to give an account of his public acts to me; that as far as the money went, my father's effects were not as great as all that, and that he had left the public treasury bankrupt so there was nothing to be got from there either; as for the tribunate, my candidacy would be illegal and was out of the question.

He thinks because I am young he can intimidate me. He is wrong. We parted on bad terms. Among the people, however, and among my father's soldiers my reception has been as warm as Antony's was cold.

Cicero was delighted at the enmity between Antony and Octavian and showed the letter to several people: 'You see how the cub tweaks the old lion's tail?' He asked me to go to Rome on his behalf on the first of June and report back what happened in the Senate meeting.

I found Rome, as everyone had warned us, teeming with soldiers, mostly Caesar's veterans whom Antony had summoned to the city to serve as his private army. They stood around on the street corners in sullen, hungry groups, intimidating anyone who looked as though they might be wealthy. As a result, the Senate was very thinly attended, and there was no one brave enough to oppose Antony's most audacious proposal: that Decimus should be removed from the governorship of Nearer Gaul and that he, Antony, should be awarded both of the Gallic provinces, together with command of their legions, for the next five years – exactly the same concentration of power that had set Caesar on the road to the dictatorship. As if this were not enough, he also announced that he had summoned home the three legions based in Macedonia that Caesar had planned to use in the Parthian campaign and placed these under his own command as well. Dolabella did not object, as might have been expected, because he was to receive Syria, also for five years; Lepidus was bought off with Caesar's old position of pontifex maximus. Finally, as this arrangement left Brutus and Cassius without their anticipated provinces, he arranged for them to be offered instead a couple of Pompey's old corn commissionerships – one in Asia, the other in Sicily; they would have no power at all; it was a humiliation; so much for reconciliation.

The bills were approved by the half-empty Senate and Antony took them to the Forum the next day to be voted on by the people. The inclement weather continued. There was even a thunderstorm halfway through proceedings – such a terrible omen that the assembly should have been dismissed at once. But Antony was an augur: he claimed to have seen no lightning and ruled that the vote could go ahead, and by dusk he had what he wanted. There was no sign of Octavian. As I turned to leave the assembly I saw Fulvia watching from a litter. She was soaked from the rain but did not seem to notice, so engrossed was she in her husband's apotheosis. I made a mental note to myself to warn Cicero that a woman who hitherto had been nothing more than a nuisance to him had just become a far more dangerous enemy.

The following morning I went to see Dolabella. He took me to the nursery and showed me Cicero's grandson, the infant Lentulus, who had just learnt to take a few wobbling steps. It was now more than fifteen months since Tullia's death, yet still

Dolabella had not repaid her dowry. At Cicero's request I began to broach the subject ('Do it politely, mind you: I can't afford to antagonise him'), but Dolabella cut me off at once.

'It's out of the question, I'm afraid. You can give him this instead in full and final settlement. It's worth far more than money.' And he threw across the table an imposing legal document with black ribbons and a red seal. 'I've made him my legate in Syria. Don't worry, tell him – he doesn't have to *do* anything. But it means he can leave the country honourably and gives him immunity for the next five years. My advice, tell him, is that he should get out as soon as he can. Things are worsening by the day and we can't be held responsible for his safety.'

I took the message back to Tusculum and relayed it verbatim to Cicero, who was sitting in the garden beside Tullia's grave. He studied the warrant for his legateship. 'So this little piece of paper has cost me a million sesterces? Does he really imagine that waving this in the face of some illiterate half-drunk legionary would deter him from sticking his sword in my throat?' He had already heard what had happened at the Senate and in the public assembly, but wanted me to recite my precis of the speeches. At the end he said, 'So there was no opposition?'

'None.'

'Did you see Octavian at all?'

'No.'

'No – of course not – why would you? Antony has the money, the legions and the consulship. Octavian has nothing but a borrowed name. As for us, we daren't even show our faces in Rome.' He slumped against the wall in despair. 'I tell you something, Tiro, between you and me – I'm starting to wish the Ides of March had never happened.'

There was to be a family conference with Brutus and Cassius

on the seventh day of June in Antium to decide their next steps: he had been invited and he asked me to accompany him.

We set off early, descending the hills just as the sun came up, and crossed the marshy land in the direction of the coast. The mist was rising. I remember the croaking of the bullfrogs, the cries of the gulls; Cicero barely spoke. Just before midday we reached Brutus's villa. It was a fine old place built right on the shoreline with steps cut into the rocks leading down to the sea. The gate was blocked by a strong guard of gladiators; others patrolled the grounds; more were visible walking on the beach – I guess there must have been a hundred armed men in all. Brutus was waiting with the others in a loggia filled with Greek statuary. He looked strained – the familiar nervous tapping of his foot was more pronounced than ever. He told us he had not left the house for two months – amazing considering he was urban praetor and not supposed to be out of Rome for more than ten days a year. At the head of the table sat his mother, Servilia; also present were his wife Porcia and his sister Tertia, who was married to Cassius. Finally there was M. Favonius, the former praetor known as Cato's Ape on account of his closeness to Brutus's uncle. Tertia announced that Cassius was on his way.

Cicero suggested I might fill in the time while we waited by giving a detailed account of the recent debates in the Senate and the public assembly, whereupon Servilia, who had ignored me up to that point, turned her fierce eye upon me and said, 'Oh, so this is your famous *spy*?'

She was a female Caesar – that is the best way I can describe her: quick-brained, handsome, haughty, bone-hard. The Dictator had presented her with lavish gifts, including estates confiscated from his enemies and huge jewels picked up on his conquests, yet when her son arranged his murder and she was given the news, her eyes stayed as dry as the gemstones he had given her. In this too she was like Caesar. Cicero was slightly awed by her.

I stammered my way through the transcript of my notes, all the while conscious of Servilia's stare, and at the end she said with great contempt, 'A grain commissionership in Asia! It was for this that Caesar was assassinated – so that my son could become a corn merchant?'

'Even so,' said Cicero, 'I think he should take it. It's better than nothing – certainly better than staying here.'

Brutus said, 'I agree with you on your last point at least. I can't stay hidden from view any longer. I'm losing respect with every day that passes. But Asia? No, what I really need to do is go to Rome and do what the urban praetor always does at this time of year – stage the Games of Apollo and show myself to the Roman people.' His sensitive face was full of anguish.

'You can't go to Rome,' replied Cicero. 'It's far too dangerous. Listen, the rest of us are more or less expendable, but not you, Brutus – your name and your honour make you the great rallying point of freedom. My advice is to take this commission, do some honourable public work far away from Italy in safety, and await more favourable events. Things will change: in politics they always do.'

At that moment Cassius arrived and Servilia asked Cicero to repeat what he'd just said. But whereas adversity had reduced Brutus to a state of noble suffering, it had put Cassius in a rage, and he started pounding on the table: 'I did not survive the massacre at Carrhae and save Syria from the Parthians in order to be made a grain collector in Sicily! It's an insult.'

Cicero said, 'Well then, what will you do?'

'Leave Italy. Go abroad. Go to Greece.'

'Greece,' observed Cicero, 'will soon be rather crowded,

whereas first of all Sicily is safe, second you'll be doing your duty like a good constitutionalist, and third and above all you'll be closer to Italy to exploit opportunities when they arise. You must be our great military commander.'

'What sort of opportunities?'

'Well, for example, Octavian could yet cause all sorts of trouble for Antony.'

'Octavian? That's one of your jokes! He's far more likely to come after us than he is to pursue a quarrel with Antony.'

'Not at all – I saw the boy when he was on the Bay of Naples, and he's not as ill-disposed towards us as you might think. "It's my legacy I want, not vengeance" – those were his very words. His real enemy is Antony.'

'Then Antony will crush him.'

'But Antony has to crush Decimus first, and that's when the war will start – when Antony tries to take Nearer Gaul away from him.'

'Decimus,' said Cassius bitterly, 'is the man who has let us down more than any other. Just think what we could have done with those two legions of his if he'd brought them south in March! But it's too late now: Antony's Macedonian legions will outnumber him two to one.'

The mention of Decimus was like the breaking of a dam. Denunciations flowed from everyone round the table, Favonius especially, who maintained he should have warned them he was mentioned in Caesar's will: 'That did more to turn the people against us than anything else.'

Cicero listened in growing dismay. He intervened to say that there was no point in weeping over past errors, but couldn't resist adding, 'Besides, if it's mistakes you're talking about, never mind Decimus – the seeds of our present plight were sown when you failed to call a meeting of the Senate, failed to rally the people to our cause, and failed to seize control of the republic.'

'Well upon my word!' exclaimed Servilia. 'I never heard anything like it – to be accused of a lack of resolution by you of all people!'

Cicero glowered at her and immediately fell silent, his cheeks burning either with fury or embarrassment, and not long after that the meeting ended. My notes record only two conclusions. Brutus and Cassius agreed grudgingly at least to consider accepting their grain commissionerships, but only after Servilia announced in her grandest manner that she would arrange for the wording of the Senate resolution to be couched in more flattering terms. And Brutus reluctantly conceded that it was impossible for him to go to Rome and that his praetorian games would have to be staged in his absence. Apart from that the conference was a failure, with nothing decided. As Cicero explained to Atticus in a letter dictated on the way home, it was now a case of 'every man for himself': *I found the ship going to pieces, or rather its scattered fragments. No plan, no thought, no method. Hence, though I had no doubts before, I am now all the more determined to escape from here, and as soon as I possibly can.*

The die was cast. He would go to Greece.

As for me, I was almost sixty and had privately resolved that the time had come for me to leave Cicero's service and live what remained of my life alone. I knew from the way he talked that he wasn't expecting us to part company. He assumed we would share a villa in Athens and write philosophy together until one or other of us died of old age. But I could not face leaving Italy again. My health was not good. And love him as I did, I was tired of being a mere appendage to his brain.

I dreaded having to tell him and kept postponing the fateful moment. He undertook a kind of farewell progress south through Italy, saying goodbye to all his properties and reliving old memories, until eventually we reached Puteoli at the beginning of July – or Quintilis, as he still defiantly insisted on calling it. He had one last villa he wished to visit, along the Bay of Naples in Pompeii, and he decided he would leave on the first leg of his journey abroad from there, hugging the coast down to Sicily and boarding a merchant ship in Syracuse (he judged it too dangerous to sail from Brundisium, as the Macedonian legions were due to start arriving any day). To convey all his books, his property and household staff, I hired three ten-oared boats. He took his mind off the voyage, which he dreaded, by trying to decide what literary composition we should undertake while at sea. He was working on three treatises simultaneously, moving between them as his reading and his inclination took him: *On Friendship, On Duties* and *On Virtues*. With these he would complete his great scheme of absorbing Greek philosophy into Latin and of turning it in the process from a set of abstractions into principles for living.

He said, 'I wonder if this would be a good opportunity for us to write our version of Aristotle's *Topics*? Let's face it: what could be more useful in this time of chaos than to teach men how to use dialectics to construct reasoned arguments? It could be in the form of a dialogue, like the *Disputations* – you playing one part and I the other. What do you think?'

'My friend,' I replied hesitantly, 'if I may call you that, I have wanted for some time to speak to you but have not been sure how to do it.'

'This sounds ominous! You'd better go on. Are you ill again?'

'No, but I need to tell you I have decided not to accompany you to Greece.'

'Ah.' He stared at me for what felt like a very long time, his jaw moving slightly as it often did when he was trying to find the right word. Finally he said, 'Where will you go instead?'

'To the farm you so kindly gave me.'

His voice was very quiet: 'I see, and when would you want to do that?'

'At any time convenient to you.'

'The sooner the better?'

'I don't mind when it is.'

'Tomorrow?'

'It can be tomorrow if you like. But that is not necessary. I don't want to inconvenience you.'

'Tomorrow then.' And with that he turned back to his Aristotle.

I hesitated. 'Would it be all right if I borrowed young Eros from the stables and the little carriage, to transport my belongings?'

Without looking up he replied, 'Of course. Take whatever you need.'

I left him alone and spent the remainder of the day and the evening packing my belongings and carrying them out into the courtyard. He did not appear for dinner. The next morning there was still no sign of him. Young Quintus, who was hoping for a place on Brutus's staff and staying with us while his uncle tried to fix an introduction, said that he had gone off very early to visit Lucullus's old house on the island of Nesis. He put a consoling hand on my shoulder. 'He asked me to tell you goodbye.'

'He didn't say more than that? Just goodbye?'

'You know how he is.'

'I know how he is. Would you please tell him I'll come back in a day or two to say a proper farewell?'

I felt quite sick, but determined. I had made up my mind. Eros drove me to the farm. It was not far, only two or three miles, but the distance seemed much greater as I moved from one world to another.

The overseer and his wife had not been expecting me so soon but nonetheless seemed pleased to see me. One of the slaves was called from the barn to carry my luggage into the farmhouse. The boxes containing my books and documents went straight upstairs into the raftered room I had selected earlier as the site for my little library. It was shuttered and cool. Shelves had been put up as I requested – rough and rustic, but I didn't care – and I set about unpacking at once. There is a wonderful line in one of Cicero's letters to Atticus in which he describes moving into a property and says: *I have put out my books and now my house has a soul.* That was how I felt as I emptied my boxes. And then to my surprise in one of them I discovered the original manuscript of *On Friendship*. Puzzled, I unrolled it, thinking I must have brought it with me by mistake. But when I saw that Cicero had copied out at the top of the roll in his shaking hand a quotation from the text, on the importance of having friends, I realised it was a parting gift:

> *If a man ascended into heaven and gazed upon the whole workings of the universe and the beauty of the stars, the marvellous sight would give him no joy if he had to keep it to himself. And yet, if only there had been someone to describe the spectacle to, it would have filled him with delight. Nature abhors solitude.*

* * *

I allowed two days to pass before I returned to the villa in Puteoli to say my proper goodbye: I needed to be sure I was strong enough in my resolve not to be persuaded out of it. But the steward told me Cicero had already left for Pompeii and I returned at once to the farm. From my terrace I had a sweeping view of the entire bay, and often I found myself standing there peering into the immense blueness, which ran from the misty outline of Capri right round to the promontory at Misenum, wondering if any of the myriad ships I could see was his. But then gradually I became caught up in the routine of the farm. It was almost time to harvest the vines and the olives, and despite my creaking knees and my soft scholar's hands, I donned a tunic and a wide-brimmed straw hat and worked outside with the rest, rising with the light and going to bed when it faded, too exhausted to think. Gradually the pattern of my former life began to fade from my mind, like a carpet left out in the sun. Or so I thought.

I had no cause to leave my property save one: the place had no bath. A good bath was the thing I missed most, apart from Cicero's conversation. I couldn't bear to wash myself only in the cold water from the mountain spring. Accordingly I commissioned the construction of a bathhouse in one of the barns. But that couldn't be done until after the harvest, and so I took to riding off every two or three days to use one of the public baths that are found everywhere along that stretch of coast. I tried many different establishments – in Puteoli itself, in Bauli and in Baiae – until I decided Baiae had the best, on account of the natural hot sulphurous water for which the area is famous. The clientele was sophisticated and included the freedmen of senators who had villas nearby; some of whom I knew. Without even meaning to, I began to pick up the latest gossip from Rome.

Brutus's games had passed off well, I discovered: no expense spared, even though the praetor himself was not present. Brutus had amassed hundreds of wild beasts for the occasion and, desperate for popular acclaim, he gave orders that every last one of them should be used up in fights and hunts. There were also musical performances and plays, including *Tereus*, a tragedy by Accius that contained copious references to the crimes of tyrants: apparently it received knowing applause. But unfortunately for Brutus, his games, although generous, were quickly overshadowed by an even more lavish set that Octavian gave immediately afterwards in honour of Caesar. It was the time of the famous comet, the hairy star that rose every day an hour before noon – we could see it even in the brilliantly sunny skies of Campania – and Octavian claimed it was nothing less than Caesar ascending into heaven. Caesar's veterans were greatly taken with this notion, I was told, and young Octavian's fame and reputation began to soar with the comet.

Not long after this I was lying one afternoon in a hot pool on a terrace overlooking the sea when some men joined me who I soon gathered by their talk were on the staff of Calpurnius Piso. He had a veritable palace about twenty miles away at Herculaneum and I suppose they must have decided to break their journey from Rome and complete their travelling the next day. I didn't consciously eavesdrop but I had my eyes closed and they may have thought I was sleeping. At any rate, I quickly pieced together the sensational intelligence that Piso, the father of Caesar's widow, had made an outspoken attack on Antony in the Senate, accusing him of theft, forgery and treason, of aiming at a new dictatorship and of setting the nation on the road to a second civil war. When one of them said, 'Aye, and there's not another man in Rome with the courage to say it, now that our so-called liberators are all either hiding or have fled abroad', I thought with a pang of Cicero, who would have hated to know that he had been supplanted as an upholder of liberty by Piso, of all people.

I waited until they'd moved on before I climbed out of the pool. I remember I thought I would have a massage while I pondered what I'd just heard. I was moving towards the shaded area where the tables were set out when a woman appeared carrying a pile of freshly laundered towels. I cannot say I recognised her at once – it must have been fifteen years since I had last set eyes on her – but a few paces after we had passed one another I stopped and looked round. She had done the same. I recognised her then all right. It was the slave girl Agathe whose freedom I had bought before I went into exile with Cicero.

This is Cicero's story, not mine; it is certainly not Agathe's. Nevertheless, our three lives were entwined, and before I resume the main part of my story I believe she deserves some mention.

I had met her when she was seventeen and a slave in the bath chambers of Lucullus's great villa in Misenum. She and her parents, by then dead, had been seized as slaves in Greece and brought to Italy as part of Lucullus's war booty. Her beauty, her gentleness and her plight all moved me. When I saw her next she was in Rome, one of six household slaves produced as witnesses at the trial of Clodius to support Lucullus's contention that Clodius, his former brother-in-law, had committed incest and adultery in Misenum with his ex-wife. After that I glimpsed her just once more, when Cicero visited Lucullus before going into exile. She seemed to me by then to be broken in spirit and half dead. Having some small savings put aside, on the night we fled Rome I gave the money to Atticus so that he could purchase her from Lucullus on my behalf and set her free. I had kept an eye out for her in Rome over the years but had never seen her.

She was thirty-six, still beautiful to me, although I could tell from her lined face and raw-boned hands that she still had to work hard. She seemed embarrassed and kept brushing back loose strands of grey hair with the back of her wrist. After a few awkward pleasantries there was a difficult silence and I found myself saying, 'Forgive me, I am keeping you from your work – you will be in trouble with the owner.'

'There will be no trouble on that score,' she replied, laughing for the first time. 'I *am* the owner.'

After that we began to talk more freely. She told me she had tried to find me when she was freed, but of course by then I was in Thessalonica. Eventually she had come back to the Bay of Naples: it was the place she knew best and it reminded her of Greece. Because of her experience in the household of Lucullus, she had found plentiful work as an overseer in the local hot baths. After ten years some wealthy clients, merchants in Puteoli, had set her up in this place, and now it belonged to her. 'But all this is because of you. How can I ever begin to thank you for your kindness?'

Live the good life, Cicero had said: *learn that virtue is the sole prerequisite for happiness*. As we sat on a bench in the sunshine, I felt I had proof of that particular piece of his philosophy, at least.

My sojourn on the farm lasted forty days.

On the forty-first, the eve of the Festival of Vulcan, I was working in the vineyard in the late afternoon when one of the slaves called out to me and pointed down the track. A carriage, accompanied by twenty men on horseback, was bouncing over the ruts, throwing up so much dust in the shafts of summer sunshine, it looked as if it was travelling on golden clouds. It drew up outside the villa and from it descended Cicero. I suppose I had always known in my heart that he would come looking for me. I was fated never to escape. As I walked towards him, I snatched off my straw hat and swore to myself that on no account would I be persuaded to return with him to Rome. Beneath my breath I whispered, 'I will not listen . . . I will not listen . . . I will not listen . . .'

I could see at once from the swing of his shoulders as he wheeled round to greet me that he was in tremendous spirits. Gone was the drooping dejection of recent times. He put his hands on his hips and roared with laughter at my appearance. 'I leave you alone for a month and see what happens! You have turned into the elder Cato's ghost!'

I arranged for his entourage to be given refreshment while we went on to the shaded terrace and drank some of last year's wine, which he pronounced to be not bad at all. 'What a view!' he exclaimed. 'What a place to live out one's declining years! Your own wine, your own olives . . .'

'Yes,' I replied carefully, 'it suits me very well. I shan't be going far. And your plans? What happened to Greece?'

'Ah well, I got as far as Sicily, whereupon the southerly winds got up and kept blowing us back into harbour and I began to wonder if the gods weren't trying to tell me something. Then, while we were stuck in Regium waiting for better weather, I heard about this extraordinary attack on Antony made by Piso. You must have heard the commotion even here. After that, letters came from Brutus and Cassius saying that Antony was definitely starting to weaken – they were to be offered provinces after all, and he had written to them saying he hoped they would soon be able to come to Rome. He has summoned the Senate for a meeting on the first of September and Brutus has sent a letter to all former consuls and praetors asking them to attend.

'So I said to myself: am I really going to run away at this of all moments, while there's still a chance? Will I go down in history as a coward? I tell you, Tiro, suddenly it was as if a thick mist that had enshrouded me for months had cleared and I saw my duty absolutely. I turned right around and sailed back the way I had come. As it happened, Brutus was at Velia, preparing to set sail, and he practically went down on his knees to thank me. He's been given Crete as his province; Cassius has Cyrene.'

I could not help pointing out that these were hardly adequate compensation for Macedonia and Syria, which was what they had been allotted.

'Of course not,' replied Cicero, 'which is why they're resolved to ignore Antony and his wretched illegal edicts and go straight to their original provinces. After all, Brutus has followers in Macedonia, and Cassius was the hero of Syria. They will raise legions and fight for the republic against the usurper. A whole new spirit has infused us – a flame pure white and sublime.'

'And you will go to Rome?'

'Yes, for the meeting of the Senate in nine days' time.'

'Then it sounds to me as though you have the most dangerous assignment of the three.'

He waved his hand dismissively. 'So what is the worst that can happen? I'll die. Very well: I'm past sixty; I've run my race. And at least this will be a good death – which as you know is the supreme objective of the good life.' He leaned forwards. 'Tell me: do I seem happy to you?'

'You do,' I conceded.

'That's because I realised when I was stuck in Regium that finally I have conquered my fear of death. Philosophy – our work together – has accomplished that for me. Oh, I know that you and Atticus won't believe me. You'll think that underneath I'm still the same timid creature I always was. But it's true.'

'And presumably you expect me to come with you?'

'No, not at all – the opposite! You have your farm and your literary studies. I don't want you to expose yourself to any more risk. But our earlier parting was not what it should have been, and I couldn't pass your gate without remedying that.' He stood and opened his arms wide. 'Goodbye, my old friend. Words are inadequate to express my gratitude. I hope we meet again.'

He clasped me to him so firmly and for so long that I could feel the strong and steady beating of his heart. Then he pulled away, and with a final wave he walked towards his carriage and his bodyguards.

I watched him go, his familiar gestures: the straightening of his shoulders, the adjustment of the folds of his tunic, the unthinking way he offered his hand to be helped into his carriage. I glanced around at my vines and my olive trees, my goats and my chickens, my dry-stone walls, my sheep. Suddenly it seemed a small world – a very small world.

I called after him: 'Wait!'

XVI

If Cicero had pleaded with me to return with him to Rome, I probably would have refused. It was his willingness to set off without me on the last great adventure of his life that piqued my pride and sent me chasing after him. Of course my change of heart did not surprise him. He knew me far too well. He merely nodded and told me to gather what I required for the journey, and to be quick about it: 'We need to make good progress before nightfall.'

I called my little household together in the courtyard and wished them luck with the harvest. I told them I would come back as soon as possible. They knew nothing of politics or Cicero. Their expressions were bewildered. They lined up to watch me leave. Just before the place disappeared from view, I turned to wave, but they had already returned to the fields.

It took us eight days to reach Rome, and every mile of the journey was fraught with peril, despite the guards that had been provided for Cicero by Brutus, and always the threat was the same: Caesar's old soldiers, who had sworn oaths to hunt down those responsible for the assassination. The fact that Cicero had known nothing of it beforehand did not concern them: he had defended it afterwards, and that was enough to render him guilty in their eyes. Our route took us across the fertile plains that had been given to Caesar's veterans to farm, and at least twice – once when we passed through the town of Aquinum and then soon afterwards at Fregellae – we were warned of ambushes up ahead and had to halt and wait until the road was secured.

We saw burnt-out villas, scorched fields, slaughtered livestock; even once a body hanging from a tree with a placard reading 'Traitor' round its neck. Caesar's demobbed legionaries roamed Italy in small bands as if they were back in Gaul, and we heard many stories of looting, rape and atrocities. Whenever Cicero was recognised by the ordinary citizens, they flocked to him, kissed his hands and clothes and pleaded with him to deliver them from terror. Nowhere was the common population's devotion more evident than when we reached the gates of Rome on the day before the Senate was due to meet. His welcome was even warmer than when he returned from exile. There were so many deputations, petitions, greetings, handshakes and sacrifices of thanks to the gods that it took him nearly all day to cross the city to his house.

In terms of reputation and renown I guess he was now the pre-eminent figure in the state. All his great rivals and contemporaries – Pompey, Caesar, Cato, Crassus, Clodius – had died violent deaths. 'They are not cheering me as an individual so much as the memory of the republic,' he said to me when finally we got inside. 'I don't flatter myself – I'm merely the last left standing. And of course demonstrating in support of me is a safe way of protesting against Antony. I wonder what *he* makes of today's outpouring. He must want to *crush* me.'

One by one the leaders of the opposition to Antony in the Senate trooped up the slope to pay their respects. There were not many but I must mention two in particular. The first was

P. Servilius Vatia Isauricus, the son of the old consul who had recently died aged ninety: he had been a strong supporter of Caesar and had only just returned from governing Asia – a difficult and arrogant man, he was deeply envious of Antony's dominant position in the state. The second opponent of Antony I have already mentioned: Lucius Calpurnius Piso, the father of Caesar's widow, who had been the first to raise his voice against the new regime. He was a sallow, stooping, hairy-faced old man with very bad teeth who had been consul at the time Cicero went into exile: for years he and Cicero had hated one another, but now they both hated Antony even more, and so in politics at least that made them friends. There were others present, but this was the pair who mattered most and they were of one voice in warning Cicero to stay away from the Senate the next day.

'Antony has laid a trap for you,' said Piso. 'He plans to propose a resolution tomorrow calling for fresh honours in memory of Caesar.'

'Fresh honours!' cried Cicero. 'The man is already a god. What other honours does he need?'

'The motion will state that every public festival of thanksgiving should henceforth include a sacrifice in honour of Caesar. Antony will demand to know your opinion. The meeting will be surrounded by Caesar's veterans. If you support the proposal, your return to public life will be destroyed before it even starts – all the crowds who cheered you today will jeer you as a turncoat. If you oppose it, you will never reach home alive.'

'But if I refuse to attend I'll look like a coward, and what sort of leadership is that?'

Isauricus said, 'Send word that you're too exhausted from your journey. You're getting on in years. People will understand.'

'None of us is going,' added Piso, 'despite his summons. We'll show him up as a tyrant whom no one will obey. He'll look like a fool.'

This was not the heroic return to public life that Cicero had planned, and he was reluctant to hide away at home. Still, he saw the wisdom of what they were saying and the following day he sent a message to Antony pleading tiredness as his excuse for not attending the session. Antony's response was to fly into a rage. According to Servius Sulpicius, who gave Cicero a full report, in front of the Senate he threatened to send a team of workmen and soldiers round to Cicero's house to tear down his door and drag him to the meeting. He was only deterred from such extreme action when Dolabella pointed out that Piso, Isauricus and a few others had also stayed away: he could hardly round up all of them. The debate went ahead and Antony's proposal to honour Caesar was passed, but only under duress.

Cicero was outraged when he heard what Antony had said. He insisted he would go to the Senate the next day and make a speech, regardless of the risk: 'I haven't returned to Rome in order to cower under my blankets!' Messages went back and forth between him and the others, and in the end they agreed to attend together, reasoning that Antony wouldn't dare to massacre them all. The following morning, shielded by bodyguards, they walked down in a phalanx from the Palatine – Cicero, Piso, Isauricus, Servius Sulpicius and Vibius Pansa (Hirtius could not join them because he really was ill) – right the way through the cheering crowds to the Temple of Concordia on the far side of the Forum, where the Senate was due to meet. Dolabella was waiting on the steps with his curule chair. He came over to Cicero and announced that Antony was sick and that he would be presiding in his place.

Cicero laughed. 'So much illness going around at the moment – the entire state seems to be ailing! One might almost imagine that Antony shares the common characteristic of all bullies: eager to dish out punishment, unable to take it.'

Dolabella replied coldly: 'I trust you won't say anything today that will put our friendship in jeopardy: I've reconciled with Antony and any attack on him I'd regard as an attack on myself. Also I'd remind you that I did give you that legateship on my staff in Syria.'

'Yes, although actually I'd prefer the return of my dear Tullia's dowry, if you don't mind. And as far as Syria is concerned – well, my young friend, I should make haste to get there, or Cassius might be in Antioch before you.'

Dolabella glared at him. 'I see you have abandoned your usual affability. Very well, but be careful, old man. The game is getting rougher.'

He stalked away. Cicero watched him go with satisfaction. 'I have wanted to say that for a long time.' He was like Caesar, I thought, sending his horse to the rear before a battle: he would either win where he stood or die.

The Temple of Concordia was the place where Cicero had convened the Senate as consul all those years before, in order to debate the punishment of the Catiline conspirators; from here he had led them to their deaths in the Carcer. I had not set foot in it since and I felt the oppressive presence of many ghosts. But Cicero seemed immune to such memories. He sat on the front bench between Piso and Isauricus and waited patiently for Dolabella to call him – which he did, as late in proceedings as he could and with insulting offhandedness.

Cicero started quietly, as was his way: 'Before I begin to speak on public affairs, I will make a brief complaint of the wrong done to me yesterday by Antony. Why was I so bitterly denounced? What subject is so urgent that sick men should be carried to this chamber? Was Hannibal at the gates? Who ever heard of a senator being threatened with having his house attacked because he failed to appear to discuss a public thanksgiving?

'And in any case, do you think I would have supported his proposal if I had been here? I say: if a thanksgiving is to be given to a dead man, let it be given to the elder Brutus, who delivered the state from the despotism of kings and who nearly five hundred years later has left descendants prepared to show similar virtue to achieve a similar end!'

There was a gasp. Men's voices are supposed to weaken as they age; but not Cicero's on that day.

'I am not afraid to speak out. I am not afraid of death. I am grieved that senators who have achieved the rank of consul did not support Lucius Piso in June, when he condemned all the abuses now widespread in the state. Not one single ex-consul seconded him by his voice – no, not even by a look. What is the meaning of this slavery? I say these men have fallen short of what their rank requires!'

He put his hands on his hips and glared around him. Most senators could not meet his eye.

'In March I accepted that the acts of Caesar should be recognised as legal, not because I agreed with them – who could do that? – but for the sake of reconciliation and public harmony. Yet any act that Antony disagrees with, such as that which limits provincial commands to two years, has been repealed, while other decrees of the Dictator have been miraculously discovered and posted after his death, so that criminals have been brought back from exile – by a dead man. Citizenship has been given to whole tribes and provinces – by a dead man. Taxes have been imposed – by a dead man.

'I wish Mark Antony were here to explain himself – but apparently he is unwell: a privilege he did not grant me yesterday. I hear he is angry with me. Well, I will make him an offer – a fair one. If I say anything against his life and character, let him declare himself my most bitter enemy. Let him keep an armed guard if he really feels he needs it for his own protection. But don't let that guard threaten those who express their own free opinions on behalf of the state. What can be fairer than that?'

For the first time his words drew murmurs of agreement.

'Gentlemen, I have already reaped the reward of my return simply by making these few remarks. Whatever happens to me, I have kept faith with my beliefs. If I can speak again here safely, I shall. If I can't, then I shall hold myself ready in case the state should call me. I have lived long enough for years and for fame. Whatever time remains to me will not be mine, but will be devoted to the service of our commonwealth.'

Cicero sat to a low rumble of approval and some stamping of feet. The men around him clapped him on the shoulder.

When the session ended, Dolabella swept out with his lictors, no doubt heading straight to Antony's house to tell him what had happened, while Cicero and I went home.

For the next two weeks the Senate did not meet and Cicero stayed barricaded in his house on the Palatine. He recruited more guards, bought a ferocious new watchdog, and fortified the villa with iron shutters and doors. Atticus lent him some scribes, and these I set to work making copies of his defiant speech to the Senate, which he sent to everyone he could think of – to Brutus in Macedonia, to Cassius en route to Syria, to Decimus in Nearer Gaul, to the two military commanders in Further Gaul, Lepidus and L. Munatius Plancus, and to many others. He called it, half seriously and half in self-mockery, his Philippic, after the famous series of orations Demosthenes had delivered in opposition to the Macedonian tyrant Philip II. A copy must have reached Antony: at any rate, he made known his intention to reply in the Senate, which he summoned to meet on the nineteenth day of September.

There was never any question of Cicero attending in person: being unafraid of death was one thing, committing suicide another. Instead he asked if I would go and make a record of what Antony said. I agreed, reasoning that my natural anonymity would protect me.

The moment I entered the Forum, I thanked the gods that Cicero had stayed away, for Antony had filled every corner with his private army. He had even stationed a squadron of Iturean archers on the steps of the Temple of Concordia – wild-looking tribesmen from the borders of Syria, notorious for their savagery. They watched as each senator entered the temple, occasionally fitting arrows into their bows and pretending to take aim.

I managed to squeeze in at the back and take out my stylus and tablet just as Antony arrived. In addition to Pompey's house in Rome, he had also commandeered Metellus Scipio's estate at Tibur, and it was there that he was said to have composed his speech. He looked badly hungover as he passed me, and when he reached the dais, he leaned forward and vomited a thick stream into the aisle. This drew laughter and applause from his supporters: he was notorious for being sick in public. Behind me his slaves locked and barred the door. It was against all custom to take the Senate hostage in this manner, and clearly intended to intimidate.

As to his harangue against Cicero, it was in essence a continuation of his vomit. He spewed forth years of swallowed bile. He gestured around the temple and reminded senators that it was in this very building that Cicero had arranged for the illegal execution of five Roman citizens, among them P. Lentulus Sura, Antony's own stepfather, whose body Cicero had refused to return to his family for a decent burial. He accused Cicero ('this bloodstained butcher who lets others do his killing') of having masterminded the assassination of Caesar, just as he had the murder of Clodius. He maintained that it was Cicero who had artfully poisoned the relations between Pompey and Caesar that had led to civil war. I knew the charges were all lies, but also that they would be damaging, as would the more personal accusations he made – that Cicero was a physical and moral coward, vain and boastful and above all a hypocrite, forever twisting this way and that to keep in with all factions, so that even his own brother and nephew deserted him and denounced him to Caesar. He quoted from a private letter Cicero had sent him when he was trapped in Brundisium: *I shall always, without hesitation and with my whole heart, do anything that I can to accord with your wishes and interests.* The temple rang with laughter. He even dragged up Cicero's divorce from Terentia and his subsequent marriage to Publilia: 'With what trembling, debauched and covetous fingers did this lofty philosopher undress his fifteen-year-old bride on her wedding night, and how feebly did he perform his husbandly duties – so much so that the poor child fled from him in horror soon afterwards and his own daughter preferred to die rather than live with the shame.'

It was all horribly effective, and when the door was unlocked and we were released into the light, I dreaded having to return to Cicero and read it back to him. However, he insisted on hearing it word for word. Whenever I tried to miss out a passage or a phrase, he spotted it at once and made me go back and put it in. At the end he looked quite crumpled. 'Well, that's politics,' he said, and tried to shrug it off. But I could tell he was shaken. He knew he would have to retaliate in kind or retire humiliated. Trying to do so in person in the Senate, controlled as it was by Antony and Dolabella, would be too dangerous. Therefore his counter-charge would have to be made in writing, and once it was published there could be no going back. Against such a wild man as Antony, it was a duel to the death.

Early in October, Antony left Rome for Brundisium, in order to secure the loyalty of the legions he had brought over from Macedonia, and which were now bivouacked just outside the town. With Antony gone, Cicero also decided to retire from Rome for a few weeks and devote himself to composing his riposte, which he was already calling his Second Philippic. He headed off to the Bay of Naples and left me behind to look after his interests.

It was a melancholy season. As always in late autumn, the skies above Rome were darkened by countless thousands of starlings arriving from the north, and their chattering shrieks seemed to warn of some imminent calamity. They would nestle in the trees beside the Tiber only to rise in huge black flags that would unfurl overhead and sweep back and forth as if in panic. The days became chilly; the nights longer; winter approached and with it the certainty of war. Octavian was in Campania, very close to where Cicero was staying, recruiting troops in Casilinum and Calatia from among Caesar's veterans. Antony was trying to bribe the soldiers in Brundisium. Decimus had raised a new legion in Nearer Gaul. Lepidus and Plancus were waiting with their forces beyond the Alps. Brutus and Cassius had hoisted their standards in Macedonia and in Syria. That made a total of seven armies, formed or forming. It was merely a question of who would strike first.

In the event, that honour, if honour is the word, fell to Octavian. He had mustered the best part of a legion by promising the veterans a staggering bounty of two thousand sesterces a head – Balbus had guaranteed the money – and now he wrote to Cicero begging his advice. Cicero sent the sensational news to me to pass on to Atticus.

His object is plain: war with Antony and himself as commander-in-chief. So it looks to me as though in a few days' time we shall be in arms. But who are we to follow? Consider his name; consider his age. He wanted my advice as to whether he should proceed to Rome with three thousand veterans or hold Capua and block Antony's route or go to join the three Macedonian legions now marching along the Adriatic coast, which he hopes to have on his side. They refused to take a bounty from Antony, so he says, booed him savagely, and left him standing as he tried to harangue them. In short, he proffers himself as our leader and expects me to back him up. For my part I have recommended him to go to Rome. I imagine he will have the city rabble behind him, and the honest men too if he convinces them of his sincerity.

Octavian followed Cicero's recommendation and entered Rome on the tenth day of November. His soldiers occupied the Forum. I watched as they deployed across the centre of the city, securing the temples and the public buildings. They remained in position throughout that night and the whole of the following day while Octavian set up his headquarters in Balbus's house and tried to arrange a meeting of the Senate. But the senior magistrates were all gone: Antony was trying to win over the Macedonian legions; Dolabella had left for Syria; half the praetors, including Brutus and Cassius, had fled Italy – the city was leaderless. I could see why Octavian was pleading with Cicero to join him on his adventure, writing to him once and sometimes twice a day: Cicero alone might have had the moral authority to rally the Senate. But he had no intention of putting himself under the command of a mere boy leading an armed insurrection with precarious chances of success; prudently he stayed away.

In my role as Cicero's eyes and ears in Rome, I went down to the Forum on the twelfth to hear Octavian speak. By this time he had abandoned his attempts to summon the Senate and instead had persuaded a sympathetic tribune, Ti. Cannutius, to convene a public assembly. He stood on the rostra under a grey sky waiting to be called – slender as a reed, blond, pale, nervous; it was, as I wrote to Cicero, 'a scene both ridiculous and yet oddly compelling, like an episode from a legend'. He was not a bad speaker, either, once he got started, and Cicero was delighted by his denunciation of Antony ('this forger of decrees, this subverter of laws, this thief of rightful inheritances, this traitor who is even now seeking to make war upon the entire state . . .'). But he was less pleased when I reported how Octavian had pointed to the statue of Caesar that had been set up on the rostra and praised him as 'the greatest Roman of all time, whose murder I shall avenge and whose hopes in me I swear to you by all the gods I shall fulfil'. With that he came down from the platform to loud applause and soon afterwards left the city, taking his soldiers with him, alarmed at reports that Antony was approaching with a much larger force.

Events now moved with great rapidity. Antony halted his

army – which included Caesar's famous Fifth Legion, 'the Larks' – a mere twelve miles from Rome at Tibur and entered the city with a bodyguard of a thousand men. He summoned the Senate for the twenty-fourth and let it be known that he expected them to declare Octavian a public enemy. Failure to attend would be regarded as condoning Octavian's treason and punishable by death. Antony's army was ready to move into the city if his will was thwarted. Rome was gripped by the certainty of a massacre.

The twenty-fourth arrived, the Senate met – but Antony himself did not appear. One of the Macedonian legions that had booed him, the Martian, encamped sixty miles away at Alba Fucens, had suddenly declared itself for Octavian, in return for a bounty five times the size of that Antony had offered them. He raced off to try to win them back, but they mocked him openly for his stinginess. He returned to Rome, summoning the Senate for the twenty-eighth, this time to meet in an emergency session at night. Never before in living memory had the Senate gathered in darkness: it was contrary to all custom and the sacred laws. When I went down to the Forum intending to make my report for Cicero, I found it full of legionaries drawn up in the torchlight. The sight was so sinister I lost my nerve and did not dare to enter the temple, but instead stood around with the crowd outside. I saw Antony arrive, hotfoot from Alba Fucens, accompanied by his brother Lucius, an even wilder-looking character than him, who had fought as a gladiator in Asia and slit a friend's throat. And I was still there an hour later to see them both leave in a hurry. Never will I forget the rolling-eyed look of panic on Antony's face as he rushed down the temple steps. He had just been told that another legion, the Fourth, had followed the example of the Martian and had also declared for Octavian. Now he was the one who risked being outnumbered.

Antony fled the city that same night and went to Tibur to rally his army and raise fresh recruits.

While all this was going on, Cicero finished his so-called Second Philippic and sent it to me with instructions to borrow twenty scribes from Atticus and ensure it was copied and circulated as soon as possible. It took the form of a long speech – had it been delivered, it would have lasted a good two hours – and therefore rather than set each man to work making a single copy, I divided the roll into twenty parts and shared the pieces between them. In this way, once their completed sections were glued together, we were able to turn out four or five copies a day. These we sent to friends and allies with a request that they either make copies themselves or at least hold meetings at which the speech could be read aloud.

News of it soon spread. On the day after Antony withdrew from the city, it was posted in the Forum. Everyone wanted to read it, not least because it was filled with the most venomous gossip, for example that Antony had been a homosexual prostitute in his youth and was always falling down drunk and had kept a nude actress as his mistress. But I ascribe its phenomenal popularity more to the fact that it was also full of detailed information no one had dared disclose before – that Antony had stolen seven hundred million sesterces from the Temple of Ops and had used part of it to pay off personal debts of forty million; that he and Fulvia had forged Caesar's decrees to extort ten million sesterces from the king of Galatia; that the pair had seized jewels, furniture, villas, farms and cash and had divided it all up among themselves and their entourage of actors, gladiators, soothsayers and quacks.

On the ninth day of December, Cicero finally returned to Rome. I had not been expecting him. I heard the watchdog barking and went out into the passage to discover the master of the house standing there with Atticus. He had been away for nearly two months and looked to be in exceptionally good health and spirits. Without even taking off his cloak and hat he handed me a letter he had received the previous day from Octavian:

I have read your new Philippic and think it quite magnificent – worthy of Demosthenes himself. I only wish I could see the face of our latter-day Philip when he reads it. I learn he has decided against attacking me here, no doubt nervous that his men would refuse to take the field against Caesar's son, and instead is marching his army rapidly to Nearer Gaul with the intention of wresting that province from your friend Decimus.

My dear Cicero, you must agree my position is stronger than we ever could have dreamed of when we met at your house in Puteoli. I am here now in Etruria seeking fresh recruits. They are flocking to me. And yet as ever I am in sore need of your wise advice. Can we not contrive a meeting? There is no man in all the world I would sooner speak with.

'Well,' said Cicero with a grin, 'what do you think?'

I replied, 'It's very gratifying.'

'Gratifying? Come now – use your imagination! It's more than that! I've been thinking about it ever since I got it.'

After a slave had helped him out of his outdoor clothes, he beckoned me and Atticus to follow him into his study and asked me to close the door.

'Here is the situation as I see it. Were it not for Octavian, Antony would have taken Rome and our cause would be finished by now. But fear of Octavian forced the wolf to drop his prey at the last moment and now he's slinking north to devour Nearer Gaul instead. If he defeats Decimus this winter and takes the province – which he probably will – he will have the financial base and the forces to return to Rome in the spring and finish us off. All that stands between us and him is Octavian.'

Atticus said sceptically, 'You really think Octavian has raised an army in order to defend what's left of the republic?'

'No, but equally is it in his interests to allow Antony to take control of Rome? Of course not. Antony at this juncture is his real enemy – the one who has stolen his inheritance and denies his claims. If I can persuade Octavian to see that, we may yet save ourselves from disaster.'

'Possibly – but only to deliver the republic from the clutches of one tyrant into those of another; and a tyrant who calls himself Caesar at that.'

'Oh, I don't know if the lad is a tyrant – I think I may be able to use my influence to keep him on the side of virtue, at least until Antony is disposed of.'

'His letter certainly seems to suggest he would listen to you,' I said.

'Exactly. Believe me, Atticus, I could show you thirty such letters if I could be bothered to find them, going all the way back to April. Why is he so eager for my counsel? The truth is the boy lacks a father figure – his natural father is dead; his stepfather is a goose; and his adopted father has left him the greatest legacy in history but no guidance on how to gain hold of it. Somehow I seem to have stepped into the paternal role, which is a blessing – not so much for me as for the republic.'

Atticus said, 'So what are you going to do?'

'I shall go and see him.'

'In Etruria, in the middle of winter, at your age? It's a hundred miles away. You must be mad.'

I said, 'But you can hardly expect Octavian to come to Rome.'

Cicero waved away these objections. 'Then we'll meet halfway. That villa you bought the other year, Atticus, on Lake Volsinii – that would suit the purpose admirably. Is it occupied?'

'No, but I can't vouch for its comfort.'

'That doesn't matter. Tiro, draft a letter from me to Octavian proposing a meeting in Volsinii as soon as he can manage it.'

Atticus said, 'But what about the Senate? What about the consuls-designate? You have no power to negotiate on behalf of the republic with anyone, let alone with a man at the head of a rebel army.'

'Nobody is wielding power in the republic any more. That's the point. It's lying in the dust waiting for whoever dares to pick it up. Why shouldn't I be the one to seize it?'

Atticus had no answer to that and Cicero's invitation went off to Octavian within the hour. After three days of anxious waiting Cicero received his reply: *Nothing would give me greater pleasure than to see you again. I shall meet you in Volsinii on the sixteenth as you propose unless I hear that that has become inconvenient. I suggest we keep our rendezvous secret.*

To ensure that no one would guess what he was up to, Cicero insisted we left in the darkness long before dawn on the morning of the fourteenth of December. I had to bribe the sentries to open the Fontinalian Gate especially for us.

We knew we would be venturing into lawless country, full of roaming bands of armed men, and so we travelled in a closed carriage escorted by a large retinue of guards and attendants.

Once across the Mulvian Bridge we turned left along the bank of the Tiber and joined the Via Cassia, a road I had never travelled before. By noon we were climbing into hilly country. Atticus had promised me spectacular views. But the dismal weather Italy had endured ever since Caesar's assassination continued to curse us, and the distant peaks of the pine-covered mountains were draped in mist. For the entire two days we were on the road it barely seemed to get light.

Cicero's earlier ebullience had faded. He was uncharacteristically quiet, conscious no doubt that the future of the republic might depend on the coming meeting. On the afternoon of the second day, as we reached the edge of the great lake and our destination came into view, he began to complain of feeling cold. He shivered and blew on his hands, but when I tried to cover his knees with a blanket, he threw it off like an irritable child and said that although he might be ancient, he was not an invalid.

Atticus had bought his property as an investment and had only visited it once; still, he never forgot a thing when it came to money and he quickly remembered where to find it. Large and dilapidated – parts of it dated back to Etruscan times – the villa stood just outside the city walls of Volsinii, right on the edge of the water. The iron gates were open. Drifts of dead leaves had rotted in the damp courtyard; black lichen and moss covered the terracotta roofs. Only a thin curl of smoke rising from the chimney gave any sign it was inhabited. We assumed from the deserted grounds that Octavian had not yet arrived. But as we descended from the carriage, the steward hurried forward and said that a young man was waiting inside.

He was sitting in the tablinum with his friend Agrippa and he rose as we entered. I looked to see if the spectacular change in his fortunes was reflected at all in his manner or person, but he seemed exactly as before: quiet, modest, watchful, with the same unstylish haircut and youthful acne. He had come without any escort, he said, apart from two chariot drivers, who had taken their teams to be fed and watered in the town. ('No one knows what I look like, so I prefer not to draw attention to myself; it is better to hide in plain sight, don't you think?') He clasped hands very warmly with Cicero. After the introductions were over, Cicero said, 'I thought Tiro here could make a note of anything we agree on and then we could each have a copy.'

Octavian said, 'So you're empowered to negotiate?'

'No, but it would be useful to have something to show to the leaders of the Senate.'

'Personally, if you don't mind, I would prefer it if nothing were written down. That way we can talk more freely.'

There is therefore no verbatim record of their conference, although I wrote up an account immediately afterwards for Cicero's personal use. First Octavian gave a summary of the military situation as he understood it. He had, or would have shortly, four legions at his disposal: the veterans from Campania, the levies he was raising in Etruria, the Martian and the Fourth. Antony had three legions, including the Larks, but also another entirely inexperienced, and was closing in on Decimus, whom he understood from his agents had retreated to the city of Mutina, where he was slaughtering and salting cattle and preparing for a long siege. Cicero said that the Senate had eleven legions in Further Gaul: seven under Lepidus and four under Plancus.

Octavian said, 'Yes, but they are the wrong side of the Alps and are needed to hold down Gaul. Besides, we both know the commanders are not necessarily reliable, especially Lepidus.'

'I shan't argue with you,' said Cicero. 'The position boils down to this: you have the soldiers but no legitimacy; we have the legitimacy but no soldiers. What we do both have, however, is a common enemy – Antony. And it seems to me that somewhere in that mixture must be the basis for an agreement.'

Agrippa said, 'An agreement you've just told us you have no authority to make.'

'Young man, take it from me, if you want to make a deal with the Senate, I am your best hope. And let me tell you something else – it will be no easy task to convince them, even for me. There'll be plenty who'll say, "We didn't get rid of one Caesar to ally ourselves with another."'

'Yes,' retorted Agrippa, 'and plenty on our side who'll say, "Why should we fight to protect the men who murdered Caesar? This is just a trick to buy us off until they're strong enough to destroy us."'

Cicero slammed his hands on the armrests of his chair. 'If that is how you feel, then this has been a wasted journey.'

He made as if to rise, but Octavian leaned across and pressed down on his shoulder. 'Not so fast, my dear friend. No need to take offence. I agree with your analysis. My sole objective is to defeat Antony, and I would much prefer to do that with the legal authority of the Senate.'

Cicero said, 'Let us be clear: you would prefer it even if – and this is what it *would* mean – you have to go to the rescue of Decimus, the very man who lured your adopted father to his death?'

Octavian fixed him with his cold grey eyes. 'I have no problem with that.'

From then on, there was no doubt in my mind that Cicero and Octavian would make a deal. Even Agrippa seemed to relax a little. It was agreed that Cicero would propose in the Senate that Octavian, despite his age, be given imperium and the legal authority to wage war against Antony. In return, Octavian would place himself under the command of the consuls. What might happen in the longer term, after Antony was destroyed, was left vague. Nothing was written down.

Cicero said, 'You will be able to tell if I have fulfilled my side of my bargain by reading my speeches – which I shall send you – and in the resolutions passed by the Senate. And I shall know from the movements of your legions if you are fulfilling yours.'

Octavian said, 'You need have no doubts on that score.'

Atticus went off to find the steward and came back with a jug of Tuscan wine and five silver cups which he filled and handed round. Cicero felt moved to make a speech. 'On this day youth and experience, arms and the toga, have come together in solemn compact to rescue the commonwealth. Let us go forth from this place, each man to his station, resolved to do his duty to the republic.'

'To the republic,' said Octavian, and raised his cup.

'To the republic!' we all echoed, and drank.

Octavian and Agrippa politely refused to stay the night: they explained that they needed to reach their nearby camp before darkness as the next day was Saturnalia and Octavian was expected to distribute gifts to his men. After much mutual back-slapping and protestations of undying affection, Cicero and Octavian said goodbye to one another. The young man's parting phrase I still remember: 'Your speeches and my swords will make an unbeatable alliance.' When they had gone, Cicero went out on to the terrace and walked around in the rain to calm his nerves while I out of habit cleared away the wine cups. Octavian, I noticed, had not touched a drop.

XVII

Cicero had not expected to have to address the Senate until the first day of January, when Hirtius and Pansa were due to take over as consuls. But on our return we discovered the tribunes had summoned an emergency meeting to be held in two days' time to discuss the looming war between Antony and Decimus. Cicero decided that the sooner he made good on his promise to Octavian the better. Accordingly he went down to the Temple of Concordia early in the morning to show his intention of speaking. As usual I went with him and stood at the door to record his remarks.

Once word spread that Cicero was in his place, people began pouring into the Forum. Senators who might not otherwise have attended also decided they had better come to hear what he had to say. Within an hour the benches were packed. Among those who changed his plans was the consul-designate, Hirtius. He rose from his sickbed for the first time in weeks, and his appearance when he walked into the temple drew gasps. The plump young gourmet who had helped write Caesar's *Commentaries* and who used to entertain Cicero to dinners of swan and peacock had shrivelled to barely more than a skeleton. I believe he was suffering from what Hippocrates, the father of Greek medicine, calls a *carcino*; he had a scar on his neck where a growth had been recently removed.

The tribune who presided over the session was Appuleius, a friend of Cicero. He began by reading out an edict issued by Decimus denying Antony permission to enter Nearer Gaul, reiterating his determination to keep the province loyal to the Senate and confirming that he had moved his forces into Mutina. That was the town where I had delivered Cicero's letter to Caesar all those years before, and I recalled its stout walls and heavy gates: much would depend on whether it could hold out against a long siege by Antony's superior forces. When he had finished reading, Appuleius said, 'Within days – perhaps even already – the republic will be gripped once more by civil war. The question is: what are we to do? I call on Cicero to give us his opinion.'

Hundreds of men leaned forwards in anticipation as Cicero rose.

'This meeting, honourable gentlemen, comes not a moment too soon in my opinion. An iniquitous war against our hearths and altars, our lives and fortunes, is no longer just being prepared but is actually being waged by a profligate and wanton man. It is no good our waiting for the first day of January before we act. Antony does not wait. He's already attacking the eminent and remarkable Decimus. And from Nearer Gaul he threatens to descend on us in Rome. Indeed, he would have done so before now had it not been for a young man – or almost rather a boy, but one of incredible and near-godlike intelligence and courage – who raised an army and saved the state.'

He paused to allow his words to register. Senators turned to their neighbours to check they had heard correctly. The temple became a hubbub of surprise mingled with some notes of indignation and gasps of excitement. Did he just say the boy had saved the state? It was a while before Cicero could continue.

'Yes, this is my belief, gentlemen, this is my judgement: had not a single youth stood up to that madman, this commonwealth would have utterly perished. On him today – and we are here today, free to express our views, only because of him – on him we must confer the authority to defend the republic, not as something merely undertaken by him, but as a charge *entrusted to him by us*.'

There were a few cries of 'No!' and 'He's bought you!' from Antony's supporters but these were drowned by applause from the rest of the Senate. Cicero pointed to the door. 'Do you not see the packed Forum and how the Roman people are encouraged to hope for the recovery of their liberty? That now, after a long interval, when they see us assembled here in such numbers, they hope we have met together as free men?'

Thus opened what became known as the Third Philippic. It tuned Roman politics on its axis. It lavished praise on Octavian, or Caesar, as Cicero now called him for the first time. ('Who is more chaste than this young man? Who more modest? What brighter example have we among youth of old-world purity?') It pointed the way to a strategy that might yet lead to the salvation of the republic. ('The immortal gods have given us these safeguards – for the city, Caesar; Decimus for Gaul.') But perhaps even more important, for tired and careworn hearts, after months and years of supine acquiescence, it fired the Senate with fighting spirit.

'Today for the first time after a long interval we set our feet in possession of liberty. It is to glory and to liberty we were born. And if the final episode in the long history of our republic has arrived, then let us at the least behave like champion gladiators: they meet death honourably; let us see to it that we too – who stand foremost of all nations on the earth – fall with dignity rather than serve with ignominy.'

Such was the effect that when Cicero sat down a large part of the Senate immediately stood and rushed to crowd around him with their congratulations. It was clear that for the time being he had carried all before him. At Cicero's behest a motion was proposed thanking Decimus for his defence of Nearer Gaul, praising Octavian for his 'help, courage and judgement', and promising him future honours as soon as the consuls-elect convened the Senate in the new year. It passed overwhelmingly. Then, most unusually, the tribunes invited Cicero rather than a serving magistrate to go out into the Forum and report to the people on what the Senate had decided.

He had told us before he went to meet Octavian that power in Rome was lying in the dust merely waiting for someone to pick it up. That was what he did that day. He climbed on to the rostra, watched by the Senate, and turned to face all those thousands of citizens. 'Your incredible numbers, Romans,' he bellowed at them, 'and the size – the greatest I can ever remember – of this assembly, inspire me to defend the republic and give me the hope of re-establishing it!

'I can tell you that Gaius Caesar, who has protected and is protecting the state and your liberty, has just been thanked by the Senate!' A great swell of applause arose from the crowd. 'I commend,' shouted Cicero, struggling to make his voice heard, 'I commend you, Romans, for greeting with the warmest applause the name of a most noble young man. Divine and immortal honours are due for his divine and immortal services!

'You are fighting, Romans, against an enemy with whom no peace terms are possible. Antony is not just a guilty and villainous man. He is a monstrous and savage animal. The issue is not on what terms we shall live, but whether we shall live at all, or perish in torture and ignominy!

'As for me, I shall spare no efforts on your behalf. We have today, for the first time after a long interval, with my counsel and at my instance, been fired by the hope of liberty!'

With that he took a pace backward to signal that his speech was over, the crowd roared and stamped their feet in approval, and the last and most glorious phase of Cicero's public career began.

From my shorthand notes I made a transcript of both speeches, and once again a team of scribes worked in relays to make copies. These were variously posted up in the Forum and dispatched to Brutus, Cassius, Decimus and the other prominent men in the republican cause. Naturally they were also sent to Octavian, who read them at once and replied within a week:

From G. Caesar to his friend and mentor M. Cicero.

Greetings!

I enjoyed your latest Philippics very much. 'Chaste . . . modest . . . purity . . . godlike intelligence' – my ears are burning! Seriously, don't lay it on too thick, mon vieux, *as I can only be a disappointment! I would love one day to talk to you about the finer points of oratory – I know how much I could learn from you, on this as on other matters. And so – onwards! As soon as I hear word from you that my army has been made legal and I have the necessary authority to wage war, I shall move my legions north to attack Antony.*

All men now waited anxiously for the next meeting of the Senate, due to be held on the first day of January. Cicero fretted that they were wasting precious time: 'It is the most important rule in politics always to keep things moving.' He went to see Hirtius and Pansa and urged them to bring the session forward; they refused, saying they did not have the legal authority. Still, he believed he had their confidence and that the three of them would present a united front. But when the new year dawned, and the sacrifices had been conducted on the Capitol in accordance with tradition, and the Senate retired to the Temple of Jupiter to debate the state of the nation, he received a nasty shock. Both Pansa, who presided and made the opening speech, and Hirtius, who spoke next, expressed the hope that, grave though the situation was, it might still be possible to find a peaceful solution with Antony. This was not at all what Cicero wanted to hear.

As the senior ex-consul, he had expected to be called next and rose accordingly. But instead Pansa ignored him in favour of his father-in-law, Quintus Calenus, an old supporter of Clodius and a crony of Antony, who had never been elected consul but had only been appointed to the office by the Dictator. He was a stocky, burly figure, built like a blacksmith, and no great speaker, but he was blunt and heard with respect.

'This crisis,' he said, 'has been made out by the learned and distinguished Cicero to be a war between the republic on the one side and Mark Antony on the other. That's not correct, gentlemen. It's a war between three different parties: Antony, who was made governor of Nearer Gaul by a vote of this house and by the people; Decimus, who refuses to surrender his command; and a boy who has raised a private army and is out for all he can get. Of the three, I know and personally favour Antony. Perhaps as a compromise we should offer him the governorship of Further Gaul instead? But if that's too much for the rest of you, I propose we should at the very least stay neutral.'

When he sat, Cicero stood again. But again Pansa ignored him and called Lucius Piso, Caesar's ex-father-in-law, whom Cicero had also naturally counted as an ally. Instead Piso made a long speech, the gist of it being that he had always regarded Antony as a danger to the state, and still did, but having lived through the last civil war, he had no desire to live through another and believed the Senate should make one last attempt at peace by sending a delegation to Antony to offer him terms. 'I propose that he should submit himself to the will of the Senate and people, abandon his siege of Mutina and withdraw his army to the Italian side of the Rubicon but no closer to Rome than two hundred miles. If he does that, then even at this late stage war may be averted. But if he does not, and war does come, at least the world will have no doubt who bears the blame.'

When Piso had finished, Cicero did not even bother to stand, but sat with his chin sunk on his chest, glowering at the floor. The next speaker was his other supposed ally, P. Servilius Vatia Isauricus, who delivered himself of a great many platitudes and spoke bitterly of Antony, but even more bitterly of Octavian. He was a relative by marriage of Brutus and Cassius and raised a question that was in many minds: 'Ever since he arrived in Italy Octavian has made the most violent speeches, swearing to avenge his so-called father by bringing his killers to justice. In so doing he threatens the safety of some of the most illustrious men in the state. Have they been consulted about the honours now being contemplated for Caesar's adopted son? What guarantees do we have that if we proceed to make this ambitious and immature would-be warlord the "sword and shield of the Senate" – as the noble Cicero suggests – he won't turn round and use his sword against *us*?'

These five speeches, coming after the ceremonial opening, took up all of the short January day, and Cicero returned home with his prepared oration undelivered. 'Peace!' He spat out the word. Always in the past he had been an advocate of peace; no longer. He jutted his chin in belligerence as he complained bitterly of the consuls: 'What a pair of spineless mediocrities. All those hours I spent teaching them how to speak properly! And to what end? I would have been better employed teaching them how to think straight.' As for Calenus, Piso and Isauricus, they were 'addle-headed appeasers', 'faint hearts', 'political monstrosities' – after a time I stopped making a note of his insults. He retired to his study to rewrite his speech and the next morning sallied forth for the second day of the debate like a warship in full battle array.

From the moment the session began he was on his feet, and stayed there, signalling that he expected to be called next and would not take no for an answer. Behind him his supporters chanted his name, and eventually Pansa had no option but to indicate by his gestures that Cicero had the floor.

'Nothing, gentlemen,' Cicero began, 'has ever seemed longer to me in coming than the beginning of this new year and with it this meeting of the Senate. *We* have waited – but those who wage war against the state have not. Does Mark Antony desire peace? Then let him lay down his arms. Let him ask for peace. Let him appeal to our mercy. But to send envoys to a man on whom thirteen days ago you passed the heaviest and severest judgement is beyond a joke and is – if I must give my real opinion – madness!'

One by one, like the impact of missiles thrown by some mighty ballista, Cicero demolished the arguments of his opponents. Antony did not have any legal title to be governor of

Nearer Gaul: his law was pushed through an invalid assembly in a thunderstorm. He was a forger. He was a thief. He was a traitor. To give him the province of Further Gaul would be to give him access to 'the sinews of war: unlimited money' – the idea was absurd. 'And it is to this man, great heavens, that we are pleased to send envoys? He will never obey anybody's envoys! I know the fellow's madness and arrogance. But time meanwhile will be wasted. The preparations for war will cool – they have already been dragged out by slowness and delay. If we had acted sooner we should not now be having a war at all. Every evil is easily crushed at birth; allow it to become established and it always gathers strength.

'So I propose, gentlemen, that we should send no envoys. I say instead that a state of emergency should be declared, that the courts should be shut, that military dress should be worn, that recruitment should be started, that exemptions from military service should be suspended throughout Rome and the whole of Italy, and that Antony be declared a public enemy . . .'

A spontaneous roar of applause and stamping feet drowned out the remainder of his sentence but he carried on speaking through it:

'. . . if we do all that, he will feel that he has begun a war against the state. He will experience the energy and strength of a Senate with one mind. He says this is a war of parties. What parties? This war has not been stirred up by any parties but by him alone!

'And now I come to Gaius Caesar, upon whom my friend Isauricus heaped such scorn and suspicion. Yet if he had not lived, who of us could have been alive now? What god presented to the Roman people this heaven-sent boy? By his protection the tyranny of Antony was thwarted. Let us therefore give

Caesar the necessary command, without which no military affairs can be administered, no army held together, no war waged. Let him be pro-praetor with the maximum power of a regular appointment.

'On him our hope of liberty rests. I know this young man. Nothing is dearer to him than the republic, nothing more important than your authority, nothing more desirable than the opinion of good men, nothing sweeter than genuine glory. I shall even venture to give you my word, gentlemen – to you and to the Roman people: I promise, I undertake, I solemnly pledge that Gaius Caesar will always be such a citizen as he is today, the citizen that we all most earnestly wish and pray that he should be.'

That speech, and in particular that guarantee, changed everything. I believe it can truly be asserted – and it is a rare boast for any oration – that if Cicero had not delivered his Fifth Philippic, then history would have been different, for opinion in the Senate was almost evenly divided, and until he spoke, the debate was running Antony's way. Now his words stemmed the tide and the votes started to flow back in favour of war. Indeed, Cicero might have won on every point if a tribune named Salvius had not interposed his veto, prolonging the debate into a fourth day, and giving Antony's wife Fulvia the chance to appear at the door of the temple to plead for moderation. She was accompanied by her infant son – the one who had been sent up to the Capitol as a hostage – and by Antony's elderly mother, Julia, who was a cousin of Julius Caesar and greatly admired for her noble bearing. They were all dressed in black and made a most affecting spectacle, three generations walking down the aisle of the Senate with their hands clasped in supplication. Every senator was aware that if Antony was to be named a public enemy, all his property would be seized and they would be thrown out on to the streets.

'Spare us this humiliation,' cried out Fulvia, 'we beseech you!'

The vote to declare Antony an enemy of the state was duly lost, while the motion to send a delegation of envoys to make him a final peace offer was carried. The rest, however, was all for Cicero: Octavian's army was recognised as legitimate and incorporated with Decimus's under the standard of the Senate; Octavian was made a senator, despite his youth, and also awarded a pro-praetorship with power of imperium; as a nod to the future, the age requirement for the consulship was lowered by ten years (although it would still be another thirteen before Octavian was eligible to stand); the loyalty of Plancus and Lepidus was bought, the one being confirmed as consul for the following year, the other being honoured by a gilded equestrian statue on the rostra; and the raising of new armies and the imposition of a state of military preparedness in Rome and all across Italy was ordered to begin immediately.

Once again the tribunes asked Cicero, rather than the consuls, to convey the Senate's decisions to the thousands gathered in the Forum. When he told them that peace envoys were to be sent to Antony, a collective groan went up. Cicero made a soothing gesture with his hands. 'I gather, Romans, that this course is also repudiated by you, as it was by me, and with good reason. But I urge you to be patient. What I did earlier in the Senate I will do before you now. I predict that Mark Antony will ignore the envoys, devastate the land, besiege Mutina and raise more troops. And I am not afraid that when he hears what I have said, he will change his plans and obey the Senate in order to refute me: he is too far gone for that. We shall lose some precious time, but never fear: we shall have victory in the end.

Other nations can endure slavery, but the most prized possession of the Roman people is liberty.'

The peace delegation left the next day from the Forum. Cicero went with an ill grace to see them off. The chosen envoys were three ex-consuls: Lucius Piso, who had come up with the idea in the first place and so could hardly refuse to take part; Marcus Philippus, Octavian's stepfather, whose participation Cicero called 'disgusting and scandalous'; and Cicero's old friend Servius Sulpicius, who was in such poor health that Cicero begged him to reconsider: 'It's two hundred and fifty miles in midwinter, through snow and wolves and bandits, and with only the amenities of an army camp at the end of it. For pity's sake, my dear Servius, use your illness as an excuse and let them find someone else.'

'You forget I was at Pompey's side at Pharsalus. I stood and watched the slaughter of the best men in the state. My last service to the republic will be to try to stop that happening again.'

'Your instincts are as noble as ever, but your hold on reality is poor. Antony will laugh in your face. All that your suffering will accomplish is to help prolong the war.'

Servius looked at him sadly. 'What happened to my old friend who hated soldiering and loved his books? I rather miss him. I certainly preferred him to this rabble-rouser who stirs up the crowd for blood.'

With that he climbed stiffly into his litter and was borne away with the others to begin the long journey.

Preparations for war now slowed to a half-hearted pace, as Cicero had warned they would, while Romans awaited the outcome of the peace mission. Although levies took place across Italy to recruit four new legions, there was no great sense of urgency now that the immediate threat seemed to have been lifted. In the meantime, the only legions the Senate could draw on were the two encamped near Rome that had declared for Octavian – the Martian and the Fourth – and after receiving permission from Octavian, these agreed to march north to relieve Decimus under the command of one of the consuls. Lots for the office had to be drawn in accordance with the law, and by a cruel jest of the gods it went to the sick man, Hirtius. Watching this ghostly figure in his red cloak painfully ascend the steps of the Capitol, perform the traditional sacrifice of a white bull to Jupiter and then ride off to war filled Cicero with foreboding.

It was to be almost a month before the city's herald announced that the returning peace envoys were approaching the city. Pansa summoned the Senate to hear their report that same day. Only two of them came into the temple – Piso and Philippus. Piso stood and in a grave voice announced that the gallant Servius had no sooner reached Antony's headquarters than he had died of exhaustion. Because of the distance involved, and the slowness of winter travel, it had been necessary to cremate him on the spot rather than bring the body home.

'I have to tell you, gentlemen, that we found that Antony has surrounded Mutina with a very powerful system of siege works, and throughout our time in his camp he continued to pound the town with missiles. He refused to allow us safe passage through his lines to talk to Decimus. As to the terms you had empowered us to offer him, he rejected them in favour of terms of his own.' Piso produced a letter and began to read. 'He will give up his claim to the governorship of Nearer Gaul but only if he is compensated by the award instead of Further Gaul for five years together with the command of Decimus's army, raising his total strength to six legions. He demands that all the decrees he has issued in Caesar's name should be declared legal; that there should be no further investigation into the disappearance of the state's treasury from the Temple of Ops; that his followers should be given an amnesty; and finally that his soldiers should be paid what they are owed and also awarded land.'

Piso rolled up the document and tucked it into his sleeve. 'We have done our best, gentlemen. I am disappointed, I will not hide it. I fear this house must recognise that a state of war exists between the republic and Mark Antony.'

Cicero got to his feet, but yet again Pansa called his father-in-law, Calenus, to speak first. He said: 'I deplore the use of the word "war". On the contrary, I believe we have here, gentlemen, the basis for an honourable peace. It was my suggestion, first made in this Senate, that Antony should be offered Further Gaul, and I am glad that he has accepted it. Our main points are all met. Decimus remains as governor. The people of Mutina are spared any further misery. Roman does not take up arms against Roman. I can see by the way he shakes his head that Cicero does not like what I am saying. He is an angry man. But more than that, I venture to say that he is an angry *old* man. Let me remind him that it will not be men of our age who die in this new war. It will be his son, and my son, and yours, gentlemen – and yours, and yours, and yours. I say let us have a truce with Antony and reconcile our differences peacefully as our gallant colleagues Piso, Philippus and the lamented Servius have shown us how to do.'

Calenus's speech was warmly received. It was clear that Antony still had his supporters in the Senate, including his legate, the diminutive Cotyla, or 'Half-Pint', whom he had sent south to report on the mood in Rome. As Pansa called speaker after speaker – including Antony's uncle, Lucius Caesar, who said he felt duty-bound to defend his nephew – Cotyla ostentatiously made notes of their remarks, presumably so that he could report them back to his master. It had an oddly unnerving effect, and at the end of the day, a majority of the house, including Pansa, voted to remove the word 'war' from the motion and declare instead that the country was in a state of 'tumult'.

Pansa did not call Cicero until the following morning. But once again this worked to Cicero's advantage. Not only did he rise in an atmosphere of intense expectation; he was able to attack the arguments of the previous speakers. He started with Lucius Caesar: 'He excuses his vote because of his family connections. He is an uncle. Fair enough. But are the rest of you uncles too?'

And once he had his audience laughing – once he had softened the ground, so to speak – he proceeded to pulverise them with a cataract of invective and derision. 'Decimus is being attacked – there is no war. Mutina is being besieged – not even this is war. Gaul is being laid waste – what could be more peaceful? Gentlemen, this is a war such as has never been seen before! We are defending the temples of the immortal gods, our walls, our homes, and the birthrights of the Roman people, the altars, hearths and tombs of our ancestors; we are defending our laws, law courts, liberty, wives, children, fatherland. On the other side, Mark Antony fights to wreck all this and plunder the state.

'At this point my brave and energetic friend Calenus reminds me of the advantages of peace. But I ask you, Calenus: what do you mean? Do you call slavery peace? Heavy fighting is in progress. We have sent three leading members of the Senate to intervene. These Antony has repudiated with contempt. Yet you remain his most constant defender!

'With what dishonour did yesterday dawn upon us! "Oh, but what if he were to make a truce?" A truce? In the presence, before the very eyes of the envoys he pounded Mutina with his engines. He showed them his works and his siege train. Not for a moment, although the envoys were there, did the siege find a breathing space. Envoys to this man? Peace with this man?

'I will say it with grief rather than with insult: we are deserted – deserted, gentlemen – by our leaders. What concessions have we not made to Cotyla, the envoy of Mark Antony? Though by rights the gates of this city should have been closed to him, yet this temple was open. He came into the Senate. He entered in his notebooks your votes and everything you said. Even those who had filled the highest offices were currying favour with him to the disgrace of their dignity. Ye immortal gods! Where is the ancient spirit of our ancestors? Let Cotyla return to his general but on condition that he never returns to Rome.'

The Senate sat stunned. They had not been shamed in such a fashion since Cato's day. At the end, Cicero laid a fresh motion: that those fighting with Antony would be given until the Ides of March to lay down their arms; after that, any who continued in his army, or who went to join him, would be regarded as traitors. The proposal passed overwhelmingly. There was to be no truce, no peace, no deal; Cicero had his war.

A day or two after the first anniversary of Caesar's assassination – an occasion that passed without notice apart from the laying of flowers on his tomb – Pansa followed his colleague Hirtius into battle. The consul rode off from the Field of Mars at the head of an army of four legions: almost twenty thousand men scoured from every corner of Italy. Cicero watched with the rest of the Senate as they paraded past. As a military force it was less impressive than it sounded. Most were the rawest of recruits – farmers, ostlers, bakers and laundrymen who could barely even march in time. Their real power was symbolic. The republic was in arms against the usurper Antony.

With both consuls gone, the most senior magistrate left behind in the city was the urban praetor, Marcus Cornutus – a soldier picked by Caesar for his loyalty and discretion. He now found himself required to preside over the Senate even though he had minimal experience of politics. He soon placed himself entirely in the hands of Cicero, who thus, at the age of sixty-three, became the effective ruler of Rome for the first time since his consulship twenty years before. It was to Cicero that all the imperial governors addressed their reports. It was he who decided when the Senate should meet. It was he who made the main appointments. His was the house that was packed all day with petitioners.

He sent an amused account of his *redux* to Octavian:

I do not think I boast when I say that nothing can happen in this city these days without my approval. Indeed it is actually better than a consulship because no one knows where my power begins or ends; therefore rather than run the risk of offending me, everyone consults me on everything. Actually it is even better, come to think of it, than a dictatorship, because nobody holds me to blame when things go wrong! It is proof that one should never mistake the baubles of office for actual power – another piece of avuncular advice for your glittering future, my boy, from your devoted old friend and mentor.

Octavian wrote back at the end of March to report that he was doing as he had promised: his army of nearly ten thousand men was striking camp just south of Bononia, beside the Via Aemilia, and moving off to join the armies of Hirtius and Pansa in relieving the siege of Mutina:

> *I am placing myself under the command of the consuls. We are expecting a great battle with Antony within the next two weeks. I promise that I shall endeavour to perform as valiantly in the field as you have in the Senate. What was it that the Spartan warriors said? 'I shall return either with my shield, or on it.'*

Around this time, word began to reach Cicero of events in the east. From Brutus in Macedonia he learned that Dolabella – heading for Syria at the head of a small force – had reached as far as Smyrna on the eastern shores of the Aegean, where he had encountered the governor of Asia, Trebonius. Trebonius had treated him civilly enough and even allowed him to proceed on his way. But that night Dolabella had secretly turned back, entered the city, seized Trebonius while he was asleep, and subjected him to two days and nights of intensive torture, using whips, the rack and hot irons, to force him to disclose the whereabouts of his treasury. After that, on Dolabella's orders, his neck was broken. His head was cut off and Dolabella's soldiers kicked it back and forth through the streets until it was completely crushed, while his body was mutilated and placed on public display. 'Thus dies the first of the assassins who murdered Caesar,' Dolabella was said to have declared. 'The first – but he will not be the last.'

Trebonius's remains were shipped to Rome and subjected to a post-mortem examination to confirm the manner of his death before being passed to his family for cremation. His grisly fate had a salutary effect on Cicero and the other leaders of the republic. They knew now what to expect if they fell into the hands of their enemies, especially when Antony issued an open letter to the consuls pledging his loyalty to Dolabella and expressing his delight at Trebonius's fate: *That a criminal has paid the penalty is a matter for rejoicing.* Cicero read the letter out loud in the Senate: it strengthened men's determination not to compromise. Dolabella was declared a public enemy. It was a particular shock to Cicero that his former son-in-law should have exhibited such cruelty. He lamented to me afterwards: 'To think that such a monster stayed under my roof and shared a bed with my poor dear daughter; to think that I actually *liked* the man . . . Who knows what animals lurk within the people who are close to us?'

The nervous strain under which he lived during those early days of April, while waiting for word from Mutina, was indescribable. First there would be good news. After months without contact, Cassius at last wrote to say that he was taking complete control of Syria: that all sides – Caesareans, republicans and the last remaining Pompeians – were flocking to him and that he had under his command a united army of no fewer than eleven legions. *I want you to know that you and your friends at the Senate are not without powerful support, so you can defend the state in the best interests of hope and courage.* Brutus also was meeting with success and had raised a further five legions, some twenty-five thousand men, in Macedonia. Young Marcus was with him, recruiting and training cavalry: *Your son earns my approval by his energy, endurance, hard work and unselfish spirit, in fact by every kind of service.*

But then would come more ominous dispatches. Decimus was

in desperate straits after more than four months trapped in Mutina. He could only communicate with the outside world by carrier pigeon, and the few birds that got through brought news of starvation, disease and low morale. Lepidus meanwhile was moving his legions closer to the scene of the impending battle with Antony, and he urged Cicero and the Senate to consider a fresh offer of peace talks. Cicero was so incensed by this weak and arrogant man's presumption that he dictated to me a letter that went off that same night:

Cicero to Lepidus.

I rejoice at your desire to make peace among citizens but only if you can separate that peace from slavery. Otherwise you should understand that all men of sense have taken a resolution to prefer death to servitude. You will act more wisely in my judgement if you meddle no further in this affair, which is not acceptable either to the Senate or the people, or to any honest man.

Cicero was under no illusions. The city and the Senate still harboured hundreds of Antony's supporters. If Decimus surrendered, or if the armies of Hirtius, Pansa and Octavian were defeated, he knew he would be the first to be seized and murdered. As a safety precaution he ordered home two of the three legions stationed in Africa to defend Rome. But they would not arrive until the middle of the summer.

It was on the twentieth day of April that the crisis finally broke. Early that morning, Cornutus, the urban praetor, hurried up the hill. With him was a messenger who had been dispatched by Pansa six days earlier. Cornutus's expression was grim. 'Tell Cicero,' he said to the messenger, 'what you've just told me.'

In a trembling voice the messenger said, 'Vibius Pansa regrets to report a catastrophic defeat. He and his army were surprised by the forces of Mark Antony at the settlement of Forum Gallorum. The lack of experience of our men was immediately evident. The line broke and there was a general slaughter. The consul managed to escape but is himself wounded.'

Cicero's face turned grey. 'And Hirtius and Caesar? Any news of them?'

Cornutus said, 'None. Pansa was on his way to their camp but was attacked before he could join them.'

Cicero groaned.

Cornutus said, 'Should I summon a meeting of the Senate?'

'Dear gods, no!' To the messenger Cicero said, 'Tell me the truth – does anyone else in Rome yet know about this?'

The messenger bowed his head. 'I went first to the consul's home. His father-in-law was there.'

'Calenus!'

Cornutus said grimly, 'He knows it all, unfortunately. He's in the Portico of Pompey at this very moment, on the exact spot where Caesar was struck down. He's telling anyone who'll listen that we're paying the price for an impious killing. He accuses you of planning to seize power as dictator. I believe he's gathering quite a crowd.'

I said to Cicero, 'We ought to get you out of Rome.'

Cicero shook his emphatically. 'No, no. *They're* the traitors, not I. Damn them, I'll not run away. Find Appuleius,' he ordered the urban praetor briskly, as if he were his head steward. 'Tell him to call a public assembly and then to come and fetch me. I'll speak to the people. I need to steady their nerves. They must be reminded that there's always bad news in war. And you,' he said to the messenger, 'had better not breathe a word of this to another soul, do you understand, or I'll have you put in chains.'

I never admired Cicero more than I did that day, when he stared ruin in the face. He went into his study to compose an oration, while I, from the terrace, watched the Forum begin to fill with citizens. Panic has its own pattern. I had learned to recognise it over the years. Men run from one speaker to another. Groups form and dissolve. Sometimes the public space clears entirely. It is like a cloud of dust drifting and whirling before the onset of a storm.

Appuleius came toiling up the hill as requested and I took him in to see Cicero. He reported that the current rumour going round was that Cicero was to be presented with the fasces of a dictator. It was a trick, of course – a provocation that would be the pretext for his murder. The Antonians would then ape the tactics of Brutus and Cassius and seize the Capitol and try to hold it until Antony arrived in the city to relieve them.

Cicero asked Appuleius, 'Will you be able to guarantee my security if I come down to address the people?'

'I can't give an absolute guarantee, but we can try.'

'Send as big an escort as you can. Allow me one hour to get myself ready.'

The tribune went away, and to my astonishment Cicero then announced that he would have a bath and be shaved, and change into a fresh set of clothes. 'Make sure you write all this down,' he said to me. 'It will make a good end for your book.'

He went off with his body slaves, and by the time he came back an hour later, Appuleius had assembled a strong force out in the street, consisting mostly of gladiators along with his fellow tribunes and their attendants. Cicero braced his shoulders, the door was opened, and he was just about to cross the threshold when the lictors of the urban praetor came hurrying up the road, clearing a path for Cornutus. He was holding a dispatch.

His face was wet with tears. Too out of breath and emotional to speak, he thrust the dispatch into Cicero's hands.

From Hirtius to Cornutus. Before Mutina.

I send you this in haste. Thanks be to the gods, we have this day retrieved an earlier disaster and won a great victory over the enemy. What was lost at noon has been recouped at sunset. I led out twenty cohorts of the Fourth Legion to relieve Pansa and fell upon Antony's men when they were celebrating prematurely. We have captured two eagles and sixty standards. Antony and the remnants of his army have retreated to his camp, where they are trapped. Now it is his turn to taste what it is like to be besieged. He has lost the greater part of his veteran troops; he has only cavalry. His position is hopeless. Mutina is saved. Pansa is wounded but should recover. Long live the Senate and people of Rome. Tell Cicero.

XVIII

What followed was the greatest day of Cicero's life – more hard-won than his victory over Verres, more exhilarating than his election to the consulship, more joyful than his defeat of Catilina, more historic than his return from exile. All those triumphs dwindled to nothing in comparison to the salvation of the republic.

That day I reaped the richest of rewards for my many days of labour and sleepless nights, wrote Cicero to Brutus. *The whole population of Rome thronged to my house and escorted me up to the Capitol, then set me on the Speakers' Platform amid tumultuous applause.*

The moment was all the sweeter for having been preceded by such bitter despair. 'This is your victory!' he shouted from the rostra to the thousands in the Forum. 'No,' they called back, 'it is *your* victory!' The following day in the Senate he proposed that Pansa, Hirtius and Octavian should be honoured by an unprecedented fifty days of public thanksgiving, and a monument erected to the fallen: 'Brief is the life given us by nature; but the memory of a life nobly sacrificed is everlasting.' None of his enemies dared oppose him: either they stayed away from the session or voted tamely as he asked. Every time he stepped out of doors he was cheered. He was at his zenith. All he needed now was the final official confirmation that Antony was dead.

A week later came a dispatch from Octavian:

From G. Caesar to his friend Cicero.

I am scribbling this by lamplight in my camp on the evening of the twenty-first. I wanted to be the first to tell you that we have won a second great victory over the enemy. For a week, my legions, in close alliance with those of the gallant Hirtius, probed the defences of Antony's camp for weaknesses. Last night we found a suitable place and this morning we attacked. The fighting was bloody and obstinate, the slaughter great. I was in the midst of it. My standard-bearer was killed beside me. I shouldered the eagle and carried it. This rallied our men. Decimus, seeing that the decisive moment had arrived, at last led his forces out of Mutina and joined the battle. The greater part of Antony's army was destroyed. The villain himself, with his cavalry, has fled, and judging by the direction of his flight he means to cross the Alps.

So much is wonderful. But now I must tell you the hard part. Hirtius, despite his failing health, advanced with great spirit into the very heart of the enemy camp and had reached Antony's own tent when he was struck down by a fatal sword thrust to his neck. I have retrieved his body and will return it to Rome, where I am sure you will see that he receives the honours due to a brave consul. I shall write again when I can. Perhaps you will tell his sister.

When he had finished reading, Cicero passed me the letter, then clenched his fists together and raised his eyes to heaven. 'I thank the gods I have been allowed to see this moment.'

'Though it is a pity about Hirtius,' I added. I was thinking of all those dinners under the stars in Tusculum.

'True – I am very sorry for his sake. Still: how much better to die swiftly and gloriously in battle rather than lingeringly and squalidly on a sickbed. This war has been waiting for a hero. I shall make it my business to put Hirtius on the vacant plinth.'

He took Octavian's letter with him to the Senate that morning, intending to read it aloud, to deliver 'the eulogy to end all eulogies' and to propose a state funeral for Hirtius. It was a measure of his buoyant spirits that he could take the loss of a consul so lightly. On the steps of the Temple of Concordia he met the urban praetor, who was also just arriving. Senators were streaming in to take their places. The auspices were being taken. Cornutus was grinning. He said, 'I surmise by your expression that you too have heard the news of Antony's final defeat?'

'I am in raptures. Now we must make sure the villain doesn't escape.'

'Oh, take it from an old soldier – we have more than enough men to cut him off. A pity, though, that it cost us the life of a consul.'

'Indeed – a wretched business.' Side by side the two men began to climb the steps towards the entrance. Cicero said, 'I thought I would deliver a eulogy, if that is all right by you.'

'Of course, although Calenus has already asked me if *he* might say something.'

'Calenus! What business is it of his?'

Cornutus stopped and turned to Cicero. He looked surprised. 'Well, because Pansa was his son-in-law . . .'

'What are you talking about? You've got it the wrong way round. Pansa isn't dead; it's Hirtius who has died.'

'No, no. It's Pansa, I assure you. I received a message from Decimus last night. Look.' And he gave the dispatch to Cicero. 'He says that once the siege was lifted, he set off directly for Bononia to consult with Pansa on how they should best pursue

Antony, only to discover that he had succumbed to the wounds he received in the first battle.'

Cicero refused to believe it. Only when he read Decimus's letter did he have to concede there was no doubt. 'But Hirtius is dead as well – killed while storming Antony's camp. I have a letter here from young Caesar confirming that he has taken custody of the body.'

'*Both* consuls are dead?'

'It's unimaginable.' Cicero appeared so dazed by the news, I thought he might topple backwards down the steps. 'In the entire existence of the republic, only eight consuls have died during their year in office. Eight – in nearly five hundred years! And now we lose two in the same week!'

Some of the passing senators had stopped to look at them. Conscious that they were being overheard, Cicero drew Cornutus to one side and spoke to him in a quiet, urgent voice. 'This is a dark moment, but we must live through it. Nothing can be allowed to impede our pursuit and destruction of Antony. That is the alpha and omega of our policy. There are plenty of our colleagues who will try to exploit this tragedy to create mischief.'

'Yes, but who will command our forces in the absence of the consuls?'

Cicero made a sound that was something between a groan and a sigh and put his hand to his brow. What a mess this made of all his careful planning, of all his delicate balancing of power! 'Well, I suppose there's no alternative. It will have to be Decimus. He's the senior in age and experience, and he's the governor of Nearer Gaul.'

'What about Octavian?'

'Leave Octavian to me. But we will need to vote him the most extraordinary thanks and honours if we're to keep him in our camp.'

'Is it wise to make him up to be so mighty? One day he'll turn on us, I'm sure of it.'

'Perhaps he will. But we can deal with him later. He can be raised, praised and erased.'

It was the sort of cynical remark Cicero often made for effect: a play on words; a knowing joke, nothing more. Cornutus said, 'Very good, I must remember that – *raised, praised, erased.*' Then the two discussed how best to break the news to the Senate, what motions should be proposed and how the votes should be taken, and after that they proceeded into the temple.

'The nation has sustained a triumph and a tragedy in the same breath,' Cicero told the silent Senate. 'A mortal danger has been lifted but only at a mortal price. The news has just been received that we have won a second and decisive victory at Mutina. Antony is in flight with his few remaining followers, to where we do not know – to the north, to the mountains, to the gates of hell itself for all we care!' (My notes record cheers at this point.) 'But gentlemen, I have to tell you: Hirtius is dead. Pansa is dead.' (Gasps, cries, protests.) 'The gods demanded a sacrifice in expiation for our weakness and our folly over recent months and years, and our two gallant consuls have paid it in full measure. In due course their earthly remains will be returned to the city. We will lay them to rest with solemn honours. We will build a great monument to their valour that men will gaze upon for a thousand years. But we will honour them best by finishing the task they so nearly completed and extirpating Antony once and for all. (Applause.)

'I propose that in the light of the loss of our consuls at Mutina, and mindful of the need to prosecute the war to its end, Decimus

Junius Albinus be appointed commander-in-chief of the Senate's armies in the field and that Gaius Julius Caesar Octavianus should be his deputy in all matters; and that in recognition of their brilliant generalship, heroism and success, the name of Decimus Junius Albinus should be added to the Roman calendar to mark his birthday for eternity, and that Gaius Julius Caesar Octavianus should be awarded the honour of an ovation as soon as it is convenient for him to come to Rome to receive it.'

The ensuing debate was full of mischief. As Cicero wrote to Brutus, *That day I realised that gratitude has considerably fewer votes in the Senate than spite.* Isauricus, as jealous of Octavian as he had been of Antony, objected to the idea of awarding him an ovation, which would allow him to parade with his legions through Rome. In the end Cicero was only able to carry his proposal by agreeing to give Decimus the even greater honour of a triumph. A commission of ten men was set up to settle the remuneration, in cash and land, of all the soldiers: the idea was to draw them away from Octavian, reduce their bounty and put them on the payroll of the Senate. To add insult to this injury, neither Octavian nor Decimus was invited to join the commission. Calenus, dressed in mourning, also demanded that his son-in-law's doctor, Glyco, be arrested and examined under torture if necessary to determine whether Pansa's death was murder: 'Remember we were assured to begin with that his injuries were not serious, but now we can see that certain persons stand to gain greatly by his removal' – an obvious reference to Octavian.

All in all it was a bad day's work, and Cicero had to sit down that night and explain to Octavian what had happened.

I am sending you by the same courier the resolutions that have today been agreed by the Senate. I hope you will accept the logic of our placing you and your soldiers under the command of Decimus, just as you were previously subordinate to the consuls. The Commission of Ten is a bit of nonsense I shall try to have rescinded: give me time. You should have been there, my dear friend, to hear the encomia! The rafters rang with praise of your daring and loyalty, and I am glad to say that you will be the youngest commander in the history of the republic to be granted the distinction of an ovation. Press on with your pursuit of Antony, and keep that place in your heart for me that I keep in mine for you.

After that there was silence.

For a long time Cicero heard nothing from the theatre of operations. That was not surprising. It was remote, inhospitable country. He comforted himself by imagining Antony with his lonely band of followers struggling along the inaccessible narrow mountain passes while Decimus raced to try to cut him off. It was not until the thirteenth day of May that news arrived from Decimus – and then, as is often the way with these things, not one but three dispatches arrived all at once. I took them straight to Cicero in his study; he opened the document case greedily and read them aloud in order. The first was dated the twenty-ninth of April and put Cicero on his guard at once: *I shall try to ensure that Antony is unable to maintain himself in Italy. I shall be after him immediately.*

'Immediately?' said Cicero, checking again the date at the head of the letter. 'What is he talking about? He's already writing eight days after Antony fled Mutina . . .'

The next dispatch was written a week later, when Decimus was finally on the march:

The reasons, my dear Cicero, why I was unable to pursue Antony at once are these. I had no cavalry, no pack animals. I did not know of Hirtius's death. I did not trust Caesar until I had met and talked to him. So the first day passed. Early on the next I had a message from Pansa summoning me to Bononia. As I was on my way, I received the report of his death. I hastened back to my own apology for an army. It is most sadly reduced and in very bad shape through lack of all the necessities. Antony got two days' start of me and made far longer marches as the pursued than I as the pursuer, for he went helter-skelter, while I moved in regular order. Wherever he went he opened up the slave barracks and carried off the men, stopping nowhere until he reached Vada. He seems to have made up a pretty sizeable body. He may go to Lepidus.

If Caesar had listened to me and crossed the Apennines I should have put Antony in so tight a corner that he would have been finished by lack of supplies rather than cold steel. But there is no giving orders to Caesar, nor by *Caesar to his army – both very bad things. What alarms me is how this situation can be straightened out. I cannot any longer feed my men.*

The third letter was written a day after the second and dispatched from the foothills of the Alps: *Antony is on the march. He is going to Lepidus. Please look to future action in Rome. You will counter the world's malice towards me if you can.*

'He has let him get away,' said Cicero, resting his head in his hand and reading the letters through again. '*He has let him get away!* And now he says that Octavian can't or won't obey him as commander-in-chief. Well, this is a pretty mess!'

He wrote a letter at once for the courier to take back to Decimus:

From what you write, the flames of war, so far from having been extinguished, seem to be blazing higher. We understood that Antony had fled in despair with a few unarmed and demoralised followers. If in fact his condition is such that a clash with him will be a dangerous matter, I do not regard him as having fled from Mutina at all but as having shifted the war to another theatre.

The next day, the funeral cortège of Hirtius and Pansa reached Rome, escorted by an honour guard of cavalry sent by Octavian. It passed through the streets to the Forum at dusk, watched by hushed and sombre crowds. At the base of the rostra the Senate, all in black togas, waited by torchlight to receive it. Cornutus gave a eulogy that Cicero had written for him, and then the vast assembly walked behind the biers to the Field of Mars, where the pyres had been prepared. As a mark of patriotic respect the undertakers, actors and musicians refused to take any payment; Cicero joked that when an undertaker won't take your money, you know you are a hero. But beneath his public show of bravado, in private he was profoundly troubled. As the torches were put to the base of the pyres, and the flames shot up, Cicero's face in the firelight looked old and hollowed with worry.

Almost as worrying as the fact that Antony had escaped was that Octavian either would not or could not obey Decimus's order. Cicero wrote to him, pleading with him to abide by the Senate's edict and place himself and his legions under the governor's command: *Let any differences be sorted out after victory has been attained; believe me, the surest way to achieve the highest honour in the state will be to play the fullest part now in destroying its greatest enemy.* Ominously, he received no reply.

Then Decimus wrote again:

Labeo Segulius tells me that he has been with Octavian and that a good deal of talk about you took place. Octavian to be sure made no complaints about you, he says, except for a remark which he attributed to you: 'The young man should be raised, praised and erased.' He added that he had no intention of letting himself be erased. As for the veterans, they are grumbling viciously about you and you are in danger from them. They mean to terrorise you and replace you with the young man.

I had long warned Cicero that his fondness for making puns and amusing asides would one day land him in trouble. But he couldn't help himself. He had always enjoyed a reputation as a caustic wit, and as he grew older he had only to open his mouth and people would flock around him, eager to laugh. The attention flattered him and served to inspire him to make ever more cutting remarks. His dry observations were quickly repeated; sometimes phrases were attributed to him he had never even uttered: indeed, I have compiled a whole book of these apocrypha. Caesar used to delight in his barbs, even when he was himself the target – for example, when as dictator he changed the calendar and someone enquired whether the Dog Star would still rise on the same date, Cicero replied, 'It will do as it is told.' Caesar was said to have roared with laughter. But his adopted son, whatever his other merits, was deficient when it came to a sense of humour, and for once Cicero took my advice and wrote a letter of apology.

I gather that confounded fool Segulius is going round telling all and sundry about some joke I am supposed to have made, and that now word of it has reached your ears. I cannot remember making the remark but I shall not disown it, for it sounds the sort of thing I might have said – lightly delivered, meant for the moment, not fit to be examined as a serious statement of policy. I know I do not need to tell you how fond I am of you, how zealously I guard your interests, how determined I am that you should play the leading part in our affairs in the years to come; but if I have caused offence, I am truly sorry.

His letter drew this response:

From G. Caesar to Cicero.

My feelings for you are unchanged. No apology is needed, although if it pleases you to make one, naturally I accept it. Unfortunately my supporters are not so easy-going. They warn me every day that I am a fool to put my faith in you and in the Senate. Your unguarded remark was catnip to them. Really – that Senate edict! How could I have been expected to place myself under the command of the man who lured my father to his death? My relations with Decimus are civil but we never can be friends, and my men, who are my father's veterans, will never follow him. There is only one circumstance, they say, that would make them fight for the Senate without reservation: if I am made consul. Is that impossible? Both consulships are vacant after all, and if I can be pro-praetor at nineteen, why not consul?

This letter made Cicero blanch. He wrote back at once to say that, divinely inspired though Octavian was, the Senate would never agree to a man not yet even twenty becoming consul. Octavian replied equally swiftly:

My youth, it seems, is not an impediment to my leading an army on the field of battle but it is to my becoming consul. If age is the only issue, could I not have as a consular colleague someone who is as old as I am young, and whose political wisdom and experience would make up for my lack of it?

Cicero showed the letter to Atticus. 'What do you make of this? Is he suggesting what I think he is?'

'I'm sure that's what he's implying. Would you do it?'

'I can't pretend the honour would be meaningless to me – very few men have been consul twice; that would mean immortal glory, and I'm doing the job in all but name in any case. But the price! We've already had to confront one Caesar with an army at his back demanding an illegal consulship, and we ended up fighting a war to try to stop him. Do we now have to confront another, and this time tamely surrender to him? How would it look to the Senate, and to Brutus and Cassius? Who is planting these ideas in the young man's head?'

'Perhaps he doesn't need anyone to plant them there,' Atticus replied. 'Perhaps they arise quite spontaneously.'

Cicero made no reply. The possibility did not bear contemplating.

Two weeks later, Cicero received a letter from Lepidus, who was encamped with his seven legions at Pons Argenteus in southern Gaul. After he had read it, he leaned forwards and rested his head on his desk. With one hand he pushed the letter towards me.

We have long been friends but I have no doubt that in the present violent and unexpected political crisis my enemies have brought you false and unworthy reports about me, designed to give your patriotic heart no small disquiet. I have one earnest request to make of you, dear Cicero. If previously my life and endeavour, my diligence and good faith in the conduct of public affairs have to your knowledge been worthy of the name I bear, I beg you to expect equal or greater things in time to come, as your kindness places me further and further in your debt.

'I don't understand,' I said. 'Why are you so upset?'

Cicero sighed and sat up straight. To my alarm I saw that he had tears in his eyes. 'Because it means he intends to join forces with Antony and is providing himself with an alibi in advance. His duplicity is so clumsy it's almost endearing.'

He was right of course. On that very day, the thirtieth of May, when Cicero was receiving Lepidus's false assurances, Antony himself – long-haired and bearded after almost forty days on the run – was arriving on the riverbank opposite Lepidus's camp. He waded chest-deep through the water wearing a dark cloak, went up to the palisade and began talking to the legionaries. Many recognised him from the Gallic and the civil wars; they flocked to hear him. The next day he brought all his forces over the river and Lepidus's men welcomed them with outstretched arms. They tore down their fortifications and let Antony stroll unarmed into the camp. He treated Lepidus with the greatest respect, called him by the title 'Father' and insisted that if he joined his cause he would retain the rank and honours of a general. The soldiers cheered. Lepidus agreed.

Or that at least was the story they cooked up together. Cicero was sure they had been partners from the start and that their rendezvous had been arranged in advance. It simply made Lepidus seem less of the traitor he was if he could pretend he had bowed to *force majeure*.

It took nine days for Lepidus's dispatch announcing this shattering turn of events to reach the Senate, although panicky rumours ran ahead of his messenger. Cornutus read it out in the Temple of Concordia:

> *I call on gods and men to witness how my heart and mind have ever been disposed towards the commonwealth and freedom. Of this I should shortly have given you proof, had not Fortune wrested the decision out of my hands. My entire army, faithful to its inveterate tendency to conserve Roman lives and the general peace, has mutinied; and, truth to tell has compelled me to join them. I beg and implore you, do not treat the compassion shown by myself and my army in a conflict between fellow countrymen as a crime.*

When the urban praetor finished reading, there was a great collective sigh, a groan almost, as if the whole chamber had been holding its breath in the hope that the rumours would turn out not to be true. Cornutus gestured to Cicero to open the debate. In the ensuing silence as Cicero rose to his feet one could feel an almost childlike yearning for reassurance. But Cicero had none to offer.

'This news from Gaul, which we have long suspected and dreaded, comes as no surprise, gentlemen. The only shock is the impudence of Lepidus in taking us all to be idiots. He begs us, he implores us, he entreats us – this creature! No, not even that: these bitter, squalid dregs of a noble line that merely assume the form of a human being! – he begs us not to regard his treachery as a crime. The cowardice of the fellow! I would have more respect for him if he came right out and told the truth: that he sees an opportunity to further his monstrous ambitions and has found a fellow thief to be his partner in crime. I propose that he be declared a public enemy forthwith and that all his property and estates be confiscated to help us pay for the fresh legions we shall require to replace those he has stolen from the state.'

This drew loud applause.

'But it will take us a while to raise new forces, and in the meantime we must face the salutary fact that our strategic situation is perilous in the extreme. If the fires of rebellion in Gaul spread to Plancus's four legions – and I fear we must brace ourselves for that possibility – we may have the best part of sixty thousand men ranged against us.'

Cicero had decided beforehand that he would not try to disguise the extent of the crisis. Silence gave way to murmurs of alarm.

'We should not despair,' he continued, 'not least because we have that number of soldiers ourselves, assembled by the noble and gallant Brutus and Cassius – but they are in Macedonia; they are in Syria; they are in Greece; they are not in Italy. We also have one legion of new recruits in Latium, and the two African legions that are even now at sea and on their way home to defend the capital. And then there are the armies of Decimus and Caesar – although the one is enfeebled and the other truculent.

'We have every chance, in other words. But there is no time to be lost.

'I propose that this Senate orders Brutus and Cassius immediately to send back to Italy sufficient forces to enable us to defend Rome; that we intensify our levies to raise new legions; and that we impose an emergency tax on property of one per cent to enable us to purchase arms and equipment. If we do all of this, and if we draw strength from the spirit of our ancestors and the justice of our cause, it remains my confident belief that liberty will triumph in the end.'

He delivered his closing remarks with all his usual force and vigour. But when he sat down, there was scant applause. The dreadful stench of likely defeat hung in the air, as acrid as burning pitch.

Isauricus rose next. Hitherto this haughty and ambitious patrician had been the staunchest senatorial opponent of the presumptuous Octavian. He had denounced his elevation to a special praetorship; he had even tried to deny him the relatively modest honour of an ovation. But now he delivered a paean of praise to the young Caesar that amazed everyone. 'If Rome is to be defended against Antony's ambitions, backed up now by the forces of Lepidus, then I have come to believe that Caesar is the man upon whom we must chiefly rely. His is the name that can conjure armies from thin air and make them march and fight. His is the shrewdness that can bring us peace. As a symbol of my faith in him, I have to tell you, gentlemen, that I have lately offered him the hand of my daughter in marriage, and I am gratified to be able to tell you he has accepted.'

Cicero twitched suddenly in his seat as if he had been caught by some invisible hook. But Isauricus hadn't finished yet: 'To bind this excellent young man to our cause still further, and to encourage his men to fight against Mark Antony, I propose the following motion: that in view of the grave military situation created by the treachery of Lepidus, and mindful of the service he has already rendered to the republic, the constitution be so amended that Gaius Julius Caesar Octavianus may be permitted to stand for the office of consul *in absentia*.'

Afterwards Cicero cursed himself for not having seen this coming. It was obvious, once one stopped to think about it, that if Octavian could not persuade Cicero to stand for the consulship as his partner, then he would ask someone else. But occasionally even the shrewdest statesman misses the obvious, and now Cicero found himself in an awkward spot. He had to assume that Octavian had already done a deal with his putative father-in-law. Should he accept it with good grace or should he oppose it? He had no time to think. All around him the benches were abuzz with speculation. Isauricus was sitting with his arms folded, looking very pleased with the sensation he had created. Cornutus called upon Cicero to respond to the proposition.

He stood slowly, adjusting his toga, glancing around, clearing his throat – all his familiar delaying tactics to purchase some time to think. 'May I first of all congratulate the noble Isauricus on the excellent family connection he has just announced? I know the young man to be honourable, moderate, modest, sober, patriotic, valiant in war and of calm good judgement – everything in short that a son-in-law should be. He has had no stronger advocate in this Senate than I. His future career in the republic is both glittering and assured. He will be consul, I am sure. But whether he should be consul when he is not yet twenty and solely because he has an army is a different matter.

'Gentlemen, we embarked upon this war with Antony for a principle: the principle that no man – however gifted, however powerful, however ambitious for glory – should be above the law. Whenever in the course of my thirty years in the service of the state we have yielded to temptation and ignored the law, often for what seemed at the time to be good reasons, we have slipped a little further toward the precipice. I helped to pass the special legislation that gave Pompey unprecedented powers to fight the war against the pirates. The war was a great success. But the most lasting consequence was not the defeat of the pirates: it was to create the precedent that enabled Caesar to rule Gaul for almost a decade and to grow too mighty for the state to contain him.

'I do not say that the younger Caesar is like the elder. But I do say that if we make him consul, and in effect give him control of all our forces, then we will betray the very principle for which we fight: the principle that drew me back to Rome when I was on the point of sailing to Greece – that the Roman Republic, with its division of powers, its annual free elections for every magistracy, its law courts and its juries, its balance between Senate and people, its liberty of speech and thought, is mankind's noblest creation, and I would sooner lie choking in my own blood upon the ground than betray the principle on which all this stands – that is, first and last and always, the rule of law.'

His remarks elicited warm applause and entirely set the course of the debate – so much so that Isauricus, with icy formality and a glare at Cicero, later withdrew his proposal and it was never voted upon.

I asked Cicero if he intended to write to Octavian to explain his stand. He shook his head. 'My reasons are in my speech and he will have it in his hands soon enough – my enemies will see to that.'

In the days that followed he was as busy as he had ever been – writing to Brutus and Cassius to urge them to come to the aid of the tottering republic (*the commonwealth is in the gravest peril because of the criminal folly of M. Lepidus*), overseeing the tax inspectors as they set about raising revenue, touring the blacksmiths' yards to cajole them into making more weapons, inspecting the newly raised legion with Cornutus, who had been appointed military defender of Rome. But he knew the cause was hopeless, especially when he saw Fulvia being carried openly in a litter across the Forum, accompanied by a large entourage.

'I thought we were rid of that shrew, at least,' he complained over dinner, 'yet here she is, still in Rome and flaunting herself around, even though her husband has at last been declared a public enemy. Is it in any wonder we're in such desperate straits? How is it possible, when all her property is supposed to have been seized?'

There was a pause and then Atticus said quietly, 'I lent her some money.'

'You?' Cicero leaned across the table and peered at him as if he were some mysterious stranger. 'Why on earth would you do that?'

'I felt sorry for her.'

'No you didn't. You wanted to put Antony under an obligation to you. It's insurance. You think we're going to lose.'

Atticus did not deny it, and Cicero left the table.

At the end of that wretched month, 'July', reports reached the Senate that Octavian's army had struck camp in Nearer Gaul, crossed the Rubicon, and was marching on Rome. Even though he had been half expecting it, the news still struck Cicero as a tremendous blow. He had given his word to the Roman people that if 'the heaven-sent boy' was given imperium, he would be a model citizen. *Every imaginable evil chance has dogged us in this war*, he lamented to Brutus. *As I write, I am in great distress, because it hardly looks as though I can make good my promises in respect to the young man, boy almost, for whom I went bail to the republic.* It was then he asked me if I thought he was honour-bound to kill himself, and for the first time I saw that he was not saying it for effect. I replied that I did not think it had come to that yet.

'Perhaps not, but I must be ready. I don't want these veterans of Caesar's torturing me to death as they did Trebonius. The question is how to do it. I'm not sure I could face a blade – do you think posterity will reckon the less of me if I choose Socrates's method and take hemlock instead?'

'I am sure not.'

He asked me to acquire some of the poison on his behalf and I went to see his doctor that same day, who gave me a small jar. He did not ask why I wanted it; I suppose he knew. Despite the wax seal, I could smell its rank odour, like mouse droppings. 'It's made from the seeds,' he explained, 'the most poisonous part of the plant, which I have crushed into a powder. The smallest dose, no more than a pinch, swallowed with water, should do the trick.'

'How long does it take to work?'

'Three hours or thereabouts.'

'Is it painful?'

'It induces slow suffocation – what do you think?'

I put the jar into a box in my room, and placed the box inside a locked chest, as if by hiding it away, death itself could be postponed.

The next day, gangs of Octavian's legionaries began to appear in the Forum. He had sent four hundred on ahead of his main army, with the aim of intimidating the Senate into granting him the consulship. Whenever they saw a senator, they surrounded him and jostled him and showed him their swords, although they never actually drew their weapons. Cornutus, as an old soldier, refused to be threatened. Determined to visit Cicero on the Palatine, the urban praetor pushed and shoved them back until they let him through. But he advised Cicero that on no account should he venture out himself unless he had a strong escort: 'They hold you as much responsible for Caesar's death as they do Decimus or Brutus.'

'If only I *had* been responsible! Then we would have taken care of Antony at the same time and we wouldn't be in the mess we are today.'

'Well here is some better news for you: the African legions arrived last night, and we didn't lose a single ship. Eight thousand men and a thousand cavalry are disembarking at Ostia even as I speak. That should be enough to hold off Octavian, at least until Brutus and Cassius send us help.'

'But are they loyal?'

'So their commanders assure me.'

'Then bring them here as quickly as possible.'

The legions were only a day's march from Rome. As they approached the city, Octavian's men slipped away into the surrounding countryside. When the vanguard reached the salt warehouses, Cornutus ordered the column to parade through the Trigemina Gate and across the Forum Boarium in full view of the crowds in order to steady civilian morale. Then they took up position on the Janiculum. From these strategic heights they controlled the western approaches to Rome and could deploy rapidly to block any invading force. Cornutus asked Cicero if he would come out and inspire the men with a rousing speech. Cicero agreed, and he was carried out of the city gates in a litter accompanied by fifty legionaries on foot. I rode on a mule.

It was a hot, muggy day without a tremor of wind. We crossed the River Tiber over the Sublician Bridge and traipsed along a road of dried mud through the shanty towns that have for as long as I can remember filled the flat plain of the Vaticanum. It was notoriously malarial in the summer, and swarming with hostile insects. Cicero's litter had the protection of a mosquito net but I did not, and the insects whined in my ears. The whole place stank of human filth. Children, pot-bellied with hunger watched us listlessly from the doorways of tumbling shacks, while all around them, disregarded and pecking away at the rubbish, were hundreds of the crows that nest in the nearby sacred grove. We passed through the gates of the Janiculum and went up the hill. The place was teeming with soldiers. They had pitched their tents wherever they could find some space.

On the flatter ground at the top of the slope Cornutus had drawn up four cohorts – almost two thousand men. They stood in lines in the heat. The light on their helmets dazzled as brightly as the sun, and I had to shield my eyes. When Cicero stepped out of his litter there was absolute silence. Cornutus conducted him to a low platform beside an altar. A sheep was sacrificed. Its guts were pulled out and examined by the haruspices and declared propitious: 'There is no doubt of ultimate victory.' The crows circled overhead. A priest read a prayer. Then Cicero spoke.

I cannot remember exactly what he said. All the usual words were there – liberty, ancestors, hearths and altars, laws and temples – but for once I listened without hearing. I was looking at the faces of the legionaries. They were sunburnt, lean, impassive. Some were chewing mastic. I saw the scene through their eyes. They had been recruited by Caesar to fight against King Juba and the army of Cato. They had slaughtered thousands and had been stuck in Africa ever since. They had travelled hundreds of miles crammed together in boats. They had been force-marched for a day. Now they were lined up in the heat in Rome and an old man was talking at them about liberty, ancestors, hearths and altars – and it meant nothing.

Cicero finished speaking. There was silence. Cornutus ordered them to give three cheers. The silence continued. Cicero stepped off the platform and got back into his litter and we returned down the hill, past the saucer-eyed starving children.

Cornutus came to see Cicero the following morning and told him that the African legions had mutinied overnight. It seemed that Octavian's men had crept back from the countryside in the darkness, infiltrated the camps and promised the soldiers twice as much money as the Senate could afford to pay them. Meanwhile Octavian's main army was reported to be moving south along the Via Flaminia and was barely a day's march away.

'What will you do now?' Cicero asked him.

'Kill myself,' came the reply, and he did, that same evening, pressing the tip of his sword to his stomach and falling upon it heavily rather than surrender.

He was an honourable man and deserves to be remembered, not least because he was the only member of the Senate who took that course. When Octavian was close to the city, most of the leading patricians went out to meet him on the road to escort him into Rome. Cicero sat in his study with the shutters closed. The air was so close it was hard to breathe. I looked in from time to time but he did not seem to have moved. His noble head, staring straight ahead and silhouetted against the faint light from the window, was like a marble bust in a deserted temple. Finally he noticed me and asked where Octavian had set up his headquarters.

I replied that he had moved into the home of his mother and stepfather on the Quirinal.

'Perhaps you could send a message to Philippus and ask him what he suggests I should do.'

I did as he requested and the courier returned with a scrawled reply that Cicero ought to go and talk to Octavian: 'You will find him, I am sure, as I did, disposed to mercy.'

Wearily Cicero got to his feet. The big house, usually thronged with visitors, was empty. It felt as if no one had lived in it for a long time. In the late summer afternoon sun the silent public rooms glowed as if made of gold and amber.

We went together, in a pair of litters accompanied by a small escort, to the house of Philippus. Sentries guarded the street and the front door but they must have been given orders to let Cicero through, for they parted at once. As we crossed the threshold, Isauricus was just leaving. I had expected him, as Octavian's future father-in-law, to give Cicero a smile of condescension or of triumph; instead he scowled at him and hurried past us.

Through the heavy open door we could see Octavian standing in a corner of the tablinum dictating a letter to a secretary. He beckoned to us to enter. He seemed in no hurry to finish. He was wearing a simple military tunic. His body armour, helmet and sword lay scattered on a couch where he had flung them. He looked like a young recruit. Finally he ended his dictation and sent the secretary away.

He scrutinised Cicero in an amused way that reminded me of his adopted father. 'You are the last of my friends to greet me.'

'Well, I imagined you would be busy.'

'Ah, is that it?' Octavian laughed, revealing those terrible teeth of his. 'I was presuming that you disapproved of my actions.'

Cicero shrugged. 'The world is as it is. I have given up the habit of approving and disapproving. What's the point? Men do as they please, whatever I think.'

'So what is it you want to do? Do you want to be consul?'

For the merest fraction of a moment Cicero's face seemed to flood with pleasure and relief, but then he understood that Octavian was joking and immediately the light went out of it again. He grunted, 'Now you're toying with me.'

'I am. Forgive me. My colleague as consul will be Quintus Pedius, an obscure relative of mine of whom you will never have heard, which is the whole point of him.'

'So not Isauricus?'

'No. There seems to have been some misunderstanding there. I shan't be marrying his daughter either. I shall spend some time here settling matters and then I must go and confront Antony and Lepidus. You can leave Rome too if you like.'

'I can?'

'Yes, you can leave Rome. You can write philosophy. You can go anywhere you please in Italy. However, you cannot return to Rome in my absence, nor can you attend the Senate. You cannot write your memoirs or anything political. You cannot leave the country and go to Brutus or Cassius. Is that acceptable? Will you give me your word? I can assure you my men would not be so generous.'

Cicero bowed his head. 'It is generous. It is acceptable. I give you my word. Thank you.'

'In return I will guarantee your safety, in recognition of our past friendship.' He picked up a letter to signal that the audience was at an end. 'One last thing,' he said as Cicero turned to leave. 'It makes no difference, but I would like to know: was it a joke, or would you really have erased me?'

'I believe I would have done exactly the same as you are doing now,' replied Cicero.

XIX

After that, he seemed to become an old man very suddenly. He retired to Tusculum the next day and immediately started complaining about his eyesight. He refused to write or even read: he said it gave him a headache. He took no solace from his garden. He visited no one and no one visited him, apart from his brother. They would sit together for hours on a bench in the Lyceum, mostly in silence. The only subject Quintus could tempt him to discuss was the distant past – their shared memories of childhood and of growing up in Arpinum – and for the first time I heard Cicero talk at length about his father and mother. It was unnerving to see him, of all men, so disconnected from the world. Throughout his life he had demanded to know the latest news from Rome. Now, when I told him what I had heard was happening – that Octavius had set up a special court to try the assassins of Caesar, or even that he had left the city at the head of an army of eleven legions to fight Antony – he made no comment, save that he preferred not even to think about it. A few more weeks of this, I thought to myself, and he will die.

People often ask me why he did not try to run away. After all, Octavian did not yet have any firm control of the country. The weather was still clement. The ports were not watched. Cicero could have slipped out of Italy to join his son in

Macedonia: I am sure Brutus would have been only too pleased to offer him sanctuary. But the truth was he lacked the will to do anything so decisive. 'I am finished with running,' he sighed to me. He couldn't even summon the energy to go down to the Bay of Naples. Besides, Octavian had guaranteed his safety.

I guess it must have been about a month after our retreat to Tusculum that he sought me out one morning and told me he would like to review his old letters: 'This constant talk with Quintus about my early years has stirred the sediment of my memory.' I had preserved them all, however fragmentary, incoming and outgoing, over more than three decades, and had sorted them by correspondent and arranged them on rolls chronologically. I carried the cylinders into his library and he lay on the couch while one of his secretaries read them out. It was all there, an entire life, from his early struggles to gain election to the Senate, through the hundreds of legal cases he took to make his name famous and which culminated in the epic prosecution of Verres, his election to aedile and then to praetor and finally to consul, his struggles with Catilina and Clodius, his exile and return, his relations with Caesar and Pompey and Cato, the civil war, the assassination, his return to power, Tullia and Terentia . . .

For more than a week he relived his life, and at the end he had recovered something of his old self. 'What an adventure it has been,' he mused, stretching out on the couch. 'It has all come back to me, the good and the bad, the noble and the base. I truly believe I can say, without being immodest, that these letters add up to the most complete record of an historical era ever assembled by a leading statesman. And what an era! No one else saw so much, and wrote about it while it was still fresh. This is history composed without any benefit of hindsight. Can you think of anything to compare with it?'

'It will be of immense interest a thousand years from now,' I said, trying to encourage his new good mood.

'Oh, it's more than merely of interest! It's the case for my defence. I may have lost the past and lost the present, but I wonder if with this I might not yet win the future.'

Some of the letters showed him in a bad light – vain, duplicitous, greedy, wrong-headed – and I expected him to weed out the most egregious examples and order me to destroy them. But when I asked him which letters he wished me to discard, he replied, 'We must keep them all. I can't present myself to posterity as some improbable paragon – no one will believe it. If this archive is to have the necessary authenticity, I must stand before the muse of history as naked as a Greek statue. Let future generations mock me for my follies and pretensions however much they like – the important thing is that they will have to read me, and in that will lie my victory.'

Of all the sayings associated with Cicero, the most famous and characteristic is: 'While there is life there is hope.' He still had life – or the semblance of it, at least; and now he had the faintest gleam of hope.

Beginning that day, he concentrated what remained of his strength on the task of ensuring his papers survived. Atticus eventually agreed to help, on condition he was allowed to retrieve every letter he had ever written to Cicero. Cicero rather despised him for his caution but in the end agreed: 'If he wants to be a mere shadow in history, that's his lookout.' With some reluctance I returned the correspondence I had carefully assembled over so many years and watched as Atticus lit a brazier and – not trusting the task to a servant – burnt with his own hand all the rolls on which his letters had been preserved. Then he put his scribes to work. Three complete sets of the collected letters were produced.

Cicero kept one, Atticus another and I the third. I sent mine down to my farm along with locked boxes containing all my shorthand notes recording thousands of meetings, speeches, conversations, witticisms and barbed remarks, as well as the dictated drafts of his books. I told the overseer that it all should be hidden in one of the barns and that if anything happened to me he should give it to Agathe Licinia, the freedwoman who owned the baths of Venus Libertina at Baiae. Quite what she would do with it, I was not sure, but I sensed that I could trust her above all people in the world.

At the end of November, Cicero asked me if I would go back to Rome to make sure the last of his papers had been removed from his study, and to carry out a final general inspection. The house was being sold on his behalf by Atticus, and much of the furniture had already gone. It was the start of winter. The morning was chilly, the light gloomy. I wandered between the empty rooms as if I were an invisible spirit, and in my imagination I re-peopled them. I saw the tablinum once again filled with statesmen discussing the future of the republic, heard Tullia's laughter in the dining room, saw Cicero bent over his books of philosophy in the library attempting to explain why fear of death was illogical . . . My eyes were blurred with tears; my heart ached.

Suddenly a dog began to howl – so loudly and frantically that my bittersweet fantasies vanished in an instant. I stopped to listen. Our old dog had gone. This had to be a neighbour's. It was a most piteous wailing and it set off others. I went out on to the terrace. The sky was dark with swirls of starlings, and all across Rome dogs were howling like wolves. Indeed it was later said that at this very moment a wolf was seen darting across the Forum; that statues sweated blood and a newly born baby spoke. I heard the sound of running feet and looking down saw a group of men whooping with delight, racing towards the rostra and tossing to one another what I thought at first was a football but then realised was a human head. A woman started screaming in the street. Without thinking what I was doing I went out to see who it was and found the wife of our elderly neighbour, Caesetius Rufus, crawling on her knees in the gutter, while behind her the trunk of a corpse gushed blood from its neck across the threshold. Her steward, who I knew quite well, was running hopelessly to and fro. Panicking, I grabbed his arm and shook him until he told me what had happened – Octavian, Antony and Lepidus had joined forces and had published a list of hundreds of senators and equestrians who were to be killed and their fortunes seized. There was a bounty of a hundred thousand sesterces for each head that was brought to them. Both of the Cicero brothers were named on the list, and Atticus.

'That cannot be true,' I assured him. 'We have a solemn promise.'

'It's true,' he cried. 'I've seen it.'

I ran back to the house, where the few remaining slaves were gathered, frightened, in the atrium. 'Everyone must scatter,' I told them. 'If they catch us they will torture us to try to make us reveal the whereabouts of the master. If it comes to it, say he is in Puteoli.' I scribbled out a message to Cicero: *You and Quintus and Atticus are proscribed – Octavian has betrayed you – the death squads are looking for you – make at once for your house on the island – I will find you a boat.* I gave it to the ostler and told him to take it by his fastest horse to Cicero in Tusculum. Then I went to the stables and found my carriage and driver and ordered him to set off for Astura.

Even as we clattered down the hill, gangs of men armed with

knives and staves were running up on to the Palatine, where the richest human pickings would be found, and I banged my head against the side of the carriage in my anguish that Cicero hadn't made good his escape from Italy while he had the chance.

I made that unfortunate driver whip his poor pair of horses until their flanks bled so that we could arrive in Astura before nightfall. We found the boatman in his hut, and even though the sea was beginning to get up and the light was dim, he rowed us the hundred yards over to the little island where Cicero's villa stood secluded in the trees. It had not been visited by him for months, and the slaves were amazed to see me, and not a little resentful at having to light fires and heat the rooms. I lay down on my damp mattress and listened to the wind buffeting around the roof and rustling the trees. As the waves crashed against the rocky shore and the house creaked, I was full of terror, imagining that every sound might be the arrival of Cicero's murderers. If I had brought that jar of hemlock, I almost think I might have taken it.

The next morning the weather was calmer, although when I walked through the trees and contemplated the huge expanse of grey sea with the lines of white waves running in to the shore, I felt utterly desolate. I wondered if this was a foolish plan and that we would do better to make directly for Brundisium, which at least was on the right side of Italy for a voyage east. But of course news of the proscriptions and the vast bounty for a severed head would race ahead of us, and nowhere would be safe. Cicero would never reach the harbour alive.

I sent my driver off in the direction of Tusculum with a second letter for Cicero, saying that I had arrived 'on the island' – I kept it vague in case the message fell into the wrong hands – and urging him to make all speed. Then I asked the boatman to go to Antium to see if he could charter a vessel to carry us down the coast. He looked at me as if I were mad to make such a request in winter, when the weather was so treacherous, but after some grumbling he went away, and came back the following day to say that he had procured a ten-oared boat with a sail that would be with us as soon as they could row the seven miles from Antium. After that there was really nothing I could do except wait.

The wooded islet of Astura was the place where Cicero had gone to ground after Tullia had died. He had found the absolute silence, except for the sounds of Nature, soothing; I found the opposite: they jangled my nerves, especially as day after day passed when nothing happened. I kept a regular lookout, but it wasn't until late in the afternoon on the fifth day that there was a sudden eruption of activity on the shoreline. Two litters arrived through the trees accompanied by a retinue of slaves. The boatman rowed me over to take a look, and as we drew closer, I saw that on the beach stood Cicero and Quintus. When I hurried over the sand to greet them, I was shocked by their appearance. Neither had changed his clothes or shaved; both were red-eyed from crying. A light rain was falling. Drenched, they looked like a pair of indigent old men. Quintus, if anything, was in a worse state than Cicero. After a sorrowful greeting, he took one look at the boat I had hired, pulled up on to the beach, and announced he would not set foot in it for a moment.

He turned to Cicero. 'My dear brother, this is hopeless. I don't know why I've let you drag me here, except that all my life I have done what you have told me. Look at us! Old men, we're in failing health. The weather is poor. We have no money. We would be better off following Atticus's example.'

I asked, 'Where is Atticus?'

Cicero said, 'He's gone into hiding in Rome.' He started to cry. He made no attempt to disguise it. And then, as quickly as he had started, he stopped and continued speaking as if nothing had happened. 'No, I'm sorry, Quintus, I can't live in someone's cellar, trembling every time there's a knock at the door. Tiro's plan is as good as any. Let's see how far we can get.'

Quintus said, 'Then I'm afraid that we must part, and I shall pray to meet you again – if not in this life then the next.'

They fell into one another's arms and clung to each other tightly, then Quintus broke away. He embraced me. None of those watching the scene could restrain their tears. Certainly I was overcome by the sadness of it all. After that, Quintus climbed back into his litter and was borne away up the track and into the trees.

It was too late for us to set off that day, and so we were rowed over to the villa. While Cicero dried himself at the fire, he explained that he had lingered for two days in Tusculum, unable to believe that Octavian had betrayed him, sure that there must have been some mistake. This much he had discovered: that Octavian had met Antony and Lepidus in Bononia, on an island in the middle of the river – just the three of them, with a couple of secretaries: they had left their bodyguards behind and had searched one another for concealed weapons – and that over the next three days, working from dawn till dusk, they had divided up the carcass of the republic between them, and to pay their armies had compiled a death list of two thousand wealthy men, including two hundred senators, whose property would be seized. 'I am told by Atticus, who heard it from the consul Pedius, that each of the criminals, as a token of good faith, was required to mark for death someone who was precious to them. Thus

Antony gave up his uncle, Lucius Caesar, even though he spoke in his defence in the Senate; Lepidus yielded his brother, Aemilius Paullus; and Octavian offered me – Antony insisted, although Pedius maintained the boy had been reluctant to agree.'

'Do you believe it?'

'Not particularly. I have looked into those pale grey soulless eyes of his once too often. He is no more affected by the death of a man than he is by the death of a fly.' He let out a sigh that seemed to shake his entire body. 'Oh Tiro, I am so tired! To think that I, of all people, have been outwitted at the last by a young man who has barely started to shave! Do you have that poison I asked you to get?'

'It's in Tusculum.'

'Well then, I can only pray to the immortal gods to allow me to die tonight in my sleep.'

But he did not die. He woke depressed, and the next morning, when we were standing on the little quay waiting for the sailors to pick us up, he suddenly announced that he would not leave after all. Then when the boat came within earshot, one of the sailors shouted up to us that he had just seen a unit of legionaries on the road from Antium, heading in our direction, led by a military tribune. That immediately shook Cicero out of his lethargy. He held out his hand and the sailors helped him down into the boat.

Our voyage quickly began to repeat the pattern of our first flight into exile. It was as if Mother Italy could not bear to allow her favourite son to leave her. We had gone about three miles, hugging close to the shore, when the grey sky began to fill with immense black clouds rolling in from the horizon. A wind got up, stirring the sea into steep waves, and our little boat seemed to rise almost to the perpendicular, only to crash down again, bow first, and saturate us with salt water. If anything, it was worse than before, because this time there was no shelter. Cicero and I sat huddled in hooded cloaks while the men tried to row us crosswise into the oncoming waves. The hull began to fill and the vessel became dangerously low. We all had to help bail, even Cicero, frantically scooping up the freezing water with our hands and tipping it over the side to stop ourselves sinking. Our limbs and faces were numb. We swallowed salt. The rain blinded us. Eventually, after rowing bravely for many hours, the sailors were exhausted, and told us they needed to rest. We rounded a rocky promontory and headed towards a cove, rowing as close to the beach as we could before we all had to jump out and wade ashore. Cicero sank in almost to his waist and four of the sailors had to carry him on to the land. They laid him down and went back to help their crewmates with the boat, hauling it right up on to the beach. They laid it on its side and propped it up using branches cut from the nearby myrtle trees, and with the sail and the mast they built a makeshift shelter. They even managed to light a fire, although the wood was wet, and the wind blew the smoke this way and that, choking us and making our eyes smart.

Darkness soon came, and Cicero, who had not uttered a word of complaint, appeared to sleep. Thus ended the fifth day of December.

I woke at dawn on the sixth after a fitful night to find calmer skies. My bones were chilled, my damp clothes stiff with salt and sand. I stood with difficulty and looked about me. Everyone was still asleep, except for Cicero. He had gone.

I looked up and down the beach and peered out to sea, then turned to scan the trees. There was a small gap, which turned out to lead to a path, and I set off, calling his name. At the top of the path was a road. Cicero was lurching along it. I called to him again but he ignored me. He was making slow and unsteady progress in the direction from which we had come. I caught him up and fell in beside him and spoke to him with a calmness I did not feel.

'We need to get back in the boat,' I said. 'The slaves in the house may have told the legionaries where we are headed. They may not be far behind us. Where are you going?'

'To Rome.' He did not look at me but kept on walking.

'To do what?'

'To kill myself on Octavian's doorstep. He will die of shame.'

'He won't,' I said, and caught his arm, 'because he has no shame, and the soldiers will torture you to death like they did Trebonius.'

He glanced at me and stopped walking. 'Do you think so?'

'I know it.' I took him by the arm and tugged him gently. He did not resist but lowered his head and allowed me to lead him like a child back through the trees to the beach.

How melancholy it is to relive all of this! But I have no choice if I am to fulfil my promise to him and tell the story of his life.

We put him back on to the boat and launched it once more into the waves. The day was grey and vast, as at the dawn of time. We rowed on for many hours, assisted by a breeze that filled the sail, and by the end of the afternoon had covered, by my reckoning, a further twenty-five miles or thereabouts. We passed the famous Temple of Apollo that stands a little above the sea on the headland at Caieta, and Cicero, who had been slumped, staring vacantly towards the shore, suddenly recognised it, sat up straight and said, 'We are nearly at Formiae. I have a house here.'

'I know you do.'

'Let us put in here for the night.'

'It's too risky. You're well known to have a villa at Formiae.'

'I don't care about that,' replied Cicero with something of his old firmness. 'I want to sleep in my own bed.'

And so we rowed towards the shore and tied up at the jetty that was built out into the sea a little way from the villa. As we moored, a great flock of crows rose cawing from the nearby trees as if in warning, and I asked Cicero at least to allow me to make sure his enemies weren't lying in wait for him before he disembarked. He agreed, and I set off up the familiar path through the trees, accompanied by a couple of the sailors. The path led us to the Via Appia. By now it was almost dusk. The road was empty. I walked about fifty paces to where Cicero's villa stood behind a pair of iron gates. I went up the drive and knocked firmly on the oak door, and after a short interval and a great noise of bolts drawn back, the porter appeared. He was startled to see me. I looked past his shoulder and asked if any strangers had come looking for the master. He assured me they had not. He was a good-hearted, simple fellow. I had known him for years, and I believed him.

I said, 'In that case, send four slaves with a litter down to the jetty to pick up the master and bring him to the villa, and meanwhile have a hot bath drawn for him and fresh clothes and food prepared, for he is in a poor state.'

I also sent two other slaves with fast horses to keep a lookout along the Via Appia for this mysterious and ominous detachment of legionaries that seemed to be on our trail.

Cicero was carried into the villa, and the gate and door were locked behind him.

I saw little of him after that. As soon as he had had his bath, he took a little food and wine in his room and then retired to sleep.

I slept myself – and very deeply, despite my anxieties, for such was my exhaustion – and the following morning had to be roughly woken by one of the slaves I had stationed along the Via Appia. He was out of breath and frightened. A force of thirty legionaries on foot, with a centurion and a tribune on horseback, was marching towards the house from the north-west. They were less than half an hour away.

I ran to wake Cicero. He had the covers up to his chin and refused to stir, but I tore them off him anyway.

'They are coming for you,' I said, bending over him. 'They're almost here. We have to move.'

He smiled at me, and laid his hand on my cheek. 'Let them come, old friend. I am not afraid.'

I pleaded with him: 'For my sake, if not for yours – for the sake of your friends and for Marcus – please *move*!'

I think it was the mention of Marcus that did it. He sighed. 'Very well, then. But it is quite pointless.'

I withdrew to let him dress and ran around issuing orders – a litter to be ready immediately, the boat prepared to sail with the sailors at their oars, the gate and the door to be locked the moment we were out of the villa, the household slaves to vacate the premises and hide wherever they could.

In my imagination I could hear the steady tramp of the legionaries' boots becoming louder and louder . . .

At length – far too great a length! – Cicero appeared looking as immaculate as if he were on his way to address the Senate. He walked through the villa saying goodbye to everyone. They were all in tears. He took a last look around as if saying farewell to the building and all his beloved possessions, and then climbed into the litter, closed the curtains so that no one could see his face, and we set off out of the gate. But instead of the slaves all making a run for it, they seized such weapons as they could find – rakes, brooms, pokers, kitchen knives – and insisted on coming with us, forming a homely rustic phalanx around the litter. We went the short distance along the road and turned down the path into the woods. Through the trees I could glimpse the sea shining in the morning sun. Escape seemed close. But then, at the bottom of the path, just before it opened out on to the beach, a dozen legionaries appeared.

The slaves at the front of our little procession cried out in alarm, and those carrying the litter scrambled to turn it round. It swayed dangerously and Cicero was almost pitched to the ground. We struggled back the way we had come, only to discover that more soldiers were above us, blocking access to the road.

We were trapped, outnumbered, doomed. Nevertheless, we determined to make a fight. The slaves set the litter down and surrounded it. Cicero drew back the curtain to see what was going on. He saw the soldiers advancing rapidly towards us and shouted to me: 'No one is to fight!' Then to the slaves he said: 'Everyone lay down your weapons! I am honoured by your devotion, but the only blood that needs to be shed here is mine.'

The legionaries had their swords drawn. The military tribune leading them was a hirsute, swarthy-looking brute. Beneath the ridge of his helmet his eyebrows merged together to form a continuous thick black line. He called out, 'Marcus Tullius Cicero, I have a warrant for your execution.'

Cicero, still lying in his litter, his chin in his hand, looked him up and down very calmly. 'I know you,' he said, 'I'm sure of it. What's your name?'

The military tribune, plainly taken aback, said, 'My name, if you must know it, is Caius Popillius Laenas, and yes, we do know one another: not that it will save you.'

'Popillius,' murmured Cicero, 'that's it,' and then he turned to me. 'Do you remember this man, Tiro? He was our client – that fifteen-year-old who murdered his father, right at the beginning of my career. He'd have been condemned to death for parricide if I hadn't got him off – on condition he went into the army.' He laughed. 'This is a kind of justice, I suppose.'

I looked at Popillius and indeed I did remember him.

Popillius said, 'That's enough talk. The verdict of the Constitutional Commission is that the death sentence should be carried out immediately.' He gestured to his soldiers to drag Cicero from his litter.

'Wait,' said Cicero, 'leave me where I am. I have it in mind to die this way,' and he propped himself up on his elbows like a defeated gladiator, threw back his head and offered his throat to the sky.

'If that's what you want,' said Popillius. He turned to his centurion. 'Let's get it over with.'

The centurion took up his position. He braced his legs. He swung his sword. The blade flashed, and in that instant for Cicero the mystery that had plagued him all his life was solved, and liberty was extinguished from the earth.

Afterwards they cut off his head and hands and put them in a sack. They made us sit down and watch them while they did it. Then they marched away. I was told that Antony was so delighted with these extra trophies that he gave Popillius a bonus of a million sesterces. It is also said that Fulvia pierced Cicero's tongue with a needle. I do not know. What is certainly true is that on

Antony's orders the head that had delivered the Philippics and the hands that had written them were nailed up on the rostra, as a warning to others who might think of opposing the Triumvirate, and they stayed there for many years, until finally they rotted and fell away.

After the killers had gone, we carried Cicero's body down to the beach and built a pyre, and at dusk we burned it. Then I made my way south to my farm on the Bay of Naples.

Little by little I learned more of what had happened.

Quintus was soon afterwards captured with his son and put to death.

Atticus emerged from hiding and was pardoned by Antony because of the help he had given Fulvia.

And much, much later, Antony committed suicide together with his mistress Cleopatra after Octavian defeated them in battle. The boy is now the Emperor Augustus.

But I have written enough.

Many years have passed since the episodes I have recounted. At first I thought I would never recover from Cicero's death. But time wipes out everything, even grief. Indeed, I would go so far as to say that grief is almost entirely a question of perspective. For the first few years I used to sigh and think, 'Well, he would still be in his sixties now,' and then a decade later, with surprise, 'My goodness, he would be seventy-five,' but nowadays I think, 'Well, he would be long since dead in any case, so what does it matter how he died in comparison with how he lived?'

My work is done. My book is finished. Soon I will die too.

In the summer evenings I sit on the terrace with Agathe, my wife. She sews while I look at the stars. Always at such moments I think of Scipio's dream of where dead statesmen dwell in *On the Republic*:

> *I gazed in every direction and all appeared wonderfully beautiful. There were stars which we never see from earth, and they were all larger than we have ever imagined. The starry spheres were much greater than the earth; indeed the earth itself seemed to me so small that I was scornful of our empire, which covers only a single point, as it were, upon its surface.*

'If only you will look on high,' the old statesman tells Scipio, 'and contemplate this eternal home and resting place, you will no longer bother with the gossip of the common herd or put your trust in human reward for your exploits. Nor will any man's reputation endure very long, for what men say dies with them and is blotted out with the forgetfulness of posterity.'

All that will remain of us is what is written down.

DRAMATIS PERSONAE

AFRANIUS, LUCIUS an ally of Pompey's from his home region of Picenum; one of Pompey's army commanders in the war against Mithradates; consul in 60 BC

AGRIPPA, MARCUS VIPSANIUS Octavian's closest associate, aged twenty

AHENOBARBUS, LUCIUS DOMITIUS patrician senator; praetor in 58 BC; married to Cato's sister; a determined enemy of Caesar

ANTONY, MARK (MARCUS ANTONIUS) renowned as a brave and enterprising soldier under Caesar's command in Gaul; grandson of a famous orator and consul; stepson of one of the Catiline conspirators executed by Cicero

ATTICUS, TITUS POMPONIUS Cicero's closest friend; an equestrian, an Epicurean, immensely wealthy; brother-in-law to Quintus Cicero, who is married to his sister, Pomponia

BALBUS, LUCIUS CORNELIUS wealthy Spaniard originally allied to Pompey and then to Caesar, whose *homme d'affaires* he became in Rome

BIBULUS, MARCUS CALPURNIUS Caesar's colleague as consul in 59 BC, and his staunch opponent

BRUTUS, MARCUS JUNIUS direct descendant of the Brutus who drove the kings from Rome and established the republic in the sixth century BC; son of Servilia, nephew of Cato; the great figurehead of the constitutionalists

CAESAR, GAIUS JULIUS former consul; a member of the 'triumvirate' with Pompey and Crassus; governor of three Roman provinces – Nearer and Further Gaul and Bithynia; six years Cicero's junior; married to Calpurnia, daughter of L. Calpurnius Piso

CALENUS, QUINTUS FUFIUS an old crony of Clodius and Antony; a supporter of Caesar and an enemy of Cicero; father-in-law of Pansa

CASSIUS, GAIUS LONGINUS senator and able soldier; married to Servilia's daughter, Junia Tertia, and thus Brutus's brother-in-law

CATO, MARCUS PORCIUS half-brother of Servilia; uncle of Brutus; a Stoic and a stern upholder of the traditions of the republic

CICERO, MARCUS TULLIUS JUNIOR Cicero's son

CICERO, QUINTUS TULLIUS Cicero's younger brother; senator and soldier; married to Pomponia, the sister of Atticus; governor of Asia, 61–58 BC

CICERO, QUINTUS TULLIUS JUNIOR Cicero's nephew

CLODIA daughter of one of the most distinguished families in Rome, the patrician Appii Claudii; the sister of Clodius; the widow of Metellus Celer

CLODIUS PULCHER, PUBLIUS scion of the leading patrician dynasty, the Appii Claudii; a former brother-in-law of L. Lucullus; the brother of Clodia, with whom he is alleged to have had an incestuous affair; at his trial for sacrilege Cicero gave evidence against him; transferred to the plebs at the instigation of Caesar and elected tribune

CORNUTUS, MARCUS one of Caesar's officers, appointed urban praetor in 44 BC

CRASSIPES, FURIUS Tullia's second husband; a senator; a friend of Crassus

CRASSUS, MARCUS LICINIUS former consul; member of the 'triumvirate'; brutal suppressor of the slave revolt led by Spartacus; the richest man in Rome; a bitter rival of Pompey

CRASSUS, PUBLIUS son of Crassus the triumvir; cavalry commander under Caesar in Gaul; an admirer of Cicero

DECIMUS properly styled BRUTUS, DECIMUS JUNIUS ALBINUS, but not to be confused with BRUTUS (above); brilliant young military commander in Gaul; a protégé of Caesar

DOLABELLA, PUBLIUS CORNELIUS Tullia's third husband; one of Caesar's closest lieutenants – young, charming, precocious, ambitious, licentious, brutal

FULVIA wife of Clodius; subsequently married to Mark Antony

HIRTIUS, AULUS one of Caesar's staff officers in Gaul, groomed for a political career; a noted gourmet, a scholar who helped Caesar with his *Commentaries*

HORTENSIUS HORTALUS, QUINTUS former consul, for many years the leading advocate at the Roman bar, until displaced by Cicero; a leader of the patrician faction; immensely wealthy; like Cicero, a civilian politician and not a soldier

ISAURICUS, PUBLIUS SERVILIUS VATIA a patrician, son of one of the grand old men of the Senate, who nevertheless chose to support Caesar; elected praetor in 54 BC

LABIENUS, TITUS a soldier and former tribune from Pompey's home region of Picenum; one of Caesar's ablest commanders in Gaul

LEPIDUS, MARCUS AEMILIUS patrician senator, married to a daughter of Servilia; member of the College of Pontiffs

MILO, TITUS ANNIUS a tough street-wise politician, an owner of gladiators

NEPOS, QUINTUS CAECILIUS METELLUS consul at the time of Cicero's return from exile

OCTAVIAN, GAIUS JULIUS CAESAR Caesar's great-nephew and heir

PANSA, GAIUS VIBIUS one of Caesar's commanders in Gaul

PHILIPPUS, LUCIUS MARCIUS consul soon after Cicero's return from exile; married to Caesar's niece, Atia, and thus the stepfather of Octavian; owner of a villa next door to Cicero's on the Bay of Naples

PHILOTIMUS Terentia's business manager, of questionable honesty

PISO, LUCIUS CALPURNIUS consul at the time of Cicero's exile, and thus an enemy of Cicero's; Caesar's father-in-law

PLANCIUS, GNAEUS quaestor of Macedonia; his family were friends from the same region of Italy as the Ciceros

PLANCUS, LUCIUS MUNATIUS close lieutenant of Caesar, appointed governor of Further Gaul in 44 BC

POMPEY, GNAEUS MAGNUS born in the same year as Cicero; for many years the most powerful man in the Roman world; a former consul and victorious general who has already triumphed twice; a member of the 'triumvirate' with Caesar and Crassus; married to Caesar's daughter, Julia

RUFUS, MARCUS CAELIUS Cicero's former pupil; the youngest senator in Rome – brilliant, ambitious, unreliable

SERVILIA ambitious and politically shrewd half-sister of Cato; the long-term mistress of Caesar; the mother of three daughters and a son Brutus, by her first husband

SERVIUS SULPICIUS RUFUS contemporary and old friend of Cicero, famed as one of the greatest legal experts in Rome; married to Postumia, a mistress of Caesar

SPINTHER, PUBLIUS CORNELIUS LENTULUS consul at the time of Cicero's return from exile; an enemy of Clodius and friend of Cicero

TERENTIA wife of Cicero; ten years younger than her husband, richer and of nobler birth; devoutly religious, poorly educated, with conservative political views; mother of Cicero's two children, Tullia and Marcus

TIRO Cicero's devoted private secretary, a family slave, three years younger than his master, the inventor of a system of shorthand

TULLIA Cicero's daughter

VATINIUS, PUBLIUS a senator and soldier famed for his ugliness; a close ally of Caesar

GLOSSARY

aedile an elected official, four of whom were chosen annually to serve a one-year term, responsible for the running of the city of Rome: law and order, public buildings, business regulations, etc

auspices supernatural signs, especially flights of birds and lightning-flashes, interpreted by the **augurs**; if ruled unfavourable no public business could be transacted

Carcer Rome's prison, situated on the boundary of the Forum and the Capitol, between the Temple of Concord and the Senate house

century the unit in which the Roman people cast their votes on the Field of Mars at election time for consul and praetor; the system was weighted to favour the wealthier classes of society

chief priest see **pontifex maximus**

consul the senior magistrate of the Roman Republic, two of whom were elected annually, usually in July, to assume office in the following January, taking it in turns to preside over the senate each month

comitium the circular area in the Forum, approximately 300 feet across, bounded by the senate house and the rostra, traditionally the place where laws were voted on by the people, and where many of the courts had their tribunals

curule chair a backless chair with low arms, often made of ivory, possessed by a magistrate with imperium, particularly consuls and praetors

dictator a magistrate given absolute power by the senate over civil and military affairs, usually in a time of national emergency

equestrian order the second most senior order in Roman society after the Senate, the 'Order of Knights' had its own officials and privileges, and was entitled to one-third of the places on a jury; often its members were richer than members of the Senate, but declined to pursue a public career

Gaul divided into two provinces: **Nearer Gaul**, extending from the River Rubicon in northern Italy to the Alps, and **Further Gaul**, the lands beyond the Alps roughly corresponding to the modern French regions of Provence and Languedoc

haruspices the religious officials who inspected the entrails after a sacrifice in order to determine whether the omens were good or bad

imperator the title granted to a military commander on active service by his soldiers after a victory; it was necessary to be hailed imperator in order to qualify for a triumph

imperium the power to command, granted by the state to an individual, usually a consul, praetor or provincial governor

legate a deputy or delegate

legion the largest formation in the Roman army, at full strength consisting of approximately 5,000 men

lictor an attendant who carried the fasces – a bundle of birch rods tied together with a strip of red leather – that symbolised a magistrate's imperium; consuls were accompanied by twelve lictors, who served as their bodyguards, praetors by six; the senior lictor, who stood closest to the magistrate, was known as the proximate lictor

manumission the emancipation of a slave

Order of Knights see **equestrian order**

pontifex maximus the chief priest of the Roman state religion, the head of the fifteen-member College of Priests, entitled to an official residence on the Via Sacra

praetor the second most senior magistrate in the Roman republic, eight of whom were elected annually, usually in July, to take office the following January, and who drew lots to determine which of the various courts – treason, embezzlement, corruption, serious crime, etc – they would preside over; see also **urban praetor**

prosecutions as there was no public prosecution system in the Roman Republic, all criminal charges, from embezzlement to treason and murder, had to be brought by private individuals

public assemblies the supreme authority and legislature of the Roman people was the people themselves, whether constitued by **tribe** (the *comitia tributa*, which voted on laws, declared war and peace, and elected the tribunes) or by **century** (the *comitia centuriata*, which elected the senior magistrates)

quaestor a junior magistrate, twenty of whom were elected each year, and who thereby gained the right of entry to the Senate; it was necessary for a candidate for the quaestorship to be over thirty and to show wealth of one million sesterces

rostra a long, curved platform in the Forum, about twelve feet high, surmounted by heroic statues, from which the Roman people were addressed by magistrates and advocates; its name derived from the beaks (*rostra*) of captured enemy warships set into its sides

Senate *not* the legislative assembly of the Roman Republic – laws could only be passed by the people in a tribal assembly – but something closer to its executive, with 600 members who could raise matters of state and order the consul to take action or to draft laws to be placed before the people; once elected via the quaestorship (see **quaestor**) a man would normally remain a senator for life, unless removed by the censors for immorality or bankruptcy, hence the average age was high (*senate* derived from *senex* = old)

tribes the Roman people were divided into thirty-five tribes for the purposes of voting on legislation and to elect the tribunes; unlike the system of voting by **century**, the votes of rich and poor when cast in a tribe had equal weight

tribune a representative of the ordinary citizens – the plebeians – ten of whom were elected annually each summer and took office in December, with the power to propose and veto legislation, and to summon assemblies of the people; it was forbidden for anyone other than a plebeian to hold the office

triumph an elaborate public celebration of homecoming, granted by the Senate to honour a victorious general, to qualify for which it was necessary for him to retain his military imperium – and as it was forbidden to enter Rome whilst still possessing military authority, generals wishing to triumph had to wait outside the city until the Senate granted them a triumph

urban praetor the head of the justice system, senior of all the praetors, third in rank in the republic after the two consuls

ACKNOWLEDGMENTS

My greatest debt over the twelve years it has taken to write this novel and its two predecessors is to the Loeb edition of Cicero's collected speeches, letters and writings, published by Harvard University Press. I have been obliged to edit and compress Cicero's words, but wherever possible I have tried to let his voice come through. Loeb has been my Bible.

I have also made constant use of the great nineteenth-century works of reference edited by William Smith: his *Dictionary of Greek and Roman Antiquities, Dictionary of Greek and Roman Biography and Mythology* (three volumes) and *Dictionary of Greek and Roman Geography* (two volumes); these are now freely available online. *The Magistrates of the Roman Republic, Volume II, 99 BC – 31 BC* by T. Robert S. Broughton was also invaluable, as was *The Barrington Atlas of the Greek and Roman World* edited by Richard J. A. Talbert. Again, wherever possible I have followed the facts and descriptions offered in the original sources – Plutarch, Appian, Sallust, Caesar – and I thank all those scholars and translators who have made them accessible and whose words I have used.

Biographies of, and books about, Cicero, which have given me numberless insights and ideas, include: *Cicero: A Turbulent Life* by Anthony Everitt, *Cicero: A Portrait* by Elizabeth Rawson, *Cicero* by D. R. Shackleton Bailey, *Cicero and his Friends* by Gaston Bossier, *Cicero: The Secrets of his Correspondence* by Jérôme Carcopino, *Cicero: A Political Biography* by David Stockton, *Cicero: Politics and Persuasion in Ancient Rome* by Kathryn Tempest, *Cicero as Evidence* by Andrew Lintott, *The Hand of Cicero* by Shane Butler, *Terentia, Tullia and Publia: the Women of Cicero's Family* by Susan Treggiari, *The Cambridge Companion to Cicero* edited by Catherine Steel, and – still thoroughly readable and useful – *The History of the Life of Marcus Tullius Cicero*, published in 1741 by Conyers Middleton (1683-1750).

Biographies of Cicero's contemporaries which I have found particularly useful include: *Caesar* by Christian Meier, *Caesar* by Adrian Goldsworthy, *The Death of Caesar* by Barry Strauss, *Pompey* by Robin Seager, *Marcus Crassus and the Late Roman Republic* by Allen Ward, *Marcus Crassus, Millionaire* by Frank Adcock, *The Patrician Tribune: Publius Clodius Pulcher* by W. Jeffrey Tatum and *Catullus: A Poet in the Rome of Julius Caesar* by Aubrey Burl.

For the general ambience of Rome – its culture, society and political structure – I have drawn on three works by the incomparable Peter Wiseman – *New Men in the Roman Senate, Catullus and His World* and *Cinna the Poet and other Roman essays*. To these I must also add *The Crowd in Rome in the Late Republic* by Fergus Millar, which analyses how politics might have operated in Cicero's Rome. Also valuable were *Intellectual Life in the Late Roman Republic* by Elizabeth Rawson, *The Constitution of the Roman Republic* by Andrew Lintott, *The Roman Forum* by Michael Grant, *Roman Aristocratic Parties and Families* by Friedrich Münzer (translated by Thérèse Ridley) and (of course) *The Roman Revolution* by Ronald Syme and Theodore Mommsen's *History of Rome*.

For the physical recreation of Republican Rome I relied on the scholarship of *A New Topographical Dictionary of Ancient Rome* by L. Richardson jr, *A Topographical Dictionary of Rome* by Samuel Ball Platner, the *Pictorial Dictionary of Ancient Rome* (two volumes) by Ernest Nash and *Mapping Augustan Rome*, the *Journal of Roman Archaeology* project directed by Lothar Haselberger.

A special word of thanks should go to Tom Holland whose wonderful *Rubicon: The Triumph and Tragedy of the Roman Republic* (2003) first gave me the idea of writing a fictional account of the friendships, rivalries and enmities between Cicero, Caesar, Pompey, Cato, Crassus and the rest.

Dictator is my fourth foray into the ancient world, a series of journeys that began with *Pompeii* (2003). One of the great pleasures of these years has been meeting scholars of Roman history who have been without exception encouraging, even to the extent of electing me a proud if notably undistinguished President of the Classical Association in 2008. For various offers of encouragement and advice over the years I would like to thank in particular Mary Beard, Andrew Wallace-Hadrill, Jasper Griffin, Tom Holland, Bob Fowler, Peter Wiseman and Andrea Carandini. I apologise to those I have forgotten, and naturally absolve all those listed above of any responsibility for what I have written.

The two publishers who first commissioned me to write about Cicero were Sue Freestone in London and David Rosenthal in New York. Like the Roman Empire, they have both moved on, but I would like to thank them for their original enthusiasm and continued friendship. Their successors, Jocasta Hamilton and Sonny Mehta, have stepped into the breach and skilfully steered the project to its conclusion. Thanks also to Gail Rebuck and to Susan Sandon, for gallantly staying the course. My agent, Pat Kavanagh, to my great sadness and that of all her authors, did not live to see the work which she represented completed; I hope she would have enjoyed it. My thanks go to my other agents, Michael Carlisle of Inkwell Management in New York, and to Nicki Kennedy and Sam Edenborough of ILA in London. The estimable Wolfgang Müller, my German translator, once again acted as an unofficial copy-editor. Joy Terekiev and Cristiana Moroni of Mondadori in Italy have shared the journey literally to Tusculum and Formiae.

Finally – *finally* – I would like to thank, as always, my wife, Gill, and also our children, Holly, Charlie, Matilda and Sam, half of whose lives have been lived in the shadow of Cicero. Despite this, or perhaps even because of it, Holly took a degree in classics and now knows far more about the ancient world than her old dad, so it is to her that this book is dedicated.

SPECIAL MESSAGE TO READERS

This book is published under the auspices of

THE ULVERSCROFT FOUNDATION

(registered charity No. 264873 UK)

Established in 1972 to provide funds for research, diagnosis and treatment of eye diseases. Examples of contributions made are: —

A Children's Assessment Unit at Moorfield's Hospital, London.

•

Twin operating theatres at the Western Ophthalmic Hospital, London.

•

A Chair of Ophthalmology at the Royal Australian College of Ophthalmologists.

•

The Ulverscroft Children's Eye Unit at the Great Ormond Street Hospital For Sick Children, London.

You can help further the work of the Foundation by making a donation or leaving a legacy. Every contribution, no matter how small, is received with gratitude. Please write for details to:

THE ULVERSCROFT FOUNDATION,
The Green, Bradgate Road, Anstey,
Leicester LE7 7FU, England.
Telephone: (0116) 236 4325

In Australia write to:
THE ULVERSCROFT FOUNDATION,
c/o The Royal Australian and New Zealand
College of Ophthalmologists,
94-98, Chalmers Street, Surry Hills,
N.S.W. 2010, Australia

John Katzenbach is the author of seven previous novels, one of which was nominated for the Edgar Award. He has been a criminal court reporter for *The Miami Herald* and *Miami News*. He lives in western Massachusetts.

THE ANALYST

'Happy fifty-third birthday, Doctor. Welcome to the first day of your death. You ruined my life. And now I fully intend to ruin yours.' Until the moment he reads those words, New York psychoanalyst Dr Frederick Starks has led a quiet and, so he believes, blameless life. But suddenly he is plunged into a dizzying battle of wits designed by a man who calls himself Rumplestiltskin. The rules: in two weeks Starks must guess his tormentor's identity and the source of his fury. If he succeeds, he goes free. If he fails, one by one, Rumplestiltskin will destroy fifty-two of Dr Starks's loved ones — unless the doctor agrees to kill himself . . .

JOHN KATZENBACH

THE ANALYST

Complete and Unabridged

CHARNWOOD
Leicester

First published in Great Britain in 2002 by
Bantam Press
London

First Charnwood Edition
published 2003
by arrangement with
Transworld Publishers, a division of
The Random House Group Limited
London

British Library CIP Data

Katzenbach, John
The analyst.—Large print ed.—
Charnwood library series
1. Psychologists—New York (State)—New York—Fiction 2. Revenge—Fiction
3. Suspense fiction
4. Large type books
I. Title
813.5′4 [F]

ISBN 0–7089–4882–0

Published by
F. A. Thorpe (Publishing)
Anstey, Leicestershire

Set by Words & Graphics Ltd.
Anstey, Leicestershire
Printed and bound in Great Britain by
T. J. International Ltd., Padstow, Cornwall

This book is printed on acid-free paper

For my fishing buddies:
Ann, Peter, Phil, and Leslie

Part One

THE UNWELCOME LETTER

1

In the year he fully expected to die, he spent the majority of his fifty-third birthday as he did most other days, listening to people complain about their mothers. Thoughtless mothers, cruel mothers, sexually provocative mothers. Dead mothers who remained alive in their children's minds. Living mothers, whom their children wanted to kill. Mr. Bishop, in particular, along with Miss Levy and the genuinely unlucky Roger Zimmerman, who shared his Upper West Side apartment and it seemed the entirety of both his waking life and his vivid dreams with a hypochondriac, manipulative, shrewish woman who seemed dedicated to nothing less than ruining her only child's every meager effort at independence — all of them used the entirety of their hours that day to effuse bitter vitriol about the women who had brought them into this world.

He listened quietly to great surges of murderous hatred, only occasionally interjecting the most modest of benign comments, never once interrupting the anger that spewed forth from the couch, all the time wishing that just one of his patients would take a deep breath and step back from their rage for an instant and see it for what it truly was: fury with themselves. He knew, through experience and training, that eventually, after years of talking bitterly in the oddly detached world of the analyst's office, all of them, even poor, desperate, and crippled Roger Zimmerman, would reach that understanding themselves.

Still, the occasion of his birthday, which reminded him most directly of his own mortality, made him wonder whether he would have enough time remaining to see any of them through to that moment of acceptance which is the analyst's eureka. His own father had died shortly after he reached his fifty-third year, heart weakened through years of chain smoking and stress, a fact that he knew lurked subtly and malevolently beneath his consciousness. So, as the unpleasant Roger Zimmerman moaned and whined his way through the final few minutes of the last session of the day, he was slightly distracted, and not paying the complete attention he should have been when he heard the faint triple buzz of the bell he'd installed in his waiting room.

The bell was his standard signal that a patient had arrived. Every new client was told prior to their first session that upon entry, they were to produce two short rings, in quick succession, followed by a third, longer peal. This was to differentiate the ring from any tradesman, meter reader, neighbor, or delivery service that might have arrived at his door.

Without shifting position, he glanced over at his daybook, next to the clock he kept on the small table behind the patient's head, out of their sight. The six P.M. entry was blank. The clock face read twelve minutes to six, and Roger Zimmerman seemed to stiffen in his position on the couch.

'I thought I was the last every day.'

He did not respond.

'No one has ever come in after me, at least not that I can remember. Not once. Have you changed your schedule around without telling me?'

Again, he did not reply.

'I don't like the idea that someone comes after me,' Zimmerman said decisively. 'I want to be last.'

'Why do you think you feel that way?' he finally questioned.

'In its own special way, last is the same as first,' Zimmerman answered with a harshness of tone that implied that any idiot would have seen the same.

He nodded. Zimmerman had made an intriguing and accurate observation. But, as the poor fellow seemed forever doomed to do, he had made it in the session's final moment. Not at the start, where they might have managed some profitable discussion over the remaining fifty minutes. 'Try to bring that thought with you tomorrow,' he said. 'We could begin there. I'm afraid our time is up for today.'

Zimmerman hesitated, before rising. 'Tomorrow? Correct me if I'm mistaken, but tomorrow is the last day before you disappear for your damn stupid August vacation the same as you do every damn year. What good will that do me?'

Again, he remained silent, letting the query remain floating in the space above the patient's head. Zimmerman snorted loudly. 'Whoever's out there's probably more interesting than I am anyway, huh?' he said bitterly. Then Zimmerman swung his feet off the couch and looked up toward the doctor. 'I don't like it when something is different,' he said sharply. 'I don't like it at all.' He tossed a quick, pointed glare at the doctor as he rose, shaking his shoulders, letting a nasty snarl creep across his face. 'It's supposed to always be the same. I come in, lie down, start talking. Last patient every day. That's the way it's supposed to be. No one likes change.' He sighed, but this time with more than a touch of anger, not resignation. 'All right. Tomorrow, then. Last session before you take off for Paris, Cape Cod, Mars, or wherever you head for and leave me all goddamn alone.' Zimmerman pivoted abruptly and strode purposely across the small office, and out the exit door without once looking back.

For a moment, he remained in his armchair, listening for the faint sound of the angry man's footsteps resounding down the exterior hallway. Then he rose, feeling some of the age that had stiffened his joints and tightened his muscles during the long and sedentary afternoon behind the couch, and made his way to the entrance, a second door that led to his modest waiting room. In some respects, this room with its odd, unlikely design, where he'd established his practice decades ago, was unique, and had been the sole reason he'd rented the apartment in the year after he'd finished his residency and the reason he'd stayed there more than a quarter century.

The office had three doors: one which led to the vestibule, which he'd reinvented as a tiny waiting room; a second, which led directly out to the apartment building corridor; and a third, which took him inside to the modest kitchen, living area, and bedroom of the remainder of the apartment. His office was a sort of personal island, with portals to these other worlds. He often regarded it as a nether-space, a bridge between different realities. He liked that, because he believed the separation of the office from the great outside helped make his own job somewhat easier.

He had no idea which of his patients had returned without an appointment. He could not immediately recall a single instance of a patient doing that, in all his years of practice.

Nor was he able to imagine which patient was in crisis sufficiently to throw such an unexpected change in the relationship between analyst and analysand. Routine was what he built on, routine and longevity, where the sheer weight of words spoken in the artificial but absolute sanctity of the analyst's office finally paved themselves into roads of understanding. Zimmerman was right about that. Change went against the grain. So he briskly crossed the room with the modestly gathered pace of anticipation, slightly unsettled at the idea that something of possible urgency had entered a life he frequently feared had become far too stolid and utterly predictable.

He opened the door to the waiting room and stared ahead.

The room was empty.

For a moment, he was confused, and thought perhaps that he'd imagined the bell ringing, but then, Mr. Zimmerman had heard it as well, and he, too, had recognized the distinctive noise signaling that someone familiar was present in the waiting room.

'Hello?' he said, although there was clearly no one there to hear him.

He could sense his forehead knitting with surprise, and he adjusted the wire-rim glasses perched on his nose. 'Curious,' he said out loud. And then he noticed the envelope left behind on the seat of the single stiff-backed chair he provided for patients waiting for their appointments. He exhaled slowly, shook his head back and forth, and thought this was a bit overly melodramatic, even for the membership of his current list of patients.

He stepped over and picked up the envelope. His name was typed on the outside.

'How unusual,' he said out loud. He hesitated before opening the letter, holding it up to his forehead the way Johnny Carson used to, when engaged in his Carnac the Magnificent routine, trying, in that instant, to guess which of his patients had left it for him. But it was an act that seemed uncharacteristic among the dozen he saw regularly. They all liked to voice their complaints about what they perceived as his many inadequacies and shortcomings directly and frequently, which while sometimes irritating, remained an integral part of the process.

He tore open the envelope and withdrew two sheets of paper filled with typing. He read only the first line:

Happy 53rd birthday, doctor. Welcome to the first day of your death.

He breathed in sharply. The stale air of the apartment seemed to make him dizzy, and he reached out quickly for the wall, to steady himself.

* * *

Dr. Frederick Starks, a man in the profession of introspection, lived alone, haunted by other people's memories.

He walked over to his small, antique maple desk, a gift fifteen years earlier from his wife. It had been three years since she passed away, and when he sat down at the desk it seemed he could still hear her voice. He spread the two sheets of the letter out in front of him on the blotter. He thought to himself that it had been a decade since he'd actually been afraid of something, and what he'd been afraid of then was the diagnosis delivered by the oncologist to his wife. Now, this new dry, acid taste on his tongue was as unwelcome as the acceleration of his heart, which he could feel racing in his chest.

He took a second or two to try to calm the rapid beating, waiting patiently until he could feel the rate settle slowly. He was acutely aware of his loneliness at that moment, hating the vulnerability that solitude created within him.

Ricky Starks — he rarely let anyone know how much he greatly preferred the playground and frat house sound of the informal abbreviation to the more sonorous Frederick — was a man of necessary routine and order. He was devoted to a regularity that bordered on religion and certainly touched obsession; by imposing so much reason on his own day-to-day life, he thought it was the only safe way to try to make sense of the turmoil and chaos that his patients brought to him daily. He was a slight man physically, an inch or two short of six feet, with a thin, ascetic body helped by a daily lunchtime course of brisk walking exercise and a steadfast refusal to indulge in the sweets and ice creams that he secretly adored.

He wore glasses, which wasn't unusual for a man his age, though he took pride in the detail that his prescription still was minimal. He took pride, as well, that although thinned, his hair still rode upright on his scalp like wheat on a prairie. He no longer smoked, and took only a rare glass of wine on an occasional evening to help him sleep. He was a man who had grown accustomed to his solitude, undaunted by eating dinner in a restaurant alone, or attending a Broadway show or current movie by himself. He thought the inventory of his body and mind to be in excellent condition. He felt far younger than his years most days. But he was acutely aware that the year he was entering was the year that his father had failed to live past, and despite that lack of logic in this observation, he had not thought that he would live past fifty-three, either, as if such an act would be unfair, or was somehow inappropriate. And yet, he thought contradictorily to himself, as he stared again at the first words of the letter, I am not yet ready to die. Then he read on, slowly, pausing over each sentence, allowing dread and disquiet to take root within him.

I exist somewhere in your past.
You ruined my life. You may not know how, or why, or even when, but you did. Brought disaster and sadness to my every second. You ruined my life. And now I fully intend to ruin yours.

Ricky Starks breathed in hard again. He lived in a world common with false threats and fake promises, but knew immediately that the words in front of him were far different from those meandering rantings he was accustomed to hearing daily.

At first, I thought I should simply kill you to settle the score. Then I realized that was simply too easy. You are a pathetically facile target, doctor. You do not lock your doors during the day. You take the same walk on the same route Monday through Friday. On weekends, you remain wondrously predictable, right down to the trip out on Sunday morning to pick up the Times*, an onion bagel, and a hazelnut coffee, two sugars, no milk, at the trendy coffee bar two blocks to your south.*

Far too easy. Stalking and killing you wouldn't have been much of a challenge. And, given the ease with which this murder could be accomplished, I wasn't certain that it would deliver the necessary satisfaction. I've decided I would prefer you to kill yourself.

Ricky Starks shifted uncomfortably in his seat. He could feel heat rippling up from the words in front of him, like fire catching in a woodstove, caressing his forehead and cheeks. His lips were dry, and he fruitlessly ran his tongue over them.

Kill yourself, doctor.

Jump from a bridge. Blow your brains out with a handgun. Step in front of a midtown bus. Leap in front of a subway train. Turn on the gas stove and blow out the pilot light. Find a convenient beam and hang yourself. The method you choose is entirely up to you.

But it is your best chance.

Your suicide will be far more appropriate, given the precise circumstances of our relationship. And certainly a far more satisfying method for you to pay off your debt to me.

So, here is the game we are going to play: You have exactly one fortnight, starting tomorrow morning at six A.M.*, to discover who I am. If you succeed, you must purchase one of those tiny one-column ads that run along the bottom of the daily* New York Times *front page, and print my name there. That's all: Just print my name.*

If you do not, then . . . well, this is the fun part. You will take note that the second sheet of this letter contains the names of fifty-two of your relatives. They range in age from a newborn, barely six months old, the child of your great-grandniece, to your cousin the Wall Street investor, and capitalist extraordinaire, who is as dried-up and dull as you. If you are unable to purchase the ad as described, then you have this choice: Kill yourself immediately or I will destroy one of these innocent people.

Destroy.

What an intriguing word. It could mean financial ruin. It could mean social wreckage. It could mean psychological rape.

It could also mean murder. That's for you to wonder about. It could be someone young, or someone old. Male or female. Rich or poor.

All I promise is that it will be the sort of event that they — or their loved ones — will never recover from, no matter how many years they might spend in psychoanalysis.

And whatever it is, you will live every remaining second of every minute you have left on this earth with the knowledge that you alone caused it.

Unless, of course, you take the more honorable approach and kill yourself first, saving whichever target I have selected from their fate.

There's your choice: my name or your obituary. In the same paper, of course.

As proof of the length of my reach, and the extent of my planning, I have this day contacted one of the names on the list with a most modest little message. I would urge you to spend the remainder of this evening ferreting out who was touched, and how. Then you can begin on the true task before you without delay in the morning.

I do not, of course, truly expect you to be able to guess my identity. So, to demonstrate that I am a sporting type, I've decided that from time to time over the next fifteen days I will provide you with a clue or two. Just to make things more interesting, although a clever, intuitive sort, such as yourself, should assume that this entire letter is filled with clues. Nevertheless, here is a preview, and it comes for free.

In the past, life was fun and wild,
Mother, father, and young child.
But all the good times went astray,
When my father sailed away.

Poetry is not my strong suit.

Hatred is.

Remember: You may ask three questions. Yes or No answers, please.

Use the same method, the front-page ads in the New York Times.

I will reply in my own style within twenty-four hours.

Good luck. You might also try to find time now to make your funeral arrangements. Cremation is probably preferable to an elaborate burial service. I know how much you dislike churches. I don't think it would be a smart idea to contact the police. They would probably mock you, which I suspect your conceit would have difficulty handling. And it would likely enrage me more, and, right now, you must be a little uncertain as to how unstable I actually am. I might respond erratically, in any number of quite evil ways. But of one thing of which you can be absolutely certain: My anger knows no limits.

The letter was signed in all-capital letters:
RUMPLESTILTSKIN

Ricky Starks sat back hard in his chair, as if the fury emanating from the words on the page in front of him had been able to strike him in the face like a fist. He pushed himself to his feet, walked over to the window and cracked it open, allowing the city sounds to burst into the quiet of the small room, carried by an unexpected late July breeze that promised an evening thunderstorm might be tracking the city. He breathed in, looking for something in the air to give him a sense of relief from the heat that had overcome him. He could hear the high-pitched caterwaul of a police siren a few blocks distant, and the steady cacophony of car horns that is like white noise in Manhattan. He took two or three deep breaths, then pulled the window closed, shutting away all the outside sounds of normal urban life.

He turned back to the letter.

I am in trouble, he thought. But how much, he was initially unsure.

He realized that he was being deeply threatened, but the parameters of that threat were still unclear. A significant part of him insisted he ignore the document on the desktop. Simply refuse to play what didn't sound like much of a game. He snorted once, allowing this thought to flourish. All his training and experience suggested that doing nothing was the most reasonable course of action. After all, often the analyst finds that maintaining silence and a failure to respond to the most provocative and outrageous behavior by a patient is the cleverest way to get to the psychological truth of those actions. He stood up and walked around the desk twice, like a dog sniffing at an unusual smell.

On the second pass, he stopped and stared down at the page of words again.

He shook his head. That won't work, he realized. For a moment he had a shot of admiration for the writer's sophistication. Ricky understood he would probably have greeted the 'I'm going to kill you' threat with a detachment closing on boredom. After all, he had lived long, and quite well, he thought, so threatening to kill a man in his middle years didn't really amount to much. But that wasn't what he was facing. The threat was more oblique. Someone else was slated to suffer if he did nothing. Someone innocent, and in all likelihood, someone young, because the young are far more vulnerable.

Ricky swallowed hard. I would blame myself and I would live out my remaining time in true agony.

Of that, the writer was absolutely correct.

Or else kill myself. He could taste a sudden bitterness on his tongue. Suicide would be the antithesis of everything he'd stood for, his entire life. He suspected the person who signed his name *Rumplestiltskin* knew that.

He felt abruptly as if he'd been placed on trial.

Again he began to pace around his office, assessing the letter. A great voice within him wanted to be dismissive, to shrug the entire message off, to anoint it an exaggeration and a fantasy without any basis in reality but found that he was unable to. Ricky berated himself: *Just because something makes you uncomfortable, doesn't mean you should ignore it*.

But he didn't really have a good idea how to respond. He stopped pacing and returned to his seat. Madness, he thought. But madness with a distinctly clever touch, because it will cause me to join in the madness.

'I should call the police,' he said out loud. Then he stopped. And say what? Dial 911 and tell some dull and unimaginative desk sergeant that he'd received a threatening letter? And listen to the man tell him *So what*? As best as he could tell, no law had been broken. Unless suggesting that someone kill themselves was a violation of some sort. Extortion? What sort of homicide could it be? he wondered. The idea crossed his mind to call an attorney, but then he understood that the situation posed by Rumplestiltskin's letter wasn't legal. He had been approached on the playing field that he knew. The game suggested was one of intuitiveness, and psychology; it was about emotions and fears. He shook his head and told himself: I can play in that arena.

'What do you know already?' he spoke to himself in the empty room.

Someone knows my routine. Knows how I let patients into my office. Knows when I break for lunch. What I do on the weekends. Was also clever enough to ferret out a list of relatives. That took some ingenuity.

Knows my birthday.

He breathed in sharply, again. I have been studied.

I did not know it, but someone has been watching me. Measuring me. Someone has devoted considerable time and effort to creating this game and not left me much time for countermoves.

His tongue remained dry and his lips parched. He was suddenly very thirsty, but unwilling to leave the sanctity of his office for the kitchen and a glass of water.

'What did I do to make someone hate me so?' he asked.

This question was like a quick punch in the stomach. Ricky knew he enjoyed the arrogance of many caregivers, thinking that he had delivered good to his small corner of the world through understanding and acceptance of one's existence. The idea that he'd created some monstrous infection of hatred in someone somewhere was extremely unsettling.

'Who are you?' he demanded of the letter. He immediately started to race through the catalog of patients, stretching back over decades, but, just as swiftly, stopped. He understood he might have to do this eventually, but he would need to be systematic, disciplined, dogged, and he wasn't ready to take that step yet.

Ricky didn't think of himself as very qualified to be his own policeman. But then he shook his head, realizing that, in a unique way, that was untrue. For years he'd been a sort of detective. The difference was truly the nature of the crimes he'd investigated and the techniques he'd used. Buttressed slightly by this thought, Ricky Starks sat back down at his desk, reached into the top right-hand drawer and removed an old, leather-bound address book so frayed around the edges that it was held together by a rubber band. For starters, he told himself, we can find the relative who has been contacted by this person. It must be some former patient, he told himself, one who cut his analysis short and plunged into depression. One who has harbored a near-psychotic fixation for a number of years. He guessed that with a little bit of luck and perhaps a nudge or two in the right direction from whichever of his relatives had been contacted, he would be able to identify the disgruntled ex-patient. He tried to tell himself, empathetically, that the letter writer — Rumplestiltskin — was really reaching out to him for help. Then, almost as quickly, he discarded this wishy-washy thought. Holding the address book in his hand, Ricky thought about the fairy tale character whose name the letter writer had signed. Cruel, he told himself. A magical gnome with a black heart that isn't outfoxed, but loses his contest through sheer bad luck. This observation did not make him feel any better.

The letter seemed to glow on the desktop in front of him.

He nodded slowly. It tells you much, he insisted. Blend the words on the page with what the writer has already done, and you're probably halfway to figuring out who it is.

So, he pushed the letter to the side and opened up the address book, searching for the number for the first person on the list of fifty-two. He grimaced a little and he started to punch the numbers onto the telephone keypad. In the past decade, he had had little contact with any of his relatives, and he suspected none of them would be very eager to hear from him. Especially given the nature of the call.

2

Ricky Starks thought himself singularly ill suited at prying information from relatives surprised to hear his voice. He was accustomed to internalizing everything he heard from patients in his office, keeping close reins on all observation and insight. But as he dialed number after number, he found himself in unfamiliar and uncomfortable territory. He was incapable of designing a verbal script that he could follow, some standard salutation followed by a brief explanation of why he was calling. Instead, all he could hear was hesitation and indecision in his voice, as he stumbled through hackneyed greetings and tried to extricate an answer to the stupidest question: Has something unusual happened to you?

Consequently, his evening was filled with a series of genuinely irritating telephone conversations. His relatives either were unpleasantly surprised to hear from him, unhappily curious as to why after so much time had passed he would be telephoning out of the blue, busy with some other activity that he was interrupting, or simply rude. There was a brusque quality to each contact, and more than once he was dismissed sharply. There were more than a few terse 'What the hell is this all about?' questions, to which he lied that a former patient had somehow managed to obtain a list of his relatives' names and he was concerned that they might be contacted. He left out the possibility that someone might be facing a threat, which, he wondered was probably the biggest lie of all.

It was already approaching ten P.M., which was closing in on his bed-time and he still had more than two dozen names on the list. So far, he had been unable to discern anything enough out of the ordinary in any of the lives he'd checked to warrant further investigation. But, at the same time, he was doubtful of his own questioning abilities. The odd vagueness of Rumplestiltskin's letter made him fear that he might have simply missed the connection. And, it was equally possible that in any one of the brief conversations he'd experienced that evening that the person contacted by the letter writer had not told Ricky the truth. And, mingled in with the phone calls had been several frustrating nonanswers. Three times he'd had to leave stilted and cryptic messages on answering machines.

He refused to allow himself the belief that the letter delivered that day had been a mere charade, although that would have been nice. His back had stiffened up. He had not eaten and was hungry. He had a headache. He rubbed a hand through his hair, and then stroked his eyes before dialing the next number, feeling a sort of exhaustion that bordered on tension pounding behind his temples. He considered the pain of his headache to be a small penance for the realization that he was being greeted with: that he was isolated and estranged from the majority of his family.

The wages of neglect, Ricky thought to himself, as he readied to dial the twenty-first name on the list provided by Rumplestiltskin. It is probably unreasonable to expect one's relatives to embrace sudden contact after so many years of silence, especially distant relatives, with whom there was little he shared. More than one had paused when he said his name, as if trying to place precisely who he was. These pauses made him feel a little like some ancient hermit coming down off a mountaintop, or a bear in the first minutes after a long winter's hibernation.

The twenty-first name seemed only vaguely familiar. He concentrated hard, trying to put a face and then a status to the letters on the sheet in front of him. A slow picture formed in his head. His older sister who'd passed away a decade before had two sons, and this was the elder of the two. This made Ricky an uncle of little substance. He had had no contact with any niece or nephew since the sister's funeral. He racked his brain, trying to remember more than appearance, but something about the name. Did the name on the list have a wife? A family? A career? Who was he?

Ricky shook his head. He had drawn a blank. The person he needed to contact had little more personality than a name plucked from a telephone book. He was angry with himself. That's not right, he insisted to himself, you should remember something. He pictured his sister, fifteen years older than he, an age chasm that had made them members of the same family growing up, but revolving in far different orbits. She was the eldest; he was a child of accident, destined always to be the baby of the family. She had been a poet, graduating from a well-to-do women's college during the Fifties, who first worked in publishing, then married successfully — a corporate attorney from Boston. Her two sons lived in New England.

Ricky looked at the name on the sheet in front of him. There was an address in Deerfield, Massachusetts, in the 413 area code. A burst of memory flooded him. The son was a professor at the private school located in that town. What does he teach? Ricky demanded of himself. The answer came in a few seconds: history. United States history. He squeezed his eyes shut for a moment, and came up with a mental image: a short, wiry man in a tweed jacket, with horn-rimmed glasses and rapidly thinning sandy hair. A man with a wife who was easily two inches taller than he was.

He sighed, and equipped at least with a small parcel of information, reached for the telephone.

He dialed the number and listened while the phone rang a half-dozen times before being answered by a voice that had the unmistakable tone of youth. Deep, but eager.

'Hello?'

'Hello,' Ricky, said. 'I'm trying to reach Timothy Graham. This is his Uncle Frederick. Doctor Frederick Starks . . . '

'This is Tim Junior.'

Ricky hesitated, then continued, 'Hello there, Tim Junior. I don't suppose we've ever met . . . '

'Yes, we did. Actually. One time. I remember. At grandmother's funeral. You sat right behind my parents in the second pew of the church and you told my dad that it was a kind thing that grandma didn't linger. I remember what you said, because I didn't understand it at the time.'

'You must have been . . . '

'Seven.'

'And now you're . . . '

'Almost seventeen.'

'You have a good memory to recall a single meeting.'

The young man considered this statement, then replied, 'Grandmother's funeral made a big impression on me.' He did not elaborate, but changed course. 'You want to speak with my dad?'

'Yes. If possible.'

'Why?'

Ricky thought this an unusual question coming from someone young. Not so much that Timothy Junior would want to know why, for that was a natural state of the young. But in this context the question had a slightly protective air to it. Ricky thought most teenagers would have simply bellowed for their father to pick up the telephone and then returned to whatever they were doing, whether watching TV or doing homework or playing video games, because an out-of-the-blue phone call from an old and distant relative wasn't something they would ordinarily add to the list of relevancies in their lives.

'Well, it's something a little strange,' he said.

'It's been a strange day here,' the teenager responded.

This statement grabbed Ricky's attention. 'How so?' he asked.

But the teenager didn't answer this question. 'I'm not sure my dad will want to talk right now, unless he knows what it's all about.'

'Well,' Ricky said carefully, 'I think he might be interested in what I have to tell him.'

Timothy Junior absorbed this. Then answered: 'My dad's tied up right now. The cops are still here.'

Ricky inhaled swiftly. 'The police? Is something wrong?'

The teenager ignored this question to pose one of his own. 'Why are you calling? I mean, we haven't heard from you in . . . '

'Many years. At least ten. Not since your grandmother's funeral.'

'So, right. That's what I thought. Why all of a sudden now?'

Ricky thought the boy right to be suspicious. He launched into his set speech. 'A former patient of mine — you recall I'm a doctor, Tim, right? — may try to contact some of my relatives. And even though we haven't been in touch in all these years, I wanted to alert people. That's why I'm calling.'

'What sort of patient? You're a shrink, right?'

'A psychoanalyst.'

'And this patient, is he dangerous? Or crazy? Or both?'

'I think I ought to speak about this with your dad.'

'I told you, he's talking to the police right now. I think they're getting ready to leave.'

'Why is he speaking with the police?'

'It has to do with my sister.'

'What has to do with your sister?' Ricky tried to

remember the girl's name and tried to picture her in his head, but all he could recall was a small blond-haired child, several years younger than her brother. He remembered the two of them sitting to the side of the reception after his sister's funeral, uncomfortable in stiff, dark clothes, quiet but impatient, eager for the somber tone of the gathering to dissipate and life to return to normal.

'Someone followed . . . ' the teenager started, then stopped. 'I think I'll get my father,' he said briskly. Ricky heard the phone clatter to a table-top, and muffled voices in the background.

In a moment the phone was picked up and Ricky heard a voice that seemed the same as the teenager's, but with a deeper weariness attached. At the same time the voice had a harried urgency to it, as if the owner were being pressured, or caught at a moment of indecision. Ricky liked to think himself an expert on voices, on inflection and tone, choices of words and pacing, all of which were telltale signals or windows on what was concealed within. The teenager's father spoke without introduction.

'Uncle Frederick? This is most unusual and I'm in the middle of a little family crisis here, so I hope this is truly important. What can I do for you?'

'Hello, Tim. I apologize for barging in like this . . . '

'That's all right. Tim Junior said you had a warning . . . '

'In a way. I received a cryptic letter from what might be a former patient today. It had what some might consider a threatening tone. That was directed primarily at me. But it also indicated that the letter writer might contact one of my relatives. I have been calling around the family to alert people, and to determine if anyone has already been approached.'

There was a deadly, cold silence on the phone that lasted nearly a minute.

'What sort of patient?' Tim Senior asked sharply, echoing his son's query. 'Is this someone dangerous?'

'I don't know who it is exactly. The letter wasn't signed. I'm only presuming it is an ex-patient but I don't really know for certain. In fact, it might not be. The truth is, I don't know anything yet, for certain.'

'That sounds vague. Exceedingly vague.'

'You are correct. I'm sorry.'

'Do you think this threat is real?'

Ricky could hear a harsh, hard edge lining the man's voice.

'I don't know. Obviously it concerned me enough to make some calls.'

'Have you spoken with the police?'

'No. Sending me a letter doesn't seem to break the law, does it?'

'That's exactly what the bastards just told me.'

'I beg your pardon?' Ricky said.

'The cops. I called the cops and then they came all the way over here to tell me they couldn't do anything.'

'Why did you call the police?'

Timothy Graham didn't immediately answer. He seemed to take in a long breath of air, but instead of calming himself, this had the opposite effect, as if releasing a spasm of pent-up rage.

'It was disgusting. Some sick fuck. Some slimy sick motherfucker. I'll kill him if I ever get my hands on him. Kill him with my bare hands. Is your ex-patient a sick fuck, Uncle Frederick?'

The sudden outburst of obscenity took Ricky aback. It seemed dramatically out of the ordinary for a quiet, well-mannered, and unprepossessing history professor at an exclusive and conservative prep school. Ricky paused, at first a little unsure how to reply.

'I don't know,' he said. 'Tell me what has happened that has made you so upset.'

Tim Senior hesitated again, breathing in deeply, the

noise making a snakelike hissing sound over the telephone line. 'On her birthday, if you can believe it. On her fourteenth birthday, of all days. That's just disgusting . . .'

Ricky stiffened in his seat. A memorylike explosion burst behind his eyes. He realized he should have seen the connection right away. Of all his relatives, only one by the greatest of coincidences, shared his birthday. The little girl whose face he had so much trouble recalling, and whom he'd met only once, at a funeral. He berated himself: *This should have been your first phone call.* But he did not let this observation creep into his own voice.

'What happened?' he asked bluntly.

'Someone left a birthday card for her inside her locker at school. You know, one of those nice, oversized, tritely sentimental cards that you buy at the mall. I still can't figure out how the bastard got in there and got the locker opened without being seen by someone. I mean, where the hell was security? Unbelievable. Anyway, when Mindy got to school, she found the card, figured it was from one of her friends, and opened it. Guess what? The card was stuffed with disgusting pornography. Full-color, leave nothing to the imagination porn. Pictures of women tied up in ropes and chains and leathers and penetrated in every imaginable fashion by every conceivable device. Real hard-core, triple-X stuff. And the person wrote on the card: *This is what I intend to do to you as soon as I can catch you alone . . .*'

Ricky shifted about in his seat. Rumplestiltskin, he thought.

But what he asked was, 'And the police? What do they tell you?'

Timothy Graham snorted with a dismissive burst that Ricky imagined had been used on slacker students for years and was likely to freeze them with fear but in this context spoke more of impotence and frustration.

'The local police,' he said briskly, 'are idiots. Complete idiots. They blithely tell me that unless there exists substantial and credible evidence that Mindy is actively being stalked by someone, there's nothing they can do. They want some sort of overt act. In other words, she has to actually be attacked first. Idiots. They believe that the letter and the enclosures are practical jokes. Probably upperclassmen at the academy. Maybe somebody I gave a lousy grade to last term. Of course, that's not outside the realm of possibility around here, but . . . ' The history professor paused. 'Why don't you tell me about your former patient? Is he a sex criminal?'

Ricky hesitated himself, then said, 'No. Not at all. This doesn't sound like him at all. Really, he's harmless. Just irritating.'

He wondered if his nephew would hear the lies in his voice. He doubted it. The man was furious, flustered, and outraged, and was unlikely to have the ability to recognize a departure from the truth for some time.

Timothy Graham was silent for a moment. 'I will kill him,' he said coldly. 'Mindy has been in tears all day. She thinks there's someone out there who wants to rape her. She's just fourteen and never hurt a soul in her life and is impressionable as hell and she's never been exposed to that sort of filth before. It seems like only yesterday she was still into teddy bears and Barbie dolls. I doubt she'll sleep much tonight, or for the next couple of days. I just hope that the fright hasn't changed her.'

Ricky didn't say anything, and the history teacher continued after pausing to catch his breath.

'Is that possible, Uncle Frederick? You're the damn expert. Can someone have their life changed that quickly?'

Again he didn't reply, but the question echoed within him.

' . . . It's awful, you know. Just awful,' Timothy Graham burst out. 'You try so hard to protect your children from how sick and evil the world really is, then let your guard down for a second and blam! It hits you. Maybe this isn't the worst case of lost innocence you've ever heard of Uncle Frederick, but, then, you're not listening to your beloved little girl who never hurt a single soul in her entire life, crying her eyes out on her fourteenth birthday because someone somewhere means her harm.'

And with that, the history professor hung up the telephone.

* * *

Ricky Starks leaned back at his desk. He let a long, slow breath of air whistle between his front teeth. In a way, he was both upset and intrigued by what Rumplestiltskin had done. He sorted through it rapidly. There was nothing spontaneous about the message he'd sent to the teenage girl; it was calculated and effective. He'd obviously put in some time studying her as well. It also showed some skills that Ricky guessed he would be wise to take note of. Rumplestiltskin had managed to avoid security at a school, and had the burglar's ability to open a lock without destroying it. He was able to leave the school equally undetected and then travel straight down the highway from Western Massachusetts to New York City to leave his second message in Ricky's waiting room. The timing wasn't difficult; the drive wasn't long, perhaps four hours. But it denoted planning.

But that wasn't what bothered Ricky. He shifted about in his seat.

His nephew's words seemed to echo about in the office, rebounding off the walls, filling the space around him with a sort of heat: *lost innocence*.

Ricky thought about these words. Sometimes, in the course of a session, a patient would say something that had an electric quality, because they were moments of understanding, flashes of comprehension, insights that were bristling with progress. These were the moments any analyst searched for. Usually they were accompanied by a sense of adventure and satisfaction, because they signaled achievements along the path of treatment.

Not this time.

Ricky felt an unruly despair within him, one that walked at the side of fear.

Rumplestiltskin had attacked his great-niece at a moment of childish vulnerability. He had taken a moment that should be filed in the great vault of memories as one of joy, of awakening — her fourteenth birthday. And then he'd rendered it ugly and frightening. It was as profound a threat as Ricky could imagine, as provocative as he could envision.

Ricky lifted a hand to his forehead as if he suddenly felt feverish. He was surprised not to find sweat there. He thought to himself: We think of threats as something that compromises our safety. A man with a gun or a knife and a sexual obsession. Or a drunk driver behind the wheel of a car accelerating down the highway carelessly. Or some insidious disease, like the one that killed his wife, starting to worry away at our insides.

Ricky rose from his chair and started pacing nervously about.

We fear being killed. But what is far worse is being ruined.

He glanced over at Rumplestiltskin's letter. *Ruined*. He'd used that word, right alongside *destroy*.

His adversary was someone who understood that often what truly threatens us and is hardest to combat is something that stems from within. The impact and pain of nightmare can be far greater than being struck by a fist. And equally, sometimes it is not so much that fist, but the emotion behind it, that creates pain. He stopped abruptly, and turned toward the small bookcase that rested against one of the sidewalls of the office. There were rows of texts arranged there — medical texts, for the most part, and professional journals. Collected in those books were literally hundreds of thousands of words that clinically and coldly dissected human emotions. In an instant, he understood that all that knowledge was likely useless to him.

What he wanted was to pluck a textbook from one of those shelves, flip to the index, find an entry under *R* for Rumplestiltskin, then open to a page that gave a dry and straightforward description of the man who'd written him the letter. He felt a surge of fear, knowing that there was no such entry. And he found himself turning away from the books that had to this moment defined his career, and what he remembered instead was a sequence from a novel that he had not read since his college days. *Rats*, Ricky thought. *They put Winston Smith in a room with rats because they knew that was the only thing on this earth that truly frightened him. Not death. Not torture. Rats*.

He looked around his apartment and office, a place that he thought did much to define him, where he'd been comfortable and happy for many years. He wondered, in that second, whether it was all about to change and wondered if it suddenly was about to become his own fictional Room 101. The place where they kept the worst thing in the world.

3

It was now just midnight, and he felt stupid and utterly alone.

His office was strewn with manila folders and scraps of paper, stacks of stenographer's notebooks, sheets of foolscap and an old-fashioned microcassette tape deck that had been out of date for a decade resting at the bottom of a small pile of minicassette tapes. Each grouping represented the meager documentation that he had accumulated on his patients over the years. There were notes about dreams, scribbled entries listing critical associations that patients made, or that occurred to him, during the course of treatment — telltale words, phrases, memories. If any sculpture was designed to express the belief that analysis was as much art as medicine, it could do no better than the disarray surrounding him. There were no orderly forms, listing height, weight, race, religion, or place of national origin. He had no cleverly alphabetized documents delineating blood pressure, temperature, pulse rate, and urine output. Nor did he even have organized and accessible charts, listing patients' names, addresses, next of kin, and diagnosis.

Ricky Starks was not an internist or a cardiologist or a pathologist who approached each patient seeking a clearly defined answer to an ailment, and who kept copious and detailed notes on treatment and progress. His chosen specialty defied the science that preoccupied other forms of medicine. It was this quality that made the analyst something of a medical outsider, and why most of the men and women attracted to the profession found it.

But at this moment, Ricky stood in the center of the

growing mess and felt like a man emerging from an underground shelter after a tornado has swept overhead. He thought he had ignored what chaos his life really was until something big and disruptive had torn through, unsettling all the careful balances he'd created. Trying to sort his way through decades of patients and hundreds of daily therapies was probably hopeless.

Because he already suspected that Rumplestiltskin wasn't there.

At least, not in readily identifiable form.

Ricky was absolutely certain that if the person who'd written the letter had ever graced his couch for any measurable length of treatment he would have recognized him. Tone. Style of writing. All the obvious moods of anger, rage, and fury. These elements would have been as distinctive and unmistakable to him as a fingerprint to a detective. Telltale clues that he would have been alert to.

He knew that this supposition contained a certain amount of arrogance. And, he thought it would be a poor idea to underestimate Rumplestiltskin until he knew much more about the man. But he was certain that no patient that he'd ever had in any usual course of analysis would return, bitter and enraged, years later, so changed that they could hide their identity from him. They might return, still inwardly bearing the scars that had caused them to seek him out in the first place. They might return frustrated and acting out, because analysis is not some sort of antibiotic for the soul; it doesn't eradicate the infections of despair that cripple some people. They might be angry, feeling that they had wasted years in talk and nothing much had changed for them. These were all possibilities, though in Ricky's nearly three decades as an analyst, few such failures had ever happened. At least not that he knew of. But he wasn't so conceited to believe that every treatment, no matter how long it lasted, was always completely successful. There were bound to be therapies that were less victorious than others.

There had to be people he hadn't helped. Or had helped less. Or had lapsed from the understanding that analysis brings, back to some prior state. Crippled again. In despair again.

But Rumplestiltskin presented a far different portrait. The tone of his letter and the message relayed to his fourteen-year-old great-niece showed a calculating, aggressive, and perversely confident person. A psychopath, Ricky thought, giving a clinical term to someone still unclear in his mind. This was not to say that he didn't think that perhaps once or twice over the decades of his career he hadn't treated individuals with psychopathic tendencies. But none who had ever displayed the depth of hatred and fixation that Rumplestiltskin did. Yet someone whom he'd treated less than successfully was connected to the letter writer.

The trick, he realized, was determining who these ex-patients were, and then tracing them to Rumplestiltskin. Because that was clearly, now that he had thought about it for a few hours, where the connection rested. The person who wanted him to kill himself was someone's child, spouse, or lover. The first task, Ricky thought aggressively, was determining what patient had left his treatment on the shakiest of circumstances. Then he could start backtracking.

He maneuvered amid the mess he'd created back to his desk and picked up Rumplestiltskin's letter. *I exist somewhere in your past*. Ricky stared hard at the words, then looked back at the piles of notes scattered about the office.

All right, he said to himself. The first task is to organize my professional history. Find the segments that can be eliminated.

He sighed out loud. Did he make some mistake as a hospital resident more than twenty-five years earlier that was now returning to haunt him? Could he even remember those first patients? While he was undergoing his own analytic training he had been engaged in a study of paranoid schizophrenics who had been committed to the psychiatric wards at Bellevue Hospital. The study had been about determining predictability factors for violent crimes and had not been a clinical success. But he'd come to know and been involved in some treatment plans for men who went on to commit serious crimes. It had been the closest he'd ever come to forensic psychiatry and he hadn't liked it much. When his work with the study was finished, he'd immediately retreated back into the far safer and physically less demanding world of Freud and his followers.

Ricky felt a sudden thirst, as if his throat were parched by heat.

He realized he knew absolutely next to nothing about crime and criminals. He had no special expertise in violence. Indeed, he had little interest in that field. He doubted that he even knew any forensic psychiatrists. None were included in his extremely small circle of occasional friends and professional acquaintances with whom he kept current.

He glanced over at the textbooks lining his shelves. Krafft-Ebing was there, with his seminal work on sexual psychopathology. But that was it, and he rather doubted that Rumplestiltskin was a sexual psychopath, even with the pornographic message he'd sent to Ricky's great-niece.

'Who are you?' he said out loud.

Then he shook his head.

'No,' he said slowly. 'First, what are you?' And then, he told himself, after I can answer that, I will determine who you are.

I can do this, Ricky thought, trying to bolster his own confidence. Tomorrow I will sit down and rack my memory and create a list of former patients. I will divide them into categories that represent all the stages of my professional life. Then I will start to investigate. Find the failure that will connect me to this fellow, Rumplestiltskin.

Exhausted, not at all certain that he had accomplished anything, Ricky stumbled out of his office and into his small bedroom. It was a simple, monklike room with a bed stand, a chest of drawers, a modest closet, and a single bed. Once there had been a double bed with an ornate headboard and colorful paintings on the walls, but after his wife's death he'd given away their bed, choosing something simpler and narrower. The bright knickknacks and artwork that his wife had once decorated the room with were mostly gone as well. Her clothing he'd given to charity, her jewelry and personal items had been sent to her sister's three nieces. He kept a photograph of the two of them on the bureau, taken fifteen years earlier outside their farmhouse in Wellfleet on a clear, azure summer morning. But since her death he'd systematically erased most of the other, outward signs of her onetime presence. A slow and painful death followed by a three-year erasure.

Ricky slid out of his clothes, taking time to carefully fold his slacks and hang up his blue blazer. The button-down shirt he wore went into a laundry hamper. He dropped his tie on the bureau surface. Then he plopped down on the edge of the bed in his underwear, thinking that he wished he had more energy. In the bedside drawer, he kept a vial of rarely used sleeping tablets. They were significantly past their expiration date, but he guessed that they would still be potent enough for him that night. He swallowed one and a tiny piece of another, hoping that they would quickly deliver a deep and deadening sleep.

He sat for a moment running his hand across the

rough cotton sheets and thought it oddly hypocritical for an analyst to face the night and desperately long that his rest not be marred by dreams. Dreams were important, unconscious riddles that mirrored the heart. This he knew, and they were generally welcome avenues to travel. But this night he felt overwhelmed, and he lay back dizzily, feeling his pulse still moving swiftly within him, eager for the medications to push him beneath the veil of dark. Utterly exhausted by the impact of a single threatening letter, he felt far older in that moment than the accumulation of his fifty-three years.

* * *

His first patient on this final day before his projected monthlong August vacation arrived promptly at seven A.M., signaling her arrival with the three distinctive peals of his waiting room buzzer. The session went well, he thought. Nothing particularly exciting, nothing dramatic. But some steady progress. The young woman on the couch was a third-year psychiatric social worker, seeking to gain her psychoanalytic certificate while by-passing medical school. It was neither the most efficient, nor the easiest route to becoming an analyst, and was a course frowned on by some of his stodgier colleagues because it didn't include the traditional medical degree, but was a method he'd always admired. It took real passion for the profession, a single-minded devotion to the couch and what it could accomplish. He often conceded to himself that it had been years since he'd been called upon to utilize the M.D. that followed his name. The young woman's therapy centered around a set of overly aggressive parents who'd created an atmosphere in her childhood charged with accomplishment, but lacking in affection. Consequently, in her sessions with Ricky, she was frequently impatient, eager for insights that dovetailed with her textual readings and course work at the midtown Institute for Psychoanalysis. Ricky was forever reining her in, trying to get her to see that knowing facts is not necessarily the same as understanding.

When he coughed slightly, shifted in his seat, and said, 'Well, I'm afraid that's all the time we have for today,' the young woman, who had been describing a new boyfriend of questionable potential, sighed. 'Well, we'll see if he's still around a month from now . . . ' — which made Ricky smile.

The patient swung her feet off the couch and said, 'Have a nice vacation, doctor. I'll see you after Labor Day.' Then she gathered her pocket-book and briskly exited the treatment room.

The entire day seemed to fall together in routine normalcy.

Patient after patient entered the office, bearing little in the way of emotional adventure. They were mostly veterans of vacation time, and he suspected more than once that they unconsciously believed it wise to withhold feelings that were going to be delayed a month in examination. Of course, what was held back was as intriguing as what might have been said, and with each patient he was alert to these holes in the narrative. He had immense trust in his ability to precisely remember words and phrases uttered beside him that might lurk profitably over the month hiatus.

In the minutes between sessions, he busily started to backtrack over his own years, starting to create a list of patients, jotting down names on a blank steno pad. As the day lengthened, so did the list. His memory, he thought, was still acute, which encouraged him. The only decision he had to make that day was at lunchtime, when he ordinarily would have stepped out on his daily walk, just as Rumplestiltskin had described. This day, he paused, part of him wanting to break the routine that the letter writer had so accurately portrayed, as some sort of act of defiance. Then, he'd realized that it was far more defiant to stick to the routine, and hope that the person watching him saw that he was uncowed by the letter. So out he went at noontime, walking the same path as always, putting his feet down in the same sidewalk squares, taking breaths of heavy city air with the same regularity as he did each day. He was unsure whether he wanted Rumplestiltskin to follow him, or not. But he discovered that every pace he took seemed to be echoed, and more than once he had to fight the urge to pivot quickly and see if he was being trailed. When he returned to his apartment, he was breathing heavily with relief.

The afternoon patients followed the same pattern as the morning group.

A few had some bitterness toward the upcoming vacation; this was as he expected. Some expressed a bit of fear and more than a little anxiety. The routine of daily fifty-minute sessions was powerful, and it was unsettling for several to know that even for a short time they would be without that particular anchor. Still, they and he knew that the time would pass, and as with everything in analysis, the time spent away from the couch could lead to insights about the process. Everything, every moment, anything during the day-to-day of life, might be associated with insight. It was what made the process fascinating for both patient and doctor.

At one minute before five, he glanced out his window. The summer day was still dominating the world outside the office: bright sun, temperatures creeping up into the nineties. The city heat had an insistence to it, demanding to be acknowledged. He listened to the hum of the air conditioner, and suddenly recalled what it was like when he was first starting out, and an open window and a rattling old oscillating fan was all the relief he could afford from the hazy, stultifying atmosphere of the city in July. Sometimes, he thought, it seems as if there is no air anywhere.

He tore his eyes away from the window when he heard the three peals of the buzzer. He pushed himself to his feet, and walked over to the door, pulling it open quickly to allow Mr. Zimmerman with all his impatience to enter immediately. Zimmerman did not like to wait in the anteroom. He showed up seconds before the session was to begin, and expected to be admitted instantaneously. Ricky had once spied the man marching up and down the sidewalk outside the apartment building on a bitter winter evening, furiously glancing at his watch every few seconds, trying to will the time to pass so that he did not have to wait inside. On more than one occasion, Ricky had been tempted to let the man cool his heels for a few minutes, to see if he could stimulate some understanding on Zimmerman's part as to why being so precise was so important. But he had not done this. Instead, Ricky swung open the door at exactly five o'clock every weekday, so that the angry man could barrel into the treatment room, toss himself down on the couch, and launch immediately into sarcasm and fury over all the wrongs that had been perpetrated on him that day. Ricky took a deep breath as he opened his door, and adopted his best poker face. Regardless of whether Ricky felt inside he was holding a full house or a jack-high bust, Zimmerman got the same noncommittal look each day.

'Good afternoon,' he started, his standard greeting.

But it was not Roger Zimmerman in the waiting room.

Instead, Ricky was suddenly eye-to-eye with a striking and statuesque young woman.

She wore a long black belted raincoat that dropped to her shoes, far out of place on the hot summer day, dark sunglasses, which she removed quickly, revealing penetrating vibrant green eyes. He would have guessed her age at somewhere just on the better side of thirty. A woman whose considerable looks were at their peak and whose understanding of the world had sharpened past youth.

'I'm sorry . . . ' Ricky said hesitantly. 'But . . . '

'Oh,' the young woman replied airily, shaking shoulder-length blond hair and gesturing smoothly with her hand. 'Zimmerman won't be here today. I came instead.'

'But he . . . '

'He won't be needing you any longer,' she continued. 'He decided to conclude his treatment at precisely two-thirty-seven this afternoon. Curiously enough, he was at the 92nd Street subway station when he reached this decision after the briefest of conversations with Mr. R. It was Mr. R. who persuaded him that he no longer needed or desired your services. And to our surprise, it wasn't all that difficult for Zimmerman to reach that conclusion, either.'

And then she pushed past the startled doctor into his office.

4

'So,' the young woman said breezily, 'this is where the mystery unfolds.'

Ricky had wordlessly trailed her into his office, where he watched as she surveyed the small room. Her eyes lingered on the couch, his chair, his desk. She walked over and inspected the books he had on the shelves, nodding her head as she absorbed the thick and stodgy titles. She ran a finger along the spine of one text, then noted the dust that came away on her fingertip, causing her to shake her head. 'Not used much . . . ,' she muttered. She lifted her eyes to his once, saying reproachfully, 'What? Not a single volume of verse, or work of fiction?' Then she approached the cream-colored wall where he'd hung his diplomas and several small pieces of art, alongside a modestly sized oak-framed portrait of the great man himself. In the picture he was holding his ubiquitous cigar, staring balefully out with his deeply recessed eyes, white beard covering the precancerous jaw that would prove to be so unbearably painful in his last years. She tapped the glass over the portrait with a long finger, tipped with nails painted a fire-engine red.

'Isn't it interesting how every profession seems to have some icon hanging on the wall. I mean, if I went to see a priest, he'd have a Jesus on a crucifix somewhere. A rabbi would have a Star of David, or a menorah. Every two-bit politician puts up a picture of Lincoln or Washington. There really ought to be a law against that. Medical doctors like to have those little plastic cutaway models of a heart or a knee or some other organ within easy reach. For all I know, a computer programmer out in Silicon Valley nails up a portrait of Bill Gates on the wall of his cubicle where he worships daily. A psychoanalyst like you, Ricky, needs the picture of Saint Sigmund. It lets everyone who enters here know who truly created the ground rules. And it gives you a tiny little bit of legitimacy that might otherwise be called into question, I suppose.'

Ricky Starks silently picked up an armchair and moved it to the space in front of his desk. Then he maneuvered to the opposite side, and gestured to the young woman to take a seat.

'What?' she asked briskly, 'I don't get to use the famous couch?'

'That would be premature,' he replied coldly. He gestured a second time. The young woman swept her vibrant green eyes over the room again, as if trying to memorize everything contained within, then she plopped herself down in the chair. She slumped in the seat languidly, simultaneously reaching into a pocket of the black raincoat and removing a package of cigarettes. She removed one, stuck it between her lips, ignited a flame from a clear butane lighter, but stopped the fire just inches away from the cigarette tip.

'Ah,' she said, a slow smile lingering across her face, 'how rude of me. Would you care for a smoke, Ricky?'

He shook his head. Her smile remained.

'Of course not. When was it you quit? Fifteen years ago? Twenty? Actually, Ricky, I think it was 1977, if Mr. R. informs me correctly. A brave time to stop smoking, Ricky. An era when many people lit right up without thinking, because, although the tobacco companies denied it, people actually did know that it was bad for you. Killed you, no lie. So people pretty much preferred not to think about it. The ostrich approach to health: Stick your head in a hole and ignore the obvious. And there was so much else happening, anyway, back then. Wars and riots and scandals. I'm told it was a most wondrous time to be alive. But Ricky the young doctor-in-training managed to quit smoking when it was ever so popular a habit and not nearly as socially unacceptable as today. That tells me something.'

The young woman lit the cigarette, took a single long puff, and languidly blew smoke out into the room.

'An ashtray?' she asked.

Ricky reached into a desk drawer and removed the one he kept hidden there. He put it on the edge of the desktop. The young woman immediately stubbed the cigarette out.

'There,' she said. 'Just enough of a pungent, smoky smell to remind us of that time.'

Ricky waited a moment, before asking, 'Why is it important to remember that time?'

The young woman rolled her eyes, tossed her head back, and let loose with a long, blaring laugh. The harsh sound was out of place, like a guffaw in a church or a harpsichord in an airport. When her laugh faded, the young woman fixed Ricky with a single, penetrating glare. 'Everything is important to remember. Everything about this visit, Ricky. Isn't that true for every patient? You don't really know what it is they'll say or when they'll say it that will open up their world to you, do you? So you have to be alert at all times. Because you never precisely know when the door might open to reveal the hidden secrets. So, you must always be ready and receptive. Attentive. Always vigilant for the word or the story that is slipped loose and tells you much, right? Isn't that a fair assessment of the process?'

He nodded in reply.

'Good,' she said brusquely. 'Why would you think that this visit today is any different from any other? Even though it obviously is.'

He did not reply. Again, he remained quiet for a second or two, just eyeing the young woman, hoping to unsettle her. But she seemed oddly cold-blooded and even-tempered, and silence, which he knew is often the most disturbing sound of all, seemed to not affect her. Finally, he spoke quietly, 'I am at a disadvantage. You seem to know much about me, and at least a little something about what happens here in this room, and I don't even know your name. I would like to know what you mean when you say Mr. Zimmerman has ended his treatment, because I have had no contact from Mr. Zimmerman, which is extremely unlikely. And I would like to know what your connection is to the individual you call Mr. R. and whom I presume is the same person who sent me the threatening letter signing it Rumplestiltskin. I would like the answers to these questions promptly. Otherwise, I will call the police.'

She smiled again. Unflustered.

'Practicality intrudes?'

'Answers,' he replied.

'Isn't that what we're all searching for, Ricky? Everyone who steps through that door into this room. Answers?'

He did not respond. Instead he reached for the telephone.

'Do you not imagine that in his own way, that is what Mr. R. wants, as well? Answers to questions that have plagued him for years. Come now, Ricky: Don't you agree that even the harshest sort of revenge starts with a simple question?'

This was intriguing, Ricky thought. But the interest he might have had in the observation was overcome by his growing irritation with the young woman's manner. She displayed nothing except a confident arrogance. He put his hand on the receiver. He was at a loss for anything else to do.

'Please respond promptly to my questions,' he said. 'Otherwise I will turn all this over to the police and let them sort it out.'

'No sense of sport, Ricky? No interest in playing the game?'

'I fail to see what sort of game is involved with sending disgusting, threatening pornography to an impressionable girl. Nor do I see the game in demanding that I kill myself.'

'But, Ricky,' the woman grinned, 'wouldn't that be the biggest game of all? Outplaying death?'

This made him pause, hand still hovering over the telephone. The young woman pointed at his hand. 'You can win, Ricky. But not if you pick up that telephone and dial 911. Then someone, somewhere, will lose. That promise has been made, and trust me, it will be kept. Mr. R. is, if nothing else, a man of his word. And when that someone loses, you lose, too. This is only Day One, Ricky. To give up now would be like conceding defeat right after the opening kickoff. Before you've even had time to run a single play from scrimmage.'

He pulled his hand back.

'Your name?' he asked.

'For today and for the purposes of the game, call me Virgil. Every poet needs a guide.'

'Virgil is a man's name.'

The woman who called herself Virgil shrugged broadly. 'I have a girlfriend who goes by the name Rikki. Does this make a difference?'

'No. And your connection to Rumplestiltskin?'

'He's my employer. He's extremely wealthy and able to hire all sorts of assistance. Any kind of assistance he wants. To achieve whatever means and ends he envisions for whatever plan he has in mind. Currently, he is preoccupied with you.'

'So, presumably, then as an employee, you have his name, an address, an identity which you could simply pass on to me and end this foolishness once and for all.'

Virgil shook her head. 'Alas, no, Ricky. Mr. R. is not so naive as to fail to insulate his identity from mere factotums, such as myself. And, even if I could help you, I wouldn't. Hardly be sporting. Imagine if the poet and his guide had looked up at the sign that said 'All hope abandon, ye who enter here! . . . ' and Virgil had shrugged and said, 'No shit. You don't want to go in there . . . ' Why, that would have ruined the poem. Can't write an epic about turning away at the gates of Hell, can you, Ricky? Nope. Got to walk through that doorway.'

'Why, then, are you here?'

'I told you. He thought you might doubt his sincerity — though that young lady with the stodgy and utterly predictable dad up in Deerfield who had her teenage emotions rearranged so easily should have been message enough for you. But doubts sow hesitation and you have only two weeks left to play, which is a short enough time. Hence, he sent a bona fide guide to get you jump-started. Me.'

'All right,' Ricky said. 'You keep talking about this game. Well, it is not a game to Mr. Zimmerman. He has been in analysis for slightly less than a year, and his treatment is at an important stage. You and your employer, the mysterious Mr. R., can screw around with me. That's one thing. But it is altogether something different when you involve my patients. That crosses a boundary . . . '

The young woman called Virgil held up her hand. 'Ricky, try not to sound so pompous.'

Ricky stopped and stared harshly at the woman.

She ignored this look, and with a small wave of her hand, added, 'Zimmerman was elected to become part of the game.'

Ricky must have looked astonished, because Virgil added, 'Not so eagerly at first, I'm told, but with an odd sort of enthusiasm after a short time. But I wasn't a participant in that particular conversation so I can't help you with those details. My role was different. I'll tell you who did get involved, however. A middle-aged and somewhat disadvantaged woman who calls herself

LuAnne, which is a pretty name, admittedly unusual and not very fitting given her precarious position on this planet. Anyway, Ricky, when I leave here, I think you'd be wise to have a talk with LuAnne. Who knows what you might learn? And, I'm certain you will pursue Mr. Zimmerman for an explanation, but I'm quite sure he will not be so readily available. As I said, Mr. R. is very wealthy and accustomed to getting his way.'

Ricky was about to demand a better clarification; the words were partway formed on his lips, when Virgil stood up. 'Do you mind,' she said huskily, 'if I remove my raincoat?'

He gestured widely with his hand, a motion that spoke of acceptance. 'If you like,' he said.

She smiled again, and slowly unbuttoned the front snaps and unfastened the belt around the waist. Then, in a single, abrupt motion, she shrugged the coat from her shoulders and let it drop to the floor.

She wore nothing beneath.

Virgil placed one hand on her hip and cocked her body in his direction provocatively. She pivoted about, turning her back momentarily, then swung around again, facing him. Ricky took in the entirety of her figure in a single glance, eyes working like a photographer's camera, capturing her breasts, her sex, her long legs, and then finally returning to her eyes. These glowed with anticipation.

'See, Ricky,' she said softly, 'you're not so old. Can't you feel blood rushing about inside you? A little stirring between the legs, no? I have quite a figure, don't I?' She giggled once. 'You don't have to answer. I'm well aware of the response. I've seen it before, in other men.'

Her eyes continued to lock onto his own, as if insisting that she could control the direction his vision took.

'There's always this wondrous moment, Ricky,' Virgil said, grinning widely, 'when a man first takes in the sight of a woman's body. Especially a woman's body he hasn't seen before. A view that is all adventure. His eyes simply cascade like water over a cliff, right down the front. Then, just like now, for you, where you'd rather be staring between my legs, there is this guilty bit of eye contact. It's as if the man is trying to say that he still sees me as a person, looking at my face, but in reality he's thinking like a beast, no matter how educated and sophisticated he might pretend to be. Isn't that what's happening now?'

He did not reply. He realized that it had been years since he'd been in the presence of a naked woman, a realization that seemed to be making a loud, reverberating noise deep within him. His ears rang with every word Virgil spoke and he was aware that he felt hot, as if the day's heat outdoors had burst uninvited into the office room.

She continued to smile at him. She pivoted about a second time, displaying her figure again. She held her pose, lingering first in one position, then another, like an artist's model trying to find just the correct posture. Each turn of her body seemed to increase the temperature in the office by a few more degrees. Then she slowly bent down and picked the black raincoat off the floor. She held it out in front of her for a second, as if she were reluctant to put it back on. But then, in a swift motion, she slid her arms into the sleeves and began to fasten it tightly in front of her. As her naked form disappeared, Ricky felt almost as if he were emerging from some sort of hypnotic trance, or, at least, what he thought it must feel like when a patient emerges from under an anesthetic. He started to speak, but Virgil held up her hand, stopping him.

'Sorry, Ricky,' she said curtly. 'The session has ended for today. I've given you lots of information, and now it's up to you to act. That's not something you do well, is it? What you do is listen. And then nothing. Well, those times have ended, Ricky. Now you'll have to get out into the world and do something. Otherwise . . . well, let's not think of the otherwise. When the guide points, you have to take the path. Don't get caught sitting about. Idle hands — blah, blah, blah. The early worm catches the whatever. There's some extremely good advice. Be sure you take it.'

She strode quickly toward the exit door.

'Wait,' he said impulsively. 'Will you be back?'

'Who knows?' Virgil replied with a small grin. 'Maybe from time to time. We'll see how you do.' Then she tugged open the door and exited.

He listened for a moment to the click-clack of her heels in the corridor, then he jumped up and raced over to the door. He pulled it open, but Virgil had already disappeared from the hallway. He paused a moment, then retreated back into his office, heading toward the window. He thrust himself up to the windowpane, staring out, just in time to see the young woman emerge from the front of the apartment building. As he watched, a long black limousine slithered to the front, and Virgil stepped from the curb, into the vehicle. The car slid away down the street, moving too suddenly for Ricky to observe the license plate or any other identifying characteristics even if he had been organized and clever enough to think of doing this.

* * *

Sometimes off the beaches of Cape Cod, up in Wellfleet near his vacation home, there are strong rip currents that form, and which can be dangerous, and occasionally fatal. They are created by the repetitive force of the ocean pounding against the shore, which eventually digs a bit of a furrow beneath the waves in the sandbars that guard the beach. When the space opens up, the incoming water suddenly finds a new location for its return race to the sea, pouring back through this underwater channel. On the surface, the rip current is established. When one is caught in the rip, there are a couple of tricks one must adhere to, which make the experience unsettling, perhaps scary, certainly exhausting, but primarily inconvenient. Ignore the tricks, and one is likely to die. Because the rip is narrow, one should never fight the flow. One should merely swim parallel to the shore, and within seconds the fierce tug of the current will slacken, leaving one with a simple haul to the beach. In fact, rips are generally short, as well, so one can ride them out and when the pull diminishes, adjust location accordingly and swim back to the beach. These, Ricky knew, are the simplest of instructions, and spoken on firm ground at a cocktail party, or even standing in loose and hot sand at the side of the ocean, makes it sound as if extracting oneself from a rip current is no more trouble than flicking a sand flea from the skin.

The reality, of course, is significantly harder. Being inexorably swept toward the ocean, away from the safety of the beach, creates panic instantly. Being caught in a force far stronger than any one individual is terrifying. Fear and the ocean are a lethal combination. Terror and exhaustion follow quickly. It seemed to Ricky that he read about at least one drowning every summer in the *Cape Cod Times* where the doomed swimmer had died only a few short feet from shore and safety.

Ricky tried to grip hard on his emotions, because he felt caught in a rip.

He took a deep breath and fought against the sensation that he was being tugged toward something dark and dangerous. As soon as the limousine bearing Virgil had departed from his view, he had seized his appointment book and found Zimmerman's number where he'd written it down on the front page, and then forgotten about it, never once having been forced to call the patient. He'd rapidly dialed the exchange, only to be greeted by empty ringing. No Zimmerman. No Zimmerman's overprotective mother. No answering machine or service. Just a steady, frustrating ringing.

He had, in that moment of confusion, decided he'd best speak directly with Zimmerman. And, even if the man had been somehow bribed by Rumplestiltskin to end his treatment, perhaps, Ricky thought, he could shed some light on who his tormentor was. Zimmerman was a bitter man, but not one capable of holding a secret, regardless of what he'd been told to do. Ricky slammed down the telephone in mid-unanswered ring, and seized his coat. Within seconds he was out his doorway.

The city streets were still filled with sunlight, though it was well into the dinner hour. The residue of rush-hour traffic continued to clog the roadways, though the commuting crowds jamming the sidewalks had thinned some. New York, like any great city, even though it boasts of a twenty-four-hour life, still functioned on the same rhythms as anywhere: energy in the morning, determination at midday, hunger in the evening. He ignored the packed restaurants, although more than once he caught an inviting smell as he passed one by. But this evening, Ricky Stark's hunger was of a far different sort.

He did something he almost never did. Instead of hailing a cab, Ricky set off to cross Central Park on foot. He thought the time and exertion would help him to straighten out his emotions, get a grip on what was happening to him. But despite his training, and vaunted powers of concentration, he had trouble remembering what it was that Virgil said to him, though he had no difficulty recalling every nuance of her body, from the smile playing on her lips, the curve of her breasts, to the shape of her sex.

The day's heat lingered into the early evening. Within

a few hundred yards he felt sticky sweat gathering at his neck and under his arms. He loosened his tie and removed his blazer, slinging it over his back, giving him a jaunty appearance that contradicted how he felt. The park was still filled with folks exercising, more than once he stepped aside to oblige a phalanx of joggers. He could see orderly people walking their dogs in dog-walking designated areas, and he passed a half-dozen softball games in progress. The baseball fields were all laid out so that the outfields overlapped. He noticed that often the right fielder on one team was standing more or less next to the left fielder of another, in a different game. There seemed to be an odd, city-defined etiquette to this shared space, each person trying to maintain focus on his own game, while not intruding on the other. Occasionally a ball struck by the team at bat would invade the premises of the opposite game, and those players would diligently step aside to accommodate the disruption, before resuming play. Ricky thought life was rarely that simple and infrequently that balletlike. Usually, he thought, we get in one another's ways.

It took him another quarter hour of briskly paced walking to reach the block where Zimmerman's apartment building was. By now, he was genuinely sweaty, and he wished he'd worn some old tennis shoes or runner's shoes, rather than the leather wingtips that seemed tight and threatened to give him a blister. He could feel a clammy dampness soaking through his undershirt, staining his oxford blue dress shirt. He thought his hair was matted and sticking to his forehead. Ricky hesitated in front of a store's plate glass window, trying to assess his reflection, seeing instead of the orderly, composed physician who greeted his patients poker-faced at his office door, a bedraggled, anxious man, caught up in a maze of indecision. He looked harried, disheveled, and probably a little bit frightened, he thought, and he took a few moments to try to compose himself.

Never before, in the entirety of his almost three decades of practice, had he broken from the rigid and formalized relationship between patient and analyst. Not once had he ever imagined going to a patient's home to check on them. No matter how deep the despair the client might have felt, they traveled with their depression to him. They reached out to him. If distraught and overwhelmed, they called him, and made an appointment to see him, in his office. It was an integral part of the process of getting better. As hard as it was for some people, as crippled as they might be by their emotions, the mere physical act of coming to see him was a critical step. To step outside the confines of the analyst's office was a complete rarity. It seemed cruel, sometimes, the artificial barriers and distances created by the relationship between patient and doctor, but it was out of those same distances that insight was discovered.

He hesitated on the corner, a half block from Zimmerman's apartment, a little astonished to find himself in that spot. That his hesitation was not all that different from Zimmerman's occasional pacing outside the doors to Ricky's office, was lost on him.

He took two or three steps down the block, then stopped.

He shook his head, and said, out loud, but under his breath, 'I can't do this.'

A young couple passing a few feet away must have heard his words, because the man said, 'Sure you can, fella. It's not that hard,' as if in reply. The young woman hanging on his arm burst into a laugh, then mock punched the man in the arm, as if to chastise him for being witty and rude, at the same time. They continued past him, and on into whatever their evening held for them, while Ricky stood, rocking like a boat tugging at its mooring, unable to move, but being pulled hard by wind and currents nonetheless.

'What did she say?' he whispered to himself.

Zimmerman decided to end his treatment at precisely 2:37 P.M. in a nearby subway stop.

This made no sense.

He looked back over his shoulder and saw a telephone kiosk on the corner. He strode over to the phone bank and stuck a quarter in the pay phone, rapidly punching in Zimmerman's number. Again the phone rang a dozen times, unanswered.

This time, however, Ricky felt relieved. The absence of a response at Zimmerman's house seemed to absolve him of the need to knock on the man's door, although he was surprised that Zimmerman's mother did not pick up. According to her son, she was bedridden most of the day, incapacitated and sickly, except for the unfettered and nearly inexhaustible supply of angry demands and belittling comments that she delivered nonstop.

He hung up the telephone and stepped back. He took a long look down the block where Zimmerman's apartment was, and then shook his head. He told himself: You've got to take control of this situation. The threatening letter, the child being singled out for pornography, the sudden appearance of a naked and quite stunning woman in his office, had all upset his equilibrium. He needed, he thought, to impose order back on events, and then chart a simple course through the game that he was caught up inside. What he didn't need to do, he told himself, was to throw away almost a year of analysis with Roger Zimmerman because he was frightened and acting rashly.

Telling himself these things, reassured him. He turned away, determined to head back to his home and start packing for his vacation.

His eyes, however, caught the entrance to the 92nd

Street subway station. Like so many other stations, this was nothing more than a set of stairs that descended into the earth, with a modest yellow lettered sign above. He moved in that direction, paused momentarily at the head of the stairs, then stepped down, driven suddenly by a sense of error and fear, as if something was just slowly emerging from mist and fog and becoming clear. His footsteps clattered on the steps. Artificial light hummed and buzzed and reflected off the tiles on the walls. A distant train groaned through a tunnel. A musty, aged odor, like opening a closet that has been shut for years overcame him, followed by a sense of contained heat, as if the day's temperatures had baked the station, and it was only now starting to cool. There were few people in the station at that moment, and he spotted a single black woman working in the token kiosk. He waited for a moment, for a second when she was not being harried by people making change, and then he approached. He bent toward the round, silver metal speaking filter in her Plexiglas window.

'Excuse me,' he said.

'You want change? Directions? Map's on the wall over there.'

'No,' he said, shaking his head. 'I wonder, I'm sorry this sounds strange but . . . '

'What you want, fella?'

'Well, I was wondering, did something happen down here today? This afternoon . . . '

'You gotta talk to the cops about that,' she said briskly. 'Happened before my shift.'

'But what . . . '

'I wadn't here. Didn't see nothing.'

'But what happened?'

'Guy jumped in front offa train. Or fell, I dunno. Cops been here and gone already by the time my shift begun. Cleaned up the mess and gathered up a coupla witnesses. That's it.'

'What cops?'

'Transit. Ninety-sixth and Broadway. Talk to them. I got no details at all.'

Ricky stepped back, his stomach clenched, head spinning, almost nauseous. He needed air, and there was none inside the station. A train approached, filling the station with a steady screeching noise, as if the act of slowing for the stop was torturous. The sound flooded over him, pummeling him like fists.

'You okay, mister?' the woman in the booth shouted above the racket. 'You look kinda sick.'

He nodded, and whispered a reply that she undoubtedly couldn't hear. 'I'm fine,' he said, but this was clearly a lie. Like a drunk trying to maneuver a car through twisting roads, Ricky swerved toward the exit.

5

Everything about the world Ricky entered that evening was alien to him.

The sights, sounds, and smells of the Transit Authority police station at 96th and Broadway seemed to him to represent a window on the city that he'd never before looked through and that he was only vaguely aware existed. There was a faint aroma of urine and vomit fighting the harsher odor of strong disinfectant right inside the headquarters door, as if someone had been violently ill and the cleanup had been sloppily and hastily managed in the aftermath. The pungency made him hesitate, just long enough to be overcome with a curious din, the blending of the routine and the surreal. A man was shouting unintelligible word concoctions from some hidden holding area, words that seemed to reverberate around the entranceway unconnected to everything else going on. There was an angry woman holding a crying child in front of the sergeant's thick wooden reception desk, spilling out imprecations in rapid-fire Spanish. Police officers creaked past him, their light blue shirts dampened with sweat from the day's lingering heat, their leather weapons belts making an odd counterpoint to the squeaking of their polished black shoes. A telephone rang somewhere hidden, unanswered. There were comings and goings, laughter and tears, all punctuated with bursts of obscenities emanating either from rough-edged officers or the occasional visitors, several in handcuffs, who were swept beneath the unforgiving fluorescent lights of the reception area.

Ricky swayed inside the door, assaulted by all he saw and heard, unsure what to do. An officer suddenly brushed past him in a hurry, saying 'Ouddadaway fella, coming through here . . . ' making him step forward abruptly, as if jerked by a rope.

The woman at the sergeant's desk raised her fist and shook it at the officer manning the reception area, let burst with a final cascade of words run together into a solid wall of insults, and, giving the child a shake and a twist, turned away, scowling, pushing past Ricky as if he were as insignificant as a cockroach. Ricky stumbled ahead and approached the officer behind the desk. Someone once standing approximately where Ricky took up his position had surreptitiously carved *FU* in the wood, an opinion that no one apparently cared enough to delete.

'I'm sorry,' Ricky started, only to be interrupted.

'Nobody's ever really sorry, fella. It's just what they say. Never really mean it. But hey, I'll listen to anybody. So, what is it that you think you're sorry about?'

'No, you misunderstand me. What I mean is . . . '

'No one ever says what they mean, either. Important lesson in life. It'd be helpful if more people would learn it.'

The policeman was probably in his early forties and wore an insouciant smile that seemed to indicate that he'd seen just about everything up to this point in his life worth seeing. He was a thickset man, with a solid, bodybuilder's neck and sleek black hair that was pushed slickly back from his forehead. The surface of the desk was littered with paper forms and incident reports, seemingly tossed about with no concept of organization. Occasionally the officer would grab a couple and staple them together, punching the old-fashioned desk stapler with a bang before tossing them in a wire basket.

'Let me start over,' Ricky finally stated sharply. The policeman grinned again, shaking his head.

'No one ever gets to start over — at least, not in my experience. We all say that we want to find a way to begin life all over again, but it just doesn't work out that way. But hey, give it a shot. Maybe you'll be the first. So, how can I help you, fella?'

'Earlier today there was an incident at the 92nd Street station. A man fell . . . '

'Jumped, I heard. You a witness?'

'No. But I knew the man, I believe. I was his doctor. I need information . . . '

'Doctor, huh? What sort of doctor?'

'He was in psychoanalytic treatment with me for the past year.'

'You're a shrink?'

Ricky nodded.

'Interesting job, that,' the officer said. 'You use one of those couches?'

'That's correct.'

'No shit? And people still have stuff to talk about? Me, I think I'd be looking for a catnap as soon as I put my head down. One yawn and I'd be out like a light. But people really talk up a storm, huh?'

'Sometimes.'

'Cool. Well, one guy ain't gonna be talking no more. You better speak to the detective. Head through the double doors, keep going down the corridor, office is on the left. Riggins caught the case. Or what there was of it after the Eighth Avenue express came through the 92nd Street station at about sixty miles per. You want details, that's where to go. Talk to the detective.'

The policeman gestured in the direction of a pair of doors that led into the bowels of the station. As he pointed, Ricky could hear a spiraling sound rising from some room that seemed alternately below and then above them. The desk sergeant smiled. 'That guy's gonna get on my nerves before the night is out,' he said, turning away and picking up a sheaf of papers and stapling them together with a noise like a gunshot. 'If he doesn't shut up, I'm likely to need a shrink of my own by the end of the night. What you need, doc, is a portable couch.' He laughed, made a swooping motion with his hand, the papers rustling in the breeze, shooing Ricky in the right direction.

* * *

There was a door on the left marked DETECTIVE BUREAU which Ricky Starks pushed through, entering a small office warren of grimy gray steel desks and more of the sickeningly bright overhead lighting. He blinked for a second, as if the glare stung his eyes like saltwater. A detective wearing a white shirt and red tie, sitting at the closest desk, looked up at him.

'Help you?'

'Detective Riggins?'

The detective shook his head. 'Nah, not me. She's over in the back, talking to the last of those people who got some kinda look at the jumper today.'

Ricky looked across the rooms and spotted a woman just shy of middle age wearing a man's pale blue button-down shirt and striped silk rep tie, although the tie was loosely hung around her neck, more like a noose than anything else, gray slacks which seemed to blend with the decor, and a contradictory pair of white running shoes with a Day-Glo orange stripe down the side. Her dirty-blond hair was pulled back sharply from her face in a ponytail, which made her seem a little older than the mid-thirties that Ricky might have guessed. There were wearied wrinkles at the corners of her eyes. The detective was speaking with a pair of black teenage boys, each wearing wildly exaggerated baggy blue jeans and baseball caps that were cocked at odd angles, as if glued askew on their heads. Had Ricky been slightly more aware of the ways of the world, he might have recognized this for the current style, but, as it was, he merely thought their appearance distinctly odd and a bit unsettling. Had he encountered the pair on the sidewalk, he would have undoubtedly been frightened.

The detective sitting in front of him suddenly asked, 'You here on that jumper today at 92nd Street?'

Ricky nodded. The detective picked up his phone. He gestured to a half-dozen stiff-backed wooden chairs lined up against one wall of the office. Only one chair was currently occupied, by a bedraggled, dirt-strewn woman of indistinct age, whose wiry silver gray hair seemed to explode from her head in a multitude of directions, and who appeared to Ricky to be speaking to herself. The woman wore a threadbare overcoat that she kept hugging increasingly tighter to her body, and she rocked a little bit in the seat, as if keeping rhythm with the electricity bounding about within her. Homeless and schizophrenic, Ricky diagnosed immediately. He had not seen anyone with her condition professionally since his graduate school days, although he'd hurried past many similar people over the years, picking up his pace on the sidewalk like virtually every other New Yorker. In recent years, the number of homeless street people seemed to have diminished, but Ricky always assumed that they had simply been shunted to different locations by political maneuverings so that the enthusiastic tourists and the well-heeled and well-moneyed folk making their way through midtown would not have to encounter them as frequently.

'Just have a seat over there next to LuAnne,' the detective said. 'I'll let Riggins know she's got another live one to talk with.'

Ricky stiffened when he heard the woman's name. He took a deep breath and walked over toward the row of chairs.

'May I sit here?' he asked, pointing to a seat next to the woman. She looked up at him, slightly astonished.

'He wants to know if he can sit here. What am I? The

queen of chairs? What should I say? Yes? No? He can sit where he likes . . . '

LuAnne had grimy, broken fingernails packed with dirt. Her hands were scarred and blistered and one sported a cut that seemed infected, the swollen skin turning a dark purplish color around a deep maroon scab. Ricky thought it must have been painful, but he said nothing. LuAnne rubbed her hands together like a cook spreading salt over a dish.

Ricky plopped down in the seat next to her. He shifted about, as if trying to make himself comfortable, then asked, 'So, LuAnne, you were in the subway station when the man fell on the tracks?'

LuAnne looked up into the fluorescent lighting, staring at the bright and relentless glare. She gave a little shudder with her shoulders, and then replied, 'So, he wants to know was I there when the man went in front of the train? I should tell him what I saw, all blood and people screaming, awful it was, then the police came.'

'Do you live in the subway station?'

'He wants to know do I live there, well, sometimes I should tell him, sometimes I live there.'

LuAnne finally looked away from the lights, blinking rapidly and seeming to move her head about as if recognizing ghosts throughout the room. After a moment, she finally turned toward Ricky. 'I saw,' she said. 'Were you there, too?'

'No,' he replied. 'The man who died was someone I knew.'

'Oh, sad,' she shook her head. 'So sad for you. I've known people who died. Sad for me, then.'

'Yes,' he answered. 'It's sad.' He forced a weak smile in LuAnne's direction. She smiled back. 'Tell me, LuAnne, what did you see?'

She coughed once or twice, as if trying to clear her throat. 'He wants to know what I saw,' she said, facing

Ricky but not necessarily addressing him. 'He wants to know about the man who died and then the pretty woman.'

'What pretty woman was that?' Ricky asked, trying to keep himself calm.

'He doesn't know about the very pretty woman.'

'No, I don't. But now I'm interested,' he said, trying to prod her along carefully.

LuAnne's eyes seemed to drift off into the distance, trying to focus on something beyond her vision, like a mirage, and she spoke in an offhand, friendly manner. 'He wants to know that the pretty woman came up to me, right after the man went boom! And she speaks to me very softly, saying did you see that, LuAnne? Did you see that man jump in front of the train? Did you see how he stepped right over to the edge as the train was coming through, it was the express, see, and doesn't stop, no, never stops, must get the local if you want to get on a train, and how he just jumps down! Awful, awful! She says to me, LuAnne, did you see him kill himself? No one pushed him, LuAnne, she says. No one at all. Be absolutely sure of that, LuAnne, no one pushed the man, boom! He just stepped out, the woman says. So sad. Must have wanted to die terrible bad all of a sudden, boom! And then there is a man right next to her, right next to the very pretty woman and he says, LuAnne, you must tell the police what you saw, tell them that you saw the man just step right past the other men and other ladies and jump, boom! Dead. And then the beautiful woman says to me, she says, you will tell the police, LuAnne, that is your duty as a citizen, to tell them you saw the man jump. And then she gives me ten dollars. Ten dollars all for me. But she makes me promise. LuAnne, she says, you promise to go to the police and tell them you saw the man jump good-bye? Yes, I says to her. I promise. And so I came to tell the police, just like she said and just like I promised.

Did she give you ten dollars, too?'

'No,' Ricky said slowly, 'she didn't give me ten dollars.'

'Oh, too bad,' LuAnne replied, shaking her head. 'Unlucky for you.'

'Yes. That is too bad,' Ricky agreed. 'And unlucky, as well.'

He looked up and saw the detective crossing the room toward them.

She looked even more exhausted by the day's events than Ricky had first guessed when he saw her across the room. Detective Riggins moved with a deliberateness that spoke of sore muscles, fatigue, and a spirit sapped at least in part by the day's heat and certainly by spending the afternoon laboriously helping to gather up the remains of the unfortunate Mr. Zimmerman, followed by piecing together his last few moments before stepping off the subway platform. That she managed the most meager of smiles by way of introduction surprised him.

'Hello,' she said. 'I gather you're here on Mr. Zimmerman?' But before he could reply, Detective Riggins turned toward LuAnne and added, 'LuAnne, I'm going to have an officer drive you over to the 102nd Street shelter for the night. Thank you for coming in. You were very helpful. Stay at the shelter, LuAnne, okay? In case I need to talk to you again.'

'She says stay at the shelter but she doesn't know we hate the shelter. It's filled with mean and crazy folks who'll rob you and stab you if they know you have ten dollars from a pretty woman.'

'I'll make sure that no one knows, and you'll be safe. Please.'

LuAnne shook her head, but contradictorily said, 'I'll try, detective.'

Detective Riggins pointed toward the doorway, where a pair of uniformed officers were waiting. 'Those guys will drop you off, okay?'

LuAnne rose, shaking her head.

'The car ride will be fun, LuAnne. If you like, I'll ask them to put on their lights and siren.'

This made LuAnne smile. She nodded her head with a childlike enthusiasm. The detective gestured toward the pair of uniformed cops and said, 'Guys, give our witness here the red-carpet treatment. Lights and action all the way, okay?'

Both officers shrugged, smiling. This was easy duty, and they had no complaints, as long as LuAnne was in and out of their vehicle rapidly enough so that the pungent odor of sweat, grime, and infection that she carried with her like a perfume wouldn't linger behind.

Ricky watched as the deranged woman, nodding and speaking to herself again, shuffled off toward the exit with the policemen. He turned and saw that Detective Riggins was watching her departure as well. The policewoman sighed. 'She's not nearly as bad off as some,' she said. 'And she stays pretty local. Either behind the bodega on 97th Street, in the station where she was today, or up at the entrance to Riverside Park on 96th. I mean, she's crazy and way out there, but not nasty about it, like some. I wonder who she really is. You think, doctor, maybe there's someone somewhere worrying about her? Out in Cincinnati or Minneapolis. Family, friends, relatives wondering whatever became of their eccentric aunt or cousin. Maybe she's an heiress to some oil fortune, or a lottery winner. That would be kinda neat, huh? Wonder what happened to her to have her end up like this. All those crazy little chemicals in the brain just bubbling out of control. But that's more your territory, not mine.'

'I'm not really big on medications,' Ricky said. 'Not like some of my colleagues. A schizophrenia as profound as hers genuinely needs medication, but what I do probably wouldn't help LuAnne all that much.'

Detective Riggins motioned him toward her desk, which had a chair pulled up beside it. They walked across the room together. 'You're into talking, huh? The troubled articulate, huh? All that talk, talk, talk, and sooner or later it all gets figured out?'

'That would be an oversimplification, detective. But not inaccurate.'

'I had a sister who saw a therapist after her divorce. It really helped her get her life straightened out. On the other hand, my cousin Marcie who's one of those types always got that black cloud over her head — she saw some guy for three years and ended up more authentically fucked-up than before she got started.'

'I'm sorry to hear that. Like any profession, there are wide degrees of competency.' Ricky and the detective sat down at the desk. 'But — '

Detective Riggins cut him off before he could get further with his question. 'You said you were Mr. Zimmerman's therapist, correct?'

She pulled out a notepad and pencil.

'Yes. He'd been in analysis during this past year. But . . . '

'And did you detect any heightened suicidal tendencies in the last couple of weeks?'

'No. Absolutely not,' Ricky said with determination.

The detective raised her eyebrows in modest surprise. 'Really, no? None whatsoever?'

'That's what I just said,' Ricky replied. 'In fact . . . '

'He was making progress in his analysis, then?'

Ricky hesitated.

'Well?' the detective asked abruptly. 'Was he getting better? Gaining control? Feeling more confident? More ready to take on the world? Less depressed? Less angry?'

Again, Ricky paused, before replying. 'I would say that he had not made what either you or I would consider a breakthrough. He was still struggling deeply with the issues that plagued his life.'

Detective Riggins smiled, but without humor. Her words had an edgy tone. 'So, after almost a year of near-constant treatment, fifty minutes per day, five days per week — what, forty-eight weeks per year — it would be safe to say that he was still depressed and frustrated by his life?'

Ricky bit down on his lips briefly, then nodded.

Detective Riggins wrote a few words down on her pad. Ricky could not see what she scribbled. 'Would despair be too strong a word?'

'Yes,' Ricky said with irritation.

'Even if that was the first word that his mother, whom he lived with, used? And the same word that several of his coworkers came up with?'

'Yes,' Ricky insisted.

'So, you don't think he was suicidal?'

'I told you, detective. He didn't present with any of the classic symptomology. Had he, I would have taken steps . . . '

'What sort of steps?'

'We would have tried to focus the sessions more specifically. Perhaps medication, if I actually thought the threat was sincere . . . '

'I thought you just said you didn't like prescribing pills?'

'I don't, but . . . '

'Aren't you going on vacation? Like real soon?'

'Yes. Tomorrow, at least I'm scheduled to begin, but what has that . . . '

'So, as of tomorrow, his therapeutic lifeline was going on vacation?'

'Yes, but I fail to see . . . '

The detective smiled. 'Those are interesting words for a shrink to use.'

'What words?' Ricky asked, his exasperation reaching deep within him.

' 'Fail to see . . . ,' ' Detective Riggins said. 'Isn't that pretty close to what you guys like to call a Freudian slip?'

'No.'

'So, you just don't think he committed suicide?'

'No, I do not. I just . . . '

'Have you ever lost a patient to suicide in the past?'

'Yes. Unfortunately. But in that case the signs were clear-cut. My efforts, however, weren't adequate for the depth of that patient's depression.'

'That failure stick with you for a while, doc?'

'Yes,' Ricky replied coldly.

'It would be bad for your business and real bad for your reputation if another one of your long-term patients decided to take on the Eighth Avenue express one-on-one, wouldn't it?'

Ricky rocked back in the chair, scowling.

'I don't appreciate the implication in your question, detective.'

Riggins smiled, shaking her head slightly. 'Well, let's move on, then. If you don't think he killed himself, the alternative is that someone pushed him in front of that train. Did Mr. Zimmerman ever speak about anyone who hated him, or who bore a grudge, or who might have a motive for homicide? He spoke to you every day, so presumably if he was being stalked by some unknown killer he might have mentioned it. Did he?'

'No. He never mentioned anyone who would fit the categories you suggest.'

'He never said, 'So and so wants me dead . . . '?'

'No.'

'And you'd remember if he had?'

'Of course.'

'Okay, so no one real obvious was trying to do him in. No business partner? Estranged lover? Cuckolded husband? You think someone might have pushed him in front of the express for what? Kicks? Some other mysterious reason?'

Ricky hesitated. He realized this was his opportunity to tell the police about the letter demanding he kill himself, the visit from the naked woman Virgil, the game he was being asked to play. All he had to do was to say that a crime had been committed, and that Zimmerman was a victim of an act that had nothing to do with him except his death. Ricky half opened his mouth to blurt out all these details, to let them flow forth unchecked, but what he saw instead was a bored and barely interested detective, seeking to wrap up an altogether unpleasant day with a single typewritten form which wouldn't contain a category for the information he was about to deliver.

He decided, in that second, to keep his own counsel. This was his psychoanalyst's nature. He did not share speculation or opinion easily or publicly. 'Perhaps,' he said. 'What do you know about this other woman? The woman who gave LuAnne the ten dollars?'

The detective wrinkled her forehead, as if confused by the question. 'Well, what about her?'

'Isn't her behavior in the slightest bit suspicious? Didn't it seem that she was putting words into LuAnne's mouth?'

The detective shrugged. 'I don't know that. A woman and a man accompanying her see that one of the less fortunate citizens of our great city might be an important witness to an event, so they make sure that the poor witness gets some compensation to step forward and help the police. This might be less suspicious than it is good citizenship, because LuAnne steps right up and helps us out, at least in part because of the intervention of this couple.'

Ricky paused, then asked, 'You didn't happen to find out who they were, did you?'

The detective shook her head. 'Sorry. They pointed

out LuAnne to one of the first officers on the scene, and then took off after informing the officer that they themselves were positioned poorly to see exactly what took place. And no, he didn't get a name from either of them because they weren't witnesses. Why?'

Ricky did not know whether he wanted to answer this question. A part of him screamed that he should unburden himself of everything. But he had no idea how dangerous this might be. He was trying to calculate, to guess, to assess, and to examine, but it suddenly seemed as if all the events that surrounded him were hazy and impossible to decipher, unclear and elusive. He shook his head, as if that might jog all the emotions into some sort of definition. 'I have my sincere doubts that Mr. Zimmerman would kill himself. His condition most definitely didn't seem that severe,' Ricky said. 'Write that down, detective, and put it in your report.'

Detective Riggins shrugged and grinned with an ill-disguised fatigue accented by sarcasm. 'I will do that, doctor. Your opinion, such as it is and for whatever it's worth, is noted, for the record.'

'Were there other witnesses, someone perhaps who saw Zimmerman step away from the crowd on the platform? Someone who saw him move without being pushed?'

'Just LuAnne, doctor. Everyone else only saw a part of the event. No one actually saw that he wasn't pushed. But, then, a couple of youths did see that he had been standing alone, separated from the other people waiting on the local. The eyewitness pattern, incidentally, doctor, is fairly typical for these sorts of cases. People have their eyes focused ahead, down the tunnel in the direction the train is expected. Typically jumpers move to the back end of the crowd, not the front. They're looking to do themselves in for whatever private reasons they might have, not provide a show for every other commuter in the station. So, ninety-nine times out of a hundred, they move apart from the crowd, to the back. Or pretty much precisely where Mr. Zimmerman had taken up his position.'

The detective smiled. 'Dollars to doughnuts I'll find a note in his personal belongings somewhere. Or maybe you'll get a letter in the mail this week. If you do, make a copy for my report, willya, doc? Of course, with you heading out on vacation, you may not get it before you leave. Still, it would be helpful.' Ricky wanted to reply, but he kept his own anger on a short string.

'Can I have your card, detective? In case I need to contact you in the future,' he asked as coldly as he could.

'Of course. Call me any old time.' She clearly said this in a contemptuous tone that implied the precise opposite. Then she reached into a box on her desk and removed one, which she handed over with a small flourish. Without glancing at it, Ricky put this in his pocket and rose to leave. He crossed the detective bureau rapidly, looking back only as he passed through the door, catching a single glimpse of Detective Riggins hunched over an old-fashioned typewriter, starting to peck out the words of her report on the obvious, ordinary, and seemingly inconsequential death of Roger Zimmerman.

6

Ricky Starks slammed the door to his apartment shut behind him, the noise resounding in his ears, and echoing away through the dimly lit empty building corridor. He frantically twisted the locks that he so infrequently used, double-bolting the entranceway. He pulled on the door handle, to make certain that these functioned properly. Then, still uncertain that the locks alone were sufficient, he grabbed a chair and wedged it up under the doorknob as an old-fashioned secondary barrier. It took some mental energy on his part to prevent himself from piling bureau, boxes, bookshelves — anything he could immediately lay his hands on — up against the door to barricade himself inside. Sweat stung at his eyes, and even though the air conditioner hummed along busily out of sight in the office window, he still felt flashes of sudden heat like so many lightning bolts crease his body. A soldier, a policeman, a pilot, a mountaineer — anyone versed in the various businesses of danger — would have easily recognized these for what they were: strikes of fear. But Ricky had spent so many years living away from any of those edges, that he was unfamiliar with the most obvious of signs.

He stepped away from the door, turning to survey his apartment. A single, dim overhead light above the doorway that barely overcame the night threw odd weak shadows into the corners of the waiting room. He could hear the air conditioner and beyond that, muffled street noises, but other than that, nothing but an oppressive silence.

The door to his office was open, yawning darkly. He was abruptly overcome by the sensation that when he'd left the sanctuary of his home earlier that evening in the minutes after Virgil's visit, he'd closed that door behind him, as was his usual habit. A rough-edged sense of apprehension scoured about within him, filling him with doubts. He stared at the open door, trying desperately to recall his precise steps in leaving.

He could picture himself donning his tie and jacket, pausing to double-knot his right shoelace, patting his hip to make certain that he carried his wallet, dropping the apartment key into his front pocket, then jangling it to reassure himself that it was secure. He saw himself stepping across the apartment, exiting the front door, waiting for the elevator to descend from the third floor, finding himself out on the street where the air above the sidewalk was still hot. All this was abundantly clear. It was, he thought, a departure no different from thousands of others over thousands of days. It was the return that resulted in everything seeming skewed or slightly misshapen, like staring at one's image in a circus fun-house mirror, distorted no matter which way one pivoted and turned. Inwardly he screamed at himself: *Did you close that interior door*?

He bit his lip in frustration, trying to recall the sensation of the knob in his hand, the noise of the wood shutting behind his back. The memory eluded him and he felt frozen in his position, stymied by his inability to recollect a single, simple, everyday act. And then he asked himself an even worse question, although he didn't realize it quite yet: *Why can't you remember*?

He took a deep breath and reassured himself: You must have left it open. By mistake.

Still he didn't move. He felt suddenly sapped of strength. Almost as if he'd been through a fight, or, at least, what he suspected he'd feel if he'd fought someone, because he realized abruptly that he never had. At least, not as an adult, and he discounted the occasional wrestlings of adolescent boys which seemed impossibly distant in his past.

The darkness seemed to mock him. He strained his hearing, trying to penetrate into the darkened room.

No one is there, he told himself.

But, as if to underscore the lie, he said out loud: 'Hello?'

The sound of the single word spoken in the small space had a tightening effect upon Ricky. He was overcome by a sense of being ridiculous. A child, he told himself, is frightened of shadows, not an adult. Especially one who has spent the entirety of their adult life dealing with secrets and hidden terrors, as he had.

He stepped forward, trying to regain his composure. He was home, he told himself. He was safe.

Still, he reached out quickly for the light switch on the wall, as he hesitated in the gray-black space of the doorway, groping about with his hand until he found the toggle switch, which he flicked instantly.

Nothing happened. The blackness of the room remained intact.

Ricky gasped hard, inhaling some of the darkness. He flicked the switch repeatedly, as if refusing to believe that there was no light in the room. He cursed out loud: 'Damn it to hell . . . ' but did not step inside. Instead, he allowed time for his eyes to adjust to the dark, all the time listening carefully, trying to pick out some telltale noise that might let him know that he wasn't alone. He reassured himself: When you've had as unsettling an experience as he'd had that evening, the mind naturally played all sorts of little tricks. Still, he waited a few more seconds, so that his vision had some purchase on the dark room, and he swept his eyes back and forth a few times. Then he stepped across the small space, angling for his desk and the lamp that occupied one corner. He felt not unlike a blind man, keeping his hands out in front of him, trying to feel his way across an area where there was nothing to feel. He bumped solidly into his desk, misjudging the distance slightly, banging his knee, which prompted a torrent of obscenities from his mouth. Several shits and damns and a single fuck, all of which were out of character for Ricky, who before the events of the past day, had rarely uttered an obscenity.

He sidled alongside the desk, finally finding the lamp with his hand, and locating its switch. With a relieved sigh, he clicked this, expecting light.

It, too, failed to function.

Ricky gripped the side of the desk, steadying himself. He told himself there must be some kind of power outage, caused by the heat and the citywide demand for electricity, but behind his desk he could see through the window that streetlights were burning brightly and the air conditioner continued to hum merrily along. Then he told himself that it wasn't beyond the realm of possibility that two different lightbulbs might have burned out simultaneously. Unusual, but possible.

Keeping one hand on the desk edge, he turned in the direction of the third lamp that he kept in his office. It was a standing light, a black, cast-iron design that his wife had purchased a number of years earlier to take up to the summer place in Wellfleet, but which he'd appropriated for the corner of his office, behind his chair, at the head of the couch. He used it for reading, and on rainy, dark days, to clear some of the city November gloom from the room, so that patients wouldn't be totally distracted by the weather. The lamp was perhaps fifteen feet away from where he was poised at the desk, but it was a distance that in that moment seemed much farther. He pictured his office, knowing that it was merely a few paces away and that nothing stood between him and his chair, and once there, the lamp would be easily found. He wished, in that moment, that more light from the street filtered through the windows, but what little existed seemed to stop right at the glass, as if impotent and unable to penetrate into the small room. Four strides across, he told himself. Don't bump your knee on the chair.

He stepped forward carefully, feeling the emptiness in front of him with his outstretched arms. He bent slightly at the waist, reaching for the reassuring feel of his old leather chair. It seemed to take him longer to cross the space than he would have guessed, but the chair was where it always was, and he found the arm, the back, and he lurched into the seat with a grateful welcoming squeak of leather. His hands located the small table where he kept his daybook and clock, then reached behind it for the lamp. The knob was up just beneath the bulb, and with a little twisting and fumbling, he found it. Without hesitation, he turned it with a decisive click.

The darkness remained intact.

He twisted the knob back and forth a dozen times, filling the room with clicks.

Nothing.

Ricky sat frozen in his seat, trying to arrive at some obvious and benign explanation for why none of the lights in his office functioned. This eluded him.

Breathing in deeply, he listened to the nighttime, trying to sort through the ancillary sounds of the city. His nerve ends were on edge, his hearing sharpened, every other sense gathered in an effort to determine whether he was truly alone. A part of him wanted to bolt for the front door, to escape to the corridor, and then to find someone to accompany him back into the apartment. He fought against this desire, recognizing it for the panic that it implied. He tried to force himself to remain calm.

He could hear nothing, but this did not reassure him that no one was with him in the apartment. He tried to imagine where someone might hide, which closet, which corner, beneath which table. Then he tried to concentrate on those locations, as if from the seat behind his analyst's couch, he could see into those hidden regions. But this effort, too, was unsuccessful, or, at least, he realized, unsatisfactory. He tried to remember where he might have kept a flashlight or candlesticks, guessing that if he had any, they would be in the kitchen on a shelf, probably right next to the spare lightbulbs. He stayed seated for another minute, reluctant to leave his familiar seat, managing to force himself upward only by recognizing that pursuing some sort of light was the only reasonable response.

He stepped gingerly into the center of the room, keeping his hands out in front of him again, mimicking a blind man. He was halfway across the room when the telephone on the desk rang.

The sound seared through him.

He stumbled as he pivoted toward the noise, reaching out for the sound. His hand knocked into a jar of pens and pencils he kept on his desktop, scattering them. He seized the telephone just before the sixth ring, which would have triggered his answering machine. 'Hello? Hello?'

There was no response.

'Hello? Is someone there?'

The phone went dead abruptly.

Ricky held the receiver in his hand in the darkness, cursing silently to himself, then not so silently, 'Goddamn it to hell!' he said loudly. 'Goddamn it, Goddamn it, Goddamn it . . . '

He hung up the receiver, and placed both hands on the desk surface, as if exhausted and needing to catch his breath again. He cursed again, though more softly.

The phone rang again.

He lurched back in surprise, then reached out and fumbling slightly, banging the receiver against the desktop, he grabbed the receiver and thrust it to his ear. 'This isn't funny,' he said.

'Doctor Ricky,' cooed Virgil's deep, yet kittenish voice. 'No one has ever suggested this was a joke. In fact, Mr. R. is fairly humorless, or so I'm told.'

Ricky bit back on every angry word that leapt forward to the brink of his lips. Instead, he let some silence speak for him.

After a few seconds, Virgil laughed. The sound was awful over the phone line.

'You're still in the dark, aren't you, Ricky?'

'Yes,' he said. 'You've been here, haven't you. You or someone like you broke in here while I was out and . . . '

'Ricky,' Virgil suddenly cooed, almost seductively, 'you're the analyst. When you're in the dark about something, especially something simple, what do you do?'

He didn't reply. She laughed again.

'Come on, Ricky. And you think yourself to be a master of symbolism and interpreting all sorts of mysteries? How do you shed light where there is only darkness? Why, that's your job, isn't it?'

She didn't allow him a response.

'Follow the simplest trail for an answer.'

'What?' he asked.

'Ricky, I can see you're going to need my help considerably over the next few days if you intend to make an honest effort to save your own life. Or do you prefer to sit in the dark right up to the arrival of the day that you have to kill yourself?'

He felt confused.

'I don't get it,' he said.

'You will in a moment or two,' she said firmly. Then she hung up, leaving him holding impotently on to the telephone. He took several seconds before he returned it to its cradle. The nighttime in the room seemed to envelop him, blanketing him with despair. He reviewed Virgil's words, which seemed to him to be obtuse, cryptic, and unfathomable. He wanted to scream out that he had no idea what she meant, frustrated by both the darkness that surrounded him and the sense that his private space had been disrupted and violated. Ricky ground his teeth in anger, gripping the edge of the desk, grunting with rage. He wanted to pick something up and break it.

'A simple trail,' he almost shouted out. 'There aren't any simple trails in life!'

The sound of his own words disappearing into the blackened room had the immediate effect of quieting him. He seethed, on the verge of fury.

'Simple, simple . . . ,' he said under his breath.

And then he had an idea. He was surprised that it managed to slide past his growing anger. 'It can't be . . . ' he said, as he reached out with his left hand for his desk lamp. He felt the base and found the electrical cord emerging from the side. Holding this between his fingers, he traced the wire downward to where he knew it was plugged into an extension cord that ran against the wall to the outlet. He lowered himself to his knees on the floor and within a few seconds found the plug. It had been pulled from the extension. It took another few seconds of groping around for him to find the end of the extension, but he managed. He slid the plug into the receptacle and the room around him suddenly burst with light. He rose from the floor and turned to the lamp behind the couch and immediately saw that it had been unplugged, as well. He lifted his eyes to the overhead light and guessed that the bulb behind the sconce had merely been loosened.

On his desk, the telephone rang for the third time.

He picked it up, demanding 'How did you get in here?'

'Don't you think Mr. R. can afford a capable locksmith?' Virgil said coyly. 'Or a professional burglar? Someone expert with the antique and outmoded dead-bolt locks you have on your front door, Ricky. Haven't you ever considered something more modern? Electrical locking systems with lasers and infrared motion detectors? Handprint technology, or maybe even those eyeball retina recognition systems they use at government installations. You know that sort of thing is available to the general public through slightly shady and disreputable connections. Haven't you ever had the urge to be slightly more modern in your personal security?'

'I've never needed that foolishness,' Ricky harrumphed pompously.

'Never had a break-in? Never been robbed? Not in all these years in Manhattan?'

'No.'

'Well,' Virgil said smugly, 'I guess no one ever thought you had something worth stealing. But that's not the case now, is it, doctor? My employer certainly does, and he seems more than willing to take all sorts of chances.'

Ricky did not reply. He looked up abruptly, staring out the office window.

'You can see me,' he said excitedly. 'You're looking at me right now, aren't you? How else would you know that I managed to get the lights on?'

Virgil burst into a laugh. 'Good for you, Ricky. You're making some progress when finally able to state the obvious.'

'Where are you?' Ricky asked.

Virgil paused, before replying: 'Close by. I'm at your shoulder, Ricky. I'm in your shadow. What good would it be to have a guide to Hell who wasn't there when you needed her?'

He didn't have an answer.

'Well,' Virgil continued, her voice returning to the lilting tones that Ricky was beginning to find irritating, 'let me give you a little hint, doctor. Mr. R. is a sporting type. With all the planning that has gone into this modest exercise in revenge, do you think he would be unwilling to play his game with rules that you couldn't perceive? What did you learn tonight, Ricky?'

'I learned that you and your employer are sick, disgusting people,' Ricky burst out. 'And I want nothing to do with you.'

Virgil's laugh over the telephone line was cold and flat.

'Is that what you learned? And how did you reach that particular conclusion? Now, I'm not denying it, mind you. But I'd be interested to know under what psychoanalytic or medical theory you arrived at that diagnosis when it seems to my untrained mind that you don't know us at all. Why, you and I, we've had only one session. And you still have no clue as to who Rumplestiltskin is, do you? But you're willing to jump to all sorts of conclusions. Why, Ricky, I think jumping to conclusions is dangerous for you, given the precariousness of your position. I think you should try to keep an open mind.'

'Zimmerman . . .,' he started with his own version of a mingling of cold and fury. 'What happened to Zimmerman? You were there. Did you push him off the platform? Did you give him a little shove, or maybe just a jostle, so that he lost his balance? Do you think you can get away with murder?'

Virgil hesitated, then answered bluntly, 'Yes, Ricky, I do. I think people in this day and age get away with all sorts of crimes, up to and including murder. Happens all the time. But in the case of your unfortunate patient — or should I say ex-patient? — the evidence is far stronger that he jumped. Are you absolutely sure he didn't? No secret that he was deeply troubled. What makes you think he didn't do himself in, using a fabulously inexpensive and efficient technique not all that uncommon in New York? A method you might soon be forced to consider yourself. Not all that terrible a way to go when you really think about it. A momentary feeling of fear and doubt, a decision, a single brave step off the platform, some screeching noise, a flash of light, and then blessed oblivion.'

'Zimmerman wouldn't kill himself. He showed none of the classic conditions. You or someone like you pushed him in front of that subway train.'

'I admire your certainty, Ricky. It must be a happy life to be so sure about everything.'

'I'm going to go back to the police.'

'Well, you're certainly welcome to give them another try if you think it will do you some good. Did you find them particularly helpful? Were they especially eager to listen to your analytic interpretation of events that you didn't actually witness?'

This question quieted Ricky. He waited before he said, 'All right. So, what's next?'

'There's a present for you. Over on your couch. See it?'

Ricky looked up swiftly and saw that there was a medium-sized blond manila envelope resting where his patients usually placed their heads. 'I see it,' he replied.

'Okay,' Virgil said. 'I'll wait for you to open it up.' Before he could place the telephone down on the desktop, he heard her humming a tune that he vaguely recognized, but was unable to immediately place. Had Ricky been more of a television watcher, he might have immediately determined that Virgil was using the familiar music from the quiz show *Jeopardy*. Instead, he rose, crossed the room swiftly, and seized the envelope. It was thin, and he tore it open rapidly, removing a single sheet of paper.

It was a solitary page from a calendar. A large red X had been drawn through that day's date, the first of the month of August. Thirteen days that followed were left blank. The fifteenth day was circled in red. The remaining days of the month had been blacked out.

Ricky's mouth went dry. He looked in the envelope, but there was nothing else.

He moved slowly back to the desk and lifted the receiver.

'All right,' he said. 'This isn't hard to understand.'

Virgil's voice remained even flowing and almost sweet. 'A reminder, Ricky. That's all. Something to help you get yourself started. Ricky, Ricky, I asked already: What have you learned?'

The question infuriated him and he was about to burst with outrage. But he bit back the fury gathering within him and, keeping tight rein over his emotions, replied instead, 'I've learned that there don't seem to be any boundaries.'

'Good, Ricky, good. That's progress. What else?'

'I've learned not to underestimate what is happening.'

'Excellent, Ricky. More?'

'No. That's it to this point.'

Virgil started to tsk-tsk like some caricature of a grade-school teacher. 'Not true, Ricky. What you have learned, Ricky, is that everything in this game, including the likely outcome, is being played on a field uniquely designed to accommodate you. I think that my employer has been exceptionally generous, considering his alternatives. You've been given a chance, granted a slight one, to save someone else's life and to save your own by answering a simple question: Who is he? And, because he doesn't want to be unfair, he's given you an alternative solution, less attractive for you, of course, but one that will give your sorry existence some meaning in your final days. Not many people get that sort of opportunity, Ricky. To go to their grave knowing that their sacrifice saved another from some unknown, but absolutely genuine horror. Why, this borders on sainthood, Ricky, and it's being handed to you without the delightful three miracles that the Catholic Church usually requires, although I believe they'll waive one or two on occasion for worthy candidates. How does one go about waiving a miracle, when that's the standard for acceptance in the club? Ah, well, an intriguing question we can debate at length some other moment. Right now, Ricky, you should go back to the clues you have been given, and get started. Time is wasting and there's not much of it left. Have you ever performed an analysis on deadline, Ricky? Because that is what this is all about. I'll be in touch. Remember, Virgil is never far away.'

She took a deep breath, then added: 'Got all that, Ricky?'

He remained silent, and she said it again, harsher.

'Got all that, Ricky?'

'Yes,' he said. But of course he knew that he didn't as he hung up the phone.

7

Zimmerman's ghost seemed to be laughing at him.

It was the morning after a fitful night. He had not slept much, but when he had, he had dreamed vividly, fantastically, of his dead wife sitting by his side in a vibrant red two-seater sports car that he did not recognize, but knew belonged to him. They were parked by the edge of the ocean in deep sand on a familiar beach near their vacation cottage on the Cape. It had seemed to Ricky in the dream that the gray-green Atlantic waters, the color they took on in anticipation of a storm, were sweeping ever closer to him, threatening to overtake the car in a flood tide, and he struggled madly to open the door, but when he tried to work the handle he had seen a bloodstained and grinning Zimmerman standing outside the car, holding the door closed, and he'd been trapped inside. The car would not start and somehow he knew the tires were dug down into the sand anyway. In the dream, his dead wife had seemed calm, beckoning, almost welcoming him, and he'd had little trouble interpreting all this, as he stood naked in the shower, letting lukewarm water that was neither warm nor cold flow over his head in a mildly unpleasant cascade, but one that fit his dreary mood.

Ricky dressed in faded, ratty, khaki trousers that were frayed at the cuffs and which showed all the signs of longtime use that teenagers would ordinarily have paid extra for at the mall, but which in his case were the results of years of wear and tear during the summer vacation, the only time he wore them. On his feet he placed an equally tattered pair of boat shoes and over his torso an old blue button-down shirt too worn for wear anytime other than the weekend. He dragged a comb through his hair. He looked up at his face in the mirror and thought he wore all the outward appearances of a man of accomplishments dressing down for the beginning of his vacation. He thought how for years he had awoken on the first of August and gleefully put on the old and comfortable battered clothes that signaled that for the next month he was stepping away from the carefully constructed and regimented character of the Upper East Side Manhattan psychoanalyst and into something different. Vacation was defined by Ricky as a time to get his hands dirty in the garden up in Wellfleet, to get some sand between his toes on long walks down the beach, to read popular mystery or romance novels and drink the occasional disgusting concoction called the Cape Codder, an unfortunate marriage of cranberry juice and vodka. This vacation promised no such return to routine, even though, in something he might have characterized as stubbornness, or maybe wishful thinking, he was dressed for the first day of the holiday.

He shook his head and dragged himself into the small kitchen. For breakfast, he made himself a solitary slice of dry wheat toast and some black coffee which tasted bitter no matter how many spoonfuls of sugar he dropped in. He chewed the toast with an indifference that surprised him. He had absolutely no appetite.

He carried his rapidly cooling coffee into his office where he put Rumplestiltskin's letter on the desk in front of him. Occasionally he would sneak a glance out the window, as if he hoped to catch a glimpse of the naked Virgil lurking on the sidewalk, or occupying a window from an apartment in the building across the narrow street. He knew she was somewhere close, or, at least, believed her to be, based on what she had told him.

Ricky shuddered once, involuntarily. He stared at the words of the clue.

For a moment, he felt a dizziness mingled with a flash of heat.

'What is happening?' he demanded of himself out loud.

Roger Zimmerman seemed to enter the room at that moment, as irritating and demanding in death as he was in life. As always, he wanted answers to all the wrong questions.

He dialed the dead man's apartment number again, hoping to reach someone. Ricky knew he was obliged to speak with someone about Zimmerman's death, but precisely who, eluded him. The mother was still inexplicably unaccounted for, and Ricky wished he'd had the sense to ask Detective Riggins where the woman was. He guessed with some neighbor, or in a hospital. Zimmerman had a younger brother who lived in California with whom he'd connected infrequently. The brother worked in the film industry in Los Angeles and had wanted nothing to do with taking care of the difficult and partially invalided mother, a reluctance that had caused Zimmerman to complain constantly about him. Zimmerman had been a man who reveled in the awfulness of his life, preferring to whine and complain than to change. It was this quality that made him such a poor candidate for suicide, Ricky thought. What the police and his coworkers had seen as despair, Ricky had recognized as Zimmerman's true and only joy. He lived for his hates. Ricky's task as analyst was to empower him with the ability to change. He had expected the time to eventually arrive when Zimmerman would have realized how crippled he actually was, traveling impotently from anger to anger. That moment when change was possible would have been dangerous, because Zimmerman would likely have fallen into a significant depression at the idea that he didn't need to lead his life in the way that he did. He would have been vulnerable then when the number of wasted days finally occurred to him. That understanding conceivably might have created a real and possibly lethal despair.

But that moment had been many months, and in greater likelihood, years away.

Zimmerman still had arrived at his session daily, still considering analysis to be nothing more than a fifty-minute venting opportunity, like a steam whistle on the side of an engine waiting for the conductor's tug. What little insight he'd gained he mostly used to pave new avenues of anger.

Complaining was fun for him. He wasn't boxed in and encircled by despair.

Ricky shook his head. In twenty-five years, he'd had three patients who killed themselves. Two of those had been referred to him already displaying all the classic warning signs and had been in treatment only briefly before taking their own lives. He had felt helpless on those occasions, but a helplessness that didn't carry blame. The third death, however, he did not like to think about because the person had been a longtime patient, whose downward spiral Ricky had been unable to arrest, even with prescriptions for mood elevators, a course he rarely took. It had been years since he'd thought of that patient, and he had not liked mentioning him to Detective Riggins, even if he had withheld the details of the case from the rude and only mildly inquisitive detective.

Shuddering briefly, as if the room had suddenly grown cold, Ricky thought: That was a portrait of suicide. Zimmerman wasn't.

But the idea that Zimmerman was pushed in front of a subway train to send Ricky a message was far more horrifying. It struck at his heart. It was the sort of idea that was like a spark landing in a pool of gasoline.

It was, equally, an impossible idea. He envisioned himself walking back into Detective Riggins's overbright and modestly filthy office and claiming that some strangers had deliberately murdered a person they didn't know and didn't care about in the slightest in order to force Ricky into playing some sort of death game.

He thought: It's true, but not believable, especially to some underpaid and overworked Transit Authority detective.

And, in the same moment, he realized that they knew that.

The man who called himself Rumplestiltskin and the woman who went by Virgil understood that there was no hard evidence whatsoever that might connect them to this random crime other than Ricky's bleating protests. Even if Detective Riggins didn't laugh Ricky out of her office — which she would — what incentive did she have to pursue a wild story from a physician whom she quite accurately believed would far prefer some crazy mystery novel explanation for the man's death rather than the obvious suicide that reflected so poorly on him?

He could answer that query with a single word: None.

Zimmerman's death was designed to help kill Ricky. And no one would know it, except Ricky.

The thought made him dizzy.

Sitting back hard in his chair, Ricky realized he was at a critical moment. In the hours since the letter appeared in his waiting room, he'd been caught up in a series of actions that he had absolutely no perspective upon. Analysis is about patience and he'd had none. It is about time, and there was none available. His glance caught the calendar Virgil had provided him. The fourteen days remaining seemed an impossibly brief time. For a second, he thought of a death row prisoner, told that the governor had signed his death warrant, specifying date, time, and place of execution. This was a crushing image, and he turned away from it, telling himself that even in a prison, men fought hard for life. Ricky breathed in fiercely. It is, he thought, the greatest luxury of our existence, no matter how miserable, that we don't know our allotted span of days. The calendar on his desk seemed to mock him.

'It isn't a game,' he said to no one. 'It's never been a game.'

He reached out and seized Rumplestiltskin's letter and examined the small rhyme. It's a clue, he shouted to himself. A clue from a psychopath. Look at it closely!

' . . . Mother, father, and young child . . . '

Well, he thought to himself, it's interesting that the letter writer uses the word *child*, because that doesn't specify gender.

' . . . When my father sailed away . . . '

The father left. *Sail* could be either literal or symbolic, but in either case, the father left the family. Whatever the causes of the abandonment, Rumplestiltskin must have harbored his resentment for years. It had to be further fueled by the mother, who was left behind. He had played some part in the creation of a rage that had taken years to turn murderous. But which part? That's what he needed to figure out.

Rumplestiltskin, he believed in that moment, was the child of a patient. The question was, what sort of patient?

An unhappy and unsuccessful patient, obviously. Someone who'd cut short their treatment, possibly. But which direction did the patient occupy: the mother left behind with resentment and children, or the father, who'd abandoned the family? Had he failed in his treatment of the woman cut adrift, or had he been the impetus for the man to run out on his family? He thought this was a little bit like the Japanese film *Rashomon*, where the same event is examined from diametrically different positions, with wildly disparate interpretations. Into a situation ripe for murderous anger, he'd played a role, but on which side, he couldn't tell. Regardless, Ricky thought the time frame would necessarily have happened between twenty and twenty-five years earlier, because Rumplestiltskin had to grow into the adult of means necessary to plan the elaborate details of the game.

How long, Ricky wondered, does it take to create a murderer? Ten years? Twenty years? A single instant?

He did not know, but suspected he could learn.

This gave him the first sense of satisfaction he'd felt since he'd opened the letter in his waiting room. A feeling not precisely of confidence hit him, but one of ability. What he failed to see was that he had been adrift in the real, grime-streaked world of Detective Riggins, overmatched and out of place, and that once he was functioning back within the world he knew, the world of emotion and action defined by psychology, he was comfortable.

Zimmerman, an unhappy man who needed much help that was too slow in coming, faded from his thoughts and at the same time Ricky did not make the second realization, the one that might have stopped him cold: that he had begun to play a game on the playing field designed uniquely for him, just as Rumplestiltskin told him that he would.

* * *

An analyst is not like the surgeon, who can look at the heart monitor attached to his patient and recognize success or failure from the blips on a screen. Measurements are far more subjective. Cured, a word with all sorts of hidden absolutes, isn't attached to an analytic course of treatment, even though the profession employs many medical connections.

Ricky was back at the creation of a list. He was taking a period of ten years, from 1975, when he began his residency, through 1985, and writing down the name of everyone he'd seen in treatment during that space of time. He discovered that it was relatively easy, as he went year by year, to come up with the names of the long-term patients, the ones who had engaged in traditional analyses. Those names jumped out, and he was pleased that he was able to recall faces, voices, and more than a few details about their situations. In some cases, he could recall the names of spouses, parents, children, where they worked and where they grew up, in addition to his clinical diagnosis and assessment of their problems. This was all very helpful, he thought, but he doubted that anyone who'd had a long-term course of treatment had created the person now threatening him.

Rumplestiltskin would be the child of someone whose connection had been more tenuous. Someone who left treatment abruptly. Someone who had quit coming to his office after only a few sessions.

Remembering those patients was a far more difficult enterprise.

He sat at his desk, a legal pad of paper in front of him, free-associating, month by month right through his past, trying to picture people from a quarter century earlier. This was the psychoanalytic equivalent of heavy lifting; names, faces, problems came back slowly to him. He wished that he'd kept more-organized records, but what little he'd been able to find, what few notes and documents he had from that ancient period, were all of the people who'd stuck with the course of treatment, and had, in their own way, over years of flopping down on the couch and talking, left marks in his memory.

He had to find the person who'd left a scar.

Ricky was approaching the dilemma in the only way he knew how. He recognized that it wasn't particularly efficient, but he was at a loss as to how else to proceed.

It was slow going, the morning's minutes evaporating around him in silence. The list he was creating grew haphazardly. A person staring in at Ricky would have seen him bent over slightly in his chair, pen in hand, like some blocked poet searching for an impossible rhyme to a word like *granite*.

Ricky labored hard and alone.

It was nearing noontime when the buzzer on his door rang.

The sound seemed to rip him from reverie. He straightened up abruptly, feeling the muscles in his back tighten and his throat suddenly grow dry. The buzzer rang a second time, unmistakably someone unaware of his patients' assigned ring.

He rose and crossed his office, crossed the waiting room and cautiously approached the door he so rarely locked. There was a peephole in the middle of the oaken slab, which he couldn't recall the last time he'd used, and he put his eye to the circle to stare through as the buzzer sounded one more time.

On the other side was a young man wearing a sweat-stained blue Federal Express shirt, clutching an envelope and an electronic clipboard in his hand. He looked mildly irritated and seemed about to turn away, when Ricky unlocked the door. He only loosened the dead bolts, however, leaving the chain fastened.

'Yes?' Ricky asked.

'I have a letter here for a Doctor Starks. Is that you, sir?'

'Yes.'

'I need a signature.'

Ricky hesitated. 'Do you have some identification?'

'What?' the young man asked with a grin. 'The uniform isn't enough?' He sighed and twisted his body to show a plastic encased picture identification that was clipped to his shirt. 'Can you read that?' he asked. 'All I'm looking for is a signature, then I'm out of here.'

Ricky reluctantly opened the door. 'Where do I sign?'

The deliveryman offered him the clipboard and

pointed at the twenty-second line down. 'Right there,' he said. Ricky signed. The deliveryman checked the signature, then ran an electronic tabulator across a bar code. The machine beeped twice. Ricky had no idea what that was about. Then the deliveryman handed him the small cardboard one-day express envelope. 'Have a nice day,' he said, with a tone that implied that he didn't really care one way or the other what sort of day Ricky had, but that he'd been taught to say it, and he was following designated procedure in any case.

Ricky paused in the doorway, staring down at the label on the envelope. The return address was from the New York Psychoanalytic Society, an organization that he was a longtime member of, but had had precious little to do with over the years. The society was something of a governing body for New York's psychoanalysts, but Ricky had always shunned the politicking and connecting that accompanied any such organization. He went to an occasional society-sponsored lecture, and he flipped through the society's semiannual journal to keep up with his peers and their opinions, but he avoided participating in the panel discussions the society held just as much as he avoided the holiday cocktail parties.

He stepped back into his waiting room, locking the doors behind him, wondering why the society had written to him at this point. He suspected that close to a hundred percent of the society was taking off on August vacations anyway. Like so many aspects of the process, in the psychoanalytic world, the summer month was sacred.

Ricky found the tab and pulled open the cardboard envelope. Inside there was a regular letter-sized envelope bearing the society's embossed return address in the corner. His name was typed on the envelope, and along the bottom there was a single line: BY OVERNIGHT COURIER — URGENT.

He opened the envelope and withdrew two sheets of paper. The first bore the masthead of the society. He saw immediately that the letter was from the organization's president, a physician some ten years older than he, and whom he knew only vaguely. He could not recall ever conversing with the man, other than perhaps a handshake and forgettable pleasantry.

He read swiftly:

Dear Dr. Starks:

It is my unfortunate duty to inform you that the Psychoanalytic Society is in receipt of a significant complaint concerning your relationship with a former patient. I have enclosed a copy of the complaining letter.

As per the society's bylaws, and after discussing the issue with the leadership of this organization, I have turned the entire matter over to the state's board of medical ethics investigators. You should be hearing from personnel in that office in the very near future.

I would urge you to obtain competent legal counsel at your earliest convenience. I am optimistic that we will be able to keep the nature of this complaint out of the news media, as allegations such as these throw our entire profession into disrepute.

Ricky barely glanced at the signature, as he turned to the second sheet of paper. This, too, was a letter, but addressed to the society's president, with copies to the vice president, ethics committee chairman, each doctor on the six-person ethics committee, the society's secretary, and treasurer. In fact, Ricky realized, any physician whose name was attached in any way to the society's leadership had received a copy. It read:

Dear Sir or Madam:

More than six years ago, I entered into a course of psychoanalytic treatment with Dr. Frederick Starks, a member of your organization. Some three months into a four-times-weekly series of sessions, he began to ask me what might be considered inappropriate questions. These were always about my sexual relations with the various partners I had leading up to and including a failed marriage. I assumed that these inquiries were a part of the analytic process. However, as the sessions continued, he kept demanding more and more explicit details of my sex life. The tone of these questions became increasingly pornographic. Every time I tried to change the subject matter, he invariably forced it back, always increasing the quality and quantity of description. I complained, but he countered that the root of my depression resided in my failure to fully give myself in sexual encounters. It was shortly after that suggestion that he raped me for the first time. He told me that unless I submitted, I would never feel better about myself.

Having sex during therapy sessions became a requirement for continued treatment. He was insatiable. After six months, he told me that my treatment was at an end, and that there was nothing he could do for me. He said I was so repressed that a course of drugs and hospitalization was probably required. He urged me to check into a private psychiatric hospital in Vermont, but was unwilling to even make a call to that hospital's director. He forced me to have anal sex with him the day he ended our sessions.

It has taken me several years to recover from my relationship with Dr. Starks. During this time, I have been hospitalized three times, each time for more than six months. I bear the scars of two failed suicide attempts. It is only with the constant help of a caring therapist that I have begun the process of healing. This letter to your organization is a part of that process.

For the time being, I feel I must remain anonymous, although Dr. Starks will know who I am. If you decide to pursue this matter, please direct your investigation to my attorney and/or my therapist.

The letter was unsigned, but contained the name of a lawyer with a midtown address, and a psychiatrist with a suburban Boston listing.

Ricky's hands shook. He was dizzy, and slumped against a wall of his apartment to steady himself. He felt like a prizefighter who has absorbed a pummeling — disoriented, in pain, ready to drop to the canvas when the bell leaves him utterly defeated, but still standing.

There was not a single word of truth in the letter. At least not one that he could discern.

He wondered whether that would make even the slightest bit of a difference.

8

He looked down at the lies on the page in front of him and felt a great contradiction within him. His spirits plummeted, his heart was cold with despair of his own, as if some tenacity had been sucked out of him, and at the same moment, replaced with a rage that was so far distant from his normal character that it was almost unrecognizable. His hands started to quiver, his face flushed red, and a thin line of sweat broke out on his forehead. He could feel the same heat growing at the back of his neck, in his armpits, and down his throat. He turned away from the letters, raising his eyes, looking around for something he could seize hold of and break, but he could find nothing readily available, which angered him even more.

Ricky paced back and forth across his office for a few moments. It was as if his entire body had acquired a nervous twitch. Finally, he flung himself down into his old leather chair, behind the head of the couch, and let the familiar creakings of the upholstery and the sensation of the polished fabric beneath his palms calm him, if only a little.

He had absolutely no doubt who had concocted the complaint against him. The false anonymity of the phony victim guaranteed that. The more important question, he recognized, was determining why. There was an agenda, he understood, and he needed to isolate and identify what it was.

Ricky kept a telephone on the floor next to his chair and he reached down and seized it. Within seconds he acquired the office number for the head of the Psychoanalytic Society from directory assistance. Refusing their electronic offer to dial the number for him, he furiously punched the numbers into the receiver, then leaned back, waiting for a response.

The telephone was answered by the vaguely familiar voice of his fellow analyst. But it had the tinny, emotionless, and flat quality belonging to a recording.

'Hello. You have reached the office of Doctor Martin Roth. I will be out of my office from August first to the twenty-ninth. If this is an emergency, please dial 555-1716, which will connect you with a service capable of reaching me while on vacation. You may also dial 555–2436 and speak with Doctor Albert Michaels at Columbia Presbyterian Hospital, who is covering for me this month. If you feel this is a true crisis, please call both numbers and Doctor Michaels and I will both get back to you.'

Ricky disconnected the recording and dialed the first of the two emergency numbers. He knew the second number was for a second- or third-year psychiatric resident at the hospital. The residents covered for the established physicians during vacation times, providing an outlet where prescriptions superseded the talk that was the mainstay of the analytic treatment plan.

The first number, however, was an answering service.

'Hello,' a woman's voice responded wearily. 'This is Doctor Roth's service.'

'I need to get the doctor a message,' Ricky said briskly.

'The doctor is on vacation. In an emergency, you should call Doctor Albert Michaels at — '

'I have that number,' Ricky interrupted, 'but it's not that sort of emergency and it's not that sort of message.'

The woman paused, more surprised than confused. 'Well,' she said, 'I don't know if I should call him during his vacation for just any message . . . '

'He will want to hear this,' Ricky said. It was difficult to conceal the coolness in his own voice.

'I don't know,' the woman repeated. 'We have a procedure.'

'Everyone has a procedure,' Ricky said bluntly. 'Procedures exist to prevent contact. Not help it. People with small minds and vacant imaginations fill them with schedules and procedures. People of character know when to ignore protocol. Are you that sort of person, miss?'

The woman hesitated. 'What's the message?' she abruptly demanded.

'Tell Doctor Roth that Doctor Frederick Starks . . . you had better write this down because I want you to quote me precisely . . . '

'I am writing it down,' the woman said sharply.

' . . . That Doctor Starks received his letter, reviewed the complaint contained within, and wishes to inform him that there is not a single word of truth in any of it. It is a complete and total fantasy.'

' . . . Not a single word of truth . . . okay. Fantasy. Got that. You want me to call him with that message? He's on vacation.'

'We're all on vacation,' Ricky said, just as bluntly. 'Some people just have more interesting holidays than others. This message will assuredly make his far more interesting. See that he gets it and gets it exactly the way I said it, or I'll make absolutely damn sure that you're looking for another job by Labor Day. Understand?'

'I understand,' the woman answered. She seemed undaunted by his threat. 'But I told you: We have clear-cut and defined procedures. I don't think this fits anything . . . '

'Try not to be quite so predictable,' Ricky said. 'And that way you can save your job.'

Then he hung up the telephone. He leaned back in his seat. He couldn't recall being that rude and demanding, not to mention threatening, in years. It, too, was against his nature. But then he recognized that he was likely to have to go against his nature in many ways over the next few days.

He returned his eyes to the cover letter from Dr. Roth and then read through the anonymous complaint a second time. Still inwardly battling with the outrage and indignation of the falsely accused, he tried to measure the impact of the letters and return to an answer to the question Why? He thought Rumplestiltskin clearly had in mind some specific effect, but what was it?

Some things came into focus, as he considered the question.

The complaint itself was far more subtle than one would first think, Ricky realized. The anonymous letter writer cried rape! but placed the time frame just distant enough to be beyond any legal statute of limitations. No real police detectives need be involved. Instead, it would trigger a cumbersome, ham-handed inquiry by the State Board of Medical Ethics. This would be slow, inefficient, and unlikely to get in the way of the game clock running. A complaint that involved the police would likely get an immediate response, and Rumplestiltskin clearly didn't want the police involved in any fashion, other than utterly tangentially. And, by making the complaint provocative, yet anonymous, the letter writer maintained distance. No one from the Psychoanalytic Society would call to follow up. They would hand it over, just as they had apparently done, to a third agency, washing their hands as quickly as possible to avoid what might be a real stench.

Ricky read both letters over a third time, and saw an answer.

'He wants me alone,' he blurted out loud.

For a moment, Ricky leaned back, staring at the ceiling, as if the flat white above him reflected somehow with clarity. He spoke to no one, his voice seeming to echo a little in the office space, the sound almost hollow.

'He doesn't want me to get help. He wants me to play him without even the slightest bit of assistance. And so, he took steps to make sure I couldn't talk to anyone else in the profession.'

He almost smiled at the modestly diabolical nature of what Rumplestiltskin had done. He knew that Ricky would be internally buffeted by questions surrounding Zimmerman's death. He knew Ricky was undoubtedly frightened by the invasion of his home and office in the hours that his back was turned in pursuit of Zimmerman's truth. He knew that Ricky was unsettled and uncertain, probably a little panicky and in shock at the rapid-fire series of events that had taken place. Rumplestiltskin had anticipated all that, and then speculated what Ricky's first move might be: seeking assistance. And where would Ricky have likely been willing to turn for help? He would have wanted to talk — not act — because that was the nature of his profession, and he would have turned to another analyst. A friend who could function as a sounding board. Someone who could hem and haw and listen to each detail and help Ricky sort through the wealth of things that had happened so rapidly.

But that wouldn't happen now, Ricky realized.

The complaint with its allegations of rape, including the gratuitous and ugly last portrait of the final session, was sent to everyone in the hierarchy of the Psychoanalytic Society right as they all prepared to depart on their August vacations. There was no time to forcibly deny the charge, no ready forum in which to do so effectively. The nasty nature of the charge would race through the New York analytic world like gossip at some grand Hollywood opening. Ricky was a man with many colleagues and few real friends, this he knew. And these colleagues were unlikely to want to be tainted by contact with a doctor who had violated arguably the single greatest taboo of the profession. An allegation that he'd used his position as therapist and analyst for the basest and crudest sexual favors, and then turned his back on the psychological disaster he'd created, was the psychoanalytic equivalent of the plague, and he was instantly rendered into a modern Typhoid Mary. With this allegation hanging over his head, no one was likely to step forward to help Ricky, no matter how hard he pleaded, no matter how hard he denied the charge, until it was resolved. And that would take months.

There was another, secondary effect: It created a situation where people who thought they knew Ricky, now would wonder what they knew and how they knew it. It was a wondrous lie, he thought, because the mere fact that he denied it would make people in his profession think he was covering up.

I am all alone, Ricky thought. Isolated. Adrift.

Ricky inhaled sharply, as if the air in his office had grown cold. He realized that was what he wanted. Alone.

Again he looked at the two letters. In the fake complaint the anonymous writer had included the names of a Manhattan lawyer and a Boston therapist.

Ricky couldn't help himself from shuddering. Those names were installed for me. That's the route I'm supposed to travel.

He thought of the frightening darkness in his office the night before. All he had to do was follow the simple path and plug in what had been disconnected to shed light into the room. He suspected this was more or less the same. He just didn't know where this particular path might be leading him.

* * *

He wasted the remainder of that day examining every detail of Rumplestiltskin's first letter, trying to dissect the rhymed clue further, then taking the time to write precise notes about all that had happened to him, paying as much attention as he could to each word spoken, re-creating dialogue like a reporter readying a news story, seeking a perspective that eluded him easily. He found he had the most trouble remembering exactly what the woman Virgil had said, which was disconcerting. He had no difficulty recalling the shape of her figure or the slyness in her voice, but found that her beauty was like a protective covering over her words. This troubled him, because it went against his training and his habit, and, like any good analyst, he pondered why he was so incapable of focus, when the truth was so obvious that any routinely charged teenage boy could have told him.

He was accumulating notes and observations, seeking refuge in the world he was comfortable within. But, the following morning, after he had dressed in a suit and tie, and then had taken the time to draw an X through another day in the calendar, he once again started to feel the pressure of time weighing on the situation. He thought that it was important for him to at least come up with his first question, and call the *Times* to place the question in an ad.

The morning heat seemed to mock him, and he steamed inside his suit almost immediately. He assumed he was being followed, but once again refused to turn and look. He realized he wouldn't know how to spot a person tailing him, anyway. In the movies, he thought, it was always so easy for the hero to detect the forces of evil arrayed against him. The bad guys wore the black hats and the furtive look in their eyes. In real life, he recognized, it is far different. Everyone is suspicious. Everyone is preoccupied. The man on the corner delivering items to a grocery deli, the businessman pacing rapidly down the sidewalk, the homeless man in the alcove, the faces behind the glass windows of the restaurant, or a passing car. Anyone could be watching him or not. It was impossible for him to tell. He was so accustomed to the hyperintense world of the analyst's office, where the roles were so much clearer. Out on the street, it was impossible for him to tell who might be playing the game and watching him, and who was just one of the other eight million or so beings who abruptly populated his world.

Ricky shrugged and hailed a cab at the corner. The cabbie had an unpronounceable foreign name, and was listening to an odd, Middle Eastern music station. A woman vocalist was keening in a high-pitched voice that wavered as the tempo changed. When a new tune came on, only the pace changed, the warbling vocals seemed to be the same. He couldn't make out any recognizable words, but the driver was tapping his fingers against the steering wheel in rhythmic appreciation. The cabbie grunted when Ricky gave him the address, and sped off into traffic rapidly. Ricky wondered for a moment how many people jumped into the man's cab every day. There was no way for the man behind the plastic partition to tell whether he was carrying fares to some momentous event in their life, or merely another passing minute. The cabbie punched his horn once or twice at an intersection, and drove him through the congested streets without comment.

A large white moving van blocked most of the side street where the lawyer's office was located, leaving just enough space for cars to squeeze past. Three or four burly men were moving in and out of the front doors of the modest, nondescript office building, carrying brown cardboard boxes and the occasional piece of furniture, desk chairs, sofas, and the like and walking carefully up a steel ramp into the truck to load them. A man in a blue blazer with a security badge stood to the side, keeping watch on the progress the movers made, eyeing passersby with a wariness that spoke loudly of a man with a single purpose for his presence and a rigidity that would see that purpose met. Ricky exited the cab, which sped off as soon as he slammed the door, and approached the man in the blazer.

'I'm looking for the office of a Mr. Merlin. He's an attorney . . . '

'Sixth floor, all the way to the top,' the blazer man said, without taking his eyes off the parade of movers. 'You got an appointment? Pretty busy up there with the move and all.'

'He's moving?'

The blazer man gestured. 'What you see,' he said. 'Breaking into the big time, big money, from what I hear. You can go on up, but don't get in the way.'

The elevator hummed, but thankfully no Muzak played. When the doors opened on the sixth floor, Ricky immediately saw the lawyer's office. A door was propped open and two men were struggling with a desk, lifting and angling it through the doorway, as a middle-aged woman in jeans, running shoes, and designer T-shirt watched them carefully. 'That's my desk, goddamn it, and I know every stain and scratch on it. You put a new one there, and you'll be buying me another one.'

The two movers paused, scowling. The desk slid through the door with millimeters to spare. Ricky looked past the men and saw boxes piled in the interior corridor, empty bookcases, and tables, all the items one ordinarily associated with a busy office out of place and collected for the move. From within the office there was a thudding sound and some cursing. The woman in jeans threw back her head, shaking a wild mane of auburn hair with obvious irritation. She had the look of a woman who appreciated organization and the temporary chaos of the move was almost painful for her. Ricky walked up quickly.

'I'm looking for Mr. Merlin,' he said. 'Is he around?'

The woman turned quickly. 'Are you a client? We

don't have any appointments scheduled for today. Moving day.'

'In a manner of speaking,' Ricky replied.

'Well,' the woman said stiffly, 'what manner of speaking would that be?'

'My name is Doctor Frederick Starks, and I believe it safe to say that Mr. Merlin and I have something to discuss. Is he here?'

The woman briefly looked surprised, then smiled unpleasantly, nodding her head. 'That's a name I recognize. But I don't believe Mr. Merlin was expecting a visit quite so quickly.'

'Really?' Ricky said. 'I would have guessed the exact opposite is the case.'

The woman paused as another mover emerged carrying a lamp in one hand and a box of books under another arm. She turned to him and said, 'One trip, one item. Carry too much, something just gets broken. Put one of those down and come back for it next time.'

The mover looked astonished, shrugged, and put the lamp down none too gently.

She turned back to Ricky. 'As you can see, doctor, you've arrived at a difficult moment . . . '

It seemed to Ricky that the woman was about to dismiss him, when a younger man, in his early thirties, slightly overweight and slightly balding, wearing pressed khaki slacks, an expensive designer sport shirt, and highly polished, tasseled loafers, emerged from the back of the office. It was a most curious appearance, because he was overdressed for lifting and carrying, underdressed for conducting business. The clothes he wore were ostentatious and expensive, and stated that appearance, even in genuinely informal circumstances, was somehow governed by stiff rules. What Ricky saw was that there was nothing relaxed about the man's clothes to relax in.

'I'm Merlin,' the man said, removing a folded linen

handkerchief from his pocket and wiping his hands before offering one in Ricky's direction. 'If you will forgive the chaotic nature of our surroundings, we could perhaps speak for a few moments in the conference room. Most of the furniture is still there, although for how much longer is an open question.'

The attorney gestured toward a door.

'Would you like me to take notes, Mr. Merlin?' the woman asked.

Merlin shook his head. 'I don't think we'll be all that long.'

Ricky was ushered into a room dominated by a long cherry-wood table and chairs. There was an end table at the rear of the room with a coffee machine and a jug with glasses. The attorney pointed toward a seat, then went and inspected the machine. Shrugging, he turned to Ricky.

'I'm sorry, Doctor,' Merlin said. 'No coffee left, and the water jug appears empty, too. I can't offer you anything.'

'That's all right,' Ricky replied. 'I didn't come here because I was thirsty.'

This response made the lawyer smile. 'No. Of course not,' he said. 'But I'm not sure how I can help — '

'Merlin is an unusual name,' Ricky interrupted. 'One wonders whether you're a conjuror of sorts.'

Again the lawyer grinned. 'In my profession, Doctor Starks, a name such as mine is an advantage. We are frequently asked by clients to pull the proverbial rabbit out of a top hat.'

'And can you do this?' Ricky asked.

'Alas, no,' Merlin answered. 'I have no magic wand. But, on the other hand, I have been singularly successful at forcing reluctant and recalcitrant opposition rabbits to emerge from places of concealment in all sorts of hats, relying, of course, less on magical powers than on a torrent of legal papers and a blizzard of legal demands. Perhaps in this world, these things amount to the same. Certain lawsuits seem to function in much the same way that curses and spells did for my namesake.'

'And you are moving?'

The attorney reached down and extracted a small, crafted-leather card case from a pocket. He removed a card and handed it across the table to Ricky. 'The new digs,' he said, not unpleasantly. 'Success brings a demand for expansion. Hiring new associates. Need room to stretch.'

Ricky looked at the card, with a downtown address. 'And am I to be another pelt on your wall?'

Merlin nodded, grinning not unpleasantly. 'Probably,' he said. 'In fact, it is likely. I shouldn't really be speaking with you, doctor, especially without your attorney present. Why don't you have your lawyer call me, we can go over your malpractice insurance policy . . . You are insured, aren't you, doctor? And then get this thing settled swiftly and profitably for all involved.'

'I carry insurance, but I doubt whether it would cover the complaint your client has invented. I don't think I've had a reason to read the policy in decades.'

'No insurance? That's bad . . . And *invented* is a word I might take exception to.'

'Who is your client?' Ricky demanded abruptly.

The lawyer shook his head. 'I am still not at liberty to divulge her name. She is in the process of recovery and — '

'None of this ever happened,' Ricky sliced through the lawyer's words. 'It is all a fantasy. Made up. Not a word of truth. Your real client is someone else, true?'

The attorney paused. 'I can assure you my client is real,' he said. 'As are her complaints. Miss X is a very distraught young woman . . . '

'Why not call her Miss R?' Ricky asked. '*R* as in Rumplestiltskin. Wouldn't that be more appropriate?'

Merlin looked a bit confused. 'I don't know that I follow your thinking, doctor. *X, R*, whatever. That's not really the point, is it?'

'Correct.'

'The point, Doctor Starks, is that you are in real trouble. And, trust me, you want this problem to disappear from your horizon just as quickly as humanly possible. If I have to file suit, well, then the damage will be done. Pandora's box, doctor. All the evil things will just come flying out. Everything will become a part of some public record. Allegations and denials, although, in my experience, the denial never manages to have quite the same impact as the allegation, does it? It's not the denial that sticks in people's memories, is it?' The lawyer shook his head.

'At no time have I ever abused a patient's trust in the manner alleged. I do not believe this person even exists. I have no record of such a patient.'

'Well, doc, that's dandy. I hope you're one hundred percent right about that. Because,' as he spoke, the lawyer's voice dipped an octave and the intonation of each word gained a razor-sharp edge, 'by the time I get through interviewing every patient you've had for the past decade or so, and talking with every colleague you've ever had a dispute with, and examining every facet of what you better hope is your saintlike life and certainly every second you've spent behind that couch, well, whether or not my client exists is not going to be completely relevant, because you will have absolutely no life and no reputation left. None, whatsoever.'

Ricky wanted to respond, but did not.

Merlin continued to stare directly at Ricky, not wavering even slightly.

'Do you have any enemies, doctor? How about jealous colleagues? Do you think any of your patients over the years have been less than pleased with their treatment? Have you ever kicked a dog? Maybe failed to brake when a squirrel ran out in front of your car up there at your vacation house on Cape Cod?'

Merlin smiled again, but now the smile had turned nasty.

'I already know about that place,' he said. 'A nice farmhouse in a lovely field on the edge of a forest with a garden and with just a little bit of ocean view. Twelve acres. Purchased from a middle-aged woman whose husband had just died back in 1984. Sort of took advantage of the bereaved in that transaction, huh, doc? Do you have any idea how the value of that property has increased? I'm sure you do. Let me suggest to you, Doctor Starks, one thing and one thing only. Whether or not there's the slightest bit of truth involved in my client's allegation, I'm going to own that property before this is finished. And I'm going to own your apartment, and your bank account at Chase, and the retirement account at Dean Witter that you haven't yet dipped into, and the modest stock portfolio you keep with the same brokerage firm. But I'll start with the summer place. Twelve acres. I think I can subdivide and make a killing. What do you think, doc?'

Ricky listened to the lawyer, reeling internally.

'How do you know — ' he started lamely.

'I make it my business to know,' Merlin cut him off rapidly. 'If you didn't have something I wanted, I wouldn't be bothering. But you do, and trust me on this, doc, because your lawyer will tell you the same, the fight isn't worth it.'

'My integrity is certainly worth it,' Ricky replied.

Merlin shrugged again. 'You're not seeing clearly here, doctor. I'm trying to tell you how to leave your integrity more or less intact. You rather foolishly believe that this has something to do with being right or wrong. Telling the truth rather than lying. I find this intriguing, coming from a veteran psychoanalyst such as yourself. Is the truth, in some wondrously authentic and clear-cut fashion, something that you hear often? Or are truths hidden, concealed, and covered up with all sorts of curious psychological baggage, elusive and slippery once identified? And never exactly black or white, either. More like shades of gray, brown, and even red. Isn't that what your profession preaches?'

Ricky felt foolish. The lawyer's words were battering him like so many punches in a mismatched prizefight. He took a deep breath, thinking he was stupid to have come to the office, and the smart course was to get out rapidly. He was about to rise, when Merlin added:

'Hell can take many forms, Doctor Starks. Think of me as merely one of them.'

'Come again?' Ricky said. But what he recalled was what Virgil had said in their first meeting, when she told him that she was to be his guide to Hell, and that was where her name came from.

The lawyer smiled. 'In Arthurian times,' he said not unpleasantly, with the confidence of a man who has sized up the opposition and found it distinctly lacking, 'Hell was very real in the minds of all sorts of folks, even the educated and sophisticated. They truly believed in demons, devils, possession by evil spirits, what have you. They could smell fire and brimstone awaiting the less than pious, thought that burning pits and eternal tortures were not unreasonable outcomes for poorly led lives. Today, things are more complicated, doctor, aren't they? We don't really think we're going to suffer burning tongs and eternal damnation in some fiery pit. So, what do we have instead? Lawyers. And trust me on this, doc, I can quite easily turn your life into something resembling a medieval picture etched by one of those nightmare artists. What you want is to take the easy way out, doc. The easy way. Better check that insurance policy again.'

The door to the conference room swung open right then, and two of the moving men hesitated before entering. 'We'd like to get this stuff now,' one man said. 'It's pretty much all that's left.'

Merlin rose. 'No problem. I believe Doctor Starks was just getting ready to leave.'

Ricky, too, stood. He nodded. 'Yes. I am.' He looked down at the lawyer's card. 'This is where my attorney should contact you?'

'Yes.'

'All right,' he said. 'And you'll be available . . . '

'At your convenience, doctor. I think you'd be wise to get this settled promptly. You'd hate to waste your precious vacation worrying about me, wouldn't you?'

Ricky did not reply, although he noted that he had not mentioned his vacation plans to the lawyer. He simply nodded, then turned and exited the office, not looking back for a second.

* * *

Ricky slid into a cab and told the driver to take him to the Plaza Hotel. This was barely a dozen blocks away. For what Ricky had in mind, it seemed the best selection. The cab lurched forward, racing through mid-town in that unique manner that city cabs have, accelerating quickly, surging, braking, shifting, slaloming through traffic, making no better and no worse time than a steady, contained, direct path would have. Ricky looked at the cabdriver's identification shield, which, as expected, was another unfathomable foreign name. He sat back, thinking how hard it is sometimes to get a cab in Manhattan, and wasn't it intriguing that one was so readily available as he emerged, shaken, from the attorney's office. Just as if it had been waiting for him.

The cabdriver pulled sharply to the curb outside the hotel's entrance. Ricky jammed some money through the Plexiglas partition, and exited the cab. He ignored the doorman, and jumped up the stairs and through the revolving hotel doors. The lobby was milling with guests, and he rapidly threaded his way through several parties and tour groups, dodging piles of luggage and scurrying bellhops. He launched himself to The Palm Court. On the far side of the restaurant, he paused, stared at a menu for a moment, then ducked down, hunching over slightly and headed for the corridor, moving at as quick a pace as he could muster without drawing undue attention, more like a man late for a train. He went directly to the Central Park South exit of the hotel, stepping through the doors, back onto the street.

There was a doorman flagging cabs for guests as they emerged. Ricky stepped past one family gathered at the curb. 'Do you mind,' he said to a middle-aged father dressed in a Hawaiian print shirt who was riding herd on three rowdy children all between the ages of six and ten. A mousy wife stood to the side, mother-henning the entire brood. 'I have a bit of an emergency. I don't mean to be rude, but . . . ' The father looked at Ricky crazily, as if no family trip all the way from Idaho to New York would be complete without someone stealing a cab from them, and then wordlessly gestured to the door. Ricky jumped in, slamming it behind him as he heard the wife say, 'Ralph, what are you doing? That was ours . . . '

This cabdriver, Ricky thought, at least, wasn't someone hired by Rumplestiltskin. He gave the driver the address of Merlin's office.

As he suspected, the moving van was no longer parked out front. The security guard in his blue blazer had disappeared as well.

Ricky leaned forward and knocked on the cabdriver's partition. 'I've changed my mind,' he said. 'Take me to this address, please.' He read the new address off the attorney's card. 'But when you get close, stop about a block away, okay? I don't want to pull up in front.'

The cabdriver silently shrugged and nodded.

It took a quarter hour to battle through traffic. The address on Merlin's card was near Wall Street. It reeked of prestige.

The driver did as he'd been asked, pulling to the side a block shy of the address. 'Up there,' the man said. 'You want me to drive?'

'No,' Ricky replied. 'This is fine.' He paid and tossed himself from the tight confines of the rear seat.

As he'd half guessed, there was no sign of the moving truck outside the large office building. He looked up and down the street, but saw no sign of the attorney, nor the company, nor the office furniture. He double-checked the address on the card, making certain that he had it correct, then looked into the building and saw there was a security desk just inside the front door. A single uniformed guard, reading a paperback novel, had taken up a position behind a bank of video monitors and an electronic board that showed the elevator operations. Ricky stepped into the building and first approached an office directory printed on the wall. He quickly checked and found no listing for anyone named Merlin. Ricky walked over to the guard, who looked up as he came forward.

'Help you?' he said.

'Yes,' Ricky replied. 'I seem to be confused. I have this lawyer's card, with this address, but I can't seem to find his listing. He should be moving in today.'

The guard checked the card, frowned, and shook his head. 'That's the right address,' he said, 'but we've got nobody by that name.'

'Maybe an empty office? Like I said, moving in today?'

'No one told security nothing. And there aren't any vacancies. Haven't been for years.'

'Well, that's strange,' Ricky said. 'Must be a printer's mistake.'

The guard handed back the card. 'Could be,' he said.

Ricky pocketed the card, thinking that he'd just won his first skirmish with the man stalking him. But to what advantage, he wasn't sure.

* * *

Ricky was still feeling slightly smug as he arrived at his own building. He was unsure who he'd met in the attorney's office, wondering whether the man who called himself Merlin wasn't really Rumplestiltskin himself. This was a distinct possibility, Ricky thought, because he was certain that the man at the core of the situation would want to see Ricky himself, face-to-face. He wasn't precisely certain why he believed this, but it seemed to make some sense. It was difficult to imagine someone gaining pleasure from tormenting him, without that person wanting to get a firsthand opportunity to see his handiwork.

But this observation did not even begin to color in the portrait he knew he would have to create in order to guess that man's name.

'What do you know about psychopaths?' he asked himself, as he walked up the steps to the brownstone building that housed his home office and four other apartments. Not much, he answered quietly to himself. What he knew about were the troubles and neuroses of the mildly to significantly crippled. He knew about the lies well-to-do people told themselves to justify their behavior. He didn't think he knew much about someone who would create an entire world of lies in order to bring about his death. Ricky understood that this was uncharted territory for him.

In an instant, the satisfaction Ricky had felt outmaneuvering Rumplestiltskin once, fled. He reminded himself coldly: Remember what's at stake.

He saw that the mail had been delivered, and he

opened his box. One long, thin envelope bore an official seal in the upper left-hand corner from the Transit Authority of the City of New York. He opened this first.

There was a small piece of paper clipped to a larger photocopied sheet. He read the small letter first.

Dear Dr. Starks:

Our investigation uncovered the enclosed among Mr. Zimmerman's personal effects. Because it mentions you, and seems to comment on your treatment, I send it along. Our file on this death, incidentally, is now closed.

Sincerely,

Detective J. Riggins

Ricky flipped the cover letter back and read the photocopy. It was brief, typed, and filled him with a distant dread.

To whom it may concern:

I talk and talk, but never get better. No one helps me. No one listens to the real me. I have made arrangements for my mother. These can be found along with will, insurance papers, and other documents in my desk at work. Apologies to all involved, except Dr. Starks. Goodbye to the rest.

Roger Zimmerman

Even the signature had been typed. Ricky stared at the suicide note, feeling his emotions simply drain through him.

9

Zimmerman's note, Ricky thought, could not be real.

Internally, he remained adamant: Zimmerman was no more likely to take his own life than Ricky was. He showed no signs of suicidal ideation, no inclinations to self-destruction, no propensity for self-violence. Zimmerman was neurotic and stubborn and only beginning to understand analytic insight; he was a man who still had to be pushed into doing anything, just as Ricky believed he had to have been pushed in front of that subway train. But Ricky was just starting to have trouble discerning what was real and what wasn't. Even with the detective's letter in front of him, after his visit to the subway station and the police office, he still was having difficulty accepting the reality of Zimmerman's death. It remained fixed somewhere in the surreal. He looked down at the suicide letter and realized he was the only person named. He took note, also, that it hadn't been signed by hand. Instead, the person who wrote the note had typed Zimmerman's name. Or, Zimmerman had typed his name if he had indeed written the note.

Ricky's head spun.

Any elation he felt at outmaneuvering the attorney that morning dissipated, replaced with a queasiness bordering on nausea that seemed to start in his stomach, but which he guessed was really psychosomatic. He rode the elevator to his home with the sensation of weight dragging at his heels, resting on his shoulders. The first threads of self-pity crept into his heart, the *Why me*? question dogging his slow steps. By the time he reached his office, he felt exhausted.

He threw himself down behind his desk and seized the letter from the Psychoanalytic Society. He mentally crossed off the lawyer's name, though he wasn't silly enough to think that he had heard the last from Merlin, whoever he was. The name of the Boston-based therapist that his alleged victim was seeing was included in the letter, and Ricky understood that was undoubtedly meant to be his next call. For a moment, he wanted to ignore the name, not do what he was clearly supposed to do, but then, equally, he realized that failing to vigorously protest his innocence would be considered the act of a guilty man, so, even if it was anticipated and equally useless, he had to make that call.

Still feeling sick to his stomach, Ricky reached out and dialed the therapist's number. It rang once, then, as he'd half expected, he got an answering machine: 'This is Doctor Martin Soloman. I cannot take your call at this moment. Please leave your name and number and a brief message, and I will get back to you promptly.' At least, Ricky thought, he hasn't left for vacation yet.

'Doctor Soloman,' Ricky said briskly, an actor trying to fill his voice with an element of outrage and indignation, 'this is Doctor Frederick Starks in Manhattan. I have been accused by a patient of yours of serious misconduct. I would like to inform you that these allegations are totally false. They are fantasy, without any basis in substance or reality. Thank you.'

Then he hung up. The solidity of his message restored some of his spirits. He looked at his watch. Five minutes, he thought. Ten at the most, before he calls back.

About this he was correct. At the seven-minute mark, the telephone rang.

He answered with a solid, deep, 'Doctor Starks speaking.'

The man at the other end of the line seemed to inhale sharply before saying, 'Doctor, this is Martin Soloman. I received your brief message and thought it wise if I got right back to you.'

Ricky waited for a moment or two, filling the line with silence, before continuing, 'Who is your patient, who has accused me of this reprehensible behavior?'

He was greeted with an equal space of quiet, before Soloman said, 'I don't know that I'm at liberty yet to divulge her name. She has told me that when investigators from the proper medical ethics authorities contact this office, she will make herself available. Merely voicing the complaint to the New York Psychoanalytic Society was an important first step in her recovery. She needs to proceed cautiously. But this seems incredible to me, doctor. Surely you know who your patients were such a short time ago? And claims such as hers, with the detail she has provided me over the past six months, certainly lend credence to what she's said.'

'Detail?' Ricky asked. 'What sort of detail?'

The doctor hesitated. 'Well, I don't know how much — '

'Don't be ridiculous. I don't believe for a second that this person exists,' Ricky interrupted sharply.

'I can assure you she is completely real. And her pain is substantial,' the therapist said, mimicking what Merlin the lawyer had pronounced earlier that day. 'Frankly, doctor, I find your denials less than persuasive.'

'Then what details?'

Soloman hesitated before saying, 'She has described you, physically and intimately. She has described your office. She can imitate your voice, which, I might say now, seems an uncannily accurate imitation . . . '

'Impossible,' Ricky blurted.

Doctor Soloman paused again, then asked, 'Tell me, doctor, on the wall in your office next to the portrait of Freud, is there a small blue and yellow woodcut of a Cape Cod sunset?'

Ricky almost choked. Of the few pieces of art remaining in the monastic world of his office and apartment, that was one. It had been a present to him from his wife on their fifteenth wedding anniversary, and it was one of the few items that survived his purge of her presence after she succumbed to cancer.

Soloman continued, 'It's there isn't it? My patient said that she would focus on that particular piece of art, trying to will herself into the picture, while you were abusing her sexually. Like an out-of-body experience. I've known other victims of sex crimes to do the same, to imagine themselves someplace other than reality. It's not an uncommon defense mechanism.'

Ricky swallowed hard. 'Nothing of that sort ever took place.'

'Well,' Soloman said abruptly, 'it's not me that you're going to have to convince, is it?'

Ricky paused before asking, 'How long has this patient been seeing you?'

'Six months. We've got a helluva long way to go, too.'

'Who referred her?'

'I'm sorry?'

'Who referred her to you?'

'I don't know that I recall . . . '

'You mean to tell me that a woman suffering this sort of emotional trauma simply picked your name out of a phone book?'

'I'd have to check my notes.'

'Your recollection should be sufficient.'

'I'd still have to check my notes.'

Ricky snorted. 'You'll find that no one referred her. She chose you for some obvious reason. So, I ask again: Why you, doctor?'

Soloman paused, thinking. 'I have a reputation in this city for success with victims of sex crimes.'

'What do you mean *reputation*?'

'I've had some articles written about my work in the local press.'

Ricky was thinking quickly. 'Do you often testify in court?'

'Not that often. But I am familiar with the process.'

'How often is not often?'

'Two or three times. And I know where you're going with this. Yes, they have been high-profile cases.'

'Have you ever been an expert witness?'

'Why, yes. In several civil suits, including one against a psychiatrist accused of much the same thing you are. I have a teaching position at the University of Massachusetts Medical Center, as well, where I lecture on various recovery profiles from criminal acts . . . '

'Was your name in the paper shortly before this patient approached you? Prominently?'

'Yes. A feature article in the *Boston Globe*. But I don't see why . . . '

'And you insist your patient is credible?'

'I do. I have been in therapy with her now for six months. Two sessions each week. She has been utterly consistent. Nothing she has said up to this point would make me doubt her word in the slightest. Doctor, you and I both know how close to impossible it is for someone to successfully lie to a therapist, especially over an elongated space of time.'

Ricky would have undoubtedly agreed with this statement a few days earlier. Now he was no longer quite so certain. 'And where is she now?'

'She is on vacation until the third week in August.'

'Did she happen to give you a phone number where she could be reached during August?'

'No. I don't believe so. We merely made an appointment for shortly before Labor Day and left it at that.'

Ricky thought hard, then asked another question.

'And does she have striking, extraordinary, penetrating green eyes?'

Soloman paused. When he spoke, it was with an icy reserve. 'So, you do know her then?'

'No,' Ricky said. 'I was just guessing.'

Then he hung up the phone. *Virgil*, he said to himself.

* * *

Ricky found himself staring across his office toward the painting on the wall that had figured so prominently in the false recollections of the phony patient up in Boston. There was no doubt in his mind that Dr. Soloman was real, and that he had been selected with care. There was equally no doubt, Ricky understood, that this so beautiful and so troubled young woman who had come to seek out the well-known Dr. Soloman's care would ever be seen by him again. At least not in the context that Soloman thought. Ricky shook his head. There were more than a few therapists whose conceits were so profound that they came to love the attention of the press and the devotion of their patients. They behaved as if they had some unique and altogether magical insight into the ways of the world and the workings of people, dashing off opinions and pronouncements with slipshod regularity. Ricky suspected that Soloman was closer in stripe to one of these talk-show shrinks, who embraced the image of knowledge without the actual hard work of gaining insight. It is much easier to listen to someone briefly and fly off the cuff, than it is to sit day after day, penetrating layers of the mundane and trivial in pursuit of the profound. He had nothing but contempt for the members of his profession who lent their names to opinions in courtrooms and articles in newspapers.

But, Ricky thought, the problem was, Soloman's

reputation, notoriety, and public persona would lend credence to the allegation. By fixing him on the bottom of that letter, it gained a weight that would survive just long enough for the purposes of the person who'd designed it.

Ricky asked himself: What did you learn today?

Much, he answered. But mostly that the strands of the web he found himself entangled in had been laid in place months earlier.

He looked back at the painting gracing the wall. They were here, he thought, long before the other day. His eyes cruised around the office. Nothing here was safe. Nothing here was private. *They were here months ago, and I didn't know it*.

Rage like a blow to the stomach staggered him, and his first response was to rise, stride across the office, and seize the small woodcut that the doctor from Boston had mentioned, ripping it from its hook on the wall. He took the painting and dashed it into the wastebasket by his desk, cracking the frame and shattering the glass. The sound was like a gunshot echoing in the small office space. Obscenities burst from his lips, uncharacteristic and rough, filling the air with needles. He turned and grasped the sides of his desk, as if to steady himself.

As quickly as it arrived, the anger fled, replaced by another wave of nausea which slithered through him. He felt dizzy, his head reeling, the sensation one gets when one stands up too quickly, especially with a case of the flu or a severe cold. Ricky stumbled emotionally. His breathing was tight, wheezy, and one felt as if someone had looped a rope around his chest, making it hard to breathe.

It took him several minutes to regain equilibrium, and, even when he did, he still felt weak, almost exhausted.

He continued to look around the office, but now it seemed different. It was as if all the items that decorated his life had been rendered sinister. He thought he could no longer trust anything in his sight. He wondered what else Virgil had described to the physician in Boston; what other details of his life were now on display in a complaint filed with the state board of medical ethics. He remembered times patients of his had come in distraught following a break-in or a mugging and spoken about the violation, how unsettled it made their lives. He had listened to these complaints sympathetically, with clinical detachment, but never really understanding how primal the sensation was. He had a better idea now, he told himself.

He, too, felt robbed.

Again he looked around the room. What had once seemed to him to be safe was swiftly losing that quality.

Making a lie seem real is tricky work, he thought to himself. It takes planning.

Ricky maneuvered behind his desk and saw that the red light on his answering machine was blinking steadily. A message counter was lit up, as well, also red, with the number four. He reached down and pressed the switch that would activate the machine, listening to the first of the messages. He immediately recognized the voice of a patient, a late-middle-aged journalist at the *New York Times*, a man stuck in a well-paying but fundamentally repetitive job editing stories for the science section written by younger, more energetic reporters. He was a man who longed to do more with his life, to investigate creativity and originality, but was afraid of the disruption this indulgence might bring to a carefully regimented life. Still, this patient was intelligent, sophisticated, and making significant strides in therapy, beginning to understand the connection between his rigid upbringing in the Midwest, child of dedicated academics, and his fear of adventure. Ricky quite liked the man, and thought he was a likely candidate to complete his analysis and see the freedom it would give him as an opportunity, which is a great satisfaction to any therapist.

'Doctor Starks,' the man said slowly, almost reluctantly, as he identified himself. 'I apologize for leaving a message on your machine during your vacation. I don't mean to disrupt your holiday, but this morning's mail brought a very disturbing letter.'

Ricky inhaled sharply. The voice of the patient continued slowly.

'The letter was a copy of a complaint filed against you with the state medical ethics board and the New York Psychoanalytic Society. I recognize the anonymous nature of the allegation makes it extremely hard to counter. The copy of the letter, incidentally, was mailed to me at my home, not my office, and lacked any return address or any other identifying characteristics.'

Again the patient hesitated.

'I have been placed in a substantial conflict of interest. There is little doubt in my mind that the complaint is a worthy news story, and should be turned over to someone on our city reporting staff for additional investigation. On the other hand, this act would obviously severely compromise our relationship. I am troubled deeply by the allegations, which I presume you deny . . . '

The patient seemed to catch his breath, then added with a touch of bitter anger, ' . . . Everyone always denies wrongdoing. 'I didn't do it, I didn't do it, I didn't do it . . . ' Until they're so caught by events and trapped by circumstances that they can no longer lie. Presidents. Government officials. Businessmen. Doctors. Scoutmasters and Little League coaches, for Christ's sake. Then they finally are forced to tell the truth and expect everyone to understand they had to lie, earlier, as if it's okay to keep lying until you're so goddamn caught you can't lie effectively anymore . . . '

The patient paused again, then hung up the phone.

The message seemed sliced off, short of what he wanted Ricky to respond to.

Ricky's hand shook slightly as he again pressed the Play button on the machine. The next message was merely a woman sobbing. Unfortunately, he recognized the noise, and knew it was another longtime patient. She, too, he guessed, had received a copy of the letter. He quickly fast-forwarded the tape. The two remaining messages were also from patients. One, a prominent choreographer for Broadway productions, sputtered with barely repressed rage. The other, a portrait photographer of some note, seemed as much confused as she was distraught.

Despair flooded him. Perhaps for the first time in his professional life, he didn't know what to say to his own patients. The others who hadn't yet called, he suspected, hadn't opened their mail yet.

* * *

One of the key elements to psychoanalysis is the curious relationship between the patient and the therapist, where the patient pours out every intimate detail of his life to a person who doesn't reciprocate and very rarely reacts to even the most provocative information. In the child's game Truth or Dare, trust is established by shared risk. You tell me, I'll tell you. You show me yours, I'll show you mine. Psychoanalysis skews this relationship by making it utterly one-sided. Indeed, Ricky knew, the patients' fascination with who Ricky was, what he thought and felt, how he reacted, were all dynamics of significance and were all part of the great process of transference that took place in his office, where sitting silently behind his patients' heads as they lay with their feet in the air on the couch, he symbolically became many things, but mostly, he came to symbolize to each of them something different and something troubling, and so, by taking on these different roles for each patient he could lead each of them through their problems. His silence would come to psychologically mimic one patient's mother, another's father, a third's boss. His silence would come to represent love and hate, anger and sadness. It could become loss, it could become rejection. In some respects, he understood, the analyst is a chameleon, changing color against the surface of every object he touches.

He didn't return any of the phone calls from his patients, and, by evening, all had called. The editor from the *Times* was right, he thought. We live in a society that has reformed the entire concept of the denial. Now the denial carries with it the presumption that it is merely a lie of convenience, to be recalled and subsequently tailored at some later point, when an acceptable truth has been negotiated.

Hours every day that totaled weeks that became months and turned into years with each of the patients had been savaged by a single well-constructed lie. He didn't know how to respond to his patients, whether he should respond at all. The clinician within him understood that examining each patient's response to the allegations would be fruitful, but at the same time, that seemed ineffectual.

For dinner that evening he made himself chicken soup out of a can.

Spooning the scalding mixture into his mouth, he wondered whether some of the famed medicinal and restorative powers of the concoction would flow into his heart.

He understood that he was still lacking a plan of action. Some chart that he could follow. A diagnosis, followed by a course of treatment. Up to this point, Rumplestiltskin seemed to Ricky to be like some sort of insidious cancer, attacking different parts of his persona. He still needed to define an approach. The problem was, this went against his training. Had he been an oncologist, like the men who'd unsuccessfully treated his wife, or even a dentist who was able to see the decayed tooth and pluck it out, he would have done so. But Ricky's training was far different. An analyst, although recognizing certain definable characteristics and syndromes, ultimately lets the patient invent the treatment, within the simple context of the process. Ricky was being crippled in his approach to Rumplestiltskin and his threats by the very nature that had stood him in such fine stead over so many years. The passivity that was a hallmark of his profession was suddenly dangerous.

He worried for the first time late that night that it might kill him.

10

In the morning, he crossed another day off Rumplestiltskin's calendar and composed the following inquiry:

Searching high and looking fast,
inspecting all from twenty past.
Is this year right or wrong?
(Because of time, I have not long.)
And although it seems like such a bother,
am I hunting for R's mother?

Ricky realized that he was stretching Rumplestiltskin's rules, first by asking two questions instead of one, and not exactly framing them for a simple yes or no response as he'd been instructed. But he guessed that by using the same nursery school rhyme scheme that his tormentor did, Rumplestiltskin would be prompted to ignore the violation of the rules and might answer with slightly more detail. Ricky understood that in order to deduce who had ensnared him, he needed information. Much more information. He was under no illusion that Rumplestiltskin would give away some tell-tale bit of detail that would tell Ricky precisely where to look for him, or might actually instantly provide an avenue for a name, that could then be given to the authorities — if Ricky could figure out which authorities to contact. The man had planned out his adventure in revenge too precisely for that to happen quickly, Ricky thought. But an analyst is considered a scientist of the oblique and of the hidden. He should be expert at the hidden and concealed, Ricky thought, and if he was to find the answer to Rumplestiltskin's real name, it would have to come from a slip that the man, no matter how intricately he had schemed, did not anticipate.

The lady at the *Times* who took the order for the single-column front-page ad seemed intrigued in a pleasant way by the rhyme. 'This is unusual,' she said lightly. 'Usually these are just happy fiftieth anniversary mom and dad ads, or else come-ons for some new product that someone wants to sell,' she said. 'This seems different. What's the occasion?' she asked.

Ricky, trying to be polite, replied with an efficient lie, 'It's part of an elaborate scavenger hunt. Just a summertime diversion for a couple of us who enjoy puzzles and word games.'

'Oh,' the woman replied. 'That sounds like fun.'

Ricky didn't respond to this, because there was little of fun in what he was doing. The woman at the newspaper read the rhyme back to him one last time to make certain she had the wording correctly, then took down the necessary billing information. She asked whether he wanted to be billed directly, or to put the charge on a credit card. He elected for the credit card response. He could hear her fingers clicking the computer keyboard as he read off his Visa number.

'Well,' the ad lady said, 'that's it, then. The ad will run tomorrow. Good luck with your game,' she added. 'I hope you win.'

'So do I,' he said. He thanked her and hung up the phone. He turned back to the piles of notes and records.

Narrow and eliminate, he thought. Be systematic and careful.

Rule out men or rule out women. Rule out the old, focus on the young. Find the right time sequence. Find the right relationship. That will get a name. One name will lead to another.

Ricky breathed hard. He had spent his life trying to help people understand the emotional forces that caused things to happen to them. What an analyst does is isolate blame and try to render it into something manageable, because an analyst would think of the need for revenge to be as crippling a neurosis as anyone could suffer. The analyst would want the patient to find a way past that need and beyond that anger. It wasn't uncommon for a patient to start a therapy stating a fury that seemed to demand an acting-out response. The treatment was designed to eliminate that urge, so that they could get on with their life unencumbered by the compulsive need to get even.

Getting even, in his world, was a weakness. Perhaps even a sickness.

Ricky shook his head.

As his head spun, trying to sort through what he knew and how to apply it to his situation, the telephone on the desk rang. It startled him, and he hesitated, reaching out for it, wondering whether it would be Virgil.

It was not. It was the ad lady at the *Times*.

'Doctor Starks?'

'Yes.'

'I'm sorry to call you back, but we had a little problem.'

'A problem? What sort of problem?'

The woman hesitated, as if reluctant to say, then continued, 'The Visa card number you gave me, uh, it came back canceled. Are you certain you gave me the proper number sequence?'

Ricky blushed, alone in the room. 'Canceled? That's impossible,' he said indignantly.

'Well, maybe I got the number wrong . . . '

He reached for his wallet and pulled out the card, reading off the sequence of numbers again, but slowly.

The woman paused. 'No, that's the number I submitted for approval. It came back that the card had been recently canceled.'

'I don't understand,' Ricky said with mounting frustration. 'I didn't cancel anything. And I pay off the entire balance every month . . . '

'The card companies make more mistakes than you'd think,' the woman said, apologetically. 'Have you got another card? Or maybe you'd just prefer me to send you a bill and you can pay by check?'

Ricky started to remove another card from his wallet, then abruptly stopped. He swallowed hard. 'I'm sorry for the inconvenience,' he said slowly, suddenly working hard to keep himself under control. 'I will have to contact the credit card company. In the meantime, please just send me the bill as you suggest.'

The woman mumbled an agreement, double-checking his address, then adding, 'It happens all the time. Did you lose your wallet? Sometimes thieves get numbers from old statements that are tossed away. Or you buy something and the clerk sells the number to a crook. There are zillions of ways cards get screwed up, doctor. But you better call the issuing company and get it straightened out. You don't want to end up fighting over charges you don't make. Anyway, they'll probably just overnight you a new card.'

'I'm sure,' Ricky said. He hung up the phone.

Slowly he extracted each of the credit cards from his wallet. They're all useless, he told himself. They have all been canceled. He didn't know how, but he knew by whom.

* * *

Still, he started the tedious process of calling to discover what he already knew to be true. The telephone customer service clerks at each credit card company were friendly but not very helpful. When he tried to explain that he hadn't actually canceled his cards, he was informed that he indeed had. That's what their computers showed, and whatever the computer showed, had to be right. He asked each company exactly how the card had been canceled, and each time he was told that the request had been made electronically, through the bank's Web sites. Simple transactions of that sort, the clerks dutifully pointed out, could be accomplished with a few simple swipes at a keyboard. This was, they said, a service that the bank offered, to make financial life easier for their clients, although Ricky, in his current state, might have debated that. All offered to open new accounts for him.

He told each company he would get back to them. Then he took some scissors he kept in his top drawer and cut each of the useless pieces of plastic in half. It was not lost on Ricky that this act was precisely what some patients had been forced to do, when they allowed themselves to get overextended with their credit and into debt.

Ricky did not know how far into his finances Rumplestiltskin had managed to penetrate. Nor did he know how. *Debt* is a concept close to the game the man had created, Ricky thought. He believes I owe him a payment, and not one that can be paid by check or credit card.

A visit in the morning to the local branch of his bank was in order, Ricky thought. He also placed a telephone call to the man who handled his modest investment portfolio, leaving a message with a secretary, asking that the broker call him back promptly. Then he sat back for a moment, trying to imagine how Rumplestiltskin had entered this part of his life.

Ricky was a computer idiot. His knowledge of the Internet and AOL, Yahoo, and eBay, Web sites, chat rooms, and cyberspace was limited to a vague familiarity with the words, but not the reality. His patients often spoke of life connected to the keyboard, and in that way he'd gained some appreciation of what a computer could do, but more of what a computer did to them. He had never seen any need to learn any of this himself. His own writing was scrawled in pen in notebooks. If he had to compose a letter, he used an antique electric typewriter that was more than twenty years old and kept in a closet. He owned a computer, in a way. His wife had purchased one in the first year of her disease, then upgraded it a year before her death. He had been aware that she had used the machine to electronically visit cancer support groups and to speak with other cancer victims in that curiously detached world of the Internet. He had not joined her in these sorties, thinking that he was respecting her privacy by not intruding, when another might have suggested that he was simply not showing enough interest. Shortly after she'd died, he'd taken the machine from the desk in the corner of their bedroom that she'd occupied when she was able to gather the energy to get out of bed, and packed it away in a box and stuck it in the basement storage rooms of his building. He had meant to throw it out or give it to some school or library, and had just never gotten around to it. It occurred to him that he might need it, now.

Because, he suspected, Rumplestiltskin knew how to use one.

Ricky rose from his seat, deciding in that instant to recover his dead wife's computer from the basement. In the top right-hand desk drawer, he kept a key to a padlock, which he grabbed.

He made certain to lock his front door behind him, then took the elevator down to the basement. It had been months since he'd been in the building's storage area and he wrinkled his nose at the musty, stale-smelling air in the space. It had a fetid, sickly quality to it, aged and filthy, charred by the daily cycle of heat. Just stepping out of the elevator gave him the asthmatic's sensation of tightening in his chest. He wondered why building management never cleaned the area. There was a light switch on the wall, which he flicked, throwing a little brightness into the basement from a single uncovered overhead hundred-watt bulb. Whenever he moved, he carried shadows with him, streaking grotesquely through the dark and damp. Each of the building's six apartments had a storage area, delineated by chicken wire nailed to cheap balsa wood frames, with the apartment number stenciled on the outside. It was a place of broken chairs and boxes of old papers, unused and rusty bicycles, skis and steamer trunks, and unneeded suitcases. Dust and cobwebs covered most everything, and most everything was in the category of something slightly too valuable to throw out, but not important enough to keep around every day. Things collected from time to time that just slipped into the category of better keep this because someday we might need it, but just barely.

Ricky hunched over slightly, although there was plenty of headroom. It was more the closed atmosphere that made him bend. He approached his own cubicle with the padlock key in hand.

But the lock was already open. It hung from the handle of the door like a forgotten Christmas tree ornament.

He looked closer and saw that it had been sliced open with bolt cutters.

Ricky stepped back a single stride, shocked, as if a rat had suddenly run in front of him.

His first instinct was to turn and run, his second to move forward. This is what he did, walking slowly to the chicken wire door and pulling it open. What he saw immediately was that exactly what he came down to the basement searching for, the box containing his wife's computer, was missing. He moved deeper inside the storage area. The overhead light was partially blocked by his own body, so that only swordlike streaks of illumination carved through the area. He glanced about and saw that another box was absent. This was a large plastic file container that kept copies of his completed tax returns.

The rest of his near-trash seemed to be intact, for what it was worth.

Almost staggered by an overwhelming sense of defeat, Ricky turned and headed back to the elevator. It was not until he rose out of the basement, back into the midday light, clearer air, and away from the grime and dust of memories stored below that he allowed himself to think about the impact that the missing computer and tax returns might have.

What was stolen? he asked himself.

He shuddered suddenly. He answered his own question: Perhaps everything.

The missing tax returns made his stomach churn with an evil, acid sensation. No wonder the attorney Merlin knew so much about his assets. He probably knew everything about Ricky's modest finances. A tax return is like a road map, from Social Security number to charitable donations. It displays all the well-traveled routes of one's existence, without the history. Like a map, it shows someone how to get from here to there in another person's life, where the turnpikes flow and where the back roads begin. All it lacks is color and description.

The missing computer frightened Ricky just as much. He had no idea what remained on the hard drive, but he knew it was something. He tried to recall the hours that his wife had spent on the machine before the disease robbed her even of the strength to type. How much of her pain, memories, insights, and electronic travels were there, he had no idea. He knew only that skilled computer technicians could recover all sorts of past journeys from computer memory chips. He assumed that Rumplestiltskin had the necessary ability to extract from the machine whatever was there that he decided he wanted.

Ricky slumped into his apartment. The sense of violation he felt was like being sliced with a heated razor blade. He looked about him, and understood that everything he thought was so safe and private about his life was vulnerable.

Nothing was secret.

If he were still a child, Ricky realized, he would have burst into tears at that very moment.

* * *

His dreams that night were filled with dark and violent images, of being cut by knives. In one dream, he saw himself trying to maneuver through a poorly lit room, knowing all the time that if he stumbled and fell he would fall through the blackness into some oblivion, but as he traversed the dreamscape, he was uncoordinated and clumsy, grasping at vaporous walls with drunken fingers, his journey seemingly helpless. He awakened into the pitch-darkness of his bedroom filled with that momentary panic as one staggers from unconscious to conscious, sweat staining his nightshirt, his breathing shallow and his throat hoarse, as if he'd been crying out for several hours in sustained despair. For a moment he was still unsure whether he'd left the nightmare behind, and it was not until he clicked on the bedside lamp and was able to look around the familiar space of his own room that his heart began to return to a normal pace. Ricky dropped his head back onto his pillow, desperate for rest, knowing none was readily available. He had no difficulty interpreting his dreams. They were as evil as his waking life was becoming.

The ad ran in the *Times* that morning on the front page, at the bottom, as specified by Rumplestiltskin. He read it over several times, then thought that at the least, it would give his tormentor something to think about. Ricky did not know how long it would take for the man to reply, but he expected some sort of answer rapidly, perhaps in the following morning's paper. In the interim, he decided it would be best if he kept working on the puzzle.

He felt a momentary, illusory surge of success, with the ad running, as if encouraged that he had taken a step forward, and gained a temporary sense of determination. The overwhelming despair from the previous day's discovery of the missing computer and stolen tax returns was, if not exactly forgotten, at least put aside. The ad gave Ricky the sensation that this day, at least, he wasn't being a victim. He found himself focused, able to concentrate, his memory more acute and accurate. The day fled rapidly, as quickly as an ordinary day with patients would have, as Ricky plumbed his recollections and traveled steadily through his own interior landscape.

* * *

By the end of the morning, he'd created two separate working lists. Still confining himself to the ten-year period that started in 1975 and went to 1985, on the first list he identified some seventy-three people that he had seen in treatment. The courses of treatment had ranged from a high of seven years for one deeply troubled man, to a three-month burst for a woman experiencing marital difficulties. On average, most of his patients were in the three-to-five-year range. A few less. The majority of his patients were traditional Freudian-based analyses, four to five times per week, utilizing the couch and all the various techniques of the profession. A few were not; they were face-to-face encounters, more simple talk sessions, where he had behaved less as an analyst and more as an ordinary therapist, complete with opinions, pronouncements, and advice, which are, for the most part, the things an analyst strives hardest to avoid. He realized that by the mid-1980s he had weaned most of this sort of patient out of his practice, and begun to confine himself solely to the in-depth experience of psychoanalysis.

There were also, he knew, a number of patients, perhaps two dozen over that ten-year period, who had started treatments and then interrupted them. The reasons for discontinuing therapies were complex: Some hadn't the money or the necessary health insurance to cover his fees; others had been forced to relocate, because of job or school demands. A few had simply decided angrily that they weren't being helped enough, or rapidly enough, or were too angry with the world and what it promised to deliver to them to continue. These people were rare, but existed.

They comprised his second list. This was a far more difficult list to come up with.

It was, he realized swiftly, on first appearance, the far more dangerous list. They were the people who might have transformed their rage into an obsession with Ricky, and then passed that obsession on.

He placed both lists on the desk in front of him, and thought he should start the process of tracking down the names. Once he had Rumplestiltskin's reply, he thought, he could eliminate a number of people from each, then forge ahead.

All morning he had been expecting the telephone to ring, with a reply from his account executive. He was a little surprised not to have heard from the man, because in the past he'd always handled Ricky's money with a boring diligence and dependability. He dialed the number again, once again reaching the secretary.

She seemed flustered when she heard his voice. 'Oh, Doctor Starks, Mr. Williams was about to call you back.

There's been some confusion over your account,' she said.

Ricky's stomach clenched. 'Confusion?' he asked. 'How can money be confused? People can be confused. Dogs can be confused. Money cannot.'

'I'm going to connect you with Mr. Williams,' the secretary replied. There was a momentary silence, and then the not exactly familiar, but not unrecognizable voice of his account executive came on the line. Ricky's investments were all conservative, boring, mutual funds and bonds. Nothing hip-hop or aggressively modern, just modest and steady growth. Nor were they particularly substantial. Of all the professions in the medical world, psychoanalysts were among the most limited in what they could charge and the number of patients they could see. They were not like the radiologist who had three patients booked into different examining rooms for the same time slot, nor the anesthesiologist who went from assembly-line surgery to surgery. Analysts didn't often become rich and Ricky was no exception to this rule. He owned his place on the Cape and his apartment and that was it. No Mercedes. No Piper twin engine. No forty-two-foot yawl named the *Icutknees* harbored on Long Island Sound. Just some prudent investments designed to provide him enough money for retirement, if he ever decided to cut back on his patient load. Ricky spoke with his broker perhaps once or twice a year, that was it. He'd always assumed he was one of the genuinely smaller fishes in the executive's pond.

'Doctor Starks?' The executive came on the line brusque and speaking swiftly. 'I'm sorry to have kept you waiting, but we're trying to figure out a problem here . . . '

Ricky's stomach seemed empty, tight. 'What sort of problem?'

'Well,' the executive said, 'did you open up a personal trading account with one of the new online brokers? Because . . . '

'No, I haven't. In fact, I hardly know what you're talking about.'

'Well, that's the confusing part. It appears that there's been significant day-trading in your account.'

'What's day-trading?' Ricky asked.

'It's trading stocks rapidly, trying to stay ahead of market fluctuations.'

'Okay. I understand that. But I don't do this.'

'Does someone else have access to your accounts? Perhaps your wife . . . '

'My wife passed away three years ago,' Ricky said coldly.

'Of course,' the broker answered quickly. 'I remember. I apologize. But someone else, perhaps. Do you have children?'

'No. We did not have children. Where is my money?' Ricky spoke sharply, demanding.

'Well, we're searching. This may turn out to be a police matter, Doctor Starks. In fact, that's what I'm beginning to think. That is, if someone managed to illegally access your account . . . '

'Where is the money?' Ricky demanded a second time.

The broker hesitated. 'I can't say precisely. We have our internal auditors going over the account now. All I can say is that there has been significant activity . . . '

'What do you mean activity? The money has just been sitting there . . . '

'Well, not exactly. There are literally dozens maybe even hundreds of trades, transfers, sales, investments . . . '

'Where is it now?'

The broker continued, 'A truly extraordinary trail of

extremely complicated and aggressive financial transactions . . . '

'You're not answering my question,' Ricky said, exasperation filling his voice. 'My funds. My retirement account, my cash reserves . . . '

'We're searching. I've put my best people on it. I will have our head of security contact you as soon as they make some headway. I can't believe with all the activity that no one here spotted something wrong . . . '

'But all my money . . . '

'Right now,' the executive said slowly, 'there is no money. At least, none that we can find.'

'That's not possible.'

'I wish it were so,' the man continued, 'but it is. Don't worry, Doctor Starks. Our investigators will track the transactions. We'll get to the bottom of this. And your accounts are insured, at least in part. Eventually, we'll get this all straightened out. It's just going to take some time, and, as I said, we may have to involve the police or the SEC, because it seems that what you're saying is that a theft of some sort is involved.'

'How much time?'

'It's summertime and some of the staff is on vacation. I'd guess no more than a couple of weeks. At the most.'

Ricky hung up the phone. He did not have a couple of weeks.

By the end of the day he was able to determine that the only account that he owned that hadn't been raided and eviscerated by someone who'd gained access was the small checking account he kept at First Cape Bank up in Wellfleet. This was an account purely designed to make summer matters easier. There was barely ten thousand dollars in the account, money that he used to pay bills at the local fish market and grocery store, the liquor store and hardware store. He paid for his gardening tools and plants and seeds with that account. It was money to make his vacation run smoothly. A household account, for the month he spent in the vacation household.

He was a little surprised that Rumplestiltskin had not assaulted these funds as well. He felt toyed with, almost as if the man had left this parcel of money alone to tease Ricky. Regardless, Ricky thought he needed to find a way to get the funds into his hands, before they, too, disappeared into some bizarre financial limbo. He called the manager of the First Cape Bank and told him that he was going to need to close the account and was going to want the balance of the money in cash.

The manager informed Ricky that he would have to be present for that transaction, which was fine with Ricky. He wished some of the other institutions handling his money had had the same policy. He explained to the manager that there had been some trouble with other accounts, and that it was important that no one other than Ricky access the money. The manager offered to have the funds written into a cashier's check, which he would personally keep for Ricky's arrival. This was acceptable.

The problem was how to get the money.

Ignored in his desk was an open plane ticket from La Guardia to Hyannis. He wondered whether the reservation he'd made was still intact. He opened his wallet and counted out about three hundred dollars in cash. In the top drawer of his bedroom dresser he had another fifteen hundred dollars in traveler's checks. This was an anachronism; in this era of instant cash from automatic teller machines seemingly everywhere, the idea that someone would keep an emergency fund in traveler's checks was obsolete. Ricky took a small amount of pleasure in thinking that his antique ideas would prove helpful. He wondered for a moment whether that wasn't a concept he should embrace more fully.

But he didn't really have time to consider this.

He could get to the Cape. And get back, as well, he thought. It would take at least twenty-four hours. But in the same moment, he was overcome with a sudden sense of lethargy, almost as if he couldn't move his muscles, as if the synapses in the brain that issued commands to sinew and tissue throughout his body had abruptly gone on strike. A black exhaustion that mocked his age flowed through his body. He felt dull, stupid, and filled with fatigue.

Ricky rocked in his desk chair, his head leaned back, staring at the ceiling. He recognized the warning signs of a clinical depression as quickly as a mother would know a cold coming on when her child sneezed. He held out his hands in front of him, looking for some quiver or palsy. They were still steady. How much longer? he wondered.

11

Ricky got an answer in the following morning's *Times*, but not in the manner he'd expected it. His paper was delivered to his apartment door as it was every day except Sunday, when his usual habit was to walk out to the neighborhood delicatessen and buy the bulky paper before heading to a nearby coffee shop, just as Rumplestiltskin had so carefully observed in his opening threat. He had had more difficulty sleeping the night before, so when he heard the faint thump of the delivery service dropping the paper outside his apartment, he was alert, and within seconds had seized the paper and flung it open on the kitchen table. His eyes dropped immediately to the small ads on the bottom of the front page, only to see an anniversary greeting, a come-on for a computer dating service and a third small single-column box ad: SPECIALIZED OPPORTUNITIES, SEE PAGE B-16.

Ricky threw the paper across the small kitchen in frustration. It made a sound like a bird trying to fly with a broken wing as it slapped against the wall. He was enraged, almost choking and spitting with a sudden outburst of fury. He had expected a rhyme, another cryptic, teasing reply, at the bottom of the front page, just as his inquiry had been. No poem, no answer, he snarled inwardly. 'How do you expect me to beat your damn deadline when you don't reply in timely fashion?' he almost shouted, raising his voice to no one physically present but certainly occupying a significant space.

He noticed that his hands were shaking slightly as he made himself some morning coffee. The hot liquid did little to calm him. He tried to relax himself with some deep breathing exercises, but those only slowed his racing heart momentarily. He could feel his anger soaring through his body, as if it were capable of reaching into every organ beneath the surface of his skin and tightening every one. His head pounded already, and he felt as if he was trapped inside the apartment that he'd known as home. There was sweat dripping beneath his armpits, his brow felt feverish, and his throat was dry and sandy.

He must have sat at his table, outwardly immobile, inwardly churning for hours, almost trancelike, unable to imagine what his next step was. He knew that he needed to make plans, decisions, to act in certain directions, but not getting a reply when he expected one had crippled him. He thought he could hardly move, as if, suddenly, each of his joints in arms and legs had become immobile, unwilling to respond to commands.

Ricky did not have any idea how long he sat like that before lifting his eyes just slightly and fixing on the *Times* lying in a fluttered heap in disarray where he had flung it. Nor was he aware how long he stared at the clutter of pages before he noticed the small streak of bright red just ducking out from underneath the pile. And then, after taking notice of this abnormality — after all, in the past the *Times* was not called the Gray Lady for nothing — that he connected it to himself. He fixed on this small streak, and finally said to himself: There is no flagrant red ink in the *Times*. Mostly sturdy black and white delivered in seven-column, two-section format, as regular as clockwork. Even their color photographs of the president or models displaying the latest Parisian fashions seemed to automatically take on the drab and dull tinge of the paper's past.

Ricky picked himself up out of his chair and crossed the room, bending over the mess of newspaper. He reached for the splash of color and pulled it toward him.

It was page B-16. This was the obituary page.

But written in dramatic, glowing fluorescent red ink across the pictures, stories, and death notices was the following:

You're on the right track,
as you travel back.
Twenty certainly covers the base.
And my mother is the right case.
But her name will be hard to find,
unless I give you a clue in kind.
So I will tell you this, you would have
known her as a miss.
And in the days that came after,
you would never have heard her laughter.
You promised much, but delivered none.
That's why revenge is left to her son.
Father left, mother dead:
that is why I want your head.
This is where I end this rhyme,
Because I note you have little time.

Beneath the poem was a large red *R* and beneath that, this time in black ink, the man had drawn a rectangle around an obituary, with a large arrow pointing at the dead man's face and story, and the words: *You will fit perfectly right here*.

He stared at the poem and the message it contained for a moment that stretched into minutes and finally close to an hour, digesting each word the way a gourmand might a fine Parisian meal except that Ricky found this taste to be bitter and salty. It was well into the morning, another day x-ed away, when he noted the obvious: Rumplestiltskin had gained access to his paper in the moments between arrival outside his brownstone and delivery at his door. His fingers flew to the telephone, and within minutes he'd obtained the number for the delivery service. The phone rang twice, before being answered by an automated selection recording:

'New subscribers, please press one. Complaints about delivery or if you did not receive your paper, please press two. Account information, please press three.'

None of these options seemed to him to be precisely on target, but he suspected a complaint might actually draw a human response, so he tried two. This created a ringing, followed by a woman's voice:

'What address, please?' she said without introduction.

Ricky hesitated and then gave the address of his home.

'We show all deliveries made to that location,' she said.

'Yes,' Ricky said, 'I received a paper, but I want to know who delivered it . . . '

'What is the problem, sir? You don't need a second delivery?'

'No . . . '

'This line is for people who didn't get their paper delivered . . . '

'I understand,' he said, starting to become exasperated. 'But there was a problem with the delivery . . . '

'They were not on time?'

'No. Yes, they were on time . . . '

'Did the delivery service make too much noise?'

'No.'

'This line is for people with complaints about their delivery.'

'Yes. You said that. Or, not exactly that, and I understand . . . '

'What is your problem, sir?'

Ricky paused, trying to find a common language to deal with the young woman on the line. 'My paper was defaced,' he said abruptly.

'Do you mean it was ripped or wet or unreadable?'

'I mean that someone tampered with it.'

'Sometimes papers come off the press with errors in pagination or folding, was this that sort of mix-up?'

'No,' Ricky said, sliding away from his defensive tones. 'What I mean to say is that someone wrote offensive language on my paper.'

The woman paused. 'That's a new one,' she said slowly. Her response almost turned her into a real person, rather than the typical disembodied voice. 'I've never heard of that. What sort of offensive language?'

Ricky decided to be oblique. He spoke quickly and aggressively. 'Are you Jewish, miss? Do you know what it would be like to get a paper that someone drew a swastika on? Or are you Puerto Rican? How would you feel if someone wrote 'Go back to San Juan!'? Are you African American? You know the word that triggers hate, don't you?'

The clerk paused, as if trying to keep up. 'Someone put a swastika on your paper?' she asked.

'Something like that,' Ricky answered. 'That's why I need to speak to the people in charge of the delivery.'

'I think you better speak with my supervisor.'

'Sure,' Ricky said. 'But first I want the name and then the phone number of the person in charge of deliveries to my building.'

The woman hesitated again, and Ricky could hear her shuffling through some papers, and then there was a series of computer keys clicking in the background. When she came back on the line, she read off the name of a route supervisor, a driver, their phone numbers and their addresses. 'I'd like you to speak with my supervisor,' she said, after giving the information.

'Have him call me,' Ricky replied before hanging up the phone. Within seconds he had called the number she had provided. Another woman answered.

'Superior news delivery.'

'Mr. Ortiz, please,' he asked politely.

'Ortiz is out by the loading dock. What's this about?'

'A delivery problem.'

'Did you call the dispatch . . . ?'

'Yes. That's how I got this number. And his name.'

'What sort of problem?'

'How about I discuss that with Mr. Ortiz.'

The woman hesitated. 'Maybe he's gone home,' she said.

'Why don't you take a look,' Ricky said coldly, 'and that way we can all avoid some unnecessary unpleasantness.'

'What sort of unpleasantness?' the woman asked, still protective.

Ricky bluffed. 'The alternative would be me showing up with a policeman or two and perhaps my attorney in tow.' He spoke, adopting the most patrician 'I'm a rich white male and I own the world' tone.

The woman paused, then said, 'You hold. I'll get Ortiz.'

A few seconds later a Hispanic-accented man picked up the phone. 'This is Ortiz. Wha's this about?'

Ricky didn't hesitate. 'At approximately five-thirty this morning you delivered a copy of the *Times* outside my door, just as you do most every weekday and Saturday morning. The only difference was that today someone needed to place a message inside that newspaper. That's what I'm calling about.'

'No, this I don't know about . . . '

'Mr. Ortiz, you haven't broken any laws here, and it is not you that I am interested in. But if you do not cooperate with me, I will make a significant stink over this. In other words, you do not have a problem yet, but I will make one for you, unless I start hearing a few more helpful responses.'

The deliveryman paused, digesting Ricky's threat.

'I didn't know there was a problem,' he said. 'The dude said there wouldn't be no problem.'

'I think he lied. Tell me,' Ricky said quietly.

'I pull up the street, we got deliveries in six buildings that block, me and Carlos, my nephew, that's our route. There's a big ol' black limo parked outside, middle of the street, motor running, jus' waiting for us. Man gets right out, soon as he sees the truck, asks who's going into your building. I asks 'Why?' and he tells me none of my business, then gives a little smile, says it's no big deal, just wants to make a little birthday surprise for an old friend. Wants to write something in the paper for him.'

'Go on.'

'Tells me which apartment. Which door. Then takes out the paper and a pen and writes right on the page. Puts the paper down flat on the hood of the limo, but I can't see what he's writing . . . '

'Was there anyone else there?'

Ortiz paused, considering. 'Well, got to be a driver behind the wheel. That's one, for sure. Windows of the limo all blacked out, but maybe there's somebody else there, too. Man looked back in, like he was checking with someone was he doing it right, then finished up. Hands me back the paper. Gives me a twenty . . . '

'How much?'

Ortiz hesitated. 'Maybe it was a hundred . . . '

'And what then?'

'I did like the man says. Toss that paper right outside the right door real special.'

'Was he waiting for you outside when you finished up?'

'No. Man, limo, all gone.'

'Can you describe the man you dealt with?'

'White guy, wearing a dark suit, maybe blue. Tie. Real nice clothes, got hisself plenty of cash. Peeled that hundred off a roll like it was a quarter you gonna drop in some homeless guy's cup.'

'And what did he look like?'

'He had those tinted glasses, not too tall, hair that's

pretty funny, like it was sitting on his head screwy . . . '

'Like a wig?'

'Yeah. That's right. Coulda been a wig. And a little beard, too. Maybe that's a fake, too. Not a big guy. Definitely had a few too many meals, though. Maybe thirty years old . . . '

Ortiz hesitated.

'What?'

'I remember seeing the streetlights reflecting off those shoes. They was real polished. Real expensive. Those loafers with the little tassels on the front. What you call those?'

'I don't know. Think you could recognize him again?'

'I dunno. Maybe. Probably not. Real dark on the street. Streetlights, that's all. And maybe I was lookin' at that hundred a little closer than I was at him.'

This made sense to Ricky. He tried a different tack.

'Did you by any chance get a plate number on the limo?'

The delivery driver paused, before replying.

'No, man, didn't think of it. Shit. That woulda been smart, right?'

'Yeah,' Ricky said. But he knew this was not necessary, because he'd already met the man who had been in the street that morning waiting for the delivery truck after Ricky had placed the ad in the newspaper. Ricky was certain that it was the lawyer who'd called himself Merlin.

* * *

Midmorning, he received a telephone call from the vice president of the First Cape Bank, the same man who was holding his remaining cash in a cashier's check for Ricky. The bank executive sounded nervously upset on the telephone. As he spoke, Ricky tried to place the man's face, but was unable, although he was sure that he'd met him before.

'Doctor Starks? This is Michael Thompson at the bank. We spoke the other day . . . '

'Yes,' Ricky replied. 'You're holding some funds for me . . . '

'I am. They are locked in my desk drawer. That's not why I'm calling. We had some unusual action on your account. An event, one might say.'

'What sort of unusual action?' Ricky asked. The man seemed to mentally fidget for a second or two before answering.

'Well, I don't like to speculate, but it seems there was an unauthorized effort to access your account.'

'What sort of unauthorized effort?'

Again the man seemed hesitant. 'Well, as you know, just in recent years we've gone over to electronic banking, like everybody else. But because we're a smaller institution and more localized, well, you know we like to consider ourselves old-fashioned in a lot of ways . . . '

Ricky recognized this for the bank's advertising slogan. He also knew that the bank trustees would eagerly embrace any takeover effort by one of the megabanks, were a profitable enough offer one day to walk through their door. 'Yes,' he said. 'That's always been one of your strongest selling points . . . '

'Well, thank you. We like to think we give personalized service . . . '

'But the unauthorized access?'

'Shortly after we closed down your account as per your instructions, someone sought to make adjustments to your account, using our electronic banking services. We only learned of these attempts because an individual telephoned after they were denied access.'

'They called?'

'Someone who identified themselves as you.'

'What did they say?'

'It was in the nature of a complaint. But as soon as they heard that the account had been closed, they hung up. It was all very mysterious and a little confusing, because our computer records show they had knowledge of your password. Have you shared that code with anyone?'

'No,' Ricky said. But he felt momentarily foolish. His password was 37383 which translated from numerals into letters as FREUD and was so blatantly obvious that he almost blushed. Using his birthday might have been slightly worse, but he doubted it.

'Well, I guess you were wise to close the account.'

Ricky thought for a moment, before asking, 'Is there any way for your security to trace back either the phone number or the computer that was used to try to access the money?'

The bank vice president paused, then said, 'Well, yes. We have that capacity. But most electronic thieves are capable of staying ahead of the investigators. They use stolen computers and illegal phone codes and that sort of thing to hide their identities. Sometimes the FBI has success, but they have the most sophisticated computer security in the world. Our local security is less advanced, and therefore less effective. And no theft took place, so the criminal liability is limited. We are required by law to report the attempt to banking regulators, but that merely becomes another entry in what I'm sorry to concede is a growing file. But I can still have our guy run that program for you. I just don't think it will lead you anywhere. These electronic bank robbers are pretty clever. Usually just leads to a dead end, somewhere.'

'Would you try, please, and get back to me. Right away. I'm under some time constraints here,' Ricky said.

'We'll give it a shot and get right back to you,' the man replied, hanging up.

Ricky sat back in his chair. For a moment, he allowed

himself the fantasy that the bank security would give him a name and telephone number and this single slip would provide him the avenue to his tormentor's identity. Then he shook his head, because he wondered whether Rumplestiltskin, so careful and cautious with everything to this point, would make an error that was so simple. Far more likely that the man had accessed that account and then made the subsequent disturbing and telltale telephone call with the precise intention of providing Ricky with a path to travel down. This thought worried him greatly.

* * *

Still, Ricky realized as the day began to flee from beneath him, that he now knew much more about the man stalking him. Rumplestiltskin's clue within a poem had been curiously generous, especially for someone who had first insisted that his questions be answerable with a *yes* or *no*. The response had narrowed the distance between Ricky and a guess of the man's name considerably, he thought. Twenty years, give or take a couple, put him into a range from 1978 through 1983. And his patient was a single woman, which eliminated a significant number of people. Now he had a framework that he could function with.

What he needed to do, Ricky told himself, was re-create five years of therapies. Examine every female patient in the time frame. Somewhere in that mix would be the woman wearing the right combination of neuroses and troubles that would have been subsequently directed at the child. Find the psychosis in flower, he thought.

As was Ricky's training and habit, he sat, trying to focus, eliminating the sounds of the world around him, trying to remember. Who was I twenty years ago? he asked himself. And who was I treating? There is a tenet to psychoanalysis that helps form the foundation of the therapy: Everyone remembers everything. One might not remember it with journalistic accuracy or religious detail, perceptions and responses may be clouded or colored by all sorts of emotional forces, events recalled with clarity may actually be murky, but, when it is finally sorted through, everyone remembers everything. Hurts and fears can lurk deeply concealed under layers of stress, but they are there and can be found, no matter how powerful the psychological forces of denial can be. In his practice, he was adept at this process of peeling away, skinning memories down to the bone, to find the hard layer underneath.

So, alone in his office, he began to plumb his own memory. Occasionally he would glance over the shreds of notes and jotted images that constituted his record keeping, angry with himself for not being more precise. Any other physician, confronted with an issue from years past, would merely dust off some old file folder and pluck out the right name and diagnosis. His task was considerably harder, because all his file folders were invested in his memory. Still, Ricky felt a surge of confidence that he could manage this. He concentrated hard, a legal notepad on his lap, reconstructing his past.

One after another, images of people took form. It was a little like trying to converse with ghosts.

He discarded the men even though they intruded on his powers of recollection, leaving only the women. Names came slowly; oddly enough, it was almost easier to remember the complaints. Every image of a patient, every detail about a treatment, he wrote on the legal pad. It was still scattered and disjointed, inefficient and haphazard, but, at least, he thought to himself, it is progress.

When he looked up, he saw that his office had filled with shadows. Day had drifted away from him in this semireverie. On the yellow sheets of paper in front of him, he had come up with twelve separate recollections from the time period in question. At least eighteen women had been in some sort of therapy with him over that era. This was a manageable number, but he was troubled that there were others that he was blocking, unable to immediately recall. Of the group he recollected, he had only produced names for half of them. And these were the long-term patients. He had an unsettling sensation that Rumplestiltskin's mother was someone he'd seen only briefly.

Memory and recollection were like Ricky's lovers. Now they seemed elusive and fickle.

He rose from his chair, feeling stiffness and dull pain in his knees and shoulders, the tightening feeling one gets from sitting far too long in the same position. He stretched slowly, and bent down and rubbed a recalcitrant knee, as if he could warm it and reinvigorate it. He realized he had not eaten that day, not a bite, and was abruptly hungry. He knew there was little for him to fix in his own kitchen, and he turned and looked out the window at the fast-crawling night gliding across the city, realizing he would have to go out and purchase something. The thought of actually emerging from his apartment almost stifled his hunger and made his throat go dry.

He had a curious response: There had been so few fears in his life, so few doubts. Now the simple act of exiting his home made him pause. But he steeled himself to whatever thoughts might have intruded, and determined to head two blocks to the south. There was a little bar where he could get a sandwich. He did not know whether he would be watched — this was becoming a constant question for him — but he decided to ignore the feeling and proceed. And, he told himself, he had made progress.

The sidewalk heat seemed to pop into his face, like turning on a gas stove. He marched the two blocks south like a soldier, eyes front. The place he was looking for was in the middle of the block, with a half-dozen small tables set outside for the summer, and an interior that was narrow and dark, with a bar set against one wall and another ten tables packed into the space. There was an unusual mix of decorations on the walls, ranging from sports memorabilia to Broadway posters, pictures of actors and actresses and the occasional politician. It was as if the place hadn't quite managed to carve out an identity as any one particular group's hangout, and therefore tried to make a diverse collection happy, creating a sort of mishmash within. But the small kitchen, like so many similar places in Manhattan, made a more than passable hamburger or Reuben sandwich, and occasionally put some pasta on the menu, all at relatively inexpensive prices, a factor that occurred late to Ricky as he walked through the door. He no longer had a credit card that functioned, and his cash reserves were low. He made a mental note to start carrying the traveler's checks with him.

It was dark inside, and he blinked once or twice while his eyes adjusted to the dim light. There were a few people at the bar, and a table or two empty. A middle-aged waitress spotted him as he hesitated. 'You gonna have some dinner, hon?' she asked with a familiarity that seemed out of place in a bar that encouraged anonymity.

'That's right,' he said.

'All alone?' she asked. Her tone indicated that she knew he was alone, and that she already knew that he ate alone every night, but that some old-fashioned country courtesy out of place in the city required her to ask the question.

'Right again.'

'You want to sit at the bar, or a table?'

'A table, if that's okay. Preferably in the back.'

The waitress pivoted, spotted an empty seat at the

rear, and nodded. 'Follow me,' she said. She gestured toward a chair and opened a menu in front of him. 'Something from the bar?' she asked.

'A glass of wine. Red, please,' he said.

'Be right back. Special tonight is linguine with salmon. It's not bad.'

Ricky watched the waitress depart for the bar. The menu was large, wearing one of those plastic covers to protect it from stains, far larger physically than was necessary for the modest selection offered. He opened it and propped it up in front of him, staring at the list of burgers and entrées described on the pages with a flowery literary enthusiasm that sought to conceal the simplicity of their reality. After a moment, he set the menu down, expecting to see the waitress with his wine. She had disappeared, presumably into the kitchen.

Instead, Virgil stood in front of him.

In her hands were two glasses, each filled with red wine. She wore faded jeans and a purple sport shirt, and she had an expensive mahogany-colored leather portfolio pinned underneath one arm. She set the drinks down on the table, then pulled a seat up and plopped herself down across from him. She reached out and took the menu out of Ricky's hands.

'I already ordered each of us the special,' she said, with a small, seductive grin. 'The waitress is one hundred percent correct: It's not all that bad.'

12

Surprise riveted him, but Ricky did not react outwardly. Instead, he stared hard across the table at the young woman, continuing to wear the flat poker face that was so familiar to many of his patients. When he did speak, he said only, 'So, your thinking here is that the salmon will be fresh?'

'Fairly flopping around and gasping for breath,' Virgil replied breezily.

'That might seem appropriate,' Ricky said softly.

The young woman took a slow sip from the edge of her glass of wine, just moistening the outside of her lips with the dark liquid. Ricky pushed his own glass aside and gulped at water. 'Really should be drinking white with pasta and fish,' Virgil said. 'But, then again, we're not in the sort of place that adheres to the rules, are we? I can't imagine some frowning sommelier emerging to discuss with us the inadequacy of our selection.'

'No, I doubt that,' Ricky answered.

Virgil continued on, speaking rapidly, but without the nervousness that sometimes accompanies quickly spoken words. She sounded far more like a child excited on her birthday. 'On the other hand, drinking red has a kind of devil-may-care attitude, don't you think, Ricky? A cocky quality that suggests we don't really care what the conventions say — we're going to do what we want. Can you feel that, Doctor Starks? A bit of adventure and lawlessness, playing outside the rules. What do you think?'

'I think that the rules are constantly changing,' he replied.

'Of etiquette?'

‘Is that what we’re talking about?’ he answered with a question.

Virgil shook her head, causing her mane of blond hair to bounce seductively. She threw her head back slightly to laugh, revealing a long, attractive throat. ‘No, of course not, Ricky. You’re right about that.’

At that moment the waitress brought them a wicker basket filled with rolls and butter, dropping both of them into a stifling silence, a small moment of shared conspiracy. When she moved away, Virgil reached for the bread. ‘I’m famished,’ she said.

‘So, ruining my life burns calories?’ Ricky posed.

Again Virgil laughed. ‘It seems to,’ she said. ‘I like that, I really do. What shall we call it, doc? How about The Ruination Diet — do you like that? We could make a fortune together and retire just you and I to some exotic island paradise.’

‘I don’t see that as happening,’ Ricky said brusquely.

‘I didn’t think so,’ Virgil replied, generously buttering her roll, and biting into the edge with a crunching sound.

‘Why are you here?’ Ricky demanded, in a quiet, low voice, but still one that carried all the insistence he could muster. ‘You and your employer seem to have the design of my ruin all planned out. Step by step. Are you here to mock me? Perhaps add a bit of torment to his game?’

‘No one has ever described my company as a torment,’ Virgil said, adopting a look of false surprise. ‘I would think that you found it, well, if not pleasant, at least intriguing. And think of your own status, Ricky. You came here alone, old, nervous, filled with doubt and anxiety. The only people who even stared in your direction would have felt a momentary pang of pity, and then gone about the business of feeding and drinking, all the time ignoring the old man that you’ve clearly become. But everything changes when I sit down across from you. Suddenly, you're not all that predictable, are you?' Virgil smiled.

'It can't be that bad, can it?'

Ricky shook his head. His stomach had clenched into a ball and the taste in the back of his mouth was acid.

'My life . . . ,' he started.

'Your life has changed. And will continue to change. At least for a few more days. And then . . . well, that's the rub, isn't it?'

'You enjoy this, then?' Ricky asked suddenly. 'Watching me suffer. It's odd, because I wouldn't have instantly made you for such a dedicated sadist. Your Mr. R., perhaps, but I'm less sure about him, because he's still a bit distant. But getting closer, I would guess. But you, Miss Virgil, I didn't see you as possessor of the necessary psychopathology. But, of course, I could be wrong about that. And that's what this is all about, right? When I was wrong about something, correct?'

Ricky sipped his water, hoping he'd baited the young woman into revealing something. For an instant he saw the start of anger crease the corners of Virgil's eyes, the smallest of dark signals in the edges of her mouth. But then she recovered and waved her half-eaten roll in the air between them, as if dismissing his words.

'You misunderstand my role here, Ricky.'

'Better explain it again.'

'Everyone needs a guide on the road to Hell, Ricky. I told you that before.'

Ricky nodded. 'I recall.'

'Someone to steer you through the rocky shores and hidden shoals of the underworld.'

'And you're that someone, I know. You told me.'

'Well, are you in Hell yet, Ricky?'

He shrugged, trying to infuriate her. This was unsuccessful.

She grinned. 'Maybe knocking on the door to Hell, then?'

He shook his head, but she ignored this denial.

'You're a proud man, Doctor Ricky. It pains you to lose control over your life, no? Far too proud. And we all know what comes directly after pride. You know, the wine's not half-bad. You might try a sip or two.'

He took the wineglass in his hand, raised it to his lips, but spoke instead of drinking. 'Are you happy, Virgil? Happy with your criminality?'

'What makes you think I've committed a crime, doctor?'

'Everything you and your employer have done is criminal. Everything that you have planned is criminal.'

'Really? I thought your expertise was in luxury-class neurosis and upper-middle-class anxiety. But you've developed a forensic streak in recent days, I guess.'

Ricky paused. It wasn't his normal inclination to play cards. The analyst doles them out slowly, searching for reactions, trying to provoke travels down avenues of memory. But he had so little time, he thought, and as he watched the young woman across from him shift momentarily in her seat, he wasn't altogether certain that this meeting was going exactly the way the elusive Mr. R. had envisioned it. It gave him a small satisfaction to think that he was disrupting the planned outcome of events, even if only slightly. 'Of course,' he said carefully, 'so far you've committed a number of felonies, ranging from the possible murder of Roger Zimmerman . . . '

'His death has already been ruled a suicide by the police . . . '

'You managed to make a murder appear to be a suicide. Of that I am persuaded.'

'Well, if you're going to be so obstinate, I won't try to change your mind. But I thought keeping an open mind was a hallmark of your profession.'

Ricky ignored this dig and persisted, ' . . . to robbery and fraud . . . '

'Oh, I doubt there's proof anywhere of those acts. It's a little like the old saw about the tree falling in the forest: If there's no one there to witness it, does it make a sound? If there's no proof, did a crime actually take place? And if there is proof, it exists out there in cyberspace, right alongside your funds . . . '

'Not to mention your little libel with the bogus letters to the Psychoanalytic Society. That was you, wasn't it? Leading on that complete idiot up in Boston with such an elaborate fiction. Did you take your clothes off for him, as well . . . ?'

Virgil swept the hair away from her face again, leaning back slightly in her seat. 'Didn't have to. He's one of those men who acts like puppies when you reproach them. He simply rolls over on his back and exposes his genitals with pathetic little mewling sounds. Isn't it remarkable how much a person will believe when they want to believe . . . '

'I will get my reputation back,' Ricky said fiercely.

Virgil grinned. 'You need to be alive for that, and right now, I have my doubts.'

Ricky didn't answer, because he, too, had his doubts. He looked up and saw the waitress approach with their dinners. She set them down and asked if there was anything else she could bring to the table. Virgil wanted a second glass of wine, but Ricky shook his head.

'That's good,' Virgil said as the waitress departed. 'Keep a clear head.'

Ricky poked for an instant at the plate of food steaming in front of him. 'Why,' he asked abruptly, 'are you helping this man? What's in it for you? Why don't you drop all this pretense and stop acting like a fool and come with me to the police. We could put a stop to this game immediately and I'd see to it that you regained some semblance of normal life. No criminal charges. I could do that.'

Virgil kept her eyes on her plate as well, using her

fork to toy with the mound of pasta and slab of salmon. When she lifted her gaze to meet his, her eyes barely concealed anger. 'You'll see that I return to a normal life? Are you a magician? And, anyway, what makes you think there's anything so wonderful about a normal life?'

He persisted, ignoring this question. 'If you're not a criminal, why are you helping one? If you're not a sadist, why do you work for one? If you're not a psychopath, why are you joining one? And, if you're not a killer, why are you helping someone commit a murder?'

Virgil continued to stare at him. All the breezy eccentricity and liveliness in her manner had dissipated, replaced by a sudden frosty harshness that blew coldly across the table. 'Perhaps because I'm well paid,' she said slowly. 'In this day and age, many people are willing to do anything for money. Could you believe that of me?'

'Only with difficulty,' Ricky replied cautiously, although the opposite of what he said was likely the truth.

Virgil shook her head. 'So you'd like to dismiss money as my motive, although I'm not sure that you should. Another motive perhaps? What other motives could there be for me? You should be expert in that arena. Doesn't the concept 'searching for motives' pretty much define what you do? And isn't the same thing an integral part of this little exercise that we're all playing? So, c'mon, Ricky. We've now had two sessions together. If it's not money, what motivates me?'

Ricky stared hard at the young woman. 'I don't know enough about you . . . ,' he started lamely. She put down her knife and fork with a stiff deliberateness that indicated she didn't approve of this answer.

'Do better, Ricky. For my sake. After all, in my own way, I'm here to guide you. The trouble is, Ricky, the word *guide* has positive connotations that may actually be incorrect. I may need to steer you in directions that you don't want to go. But one thing is certain: Without me, you'll get no closer to an answer, which will kill either you — or someone close to you who is in a state of complete ignorance. And dying blindly is stupid, Ricky. In its own way a worse crime. So, now, answer my question: What other motives might I have?'

'You hate me. Hate me, just as this fellow R. does, only I don't know why.'

'Hate is an imprecise emotion, Ricky. Do you think you understand it?'

'It's something I hear every day, in my practice . . . '

She shook her head. 'No, no, no. You don't. You hear about anger and frustration, which are minor elements of hate. You hear about abuse and cruelty, which are bigger players on that stage, but still, only teammates. But mostly, what you hear about is inconvenience. Boring and old and dull inconvenience. And this has as little to do with pure hatred as a single dark cloud has to do with a thunderstorm. That cloud has to join others and grow precipitously, before venting.'

'But you . . . '

'I don't hate you, Ricky. Though, perhaps I could learn to. Try something else.'

He didn't believe this for a second, but, at the same moment felt almost as if he were spinning, trying to find an answer. He breathed in sharply.

'Love, then,' Ricky said abruptly.

Virgil smiled again. 'Love?'

'You perform because you're in love with this man Rumplestiltskin.'

'That's an intriguing idea. Especially when I told you I don't know who he is. Never met the fellow.'

'Yes, I recall you said that. I just don't believe it.'

'Love. Hate. Money. Are these the only motives you can come up with?'

Ricky paused. 'Perhaps fear, as well.'

Virgil nodded. 'Fear is good, Ricky. It can prompt all sorts of unusual behavior, can't it?'

'Yes.'

'Your analysis of this relationship suggests that perhaps Mr. R. has some sort of threatening hold over me? Like the kidnapper who forces his victims to fork over their money in the pathetic hope that he will return their dog or their child or whoever it is that he has snatched. Do I behave like a person being asked to perform tasks against my will?'

'No,' Ricky replied.

'Well, okay then. You know, Ricky, I think you're a man who doesn't seize opportunities when they arise. Here, now, this is the second time I've sat across from you, and instead of trying to help yourself, you plead with me to help you, when you've done nothing to deserve my assistance. I should have predicted this, but I did have hope for you. Really, I did. Not much anymore, though . . . '

She waved her hand in the air above the table, dismissing a reply before he could come up with one. ' . . . On to business. You got the reply to your questions in your paper this morning?'

Ricky paused, then answered: 'Yes.'

'Good. That's why he sent me here this evening. To double-check. Wouldn't be fair, he thought, if you didn't get the answers you were searching for. I was surprised, of course. Mr. R. decided to put you much closer to him. Closer than I'd have thought prudent. Pick your next questions wisely, Ricky, if you want to win. It seems to me that he's given you a big opportunity. But as of tomorrow morning, you have only a single week left. Seven days and two remaining questions.'

'I'm aware of the time.'

'Are you? I think you don't get it. Not yet. But, as long as we've been talking about motivation, Mr. R. sent along something to help you pick up the pace of your investigation.'

Virgil bent down and lifted the small leather portfolio that she'd carried beneath her arm when she'd first approached Ricky, and which she'd subsequently placed on the floor. She deliberately opened the satchel and removed a manila envelope, similar to others Ricky had seen. She handed this across the table to him. 'Open it up,' she said. 'It's just filled with motivation.'

He undid the clasp and opened the envelope. Inside were a half-dozen eight-by-ten black-and-white photographs. He removed these and examined them. There were three different subjects, each in the center of two photographs. The first shots were of a young woman, perhaps sixteen or seventeen years old, wearing blue jeans and sweat-stained T-shirt, with a carpenter's leather belt around her waist, wielding a large hammer. She appeared to be working at some construction site. The next two photographs were of another child, younger, a girl perhaps twelve years old, seated in the bow of a canoe, paddling across a lake in a wooded region. The first shot seemed slightly grainy, the second, seemingly taken from a distance with an extremely long lens, was a close-up, near enough to show the girl's braces as she grinned with the exertion of paddling. Then there was a third set of another teenager, a boy with longish hair and an insouciant smile, gesturing with a street vendor in what appeared to be a street in Paris.

All six pictures seemed to be taken without the knowledge of the subjects. It was clear that the photographer had snapped them off unnoticed by the three young people.

Ricky examined the pictures carefully, then looked up at Virgil. She no longer smiled.

'Recognize anyone?' she asked coldly.

He shook his head.

'You live in such splendid isolation, Ricky. It makes all this so damn simple. Look harder. Do you know who those young people are?'

'No. I do not.'

'Those are pictures of some of your distant relatives. Each one of those children is on the list of names Mr. R. sent you at the beginning of your game.'

Ricky looked again at the pictures.

'Paris, France, Habitat for Humanity, Honduras, and Lake Winnipesaukee in New Hampshire. Three kids on their summer vacations. Just like you.'

He nodded.

'Do you see how vulnerable they are? Do you think it was hard to take these photographs? Could one replace a camera with a high-powered rifle or a handgun, perhaps? How easy would it be to simply remove one of these children from the benign environment they're enjoying? Do you think any of them has any idea how close to death they might be? Do you imagine any of them have even the vaguest notion that life might just come to a sudden, bloody, screeching halt in seven short days?'

Virgil pointed at the photographs.

'Take another long look, Ricky,' she said. She waited while he absorbed the images. Then she reached across the table to take the pictures from his hands. 'I think all that we need to leave you with are the mental portaits, Ricky. Put the smiles those children wear into your head. Try to imagine the smiles they might enjoy in the future as they grow into adulthood. What sort of lives might they lead? What sort of people would they grow into? Will you rob the future from one of them — or someone like them — by obstinately clinging to your own pathetically few years remaining?'

Virgil paused, then with snakelike speed, she grabbed the photographs from his hands. 'I'll take these,' she said as she returned the photographs to her satchel. She pushed back from the table, simultaneously dropping a single hundred-dollar bill on top of her half-eaten plate of food. 'You've stolen my appetite,' she said. 'But I know your financial situation has deteriorated. So I'll pay for dinner.'

She turned toward the waitress, hovering at a nearby table. 'Do you have some chocolate cake?' she asked.

'A chocolate cheesecake,' the woman replied. Virgil nodded.

'Bring a piece for my friend, here,' she said. 'His life has suddenly turned bitter and he needs some sweetness to get him through the next few days.'

Then she pivoted and walked out, leaving Ricky alone. He reached for a glass of water and noticed that his hand shook slightly, rattling the ice cubes in the glass.

* * *

He walked home in the growing city darkness, his isolation nearly complete.

The world around him seemed a rebuke filled with connections, a near constant tease of people meeting people in the commerce of existence. He felt almost invisible walking down the streets back to his apartment. In a curious way, Ricky realized, he was almost transparent. No one who walked or drove past him, not one person, would register him on their view of the world. His face, his appearance, his very being, did not mean anything to anyone except the man stalking him. His death, on the other hand, was of critical importance to some anonymous relative. Rumplestiltskin, and by proxy Virgil and the lawyer Merlin and probably some other characters he hadn't yet met, were the bridges between living and dying. It seemed to Ricky that he had entered into the netherworld occupied by the people who are given the worst diagnosis by a doctor or assigned a date of execution by their judge: the few who know the date of their death. He could feel a cloud of despair hovering just over his head. He was reminded of the famous cartoon character he remembered from his own youth, Al Capp's great creation of Joe Bflspk, doomed to walk beneath a personal rain cloud dripping dampness and bolts of lightning wherever he went.

The faces of the three young people in the photographs were like ghosts to him — vaporous, filmy. He knew he had to create substance around them, so that they would be real to him. He wished he knew their names, knew also that he had to take some steps to protect them. As he fixed their faces in the near part of his memory, his pace picked up. He saw the braces in one smile, the longish hair, the sweat of selfless exertion, and as he saw each photograph, as clearly as he had when Virgil thrust them across the restaurant table, his stride lengthened, his muscles tightened, and he began to hurry. He could hear his shoes slapping against the sidewalk, almost as if the sound was coming from somewhere outside his own life, until he looked down and saw that he was nearly running. Something loosened within him, and he gave in to a sensation he didn't recognize, but to anyone stepping aside on the sidewalk to let him pass, must have seemed like a full-blown panic.

Ricky ran, breath heaving in his chest, rasping between his lips. One block, then another, not stopping as he crossed streets, leaving a blast of taxicab horns and obscenities in his wake, not seeing, not hearing, his head filled only with images of death. He did not slow until he was within sight of the entranceway to his home. He heaved to a stop, bending over, gasping for breath, stinging moisture dripping into his eyes. He remained like that, regaining his wind, for what seemed like several minutes, blocking everything out except the heat and the pain of sudden motion, hearing nothing except his own labored breath.

When he did lift his eyes, he thought: I am not alone.

This was no different a sensation than the other moments in the past few days when he'd been overcome by the same observation. It was almost predictable, based on nothing except abrupt paranoia. He tried to control himself, not give in to the sensation, almost as if he wanted to not indulge a secret passion, a craving for a sweet or a smoke. He was unable.

He pivoted sharply, trying to spot whoever was watching him, although he knew this action was useless. His eyes raced from candidates leisurely walking down the street, to empty windows in buildings nearby. He spun about, as if he could catch some telltale motion that might tip him to the person employed to watch him, but every possibility seemed slight, elusive.

Ricky turned back and stared at his own building. He was overcome with the thought that someone had been in his apartment while he was out bantering with Virgil. He leapt forward, then stopped. With an immense summoning of willpower, he forced himself to loop tendrils of control over emotions that were ricocheting around within him, telling himself to be calm, to be centered, to keep his wits about him. He took a long, deep breath and told himself that the likelihood was strong that any moment he emerged from within his apartment, regardless of the reason, Rumplestiltskin, or one of his henchmen, was slipping in behind him. That vulnerability couldn't be solved with a request to a locksmith, and had been proven the other day when he'd come home to a house without lights.

Ricky's stomach was tight, like an athlete's in the moment after a race. He thought everything that had happened to him functioned on two levels. Every message from the man was both symbolic and literal.

His home, Ricky thought, was no longer safe.

Stopped on the street outside the apartment he'd lived most of his adult life within, Ricky was almost overcome by the recognition that there might not be even one corner of his existence that the man stalking him hadn't penetrated.

For the first time, he thought: I must find a safe spot.

Not having any idea where he might uncover this location — either internally or externally — Ricky trudged up the steps to his home.

* * *

To his astonishment, there were no obvious signs of disruption. The door wasn't ajar. The lights functioned normally. The air conditioner hummed in the background. No overwhelming sense of dread or sixth-sense perception that someone had been inside. He closed and locked the door behind him feeling a momentary surge of relief. Still, his heart continued to race, and he also felt the quiver in his hand that he'd experienced in the restaurant when Virgil had left his side. He held up his hand in front of his face, inspecting it for twitching nervousness, but it was deceptively steady. He no longer trusted this; it was almost as if he could feel within the muscles and tendons of his body that a looseness had taken place, and that at any given second, he would lose control.

Exhaustion pummeled him, reaching into every crevice of his body and pounding away. He was breathing hard, but couldn't understand why, because the demands on his own physique were modest.

'You need a good night's sleep,' he told himself, speaking out loud, recognizing the tones that he might use for a patient, directed at himself. 'You need to rest, collect your thoughts, and make progress.' For the first time, he considered finding his prescription pad and writing out a scrip for himself, some medication to help him relax. He knew he needed to focus, and it seemed to him that this was becoming increasingly difficult. He hated pills, but thought just this once they might be necessary. A mood elevator, he thought. A sleeping agent to get him some rest. Then, perhaps, some amphetamine to help him concentrate in the morning, and over the course of his remaining week before meeting Rumplestiltskin's deadline.

Ricky kept a rarely used *Physician's Desk Reference* guide to drugs in his desk, and he steered himself in that direction, thinking that the all-night pharmacy two blocks away would deliver anything he called in. He wouldn't even have to venture out.

Sitting in his desk chair, quickly examining the entries in the *PDR*, it did not take Ricky long to determine what he needed. He found his prescription pad and called the pharmacy, reading off his DEA number for the first time, it seemed to him, in years. Three different drugs.

'The patient's name?' the pharmacist asked.

'They're for me,' Ricky said.

The pharmacist hesitated. 'These aren't real good medications to be mixing, Doctor Starks,' he said. 'You should be very careful about the dosages and combinations.'

'Thank you for your concern. I'll be careful . . . '

'I just wanted you to know that overdoses could be lethal.'

'I'm aware of that,' Ricky said. 'But too much of anything can kill you.'

The pharmacist considered this a joke and laughed. 'Well, I suppose so, but with some things, at least we'd go out with a smile on our face. My delivery guy will be over with these within the hour. You want me to put these on your account? It's been a while since you used it.'

Ricky thought for a moment, then said, 'Yes.

Absolutely.' He felt an abrupt twinge of pain within him, as if the man had inadvertently sliced Ricky's heart with the most innocent of questions. Ricky knew the last time he'd used the account at the pharmacy had been for his wife, as she lay dying, for morphine to help mask her pain. That had been at least three years earlier.

He stepped on the memory, trying to mentally crush it beneath his sole. He took a deep breath and said, 'And have the deliveryman ring the doorbell in exactly this fashion, please: three short rings, three long rings, three short rings. That way I'll know it's him and open up.'

The pharmacist seemed to think for an instant, before asking, 'Isn't that Morse code for S.O.S.?'

'Correct,' Ricky answered.

He hung up the telephone and sat back hard, his head filling with visions of his wife in her final days. This was too painful for him, so he turned slightly and his eyes traveled down to the desktop. He noticed that the list of relatives that Rumplestiltskin had sent him was prominently placed in the center of his blotter and in a dizzying moment of doubt, Ricky did not recall leaving it in that location. He reached out slowly, pulling the sheet of paper toward him, suddenly filling with the images of the young people in the pictures that Virgil had thrust across the dinner table at him. He started to examine the names on the page, trying to connect the faces with the letters waving like heat above a highway in front of him. He tried to steel himself, knowing that he needed to make the connection, that this was important, that someone's life might be in a balance that they knew nothing about.

As he tried to focus, he looked down.

A sensation of confusion slid through him. He started to look about, his eyes darting back and forth rapidly, as an unsettling surge quickened within him. He felt his mouth go dry and his stomach churned with sudden nausea.

He picked up notes, paper pads, and other debris from his desk, searching.

But in the same instant, he knew that what he wanted was gone.

Rumplestiltskin's first letter, describing the parameters of the game and containing the first clue, had been removed from his desktop. The physical evidence of the threat to Ricky had disappeared. All that remained, he knew immediately, was the reality.

13

He drew another X through a day on the calendar and then wrote down two telephone numbers on a pad in front of him. The first number was for Detective Riggins of the New York City Transit Authority Police. The second was a number he had not used in years, and had his doubts that it was still functional, but it was a number he had decided to call regardless. It was for Dr. William Lewis. Twenty-five years earlier, Dr. Lewis had been his training analyst, the physician who undertook Ricky's own analysis, while Ricky was obtaining his certificate. It is a curious facet of psychoanalysis that everyone who wants to practice the treatment must undergo the treatment. A heart surgeon would not offer up his own chest to a scalpel as part of his training, but an analyst does.

The two numbers, he thought, represented polar opposites of help. He was unsure whether either would actually be able to provide any, but despite Rumplestiltskin's recommendation that he keep all the events to himself, he was no longer sure he could do that. He needed to talk to someone. But who? was an elusive question.

The detective answered her phone on the second ring simply by brusquely speaking her last name: 'Riggins.'

'Detective, this is Doctor Frederick Starks. You will recall we spoke last week about the death of one of my patients . . . '

There was a momentary hesitation, not one defined by difficulty in recognition, but more a pause created by surprise. 'Sure, doctor. I sent you over a copy of the suicide note we uncovered the other day. I thought that made things pretty clear-cut. What's bothering you now?'

'I wonder if I might speak with you about some of the circumstances surrounding Mr. Zimmerman's death?'

'What sort of circumstances, doctor?'

'I'd prefer not to speak on the phone.'

The detective laughed briefly, as if amused. 'That sounds terribly melodramatic, doctor. But sure. You want to come here?'

'I presume there's a location there where we can speak privately?'

'Of course. We have a nasty little interview room where we extract confessions from various criminal suspects. More or less the same thing you do in your office, just a little less civilized and a lot more rapid . . .'

Ricky flagged a cab on the corner, which he had take him north some ten blocks, dropping him at the corner of Madison and 96th Street. He walked into the first store he could see, a women's shoe store, spent exactly ninety seconds examining the shoes, simultaneously peering through the plate glass window surreptitiously, awaiting the light on the corner to change. As soon as it did, he exited, walked across the street and flagged down another cab. He instructed this driver to head south, all the way to Grand Central Station.

Grand Central wasn't particularly crowded for midday in the summer. A steady flow of people dispersed through the cavernous interior toward commuter trains or subway connections, avoiding the occasional singing or mumbling homeless person wandering about near the entranceways, ignoring the large vibrant advertisements that seemed to fill the station with an otherworldly light. Ricky entered the stream of people trying to hesitate as little as possible in their transit through the way station. It was a place where people tried not to show indecision, and he joined that parade of determined, directed folks, all wearing that midtown steel-and-iron look, that seemed to armor them from all the other people, so that everyone traveling was like a little emotional island all to themselves, inwardly anchored, not adrift, not floating, but moving steadily with a distinct and recognizable current. He, on the other hand, was inwardly aimless, but pretending. He took the first subway train to arrive, heading west, rode it a single stop, then bounded from the train swiftly, rising out from the stifling underground into the questionable superheated air of the street and again flagging the first cab he could spot. He made certain that the cab was pointed south, which was the opposite from where he was heading. He wanted the cabbie to make an around-the-block trip, heading down a side street, dodging through delivery trucks, all the time with Ricky peering through the rear window, watching who might come up behind him.

He thought if Rumplestiltskin or Virgil or Merlin or whoever else might be working for the man pursuing him was able to follow that path undetected, then he was without any chance whatsoever. Ricky scrunched down in the seat, and rode in silence to the Transit Authority Police substation at 96th Street and Broadway.

Riggins stood up as he walked through the door to the detective bureau. She looked significantly less exhausted than she had the first time they met, although her outfit had not changed much: fashionable dark slacks above contradictory running shoes, a man's pale blue button-down shirt with a red tie loosely fastened around her neck. The tie flopped to the side of the brown leather shoulder harness she wore, with a small automatic pistol riding to the left of her breast. It was a most curious appearance, Ricky thought. The detective combined men's clothing with a feminine streak, she wore makeup and perfume to contradict the masculinity of her apparel. Her hair fell in languid waves to her shoulders, but her running shoes spoke of urgency and immediacy.

She offered her hand in a firm shake. 'Doc, glad to see you, although I must say this is a bit unexpected.' She seemed to assess his appearance rapidly, measuring up and down like a tailor inspecting a poorly conditioned gentleman who wants to squeeze into a stylish and modern suit.

'Thank you for agreeing — ' he started, but she cut him off.

'You look lousy, doc. Maybe you're taking Zimmerman's little confrontation with a subway train a little hard.'

He shook his head, smiling a little. 'Not sleeping much,' Ricky admitted.

'No shit,' Riggins replied. She gestured with a wave of her arm toward a side room, which was the interview area that she'd mentioned earlier.

The interview room was bleak and unforgiving, a narrow space devoid of any adornment, with a single metal table in the center and three steel folding chairs. A fluorescent overhead light filled the room with glare. The table had a linoleum surface, marred by scratch marks and ink stains. He thought about his own office and in particular the couch, and how each item within a patient's view had an impact on the process of confession. He thought that this room, as barren as a moonscape, was an awful place to come to the act of explanation, but, then, he understood, the explanations that emerged in that particular place were terrible to begin with.

Riggins must have noticed the way he was assessing the room, and she said, 'The city's decorating budget is very lean this year. We had to give up all the Picassos on the walls and the Roche Bobois furniture.' She gestured at one of the steel seats. 'Pull up a chair, doctor. Tell me what's bothering you.' Detective Riggins tried to suppress a grin. 'Isn't that more or less what you would say?'

'More or less,' Ricky answered. 'Although I'm at a loss as to what you find so amusing.'

Riggins nodded, losing some, but not all, of the edgy humor from her voice. 'I apologize,' she said. 'It's just the role reversal, Doctor Starks. We don't usually get prominent, uptown professional folks such as yourself in here. Transit police deal with pretty routine and ugly crimes. Muggings mostly. Gang stuff. Homeless folks get into fights that become homicides. What's troubling you so much? And I promise to try to take it extremely seriously.'

'It amuses you to see me . . . '

'Under stress. Yes, I'll admit it does.'

'You don't care for psychiatry?'

'No. I had a brother who was clinically depressed and schizophrenic and in and out of every mental facility in the city and all the doctors just gabbed and gabbed his life away, never helping him in the slightest. This experience prejudiced me. Let's leave it at that.'

Ricky paused, then said, 'Well, my wife died several years ago of ovarian cancer, but I didn't hate the oncologists who were unable to help her. I hated the disease.'

Riggins nodded again. 'Touché,' she said.

Ricky was unsure where to begin, but he decided Zimmerman was as good a location as any. 'I read the suicide note,' he said. 'To be frank, it didn't sound much like my patient. I wonder if you could tell me where you discovered it.'

Riggins shrugged slightly. 'Sure. It was found on the pillow of his bed in his own apartment. Folded nicely and neatly and impossible to miss.'

'Who found it?'

'Actually, I did. After dealing with the witnesses and

talking with you and finishing the paperwork, I went over to Zimmerman's apartment the following day and saw it as soon as I went into his bedroom.'

'Zimmerman's mother, she's an invalid . . . '

'She was so distraught after getting the initial phone call, I had to send paramedics over to transfer her to a hospital for a couple of nights. I gather she's going to be moved to an assisted-living center in Rockland County within the next day or so. The brother's handling those arrangements. By phone from California. I gather he's not terribly bent out of shape by all that took place and doesn't seem to possess much of the milk of human kindness, especially where his mother is concerned.'

'Let me get this right,' Ricky said. 'The mother is transported to the hospital and the following day you find the note . . . '

'Correct.'

'So you have no way of knowing when that note was placed in that room, do you? The apartment was empty for a significant amount of time?'

Detective Riggins smiled wanly. 'Well, I know Zimmerman didn't put it there sometime after three P.M. because that's when he caught that train significantly before it slowed down, which is an altogether poor idea.'

'Someone else could have put it there.'

'Sure. If you're the type that sees conspiracies in the woodwork. The grassy knoll approach to investigations. Doctor, he was unhappy and he jumped in front of a train. It happens.'

'That note,' Ricky started, 'it was typed, right. And unsigned, except for the typed signature.'

'Yes. You're correct about that.'

'Written on a computer, I presume.'

'Yes, again. Doctor, you're beginning to sound like a detective.'

Ricky thought for a moment. 'I seem to remember

from somewhere that typewriters could be traced, that the way each struck a key against a piece of paper was distinct and recognizable. Is the same true for a computer printer?'

Riggins shook her head. 'No.'

Ricky paused. 'I don't know much about computers,' he said. 'Never really had the need in my line of work . . . ' He stared across at the detective, who seemed to have grown slightly uncomfortable with his questions. 'But don't they internally keep a record of everything that was written on them?'

'You're correct about that, too. On the hard drive, usually. And I see where you're going with this. No, I did not check Zimmerman's computer to make certain that he actually wrote the note on the computer he kept in his bedroom. Nor did I check his computer at work. A guy jumps in front of a train and I find a suicide note on his pillow at home. This scenario pretty much discourages any further inquiries.'

'That computer at work, a lot of people would have access to it, right?'

'I'm guessing he had a password to protect his files. But the short answer is yes.'

Ricky nodded, then sat silently for a moment.

Riggins shifted about in her seat, before continuing, 'Now you said there were 'circumstances' around the death that you wanted to speak about. What are they?'

Ricky took a deep breath before replying. 'A relative of a former patient has been threatening me and my family members with some unspecified harm. To this end, they have taken some steps to disrupt my life. These steps include bogus charges against my professional integrity, electronic assaults on my financial status, break-ins at my home, invasions of my personal life, and the suggestion that I take my own life. I have reason to believe that Zimmerman's death was part of this system of harassment that I have been undergoing in the past week. I don't believe it was a suicide.'

Riggins's eyebrows had shot up. 'Jesus, Doctor Starks. Sounds like you're in some sort of mess. A former patient?'

'No. The child of one. I don't know which one quite yet.'

'And you think this person who has it in for you persuaded Zimmerman to jump in front of the train?'

'Not persuaded. Perhaps he was pushed.'

'It was crowded and no one saw a push. No one whatsoever.'

'The lack of an eyewitness doesn't preclude it happening. As the train approached, wouldn't everyone in the station naturally have looked in the direction the subway train was traveling? If Zimmerman was at the rear of the crowd, which is suggested by the lack of precise eyewitness testimony, how hard would it have been to give him the necessary nudge or shove?'

'Well, of course, doctor, that's correct. Not hard. Not hard at all. And certainly the scenario that you describe is one we are familiar with. We've had a few killings that fit that pattern over the years. And you are also correct that people's heads naturally go in one direction when a train approaches, allowing almost anything to happen at the rear of the platform more or less unnoticed. But here we have LuAnne who says he jumped, and even if she's not terribly reliable, she's something. And we have a suicide note and a depressed and angry and unhappy man in a difficult relationship with his mother, staring at a life that many would consider to be something of a disappointment . . .'

Ricky shook his head. 'Now you're the one sounding like you are making excuses. More or less what you accused me of when we first spoke.'

This comment quieted Detective Riggins. She fixed Ricky with a long stare, before continuing. 'Doctor, it seems to me that you should take this story to someone who can help you.'

'And who might that be?' he asked. 'You're a police detective. I've told you about crimes. Or what might be crimes. Shouldn't you make a report of some sort?'

'Do you want to make a formal complaint?'

Ricky looked hard at the policewoman. 'Should I? What happens then?'

'I present it to my supervisor, who's going to think it's crazy, and then channel it through police bureaucracy and in a couple of days you're going to get a call from some other detective who's going to be even more skeptical than I am. Who have you told about these other events?'

'Well, the banking authorities and the Psychoanalytic Society . . .'

'If they determine there is criminal activity, don't they routinely refer matters to either the FBI or state investigators? Sounds to me like you need to be talking to someone in the extortion and fraud bureaus of the NYPD. And, if it were me, I might be looking to hire a private detective. And a damn good lawyer, because you might need them.'

'How do I go about doing that? Contacting the NYPD . . . ?'

'I'll give you a name and number.'

'You don't think that you should look into these things. As a follow-up on the Zimmerman case?'

This question made Detective Riggins pause. She had not taken any notes during the conversation. 'I might,' she said carefully. 'I need to think about it. It's hard to reopen a case once it has received a closed status.'

'But not impossible.'

'Difficult. But not impossible.'

'Can you get authority from your superior . . . ,' Ricky started.

'I don't think I want to open that door quite yet,' the

detective said. 'As soon as I tell my boss there's an official problem, then all sorts of bureaucratic stuff has to occur. I think I'll just poke around myself. Maybe. Tell you what, doctor, why don't I look at a few things, then get back to you. At the least, I can go check that computer Zimmerman had in his bedroom. There might be a time stamp on the file that contains the suicide note. I'll do it tonight or tomorrow. How would that be?'

'Fine,' Ricky said. 'Tonight would be better than tomorrow. I'm under some time restraints. And you might pass on the name and number of the right people at the NYPD at the same time . . . '

This seemed like a reasonable arrangement. The detective nodded. Ricky took some inward pleasure in the observation that her mildly mocking and sarcastic tone had changed, shortly after he had raised the possibility that she had screwed up. Even if she thought this possibility remote, in a world where promotions and raises were so carefully connected to successful completions of investigations, the idea that she had overlooked a murder and defined it as a suicide was the sort of mistake that any bureaucrat was especially scared of. ' . . . I'll expect your call at your earliest convenience,' he said.

Then Ricky rose, feeling as if he'd just struck a blow for himself. Not a victorious sensation, but, at least, one that made him feel a little less alone in the world.

* * *

Ricky took a cab to Lincoln Center, to the Metropolitan Opera House, which was empty except for a few tourists and some security guards. There was a bank of pay telephones outside the men's and women's rooms that he was familiar with. The advantage of the phones was that from that location he could make a phone call, while at the same time keep an eye on anyone who might try to follow him into the opera house. He doubted that anyone would be able to get close enough to determine who he was calling.

The number he had for Dr. Lewis had been changed, as he'd expected. But he was connected to a second number with a different area code. He used most of the spare quarters he had to connect to that number. As the phone rang, he thought Dr. Lewis was now probably well into his eighties, and he was uncertain whether he would be of any assistance. But Ricky knew that this was the only way he could get some perspective on his situation, and with a desperate quality to his every step, it was one he should take.

The receiver rang at least eight times before being answered.

'Yes?'

'Doctor Lewis, please.'

'This is Doctor Lewis.'

It was a voice Ricky had not heard in twenty years, yet filled him with a rush of emotion that surprised him. It was as if a torrent of hates, fears, loves, and frustrations suddenly was loosed within him, and he forced himself, struggling, to maintain some composure.

'Doctor Lewis, this is Doctor Frederick Starks . . . '

Both men were silent for a moment, as if the mere meeting on the telephone after so many years was overwhelming.

Dr. Lewis spoke first. 'Well, I'll be darned. It is nice to hear from you, Ricky, even after so many years. I am quite taken aback.'

'I'm sorry, doctor, to be so abrupt. But I didn't know where else to turn.'

Again there was a brief silence.

'You are troubled, Ricky?'

'Yes.'

'And the tools of self-analysis are inadequate?'

'Yes. I was hoping you might lend me some time to talk.'

'I do not really see patients anymore,' Lewis said. 'Retirement. Age. Infirmity. Getting older, which is terrible. All sorts of things simply sliding away.'

'Will you see me?'

The old man paused. 'Your voice seems quite urgent. This is important? You are deeply troubled?'

'I am in great danger, and I have little time.'

'Well, well, well.' Ricky could sense a smile on the old analyst's face. 'That sounds genuinely intriguing. You think I can help you?'

'I don't know. But you might be able to.'

The old analyst digested this momentarily, before replying, 'Spoken like someone in our calling. You will have to come out here, I'm afraid. No more midtown office.'

'Where's here?' Ricky asked.

'Rhinebeck,' Dr. Lewis said, adding an address on River Road. 'A wonderful place to be retired, except damn cold and icy in the winter. But lovely now. You can get a train from Pennsylvania Station.'

'If I get there this afternoon . . . '

'I will see you whenever you arrive. That is one of the sole advantages to retirement. A distinct lack of pressing appointments. Take a cab from the station and I will be expecting you around dinnertime.'

* * *

He scrunched into a corner seat as far to the rear of the train as he could find and spent most of the afternoon staring out the window. The train traveled directly north following the course of the Hudson, sometimes so close to the river's edge that the water was only yards away. Ricky found himself staring out across the expanse, fascinated by the different shades of blue-green that the river engaged, a seemingly deep near-black close to the banks, stretching into a lighter, vibrant blue in the deep center. Sail-boats carved through the water, tossing white sheets of spray from their bows, and an occasional ungainly, huge container ship wallowed through the deepest channel. In the distance, the Palisades rose harshly, gray-brown columns of rock, topped with stands of dark green trees. There were mansions dotting wide lawns, houses so huge that the wealth enclosed seemed impossible to envision. At West Point he caught a glimpse of the military academy high on a hill, overlooking the river; he thought the stolid buildings as gray and taut as the uniformed lines of cadets. The river was wide and glassy, and he found it easy to imagine the explorer who gave the water its name five hundred years earlier. He watched the water surface for a bit, unsure in his own mind which way the current flowed, whether it dropped down back toward the city and the ocean beyond, or whether it climbed north, pushed by the tides and the spin of the earth. This troubled him slightly, not knowing, being unable to tell which direction the water traveled from staring at its surface.

Only a small group of people got off the train in Rhinebeck and Ricky lingered on the platform inspecting each, still worried that despite his efforts, someone had managed to follow him. There were a couple of young people, college-age kids in jeans or shorts, laughing among themselves; a middle-aged mother towing three children in a pack, trying to show patience with one wandering blond-headed boy; a harried pair of businessmen already working their cell phones as they headed up to the station. None of the folks getting off the train even glanced in Ricky's direction, except for the little boy, who paused and made a face in his direction before racing up the long flight of stairs leading away from the tracks. Ricky waited until the train started to edge out, making large metallic grunting sounds as it gathered momentum. Convinced there was no one else who had departed, Ricky ascended into the station. It was an old, brick building, with a tiled floor that echoed his footsteps as he paced through, filled with cool air that defied the late afternoon heat. A single sign with a red arrow above a wide double door read: TAXIS. He exited the station and saw only a single bedraggled white sedan, bearing a medallion on the side and an unlit emblem on its roof and a large dent in the front quarter panel. The driver seemed about ready to leave, but spotted Ricky, and sharply pulled back to the curb.

'You need a ride, fella?' the driver asked.

'Yes, please,' Ricky answered.

'Well, I'm the only guy left. I was just about to take off when I sees you coming through the door. Jump in.'

Ricky did as he was told, and gave the man Dr. Lewis's address.

'Ah, prime real estate that,' the driver said, accelerating, the tires complaining slightly as they pulled out of the station.

The road to the old analyst's house was a meandering, narrow two-lane drive through the countryside. Stately oaks created a canopy of shade above the macadam, so that the weak summer evening light seemed to slowly flow to the earth like flour through a sieve, sifting shadows right and left. The countryside rolled with gentle hills, like swells on a modest ocean. He could see clusters of horses standing in some fields, and in the distance large, imposing mansions. The homes closer to the roadway were antique, often clapboard, with small square date-signs prominently displayed, so that the passerby would know that this house was constructed in 1788, or this one in 1802. He saw flower gardens streaked with color, and more than one T-shirted homeowner astride a small tractor lawn mower, aggressively clipping some immaculate swath of green grass. It was an area that spoke of escape, he thought. He guessed that most of the residents thought their primary life was in the caverns of Manhattan, working with money, power, or prestige, and quite frequently with all of them. These were weekend homes and summer getaways, fantastically expensive, but with genuine cricket sounds at night.

The cabdriver saw his inspecting, and said, 'Not bad, huh? Some of these places will set you back a buck or two.'

'Can't get a seat in a restaurant on the weekend, I'll bet,' Ricky replied.

'Not in the summer, or around the holidays, you got that right. But not everybody's a city person. There's some folks that put down roots. Just enough to keep it from being a ghost town. It's a pretty place.' He slowed the car and then took a sharp left into a driveway. 'The trouble is, it's just a little bit too damn convenient to the city. Anyway, here you are. This is the place,' he said.

Dr. Lewis's home was one of the old, reconditioned farmhouses, a simple two-story Cape design, painted a vibrant, glowing white, with a placard that read 1791 in one corner. It wasn't by any means the largest of the homes Ricky had passed. There was a trellis covered with vines, and flowers planted by the entranceway, and a small fish pond by the edge of the yard. A hammock and some Adirondack chairs that were peeling white paint stood to the side. A ten-year-old blue Volvo station wagon was parked in front of a onetime stable, that now clearly served as a garage.

The cab pulled away behind him, and Ricky paused on the edge of the gravel drive. He was suddenly, acutely aware that his hands were empty. He had no bag, no simple gift, or the ubiquitous bottle of midpriced white wine to bring with him. He breathed in sharply, feeling a rush of conflicting emotions within him. It wasn't quite right to characterize what he felt as fear, but it was the sensation that a child feels knowing that he needs to bring some transgression to the attention of a parent. Ricky wanted to smile to himself, recognizing that the burst of feelings that had turned his feet so leaden and accelerated his heart rate were normal; the relationship between analyst and analysand is deep and provocative, and functions in many different ways, not the least of which is like an authority and a child. This, he knew, was an integral part of the process of transference, wherein the analyst engaged in the process slowly takes on different roles, all ultimately leading to understanding. Still, Ricky thought, not many physicians have such an impact on their patients. An orthopedist would probably not even recall the knee or hip that he operated on after so many years and so many joints. But the analyst is likely to remember if not everything, then much, the mind being more sophisticated than the knee, if sometimes not quite as efficient.

He stepped forward slowly, his eyes sweeping over the entranceway, absorbing all he could see. He reminded himself that this is another of the keys to analysis; the doctor knows virtually every emotional and sexual intimacy of the patient, who, in turn, knows next to nothing about the therapist. The mystery mimics the essential mysteries of life and family; and there is always a sense of fascination and trepidation about entering the unknown. He thought: Dr. Lewis knows about me, and now I will know something about him, and this changes things. The observation made him sweat nervously.

Ricky was halfway to the front steps, when the front door swung open. He heard the voice before he saw the man: 'Slightly uncomfortable, I will wager.'

Ricky replied: 'You read my mind,' which was something of an analyst joke.

He was ushered into a study, right off the

entranceway to the old house. He found his eyes swinging from side to side, absorbing, imprinting details on his imagination. Books on a shelf. Tiffany lampshade. Oriental carpet. Like many older houses, the interior had a dark hue, contradicted by vibrant white walls; it seemed to him to be cool within, not stuffy, but fresh, as if the windows had been open to the night before and the home had retained the memory of the lower temperatures. He could smell a faint odor of lilac and there was a distant sound of cooking coming from the rear of the house.

Dr. Lewis was a slight man, bent a little at the shoulders, bald, with aggressive tufts of hair bursting from his ears, which gave him a distinctly odd appearance. He wore glasses perched down far on his nose, so that he rarely seemed to actually look through them. There were some age spots on the backs of his hands, and the slightest shakiness in his fingers. He moved slowly, limping a little, finally settling into a large red leather, overstuffed wing chair, gesturing to Ricky to seat himself in a slightly lesser armchair a few feet away. Ricky sunk down into the cushions.

'I am delighted to see you, Ricky, even after so many years. How long has it been?'

'More than a decade, certainly. You're looking well, doctor.'

Dr. Lewis grinned and shook his head. 'Probably should not start this out with such an obvious lie, although at my age one appreciates lies much more than the truth. The truths are always so damn inconvenient. I need a new hip, a new bladder, a new prostate, two new eyes and ears, and some new teeth. New feet would be helpful, as well. Probably need a new heart, too, but I will not be getting any of these things. I could use a new car in the garage and the house could use new plumbing. Come to think of it, so could I. The roof is fine, though.' He tapped his forehead. 'Mine, too.' Then he cackled again. 'But I am sure you did not track me down to find out about me. I have forgotten both my training and my manners. You will join me, of course, for dinner, and I have had the guest bedroom made up for you. And now, I should keep my mouth shut, which is what we in our profession believe we do so well, and have you tell me why you are here.'

Ricky paused, not precisely certain where to begin. He stared across at the old man swallowed up in the wing chair, and felt as if a string within him suddenly broke. He could feel his control sliding away, and what he said choked out past lips that quivered. 'I believe I have only a single week left to live,' he said.

Dr. Lewis's eyebrows arched upward.

'You are ill, Ricky?'

Ricky shook his head.

'I think I must murder myself,' he answered.

The old analyst leaned forward. 'That is a problem,' he said.

14

Ricky must have spoken nonstop for more than an hour, uninterrupted by even the slightest comment or question from Dr. Lewis, who sat almost motionless in his seat, balancing his chin in the palm of his hand. Once or twice Ricky rose, pacing swiftly around the perimeter of the room as if the movement in his feet would propel his story along quicker, before returning to the overstuffed armchair and continuing with his tale. On more than one occasion he could feel sweat dripping down beneath his armpits, although the room was pleasantly cool, the windows open to the early Hudson Valley evening.

He heard some distant thunder coming from the Catskills, miles away across the river, deep explosive rolls of noise like artillery. He recalled that local legend thought the sound to be the noise made by supernatural dwarves and elves, bowling in the green hollows. He told Dr. Lewis of receiving the first letter, the poetry and threats, the stakes of the game. He described Virgil and Merlin and the attorney's office that didn't exist. He tried to leave out nothing, from the electronic assaults on his bank and brokerage accounts, to the pornographic message sent to his distant relative on the birthday they shared. He went on at length about Zimmerman, his treatment, his death, and the two visits to Detective Riggins. He spoke about the false accusation of sexual impropriety lodged against him with the medical board, his face turning slightly red as he did so. Sometimes he rambled, as when he spoke about the break-ins at his office and the odd violation he felt, or when he described his first effort in the *Times* and Rumplestiltskin's response. He ended slightly out of chronology, talking about the impact of the photographs of the three young people shown to him by Virgil. Then he leaned back, grew silent, and for the first time actually stared across the room at the old analyst, who by now had lifted both hands to his chin, supporting his head in thought, as if trying to assess the totality of the evil that had descended upon Ricky.

'Most intriguing,' Dr. Lewis finally said, leaning back and emitting a long sigh. 'I wonder if your Rumplestiltskin fellow is a philosopher. Was it not Camus who argued that the only real choice any man had in life was whether or not to commit suicide? The ultimate existential question.'

'I thought that was Sartre,' Ricky replied. He shrugged.

'I suppose that is the central question here, Ricky, the first and most important question Rumplestiltskin has posed.'

'I'm sorry, what . . . '

'Will you kill yourself to save another, Ricky?'

Ricky was taken aback by the question. 'I'm not sure,' he stammered. 'I don't think that I've really considered that alternative.'

Dr. Lewis shifted in his seat. 'It is really not all that unreasonable a question,' he said. 'And I am certain that your tormentor here has spent many hours wondering what your response would be. What sort of man are you, Ricky? What sort of physician? Because, when all is said and done, that is the essence of this game: Will you kill yourself? He appears to have proven the sincerity of his threats, or, at least made you believe that he has already committed one killing, so another is probably not beyond him. And these are, if you will permit me, Ricky, to sound callous, extremely easy murders to perform. The subjects mean nothing to him. They are merely vessels that assist him in getting to you. And they have the added advantage of being homicides that probably no FBI agent or police detective in the world, not even a Maigret or Hercule Poirot or Miss Marple or one of Mickey Spillane's or Robert Parker's creations could effectively solve. Think about it, Ricky, for it is truly devilish and wondrously existential: An act of killing takes place in Paris, Guatemala City, or Bar Harbor, Maine. It is sudden, spontaneous, and the person being killed has no rhyme or reason that it is coming. They are simply executed one second. Like being felled by a bolt of lightning. And the person supposed to directly suffer from this killing is hundreds, thousands of miles away. A nightmare for any police authority, who would have to find you, find the killer created in your past, then somehow connect them to this event in some distant country, with all the red tape and diplomatic hassles that involves. And that is assuming that they can find the killer. Probably so insulated by fake identities and red herrings of all sorts that it will be impossible. Police have enough trouble obtaining convictions when they have confessions and DNA evidence and eyewitnesses. No, Ricky, my guess is that this would be a crime that is way beyond their capacities.'

'So, what you're saying is . . . '

'Your choice, it seems to me, is relatively simple: Can you win? Can you determine the identity of the man called Rumplestiltskin in the few days you have remaining? If not, then will you kill yourself to save another? This is the most interesting question to pose to a physician. We are, after all, in the business of saving lives. But our resources for salvation are medicines, knowledge, skill with a scalpel. In this instance, your life is perhaps someone's cure. Can you make that sacrifice? And, if unwilling to do that, will you be able to live with yourself afterward? On the surface, at least, it is not all that complicated. The complicated part is, well, internal.'

'You're suggesting . . . ' Ricky started to speak, stammering slightly. He looked across the room and saw that the old analyst had sat back in his chair, so that a shadow from a table lamp's light seemed to bisect his face. Dr. Lewis gestured with a hand that seemed clawlike, long, elongated fingers thinned by age.

'I am not suggesting anything. I am merely pointing out that doing precisely what this gentleman has requested is a viable alternative. People sacrifice themselves so that others may live all the time. Soldiers in combat. Firemen in a burning building. Policemen on city streets. Is your life so sweet and so productive and so important that we can automatically assume it is more valuable than the life it might cost?'

Ricky shifted in his chair, as if the soft upholstery had grown wooden beneath him. 'I can't believe . . . ,' he started, then he stopped.

Dr. Lewis looked at him and lifted his shoulders. 'I am sorry. Of course you have not considered this consciously. But I wonder if you have not asked yourself these same questions in your unconscious, which is what prompted you to find me.'

'I came for help,' Ricky said perhaps far too swiftly. 'I need help playing this game.'

'Really? Perhaps on one level. Perhaps, on another, you came for something else. Permission? Benediction?'

'I need to probe the era in my past where Rumplestiltskin's mother was my patient. I need you to help me do that, because I have blocked that segment of my life. It's like it's just out of reach, just beyond my touch. I need you to help me steer through it. I know I can identify the patient who is connected to Rumplestiltskin, but I need assistance, and I believe that the patient who connects me to this man was someone I was seeing at the same time that I was in treatment with you, when you were my training analyst. I must have mentioned this person to you during our sessions together. So what I need is a sounding board. Someone to bounce those old memories off of. I'm sure I can talk the name out of my unconscious.'

Dr. Lewis nodded again. 'Not an unreasonable request, and clearly an intelligent approach. The analyst's approach. Talk is a cure, not action. Do I sound cruel, Ricky? I guess that I have become irascible and outrageous in my old age. Of course, I will help. But, it seems to me, as we dissect, it would be wise to look at the present, as well, because eventually you will need to find answers both in your past and in your present. Perhaps, too, in your future. Can you do that?'

'I don't know.'

Now it was Dr. Lewis's turn to grin unpleasantly. 'There is a classic analyst's response. A football player or a lawyer or a modern businessman would say 'Damn straight, I can!' But we analysts always hedge our bets, do we not. Certainty is something we are uncomfortable with, no?' He took a deep breath and shifted about for a moment. 'The problem is, this fellow who wants your head on a platter does not seem quite as indecisive or uncertain about things, does he?'

Ricky answered swiftly: 'No. He seems to have everything well planned and thought out in advance. I have the sensation that he's anticipated every single move I've made, almost as if he'd charted them all out beforehand.'

'I am sure he has.'

Ricky nodded to the truth of this observation. Dr. Lewis continued with his questions.

'He is, you would say, psychologically astute?'

'That's my impression.'

Dr. Lewis nodded. 'In some games, that is the essence of play. Football, perhaps. Certainly chess.'

'You're suggesting . . . '

'To win a game of chess, you must plan further ahead than your opponent. That single move beyond the scope of what he has envisioned is what creates checkmate and defines victory. I think you should be doing the same.'

'How do I . . . '

Dr. Lewis rose. 'That is what we should figure out over a modest dinner, and the remainder of the evening.' He smiled again, with a just slightly wry twitch at the corner of his mouth. 'Of course, you are assuming one great factor.'

'What is that?' Ricky asked.

'Well, it seems quite obvious that this fellow Rumplestiltskin has spent months, probably years, planning everything that has happened to you. It is a revenge that takes many items into consideration, and as you quite accurately point out, he has anticipated virtually every move you have made.'

'Yes. All true.'

'I wonder, then,' Dr. Lewis said slowly, 'why you assume and why you believe that he has not already enlisted me, perhaps through threats or outside pressure of some other sort, to help him achieve his desire. Maybe he paid me off somehow. Why, Ricky, do you presume I am on your side in all this?'

Then with a sweeping gesture for Ricky to accompany him instead of answering the question, the old analyst slowly led the way into the kitchen, limping slightly as he traveled forward.

* * *

Two places had been set at an antique two-board table in the center of the kitchen. A jug of ice water and some sliced wheat bread in a wicker hamper graced the center of the table. Dr. Lewis crossed the room and lifted a casserole from the oven, placed it on a trivet, then took a modest salad out of the refrigerator. He hummed slightly as he finished setting the table. Ricky recognized a few strains of Mozart.

'Have a seat, Ricky. The concoction that stands before us is chicken. Please help yourself.'

Ricky hesitated. He reached out and poured himself a tall glass of water, then gulped at it like a man who had just crossed some desert. The drink barely quenched his sudden thirst.

'Has he?' he demanded abruptly. Ricky could hardly recognize his own voice. It seemed high-pitched and shrill.

'Has he what?'

'Has Rumplestiltskin approached you? Are you a part of this?'

Dr. Lewis sat down, carefully spreading a napkin on his lap, then helping himself to a generous portion of casserole and salad before replying. 'Let me ask you this, Ricky,' he said slowly. 'What difference would it make?'

Ricky stammered his reply: 'All the difference in the world. I need to know I can trust you.'

Dr. Lewis nodded. 'Really? Trust, I think, in this world is overrated. Regardless, what have I done, so far, to relinquish the trust you have in me that brought you here in the first place?'

'Nothing.'

'Then you should eat. The casserole is made by my housekeeper, and I assure you it is quite good, although not as good, alas, as that my wife used to make before she passed away. And you appear pale, Ricky, as if you have not been taking care of yourself.'

'I need to know. Has Rumplestiltskin enlisted you?'

Dr. Lewis shook his head, but this wasn't a negative reply to Ricky's question, more a comment on the situation. 'Ricky, it seems to me that what you need is knowledge. Information. Understanding. Nothing you have described, so far, about what this man has done is designed to mislead you. When has he lied? Well, perhaps the attorney whose office was not where it was supposed to be, but that seems like a pretty simple and necessary deception. In reality, everything he has done so far is designed to lead you to him. At least it could be construed that way. He gives you clues. He sends an attractive young woman to assist you. Do you think he truly wants you to be unable to determine who he is?'

'Are you helping him?'

'I am trying to help you, Ricky. Helping you might be helping him, as well. It is a possibility. Now, sit down and eat. That is eminently good advice.'

Ricky pulled out a chair, but his stomach clenched at the thought of putting food inside.

'I need to know that you are on my side.'

The old analyst shrugged. 'Will not the answer to that question come at the end of the contest?' He poked at the casserole, then stuffed a large forkful into his mouth.

'I came to you as a friend. As a former patient. You were the man who helped train me, for Christ's sake. And now . . . '

Dr. Lewis waved his fork in midair, like a conductor with a baton, facing an out-of-synch orchestra. 'The people you treat, do you consider them friends?'

Ricky stopped, shook his head. 'No. Of course not. But the role of training analyst is different.'

'Really? Don't you have a patient or two now in more or less the same situation?'

Both men were silent as this question hovered in the air. Ricky knew the answer to the question was yes, but wouldn't speak the word out loud. After a moment or two, Dr. Lewis waved his hand, dismissing the question.

'I need to know,' Ricky demanded sharply in response.

Dr. Lewis wore an infuriating blank look on his face, appropriate for a poker table. Inwardly, Ricky steamed, recognizing the vacant appearance for what it was: the same noncommittal look that spoke neither of approval or disapproval, shock, nor surprise, nor fear, nor anger that he used with his own patients. It is the analyst's stock in trade, an essential part of his armor. He remembered it from his own treatment a quarter century earlier and bristled to see it again.

The old man shook his head slowly. 'No you do not, Ricky. You need to know only that I am willing to help you. My motives are irrelevant. Perhaps Rumplestiltskin has something on me. Perhaps he does not. Whether he wields a sword over my head or perhaps over one of my family members, is extraneous to your situation. The question always exists in our world, does it not? Is anyone safe? Is any relationship without danger? Are we not often hurt the most by those we love and respect more than those we hate and fear?'

Ricky did not reply, but Dr. Lewis did, for him.

'The answer you are currently unable to articulate is: yes. Now, eat some dinner. I anticipate a long night ahead.'

* * *

The two physicians ate their meal in relative silence. The casserole was excellent, and followed by a homemade apple pie that had a touch of cinnamon in it. There was black coffee, as well, served hot and seemingly speaking of hours ahead that needed to be energized. Ricky thought that he had never had such an ordinary, yet strange meal. He was equally famished and infuriated. The food tasted wondrous one instant, then would go chalky and cold on his tongue, another. For the first time in what seemed to him years, he remembered meals he'd eaten alone, minutes stolen away from his wife's bedside in moments when pain medication had sent her into some half-sleep reverie, in the final days of her dying. The taste, he thought, of this dinner was much the same.

Dr. Lewis removed the plates to a sink, leaving them stacked and dirty. He refilled his coffee cup a second time, then gestured for Ricky to return to the study. They went back to the seats they had occupied earlier, facing across from each other.

Ricky fought his anger at the older physician's oblique and elusive character. He told himself to use the frustration to his own benefit. This was easier said than done. He shifted about in the armchair, feeling like a child who is being reprimanded for something he wasn't to blame for.

Dr. Lewis stared across at him, and Ricky knew the old man was perfectly aware of every feeling coursing through him, just as clever as some sideshow psychic. 'So, Ricky, where would you like to begin?'

'In the past. Twenty-three years ago. When I first came to you.'

'I recall you were filled with theory and enthusiasm.'

'I believed I had the ability to save the world from despair and madness. Single-handed.'

'And did it work out that way?'

'No. You know that. It never does.'

'But you saved some?'

'I hope so. I believe so.'

Dr. Lewis smiled, catlike. 'Again, the practicing analyst's answer. Noncommittal and slippery. Age, such as I have reached, of course brings other interpretations. Our veins harden, and so do our opinions. Let me ask you a more specific question: Whom did you save?'

Ricky hesitated, as if chewing his response. He wanted to stifle his first reply, but was unable, the words falling from his tongue as if coated with oil. 'I couldn't save the person I cared the most for.'

Dr. Lewis nodded. 'Continue, please.'

'No. She doesn't have anything to do with this.'

The old analyst's eyebrows arched slightly. 'Really? I

presume we are speaking of your wife?'

'Yes. We met. We fell in love. We married. We were inseparable for years. She grew ill. We had no children because of her sickness. She died. I continued on all alone. End of tale. She isn't connected to this.'

'Of course not,' Dr. Lewis said. 'But you and she met, when?'

'Shortly before we began treatment. We met at a cocktail party. We were both newly minted; she an attorney, me a physician. Our courtship took place while I was in analysis with you. You should recall that.'

'I do. And what was her profession?'

'She was an attorney. I just said that. You should remember that, as well.'

'Again, I do. But what sort of attorney? Specifically.'

'Well, at the time we met, she had just joined with the Manhattan Office of the Public Defender as a low-grade criminal defense attorney. She worked her way steadily up into the felony divisions, but then tired of seeing all her clients go to prison, or worse, not go to prison. So she went from there into a most unique and modest private practice. Mostly civil rights litigation and work for the ACLU. Suing slum landlords and filing appellate briefs for wrongfully convicted prisoners. She was a liberal do-gooder who did good. She liked to joke that she was one of the small minority of Yale Law graduates that never made money.' Ricky smiled at this, hearing in his mind's ear his wife's own words. It was a joke they shared happily for many years, he thought.

'I see. In the course of the time you started your treatment, the same time that you met and courted your wife, she was involved in defending criminals. She followed this up dealing with many angry fringe types whom, no doubt, she further enraged by bringing legal action against them. And now, you seem involved with someone who fits the category of criminal, albeit seemingly far more sophisticated than those she must have known. But you think there can be absolutely no possible link?'

Ricky stopped, mouth open to reply. This thought chilled him.

'Rumplestiltskin has not mentioned . . .'

'I merely wonder,' Dr. Lewis said, waving a hand in the air. 'Food for thought.'

Ricky paused, memory working hard. Silence grew around the two men. Ricky began to picture himself as a young man. It was as if abruptly some fissure in some granitelike brick within him had opened. He could see himself: far younger, filled with energy. At a moment when the world was opening for him. It was a life that bore little resemblance and little connection to his current existence. That discrepancy, so denied and ignored, suddenly frightened him.

Dr. Lewis must have seen this in his face, for he said, 'Let us speak of who you were twenty-odd years ago. But not the Ricky Starks looking forward to his life, his career, and marriage. The Ricky Starks who was filled with doubts.'

He wanted to respond swiftly, dismiss this idea with a quick brush of the hand, but stopped himself sharply. He plunged into a deep memory, recalling indecision and anxiety, remembering the first day he walked through the door to Dr. Lewis's Upper East Side office. He glanced over at the old man sitting across from him, seemingly studying every flinch and twitch in Ricky's posture and thought how much the man had aged and then wondered if the same was true for himself. Trying to recollect the psychological pains that stirred one to a psychoanalyst so many years earlier was a little like the phantom pain that an amputee feels; the leg missing, but the hurt remaining, emanating from a surgical emptiness, both real and unreal at the very same instant. Ricky thought: Who was I then?

But he answered carefully: 'It seems to me that there

were two sets of doubts, two sets of anxieties, two sets of fears, any of which threatened to cripple me. The first set of each category were those about myself and stemmed from an overly seductive mother, a demanding and cold father who died young, and a childhood filled with accomplishments instead of affection. I was, by far, the youngest in my family, but instead of treating me like some precious baby, I was given impossible standards to uphold. At least, that's it in total simplicity. That was the set that you and I examined over the course of treatment. But the overflow from these neuroses impacted the relationships I had with my patients. During the course of my own treatment I saw patients in three venues: at the outpatient clinic at Columbia Presbyterian Hospital; a brief stint with the severely compromised at Bellevue . . . '

'Yes,' Dr. Lewis nodded. 'A clinical study. I recall you did not particularly enjoy treating the truly mentally ill . . . '

'Yes. Correct. Dispensing psychotropic medications and trying to keep people from harming themselves or others.' Ricky thought Dr. Lewis's statement had a provocative quality to it, a bait he didn't rise to. ' . . . And then, over the course of those years, perhaps twelve to eighteen patients in therapies that became my first analyses. Those were the cases you heard about, while I was in therapy with you.'

'Yes. Yes. These are figures I would agree with. Did you not have a supervising analyst, a gentleman who watched your progress with those patients?'

'Yes. A Doctor Martin Kaplan. But he . . . '

'He died,' the old analyst interrupted. 'I knew the man. A heart attack. Very sad.'

Ricky started to continue, then thought there was an oddly impatient tone to Dr. Lewis's voice. He took note of this, then went on. 'I'm having trouble connecting names and faces.'

'They are blocked?'

'Yes. I should have excellent recall, and yet, I find, I cannot connect faces and names. I will recall a face, and a problem, but not be able to remember a name. Or vice versa.'

'Why do you think this is?'

Ricky paused, then replied, 'Stress. It is simple. Under the sort of tension I've been placed, simple things become impossible to recall. Memory gets all turned around and twisted.'

The old analyst nodded again. 'Do you not think that Rumplestiltskin knows that? Do you not think that he is somewhat expert at the psychology of stress? Perhaps, in his way, far more sophisticated than you, the physician. And would this not tell you much about who he might be?'

'A man who knows how people react to pressure and anxiety?'

'Of course. A soldier? A policeman? A lawyer? A businessman?'

'Or a psychologist.'

'Yes. Someone in our own profession.'

'But a doctor would never . . . '

'Never say never.'

Ricky leaned back chastened. 'I'm not being specific enough,' he said. 'Rule out the people I saw at Bellevue, because they were crippled far too immensely to produce someone this evil. That leaves my private practice and the people I treated in the clinic.'

'The clinic, then, first.'

Ricky closed his eyes for a moment as if this might help him picture the past. The outpatient clinic at Columbia Presbyterian was a warren of small offices on the ground floor of the immense hospital, not far from the emergency entrance. The majority of the clientele traveled up from Harlem or down from the South Bronx. They were mostly poor and struggling, working-class folks of a variety of colors and hues and prospects, all of whom saw mental illness and neurosis as oddly exotic and distant. They occupied the no-man's-land of mental health, between the middle class and the homeless. Their problems were real; he saw drug abuse, sexual abuse, physical abuse. He saw many more than one mother abandoned by some husband, with cold-eyed and hardened children, whose career goals appeared to be limited to joining a street gang. In this crowd of the desperate and disadvantaged, Ricky knew, were more than a few people who had grown into criminals of significant proportions. Drug dealers, pimps, robbers, and killers. He remembered that there were some clients who came to the clinic who exuded a sense of cruelty about them, almost like a distant smell. They were the mothers and fathers diligently helping to create the next generation of inner-city criminal psychopaths. But he knew, as well, that these were heartless people who would direct their anger against their own. If they lashed out at someone from a different economic strata, it was by chance, not design. The business executive in his Mercedes who breaks down on the Cross Bronx Expressway on the way home to Darien after working late in the midtown office, the well-heeled tourist from Sweden who takes the wrong subway line at the wrong hour in the wrong direction.

He thought: I saw much evil. But I moved away from it.

'I can't tell,' Ricky said, finally in response. 'The people I saw at the clinic were all disadvantaged. People on the fringes of society. I would guess that the person I'm seeking is amongst the first patients I had in analysis. Not these others. And Rumplestiltskin has already told me that it is his mother. But she went by her maiden name. 'A miss,' he said.'

'Interesting,' Dr. Lewis said. His eyes seemed to

flicker with intrigue at what Ricky said. 'I can see why you would think that way. And I believe it is important to limit the spheres of one's investigation. So, of all those patients, how many were single women?'

Ricky thought hard, picturing a handful of faces. 'Seven,' he said.

Dr. Lewis paused. 'Seven. Good. And now comes time for the leap of faith, Ricky, does it not? The first moment where you really must make a decision.'

'I don't know that I follow you.'

Dr. Lewis smiled wanly. 'Up to this point, Ricky, it seems to me that you have been merely reacting to the horrendous situation you discover yourself trapped within. So many fires that need to be stamped on and extinguished. Your finances. Your professional reputation. Your current patients. Your career. Your relatives. Out of this mess, you have managed to come up with a single question for your tormentor, and this has provided you with a direction: a woman who created the child who has grown into the psychopath who wants you to kill yourself. But the leap you must make is this: Have you been told the truth?'

Ricky swallowed hard.

'I have to assume so.'

'Is this not a dangerous assumption?'

'Of course it is,' Ricky answered slightly angrily. 'But what option do I have? If I think that Rumplestiltskin is steering me in some totally wrong direction, then I have no chance at all, do I?'

'Did it occur to you that maybe you are not supposed to have a chance?'

This was a statement so blunt and terrifying that he felt sweat break out on his neck. 'If that's the case, then I should just kill myself.'

'I suppose so. Or do nothing, live, and see what happens to someone else. Maybe it is all a bluff, you know. Perhaps nothing will happen. Maybe your patient, Zimmerman, did jump in front of that train — at an inopportune moment for you and an advantageous one for Rumplestiltskin. Maybe, maybe, maybe. Perhaps the game is: You have no chance. I am just wondering out loud, Ricky.'

'I can't open that door to that possibility,' Ricky said.

'An interesting response for a psychoanalyst,' Dr. Lewis said briskly. 'A door that cannot be opened. Goes against the grain of everything we stand for.'

'I mean I don't have the time, do I?'

'Time is elastic. Maybe you do. Maybe you do not.'

Ricky shifted about uncomfortably. His face was flushed, and he felt a little like a teenager, with adult thoughts and adult feelings, who is still considered a child.

Dr. Lewis rubbed a hand across his chin, still thinking. 'I do think your tormentor is a psychologist of sorts,' he said, almost idly, as if making an observation about the weather. 'Or in a profession close to it.'

'I think I agree,' Ricky said. 'But your reasoning — '

'The game, as defined by Rumplestiltskin, is like a session on the couch. It just lasts a little longer than fifty minutes. In any given psychoanalytic hour, you must sort your way through a dizzying series of truths and fictions.'

'I have to work with what I have.'

'Is that not always the issue? But our job is often to see what the patient *is not* saying.'

'True enough.'

'So . . . '

'Maybe it is all a lie. I'll know in a week. Right before I kill myself, or buy another ad in the *Times*. One or the other.'

'It is an interesting idea.' The old doctor seemed to be musing. 'He could achieve the same end and protect himself from ever being traced by a cop or some other authority simply by lying. No one could sort their way through, could they? And you would be dead or ruined. This is diabolical. And nifty, too, in its own way.'

'I don't think this speculation is helping me,' Ricky said. 'Seven women in treatment, one of whom mothered a monster. Which one?'

'Recall them for me,' Dr. Lewis said, gesturing slightly with his hand toward the outdoors and the night that seemed to enclose them tightly, as if he were trying to usher Ricky's memory out of darkness, into the well-lit room.

15

Seven women.

Of the seven who sought him out at that time for treatment, two were married, three others were engaged or in steady relationships, and two were sexually adrift. They ranged in age from their early twenties to early thirties. All were what used to be called 'career women' in that they were brokers, executive secretaries, lawyers, or businesswomen. There was an editor and a college professor in that mix, as well. As Ricky concentrated, he began to remember the array of neuroses that brought each of them to his door. As these illnesses began to formulate in his memory, so did the treatment.

Slowly, voices returned to him, words spoken in his office. Specific moments, breakthroughs, understandings, all forced themselves back into his consciousness, prodded by the simple, direct questioning of the old doctor perched crowlike on the edge of his chair. The night swept around the two physicians, closing off everything save the small room and Ricky Starks's recollections. He wasn't sure how much time had passed in the process, but he knew the hour was late. Ricky paused, almost in midrecall, suddenly staring at the man across from him. Dr. Lewis's eyes still gleamed with an otherworldly energy, fueled, Ricky thought, in part by the black coffee, but more by the array of memory or perhaps something else, some other hidden source of eagerness.

Ricky felt a damp sweat on his neck. He attributed it to the humid air that had crept in through the open windows, promising a cooling shower, but not delivering the same.

'She is not there, is she, Ricky?' Dr. Lewis suddenly asked.

'These were the women in treatment,' he replied.

'And all treated more or less successfully, too, from what you say and what I recall your telling me in our own sessions. And, I will wager, all still living relatively productive lives. A detail, I might add, that a little bit of detective work would uncover.'

'But what . . . '

'And you remember every one. With precision and detail. And that is the flaw, is it not? Because the woman you seek in your memory is someone who does not stand out. Someone who is blocked from your powers of recollection and lost.'

Ricky started to stammer a reply, then stopped, because the truth of this statement was equally apparent to him.

'Can you not recall any failures, Ricky? Because that is where you must find your link to Rumplestiltskin. Not in successes.'

'I think I helped all those women sort their way through the various problems they were facing. I can't remember anyone who left in turmoil.'

'Ah, a touch of hubris there, Ricky. Try harder. What did Mr. R. tell you in his clue?'

Ricky was startled slightly when the old analyst used the same abbreviation that Virgil liked to employ. He rapidly tried to remember whether he had used the phrase *Mr. R.* throughout the evening, but was unable to recall a single instance. But of this, he suddenly wasn't certain. He thought he might have. Indecision, inability to be sure, loss of conviction, were like contrary winds within him. He felt buffeted, and dizzy, wondering where his ability to remember a simple detail had so precipitously disappeared. He shifted about in his seat, hoping that the alarm he felt within wasn't visible on his face, or in his posture.

'He told me,' Ricky said coldly, 'that the woman I was searching for was dead. And that I promised her something that I could not deliver.'

'Well, focus on that second part. Were there any women whom you declined to treat, who came to you in this time frame? Perhaps briefly, a dozen or so sessions, then dropping out? You continue to want to examine the women who were the start of your private practice. Perhaps someone in the clinic where you worked?'

'I'm sure that's possible, but how would I — '

'This other group of patients, they were somehow lesser, in your mind, were they not? Less affluent? Less accomplished? Less educated? And perhaps they did not register quite as firmly on the young Doctor Starks's radar screen.'

Ricky bit back any answer, because he could see both truth and prejudice in what the old physician was saying.

'Is it not more or less the essence of a promise when a patient enters the door and begins to speak? To unburden themselves. You, as analyst, are you not simultaneously making a claim? And subsequently a promise? You hold out the hope for improvement, for adjustment, for relief from torment, just like any other doctor.'

'Of course, but . . . '

'Who came, but stopped coming?'

'I don't know . . . '

'Who did you see for fifteen sessions, Ricky?' The old analyst's voice was suddenly demanding and insistent.

'Fifteen? Why fifteen?'

'How many days did Rumplestiltskin give you to uncover his identity?'

'Fifteen.'

'A fortnight plus one. An unusual and antique construction of time. I think you might have been more sensitive to the number, because there is the connection. And what is it he wants you to do?'

'Kill myself.'

'So, Ricky, who saw you for fifteen sessions and then killed herself?'

Ricky reeled, shifting about, his head suddenly aching. I should have seen it, he thought to himself. I should have seen it because it is so obvious.

'I don't know,' he stammered again.

'You do know,' the old analyst said, a little anger in his voice. 'You just do not want to know. There is a substantial difference.'

Dr. Lewis rose then. 'It is late and I am disappointed. I have had the guest bedroom made up for you. Up the stairs and to the right. I have a few remaining items of a peripheral nature that I am obligated to deal with this evening. Perhaps in the morning, after you have done some additional reflection, we can make some legitimate progress.'

'I think I need more help,' Ricky said weakly.

'You have been helped,' Dr. Lewis replied. He pointed toward the stairwell.

* * *

The bedroom was tidy, well appointed, with a sterile, hotel-room quality to it that made Ricky think instantly that it was infrequently used. There was a bath off the hallway with a similar feel. Neither space provided much window on Dr. Lewis or his life. No vials of medicines in the bathroom cabinet, no magazines stacked by the bed, no books cluttering a shelf, no pictures of family on the walls. Ricky stripped to his underwear and threw himself into the bed, after a single glance at his watch showed him that it was well past midnight. He was exhausted and in need of sleep, but he did not feel safe, his mind churning, and so sleep initially eluded him. The country sounds of crickets and the occasional moth or june bug bumping up against the window screen were twice the racket that the city created. As he lay in the bed in the dark, he slowly filtered noise away and could just make out the distant telltale sound of Dr. Lewis's voice. Ricky tried to concentrate, determining after a moment that the old analyst was angry about something, that his tone, so even and modulated in the hours spent with Ricky, was now raised in tempo and tenor. Ricky strained against the other noises to make out the words, but was unable. Then he heard the unmistakable clattering of the phone being forcefully slammed into its cradle. A few seconds later he heard the old doctor's steps on the stairs, and then a door opening and closing rapidly.

His eyes battled to remain open to the dark. Fifteen sessions and then death, he thought. Who was it?

He was not aware when he plunged into sleep, but he awakened to shafts of bright sunlight slicing through the window and striking his face. The summer morning might have seemed perfect, but Ricky dragged with the weight of memory and disappointment. He had hoped that the old physician would have been able to steer him directly to a name, and instead, he felt as adrift in the wild sea of recollection as ever before. This sense of failure was like a hangover, pounding at his temples. He pulled on his slacks, shoes, and shirt, grabbed his jacket, and after dashing water on his face and running his fingers through his hair to try to make himself mildly presentable, headed downstairs. He paced with a singleness of purpose, thinking that the only thing he would focus on was the elusive name of Rumplestiltskin's mother. He was armed with the sensation that Dr. Lewis's observation, connecting days and sessions, was accurate. What remained hidden, Ricky realized, was the context that the woman existed within. He told himself that he had far too quickly and arrogantly dismissed the less well heeled women he'd seen in the psychiatric clinic, preferring to center upon the women who became his first analysands. He thought to himself that he had seen the woman right at the moment that he had himself been making choices: about his career path, about becoming an analyst, about falling in love and marrying. It was a time when he was looking directly ahead in a single path, and his failure had taken place in a world he wanted to dismiss.

That was why he was so blocked, he thought. His step down the stairs was energized by the idea that he could assault these memories like some World War II dam buster; simply lob a big enough explosion at the concrete of repressed history and it will all burst through. He was confident that with Dr. Lewis's help he could perform this attack.

The country sunlight and warmth infiltrating the house seemed to dispel all the doubts and questions that he might have had about the old analyst. The unsettling aspects of their prior conversation dissipated in the morning brightness. Ricky poked his head into the study area, searching for his host, but saw the room was empty. He walked down the center corridor of the old farmhouse toward the kitchen, where he could smell the aroma of coffee.

Dr. Lewis wasn't there.

Ricky tried a 'hello?' out loud, but there was no response. He looked at the coffeemaker and saw that a fresh pot was warming on the hot plate, and that a single cup had been left out for him. A folded piece of paper was propped up, with his name written in pencil on the outside. Ricky poured himself a cup of coffee and opened up the note as he sipped at the bitter, hot liquid. He read:

Ricky:

I have been called away unexpectedly and do not expect a return within your time frame. I believe you should examine the arena you left for the critical person, not the arena you entered. I wonder, as well, whether by winning the game you will not lose, or, conversely, by losing, you can win. Consider strongly the alternatives that you have.

Please never contact me again for any reason or any purpose.

S/M. Lewis, M.D.

He reeled back sharply, almost as if he'd been slapped in the face.

The coffee seemed to scald his tongue and throat. He flushed, filling instantly with confusion and anger. He read through the words on the page three times, but each successive instance they grew fuzzy and less distinct, when he thought they should have sharpened. He finally crumpled the page of notepaper and stuffed it into his pocket. He walked deliberately to the sink and saw that the pile of dishes from the prior evening had been cleaned and stacked in an orderly fashion on the counter. He dumped the coffee into the white porcelain basin and then ran the water and watched the brown mess swirl down the drain. He rinsed the cup and set it to the side. For a second, he gripped the edges of the counter, trying to steady himself. In that moment, he heard the sound of a car coming up the gravel driveway.

His first thought was that this was Dr. Lewis, returning with an explanation, so he half ran to the front door. But what he saw, instead, surprised him.

Pulling to the front was the same cabdriver who had picked him up the day before at the Rhinebeck station. The driver gave him a little wave and rolled down his window as the taxi stopped.

'Hey, doc, how you doing? Look, we better get a move on if you're gonna catch your train.'

Ricky hesitated. He half turned back toward the house, thinking he needed to do something, leave a note, speak with someone, but as best as he could tell the house was empty. A glance at the reconditioned stable told him that Dr. Lewis's car was gone, as well.

'Seriously, doc, there's not all that much time, and the next train isn't until late this afternoon. You'll be sitting around all day if you miss this one. Jump in, we gotta make tracks.'

'How did you know to pick me up?' Ricky asked. 'I didn't call . . . '

'Well, someone did. Probably the guy who lives here. I got a message on my beeper says get right over here and pick up Doctor Starks pronto and make certain you make the nine-fifteen. So I burn rubber and here I am, but if you don't toss yourself in the back there, you ain't making that train and trust me, doc, there ain't a lot to do around here to keep you occupied for the whole day.'

Ricky paused one more moment, then grabbed the door handle and thrust himself into the backseat. He felt a momentary pang of guilt for leaving the house wide open, then dismissed this with an inward screw you. 'Okay,' he said. 'Let's go.'

The driver accelerated sharply, kicking up some rocks, gravel, and dust.

Within a few minutes, the cab reached the intersection where the access road to the Kingston-Rhinecliff Bridge that crosses the Hudson cuts across River Road. A New York state trooper was standing in the center of the roadway, blocking travel on the winding country road. The trooper, a young man with a Smokey the Bear hat and gray tunic, had a typically steely-eyed, seen-it-all look on his face that contradicted his youth, immediately began waving the cab to the left. The driver rolled down his window and shouted across the roadway to the trooper, 'Hey, officer! Can't I get through? Gotta make the train!'

The trooper shook his head. 'No way. Road's blocked about a half mile down until rescue and the wrecker get finished. You need to drive around. You hurry, you'll make it.'

'What happened?' Ricky asked from the backseat. The cabbie shrugged.

'Hey, trooper!' the driver called out. 'What happened?'

The trooper shook his head. 'Some old guy in a rush lost it on one of the turns. Wrapped himself around a tree. Maybe had a heart attack and blacked out.'

'He dead?' the cabdriver asked.

The trooper shook his head as if to signify that he wasn't sure. 'Rescue's there now. They called for the jaws of life.'

Ricky sat forward sharply. 'What kind of car?' he asked. He leaned forward, shouting through the driver's window. 'What kind of car?'

'Old blue Volvo,' the trooper said as he waved the cabbie to get moving to the left. The driver accelerated.

'Damn,' he said. 'We gotta go around. Gonna be tight on that train.'

Ricky squirmed in the seat. 'I've got to see!' he said. 'The car . . . '

'We stop to sightsee, ain't gonna make the train.'

'But that car, Doctor Lewis . . . '

'You think that's your friend?' the driver asked, continuing to pull away from the site of the wreck, tantalizingly out of Ricky's sight.

'He drove an old blue Volvo . . . '

'Hell, there's dozens of those cars around here.'

'No, it can't . . . '

'The cops won't let you down there. And even if they would, what you gonna do?'

Ricky didn't have an answer. He slumped back in the seat, as if he'd been slapped. The cabdriver nodded, pushing the car so that the carriage rattled and the engine roared. 'You get back to the city, then call the Rhinebeck State Trooper barracks. They'll have some details. Call emergency at the hospital, they'll fill you in. Unless you want to go there now, but I wouldn't advise it. Just sit around waiting out the ER doctors and maybe the undertaker and the cop doing the investigation and still not know much more than you do right now. Haven't you got someplace important to be?'

'Yes,' Ricky said, although he was unsure of this.

'The guy with the car, he a real good friend?'

'No,' Ricky replied. 'Not a friend at all. Just someone I knew. I thought I knew.'

'Well,' the driver said, 'there you have it. I think we're going to make the station on time.' He accelerated again, pushing the cab through a yellow light, just as it turned red, then laughing a little, as they plowed ahead. Ricky leaned back in the seat, just once glancing over his shoulder through the rear window, where the accident and whoever it involved remained hidden, tormentingly out of sight. He strained to see flashing lights, and tried to hear sirens, but they all eluded him.

* * *

He made the train with a minute or two to spare. The need to hurry seemed to obscure any opportunity to assess what had happened to him on the visit to the old analyst. He ran frantically through the empty station, his shoes making a clattering echo, as the train pulled down to the platform with the assaulting sound of its air brakes. As when he rode the train north, there were only a handful of people waiting for the midweek, midmorning trip back to New York City. A couple of businessmen speaking on cell phones, three women apparently on a shopping trip, some teenagers in jeans — that was all. The growing summer heat seemed to demand a leisurely pace that was alien to him. He thought that there was an urgency to the day that was out of place, and wouldn't seem normal until he returned to the city.

The train car was almost empty, with just a smattering of folks spread out through the rows of seats. He went to the rear and scrunched himself into a corner, immediately turning his head and pressing his cheek to the window, watching the countryside slide by, once again sitting on the side where he could inspect the Hudson River.

Ricky felt like a buoy cut loose from its mooring, what was once a sturdy and critical marker of shoals and dangerous currents, now adrift and vulnerable. He did not precisely know what to make of the trip to see Dr. Lewis. He believed he had made some progress, but wasn't certain what that progress was. He felt no closer to breaking through and recognizing his link to the man pursuing him than he had before he traveled up the river. Then, in a second thought, he realized this wasn't true. The problem he understood was that there was some mental block between him and the right memory. The right patient, the right relationship seemed to be just out of his reach, no matter how hard he stretched for it.

Of one thing, he was sure: All that he'd become in his life was irrelevant.

The mistake he'd made, that lay at the core of Rumplestiltskin's anger, came from his initial foray into the world of psychiatry and psychoanalysis. It came right from the moment that he'd turned his back on the difficult and frustrating business of treating the disadvantaged, and headed into the intellectually stimulating business of treating the intelligent and wealthy. The neurotic rich, as one doctor he knew used to term his clientele. The worried well.

This observation enraged him. Young men make mistakes. This is inevitable, in any profession. Now he was no longer young, and he wouldn't have made the same error, whatever it was. He was infuriated at the idea that he was being held accountable for something he'd done more than twenty years earlier and a choice that he'd made that was no different from the choices made by dozens of other physicians in his same circumstances. This seemed unfair and unreasonable. Had Ricky not been so battered by all that had happened, he might have seen that his entire profession was more or less based on the concept that time only exacerbates the injuries done to the psyche. It rechannels these injuries. It never heals them.

Outside the train window, the river flowed past. He was at a loss as to what his next step would be, but of one thing he was certain: He wanted to get back to his apartment. He wanted to be someplace safe, if only momentarily.

Ricky continued to stare through the window, throughout the trip, almost trancelike. At the various stops, he barely looked up and hardly shifted in his seat. The last stop before the city was Croton-on-Hudson, perhaps fifty minutes from Pennsylvania Station. The train car was still ninety percent empty, with dozens of vacant seats, so Ricky was startled when another passenger came up from behind and slipped in beside him, dropping into the seat with a heavy thud.

Ricky turned sharply, astonished.

'Hello, doctor,' the attorney Merlin said briskly. 'Is this seat taken?'

16

Merlin's breathing seemed a little labored and his face a touch flushed, like a man who'd had to run the last fifty yards in order to catch the train. A slight line of perspiration marked his forehead, and he reached inside the breast pocket of his suit coat and removed a white linen handkerchief, which he dabbed at his face. 'Almost missed the train,' he said providing an explanation where none was needed. 'I need to do more exercise.'

Ricky paused to take a deep breath, before asking, 'Why are you here?' although he thought this was a fairly stupid question, given his circumstances.

The attorney finished drying his face with the handkerchief, then slowly spread it out on his lap, smoothing it before folding and returning it to his breast pocket. Then he stowed his leather briefcase and a small waterproof carryall in the area at his feet. He cleared his throat, and replied, 'Why, to encourage you, Doctor Starks. Encourage you.'

Ricky discovered that his initial surprise at the lawyer's appearance had fled. He shifted about, trying to get a better look at the man sitting next to him. 'You lied to me, before. I went to your new address . . . '

The attorney looked mildly bemused. 'You went to the new offices?'

'Directly after we spoke. They hadn't heard of you. No one in the building had. And certainly they had no office space being rented to anyone named Merlin. So, who are you, Mr. Merlin?'

'I am who I am,' he said. 'This is most unusual.'

'Yes,' Ricky said briskly. 'Most unusual.'

'And a bit confusing. Why did you go to my new

office space after we'd spoken? What was the purpose of that visit, Doctor Starks?' The train picked up some speed as Merlin talked, lurching slightly so that the two men rubbed shoulders together in an uncomfortable intimacy.

'Because I didn't believe you were who you said you were, nor did I believe anything else you said. A suspicion I shortly discovered to be true, because when I arrived at the location printed on your business card . . . '

'I gave you a card?' Merlin shook his head, and broke into a small smile. 'On moving day? That explains much.'

'Yes,' Ricky said with irritation. 'You did. I'm sure you recollect that . . . '

'It was a difficult day. Disorienting. What is it they say? Death, divorce, and moving are the three most stressful events for your heart. And your psyche, too, I'll wager.'

'So I've heard.'

'Well, the first batch of business cards I ordered from the printer came back with the wrong address embossed on them. The new offices are a single block over. The fellow in the shop got one digit wrong and I'm afraid we didn't notice right away. I must have handed out a dozen or so before recognizing the error. These things happen. I understand the poor guy got fired from his job, because the printing company had to eat the entire order and do up new cards.' Merlin reached into his jacket and removed a small leather card case. 'Here,' he said. 'This one is right.' He handed it to Ricky, who stared at it dully, then made a sweeping gesture of refusal.

'I don't believe you,' Ricky said. 'I'm not going to believe anything you say. Not now, not ever. You were also there, outside my apartment, with the message in the *Times* a couple of days later. I know it was you.'

'Outside your apartment? How strange. When was this?'

'At five in the morning.'

'Remarkable. How can you be so certain it was me?'

'The deliveryman described your shoes perfectly. And the rest of you adequately.'

Merlin again shook his head. He smiled, with a catlike quality that Ricky remembered from their first meeting. It was the sensation that the attorney was confident in his ability to remain just slippery enough so that he couldn't be pinned down. An important capability for any lawyer. 'Well, I suppose I like to think that my dress and my appearance are unique, Doctor Starks, but I imagine the truth is a little bit more mundane. My shoes, nice as they might be, are available at dozens of shoe stores and not all that uncommon in midtown Manhattan. My suits are off-the-rack blue pinstriped standard business in the city fare. Nice, but still available to you or anyone else with five hundred bucks in their pocket. Perhaps in the near future, I will join the custom-tailored crew. I have aspirations in that direction. But, at least for now, I'm still in the fourth floor, men's wear segment of our populace. Was this deliveryman able to describe my face? How about the thinning hair, alas? No? I can tell from your look what the answer is. So, I would have my doubts about any identification you think someone made standing up under any professionally intense scrutiny. Certainly an identification that has persuaded you so completely. I think this is more a byproduct of your profession, doctor. You take what people tell you and value it too highly. You see words spoken as a means of getting to truths. I see them as methods of obscuring truths.'

The attorney eyed Ricky with a half grin. Then he added, 'You seem under pressure, doctor.'

'You would know about that, Mr. Merlin. Because it is either you or your employer who has created this.'

'I am employed by a young woman that you took advantage of, as I've said before, doctor. Really, that is what has brought me into contact with you.'

'Sure. You know what, Mr. Merlin?' Ricky said with the first harsh tones of anger sliding into his voice. 'You know what? Go find another seat. That seat is being used. By me. I don't want to speak with you anymore. I dislike being lied to as much as you do, and I won't listen to any more. There are plenty of seats on this train . . . ' Ricky gestured wildly at the nearly empty car, ' . . . take one of those and leave me alone. Or at least stop lying to me.'

Merlin did not budge.

'That would not be wise,' he said slowly.

'Perhaps I'm tired of behaving wisely,' Ricky said. 'Maybe I should behave rashly. Now leave me alone.' He didn't expect the attorney would act upon this demand.

'Is that how you've behaved?' Merlin asked. 'Wisely? Have you contacted an attorney as I recommended? Have you taken steps to protect yourself and your possessions from lawsuit and embarrassment? Have you been rational and intelligent about your choices?'

'I've taken steps,' Ricky answered. He wasn't certain that this was accurate.

The attorney obviously didn't believe him. He smiled. 'Well, I'm delighted to hear that. Perhaps we can discuss a settlement, then. You, your attorney, and I?'

Ricky lowered his voice. 'You know what the settlement demand is, don't you, Mr. Merlin, or whatever your real name is. So, please, can we dispense with the charade you persist in employing, and get to the reason you are on this train and sitting beside me?'

'Ah, Doctor Starks. I detect some desperation in your voice, as well.'

'Well, Mr. Merlin, just how much time do you think I have remaining?'

'Time, Doctor Starks? Time? Why all the time you need . . . '

'Indulge me, Mr. Merlin, by either moving or quit lying. You know what I'm saying.'

Merlin eyed Ricky closely, the same Cheshire cat grin playing around the corners of his mouth. But despite the self-satisfied smile, some pretense dropped alongside it. 'Well, doctor, ticktock, ticktock. The answer to your last question is this: I would think you have less than a week remaining.'

Ricky breathed in sharply. 'There's a truthful statement. Finally. Now, who are you?'

'Not important. Just another bit player. Someone hired to do a job. And certainly not the person you might hope I am.'

'Then why are you here?'

'I told you: encouragement.'

'All right, then,' Ricky said firmly. 'Encourage me.'

Merlin seemed to think for a moment, then answered, 'There is a line from the opening of Dr. Spock's *Baby and Child Care*, which I think is appropriate for this moment . . . '

'I never had occasion to read that book,' Ricky said bitterly.

'The line is: 'You know more than you think you do.' '

Ricky paused, considering, before replying sarcastically: 'Great. Dandy. I'll try to keep that in mind.'

'It would be worth your while.'

Ricky did not reply to this. Instead, he said, 'Deliver your message, why don't you. That's what you are, after all, right? A message boy. So get on with it. What is it that you want to get through to me?'

'Urgency, doctor. Pace. Speed.'

'How so?'

'Pick 'em up,' Merlin said, grinning, slipping into an unfamiliar vernacular. 'You need to ask your second question in tomorrow's paper. You've got to get a move on, doctor. Time is being if not exactly wasted, at least flitting past.'

'I haven't figured out my second question yet,' Ricky said.

The lawyer made a slight face, as if he was uncomfortable in his seat, or felt the twinge of a toothache coming on. 'That was the fear,' he said, 'in some circles. Hence the decision to prod you along a bit.'

Merlin reached down and lifted the leather briefcase that was beneath his feet up to his lap. He put it down and opened it up. Ricky saw that it contained a laptop computer, several manila file folders, and a portable telephone. It also contained a small, steel-blue semiautomatic pistol in a leather holster. The attorney pushed the weapon to the side, grinning when he saw Ricky stare at the weapon, and seized the phone. He flipped it open, so that it glowed with that unique electronic green that is so commonplace in the modern world. He turned to Ricky. 'Isn't there a question left over from this morning on your mind?'

Ricky continued to eye the pistol, before speaking. 'What do you mean?'

'What did you see this morning, on the way to the train?'

Ricky paused. He did not know that Merlin or Virgil or Rumplestiltskin knew about his visit to Dr. Lewis, then, in a burst, he realized that they must know, because otherwise they would not have been able to place Merlin on the train to meet him.

'What did you see?' Merlin asked again.

Ricky's face was set, his voice steely. 'An accident,' he answered.

The lawyer nodded. 'Are you certain about that, doctor?'

'Yes.'

'Certainty is such a wondrous conceit,' Merlin said. 'The advantage to being a lawyer over, say, a psychoanalyst, is that lawyers work in a world devoid of certainty. We live in the world of persuasion, instead. But now that I think about it, perhaps it isn't that different for you, doctor. After all, are you not persuaded of things?'

'Get to your point.'

The lawyer smiled again. 'I'll bet that's a phrase you've never used with a patient, is it?'

'You're not my patient.'

'True. So, you believe you saw an accident. Involving . . . ?'

Ricky was unsure how much the man knew about Dr. Lewis. It was possible he knew everything. Also possible he didn't know anything. Ricky remained silent.

The attorney finally answered his question. ' . . . involving someone you knew once and trusted, and whom you went to visit in the rather optimistic hope that he might be able to help you with your current situation. Here . . . ' He punched a series of numbers onto the phone's keypad, then handed Ricky the cell phone. 'Ask your question. Press *send* to make it work.'

Ricky hesitated, then took the phone and did as suggested. The line rang once, then a voice came on: 'State Police Rhinebeck. Trooper Johnson. How can I help you?'

Ricky paused just long enough for the trooper's voice to repeat, 'State Police. Hello?' Then he spoke.

'Hello, trooper, this is Doctor Frederick Starks calling. As I was heading toward the train station this morning on River Road there was apparently an accident. I'm concerned that it involved someone I knew. Can you fill me in on what happened?'

The trooper's reply was curious, but brisk: 'On

River Road? This morning?'

'Yes,' Ricky said. 'There was a trooper waving traffic around a detour . . . '

'You say today?'

'Yes. Not more than two hours ago.'

'I'm sorry, doctor, but we have no reports of any accidents this morning.'

Ricky sat back hard. 'But I saw . . . involving a blue Volvo? The victim's name was Doctor William Lewis. He lives on River Road . . . '

'Not today. In fact we haven't had an accident investigation around here in weeks, which is pretty unusual for the summertime. And I've been on dispatch duty since six A.M., so any calls for police or an ambulance would come through me. Are you sure about what you saw?'

Ricky took a deep breath. 'I must have been mistaken. Thank you, trooper.'

'No problem,' the man said, disconnecting the line.

Ricky's head whirled dizzily. 'But I saw . . . ,' he started.

Merlin shook his head. 'What did you see? Really? Think, Doctor Starks. Think carefully.'

'I saw a trooper . . . '

'Did you see his patrol car?'

'No. He was standing, waving traffic around and he said . . . '

' 'He said . . . ' what a great phrase. So, 'he said . . . ' something and you took it for the truth. You saw a man dressed a little bit like a state trooper, and so you assumed it was one. Did you see him direct any other vehicles, in the time you were at that intersection?'

Ricky was forced to shake his head. 'No.'

'So, really, this could have been anybody wearing a campaign hat. How closely did you inspect his uniform?'

Ricky pictured the young man, and what he

remembered were the eyes peering out beneath the Smokey the Bear hat. He tried to recall other details, but was unable. 'He appeared to be a state trooper,' Ricky said.

'Appearances mean little. In your business, or in mine, doctor,' Merlin said. 'Now, how sure were you there was an accident? Did you see an ambulance? A fire truck? Other police or rescue squad members? Did you hear sirens? Maybe the telltale chop-chop-chop of a life flight helicopter's rotors?'

'No.'

'So, you merely took one man's word that there was an accident that possibly involved someone you had just been in close proximity to the day before, but you didn't see a need to check further? You merely fled in order to catch a train, because you believed that you needed to get back to the city, right? But what was the real urgency?'

Ricky did not reply.

'And, for all you now know, in reality there was no accident down the road at all.'

'I don't know. Perhaps not. I can't be sure.'

'No, you can't be sure,' Merlin said. 'But we can be certain of one thing: that you felt that whatever you had to do was more important than ascertaining whether someone needed help. You might keep that observation in mind, doctor.'

Ricky tried to swivel in the seat to be able to look Merlin in the eye. This was difficult. Merlin continued to smile, the irritating appearance of someone in utter control. 'Perhaps you should try to telephone the person you went to visit?' He waved his hand at the cell phone. 'Make certain they are okay?'

Ricky quickly punched in Dr. Lewis's telephone number. The phone rang repeatedly, but there was no answer.

Surprise clouded his face, which Merlin registered.

Before Ricky could say anything, the lawyer was speaking again.

'What makes you so sure that that house truly was Doctor Lewis's place of residence?' Merlin asked with a slightly stiff formality. 'What did you see that connected the good doctor directly to that place? Were there family pictures on the walls? Did you see any signs of other folks? What papers, knickknacks, what we would call the furniture of life — what was there that persuaded you that you were actually in the good doctor's house? Other than his presence, of course.'

Ricky concentrated, but could see nothing in his memory. The study where they'd sat most of the night was a typical study. Books on the walls. Chairs. Lamps. Carpets. Some papers on the desk surface, but none that he'd inspected. But nothing that was unique and stood out in his recollection. The kitchen was simply a kitchen. The hallways connected the rooms. The guest room where he'd stayed the night was noticeably sterile.

Again, he remained silent, but he knew that his silence was as good a response as the attorney needed.

Merlin took a deep breath, his eyebrows lifted in anticipation of an answer, then lowering, relaxed, becoming part of the knowing smile he wore. Ricky had a brief memory of being in college and staring across a poker table at another student and knowing that whatever cards he held, they weren't adequate to beat his opponent.

'Let me summarize briefly, doctor,' Merlin said. 'I find that it is always wise to periodically take a moment to assess, tote up the score, and then proceed. This might be one of those moments. The only thing that you can be sure of is that you spent some hours in the presence of a physician that you knew from years ago. You don't know now whether that was indeed his home, or not, or perhaps whether he has been in an accident, or not. You don't know for certain that your onetime analyst is alive, or not, do you?'

Ricky started to reply, then stopped.

Merlin continued, lowering his voice just slightly, so that it had a conspiratorial quality to it, 'Where was the first lie? Where was the critical lie? What did you see? All these questions . . . '

He suddenly held up his hand. Then he shook his head, as one might when trying to correct a wayward child. 'Ricky, Ricky, Ricky, let me ask you this: Was there a car accident this morning?'

'No.'

'You're sure?'

'I just spoke to the state police. That guy said . . . '

'How do you know it was the state police you spoke with?'

Ricky hesitated. Merlin grinned. 'I dialed the number and handed you the phone. You pressed *send*, right? Now, I could have dialed just about any number, where just about anyone was waiting for the phone call. Maybe that's the lie, Ricky. Maybe your friend Doctor Lewis is on a slab in the Dutchess County Morgue awaiting some relative to come identify him right now.'

'But . . . '

'You're missing the point, Ricky.'

'All right,' Ricky said, snapping sharply, 'what is the point?'

The attorney's eyes narrowed just slightly, as if irritated by Ricky's brisk reply. He indicated the waterproof gym bag at his feet. 'Maybe he wasn't in an accident at all, doctor, but instead, in that bag right now I've got his severed head. Is that possible, Ricky?'

Ricky recoiled sharply in surprise.

'Is it possible, Ricky?' the lawyer probed, his voice now hissing.

Ricky's eyes fell to the bag. It was a simple duffel shape, without any external characteristics that might indicate what it contained. It was big enough to carry a person's head, and waterproof, so that it would be without stains or leakage. But as Ricky assessed these elements, he felt his throat go dry, and he was not sure what terrified him more, the idea that there was a head of a man he knew at his feet, or the idea that he didn't know.

He raised his eyes toward Merlin. 'It's possible,' he whispered.

'It is important that you understand anything is possible, Ricky. An auto accident can be faked. A sexual harassment complaint sent to your psychoanalytic governing body. Your bank accounts can be trashed and eviscerated. Your relatives or your friends or even just your acquaintances can be murdered. You need to act, Ricky. Act!'

There was a quaver in Ricky's next question. 'Don't you have any limits?'

Merlin shook his head. 'None whatsoever. That's what makes all this so intriguing for us participants. The system of the game established by my employer is one where anything can be a part of the activity. The same is true for your profession, I daresay, Doctor Starks, is it not?'

Ricky shifted in his seat. 'Suppose,' he said softly, hoarsely, 'I were to walk away right now. Leave you sitting with whatever is in that bag . . . '

Again Merlin smiled. He reached down and just turned the top of the bag slightly, revealing the letters F.A.S. embossed on the top. Ricky stared at his initials. 'Don't you think that there's something in that bag alongside the head that links you to it, Ricky? Don't you think that the bag was purchased with one of your credit cards, before they were canceled. And don't you think that the cabdriver who picked you up this morning and took you to the station will remember that the only thing you carried was a medium-sized blue gym bag? And that he will tell this to whatever homicide detective bothers to ask him?'

Ricky tried to lick his lips, find some moisture in his world.

'Of course,' Merlin continued, 'I can always take the bag with me. And you can behave as if you've never seen it before.'

'How — '

'Ask your second question, Ricky. Call the *Times* right now.'

'I don't know that I . . . '

'Now, Ricky. We're approaching Penn Station and when we head underground the phone won't work and this conversation will end. Make a choice, now!' To underscore his words, Merlin started to dial a number on the cell phone. 'There,' he said, with brisk efficiency. 'I've dialed the *Times* classified for you. Ask the question, Ricky!'

Ricky took the phone and pressed the *send* button. In a moment he was connected to the same woman who'd taken his call the prior week.

'This is Doctor Starks,' he said slowly, 'I'd like to place another front-page classified ad.' As he spoke, his mind churned swiftly, trying to formulate words.

'Of course, doctor. How's the scavenger hunt game going?' the woman asked.

'I'm losing,' Ricky replied. Then he said, 'This is what I want the ad to say . . . '

He paused, took as deep a breath as he could muster, and said:

Twenty years, it was no joke,
At a hospital I treated poor folk.
For a better job, some people I left.
Is that why you are bereft?
Because I went to treat some other,
did that cause the death of your mother?

The ad lady repeated the words to Ricky, and said, 'That seems like a pretty unusual clue for a scavenger hunt.'

Ricky answered, 'It's an unusual game.' Then he gave her his billing address again, and disconnected the line.

Merlin was nodding his head. 'Very good, very good,' he said. 'Most clever, considering the stress you're under. You can be a very cool character, Doctor Starks. Probably much more so than you even realize.'

'Why don't you simply call your employer and fill him in . . . ,' Ricky started. But Merlin was shaking his head.

'Do you not think that we are as insulated from him as you? Do you think a man with his capabilities hasn't built layers and walls between himself and the people who carry out his bidding?'

Ricky figured this was probably true.

The train was slowing, and abruptly descended beneath the surface of the earth, leaving sunlight and midday behind, lurching toward the station. The lights in the train car glowed, giving everything and everyone a pale, yellowish pall. Outside the window, dark shapes of tracks, trains, and concrete pillars slipped past. Ricky thought the sensation was similar to being buried.

Merlin rose, as the train pulled to a stop.

'Do you ever read the *New York Daily News*, Ricky? No, I suspect you're not the type for a tabloid. The nice refined upper-class crusty world of the *Times* for you. My own origins are much humbler. I like the *Post* and the *Daily News*. Sometimes they emphasize stories that the *Times* is far less interested in. You know, the *Times* covers something in Kurdistan, the *News* and the *Post*, something in the Bronx. But today, I think, your world would be well served by reading those papers, and not the *Times*. Do I make myself absolutely clear, Ricky? Read the *Post* and the *News* today, because there is a story there that you will find most intriguing. I would suggest absolutely essential.'

Merlin gave a little wave of the hand. 'This has been the most interesting ride, don't you think, doctor? The miles have simply flown past.' He pointed at the duffel bag.

'That's for you, doctor. A present. Encouragement, as I said.'

Then Merlin turned, leaving Ricky alone in the train car.

'Wait!' Ricky yelled. 'Stop!'

Merlin kept walking. A few other heads turned toward him. Another shout was halfway out of Ricky's mouth, but he stifled it. He did not want anyone to focus on him. He didn't want to gain anyone's attention. He wanted to sink back into the station's darkness and become one entity with the shadows. The duffel bag with his initials blocked his exit, like a sudden massive iceberg in his path.

He could no more leave the bag than he could take it.

Ricky's heart and hands seemed to quiver. He bent over and lifted the bag from the floor. Something within shifted position, and Ricky felt dizzy. For an instant he raised his eyes, trying to find something in the world that he could seize hold of, something normal, routine, ordinary, that would remind him and anchor him to some sort of reality.

He could see none.

Instead, he seized the long zipper on the top of the bag, hesitated, taking a deep breath and opened it slowly. He pulled back the opening and stared inside.

In the center of the bag there was a large cantaloupe. Head-sized and round.

Ricky burst into laughter. Relief filled him, unchecked, bursting out in guffaws and giggles. Sweat and nervousness dissipated. The world around him that had been spinning out of control stopped, and seemed to return to focus.

He zipped the bag back up and rose. The train was

empty, as was the platform outside, except for a couple of porters and a pair of blue-jacketed conductors.

Throwing the bag over his shoulder, Ricky proceeded down the platform. He started to think about his next move. He was sure that Rumplestiltskin would confirm the location and the situation where his mother had been in treatment with Ricky. He allowed himself the fervent hope that the clinic might actually have kept records of patients dating back two decades. The name that had proven so elusive for his memory might be on a list up at the hospital.

Ricky marched forward, his shoes clicking on the platform, echoing in the darkness around him. The core of Pennsylvania Station was ahead, and he moved steadily and swiftly toward the glow of the station lights. As he marched with military determination toward the brightly lit crowds of people, his eye picked out one of the redcaps, sitting on a hand truck, engrossed in the *Daily News* while he waited for the next train's arrival. In that single second, the man opened the paper so that Ricky could see the screaming headline on the front page, written in the unmistakable block letters that seemed to cry for attention. He read: TRANSIT COP IN HIT-RUN COMA.

And below that, the subhead: SEEK MISSING HUBBY IN MARITAL MAYHEM.

17

Ricky sat on a hard wooden bench in the middle of Pennsylvania Station with copies of both the *News* and the *Post* on his lap, oblivious to the flow of people surrounding him, hunched over like a single tree in a field bending to the force of a strong wind. Every word he read seemed to accelerate, slipping and skidding across his imagination like a car out of control, wheels locked and screeching impotently, unable to halt the careening, heading inevitably toward a crash.

Both stories had fundamentally the same details: Joanne Riggins, a thirty-four-year-old detective with the New York Transit Authority Police, had been the victim of a hit-and-run driver the night before, struck less than a half block from her home as she crossed the street. The detective remained on life support systems in a coma at Brooklyn Medical Center after emergency surgery. Prognosis questionable. Witnesses told both papers that a fire-engine red Pontiac Firebird had been seen fleeing the site of the accident. This was a vehicle similar to one owned by the detective's estranged husband. Although the vehicle was still missing, the ex-husband was being questioned by police. The *Post* reported that he was claiming his highly distinctive car had been stolen the night before the hit-and-run accident. The *News* uncovered that the man had had a restraining order taken out against him by Detective Riggins during the divorce proceedings, a second restraining order taken out by another, unnamed female police officer, who was said to have rushed to Detective Riggins's side in the seconds after the young woman was crushed by the speeding car. The paper also reported that the ex-husband had publicly threatened his wife during the final year of their marriage.

It was a tabloid dream story, filled with tawdry intimations of an unusual sexual triangle, a stormy infidelity, and out-of-control passions that eventually resulted in violence.

Ricky also knew that it was fundamentally untrue.

Not, of course, the majority of the story; only one small aspect: The driver of the car wasn't the man the police were interviewing, although he was a wondrously obvious and convenient suspect. Ricky knew that it would take them a significant amount of time to come to believe the ex-husband's protests of innocence and even longer to examine whatever alibi he claimed to have. Ricky thought the man was probably guilty of every thought and desire leading up to the act itself, and he guessed that the man who'd arranged this particular accident knew that, as well.

Ricky crushed and crumpled the *News* in anger, twisting the pages and then tossing them aside, scattering the sheets on the wooden bench, almost as if he'd wrung the neck of a small animal. He considered telephoning the detectives working the case. He considered calling Riggins's boss at the Transit Police. He tried to imagine one of Riggins's coworkers listening to his tale. He shook his head in growing despair. There was absolutely no chance whatsoever, he thought, that anyone would hear what he had to say. Not one word.

He lifted his head slowly, once again nearly overcome with the sense that he was being watched. Inspected. That his responses were being measured like the subject of some bizarre clinical study. The sensation made his skin grow cold and clammy. Goose bumps formed on his arms. He looked around the huge, cavernous station. In the course of a few seconds, dozens, hundreds, perhaps even thousands of people swept past him. But Ricky felt utterly alone.

He rose and, like a wounded man, started to make his

way out of the station, heading toward the cabstand. There was a homeless man by the station entrance begging for loose change, which surprised Ricky; most of the disadvantaged were shooed away from prominent locations by the police. He stopped and dropped whatever loose change he had in the man's empty Styrofoam coffee cup.

'Here,' Ricky said. 'I don't need it.'

'Thank you, sir, thank you,' the man said. 'Bless you.'

Ricky stared at the man for a moment, taking note of the sores on his hands, the lesions, partially hidden by a scraggly beard, that marked his face. Dirt, grime, and tatters. Ravaged by the streets and mental illness. The man could have been anywhere between forty and sixty years old.

'Are you okay?' Ricky asked.

'Yes, sir, yes, sir. Thank you. God bless you, generous sir. God bless you. Spare change?' The homeless man's head pivoted toward another person exiting the station. 'Any spare change?' He kept up the refrain, almost singsong with his voice, now ignoring Ricky, who continued to stand in front of him.

'Where are you from?' Ricky suddenly asked.

The homeless man stared at him, filled with a sudden distrust.

'Here,' he said carefully, indicating his spot on the sidewalk. 'There,' he continued, gesturing toward the street. 'Everywhere.' He concluded by sweeping his arms in a circle around his head.

'Where's home?' Ricky asked.

The man pointed at his forehead. This made sense to Ricky.

'Well, then,' Ricky said, 'have a nice day.'

'Yes sir, yes sir, God bless you, sir,' the man continued melodically. 'Spare change?'

Ricky stepped away, abruptly trying to decide whether he had cost the homeless man his life, merely by speaking with him. He walked toward the taxi stand, wondering if every person that he came in contact with would be targeted like the detective had, like Dr. Lewis might have been. Like Zimmerman. One injured, one missing, one dead. He realized: If I had a friend, I couldn't call him. If I had a lover, I couldn't go to her. If I had a lawyer, I couldn't make an appointment. If I had a toothache, I couldn't even go and get my cavity filled without putting the dentist in jeopardy. Whoever I touch is vulnerable.

Ricky stopped on the sidewalk and stared at his hands. Poison, he thought.

I've become poison.

Shaken by the thought, Ricky walked past the row of waiting cabs. He continued across town, heading up Park Avenue, the noises and flow of the city, incessant movement and sound, dropping away from him, so that he marched in what seemed to him to be complete silence, oblivious to the world around him, his own world narrowing, it seemed, with every stride he took. It was nearly sixty blocks to his apartment, and he walked them all, barely aware that he even took a breath of air on the trip.

Ricky locked himself into his apartment and slumped down into the armchair in his office. That was where he spent the remainder of that day and the entirety of the night, afraid to go out, afraid to stay still, afraid to remember, afraid to leave his mind blank, afraid to stay awake, afraid to sleep.

* * *

He must have nodded off sometime toward morning, because when he awakened the day was already blistering outside his windows. His neck was stiff and every joint in his body creaked with the irritation of spending the night in a chair. He rose gingerly and went to the bathroom, where he brushed his teeth and splashed water on his face, pausing to stare at himself in the mirror and to remark internally that tension seemed to have made inroads in every line and angle he presented to the world. He thought that not since his wife's final days had he appeared so close to despair, which, he admitted ruefully to himself, was about as emotionally close to death as one could get.

The x-ed out calendar on his desk was now more than two-thirds filled.

He tried Dr. Lewis's number in Rhinebeck again, only to get the same recording. He tried directory assistance for the same region, thinking perhaps there was a new listing, but came up with a blank. He thought of dialing the hospital or the morgue, to try to determine what was truth and what was fiction, but then stopped himself. He wasn't certain that he really wanted that answer.

The only thing he latched onto was one remark that Dr. Lewis had made during their conversation. Everything Rumplestiltskin was doing seemingly was to draw Ricky closer to him.

But to what purpose, other than death, Ricky could not guess.

The *Times* was outside his door, and he picked it up and saw his question at the bottom of the front page, next to an ad seeking men for impotency studies. The corridor outside his apartment was silent and empty. The hallway was dim, dusty. The single elevator creaked past. The other doors, all painted a uniform black with a gold number embossed in the center, remained closed. He guessed that many of the other tenants were on vacations.

Ricky quickly flipped through the pages of the newspaper, half hoping that the reply would be somewhere within, because, after all, Merlin had overheard the question and presumably had passed it on to his boss. But Ricky could find no evidence that Rumplestiltskin had toyed with his paper. This didn't surprise him. He did not think it likely that the man would employ the same technique twice, because that would make him more vulnerable, perhaps more recognizable.

The idea that he would have to wait twenty-four hours for an answer was impossible. Ricky knew that he had to make progress even without assistance. The only avenue that he thought viable was to try to find the records of the people who came to the clinic where he worked so briefly twenty years earlier. This, he believed, was a long shot, but at least would give him the sensation he was doing something other than waiting for the deadline to expire. He dressed quickly and headed to the front door of his apartment. But once standing there, his hand on the doorknob, ready to exit, he stopped. He felt a sudden wave of anxiety sweep over him, heart rate pitching high, temples starting to throb. It was as if an immense heat had dripped into the core of his body, and he saw that his hand quivered as he reached for the door. A part of him screamed internally, a massive warning, insisting that he not go out, that he was unsafe outside the doors to his apartment. And for just an instant, he heeded this, stepping back.

Ricky breathed in deeply, trying to control his runaway panic.

He recognized what was happening to him. He'd treated many patients with similar anxiety attacks. Xanax, Prozac, mood elevators of all sorts were available, and despite his reluctance to prescribe, he had been forced to do this on more than one occasion.

He bit down on his lip, understanding that it is one thing to treat, another to experience. He took another step back from the door, staring at the thick wood, imagining that just beyond, perhaps in the hallway, certainly on the street outside, that all sorts of terrors awaited him. Demons waiting on the sidewalk, like an angry mob. A black wind seemed to envelop him and he thought to himself that if he stepped outside, he would surely die.

It seemed in that immediate moment that every muscle in his body was crying to him to retreat, to hole up in his office, to hide.

Clinically, he understood the nature of his panic.

The reality, however, was far harder.

He fought the urge to step back, feeling his muscles gather, taut, complaining, like the first second that one has to lift something very heavy from the earth, when there is this instant measurement of strength versus weight versus necessity, all coming together in an equation that results either in rising up and carrying forward, or dropping back and leaving behind. This was one of those moments for Ricky and it took virtually every iota of power he had left within him to overcome the sensation of complete and utter fear.

Like a paratrooper jumping into unknown, enemy darkness, Ricky managed to force himself to open the door and step outside. It was almost painful to take a step forward.

By the time he reached the street, he was already stained with sweat, dizzy with the exertion. He must have been wild-eyed, pale and disheveled, because a young man passing by spun about and stared at him for a second, before picking up his own pace and hurrying ahead. Ricky launched himself down the sidewalk, lurching almost drunkenly toward the corner where he could more easily hail a cab working on one of the avenues.

He reached the corner, paused to wipe some of the moisture from his face, and then stepped to the curb, his hand raised. In that second, a yellow taxi miraculously pulled directly in front of him, to disgorge a passenger. Ricky reached for the door, to hold it open for whoever was inside, and in that time-honored city way, to claim the cab for himself.

It was Virgil who stepped out.

'Thanks, Ricky,' the woman said almost carelessly. She adjusted dark sunglasses on her face, grinning at the consternation he must have worn on his. 'I left the paper for you to read,' she added.

Without another word, she spun away, walking quickly down the street. Within seconds, she had turned a corner and disappeared.

'Come on, buddy, you want a ride?' the driver abruptly demanded. Ricky was caught holding the door, standing on the curb. He looked inside and saw a copy of that day's *Times* folded on the seat, and without thinking further, threw himself in. 'Where to?' the man asked.

Ricky started to reply, then stopped. 'The woman who just got out,' he said, 'where'd you pick her up?'

'She was a weird one,' the driver replied. 'You know her?'

'Yes. Sort of.'

'Well, she flags me down about two blocks away, tells me to pull over just up the street there, wait with the meter running all the time while she's sitting back there, doing nothing 'cept staring out the window and keeping a cell phone pinned to her ear, but not talkin' to nobody, just listening. All of a sudden, she says 'Pull over there!' and points to where you was. She sticks a twenty through the glass and says, 'That man's your next fare. Got it?' I says, 'Whatever you say, lady,' and does like she says. So now you're here. She was some looker, that lady. So where to?'

Ricky paused, then asked, 'Didn't she give you a destination?'

The driver smiled. 'She sure did. Damn. But she tells me I'm supposed to ask you anyways, see if you can guess.'

Ricky nodded. 'Columbia Presbyterian Hospital. The outpatient clinic at 152nd Street and West End.'

'Bingo!' the driver said, pushing down the meter flag and accelerating into the midmorning traffic.

Ricky reached for the newspaper resting on the cab's backseat. As he did so, a question occurred to him, and he leaned forward toward the plastic barrier between driver and passenger. 'Hey,' he said, 'that woman, did she say what to do if I gave you a different address? Like, someplace other than the hospital?'

The driver grinned. 'What is this, some sort of game?'

'You could say that,' Ricky answered. 'But no game you would want to play.'

'I wouldn't mind playing a game or two with that one, if you know what I mean.'

'Yes you would,' Ricky said. 'You might think you wouldn't, but trust me, you would.'

The man nodded. 'I hear ya,' he said. 'Some women, look like that one, more trouble than they're worth. Not worth the price of admission, you could say . . . '

'That's exactly right,' Ricky said.

'Anyways, I was supposed to take you to the hospital whatever you said. She tells me that you'd figure it out when we got there. Woman handed me a fifty to take you on the ride.'

'She's well financed,' Ricky said, leaning back. He was breathing hard, and sweat still clouded the corners of his eyes and stained his shirt. He leaned back in the cab and reached for the newspaper.

He found what he was looking for on page A-13, written in the same red pen in large block letters across a lingerie ad from Lord & Taylor's department store, so that the words creased across the model's slender figure and obscured the bikini underwear she was displaying.

Ricky narrows the track,
Getting closer, heading back.
Ambition, change, clouded your head,
So you ignored all the woman said.
Left her adrift, in a sea of strife,
So abandoned it cost her life.
Now the child, who saw the mistake,
Seeks revenge for his mother's sake.
Who once was poor, but now is rich,
Can fill his wishes, without a twitch.
You may find her in the records of all the sick,
But is it enough to do the trick?
Because, poor Ricky, at the end of the day,
There's only seventy-two hours left to play.

The simple rhyme, like before, seemed mocking, cynical in its childlike pattern. He thought it a bit like the exquisite torture of the kindergarten playground, with singsong taunts and insults. There was nothing childish about the results that Rumplestiltskin had in mind, however. Ricky tore out the single page from the *Times* and folded it up and slid it into his pants pocket. The remainder of the paper he thrust to the floor of the taxi. The driver was cursing mildly under his breath at traffic, carrying on a steady conversation with each and every truck, car, or the occasional bicyclist or pedestrian that crossed his path and obstructed his route. The interesting thing about the driver's conversations was that no one else could hear them. He didn't roll down the window and shout obscenities, nor did he lay on his horn, as some cabdrivers do, like some nervous reaction to the traffic web surrounding them. Instead, this man merely spoke, giving directions, challenges, maneuvering words as he steered his cab, so that in an odd way, the driver must have felt connected, or at least, as if he interacted with all that came onto his horizon. Or his crosshairs, depending, Ricky thought, how one saw it. It was an unusual thing, Ricky thought, to go through each day of life having dozens of conversations that couldn't be heard. Then he wondered if anyone was any different.

The cab dropped him on the sidewalk outside the huge hospital complex. He could see an emergency entrance down the block, with a large red-lettered sign and an ambulance in front. Ricky felt a chill sweep down his back despite the oppressive midsummer heat around him. It was a cold defined by the last time he had been at the hospital, which corresponded to visits to accompany his wife, while she was still fighting the disease that would kill her, still undergoing radiation and chemotherapy and all the other attacks against the insidious happenings within her body. The oncologists' offices were in a different part of the complex, but this still didn't remove the sense of impotence and dread that resurfaced throughout him, no different from when he'd last been on the streets outside the hospital. He looked up at the imposing brick buildings. He thought that he'd seen the hospital three times in his life: the first time, when he worked in the outpatient clinic for six months, before going into private practice; the second time when it joined the dismaying array of hospitals that his wife trudged to in her futile battle against death; and this third time, when he was returning to find the name of the patient whom he'd ignored or neglected, and who now threatened his own life.

Ricky trudged forward, heading toward the entrance, curiously hating the fact that he knew where the medical records were stored.

* * *

There was a paunchy middle-aged male clerk, wearing a garish Hawaiian print sport shirt and khaki pants stained with what might have been ink or the remains of lunch, standing at the records storage bank counter who looked at him with a bemused astonishment when Ricky first explained his request.

'You want exactly what from twenty years ago?' he said with undisguised incredulity.

'All the outpatient psychiatric clinic records from the six-month period I worked there,' Ricky said. 'Every patient who came in was assigned a clinic number and a file was opened, even if they only came in one time. Those files contain all the case notes that were worked up.'

'I'm not sure those records have been transferred to the computer,' the clerk said reluctantly.

'I'll bet they have,' Ricky said. 'Let's you and I check.'

'This will take some time, doctor,' the clerk said. 'And I've got lots of other requests . . . '

Ricky paused, then thought for a moment, finally picturing how easy it seemed for Virgil and Merlin to get folks to perform simple little acts by waving cash in their direction. There was $250 in his wallet, and he removed $200, placing it on the counter. 'This will help,' he said. 'Perhaps put me at the head of the line.'

The clerk glanced around, saw that no one else was watching, and scooped up the money from the countertop. 'Doctor,' he said, with a small grin, 'my expertise is all yours.' He pocketed the cash and then wiggled his fingers in the air. 'Let's see what we can find out,' he said, starting to click entries into the computer keyboard.

It took the remainder of the morning for the two men to come up with a viable list of case file numbers. While they were able to isolate the critical year, there was no corresponding way to determine by computer whether the file numbers represented men or women, and similarly, there wasn't a code that identified which physician had seen which patient. Ricky's six months at the clinic had run from March through the start of September. The clerk was able to eliminate files started before and after. Narrowing the selection down further, Ricky guessed that Rumplestiltskin's mother was seen sometime in the three-month period, over the summer, twenty years earlier. In that time frame, new patient files at the clinic had been opened for two hundred and seventy-nine people.

'You want to find one person,' the clerk said, 'you're gonna have to pull each file and inspect it yourself. I can get 'em out for you, but after that, you're on your own. It isn't going to be easy.'

'That's okay,' Ricky said. 'I didn't expect it would.'

The clerk showed Ricky to a small steel table off to the side of the records office. There was a stiff-backed wooden chair, where Ricky took up his position, while the clerk started to bring the relevant files to him. It took at least ten minutes to collect all 279 different files, stacking them on the floor next to Ricky. The clerk provided him with a yellow legal pad and an old ballpoint pen, then shrugged. 'Try to keep 'em in order,' he said, 'so I don't have to file 'em back one by one. And be careful with all the entries, please, like, don't get documents and notes mixed up from one file to the next. Of course, I'm not guessing that anyone will ever want to see these again anyways, and why we keep 'em is beyond me. But hey, I don't make the rules.'

The clerk looked at Ricky. 'You know who makes the rules?' he asked.

'No,' Ricky replied, as he reached for the first file. 'I don't. The hospital administration, most likely.'

The clerk guffawed, snorting contempt and laughter. 'Hey,' he said, as he walked back to his own perch by the computer, 'you're a shrink, doc. I thought your whole thing is to help people make up their own rules.'

Ricky didn't reply to this, but considered it a wise assessment of what he did. The problem was, he thought, that all sorts of people played by their own rules. Especially Rumplestiltskin. He picked the first file from the top of the first pile, and opened it. It was, Ricky thought abruptly, like opening a folder of memory.

Hours fled around him. Reading the files was a little like standing in a waterfall of despair. Each contained a patient's name, address, next of kin, and their insurance information, if there was any. Then there would be some typed notes on a diagnosis sheet, which delineated the patient's assessment. There were also suggested modes of treatment. In a clipped and quick fashion, each name was broken down to their psychological essence. The meager words in the files were unable to hide the bitter truths that lay behind each person's arrival at the clinic: sexual abuse, rage, beatings, drug addictions, schizophrenia, delusions — a Pandora's box of mental illness. The outpatient clinic at the hospital had been a vestige of 1960s activism, a do-gooder plan to help the less fortunate, opening the hospital doors to the community. *To give back* was the operative phrase of the times. The reality had been significantly harsher and substantially less utopian. The urban poor suffered from a vast array of illnesses, and the clinic had rapidly discovered that it was no more than a single finger in a dike sprouting thousands of leaks. Ricky had come to it while completing the final stages of his psychoanalytic training. At least, that had been his official reason. But when he first joined the clinic staff, he had been filled with idealism and the determination of the young. He could remember walking through the doors wearing his distaste for the elitism of the profession he was entering, determined to bring analytic techniques to the wide range of the desperate. This liberal sense of altruism had lasted about a single week.

In his first five days, Ricky had his desk rifled by one patient seeking drug samples; he'd been assaulted by a wild man hearing voices and throwing punches; he'd watched as one session with a young woman was interrupted by an outraged pimp, armed with a straight razor, who managed to slice both his estranged girlfriend across the face and the security guard across the arm before being subdued; and he'd been forced to send a preteen girl to the emergency room for treatment of cigarette burns on her arms and legs and still she would not tell Ricky who had put them there. He remembered her well enough; she was Puerto Rican and had soft, beautiful black eyes the same raven color as her hair, and she had come to the clinic knowing that someone was sick and that soon enough it would be she, as well, appreciating that abuse creates abuse in a way far more profound than any government study of clinical trials could ever understand. She had had no insurance and no way of paying and so Ricky saw her five times, which was what the state would allow, trying to pry information from her, when she knew that by talking about who was torturing her would probably cost her her life. He remembered it was hopeless. And he knew that if she survived, she was still doomed.

Ricky picked up another file and briefly wondered how he'd even managed to last six months at the clinic. He thought to himself that the entirety of his time there he'd spent feeling utterly and completely helpless. Then he recognized that the helplessness he felt at the hands of Rumplestiltskin was not all that different.

With that thought drumming his emotions onward, he tossed himself into the 279 files of the people he'd seen and treated all those years ago.

A good two-thirds of the people he'd seen had been women. Like so many married to poverty, they wore the rags of mental illness as obviously as they did the cuts and bruises of the abuse they received daily. He'd seen everything from addiction to schizophrenia, and he remembered how impotent the work had made him feel. He had fled back to the upper middle class from where he'd come, where low self-esteem, and the problems that accompanied it, could be talked into, if not cure, acceptance. He'd felt stupid trying to talk with some of his clinic patients, as if discussion could solve their mental anguish, when the reality would probably have been better served by a revolver and some guts, a selection, he remembered, a few had chosen, after coming to the recognition that one prison was preferable to another.

Ricky opened another file from that time, and spotted his handwritten notes. He pulled these out and tried to connect the name on the file with the words he had scrawled down. But the faces seemed vaporous, wavy, like distant heat above a highway on a hot summer day. Who are you? he asked himself. Then, he added a second question: What became of you?

A few feet away, the records office clerk dropped a pencil from his desk, and with a small cursed obscenity, reached down for it.

Ricky eyed the man for a moment, as the clerk bent back to the computer screen glowing in front of him. And, in that second, Ricky saw something. It was almost as if the way the man's back was hunched over slightly, the nervous tic he had of drumming a pencil against the desktop, the narrow way he slumped forward, all spoke a language Ricky should have understood from the first minute, or at least in the way the man's hand had clawed up the money Ricky offered him. But Ricky was only a tourist in this particular land, and that, he thought, explained why it had taken him some time to understand. He quietly pushed away from his table and stepped over behind the man.

'Where is it?' Ricky demanded in a low voice. As he spoke, he reached out and gripped the man's collarbone tightly.

'Whoa! What?' The clerk was taken by surprise. He

tried to shift about, but the pressure of Ricky's fingers digging into the flesh and bone limited his movement. 'Ouch! What the hell?'

'Where is it?' Ricky repeated, more sharply.

'What are you talking about? Damn it! Let me loose!'

'Not until you tell me where it is,' Ricky said. By now he'd lifted his left hand and also seized the man's throat, beginning to squeeze. 'Didn't they tell you I was desperate? Didn't they tell you how much pressure I was under? Didn't they tell you I might be unstable? That I might do anything?'

'No! Please! Ouch! No, damn it, they didn't say that! Let me go!'

'Where is it?'

'They took it!'

'I don't believe you.'

'They did!'

'All right. Who exactly took it?'

'A man and a woman. Just about two weeks ago. They come in.'

'The man was well dressed, paunchy, said he was a lawyer? The woman was a real looker?'

'Yes! Them. What the hell's this all about?'

Ricky released the clerk, who instantly pushed back from him. 'Jesus,' the man said, rubbing his collarbone. 'Jesus, what's the big deal?'

'How much did they pay you?'

'More than you did. A whole lot more. I didn't think it was so goddamned important, you know. It was just one file from way long ago that nobody'd even looked at for two decades. I mean, what's the trouble with that?'

'What did they tell you it was for?'

'Guy said it was part of a legal case, involving an inheritance. I couldn't see that, you know. The folks come to that clinic, they don't got much in the way of inheritance, generally speaking. But the man gave me his card, told me he'd return the file when they were finished with it. I didn't see the problem.'

'Especially when he handed you some cash.'

The clerk seemed reluctant, then he shrugged.

'Fifteen hundred. In new hundreds. Peeled 'em right off a wad, like some sort of old-time gangster. You know, I got to work two weeks for that sort of money.'

The coincidence of the amount was not lost on Ricky. Fifteen days' worth of hundreds. He glanced over at the stack of files and despaired at the hours of the day he'd already wasted. Then he looked back at the clerk, narrowing his glare. 'So the file I need is gone?'

'I'm sorry, doc, I didn't realize it was some big deal. You want the guy's card?'

'I've already got one.' He continued to stare at the clerk, who shifted about in his seat uncomfortably. 'So they took the file, and paid you off, but you're not that stupid, are you?'

The clerk twitched slightly. 'What do you mean?'

'I mean, you're not that stupid. And you haven't worked in a records office for all these years without learning a little bit about covering your tail, right? And so, one file in all these stacks is missing, but not before you made sure of something, right?'

'What are you talking about?'

'You didn't give up that file without copying it, did you? No matter how much the guy paid you, it occurred to you that maybe, just maybe, the someone else who just might come looking for it might have more juice than the lawyer and the woman, right? In fact, maybe they even told you someone might come in here searching for it, isn't that right?'

'They might have said that.'

'And maybe, just maybe, you thought you could make another fifteen hundred or even more, if you had the thing copied, correct?'

The man nodded. 'You gonna pay me, too?'

Ricky shook his head. 'Consider the payment the fact that I don't call your boss.'

The clerk seemed to sigh, measuring this statement, finally seeing in Ricky's face enough anger and stress to believe the threat in its entirety. 'There weren't a whole helluva lot in the file,' he said slowly. 'An intake form and a couple of pages of notes and instructions attached to a diagnosis form. That's what I got copied.'

'Hand them over,' Ricky said.

The clerk paused. 'I don't want any more trouble,' he said. 'Suppose someone else comes looking for this stuff . . . '

'I'm the only other person,' Ricky said.

The clerk bent down and opened a drawer. He reached in and produced an envelope that he handed to Ricky. 'There,' he said. 'Now leave me alone.'

Ricky glanced inside and saw the necessary documents. He resisted the urge to pore over them right there, telling himself that he needed to be by himself when he probed his past. He stood, slipping the envelope into his jacket. 'This is it?' he asked.

The clerk paused, then reached down and plucked another, smaller envelope from the desk drawer. 'Here,' he said. 'This goes with it. But it was attached to the outside of the file, you know, clipped on. I didn't give it to the guy. I don't know why. Figured he had it, because he seemed to know all about the case.'

'What is it?'

'A police report and a death certificate.'

Ricky breathed in sharply, filling his lungs with the stale hospital basement air.

'What's so important about some poor woman who showed up at the hospital twenty years ago?' the clerk abruptly asked.

'Someone made a mistake,' Ricky answered.

The clerk seemed to accept this explanation. 'So now someone's got to pay?' he asked.

'It would seem so,' Ricky replied, as he gathered himself to leave.

18

Ricky walked out of the hospital building, still feeling a tingling in his hands, especially in the fingertips that he'd dug deeply into the clerk's collarbone. He was unable to recall a moment in his life when he'd used force to accomplish something. He thought he lived in a world of persuasion and discussion; the idea that he'd used physical strength to threaten the clerk, even if so modestly, told him that he was crossing some sort of odd barrier, or stepping past some unspoken point of demarcation. Ricky was a man of words, or, at least, had thought so until he'd received the letter from Rumplestiltskin. In his pocket was the name of the woman he'd treated at a moment of transition in his own life. He wondered if he had reached another such point. And, in the same moment, he wondered whether he was standing at the edge of the road to becoming something new.

He walked toward the Hudson River, heading through the huge hospital complex. There was a small courtyard not far from the front of the Harkness Pavilion, a branch of the facility, one that catered to the particularly wealthy and particularly sick. The buildings were huge, multistory brick and stone edifices, that spoke of solidity and sturdiness, standing defiant against the many faces of infinitesimal and puny disease organisms. He remembered the courtyard from years before as a quiet place, where one could sit on a bench and allow the city noises to fade away, alone with whatever beast of a problem yapped and gnawed at one's insides.

For the first time in nearly two weeks he found that the sensation of being followed and watched had slipped away. He was sure that he was alone. He did not expect this state to last.

It did not take him long to spot the bench, and within moments he was seated, the file and envelope provided by the clerk in the records office on his lap. To a passerby, he would have appeared to be simply another physician or relative taking a moment outside the hospital to consider some issue, or steal a bite of lunch. Ricky paused, a little uncertain what he might be opening by removing the documents, then reached into the folder.

The name of the woman patient he'd seen twenty years ago was Claire Tyson.

He stared at the letters of her name. It meant nothing to him.

No face sprang into his recollection. No voice echoed in his ear, recalled from twenty years before. No gestures, no expressions, no tones crossed the barrier of years. The chord of memory went silent, unplayed. It was simply one name out of dozens from that time period.

His inability to recall a single detail filled him with ice.

Ricky read quickly through the intake form. The woman had come to the clinic in a state of near acute depression coupled with paniclike anxiety. She had been referred to the clinic by the emergency room, where she'd gone for treatment of contusions and lacerations. There was evidence of an abusive relationship with a man, who was not the father of her three young children. Their ages were given as ten, eight, and five, but no names were included. She was only twenty-nine years old, and had given an apartment address not far from the hospital, which Ricky knew instantly was in a very nasty part of the city. She'd had no health insurance and had been working as a part-time clerk in a grocery store. She was not a native New Yorker, but had family listed in the next of kin space from a small town in northern Florida. Her Social Security number and telephone listing were the only other completed items on the intake form.

He turned to the second sheet, a diagnosis form, and saw his own handwriting. The words filled him with dread. They were clipped, curt, to the point. They lacked any passion and sympathy.

Miss Tyson presents as a twenty-nine-year-old mother of three young children in a possibly physically difficult relationship with a man not their father. She states that the children's father abandoned her several years ago to take a job working on oil rigs in the Southwest. She has no current health insurance and is able to work only part-time, as she has no funds to hire adequate child care. She receives state assistance from welfare, and federal AFDC, food stamps, and housing subsidy. She further states that she is unable to return to her native Florida, having been estranged from her mother and father by her relationship with the children's father. She additionally claims no funds available for such a move.

Clinically, Miss Tyson appears to be a woman of above average intelligence, who cares deeply about her children and their welfare. She has a high school diploma and two years of college, having dropped out when she became pregnant. She appears significantly undernourished and has developed a persistent tic in her right eyelid. She avoids eye contact when discussing her situation, only lifting her head when asked about her children, whom she states are very close. She denies hearing voices, but admits to spontaneous eruptions of tears of despair that she is unable to control. She says she remains alive only for the children, but denies any other suicidal ideation. She denies drug dependency or addiction, and no visible signs of narcotics use were seen, but a toxicology screen is warranted.

Initial diagnosis: Acute persistent depression caused by poverty. Personality disorder. Possible drug use.

Staff recommendation: Outpatient treatment to state mandated limit of five sessions.

Then he'd signed the bottom of the page. He wondered, staring at his signature, whether he had signed his own death warrant.

There was another entry, on a second sheet, showing that Claire Tyson had come back to see him in the clinic four times, and had failed to appear for her fifth and last authorized session. So, Ricky thought, at least his old mentor, Dr. Lewis, had been wrong about that. But then another thought occurred to him and he flipped open the copy of the death certificate complete with the city coroner's seal and compared that date to the initial treatment date on his own clinic form.

Fifteen days.

He sat back hard on the bench. The woman had come into the hospital, been directed to him, and half a month later she was dead.

The death certificate seemed to glow in his hand, and Ricky quickly scanned the form. Claire Tyson had hung herself in the bathroom of her apartment using a man's leather belt, looped over an exposed plumbing pipe. The autopsy revealed she had been beaten shortly before her death and that she was three months pregnant. A police report clipped to the death certificate said that a man named Rafael Johnson had been questioned about the beating, but not arrested. The three children had been handed over to the Department of Youth Services for processing.

And there it was, Ricky thought.

None of the words printed on the forms in front of him came close to conveying the lasting horror of Claire Tyson's life and death, he thought. The word *poverty* doesn't come close to capturing the world of rats, dirt, and despair. The word *depression* barely suggests the crippling black weight that must have rested on her shoulders. In the whirlpool of life that trapped young Claire Tyson there had been only one thing that gave her meaning: the three children.

The oldest, Ricky thought. She must have told the oldest that she was going to the hospital to see him and get help. Had she told him that I was her only chance? That I held out some promise of something different? What did I say that gave her some hope, which she passed on to the three children?

Whatever it was, it was inadequate, because the woman killed herself.

Claire Tyson's suicide had to have been the pivotal moment in the lives of those three children and in particular the oldest, Ricky thought. And it didn't even register on his own life in the slightest. When the woman failed to show for her final appointment, Ricky had done nothing. He couldn't remember even making a single phone call out of concern. Instead, he'd filed all the papers in a folder and forgotten about the woman. And the children.

And now, one of them was out to get him.

Find that child and you find Rumplestiltskin, he thought.

He rose from the bench, thinking he had much to do, pleased, in an odd way, that the pressures of time and deadlines were so pressing, because otherwise he would have been forced to actually consider what he had done — or not done — twenty years earlier.

* * *

Ricky spent the remainder of the day in New York City bureaucratic Hell.

Armed only with a twenty-year-old name and address, he was shunted between offices and clerks throughout the state Department of Youth Services offices in downtown Manhattan, trying to determine what happened to the three children of Claire Tyson. The frustrating thing about his assault on the world of clerkdom was that he, and all the people at all the offices he dealt with, knew there was some record somewhere of the children. Finding it, amid the inadequate computer records and rooms filled with files, proved to be impossible, at least initially. It was clearly going to take some persistent digging and hours of time. Ricky wished he were an investigative reporter or a private detective, the type of personality that had the patience for endless hours with musty records. He did not. Nor did he have the time.

Three people exist in this world who are connected to me by this fragile thread and it might cost me my life, he told himself, as he butted up against another clerk in another office. The thought gave him a shrill urgency.

He was standing across from a large, pleasant Hispanic woman in the records division of juvenile court. She had a massive flow of raven-black hair that she pulled back sharply from her face, allowing the silver-rimmed, oddly fashionable eyeglasses that she wore to dominate her appearance. 'Doctor,' she said, 'this is not much to go on.'

'It is all I have,' he replied.

'If these three children were adopted, the records were likely sealed. They can be opened, but only with a court order. Not impossible to get, but hard, you know what I mean? Mostly what we get are children all growed up, now looking for their birth parents. There's a procedure we gots to follow in those cases. But this, what you asking, is different.'

'I understand. And I'm under some time pressures . . . '

'Everybody's in a hurry. Allatime in a hurry. What so urgent after twenty years?'

'It's a medical emergency.'

'Well, a judge likely gonna listen to that, you got some papers. Get a court order. Then maybe we could make some search.'

'A court order would take days.'

'That's right. Things don't work none too fast in here. Unless you know some judge personal. Go see 'em, get something signed real quick.'

'Time is important.'

'It is to most folks. Sorry. But you know how maybe you do better?'

'How's that?'

'You get a little bit more information about these people you be looking for, get one of those fancy search programs on your computer. Maybe come up with the info. I knows some orphans looking for their past done that. Works pretty good. You hire a private investigator, that's the first thing he gonna do after he takes your money and puts it in his pocket.'

'I don't really use computers much.'

'No? Doctor, this be the modern world. My thirteen-year-old, he can find stuff like you wouldn't believe. Fact is, he tracked down my cousin Violetta, hadn't seen nor heard from her in ten years. She was working in a hospital in L.A., but he found her. Didn't take him more'n a couple of days, neither. You ought to be trying that approach.'

'I'll keep it in mind,' Ricky answered.

'Big help if you got Social Security number or something like that, too,' the clerk said. Her accented voice was melodic, and it was clear that talking to Ricky was an interesting break from her daily routine. It was almost as if, although she was telling what he was searching for was beyond his grasp, she was reluctant to let him go. It was closing in on the evening, and probably, he thought, she could leave after dealing with him, and so wanted to keep him handy for just the right amount of time. He thought he should leave, but was unsure of his next step.

'What kinda doctor you be?' she asked abruptly.

'A psychoanalyst,' Ricky said, watching the answer cause the clerk to roll her eyes.

'You able to read people's minds, doc?'

'It doesn't work like that,' he said.

'No, maybe not. That would make you some kinda witch doctor, huh?' The clerk giggled. 'But I'll bet you're good at guessing what people gonna do next, right?'

'A little bit. Not as much as you probably think.'

The woman grinned. 'Well, in this world, you get a little information, know how to hit the right keys, you can make some good guesses. That's the way it all works.' She gestured with a thick forearm toward the computer keyboard and screen in front of her.

'I suppose so.' Ricky paused, then he looked down at the sheets of paper he'd received at the hospital records office. He turned to the police report and saw something that might help. The officers who had questioned Rafael Johnson, the dead woman's abusive boyfriend, had taken down his Social Security number. 'Hey,' Ricky said, suddenly, 'if I give you a name and a Social Security number, will that computer of yours find someone for me?'

'They still live here? Vote? Get arrested maybe?'

'Probably yes to all three. Or two at least. I don't know that he votes.'

'It might. What's the name?'

Ricky showed the woman the name and number from the police report. She looked around quickly, to see if anyone else in the office was watching her. 'Not really supposed to do something like this,' she muttered, 'but you being a doctor and all, well, we'll see.'

The clerk clicked red-painted fingernails across a keyboard.

The computer whirred and made electronic beeping noises. Ricky saw an entry come up on the screen, and simultaneously, the woman's narrowly plucked eyebrows rose in surprise.

'This be some bad boy, doctor. You sure you need him?'

'What is it?'

'Well he got a robbery, another robbery, an assault, a suspect in a car theft ring, did six in Sing Sing for aggravated assault. That be some hard time. Man, some kind of very nasty record.'

The woman read further then said suddenly, 'Oh!'

'What?'

'He isn't going to be no help to you no more, doctor.'

'Why?'

'Somebody must have caught up with him.'

'And?'

'He dead. Just six months ago.'

'Dead?'

'That's right. Says *deceased* right here, and a date. Six months. Looks like a good riddance, to me. There's a report with the entry. Got a detective's name from the 41st Precinct up in the Bronx. Case still open. Seems like somebody beat Rafael Johnson to death. Oh, nasty, real nasty.'

'What's it say?'

'Seems like after they beat him, somebody strung him up over a pipe, using his own belt. That's not nice. Not nice at all.' The woman shook her head, but she wore a small grin on her face. No sympathy for Rafael Johnson, a type who'd probably passed through her door once too often.

Ricky reeled back. It wasn't hard for him to guess who'd found Rafael Johnson. And why.

* * *

From the same pay phone in the lobby he was able to track down the detective who'd filed the criminal investigation report on the death of Rafael Johnson. He did not know if the call would yield much, but thought he should make the call, regardless. The detective had a brisk, but energetic manner over the phone line, and after Ricky identified himself, seemed curious as to why he would be calling.

'I don't get many calls from midtown medical types. They don't usually travel in the same circles as the late and little-lamented Rafael Johnson. What's your interest in this case, Doctor Starks?'

'This man Johnson was connected to a former patient of mine some twenty years ago. I'm trying to get in touch with her relatives and was hoping that Johnson might be able to steer me in the right direction.'

'That's doubtful, doc, unless you'd been willing to pay. Rafi would do anything for anybody, as long as there was some cash involved.'

'You knew Johnson before he was killed?'

'Well, let's just say that he was on the radar screens of a number of cops up here. He was a bad news kinda guy. I think you'd be hard-pressed to find anyone around here who'd say one damn nice thing about him. Petty drugs. Muscle for hire. Break-ins, robberies, a sexual assault or two. Pretty much the whole sorry useless badass package. And he ended up pretty much as one might have expected, and, to be frank, doc, I'm not thinking there were too many tears shed at that man's funeral.'

'Do you know who killed him?'

'Doc, that's the million-dollar question. But the answer is, we got a pretty good idea.'

Ricky's mind leapt at this statement.

'You do?' he asked excitedly. 'Have you arrested someone?'

'No. And not likely to, either. At least not too quick.'

As quickly as he'd filled with some hope, he plummeted back to earth. 'Why is that?'

'Well, case like this, generally speaking there's not a whole lot of forensic evidence. Maybe some blood work, if there'd been a fight, but none available, because it seemed old Rafi was trussed up pretty tight when he was beaten up, and whoever worked him over was wearing gloves. So, really, what we're looking for is to squeeze one of his buddies, come up with a name, build a case that way, with one guy ratting out the next, right up the ladder to the killer.'

'Yes. I understand.'

'But no one wants to rat out the guy who we think did up Rafael Johnson.'

'Why not?'

'Ah, prison loyalty. Code from Sing Sing. We're looking at a guy that Rafael had some trouble with, while they were sharing state-sanctioned accommodations. Seems they had a real problem in prison. Probably arguing over who owned what piece of the drug trade. Tried to do one another while up there. Homemade knives. Shivs, they call 'em. Very unpleasant way to go, or so I'm told. Seems like the two bad boys carried the bad blood out to the street with 'em. This is, maybe, one of the oldest stories in the world. We'll get the guy who lit up old Rafi when we get something a little better on one of his jerk-off buddies. One of them will trip up sooner or later and then we'll wheel and deal. Need to be able to squeeze a little tighter, you see.'

'So, you think the killer was someone Johnson knew in prison?'

'Absolutely. A guy named Rogers. You ever run into anyone that name? Bad dude. Easily as bad as Rafael Johnson, and maybe even a little worse, because he's the guy still walking around and Johnson's fertilizing a plot out on Staten Island.'

'How can you be so sure he's the guy?'

'I shouldn't be telling you this . . . '

'No, I understand if you don't want to give out details,' Ricky said.

'Well, it was a little unusual,' the policeman continued. 'But I don't suppose there's no harm in your knowing, as long as you keep it to yourself. This guy Rogers left a calling card. Seems he wanted all of Johnson's buddies to know who did him up so badassed, bloody, and beaten up. A little message for the boys back in the hole, I'm thinking. The old prison mentality. Anyway, after pounding on Johnson for a good while, turning his face into a mess, breaking both his legs and six of his fingers, not nice scouts, let me tell you, and right before he strung him up by the neck, this guy took the time to carve his initial right in the middle of Johnson's chest. A big bloody goddamn *R* cut in the flesh. Right unpleasant that, but gets the message across no doubt.'

'The letter *R*?'

'You got it. Some calling card, huh?'

It was indeed, Ricky thought. And the person whom it was truly meant for just received it.

* * *

Ricky tried not to imagine Rafael Johnson's final moments. He wondered whether the ex-con and petty thug had had any idea whatsoever who it was that was delivering his death to him. Every punch that Johnson had thrown at the unfortunate Claire Tyson twenty years earlier had been repaid, with interest. Ricky told himself not to dwell on what he'd learned, but one thing was obvious: The man who called himself Rumplestiltskin had designed his revenge with considerable thought and care. And that the umbrella of that revenge spread farther than Ricky had imagined.

For the third time, Ricky dialed the number for the *New York Times* advertising department, to ask his final question. He was still standing at the pay telephone in the lobby of the courthouse building, holding a finger in one ear to try to drown out the noise of people leaving the offices. The clerk at the newspaper seemed annoyed that Ricky had just managed to beat the six P.M. deadline for the ad. The clerk's voice was curt, direct. 'All right, doctor. What do you want the ad to say?'

Ricky thought, then said:

> *Is the man I seek, one of the three?*
> *Orphaned young, but now no fool,*
> *seeking those who were so cruel?*

The clerk read the lines back to him, without making a single comment, as if he were immune to curiosity. He took down the billing information rapidly and just as quickly disconnected the line. Ricky could not imagine what the clerk had waiting for him at his home that was so compelling that Ricky's question did not even elicit the smallest comment, but he was thankful for that.

He walked out to the street and started to lift his hand to flag down a cab, then thought, oddly, that he would rather ride the subway. The streets were crowded with the evening rush hour traffic, and a steady stream of people were descending into the bowels of Manhattan to ride the trains home. He joined them, finding an odd sanctuary in the press of people. The subway was jammed, and he was unable to find a seat, so he rode north hanging from a metal rail, pummeled and jostled by the rhythm of the train and the mass of humanity. It was almost luxurious to be gripped by so much anonymity.

He tried not to think that in the morning, he would have only forty-eight remaining hours. He decided that even though he'd asked the question in the paper, he would assume that he already knew the answer, which would give him two days to come up with the names of Claire Tyson's orphaned children. He did not know whether he could manage this, but at least it was something he could focus on, a concrete bit of information that he could either acquire or not, a hard and cold fact that existed somewhere in the world of documents and courts. This was not a world he was comfortable in, as he'd amply demonstrated that afternoon. But at least it was a recognizable world, and this gave him some hope. He wracked his memory, knowing that his late wife had been friendly with a number of judges, and thinking that perhaps one of them might sign an order for him to penetrate the adoption records. He smiled, thinking that he might be able to pull that off, and that would be a maneuver that Rumplestiltskin hadn't anticipated.

The train rocked and shook, then decelerated, causing him to tighten his grip on the metal bar. It was hard to steady himself, and he pushed up against a young man with a backpack and long hair, who ignored the sudden physical contact.

The subway stop was two blocks from Ricky's home, and he rose up through the station, grateful to be out in the open again. He paused, breathing in the heat from the sidewalk, then set off rapidly down the street. He was not precisely confident, but filled with a sense of purpose. He decided that he would find his late wife's old address book in the basement storage area and start that evening calling judges she had once known. One was bound to be willing to help. It was not much of a plan, he thought, but at least it was something. As he walked rapidly forward, he was unsure whether he had reached this point in the exercise in revenge because that was what Rumplestiltskin wanted, or because he'd been clever. And, in a strange way, he felt suddenly buoyed by the idea that Rumplestiltskin had taken such a terrible revenge upon Rafael Johnson, the man who'd beaten his mother. Ricky thought that there had to be a significant distinction between the modest neglect that he'd authored, which was truly born of bureaucratic deficiencies, and the physical abuse that Johnson had delivered. He allowed himself the optimistic thought that perhaps all that had happened to him, to his career, his bank accounts, his patients, all the disruption and disarray that had been created in his life might just end there, with a name and an apology of sorts, and then he could go about the task of reconstituting his life.

He did not allow himself to dwell even for a second on the true nature of revenge, because this was not something he was in the slightest familiar with. Nor did he focus on the threat to one of his relatives that still lurked in the background.

Filled instead with if not precisely positive thoughts, at least some semblance of normalcy, and the belief that he might just have a chance to play the game successfully, Ricky turned the corner to his block, only to stop abruptly in his tracks.

In front of his brownstone, there were three police cars, lights flashing, one large red city fire truck and two yellow public works vehicles. The spinning emergency lights blended with the dimming evening atmosphere.

Ricky stumbled backward, like a drunken man, or a man rebounding from a punch to the face. He could see several policemen standing about by his front steps, jawing with workers wearing hard hats and sweat-stained coveralls. A fireman or two were on the fringe of the conversation, but then, as he stepped ahead, peeled away from the group milling about, and swung themselves up into the fire truck. With a deep engine roar mingled with a siren's harsh blare, the fire truck headed off down the street.

Ricky hurried forward, only subliminally aware that the men in front of him were lacking urgency. When he arrived in front of his home, he was almost out of breath. One of the policemen turned and faced him.

'Hey, slow down, fella,' the officer said.

'This is my home,' Ricky replied anxiously. 'What happened?'

'You live here?' the cop asked, although he'd already been given the answer to this question.

'Yes,' Ricky repeated. 'What's going on?'

The cop didn't reply directly. 'Oh, man. You better go talk to the suit over there,' he said.

Ricky looked toward another group of men. He saw one of his neighbors, a man from two stories above him, a stockbroker who headed the building's loosely confederated association, arguing and gesturing with a city Department of Public Works man, wearing a yellow hard hat. Two other men stood nearby. Ricky recognized one of them as the building supervisor, and another as the man in charge of building maintenance.

The DPW man was speaking loudly and as Ricky approached the group he overheard the man say, 'I don't give a shit what you say about inconveniencing people. I'm the guy who decides occupancy and I'm saying no fucking way!'

The stockbroker turned away in frustration, pivoting in Ricky's direction. He gave a small wave and stepped toward Ricky, leaving the other men arguing.

'Doctor Starks,' he said, holding out his hand to shake. 'I had hoped that you'd already left on vacation.'

'What is going on?' Ricky asked quickly.

'It's a mess,' the broker continued. 'One huge mess.'

'What is?'

'Didn't the policemen tell you?'

'No. What's going on?'

The broker sighed and shrugged his shoulders. 'Well, apparently there was some sort of massive plumbing failure on the third floor. Several pipes seemed to have burst wide open simultaneously because of some kind of pressure buildup. Went off like bombs. Gallons and gallons of water have flooded the first two floors and the people on the third and fourth have no utilities at all. Electric, gas, water, telephone — the works. All out.'

The broker must have seen the look of astonishment on Ricky's face, because he continued in a solicitous manner. 'I'm sorry. I know your place was one of the hardest hit. I haven't seen it, but . . .'

'My apartment . . . '

'Yes. And now this idiot from DPW wants the entire building cleared until structural engineers and contractors can get in and check out the whole place . . .'

'But, my things . . .'

'One of the DPW guys will escort you in to get what you need. They're saying the whole place is dangerously compromised. Have you got someone you can call? A place to stay? I was under the impression that you generally took August up on the Cape. I thought you'd be there . . .'

'But how?'

'They don't know. Apparently the apartment where all the trouble started was right above yours. And the Wolfsons are up in the Adirondacks for the summer. Damn, I've got to call them. I hope they've got a listed phone number up there. Do you know a good general contractor? Someone who can handle ceilings, floors, and everything in between. And you'd better call your insurance agent, but I'm not guessing he's going to be pleased to hear about this. You'll need to get him over here right away in order to clear a settlement, but there's already a couple of guys inside taking photos.'

'I still don't understand . . . '

'The guy said, it was like the plumbing simply exploded. A blockage maybe. It will be weeks before we know. Might have been some kind of a gas buildup. Whatever, it was enough to create an explosion. Like a bomb went off.'

Ricky stepped back, staring up at his home of a quarter century. It was a little like being told of a death of someone old and familiar, important and close. He had the sensation that he needed to see firsthand, to examine, to touch in order to believe. Like once when he'd stroked the cheek of his wife and felt a porcelain cold on her skin and understood fully in that moment what had finally happened. He gestured at the building maintenance man. 'Take me in,' he demanded. 'Show me.'

The man nodded unhappily. 'You ain't gonna like it,' he said. 'No sir. And those shoes gonna get ruined, I think.' The man reluctantly handed him a silver hard hat. The hat was marred with scrapes and scars.

* * *

There was still water dripping through the ceiling and leaking down the walls of the lobby as Ricky entered the building, making the paint boil up and flake off. The dampness was palpable, the atmosphere inside suddenly moist, humid, and musty, like some jungle. There was a faint odor of human waste in the air, and puddles had formed on the marble floor, making the entranceway slippery, a little like stepping out onto a frozen pond surface in the winter. The maintenance man was walking a few feet ahead of Ricky, watching carefully where he put his feet. 'You catch that smell? You don't want to pick up some kinda infection,' the man said, back over his shoulder.

They took the stairs up slowly, avoiding the standing water as best as possible, although Ricky's shoes had already begun to make squishing sounds with each step, and he could feel wetness seeping through the leather. On the second floor, two young men, wearing coveralls, rubber boots, surgical gloves, and masks, were wielding large mops, trying to get started on the bigger collections of wastewater. The mops made a slapping sound as they were dragged through the mess. The men were working slowly and deliberately. A third man, also with rubber boots and a mask, but wearing a cheap brown suit, tie loosened around his neck, was standing to the side. He had a Polaroid camera in his hands and was taking shot after shot of the destruction. The light bar flashed, making a small explosion, and Ricky saw a large bulge in one of the ceilings, like a gigantic boil about to burst, where water had collected and threatened to inundate the man taking the photographs.

The door to Ricky's apartment was open wide. The building maintenance man said, 'Sorry, we had to open it up. We were trying to find the source of the main problem . . . ' He stopped then, as if no further explanation were necessary, but added a single word, ' . . . Shit . . . ' which also didn't need expansion.

Ricky took a single step into his apartment and stopped in his tracks.

It was as if some kind of hurricane had swept through his home. Water was pooled up an inch deep. Electrical lights had shorted out, and there was a distinct odor of material that had been burned then extinguished in the air. All the furniture and carpeting were soaked, much of it clearly ruined. Huge portions of the ceiling were bowed and buckled, others had burst open, spreading white snowlike plaster dust around. Strips of Sheetrock had come loose and fallen into piles resembling papier-mâché lumps. Too many places for him to count still dripped dark, brown-tinged noxious water. As he stepped farther into the apartment, the smell of waste that had insinuated itself into the lobby increased insistently, almost overwhelming him.

Ruin was everywhere. His things were either inundated or scattered. It was a little bit as if a tidal wave had slammed into the apartment. He cautiously entered his office, standing in the doorway. A huge slab of ceiling had fallen onto the couch. His desk was beneath a curled strip of Sheetrock. There were at least three different holes in the ceiling, all dripping, all with shattered and exposed pipes hanging down like stalactites in a cave. Water covered the floor. Some of the artwork, his diplomas and the picture of Freud, had fallen, so there was shattered glass in more than one spot.

'Little like some kinda terrorist attack, ain't it?' the maintenance man said. When Ricky stepped forward, he reached out and grabbed the doctor by the arm. 'Not in there,' he said.

'My things . . .' Ricky started.

'I don't think the floor is safe no more,' the man said. 'And any of those pipes hanging down could break loose anytime. Whatever you want is likely ruined anyway. Best to leave it. This place is a helluva lot more dangerous than you think. Take a whiff, doc. Smell that? Not just the shit and stuff. I think I smell gas, too.'

Ricky hesitated, then nodded. 'The bedroom?' he asked.

'More of the same. All the clothes, too. And the bed was crushed by some huge chunk of ceiling.'

'I still need to see,' Ricky said.

'No, you don't,' the man replied. 'Ain't no nightmare you can think up gonna equal what the truth is, so best leave it and get the hell out. Insurance gonna pay for just about everything.'

'My things . . . '

'Things are just things, doc. A pair of shoes, a suit of clothes — they can be replaced pretty easy. Not worth risking sickness or injury. We need to get out of here and let the experts take over. I ain't trusting what's left of that ceiling to stay put. And I can't vouch for the floor none, either. They gonna have to gut this place, top to bottom.'

That was what Ricky felt in that second. Gutted from top to bottom. He turned and followed the man out. A small piece of ceiling fell behind him, as if to underscore what the man had said.

Back out on the sidewalk, the building maintenance man and the stockbroker, accompanied by the man from DPW, all approached him.

'Bad?' the broker said. 'Ever seen worse?'

Ricky shook his head.

'Insurance guys are already coming by,' the broker continued. He handed Ricky his business card. 'Look, call me at my office in a couple of days. In the meantime, have you got a place to go?'

Ricky nodded, pocketing the man's card. He had just one untouched place left in his life. But he did not have much hope that it would remain that way.

19

The last of the night clothed him like an ill-fitting suit, tight and uncomfortable. He pressed his cheek up against the glass of the window, feeling the coolness of the early morning hour penetrate past the barrier, almost as if it could seep directly into him, the darkness outside joining with the bleakness he felt inside. Ricky longed for morning, hoping that sunlight might help defeat the blackness of his prospects, knowing that this was a futile hope. He breathed in slowly, tasting stale air on his tongue, trying to dislodge the weight of the despair that filled him. This he could not do.

Ricky was in the sixth hour of the Bonanza Bus late-night ride from Port Authority to Provincetown. He listened to the diesel drone of the bus engine, a constant rise and fall, as the driver changed gears. After a stop in Providence, the bus had finally reached Route 6 on the Cape, and was making its slow and determined progression up the highway, discharging passengers in Bourne, Falmouth, Hyannis, Eastham, and finally his stop in Wellfleet, before heading to P-Town at the tip of the Cape.

The bus was by now only about one-third filled. Throughout the trip, all the other passengers had been young men or women, late teenage through college and just entering the workforce age, stealing a getaway weekend on Cape Cod. The weather forecast must be good, he thought. Bright skies, warm temperatures. Initially, the young people had been noisy, excited in the first hours of the trip, laughing, jabbering away, connecting in that method that youth finds so automatic, ignoring Ricky, who sat alone in the back, separated by gulfs far greater than merely his age. But the steady dull throb of the engine had done its work on virtually all the passengers, save him, and they were spread out now in various sleep positions, leaving Ricky to watch the miles slide beneath the wheels, his thoughts flowing past as quickly as the highway.

There was no doubt in his mind that no plumbing accident had destroyed his apartment. He hoped the same was not true of his summer home.

It was, he realized, pretty much all he had left.

Internally, he measured what he was heading to, a modest inventory that did more to depress than encourage: a house dusty with memories. A slightly dented and scratched ten-year-old Honda Accord that he kept in the barn behind the house solely to use during the summer vacation, not ever having needed a vehicle while living in Manhattan. Some weathered clothes, khakis, polo shirts, and sweaters with frayed collars and moth holes. A cashier's check for $10,000 (more or less) awaiting him at the bank. A career in tatters. A life in utter disarray.

And about thirty-six remaining hours before Rumplestiltskin's deadline.

For the first time in days he fixated on the choice facing him: the name or his own obituary. Otherwise someone innocent would face a punishment that Ricky could only begin to imagine. All the harsh ranges from ruin to death. He had no doubt any longer of the man's sincerity. Nor of his reach and his determination.

Ricky thought: For all my running around and speculating and trying to figure out the puzzles presented to me, the choice has never changed. I am in the same position that I was when the first letter arrived at my office.

Then he shook his head, because that wasn't quite right. His position, he realized, had worsened significantly. The Dr. Frederick Starks who had opened the letter in his well-appointed uptown office, surrounded by his carefully ordered life, in control of every minute of each day as it arrived in his palm so regularly, no longer existed. He had been a jacket-and-tie man, unruffled and every hair in place. He stared for a moment at the bus window, just catching his reflection in the dark pane of glass. The man who looked back at him barely resembled the man he thought he once was. Rumplestiltskin had wanted to play a game. But there was nothing sporting about what had happened to him.

The bus jerked slightly, and the engine decelerated, signaling another stop arriving. Ricky glanced at his wristwatch and saw that he would arrive in Wellfleet right around dawn.

⋆ ⋆ ⋆

Perhaps the most wondrous thing about starting his vacation, year in, year out, had been the greeting of routine. The ritual of arriving was the same each year, and thus became small acts that had all the familiarity of seeing an old and dear friend after too long an absence. When his wife had died, Ricky had been dogmatic about maintaining the same approach to arriving at the vacation home. Every year, on the first of August, he took the same flight from La Guardia to the small airport in Provincetown, where the same cab company picked him up and transported him on old, familiar roads the dozen or so miles to his home. The process of opening the house remained the same, from tossing the windows wide open to the clear Cape air, to folding the old, threadbare sheets that had covered the wicker and cotton furniture, and sweeping out the dust that had accumulated inside on the counters and shelves over the winter months. Once he had shared all the tasks. The past few years, he'd performed them alone, always reminded, as he went through the modest stack of mail that forever welcomed him — mostly gallery openings and invitations to cocktail parties that would be rejected — that doing these things alone that he had once shared, gave his wife a ghostly presence in his life, but he'd been comfortable with that. It had curiously made him feel less isolated.

This year, everything was different. He carried nothing in his hands, but the baggage that accompanied him was heavier than any he could ever remember, even the first summer after his wife had died.

The bus unceremoniously deposited him on the black macadam of the parking lot at the Lobster Shanty Restaurant. He had never eaten there in all the years of coming to the Cape — put off, he supposed, by the smiling lobster, wearing a bib and waving a knife and fork in its claws that adorned the sign above the restaurant entrance. There had been two cars waiting there for other passengers, both of which sped off after picking up a couple of Ricky's fellow travelers. There was a little damp chill in the morning, and some misty fog hung over some of the hills. Dawn's light was turning the world around him gray and vaporous, like a slightly out-of-focus photograph. Ricky shivered standing at the curb as he felt the morning creep beneath his shirt. He knew precisely where he was, a little over three miles from his house, a place he'd driven past hundreds of times. But to see it from the hour and the circumstances made it all seem alien, just slightly out of harmony, an instrument playing the right notes in the wrong key. He entertained the idea of calling for a cab only a minute or two, then trudged off down the highway, marching with the hesitant step of a battle-weary soldier.

It took just under an hour for Ricky to reach the dirt road that led down to his house. By this time the inevitable heat and sunlight that the August morning promised had gathered, driving away some of the mist and fog from the surrounding hillside. From where he stood by the entry to his home, he could see three black crows perhaps twenty yards away down the highway, picking aggressively at the carcass of a dead raccoon. The beast had picked the wrong, dark moment to cross the road the night before, and in that second had been turned into another animal's breakfast. The crows had a way of feeding that momentarily captured Ricky's attention: They stood by the dead animal, heads pivoting back and forth, swiveling right and left as they inspected the world for threats, as if they understood the danger of standing in the road, and no hunger, no matter how acute, would allow them to drop their wariness even for a second. Then, once persuaded that they were safe, their cruelly long beaks would dip and tear at the carcass. They pecked at one another, as well, as if reluctant to share in the abundance left behind by a speeding BMW or SUV. It was a common sight, and ordinarily Ricky would have barely noticed. But this morning, it infuriated him, as if the birds' display was meant for him. Carrion, Ricky thought angrily. Picking at the dead. He suddenly started waving his arms and gesturing wildly in their direction. But the birds ignored him until he took a few menacing steps at them. Then with a chorus of raucous alarm, they lifted up into the air, circling above the trees momentarily, then returning, seconds after Ricky retreated to his driveway. They are more determined than I, Ricky thought, almost overcome with frustration, and he turned his back on the scene, walking steadily but shakily through a tunnel of trees, his shoes kicking up small clouds of dust from the road surface.

His house was barely a quarter mile from the road, but hidden from roadside view.

Most of the new construction on the Cape wears the arrogance of money in both design and location. Large homes slapped down on every hillside and promontory, pitched to gather whatever view of the Atlantic can be acquired. And, if no water view is available, then bent so that they look upon glades, or stands of the thick tangles of wind-stunted trees that dominate the landscape. New houses are designed to look at something. Ricky's house was different. Built well over a hundred years earlier, it had once been a small farm, so it was set at the edge of fields. The fields that had once grown corn were now part of conservation land, so there was an automatic isolation to the location. The house found peace and solitude less in the vista it looked out upon, and more from an ancient connection to the land beneath its foundation. Now it was a little like an old, graying pensioner, slightly tattered and shopworn, frayed about the edges, who wore his medals on holidays, but preferred to spend his hours catnapping in the sunlight. The house had done its duty for decades, and now rested. It had none of the energy of modern homes, where relaxation is almost a demand and a pressing requirement.

Ricky walked through the shadows beneath overhanging trees until the road emerged from the modest forest and he saw the house tucked in the corner of an open field. That the house was standing almost surprised him.

He stood on the front stoop, relieved that he'd found the spare key beneath the loose gray flagstone, as expected. He paused for a moment, then unlocked the door and stepped inside. The musty smell of stale air was almost a relief. His eyes quickly absorbed the world inside. Dust and quiet.

As Ricky recognized the tasks that awaited him — tidying up, sweeping out, getting the house ready for his vacation — an almost dizzying exhaustion filled him. He walked up the narrow flight of stairs to the bedroom. The wooden floorboards, warped and worn with age, creaked beneath his tread. In his room, he opened the window so that warm air would pour over him. He kept a photo of his dead wife in a drawer of a chest, a curious place to store her picture and her memory. He went and pulled it out, and then clutching it like a child would a teddy bear, tossed himself onto the creaky double bed where he'd slept alone for the past three summers, dropping almost immediately into a deep, but unsettled sleep.

* * *

He could sense that the sun had scoured the day when he opened his eyes to the early afternoon. For a moment, he was disoriented, but then, as he awakened further, the world around him jumped into focus. The world outside was familiar and much loved, but seeing it seemed harsh, almost as if the vista that was most comforting was oddly out of his reach. It gave him no pleasure to stare at the world around him. Like the picture of his wife that he still clutched in his hand, it was distant, and somehow lost from him.

Ricky moved to the bathroom, splashing cold water on his face at the sink. His face in the mirror seemed to have aged. He placed his hands on the edge of the porcelain, and stared at himself, thinking he had much to do, not much time to do it.

He moved swiftly to the ordinary chores of summertime. A trip to the barn to pull the car cover off the old Honda, and plug in the electric battery charger that he kept in storage there precisely for this moment every summer. Then, as the car was being reenergized, he went back to the house and started to strip the furniture covers off, and run a quick few broom swipes along the floors. There was an old feather duster in the closet as well, and he got this out and immediately turned the interior of the house into a world of dust mites, spinning in shafts of sunlight.

As was his custom on the Cape, he left the front door

open, when he left. If he'd been followed, which was possible, he didn't want to force Virgil or Merlin or anyone associated with Rumplestiltskin to break in. It was as if this would somehow minimize the violation. He did not know if he could tolerate anything else in his life being broken. His home in New York, his career, his reputation, everything associated with who Ricky thought he was, and everything that he had built into his life, had systematically been ruined. He felt a sort of immense fragility descending upon his heart, as if a single crack in a windowpane, a scratch on the woodwork, a broken teacup, or a bent spoon would be more than he could manage.

He breathed a long sigh of relief when the Honda started up. He pumped the brakes and they seemed to work, as well. He backed the car out gingerly, all the time thinking: This is what it must feel like to be close to death.

* * *

A friendly receptionist pointed Ricky to the bank manager's glass-enclosed cubicle about ten feet away. The First Cape Bank was a small building, with shingle siding like so many of the older homes in the area. But the inside was as modern as any, so that the offices combined the worn with the new. Some architect had thought this to be a good idea, but the result, Ricky thought, was the creation of a place that belonged nowhere. Still, he was glad it was there, and still open.

The manager was a short, outgoing fellow, paunchy, with a bald spot on his head that had obviously been sunburned too often that summer. He shook Ricky's hand vigorously. Then stepped back, eyeing Ricky with an appraiser's glance.

'Are you okay, doctor? Have you been ill?'

Ricky paused, then replied, 'I'm fine. Why do you ask?'

The manager seemed embarrassed, waving his hand in the air dismissively, as if he could erase the question he'd uttered. 'I'm sorry. I didn't mean to pry.'

Ricky thought his appearance must show the stress of the past days. 'I've had one of those summer colds. Really knocked me for a loop . . . ,' he lied.

The manager nodded. 'They can be difficult. I trust you had yourself tested for Lyme disease. Up here, someone looks a bit under the weather, that's the first thing we think about.'

'I'm fine,' Ricky lied again.

'Well, we've been expecting you, Doctor Starks. I believe you'll find everything is in order, but I must say, this is the most unusual account closing I've ever attended.'

'Why is that?'

'Well, first there was that unauthorized attempt to access your account. That was odd enough for a place like this. Then today, a courier delivered a package here addressed to you, care of the bank.'

'A package?'

The manager handed over an overnight mail envelope. It had Ricky's name and the bank manager's name. It had been sent from New York. In the box for a return, there was a post office box number and the name: R. S. Skin. Ricky took it, but did not open it. 'Thank you,' he said. 'I apologize for the irregularities.'

The bank manager produced a smaller envelope from his desk drawer. 'Cashier's check,' he said. 'In the amount of ten thousand seven hundred and seventy-two dollars. We are sorry to lose your account, doctor. I hope you are not taking this to one of our competitors.'

'No.' Ricky eyed the check.

'Are you selling your home here, doctor? We could be of assistance in that transaction . . . '

'No. Not selling.'

The manager looked surprised. 'Then why close the account? Most times, when long-standing accounts close, it's because some great change has taken place in the household. A death or divorce. Bankruptcy sometimes. Something tragic or very difficult, that causes people to reinvent themselves. Start over again somewhere new. But this case . . . '

The manager was probing.

Ricky would not rise to answer. He stared at the check. 'I wonder, if it's not too inconvenient, could I have the amount in cash?'

The manager rolled his eyes slightly. 'It might be dangerous to carry that much cash around, doctor. Perhaps traveler's checks?'

'No thank you, but you are kind to be concerned. Cash is better.'

The manager nodded. 'I'll just get it, then. Be right back. Hundreds?'

'That would be fine.'

Ricky sat alone for a few moments. Death, divorce, bankruptcy. Illness, despair, depression, blackmail, extortion. He thought any one or perhaps all of the words could apply to him.

The manager returned and handed Ricky another envelope, containing the cash. 'Would you care to count it?' he asked.

'No, I trust you,' Ricky said, pocketing the money.

'Well, please, Doctor Starks, if we can ever be of service again, here's my card . . . '

Ricky took this as well, muttering his thanks. He turned to leave, then stopped suddenly, looking back at the manager.

'You said people usually close accounts because?'

'Well, usually something very hard has happened to them. They need to move to a new location, begin a new career. Create a new life for themselves and their families. We get many closings, the vast majority, I'd say, because elderly, longtime customers pass away, and their estates, which we've handled, get sucked up and tossed into the more aggressive money markets or Wall Street by the children who do the inheriting. I would say that almost ninety percent of our account closings are related to a death. Maybe even a higher percentage. That's why I wondered about yours, doctor. It just doesn't fit the pattern that we're accustomed to.'

'How interesting,' Ricky said. 'I don't know about that. Well, please rest assured that if I need a bank in the future, this will be the one I use.'

This placated the manager somewhat. 'We will be at your service,' he said, as Ricky, suddenly chewing on what the bank manager had told him, turned and exited into the last of the day of his last day but one.

* * *

The weightless dark of early evening had descended by the time Ricky returned to the farmhouse. In the summer, he thought, the truly thick and heavy night holds off until midnight or later. In the fields adjacent to his home, crickets chirped, and above him, the first stars of night dotted the sky. It all seems so benign, he thought. A night when one should have no cares and no worries.

He half expected Merlin or Virgil to be waiting for him inside the house, but the interior was silent and empty. He flicked on the lights and then went to the kitchen and made himself a cup of coffee. Then he sat at the wooden table where he'd shared so many meals over the years with his wife, and opened the package he'd received at the bank. Inside the overnight courier bag was a single envelope with his name printed on the outside.

Ricky tore open the envelope and removed a single

folded sheet of paper. There was a letterhead at the top of the page, giving the letter the appearance of a more or less routine business transaction. The letterhead read:

R. S. Skin
Private Investigations
'All transactions strictly confidential'
P.O. Box 66–66
Church Street Station
New York, N.Y. 10008

Beneath the letterhead was the following brief letter, written in a routine and clipped business tone:

Dear Dr. Starks:
Regarding your recent inquiry to this office, we are pleased to inform you that our operatives have confirmed that your assumptions are correct. We are unable, however, at this time, to provide any further details about the individuals in question. We understand that you are operating under significant time constraints. Consequently, barring any requests from you in the future, we will not be able to provide any additional information. Should your circumstances change, please feel free to contact our office with any additional inquiries.
Bill for services to follow within twenty-four hours.
Very truly yours,
R. S. Skin, President
R. S. Skin Private Investigations

Ricky read through the letter three times, before setting it down on the table.

It was, he thought, a truly remarkable document. He shook his head, almost in admiration, certainly in despair. The address and the bogus private investigation firm were surely complete fictions. That wasn't the genius in the letter, though. The genius lay in how insignificant the letter would seem to anyone except Ricky. Every other connection with Rumplestiltskin had been erased from Ricky's life. The little poems, the first letter, the clues and directions, all had been either destroyed or stolen back from him. And this letter told Ricky what he needed to know, but in such a manner that if someone else were to come upon it, it wouldn't attract attention. And, it would almost directly lead anyone who might be curious to an immediate and impenetrable brick wall. A trail that went nowhere instantly.

That, Ricky thought, was intelligent.

He knew who it was who wanted him to kill himself, he just didn't know their names. He knew why they wanted him to kill himself. And he knew that if he failed in that demand, they had the capacity to do precisely what they had promised to do from the very first day. The bill for services.

He knew the havoc that they had produced in his last two weeks would evaporate when Ricky met the deadline. The fiction of sexual abuse that had skewered his career, the money, the apartment, the entirety of what had befallen him over the course of fourteen days would unravel instantly, as soon as he was dead.

But beyond that, he thought, the worst thing of all: No one would care.

He had isolated himself professionally and socially over the past few years. He was, if not estranged, certainly cut off and distant from his relatives. He had no real family, and no real friends. He thought his funeral would be crowded with people in dark suits, wearing faces displaying sufficient fake concern and false regret. Those would be his colleagues. There would be some people in the church pews who were former patients whom he had helped, he thought. They would wear their emotions appropriately. But it is the cornerstone of psychoanalysis that a successful treatment would put all those folks into a realm where they were free of anxiety and depression. That was what he had designed for them, in years of daily sessions. So, it would be unreasonable to ask them to actually shed a tear on his behalf.

The only person likely to squirm on the hard wooden church bench with genuine emotion was the man who'd created his death.

I am, Ricky thought, utterly alone.

What good would it do to take the letter, circle the name *R. S. Skin* in red ink, and leave it behind for some detective with the note: This is the man who made me kill myself.

The man did not exist. At least, not in a plane where some local policeman in Wellfleet, Massachusetts, at the height of the busy summer season, where crimes were defined primarily by middle-aged folks driving home from parties drunk, domestic squabbles among the wealthy, and rowdy teenagers trying to buy any variety of illegal substances, would be capable of finding him.

And worse, who would believe it? Instead, what anyone looking at Ricky's life would discover almost instantly was that his wife had passed away, his career was in tatters due to allegations of sexual misconduct, his finances were a mess, and his home had been accidentally destroyed. A fertile groundwork for a suicidal depression.

His death would make sense to anyone glancing at it. Including every colleague he had back in Manhattan. On the surface, his death at his own hand would be an absolute textbook case. No one would pause and think it unusual for even a second.

For an instant, Ricky felt a surge of anger directed at himself: You made yourself into such an easy target. He clenched his hands into fists and placed them hard on the tabletop in front of him.

Ricky took a deep breath and spoke out loud: 'Do you want to live?'

The room around him was silent. He listened, as if half expecting some ghostly response.

'What is it about your life that is worth living?' he demanded.

Again, the only reply was the distant humming of the summer night.

'Can you live, if it costs someone else their life?'

He breathed in again, then answered his own question by shaking his head.

'Do you have a choice?'

Silence answered him.

Ricky understood one thing with a deep and crystal clarity: Within twenty-four hours Dr. Frederick Starks had to die.

20

The final day of Ricky's life was spent in fevered preparations.

At the Harbor Marine Supply store he purchased two five-gallon outboard motor fuel tanks, the fire-engine red painted type that sit in the bottom of a skiff and plug into the engine. He picked out the cheapest possible pair, after rudely asking assistance from a teenage boy who was working in the store. The boy tried to steer him toward slightly more expensive tanks, that were equipped with fuel gauges and a safety pressure release valve, but Ricky rejected these with a show of disdain. The boy also asked why he needed two, and Ricky made a point of saying that just one wouldn't do for what he had in mind. He feigned anger and insistence and was as pushy and unpleasant as he could manage, right through the moment where he paid cash from his reserve for the tanks.

As soon as the transaction was completed, Ricky stopped, as if remembering something, and abruptly demanded the teenager show him the selection of nautical flare pistols. This the boy did, bringing out a half dozen. Ricky selected the cheapest, once again, although the teenager warned him that the pistol had a very modest range, and was only likely to shoot a flare fifty or so feet into the air. He suggested that other models, just slightly more expensive, would send flares significantly higher, thus providing an extra margin for safety. Again, Ricky was dismissive and insulting, told him he only expected to use the flare a single time, and, as before, paid cash after complaining about the overall cost.

The teenager, Ricky imagined, was delighted to see him leave.

His next stop was at a large chain pharmacy. He walked to the rear of the store and asked to see the head pharmacist. The man, wearing a white jacket and a slightly officious air, emerged from the back. Ricky introduced himself.

'I need a scrip filled,' he said. He gave the pharmacist his DEA authorization number. 'Elavil. A thirty-day supply of thirty milligram tablets. Nine thousand milligrams, total.'

The man shook his head, but not in disagreement, more in minor surprise. 'I haven't filled that much in a long time, doctor. And there are some far newer drugs on the market that are more effective, with far fewer side effects, and not nearly as dangerous to take as Elavil. It's almost an antique. Hardly ever used nowadays. I mean, I've got some in storage that's still within its expiration date, but, are you certain that this is what you want?'

'Absolutely,' Ricky answered.

The pharmacist shrugged, as if saying that he'd done his best to dissuade Ricky and steer him toward some other mood elevator that was more efficient. 'What name shall I put on the label?' he asked.

'My own,' Ricky replied.

From the drugstore, Ricky went to a small stationery outlet. Ignoring the rows upon rows of prefabricated get well, condolence, new baby, happy birthday, and anniversary cards that cluttered each aisle, Ricky picked out a cheap tablet of ruled letter paper, a dozen thick envelopes, and two ballpoint pens. At the counter, where he paid for the purchases, he was also able to obtain stamps for the envelopes. He needed eleven. The young woman manning the register didn't even look him in the eye as she rang up the order.

He threw this collection of items into the backseat of

the old Honda, and quickly drove down Route 6 toward Provincetown. This town, at the end of the Cape, had an unusual relationship with the other nearby vacation spots. It catered to a far younger and considerably hipper crowd, often gay or lesbian, that seemed the polar opposites of the more conservative doctors, lawyers, writers, and academicians who were drawn to Wellfleet and Truro. These two towns were all about relaxing, drinking cocktails, and discussing books and politics and who was getting divorced and who was having an affair, and therefore had a certain near-constant stodginess and predictability about them. Provincetown in the summer had a musical beat and sexual energy. It wasn't about relaxing and finding rhythms, it was about partying and connection. It was a place where the demands of youth and energy were paramount. There was little chance that he would be seen by anyone who knew him, even tangentially. Consequently, it was the ideal spot for Ricky to acquire his next items.

At a sporting goods store he bought a small, black backpack of the type favored by students for carrying books. He also purchased the cheapest back-pocket wallet the store had to offer and a midrange pair of running shoes. These purchases he made with as little conversation as possible with the clerk, avoiding eye contact, not behaving furtively, because that might have drawn attention, but making decisions efficiently, so that his presence in the store was as routine and unnoticeable as possible.

From this store, he went to another large chain drugstore where he acquired some Grecian 5 5-Minute Haircolor in black, a pair of cheap sunglasses, and a set of adjustable aluminum crutches, not the sort that extended up under the armpit, favored by injured athletes, but the type utilized by long-term users, people crippled by some disease or another, where the handle and the semicircular brace formed a sleeve for the hand and forearm.

He had one other stop in Provincetown, at the Bonanza bus terminal, a small roadside office with a single counter, three chairs to wait in and a blacktop parking area big enough for two or three buses. He waited outside, wearing the sunglasses, until a bus arrived, depositing a flock of weekend visitors, before walking in and making his purchase rapidly.

In the Honda, heading toward his home, he thought he barely had enough time left that day. Sunlight filled the windshield, heat poured in through the open side windows. It was the point of the summer afternoon when people gathered themselves off of the sand, called for the children to get out of the surf, collected towels and coolers and brightly colored plastic buckets and shovels, and began the slightly uncomfortable trek back to their vehicles — a moment of transition, before the nighttime routine of dinner and a movie, or a party, or a quiet time spent with some dog-eared paperback novel took over. It was time that Ricky, in years past, would have luxuriated in a warm shower, and then spent with his wife just talking over ordinary things in their lives. Some particularly difficult stage with a patient, for him, a client who couldn't turn his life around for her. Little moments that filled days, and became simple yet fascinating in the scheme of living quietly together. He remembered these times, wondered a bit why he had not thought of them in the years since her death. Remembering did not make him sad, as it so often does to recall missing partners, but actually comforted him. He smiled, because, he thought, for the first time in months, he could recall the sound of her voice. For a moment he wondered whether she thought of the same things, not the big and extraordinary moments of living, but the easy, little times that bordered on the routine, and were so speedily forgotten, when she was preparing herself for death. He shook his head. He guessed that she had tried, but that the pain of the cancer was too great, and when masked by morphine, these memories would be lost to her, which was a realization that Ricky regretted.

My dying seems different, he told himself.

Far different.

He pulled into a Texaco station and stopped at the row of pumps. He stepped from the Honda and took the pair of gas tanks out of the trunk, then proceeded to fill them up to the brim with regular fuel. A teenage boy, working at the full-serve section, saw him, and called out, 'Hey, mister, you want to be leaving enough room for oil, if those are going into an outboard. Some take a mix of fifty to one, others, a hundred to one, but you gotta put it right in the tank . . .'

Ricky shook his head. 'Not for an outboard, thanks.'

The teenager persisted. 'They're outboard tanks.'

'Yeah,' Ricky said. 'But I don't own an outboard.'

The boy shrugged. He was probably year-round, Ricky thought, a local high school kid who couldn't imagine another use for the tanks other than what they were designed for, and who immediately put Ricky into the category that the Cape residents had for summer people, which was a status of mild contempt and utter persuasion that no one from New York or Boston had even the slightest idea what they were doing at any time whatsoever. Ricky paid, replaced the now filled tanks in the trunk of the car, an act even he understood to be remarkably dangerous, and set out for his home.

* * *

He set the two gasoline canisters down temporarily in the living room, and returned to the kitchen. He felt suddenly parched, as if he'd exerted a great deal of energy, and he found a bottle of spring water in the refrigerator which he gulped at rapidly. His heart seemed to have picked up pace, as the hours of this last day dwindled, and he told himself to remain calm.

Spreading the envelopes and the pad of paper out on the kitchen table, Ricky sat down, fingered one of the ballpoint pens, and wrote the following short note:

To the Nature Conservancy:

Please accept the enclosed donation. Do not seek more, because I have no more to give, and after tonight, will not be here to give it.

Sincerely yours,
Frederick Starks, M.D.

He then took a hundred-dollar bill from his stash and sealed it and the letter into one of the stamped envelopes.

Ricky then wrote similar notes and enclosed a similar amount in all the other stamped envelopes, save one. He made donations to the American Cancer Society, The Sierra Club, The Coastal Conservation Association, CARE, and the Democratic National Committee. In each case, he simply wrote the name of the organization on the outside of the envelope.

When he had finished, he looked at his wristwatch and saw that he was nearing the *Times's* evening deadline. He went to the phone and called the advertising department as he had on three other occasions.

This time, however, the message for the ad that he gave the clerk was different. No rhymes, no poems, no questions. Just the simple statement:

Mr. R.: You win. Check the Cape Cod Times.

Once that was accomplished, Ricky returned to his seat at the kitchen table and took the writing pad in hand. He chewed on the end of the pen for a moment, while he composed a final letter. Then he wrote rapidly:

To whom it may concern:

I did this because I was alone, and hate the emptiness in my life. I simply could not tolerate causing any further harm to any other person.

I have been accused of things I am innocent of. But am guilty of mistakes toward the people I loved, and that has brought me to this point to take this step. If someone would mail the various contributions I have left behind, I would appreciate it. All property and funds remaining in my estate should be sold and the proceeds turned over to these same charities. What is left of my home here in Wellfleet should become conservation land.

To my friends, if any, I hope you will forgive me.

To my patients, I hope you will understand.

And Mr. R., who helped bring me to this stage, I hope you will find your own way to Hell soon enough, because I will be waiting there for you.

He signed this letter with a flourish, sealed it in the last remaining envelope and addressed it to the Wellfleet Police Department.

Taking the hair color and his backpack in hand, he went to the upstairs shower. Ricky followed the directions for the dyeing agent, and emerged from the bathroom in moments with nearly jet-black hair. He stole a quick glance at his appearance in the mirror, thought it mildly foolish, then toweled himself dry. At his bureau, he selected some of the old and worn summer clothes he stored there, and stuffed them, along with a frayed windbreaker, into the backpack. He kept an additional change of clothes out, folded carefully and placed on top of the pack. Then he dressed back in the clothing he had worn that day. In an outside pocket of the pack, he slid the photograph of his dead wife. In another pocket he stuffed the latest message from Rumplestiltskin and the few remaining documents he had in his possession that detailed what had happened to him. The documents about the mother's death.

He took the backpack and change of clothes, the aluminum crutches, and stack of letters out to his car, leaving them on the passenger's seat next to his cheap sunglasses and running shoes. Then he returned inside and sat quietly in the kitchen for the remaining hours of the evening to pass. He was excited, a little intrigued, and occasionally riveted by a bolt of fear. He tried hard to think of nothing, humming to himself, blanking his mind. This, of course, did not work.

Ricky knew that he could not cause the death of another, even someone he didn't know, who was only related through the accidents of blood and marriage. Of this, Rumplestiltskin had been correct from the first day. Nothing about his life, his past, all of the little moments that made up who he was, who he had become, who he might yet turn out to be, amounted to anything in the face of this threat. He shook his head, thinking, Mr. R. knows me far better than I do myself. He had me pegged from the start.

Ricky did not know who he might be saving, but knew it was someone.

Think about that, he told himself.

Shortly after midnight, he rose. He allowed himself one final tour of the house, reminding himself how beloved each corner, each warp, and each creak in the floorboards truly was.

His hand shook slightly as he took the first canister of gasoline to the second floor, where he spread it liberally about on the floor. He doused the bedding.

The second canister was used the same way, throughout the ground floor.

In the kitchen, Ricky blew out the pilot lights on the

old gas stove. Then he opened every jet, so that the room filled immediately with the distinctive odor of rotten eggs, the stove hissing in alarm. It blended with the stink of gasoline which already permeated his clothes.

Seizing the marine flare pistol, Ricky walked back outside. He went to the old Honda, started it up and moved it well away from the house, pointing it down the driveway, leaving the engine running.

Then he moved to a spot opposite the windows to the living room. The smell from the gasoline spread throughout the house mixed with the smell on his hands and clothes. He thought how alien all these angry scents were, clashing with the summer warmth and mixed honeysuckle and wildflowers, with just the mildest hint of the ocean salt, that permeated every breeze that slipped innocently across the trees. Ricky took a single deep breath, tried not to dwell on what he was doing, took careful aim with the pistol, cocked the hammer back, and then fired a single flare through the center window. The flare arced through the night, leaving a streak of energetic white light in the black air between where he stood and the house. The flare crashed through the window with a tinkling of shattered glass. He half expected an explosion, but instead heard a muffled thud, followed by an immediate crackle and glow. Within a few seconds he saw the first licks of fire dancing about the floor and beginning to spread through the living room.

Ricky turned and ran back to the Honda. By the time he slipped the car in gear, the entire downstairs was glowing with flame. As he headed down the driveway, he heard an explosion, as the flames hit the gas in the kitchen.

He decided not to look back, but accelerated into the deepening night.

* * *

Ricky drove carefully and steadily to a spot he had known for years called Hawthorne Beach. It was several miles down a narrow, lonely blacktop lane, removed from any development, other than a couple of old and darkened farmhouses not unlike his own. He switched off the lights as he eased past any house that might be occupied. There were several beaches in the Wellfleet area that would have suited his purposes, he thought, but this was the most isolated, and least likely to be the site of some late-night teenage party. There was a small parking lot at the beach entrance, usually operated by the Trustees of Reservations, the Massachusetts conservation association dedicated to preserving the wildest spots in the state's landscape. The parking lot would only accommodate perhaps two dozen cars, and was usually filled by nine-thirty in the morning because it was a spectacular beach, a wide expanse of flat sand resting at the base of a fifty-foot bluff of blond sandy dirt encrusted with green sea grass thatches, with some of the strongest surf on the Cape. The combination was favored both by families who were moved by the view, and surfers who appreciated the waves and strong tidal pull, so that their sport was always mingled with a bit of danger. At the end of the parking lot, there was a warning sign: STRONG CURRENTS AND DANGEROUS UNDERTOW. DO NOT SWIM WITHOUT LIFEGUARD BEING PRESENT. BE ALERT FOR THREATENING CONDITIONS.

Ricky parked by the sign. He left the keys in the car. He placed the envelopes with the contributions on the dashboard and set the envelope with the letter addressed to the Wellfleet Police right in the center of the steering wheel.

Seizing the crutches, the backpack, running shoes, and change of clothes, he stepped away from the car.

These he placed at the top of the bluff, a few feet away from a wooden barrier that marked the narrow path down to the sand, after removing the picture of his wife from the backpack's outer pocket. This he placed in his pants pocket. He could hear the steady rhythmic crash of waves, and felt a bit of a southeasterly breeze on his face. He welcomed the noise, because it told him that the surf had picked up in the hours after sunset, and was slamming like a frustrated wrestler against the shoreline.

There was a full moon above, spreading wan light across the beach. It made his slippery, stumbling trip down the bluff to the water's edge considerably easier.

In front of him, as he had predicted to himself, the surf was roaring like a drunken man, exploding as it hit the beach and sending sheets of white froth across the sand.

A small chill carried in on a breath of wind, striking him in the chest, making him hesitate, breathe in deeply.

Then Ricky removed every article of clothing he wore, including his underwear, and folded them into a neat pile, which he carefully placed on the sand well above the high-water mark the evening tide had left behind, where the first person to stand at the top of the bluff in the morning was sure to see them. He took the vial of pills that he'd acquired that morning at the pharmacy and emptied them into his hand, sticking the plastic container with the clothes. Nine thousand milligrams of Elavil, he thought. Taken all at once it would knock a person into unconsciousness within three to five minutes. The last thing he did was put the photograph of his wife near the top of the pile, weighed down by the edge of his shoe. He thought to himself, you did much for me while you were alive. Do this one thing more.

He raised his head and looked out at the immense

expanse of black ocean before him. The stars dotted the sky above, as if it were their responsibility to mark the line of demarcation between the waves and the heavens.

It is, he told himself, a nice enough night to die.

Then, naked as the morning that was only hours away, he walked down slowly toward the fury of waves.

Part Two

THE MAN WHO NEVER WAS

21

Two weeks after the night he died, Ricky sat on the edge of a lumpy bed that creaked whenever he shifted position, listening to the sound of distant traffic filter through the thin walls of the motel room. It mingled freely with the noise of a television set in an adjacent room tuned too loudly to a ball game. Ricky concentrated on the sound for a moment and guessed that the Red Sox were at Fenway, and the season was closing down which meant that they would be close, but not close enough. For a moment, he considered turning on the set in the corner of his room, but decided against it. They will lose, he told himself, and he did not want to experience any more loss, even the transitory one provided by the eternally frustrated baseball team. Instead, he turned to the window, staring out into the evening. He had not drawn the shades, and could see headlights slicing down the nearby interstate highway. There was a red neon sign by the driveway to the motel, which informed drivers that nightly, weekly, and monthly rates were available, as were kitchenettes such as the one he occupied, although why anyone would want to stay in that location for more than a single night eluded Ricky. Anyone except himself, he thought ruefully.

He rose from his seat and went into the small bathroom. He inspected his appearance in the mirror above the sink. The black dye that had marred his light hair was fading quickly, and Ricky was beginning to regain his normal appearance. He thought this slightly ironic because he knew that even if he once again looked as the man he once was, he would never actually be that person.

For two weeks, he had barely left the confines of the motel room. At first he'd been in a sort of self-induced shock, like a junkie undergoing a forced withdrawal, shivering, sweating, twisting in pain. Then, as this initial phase dissipated, it had been replaced by an overwhelming outrage, a blinding, white-hot fury that had caused Ricky to pace angrily around the tiny confines of the room, teeth gritted, his body almost contorted by rage. More than once he'd punched the walls in frustration. Once he'd picked up a glass in the bathroom and crushed it into shards in his hand, slicing himself in the process. He'd bent over the toilet, watching blood drip into the water in the bowl, half wishing that every drop within him would simply flow out. But the pain that gathered in the ravaged palm and fingers reminded him that he remained alive, and eventually led him into another stage, where all the fear, then all the rage finally subsided, like the winds settling down after a thunderstorm. This new stage seemed to Ricky to be cool, like the touch of polished metal on a winter morning.

In this stage, he began to plan.

His motel room was a shabby, decrepit place that catered to long-haul truckers, traveling salesmen, and the local teenagers needing a few private hours away from prying adult eyes. It was located on the outskirts of Durham, New Hampshire, a place that Ricky had selected at random because it was a college town, housing a fractious population thanks to the state university. He had thought the academic atmosphere ensured him access to the out-of-town newspapers he would need, and provide a transitory world that would help to hide him. This guess on his part, as best as he could tell, had so far proven true.

At the end of his second week of death, he'd begun to make sorties out into the world. On the first few occasions, he'd limited himself to the distance his feet would carry him. He didn't speak with anyone, avoided eye contact, stuck to abandoned streets and quiet neighborhoods, almost as if he half expected to be recognized, or worse, to hear the mocking tones of Virgil or Merlin float over his shoulder from behind his back. But his anonymity remained intact, and confidence grew within him. He'd rapidly expanded his horizon, finding a bus line and riding it throughout the small city, getting off at random locations, exploring the world he'd entered.

On one of these trips, he'd discovered a secondhand clothing store, which had provided him with an oddly well-fitted, cheap, and utilitarian blue blazer and some worn slacks and button-down shirts. He'd found a used leather satchel at a nearby consignment shop. He put away his eye-glasses in favor of contact lenses, purchased at a chain eyewear outlet. These few items, worn with a tie, gave him the appearance of someone on the edge of academia, respectable, but not important. He thought he blended in nicely, and he welcomed his invisibility.

On the kitchenette table to his side in the small room were copies of the *Cape Cod Times* and the *New York Times* for the days immediately following his death. The paper on the Cape had stripped the story across the bottom of their front page, with the headline: PROMINENT PHYSICIAN AN APPARENT SUICIDE; LANDMARK FARMHOUSE DESTROYED IN BLAZE. The reporter had managed to acquire most of the details that Ricky had provided, from the gasoline purchased that morning in newly acquired containers spread throughout the home, to the suicide note and the contributions to charities. He'd also managed to discover that there had been recent 'allegations of impropriety' against Ricky, although the reporter neglected to convey the substance of the concoction invented by Rumplestiltskin and carried out so dramatically by Virgil. The article also mentioned his wife's death three years earlier and suggested that Ricky had recently undergone 'financial reversals' that also might have contributed to his entering a suicidal frame of mind. It was, Ricky thought, an excellent piece of writing, well researched and filled with persuasive details, just as he'd hoped. The *New York Times's* obituary, which appeared a day later, had been discouragingly brief, with only a suggestion or two for the reasons behind his death. He had stared at it with a sense of irritation: a little angry and put out that the entirety of his life's accomplishments seemed to be so successfully wrapped up in four paragraphs of clipped and opaque journalese. He thought that he had given more to the world, but then understood that perhaps he hadn't, which made him pause for a moment or two. The obituary also pointed out that no memorial service was planned, which, Ricky realized, was a much more important consideration. He suspected that the lack of a service honoring his life reflected Rumplestiltskin and Virgil's work with the sexual misconduct allegation. None of his colleagues in Manhattan wanted to taint themselves with attendance at some event that memorialized Ricky's work and persona when so much of that had been abruptly called into question. He guessed that there were a great number of fellow analysts in the city who saw the news of his death in the paper and thought that it was exquisite proof of the truth to Rumplestiltskin's creation and at the same time was a fortunate thing, for the profession was spared a moment of ugliness when the allegations had surfaced in the *New York Times*, as they inevitably would have. This thought created in Ricky a modest fury with the membership of his own profession, and for a moment or two he insisted to himself that he was well to be done with it.

He wondered whether up to the first day of his

vacation he had been equally as blind.

Both newspaper stories stated that his death was apparently by drowning, and that Coast Guard units were searching Cape waters for Ricky's body. The *Cape Cod Times*, though, to Ricky's relief, quoted the local commander saying that body recovery was extremely unlikely, given the strong tides in the area of Hawthorne Beach.

When he reflected upon it, Ricky thought it was as good a death as he could come up with, on such short notice.

He hoped that all the clues of his own suicide had been collected, from the prescription for the overdose he'd appeared to have taken before walking into the waves, to his unforgettable and uncharacteristic rudeness to the teenager in the marine supply store. Enough, he told himself, to satisfy the local police, even without a body to autopsy. Enough, too, he hoped, to convince Rumplestiltskin that his plan for Ricky had been successful.

The oddity of reading about one's own suicide created a turmoil within him that he was having trouble sorting through. The toil of the stress of his last fifteen days of life, from the moment Rumplestiltskin entered his life to the moment he'd walked down to the edge of the water, carefully leaving footprints in the newly scoured sand, had put Ricky through something that he thought no psychiatric text ever contemplated.

Fear, elation, confusion, relief — all sorts of contradictory emotions — had flooded him, almost from the first step, when, water licking at his toes, he'd thrown the handful of pills into the ocean, then turned and walked through the wash a hundred yards, distant enough so that the new set of footprints when he emerged from the cold water around his ankles would not be noticed by the police or anyone else inspecting the scene of his disappearance.

The hours that had followed seemed to Ricky, alone in the kitchenette, to be the stuff of memory nightmare, like those details of a dream that stick with one after waking, giving a sense of unsettled uneasiness to each daytime step. Ricky could see himself dressing on the bluff in the extra set of clothes, pulling on the running shoes in a frantic hurry to escape the beach without being spotted. He'd strapped the crutches to the backpack, then hefted it onto his shoulders. It was a six-mile run to the parking lot of the Lobster Shanty, and he'd known that he had to get there before dawn and before anyone else taking the six A.M. express to Boston arrived.

Ricky could still feel the sensation of wind burning in his lungs as he'd raced the distance. The world around was still night and filled with black air, and as his feet had pounded against the roadway, he'd thought that it was like running through what he imagined a coal mine to be like. A single set of eyes marking his presence might have destroyed the slender chance at life that he was seizing, and he had run with all that urgency driven into every step taken down the black macadam street.

The lot had been empty when he arrived, and he'd drifted into the deep shadows by the corner of the restaurant. It was there that he'd unstrapped the crutches from the backpack and slung them on his arms. Within a few moments, he'd heard a distant sound of sirens blaring. He took a small satisfaction in how long it had taken someone to notice his home burning. A few moments later, some cars began to drop people in the lot, to wait for the bus. It was a mingled group, mostly young people heading back to Boston jobs and a couple of middle-aged business types, who seemed put out by the need to ride the bus, despite the convenient quality it had. Ricky had hung back, to the rear, thinking that he was the only one of the people waiting on this damp, cool Cape morning bathed in the sweat of fear and exertion. When the bus arrived two minutes late, Ricky had crutched out into line to board. Two young men stood aside, letting him struggle up the steps, where he had handed the driver his ticket purchased the day before. Then he had sat in the back, thinking that even if Virgil or Merlin or anyone assigned by Rumplestiltskin to probe the suicide and who might have doubted the truth of his death thought to question any bus driver or passenger on that early morning trip, what they would remember was a man with dark hair and crutches, and not known that he had run to the waiting area.

There had been an hour delay before the bus to Durham. In that time he'd walked two blocks away from the South Street bus terminal, until he'd found a Dumpster outside an office building. He'd thrown the crutches into the Dumpster. Then he had returned to the station and boarded another bus.

Durham, he thought, had one other advantage: He had never been there before, knew no one who'd ever lived there, and had absolutely no connection with the city whatsoever. What he did like were the New Hampshire license plates, with the state motto: Live Free or Die. This, he thought, was an appropriate sentiment for himself.

He wondered: Did I escape?

He thought so, but he wasn't yet sure.

Ricky went to the window and again stared out into a darkness that was unfamiliar. There is much to do, he told himself. Still searching the nighttime beyond the motel room, Ricky could just make out his own reflection in the glass. Dr. Frederick Starks no longer exists, he told himself. Someone else does. He breathed in deeply, and understood that his first priority was to create a new identity for himself. Once that was accomplished, then he could find a more permanent home for the upcoming winter. He knew he would need a job to supplement the money he had left. He needed to cement his anonymity and reinforce his disappearance.

Ricky stared over at the table. He had kept the death certificate for Rumplestiltskin's mother, the police report for the murder of her onetime lover, and the copy of the file from his months in the clinic at Columbia Presbyterian, where the woman had come to him for help and he'd failed to deliver it. He thought to himself that he had paid a large price for a single act of neglect.

That payment was made, and he couldn't go back.

But, Ricky thought, his heart filled with a cold iron, now I, too, have a debt to collect.

I will find him, he insisted to himself. And then I will do to him what he did to me.

Ricky stood and walked over to the wall, where he flicked the switch for the lights, dropping the room into darkness. An occasional sweep of headlights from outside sliced across the walls. He lay down on the bed, which creaked in an unfriendly fashion beneath him.

Once, he reminded himself, I studied hard to learn to save lives.

Now I must educate myself in how to take one.

* * *

Ricky surprised himself with the sense of organization that he was able to impose on his thoughts and feelings. Psychoanalysis, the profession that he'd just departed, is perhaps the most creative of all the disciplines of medicine, precisely because of the changeable nature of the human personality. While there are recognizable diseases and established courses of treatment within the realm of therapy, ultimately they are all individualized, because no two sadnesses are precisely alike. Ricky had spent years learning and perfecting the flexibility of the therapist, understanding that any given patient could walk through his door on any given day with something the same, or something utterly different, and that he had to be prepared at all times for the wildest swings in mood and sense. The problem, he thought to himself, was how to find the strengths of the capabilities that he'd developed in his years behind the couch, and translate them into the singleness of purpose that would recover his life for him.

He would not allow himself to fantasize that he could ever go back to who he was. No daydream of hope that he could return to his home in New York and take up again the routine of his life. That wasn't the point, he understood. The point was to make the man who'd ruined his life pay for his fun.

Once that debt was paid, Ricky realized, then he would be free to become whatever he wanted. Until the specter of Rumplestiltskin was removed from his life, Ricky would never have a moment's peace, or a second's freedom.

Of this, he was unequivocally certain.

Nor was he sure, yet, that Rumplestiltskin was convinced that Ricky had killed himself. The possibility existed, Ricky thought, that he'd only bought some time for himself, for whatever innocent relative had been targeted. It was the most intriguing of situations, he knew. Rumplestiltskin was a killer. Now Ricky needed to be able to outplay the man at his own game.

He knew this: He had to become someone new and someone utterly different from the man he once was.

He had to invent this new persona without creating any telltale sign that the man once known as Dr. Frederick Starks still existed. His own past was cut off for him. He did not know where Rumplestiltskin might have put a trap, but he knew one was there, waiting for the slightest sign that he wasn't floating somewhere in the waters off Cape Cod.

He knew he needed a new name, an invented history, a believable life.

In this country, Ricky realized, what we are first and foremost are numbers. Social Security numbers. Bank account and credit card numbers. Tax identification numbers. Driver's license numbers. Telephone numbers and home addresses. Creating these was the first order of business, Ricky thought. And then he needed to find a job, a home, he needed to create a world around him that was credible and yet totally anonymous. He needed to be the smallest and most insignificant of someones, and then he could start to build the education that he needed to track down and execute the man who'd forced him to murder himself.

Creating the history and the personality of his new self didn't worry him. He was, after all, an expert in the connection between actual events and the impressions these made on the self. Of greater concern was precisely how to create the numbers that would make the new Ricky believable.

His first sortie out on this task was a failure. He went to the library at the University of New Hampshire, only to discover that he needed a college identification card to get past the security at the door. For a moment, he looked longingly at the students wandering through the stacks of books. There was, however, a second library, significantly smaller, located on Jones Street. It was a part of the county library system, and, while lacking the volume and the cavernous quiet of the university, still had what Ricky thought he would need, which was books and information. It also had a secondary advantage: Entrance was open. Anyone could walk in, read any newspaper, magazine, or book in any one of the large leather chairs interspersed throughout the low-slung, two-story brick building. To check out a book would require a card, however. The library also had another advantage: Along one wall was a long table with four different computers set up. There was a printed list of rules for operating the computers, which started with the first-come, first-available, rule. Then operating instructions.

Ricky eyed the computers, and thought to himself that perhaps they might be of assistance to him. Unsure where to start, wearing a sort of antique attitude about modern devices, Ricky, the onetime man of talk, wandered into the stacks of books, searching for a section on computers. This did not take more than a few minutes to uncover. He tilted his head slightly, to be able to read the book titles along their spines, and within moments spotted one entitled: *Getting Started in Home Computing — A Guide for the Uninitiated and Afraid*.

He dumped himself into a leather armchair and started reading. The prose in the book was irritating and cloying, directed toward true idiots, he thought. But it was filled with information, and, had Ricky been a little more astute, he would have understood that the childish word formations were designed for people such as himself, because the average American eleven-year-old already knew everything contained within the pages.

After reading for an hour, Ricky approached the rows of computers. It was midmorning, midweek, late in the summer, and the library was almost empty. He had the area to himself. He clicked on one of the machines, and drew himself up to it. On the wall, as he'd noted, were instructions, and he skipped down to the segment where it explained how to access the Internet. He followed the directions and the computer screen leapt to life in front of him. He continued clicking buttons and typing in instructions and within a few more moments had jumped full-bore into the electronic world. He opened up a search engine, as the guidebook had told him to, and typed in the phrase: *False Identity*.

Less than ten seconds later, the computer told him

there were more than 100,000 entries under that category, and Ricky started to read from the beginning.

By the end of the day, Ricky had learned that the business of creating new identities was a thriving one. There were dozens of companies spread throughout the world that would provide him with virtually every sort of false documentation, all of which was sold under the disclaimer FOR NOVELTY PURPOSES ONLY. He thought there was something transparently criminal in a French business that offered to sell a California driver's license. But while transparent, it was also not against the law.

He made lists of places and documents, putting together a fictional portfolio. He knew what he needed, but obtaining it was a bit of a problem.

He realized swiftly that people seeking fake identities already were someone.

He was not.

He still had a pocket filled with cash, and locations where he could spend it. The problem was, they all existed in the electronic world. The cash he had was useless. They wanted credit card numbers. He had none. They wanted an E-mail address. He had none. They wanted a home to deliver the material to. He had none.

Ricky refined his computer search and started reading about identity theft. He discovered that it was a thriving criminal enterprise in the United States. He read horror story after horror story about people who awakened one day to find their lives in turmoil because someone somewhere with little conscience was running up debts in their name.

It wasn't a difficult leap for Ricky to recall how his own bank and brokerage accounts had been eviscerated, and he suspected that Rumplestiltskin had accomplished all this with remarkable ease simply by acquiring a few of Ricky's numbers. It helped explain why the box containing his old tax returns was missing when he went to search for it. It wasn't particularly difficult to be someone else in the electronic world. He promised himself that whoever he managed to become, he would never again idly toss into the trash a preapproved credit card application he received unsolicited in the mail.

Ricky pushed himself away from the computer and walked outside the library. The sun was shining brightly, and the air was still filled with the heat of summer. He continued walking almost aimlessly, until he found himself in a residential area filled with modest two-story wood-frame houses and small yards often littered with bright plastic children's toys. He could hear some young voices coming from a backyard, out of sight. A dog of undetermined breed looked up from where he rested on one small lawn, restrained by a rope tied at one end to his collar and the other to a thick oak tree. The dog wagged his tail vigorously at Ricky's appearance, as if inviting him to come over and scratch its ears. Ricky looked around, at tree-lined streets, where the shadows thrown by leafy branches created dark spots on the sidewalk. A slight breeze ruffled through the canopy of green, making the streaks and splotches of darkness on the sidewalks shift position and shape, before returning to rest. He took a few more strides down the street and in the front window of one house, he saw a small, hand-lettered sign: ROOM TO RENT. INQUIRE WITHIN.

Ricky began to step forward. That's what I need, he said to himself.

Then, as abruptly, he stopped.

I have no name. No history. No references.

He made a mental note of the location of the house, and walked on, thinking to himself: I need to be someone. I need to be someone who can't be traced. Someone alone, but someone real.

A dead person can come back to life. But that creates a question, a small rend in the fabric, that can be uncovered. An invented person can suddenly rise out of imagination, but that, too, creates questions.

Ricky's problem was different from the criminals, the men seeking to run away from alimony payments, the ex-cult members afraid they were being followed, the women hiding from abusive husbands.

He needed to become someone who was both dead and alive.

Ricky thought about this contradiction, then smiled. He leaned his head back, facing into the bright sun.

He knew exactly what to do.

* * *

It did not take Ricky long to find a Salvation Army clothing store. It was located in a small, undistinguished shopping mall on the main bus route, a place of pavement, low-slung, square buildings, and bleached and peeling paint, not exactly decrepit and not precisely run-down, but a place that showed the fraying of neglect in trash cans that hadn't been emptied and cracks in the asphalt parking lot. The Salvation Army store was painted a flat, reflective white, so that it glowed in the afternoon sun. Inside, it was similar to a small warehouse, with electrical appliances like toasters and waffle irons for sale on one wall, and rows of donated clothing hanging from racks occupying the center of the store. There were a few teenagers pawing through the racks, searching for baggy, fatigue pants and other bland articles, and Ricky sidled in behind them, inspecting the same piles of clothes. It seemed to him upon first glance that no one ever donated anything to the Salvation Army that wasn't chocolate brown or black, which fit his imagination.

He quickly found what he was seeking, which was a long, ripped wool winter overcoat that reached to his ankles, a threadbare sweater, and pants two sizes too large for him. Everything was cheap, but he selected the cheapest of the offering. Also the most damaged and the most inappropriate for the still-hot last of the summer weather that gripped New England.

The cashier was an elderly volunteer, who wore thick glasses and an incongruously red sport shirt that stood out in the bleak and brown world of donated clothing. The man lifted the overcoat to his nose and sniffed.

'You sure you want this one, fella?'

'That's the one,' Ricky replied.

'Smells like it's been somewhere nasty,' the man continued. 'Sometimes we get stuff in here, it makes it to the racks, but really ought not to. There's much nicer stuff, you look a little harder. This one kinda stinks and somebody should have repaired that rip in the side before putting it out for sale.'

Ricky shook his head. 'It's exactly what I need,' he said.

The man shrugged, adjusting his glasses, peering down at the tag. 'Well, I ain't even gonna charge you the ten bucks they want for that. Say, how about three? That seems more fair. That okay?'

'You're most generous,' Ricky said.

'What you want this junk for, anyway?' the man asked, not unfriendly in his curiosity.

'It's for a theater production,' Ricky lied.

The elderly clerk nodded his head. 'Well, I hope it isn't for the star of the show, because they take one whiff of that coat, they're gonna go looking for a new prop master.' The man wheezily laughed at his joke, making small breathy sounds that sounded more labored than humored. Ricky joined in with his own false laugh.

'Well, the director said to get something ratty, so I guess it'll be on him,' he said. 'I'm just the gofer. Community theater, you know. No big budget . . . '

'You want a bag?'

Ricky nodded, and exited the Salvation Army store with the purchases under his arm. He spotted a bus pulling up to the pickup spot on the edge of the mall, and he hurried to catch it. The exertion caused him to break a sweat, and once he slapped himself down in the backseat of the bus, he reached inside and took the old sweater and dabbed at the moisture on his forehead and under his arms, wiping himself dry with the article of clothing.

Before he reached his motel room that evening, Ricky took all the purchases to a small park, where he took time to drag each one in some dirt by a stand of trees.

In the morning, he packed the new old articles of clothing back in a brown paper bag. Everything else, the few documents he had about Rumplestiltskin, the newspapers, the other items of clothing that he'd acquired, went into the backpack. He settled his bill with the clerk at the motel, telling the man he would likely be back in a few days, information that didn't make the clerk even glance up from the sports section of the newspaper that occupied him with a distinct intensity.

There was a midmorning Trailways bus to Boston, which Ricky now felt some familiarity with. As always, he sat scrunched into a seat in the back, avoiding eye contact with the small crowd of fellow passengers, maintaining his solitude and anonymity with each step. He made sure he was the last to step off the bus in Boston. He coughed when he inhaled the mingled exhaust and heat that seemed to hang above the sidewalk. But the inside of the bus terminal was air-conditioned, although even the air inside seemed strangely grimy. There were rows of brightly colored orange and yellow plastic seats bolted to the linoleum floor, many of which sported scars and markings deposited by bored folks who had hours to kill waiting for their bus to arrive or depart. There was a noticeable smell of fired food, and along one side of the terminal there was a fast-food hamburger outlet side by side with a doughnut shop. A newspaper kiosk sold stacks of the day's papers and newsmagazines along with the more main-stream of the pseudo-pornography available. Ricky wondered just how many people in the bus station were likely to buy copies of *U.S. News & World Report* and *Hustler* at the same time.

Ricky took up a seat as close to opposite the men's room as he could manage, watching for a lull in the traffic heading in. Within some twenty minutes, he was persuaded that the bathroom had emptied out, especially after a Boston policeman wearing a sweat-stained blue shirt had walked in and then emerged five minutes later, complaining to his clearly amused partner loudly about the nasty effect of a recently ingested sausage sandwich. Ricky darted in as the two policemen walked off, their black brogans clicking against the dirty floor of the station.

Moving swiftly, Ricky closed himself into a toilet stall, and stripped off the reasonable clothing he had been wearing, replacing it with the items purchased at the Salvation Army. He wrinkled his nose at the difficult combination of sweat and musk that greeted his nose as he slid into the overcoat. He packed his clothes into his backpack, along with everything else he had, including all his cash, with the exception of a hundred dollars in twenties, which he slid into a tear in the overcoat, and worked down into fabric, so that it was if not totally safe, at least secure. He had a little bit of change, which he stuffed into his pants pocket. Emerging from the stall, he stared at himself in a mirror above the sink. He had not shaved in a couple of days, and that helped, he thought.

A bank of blue metal storage lockers lined one wall of the terminal. He stuffed his backpack into a locker, although he kept the paper bag that he'd used to carry the old clothes in. He put two quarters into the lock, and turned the key. Closing away even the few items that he had made him hesitate. For a moment, he thought that finally, right at that minute, he was more adrift than he'd ever been. Now, save the small key that he held in his hand to locker number 569, there was nothing that linked him to anything. He had no identification. No connection to anyone.

Ricky breathed in hard, and pocketed the key.

He walked away fast from the bus station, pausing only once when he believed no one was watching, to scoop some dirt from the sidewalk and rub it into his hair and face.

By the time he'd walked two blocks, sweat had begun to rise beneath his arms and on his forehead, and he wiped it away with the sleeve of the overcoat.

Before he'd reached the third block, he thought: Now I look to be what I am. Homeless.

22

For two days Ricky walked the streets, a foreigner to every world.

His outward appearance was of a homeless man, someone clearly alcoholic, drug-addled, or schizophrenic, or even all three combined, although if someone had looked carefully into his eyes, they would have seen a distinct purpose, which is an unusual quality for the down-and-out. Inwardly, Ricky found himself eyeing people on the street, half fantasizing who they were, and what they did, almost envious of the simple pleasure that identity gave one. A woman bustling ahead, gray-haired, carrying shopping packages emblazoned with Newbury Street boutiques, spoke one story to Ricky, while the teenager wearing cut-off jeans and hefting a backpack, a Red Sox cap tilted on his head, said another. He spotted businessmen and taxi drivers, appliance deliverymen and computer technicians. There were stockbrokers and physicians and repairmen and a man hawking newspapers from a kiosk on one corner. Everyone, from the most destitute and abandoned, mumbling, voice-hearing madwoman to the Armani-wearing developer sliding into the backseat of a limousine, had an identity defined by what they were. Ricky had none.

There was both luxury and fear in what he was, he realized. Belonging nowhere, it was almost as if he were invisible. While there was a momentary relief, knowing that he was hidden from the man who had so successfully destroyed who he once was, he understood this was elusive. His being was inextricably wrapped up with the man he knew only as Rumplestiltskin, but who once had been a child of a woman named Claire Tyson, whom he had failed at her moment of need, and now was alone, because of that failure.

His first night was spent alone beneath the curved brick of a Charles River bridge. He wrapped himself in his overcoat, still sweating profusely with the leftover heat from the day, and thrust himself up against a wall, struggling to steal a few hours away from the night, awakening shortly after dawn with a crick in his neck, every muscle in his back and legs shouting outrage and insult. He rose, stretching carefully, trying to remember the last occasion he'd slept outdoors, and thinking it was not since his childhood. The stiffness in his joints told him that there was little to recommend it. He imagined his appearance, and thought that not even the most dedicated method actor would adopt his approach.

There was a mist rising from the Charles, gray banks of vaporous fog that hung over the edges of the slick water. Ricky emerged from the underpass, and stepped up to the bike path that mirrors the bank of the river. He stood, thinking that the water had the appearance of an old-fashioned black typewriter ribbon, satin in look, winding through the city. He stared, telling himself that the sun would have to rise much higher before the water would turn blue, and reflect the stately buildings that approached the sides. In the early morning, the river had an almost hypnotic effect upon him, and for an instant or two, he simply stood stock-still, inspecting the sight in front of him.

His reverie was interrupted by the rhythmic sound of feet slapping against the macadam of the bike path. Ricky turned to see two men running side by side, approaching fast. They wore shiny athletic shorts and the latest in running shoes. Ricky guessed they were both close in age to himself.

One of the men gestured wildly with his arm toward Ricky.

'Step aside!' the man yelled.

Ricky stepped back sharply, and the two men swept past him.

'Out of the way, fella,' one of the two said briskly, twisting so that he wouldn't make physical contact with Ricky.

'Gotta move,' the other man said. 'Christ!'

Still within earshot, Ricky heard one of the joggers say, 'Fucking lowlife. Get a job, huh?'

The companion laughed and said something, but Ricky couldn't make out the words. He took a step or two after the men, filled with a sudden anger. 'Hey!' he yelled. 'Stop!'

They did not. One man glanced back, over his shoulder, and then they accelerated. Ricky stepped a pace or two after them. 'I'm not . . . ' he started. 'I'm not what you think . . . '

But then he realized he might as well have been.

Ricky turned back toward the river. In that second, he understood, he was closer to being what he appeared than he was to what he had been. He took a deep breath and recognized that he was in the most precarious of psychological positions. He had killed who he was in order to escape the man who set out to ruin him. If he went much longer being nobody, he would get swallowed by precisely that anonymity.

Thinking he was in as much danger in those minutes as he had been when Rumplestiltskin was breathing down the back of his every action, Ricky moved forward, determined to answer the first and primary question.

* * *

He spent the day, going from shelter to shelter, throughout the city, searching.

It was a journey through the world of the

disadvantaged: an early morning breakfast of runny eggs and cold toast served in a backroom kitchen at a Catholic church in Dorchester, an hour spent outside a store-front temporary work broker on a nearby street, milling with men looking for a day's work raking leaves or emptying trash bins. He went from there to a state-operated shelter in Charlestown, where a man behind a desk insisted that Ricky couldn't enter without a document from an agency, which Ricky thought was as crazy an insistence as those delusions the truly mentally ill suffered from. He stomped angrily and went back out to the street, where a pair of prostitutes working the lunchtime crowd laughed at him when he tried to ask for directions. He continued to pound the pavement, passing alleys and abandoned buildings, occasionally muttering to himself whenever anyone came too close to him, language being the rough edge of madness, and along with his growing fetid smell, a pretty successful armor against contact with anyone other than the disenfranchised. His muscles stiffened and his feet grew sore, but he continued looking. Once a policeman eyed him cautiously, at one corner, took a step toward him, and then, obviously, thought better of it, and walked on past.

It was deep in the afternoon, with the sun still pounding down, making wavy lines of heat rise from the city streets, that Ricky spotted a possibility.

The man was rooting through a garbage can on the edge of a park, not far from the river. He was about Ricky's height and weight, with thinning streaks of dirty brown hair. He wore a knit cap, tattered shorts, but an ankle-length wool overcoat that almost reached down to one brown shoe and one black, one a pull-on loafer, the other a workman's boot. The man was muttering to himself, intent on the contents of the garbage can. Ricky moved close enough to see the lesions on the man's face and the backs of his hands. As the man worked, he coughed repeatedly, remaining unaware of Ricky's presence. There was a park bench ten yards away, and Ricky slumped into it. Someone had left a part of the day's paper behind on the seat, and Ricky grabbed this and pretended to read while he devoted himself to observing the man. After a second or two, he saw the man pull a discarded soda can from the garbage and toss it into an old steel shopping cart, but not the type that one pushes, instead, the type one pulls. The cart was almost filled with empty cans.

Ricky eyed the man as closely as he could, saying to himself: You were the doctor just weeks ago. Make your diagnosis.

The man seemed suddenly enraged when he pulled a can from the trash that had some problem, abruptly throwing it to the ground and kicking it into a nearby bush.

Bipolar, Ricky thought. And schizophrenic. Hears voices, has no medication, or at least, one that he is willing to take. Prone to sudden bursts of manic energy. Violent, too, probably, but more a threat to himself than others. The lesions could either be open sores from living on the street, but they could also be Kaposi's sarcoma. AIDS was a distinct possibility. So was tuberculosis or lung cancer, given the man's wracking cough. It could also be pneumonia, Ricky thought, although the season was wrong for it. Ricky thought the man wore equal cloths of life and death.

After a few minutes, the man determined that he'd taken everything of value from the trash, and headed to the next canister. Ricky remained seated, keeping the man in sight. After a few moments dedicated to assessing that trash, the man strode off, pulling his cart behind him. Ricky trailed after him.

It did not take long to reach a street in Charlestown that was filled with low-slung and grimy stores. It was a place that catered to the disadvantaged of all sorts. A discount furniture outlet that offered in large letters written on the windows layaways and easy credit, spelling the word E-Z. Two pawnshops, an appliance store, a clothing outlet that had mannequins in the windows all of which seemed to be missing an arm or a leg, as if crippled or scarred in some accident. Ricky watched as the man he was following headed straight to the middle of the block, to a faded yellow painted square building with a prominent sign on the front: AL'S DISCOUNT SODA AND LIQUORS. Beneath that was a second sign, in the same block print, nearly as large: REDEMPTION CENTER. This sign had an arrow pointing to the rear.

The man towing the cart filled with cans marched directly around the corner of the building. Ricky followed after.

At the back of the store was a half door, with a similar sign above the lintel: REDEEM HERE. There was a small doorbell button to the side, which the man rang. Ricky shrank back against the wall, concealing himself.

Within a few seconds a teenager appeared at the half door. The transaction itself took only a few minutes. The man handed in the collection of cans, the teenager counted them, and then peeled off a couple of bills from a wad he pulled from his pocket. The man took the money, reached into one of the large pockets of the overcoat, and pulled out a fat, old leather wallet, stuffed with papers. He put a couple of the bills into the wallet, and then handed one of them back to the teenager. The kid disappeared, then returned moments later with a bottle, which he handed to the man.

Ricky slunk down, sitting on the alley cement, waiting while the man walked past him. The bottle, which Ricky assumed was some cheap wine, had already disappeared in the folds of the overcoat. The man cast a single glance toward Ricky, but they made no eye contact, as Ricky hung his head. He breathed in hard for another few seconds, then rose, and continued to follow the man.

In Manhattan, Ricky had played the mouse to Virgil, Merlin, and Rumplestiltskin's cats. Now he was on the opposite side of the same equation. He hung back, then sped up, trying to keep the man in sight at all times, close enough to follow, distant enough to remain hidden. Armed now with the bottle concealed in his coat, the man marched ahead with purpose, like some military quick march with a destination in mind. His head pivoted about frequently, glancing in all directions, unmistakably afraid of being followed. Ricky thought that the man's paranoid behavior was well founded.

They covered dozens of city blocks, winding in and out of traffic, the neighborhood they traveled through growing seedier with every stride. The day's dwindling sun threw shadows across the roadways, and the peeling paint and decrepit storefronts seemed to mimic the appearance of both Ricky and his target.

He saw the man hesitate midblock, and as the man turned toward where Ricky was, Ricky dipped against a building, concealing himself. Out of the corner of his eye, he saw the man abruptly lurch down an alleyway, a narrow crevasse between two brick buildings. Ricky took a deep breath, then followed.

He came up to the entrance to the alleyway and cautiously peered around the edge. It was a spot that seemed to greet the night well in advance. It was already dark and closed in, the sort of confined space that never warmed in the winter, nor cooled in the summer. Ricky could just make out a collection of abandoned cardboard boxes and a green steel Dumpster at the far end. The alleyway abutted the back of another building, and Ricky guessed that it was a dead end.

A block away, he'd passed both a convenience store and a cheap liquor store. He turned, leaving his quarry, and headed in that direction. He slid one of his precious twenty-dollar bills from the lining of his coat, gripping it in his palm where it was immediately damp with sweat.

He went first to the liquor store. It was a small place, with advertised specials smeared in red paint on the front window. He stepped up and put his hand on the door to enter, only to find it locked. He looked up and saw a clerk sitting behind the register. He tried the door again, and it rattled. The clerk stared in his direction, then suddenly bent forward and spoke into a microphone. A tinny voice came out of a speaker near the door.

'Get the hell out of here, yah old fuck, unless yah got some money.'

Ricky nodded. 'I've got money,' he replied.

The clerk was a middle-aged paunchy man, probably close to his own age. Ricky saw, when he shifted position, that he wore a large pistol holstered on his belt.

'Yah got money? Sure. Let's see it.'

Ricky held the twenty-dollar bill up. The man eyed it from his spot behind the register.

'How'd you get that?' he said.

'I found it on the street,' Ricky answered.

The door buzzer went off, and Ricky pushed his way inside.

'Sure yah did,' the clerk said. 'All right, you got two minutes. Whatcha want?'

'Bottle of wine,' Ricky said.

The clerk reached behind himself to a shelf and picked out a bottle. It wasn't like any bottle of wine that Ricky had ever drunk before. It had a screw top and was labeled Silver Satin. It cost two dollars. Ricky nodded and handed over the twenty. The man put the bottle in a paper bag, opened the register, and removed a ten and two singles. He handed these to Ricky. 'Hey!' Ricky said. 'You owe me a couple more.'

Smiling nastily, placing a hand on the butt of his

revolver, the clerk replied, 'I think I gave you some credit the other day, old man. Just getting my previous kindness paid back.'

'You're lying,' Ricky said angrily. 'I've never been in here before.'

'You think we ought to really have an argument, you fucking bum?' The man clenched a fist and thrust it in Ricky's face. Ricky stepped back. He stared hard at the clerk, who laughed at him. 'I gave you some change. More'n you deserve, too. Now beat it. Get the fuck out of here, before I kick you out. And if you make me walk around this counter, then I'm gonna take my bottle back and the change back and I'm gonna kick your ass in the process. So what's it gonna be?'

Ricky moved slowly toward the door. He turned, trying to think of a proper rejoinder, only to have the clerk say, 'What? What is it? You got some problem?'

Ricky shook his head and exited, clutching the bottle, hearing the clerk laugh behind his back.

He walked down the block to the convenience store. He was greeted there with the same, 'You got some money?' demand. He showed the ten-dollar bill. Inside, he purchased a pack of the cheapest cigarettes he could find, a pair of Hostess Twinkies, a pair of Hostess Cup Cakes, and a small flashlight. The clerk in this store was a teenager, who threw the stuff into a plastic bag and said, 'Nice dinner,' sarcastically.

Ricky walked back onto the sidewalk. Night had swept the area. Wan light from the stores that remained open carved small squares of brightness from the darkness. Ricky crossed back to the alley entrance. He dipped as quietly as he could just inside, putting his back up against a brick wall, and sliding down to sit and wait, all the time thinking he'd had no idea before this night how easy it was in this world to be hated.

* * *

It seemed as if the darkness slowly enveloped him in the same way that the heat during the summer day did. It was thick, syrupy, a blackness that reached within him. Ricky allowed a couple of hours to pass. He was in a semidream state, his imagination filled with pictures of who he was once, the people who had come into his life to destroy it, and the scheme he had to build to regain it. He would have been comforted, sitting with his back against the brick in the darkened alleyway in a section of a city that he was unfamiliar with, if he could have pictured his late wife, or perhaps a forgotten friend, or maybe even a memory of his own childhood, some mental picture of a happy moment, a Christmas morning, or a graduation day or perhaps wearing his first tuxedo to a high school prom, or the rehearsal dinner on the eve of his wedding. But all these moments seemed to belong to some other existence, and some other person. He had never been much for reincarnation, but it was almost as if he had returned to earth as someone new. He could smell the growing fetid dank stench from his bum's overcoat and he held up his hand in the darkness and imagined that his fingernails were clogged with dirt. It used to be that the days his nails were filthy were happy days, because that meant he'd spent hours in the garden behind his house on the Cape. His stomach clenched and he could hear the whomping sound of the gasoline spread throughout the farmhouse catching fire. It was a memory in his ear that seemed to come from some other era, pulled from some distant past by an archaeologist.

Ricky looked up, and pictured Virgil and Merlin sitting in the alleyway across from him. He could make out their faces, envision each nuance and mannerism of the portly attorney and the statuesque young woman. A guide to Hell, that's what she told me, he thought. She'd been right, probably more right than she had any idea. He sensed the presence of the third member of the triumvirate, but Rumplestiltskin was still a collection of shadows, blending with the night that flooded the alleyway like a steadily rising tide.

His legs had stiffened. He didn't know how many miles he'd walked since his arrival in Boston. His stomach was empty, and he opened the package of cupcakes and ate them both in two or three gulps. The chocolate hit him like a low-rent amphetamine, giving him some energy. Ricky pushed himself to his feet and turned toward the pit of the alleyway.

He could hear a faint sound and he craned toward it, before recognizing it for what it was: a voice singing softly and out of key.

Ricky moved cautiously toward the noise. To his side he heard some animal, he guessed a rat, scuttling away with a scratching sound. He fingered the small flashlight in his hand, but tried to let his eyes adjust to the pitch-black in the alleyway. This was difficult, and he stumbled once or twice, his feet getting tangled in unrecognizable debris. He almost fell once, but kept his balance and continued moving forward.

He sensed he was almost on top of the man when the singing stopped.

There was a second or two of dark silence, and then he heard a question: 'Who's there?'

'Just me,' Ricky replied.

'Don't come any closer,' came the reply. 'I'll hurt you. Kill you, maybe. I've got a knife.'

The words were slurred with the looseness that drink provides. Ricky had half hoped the man would have passed out, but instead, he was still reasonably alert. But not too mobile, Ricky noted, for there had been no sounds of scrambling out of the way or trying to hide. He did not believe the man actually had a weapon, but he wasn't completely certain. He remained stock-still.

'This is my alley,' the man continued. 'Get out.'

'Now it's my alley, too,' Ricky said. Ricky took a deep

breath and launched himself into the realm he'd known he would have to find in order to communicate with the man. It was like diving into a pool of dark water, unsure what lay just beneath the surface. Welcome madness, Ricky said, trying to summon up all the education that he'd gained in his prior life and existence. Create delusion. Establish doubt. Feed paranoia. 'He told me we're supposed to speak together. That's what he told me. 'Find the man in the alleyway and ask him his name.' '

The man hesitated. 'Who told you?'

'Who do you think?' Ricky answered. 'He did. He speaks to me and tells me who to seek out, and this I need to do because he's told me to, and so I did, and here I am.' He rattled this near-gibberish out swiftly.

'Who speaks to you?' The questions came out of the dark with a fervent quality that warred with the drink that clouded the man's already crisscrossed mind.

'I'm not allowed to say his name, not out loud or where someone might hear me, shhhh! But he says that you will know why I've come, if you're the right one, and I won't have to explain any further.'

The man seemed to hesitate, trying to sort through this nonsensical command.

'Me?' he asked.

Ricky nodded in the darkness. 'If you're the right one. Are you?'

'I don't know,' was the reply. Then, after a momentary pause, the addition, 'I thought so.'

Ricky moved swiftly to buttress the delusion. 'He gives me the names, you see, and I am supposed to seek them out and ask them the questions, because I need to find the right one. That's what I do, over and over, and that's what I have to do, and are you the right one? I need to know, you see. Otherwise this is all wasted.'

The man seemed to be trying to absorb all this.

'How do I know to trust you?' the man slurred.

Ricky immediately slipped the small flashlight out and held it underneath his chin, the way a child might when trying to spook his friends around a campfire. Ricky flashed the light up, illuminating his face, then instantly swung it over at the man, taking seconds to survey the surroundings. He saw the man was lying with his back up against the brick wall, the bottle of wine in his hand. There was some other debris, and a cardboard box to his side that Ricky guessed was home. He switched off the light.

'There,' Ricky said as forcefully as he could. 'Do you need more proof?'

The man shifted. 'I can't think straight,' he moaned. 'My head is hurting.'

For an instant, Ricky was tempted to simply reach down and take what it was that he needed. His hands twitched with the seduction of violence. He was alone in a deserted alley with the man, and he thought, the people who had put him in that location wouldn't have hesitated to use force in the slightest. It was only by the greatest sense of control that he was able to fight off the urge. He knew what he wanted, only he wanted the man to give it up. 'Tell me who you are!' Ricky half whispered, half shouted.

'I want to be alone,' the man pleaded. 'I didn't do anything. I don't want to be here anymore.'

'You aren't the right one,' Ricky said. 'I can tell. But I need to be sure. Tell me who you are.'

The man sobbed. 'What do you want?'

'Your name. I want your name.'

Ricky could hear tears forming behind every word the man spoke. 'I don't want to say,' he said. 'I'm scared. Do you mean to kill me?'

'No,' Ricky said. 'I will not harm you if you prove to me who you are.'

The man paused, as if considering this question. 'I have a wallet,' he said slowly.

'Give it here!' Ricky demanded sharply. 'It's the only way to be sure!'

The man scrambled and scratched, and reached inside his coat. In the darkness, his eyes barely adjusted, Ricky could see the man holding something out in front of him. Ricky grabbed it and thrust it into his own pocket.

The man started to cry then. Ricky softened his voice.

'You don't have to worry anymore,' Ricky said. 'I will leave you alone, now.'

'Please,' said the man. 'Just go away.'

Ricky reached down and removed the bottle of cheap wine that he'd purchased at the liquor store. He also grasped a twenty-dollar bill from the lining of his coat. He thrust these to the man. 'Here,' he said. 'Here is something because you weren't the right man, but that is no fault of your own, and he wants me to compensate you for bothering you. Is that fair?'

The man clutched the bottle. He didn't reply for a moment, but then seemed to nod. 'Who are you?' he asked Ricky again, with a mingling of fear and confusion still riding every word.

Ricky smiled inwardly and thought there are some advantages to a classical education. 'Noman is my name,' he said.

'Norman?'

'No. Noman. So, if anyone asks who came to visit you this night, you can say it was Noman.' Ricky presumed that the average cop on the beat would have about the same patience for the tale that Polyphemus's cyclops brothers did, and the fiction created centuries beforehand by another man adrift in a strange and dangerous world. 'Have a drink and go to sleep, and when you wake up, all will be exactly the same for you.'

The man whimpered. But then he took a long pull from the bottle of wine.

Ricky rose, and picked his way gingerly down the alleyway, thinking that he had not exactly stolen what he needed, nor had he purchased it. What he'd done was what was necessary, he told himself, and was well within the rules of the game. Rumplestiltskin, of course, didn't know that he was still playing. But he would, soon enough. Ricky moved steadily back through the darkness toward the weak light of the city street just ahead.

23

Ricky did not open the man's wallet until after he'd reached the bus station, a trip across the city that required him to change subways twice, and after he'd retrieved his clothes from the locker where he had stored them. In the men's room, he managed to get at least partially cleaned up, scrubbing some of the dirt and grime from his face and hands, and rubbing a paper towel soaked with lukewarm water and thick-smelling antibacterial soap in his armpits and across his neck. There was little he could do about the slick greasiness that matted his hair or the overall musty odor that only a long shower would repair. He dumped his filthy bum's clothes into the nearest wastebasket and climbed into the acceptable khakis and sport shirt that he'd kept in the backpack. He inspected his appearance in the mirror and thought that he'd crossed back over some invisible line, where now, once again, he appeared to all to be a participant in life, rather than an occupant of the nether regions. A couple of strokes with a cheap plastic comb aided his look, but Ricky thought that he still was located on some edge, or close to it, and far distant from the man he once was.

He exited the men's room and purchased a ticket for a bus back to Durham. He had nearly an hour's wait, so he bought himself a sandwich and a soda and repaired to a corner of the station that was empty. After looking around to make certain that no one was watching him, Ricky unwrapped the sandwich on his lap. Then he opened up the wallet, concealing it with the food.

The first thing he saw brought a smile to his face and a sense of relief flooded him: a tattered and faded, but legible, Social Security card.

The name had been typed: Richard S. Lively.

Ricky liked this. Lively was what, for the first time in weeks, he felt. He saw an additional good fortune; he wouldn't have to learn to accommodate a new first name, the common nickname of Richard and his own Frederick, being the same.

He put his head back, staring up into the fluorescent ceiling lights. Rebirth in a bus station, he thought. He supposed there were far worse places to reenter the world.

The wallet smelled of dried sweat, and Ricky quickly searched the contents. There was not much, but what there was, he realized, was something of a gold mine. In addition to the Social Security card, there was an expired Illinois driver's license, a library card from a suburban system outside of St. Louis, Missouri, and a Triple A auto service card from the same state. None of these was a photo ID, except for the driver's license, which Ricky noted, gave details such as hair, eye color, height and weight, next to a slightly out-of-focus picture of Richard Lively. There was also a hospital clinic identification card from a Chicago facility that was marked with a red asterisk in one corner. AIDS, Ricky thought. HIV positive. He'd been right about the sores on the man's face. All the various pieces of identification had different addresses listed. Ricky removed all these and thrust them into his pocket. There were also two yellowed and tattered newspaper clippings, which Ricky unfolded carefully and read. The first was an obituary for a seventy-three-year-old woman, the other was an article about workforce layoffs in an automobile parts manufacturing plant. The first, he guessed, was Richard Lively's mother, and the second was the job the man had had before launching into the world of alcohol that had delivered him to the street where Ricky had spotted him. Ricky had no idea what had made him travel from the Midwest to the East

Coast, but recognized this was a propitious shift for his purposes. The chances of someone making a connection to the man diminished sharply.

Ricky read through the two clippings swiftly, committing the details to memory. He noted that there was only one other family member listed among the woman's survivors, apparently a housewife in Albuquerque, New Mexico. A sister, Ricky thought, who'd given up on her brother many years ago. The mother had been a county librarian and onetime school principal, which was the modest claim on the world that had prompted the obituary. It said her husband had passed away some years earlier. The plant that had once employed Richard Lively had manufactured brake pads and fallen victim to a corporate decision to shift to a location in Guatemala, which made the same item for far less in wages. Ricky thought that created a not uncommon bitterness, and was more than enough reason to let drink take over one's life. How the man had acquired the disease, he couldn't tell. Needles, he suspected. He stuffed the clippings back inside the wallet, then he tossed it into a nearby wastebasket. He thought about the hospital identification card with its telltale red marking, then reached into his pocket, pulling it out. He bent it until it tore, then ripped it in half. He stuck this in the wrappings from his sandwich, and also stuffed it down to the bottom of the wastebasket.

I know enough, he thought.

The announcement for his bus came over the loudspeaker, spoken in nearly unintelligible tones by some clerk behind a glass partition. Ricky rose, swinging his backpack over his shoulder, and putting Dr. Starks deep within some hidden crevice inside himself, and took his first step forward as Richard Lively.

* * *

His life began to take shape rapidly.

Within a week, he had acquired two part-time jobs, the first manning a register at a local Dairy Mart for five hours a day in the evening, the second stocking shelves in a Stop and Shop grocery store for another five hours in the morning, a time frame which gave Ricky the afternoons for his other needs. Neither place had asked too many questions, although the manager of the food market pointedly asked whether Ricky was in a twelve-step program, to which he'd replied affirmatively. It turned out the manager was as well, and after giving Ricky a list of churches and civic centers and all their scheduled meetings, he'd handed Ricky the ubiquitous green apron and put him to work.

He used Richard Lively's Social Security number to open a bank checking account, depositing the remainder of his cash. Once that was accomplished, Ricky found that sorties into the world of bureaucracy were relatively easy. He'd been issued a replacement Social Security card by filling out a form, one that he signed himself. A clerk at the Department of Motor Vehicles hadn't even glanced at the picture on the Illinois license when Ricky turned it in and obtained a New Hampshire driver's license, this time with his own picture and signature, his own eye color, height, and weight. He also rented a post office box at a local Mailboxes Etc. location, which gave Ricky a viable address for his bank account statements and as much other correspondence as Ricky could produce rapidly. He welcomed catalogs. He joined a video rental club and the YMCA. Anything that provided another card in his new name. Another form and a check for five dollars got him a copy of Richard Lively's birth certificate, mailed by a thoughtful county clerk outside of Chicago.

He tried not to think about the real Richard Lively.

He thought it had not been a particularly difficult task to delude a drunken, sick, and deranged man out of his wallet and his identity. While he told himself that what he had done was better than beating it out of him, it was not much better.

Ricky shrugged off the feelings of guilt as he expanded his world. He promised himself that he would return Richard Lively's ID to him when he'd managed to truly extricate himself from Rumplestiltskin. He just didn't know how long that would take.

Ricky knew he had to move out of the motel kitchenette, so he walked back to the area not far from the public library, searching for the house with the ROOM FOR RENT sign. To his relief, it was still in the window of the modest, wood-frame home.

The house had a small side yard, shaded by a large oak tree. It was littered with brightly colored plastic children's toys. An energetic four-year-old boy was playing with a dump truck and a collection of army figures in the grass, while an elderly woman sat on a lawn chair a few feet away, occupied mostly with a copy of that day's newspaper, occasionally glancing at the child, who made engine and battle sounds as he played. Ricky saw that the child wore a hearing device in one ear.

The woman looked up and saw Ricky standing on the walkway.

'Hello,' he said. 'Is this your house?'

She nodded, folding the paper in her lap and glancing toward where the child was playing. 'It is indeed,' she said.

'I saw the sign. About the room,' he said.

She eyed him cautiously. 'We usually rent to students,' she replied.

'I'm sort of a student,' he said. 'That is, I hope to be working on some advanced degrees, but I'm a little slow because I have to work for a living, as well. Gets in the way,' he said, smiling.

The woman rose. 'What sort of advanced degree?' she asked.

'Criminology,' Ricky replied off the cuff. 'I should introduce myself. My name is Richard Lively. My friends call me Ricky. I'm not from around here, in fact, only recently arrived here. But I do need a place.'

She continued to look him over cautiously. 'No family? No roots?'

He shook his head.

'Have you been in prison?' she asked.

Ricky thought the true answer to this was yes. A prison designed by a man I never met but who hated me.

'No,' he said. 'But that's not an unreasonable question. I was abroad.'

'Where?'

'Mexico,' he lied.

'What were you doing in Mexico?'

He made things up rapidly. 'I had a cousin who went out to Los Angeles and got involved in the drug trade, and disappeared down there. I went down trying to find him. Six months of stone walls and lies, I'm afraid. But that's what got me interested in criminology.'

She shook her head. Her tone of voice displayed she had some large and immediate doubts about this abrupt outlandish tale. 'Sure,' she said. 'And what got you here to Durham?'

'I just wanted to get as far away from that world as possible,' Ricky said. 'I didn't exactly make a great many friends asking questions about my cousin. I figured it had to be someplace far away from that world, and the map suggested it was either New Hampshire or Maine, and so this was where I landed.'

'I don't know that I believe you,' the woman answered. 'It sounds like some sort of story. How do I know you're reliable? Have you got references?'

'Anyone can get a reference to say anything,' Ricky replied. 'It seems to me that you'd be a lot wiser to listen to my voice and look at my face and make up your own mind after a bit of conversation.'

This statement made the woman smile. 'A New Hampshire sort of attitude,' she said. 'I'll show you the room, but I'm still not certain.'

'Fair enough,' Ricky said.

The room was a converted attic area, with its own modest bathroom, just enough space for a bed, a desk, and an old overstuffed armchair. An empty bookcase and a chest of drawers were lined on one wall. It had a nice window enclosed by a girlishly frilly pink curtain, with a half-moon top that overlooked the yard and the quiet side street. The walls were decorated with travel posters advertising the Florida Keys and Vail, Colorado. A bikini-clad scuba diver and a skier kicking up a sheet of pristine snow. There was a small alcove off the room which contained a tiny refrigerator and a table with a hot plate. A shelf screwed into the wall contained some white, utilitarian crockery. Ricky stared at the efficient space and thought it had many of the same qualities as a monk's cell, which is more or less how he currently envisioned himself.

'You can't really cook for yourself,' the woman said. 'Just snacks and pizza, that sort of thing. We don't really offer kitchen privileges . . . '

'I usually eat out,' Ricky said. 'Not a big eater, anyway.'

The owner continued to eye him. 'How long would you be staying? We usually rent for the school year . . . '

'That would be fine,' he said. 'Do you want a lease?'

'No. A handshake is usually all we require. We pay utilities, except for the phone. There's a separate line up here. That's your business. The phone company will activate it when you want. No guests. No parties. No music blaring. No late nights — '

He smiled, and interrupted her, 'And you usually rent to students?'

She saw the contradiction. 'Well, serious students, when we can find them.'

'Are you here alone with your child?'

She shook her head with a small grin. 'There's a flattering question. He's my grandson. My daughter is at school. Divorced and getting her accountant's degree. I watch the boy while she's working or studying, which is just about all the time.'

Ricky nodded. 'I'm a pretty private guy,' he said, 'and I'm pretty quiet. I work a couple of jobs, which takes up a good deal of my time. And in my free time, I study.'

'You're old to be a student. Maybe a bit too old.'

'We're never too old to learn, are we?'

The woman smiled again. She continued to eye him cautiously.

'Are you dangerous, Mr. Lively? Or are you running away from something?'

Ricky considered his reply, before speaking. 'Stopped running, Mrs . . . '

'Williams. Janet. The boy is Evan and my daughter whom you haven't met is Andrea.'

'Well, this is where I'm stopping, Mrs. Williams. I'm not fleeing from a crime or an ex-wife and her lawyer, or a right-wing Christian cult, although you might allow your imagination to race ahead in one or all of those directions. And, as for being dangerous, well, if I was, why would I be running away?'

'That's a good point,' Mrs. Williams said. 'It's my house, you see. And we're two single women with a child . . . '

'Your concerns are well founded. I don't blame you for asking.'

'I don't know how much I believe of what you've said,' Mrs. Williams responded.

'Is believing all that important, Mrs. Williams? Would it make a difference if I told you I was some alien from a different planet sent here to investigate the lifestyles of the folks of Durham, New Hampshire, prior to our invasion of the world? Or if I said I was a Russian spy, or an Arab terrorist, just a step ahead of the FBI and would it be okay if I used the bathroom to concoct bombs? There are all sorts of tales one can weave, but ultimately all are irrelevant. The truth that you need to know is whether I will be quiet, keep to myself, pay my rent on time, and generally speaking, not bother you, your daughter, or your grandson. Isn't that really what is critical here?'

Mrs. Williams smiled. 'I think I like you, Mr. Lively. I don't know that I trust you all that much yet, and certainly don't believe you. But I like the way you put things, which means you've passed the first test. But how about a month's security and first month's rent and then we'll do things on a month-to-month basis, so that if one or the other of us feels uncomfortable, we can bring things to a quick conclusion?'

Ricky smiled and took the old woman's hand. 'In my experience,' he said, 'quick conclusions are elusive. And how would you define *uncomfortable*?'

The smile on the older woman's face broadened some, and she maintained her grip on Ricky's hand. 'I would define *uncomfortable* with the numerals nine, one, and one, punched on the telephone keypad and a subsequent series of any number of unpleasantly pointed questions from humorless men in blue uniforms. Is that clear?'

'Clear enough, Mrs. Williams,' Ricky said. 'I think we have an agreement.'

'I thought so,' Mrs. Williams replied.

* * *

Routine came as quickly to Ricky's life as the fall did to New Hampshire.

At the grocery store he was swiftly given a raise and additional new responsibilities, although the manager did ask him why he hadn't seen him in any meetings, and so Ricky went to several, rising once or twice in a church basement to address the room filled with alcoholics, concocting a typical tale of life ruined by drink that brought murmurs of understanding from the collected men and women and several heartfelt embraces afterward, that Ricky felt hypocritical accepting. He liked his job at the grocery store, and got along well, if not expansively, with the other workers there, sharing the occasional lunch break, joking, maintaining a friendliness that successfully masked his isolation. Inventory was something he seemed to have a knack for, which made him think that stocking shelves with foodstuffs was not all that dissimilar to what he'd done for patients. They, too, had had to have their shelves restored and refilled.

A more important coup came in mid-October, when he spotted an ad for part-time help on the janitorial staff at the university. He quit his cash register job at the Dairy Mart and started sweeping and mopping in the science labs for four hours a day. He approached this task with a singleness of purpose that impressed his supervisor. But, more critically, this provided Ricky with a uniform, a locker where he could change clothes, and a university identification card, which in turn, gave him access to the computer system. Between the local library and the computer banks, Ricky went about the task of creating a new world for himself.

He gave himself an electronic name: Odysseus.

This gave rise to an electronic mail address and access to all the Internet had to offer. He opened various accounts, using his Mailboxes Etc. post office box as a home address.

He then took a second step, to create an entirely new person. Someone who had never existed, but who had a claim on the world, in the form of a modest credit history, licenses, and the sort of past that is easily documented. Some of this was simple, such as obtaining false identification in a new name. He once again marveled at the literally thousands of companies on the Internet that would provide fake IDs 'for novelty purposes only.' He started ordering fake driver's licenses and college IDs. He was also able to obtain a diploma from the University of Iowa, class of 1970, and a birth certificate from a nonexistent hospital in Des Moines. He also got himself added to the alumni list at a defunct Catholic high school in that city. He invented a phony Social Security number for himself. Armed with this pile of new material, he went to a rival bank to where he had already established Richard Lively's account and opened another small checking account in a second name. This name he chose with some thought: Frederick Lazarus. His own first name coupled with the name of the man raised from the dead.

It was in the persona of Frederick Lazarus that Ricky began his search.

He had the simplest of ideas: Richard Lively would be real and would have a safe and secure existence. He would be home. Frederick Lazarus was a fiction. There would be no connection between the two characters. One man was a man who would breathe the anonymity of normalcy. The other was a creation and if anyone ever came asking about Frederick Lazarus, they would discover that he had no substance other than phony numbers and imaginary identity. He could be dangerous. He could be criminal. He could be a man of risks. But he would be a fiction ultimately designed with one single purpose.

To ferret out the man who had ruined Ricky's life and repay in kind.

24

Ricky let weeks slide into months, let the New Hampshire winter envelop him, disappearing into the cold and dark that hid him from everything that had happened. He let his life as Richard Lively grow daily, while at the same time he continued to add details to his secondary persona, Frederick Lazarus. Richard Lively went to college basketball games when he had an evening off, occasionally baby-sat for his landladies who had rapidly come to trust him, had an exemplary attendance record at work, and gained the respect of his coworkers at the grocery store and the university maintenance department by adopting a kidding, joking, almost devil-may-care personality, that seemed to not take much seriously except for diligent, hard work. When asked about his past, he either made up some modest tale, nothing ever so outrageous that it wouldn't be believed, or deflected the question with a question. Ricky, the onetime psychoanalyst, found himself to be expert at this, creating a situation where people often thought that he'd been talking about himself, but in reality was talking about them. He was a little surprised at how easily all the lying came to him.

At first he did some volunteer work in a shelter, then he parlayed that into another job. Two nights each week he volunteered at a local suicide prevention hot line, working the ten P.M. to two A.M. shift, which was by far the most interesting. He spent more than the occasional midnight speaking softly to students threatened by various degrees of stress, curiously energized by the connection with anonymous but troubled individuals. It was, he thought, as good a way as any of keeping his skills as an analyst sharp. When he hung up the phone line, having persuaded some child not to be rash, but to come into the university health clinic and seek help, he thought, in a small way, that he was doing penance for his lack of attention twenty years earlier, when Claire Tyson had come to his own office in the clinic he hated so much, with complaints that he'd failed to listen to and in a danger he'd failed to see.

Frederick Lazarus was someone different. Ricky constructed this character with a coldheartedness that surprised himself.

Frederick Lazarus was a member of a health club, where he pounded out solitary miles on a treadmill, followed by attacking the free weights, gaining fitness and strength daily, the onetime lean, but essentially soft body of the New York analyst re-forming. His waistline shrank. His shoulders broadened. He worked out alone and in silence, save for an occasional grunt and the pounding of his feet against the mechanized tread. He took to combing his sandy hair back from his forehead, slicked aggressively. He started a beard. He took an icy pleasure in the exertion that he delivered to himself especially when he realized that he was no longer breathing hard as he accelerated his pace. The health club offered a self-defense class, mostly for women, but he rearranged his schedule slightly to be able to attend, learning the rudiments of body throws and quick, effective punches to the throat, face, or groin. The women in the class seemed a bit uncomfortable with him at first, but his willingness to serve as a volunteer for their efforts gained him a sort of acceptance. At least, they were willing to smash him without guilt when he wore protective clothing. He saw it as a means of toughening himself further.

On a Saturday afternoon in late January, Ricky slide-stepped through snowdrifts and icy sidewalks into the R and R Sporting Goods store, which was located well outside the university area in a low-rent strip mall, the sort that catered to discount tire stores and quick-lube auto service. R and R — there was no ready indication what the letters stood for — was a modest low-slung, square space, filled with plastic deer targets, blaze-orange hunting clothing, stacks of fishing rods and tackle, and bows and arrows. Along one wall there was a wide array of deer rifles, shotguns, and modified assault weapons that lacked even the modest beauty of the wood stocks and polished barrels of their more acceptable brethren. The AR-15s and AK-47s had a cold, military appearance, a clarity of purpose. Underneath the glass-topped counter were rows and rows of various handguns. Steel blue. Polished chrome. Black metal.

He spent a pleasant hour discussing the merits of various weapons with a clerk, a bearded and bald middle-aged man, sporting a red check hunting shirt and a holstered .38 caliber snub-nosed pistol on his expansive waistline. The clerk and Ricky debated the advantages of revolvers versus automatics, size against punch, accuracy compared with rate of fire. The store had a shooting range in the basement, two narrow lanes, side by side, separated by a small partition, a little like a dark and abandoned bowling alley. An electrically operated pulley system carried silhouette targets down to a wall some fifty feet distant that was buttressed by brown hundred-pound bags of sawdust. The clerk eagerly showed Ricky, who had never fired a weapon in his life, how to sight down the barrel, and how to stand, two hands on the weapon, holding it out in such a way that the world narrowed, and only his vision, the pressure of his finger on the trigger, and the target he had in his aim mattered. Ricky fired off dozens of rounds, ranging from a small .22 automatic, through the .357 Magnum and 9 mm that are favored by law enforcement, up to the .45 that was popularized during the Second World War and which sent a jolt right through his palm all the way into his shoulder and down to his chest when he fired it.

He settled on something in between, a .380 Ruger semiautomatic, with a fifteen-shot clip. It was a weapon that functioned in the range between the big bang preferred by police and the deadly little assassin's weapons that women and professional killers liked. Ricky chose the same weapon that he'd seen in Merlin's briefcase, on a train to Manhattan, in what seemed to him to have taken place in a different world altogether. He thought it was a good idea to be equal, if only in terms of handguns.

He filled out the permit forms under the name Frederick Lazarus, using the fake Social Security number that he'd created precisely for this purpose.

'Takes a couple of days,' the fat clerk said. 'Although we're a whole helluva lot easier than Massachusetts. How're you planning on paying for it?'

'Cash,' Ricky said.

'Antiquated commodity,' the clerk smiled. 'Not plastic?'

'Plastic just complicates your life.'

'A Ruger .380 simplifies it.'

Ricky nodded. 'That's more or less the point, isn't it.'

The clerk nodded as he finished the paperwork. 'Anyone in particular you're thinking of simplifying, Mr. Lazarus?'

'Now that's an unusual question,' Ricky responded. 'Do I look like a man with an enemy for a boss? A neighbor who has let his mutt loose on my lawn one too many times? Or, for that matter, a wife who had perhaps nagged me once too often?'

'No,' the clerk said, grinning. 'You don't. But then, we don't get too many handgun novices in here. Most of our customers are pretty regular, at least maybe so's we knows the face, if not the name.' He looked down at the form. 'This gonna fly, Mr. Lazarus?'

'Sure. Why not?'

'Well, that's more or less what I'm asking. I hate this damn regulation crap.'

'Rules are rules,' Ricky replied. The man nodded.

'Ain't that the goddamn truth.'

'How about practicing,' Ricky asked. 'I mean, what's the point of getting a fine weapon like this if I don't get real expert at handling it?'

The clerk nodded. 'You're a hundred percent right about that, Mister Lazarus. So many folks think that when they buy the gun, that's all they need for protecting themselves. Hell, I think that's where it starts. Need to know how to operate that weapon, especially when things get, shall we say, tense, like when some criminal is in the kitchen, and you're in your jammies up in the bedroom . . . '

'Precisely,' Ricky interrupted. 'Don't want to be so scared . . . '

The clerk finished his sentence for him, ' . . . that you end up blowing away the wife or the family dog or cat.' Then he laughed. 'Though maybe that wouldn't be the worst thing of all. Take that burglar out for a beer afterwards, if you was married to my old lady. And her damn fluffy, makes-me-sneeze-all-the-damn-time cat.'

'So, the shooting range?'

'You can use it anytime we're open and it ain't already being used. Targets is just fifty cents. Only thing we require is that you buy your ammo here. And you don't come walking through the front door with a loaded weapon. Keep it in the case. Keep the clips empty. Fill 'em up here, where's someone can see what you're doing. Then you can go squeeze off as many as you like. Come spring, we sets up a combat course in the woods. Maybe you'd like to try that out?'

'Absolutely,' Ricky said.

'You want me to call you when the approval comes back, Mr. Lazarus?'

'Forty-eight hours? I'll just swing on by myself. Or give you a call.'

'Either one is fine.' The clerk eyed Ricky carefully. 'Sometimes,' he said, 'these handgun permits come back rejected because of some dumb-ass glitch. You know, like maybe there's a problem or two with the numbers you gave me. Something comes up on somebody's computer, you know what I mean . . . '

'Foul-ups happen, right?' Ricky said.

'You seem like a pretty good guy, Mr. Lazarus. I'd hate you to get turned down 'cause of some bureaucratic snafu. Wouldn't be fair.' The clerk spoke slowly, almost cautiously. Ricky listened to the tone of what the man was saying. 'All depends on what sort of clerk you get looking over the application. Some guys over at the federal building, they just punch the numbers in, hardly pay attention at all. Other guys take their job real serious . . . '

'Sounds like you sure want to get that application in front of the right guy.'

The clerk nodded. 'We ain't supposed to know who's doing the checking, but I got some friends over there . . . '

Ricky removed his wallet. He placed a hundred dollars on the counter.

The man smiled again. 'That's not necessary,' he said. But his hand closed over the cash. 'I'll make sure you get the right clerk. The type of guy who processes things real quick and efficient . . . '

'Well,' Ricky said, 'that's real helpful. Real helpful. I would feel like I owed you a favor, then.'

'No big deal. We try to keep customers happy, that's all.' The clerk stuffed Ricky's cash into his pocket. 'Hey, you interested in a rifle? We got a special on a real nice .30 caliber with a scope for deer. Shotguns, too . . . '

Ricky nodded. 'Maybe,' he said. 'I'll have to check what my needs are. I mean, once I know that I'm not going to have any problem with permits, I'll be assessing my needs. Those look pretty impressive.' He pointed at the collection of assault weapons.

'An Uzi or an Ingram .45 caliber machine pistol or an AK-47 with a nice banana clip can go a long ways toward settling any dispute you might be facing,' the clerk said. 'They tend to discourage disagreement and urge compromise.'

'That's a good thing to keep in mind,' Ricky replied.

* * *

Ricky became significantly more adept at the computer.

Using his screen name, he made two different electronic searches for his own family tree, discovering with daunting speed how easy it was for Rumplestiltskin to have acquired the list of relatives that had been the fulcrum of his initial threat. The fifty-odd members of Dr. Frederick Starks's family had emerged across the Internet in only a couple of hours' worth of inquiries. Ricky was able to ascertain that armed with names, it did not take much longer to come up with addresses. Addresses turned into professions. It was not hard to extrapolate how Rumplestiltskin — who had all the time and energy he'd needed — had come up with information as to who these people were, and to find a few vulnerable members of the extended group.

Ricky sat at the computer, slightly astonished.

When his own name came up, and the second of the family tree programs that he was employing showed him as recently deceased, he stiffened in his chair, surprised, though he shouldn't have been; it was the same way that one feels a momentary surge of shock when an animal runs in front of their car wheels at night, only to disappear into the shrub brush by the side of the road. An instant of fear, swept away in the same moment.

He had worked for decades in a world of privacy, where secrets were hidden beneath emotional fogs and layers of doubts, mired in memory, obscured by logjammed years of denials and depressions. If analysis is, at best, the slow peeling away of frustrations in order to expose truths, the computer seemed to him to have the clinical equivalence of a scalpel. Details and facts simply blipped across the screen, cut free instantaneously with a few strokes on a keyboard. He hated it at the same time that it fascinated him.

Ricky also realized how antique his chosen profession appeared.

And, swiftly, he understood, as well, how little chance he'd ever had at winning Rumplestiltskin's game. When he replayed the fifteen days between the letter and his pseudodeath, he realized how easy it had been for the man to anticipate every move Ricky made. The predictability of his response at every turn was utterly obvious.

Ricky thought hard about another aspect of the game. Every moment had been designed in advance, every moment had thrust him in directions that were clearly expected. Rumplestiltskin had known him every bit as well as he had known himself. Virgil and Merlin together had been the means used to distract him from ever getting any perspective. They had created the breakneck pace, filled his last days with demands, made every threat real and palpable.

Every step in the play had been scripted. From Zimmerman's death by subway to his trip to see Dr. Lewis in Rhinebeck, through the clerk's office at the hospital where he'd once seen Claire Tyson. What does an analyst do? Ricky asked himself. He establishes the simplest yet most inviolable of rules. Once a day, five days per week, his patients showed up at his door, ringing the bell distinctively. Out of that regimen the rest of the chaos of their lives gained form. And with that, the ability to get control.

The lesson was simple, Ricky thought: He could no longer be predictable.

That was slightly incorrect, he told himself. Richard Lively could be as normal as necessary, as normal as he desired. A regular kind of guy. But Frederick Lazarus was to be someone different.

A man without a past, he thought, can write any future.

* * *

Frederick Lazarus obtained a library card, and immersed himself in the culture of revenge. Violence dripped from every page he read. He read histories, plays, poetry, and nonfiction, emphasizing the genre category of true crime. He devoured novels, ranging from thrillers written in the last year, to Gothics from the nineteenth century. He blistered through the theater, almost memorizing *Othello* and then, deeper still, to *The Oresteia*. He plucked segments from his memory and reread passages recalled from his own college days, spending time in particular with the man who donated his screen name to him and lent him the name he'd used with the derelict whose wallet he'd stolen. He absorbed the sequence where Odysseus slams shut the doors on the suitors and promptly murders all the men who presumed him dead.

Ricky had known little of crime and criminals, but fast became expert — at least, he understood, to the degree that the printed word can educate. Thomas Harris and Robert Parker taught him, as did Norman Mailer and Truman Capote. Edgar Allan Poe and Sir Arthur Conan Doyle were mixed liberally with FBI training manuals available through the Internet bookselling outlets. He read Hervey Cleckley's *The Mask of Sanity* and came away with a much better knowledge of the nature of psychopaths. He read books entitled *Why They Kill* and *The A to Z Encyclopedia of Serial Killers*. He read about mass murder and explosive killings, crimes of passion and murders thought to be perfect. Names and crimes filled his imagination, from Jack the Ripper to Billy the Kid, to John Wayne Gacy and The Zodiac Killer. From past through the present. He read about war crimes and snipers, about hit men and satanic rituals, mobsters, and confused teenagers who took assault rifles to school, searching for classmates who had teased them perhaps once too often.

To his surprise, he discovered he was able to compartmentalize all he read. When he shut the cover of yet another book detailing some of the more grisly acts one man can do to another, he put aside Frederick Lazarus and returned to Richard Lively. One man studied how to garrote an unsuspecting victim and why a knife is a poor choice for a murder weapon, the other read bedtime stories to his landlady's four-year-old grandson and memorized *Green Eggs and Ham*, which the child never tired of hearing at virtually any moment of the day or night. And, while one man studied the impact of DNA evidence in crime scene analysis, the other spent one long night talking an overdosed student down from a dangerous high.

Jekyll and Hyde, he thought.

In a perverse way, he discovered that he enjoyed the company of both men.

Maybe, curiously enough, more than the man he'd been when Rumplestiltskin entered his life.

* * *

Late one early spring night, nine months after his death, Ricky spent three hours on the telephone with a distraught, deeply depressed young woman who called the suicide prevention line in despair, a bottle of sleeping pills on the table in front of her. He spoke to her of what her life had become, and what it could become. He painted a word picture with his voice of a future free from the sorrows and doubts that had driven her to the state she was in. He wove hope into every thread of what he said, and when the two of them greeted the first dawn light, she had put aside the threatened overdose and made an appointment with a clinic physician.

When he walked out that morning, more energized than exhausted, he decided that it was time to make his first inquiry.

Later that day, when he had finished his shift in the maintenance department at the university, he used his electronic pass card to enter the computer sciences department's student study room. This was a square space cut up into study carrels, each with a computer linked to the university's main system. He booted one up, entered his own password, and slid right into the system. In a folder by his left hand, he had the small amount of information that he'd obtained in his former life about the woman he had ignored. He hesitated momentarily, before making his first electronic sortie. Ricky understood he could probably find freedom and a quiet, simple life, merely by living the rest of his days as Richard Lively. Life as a janitor wasn't that bad, he had to acknowledge. He wondered, for an instant, whether not knowing would be better than knowing, because he knew that as soon as he began the process of uncovering the identities of Rumplestiltskin, and his partners, Merlin and Virgil, he would be unable to stop. Two things would happen, he told himself. All the years spent as Dr. Starks, dedicated to the proposition that unearthing truth from deep within was a valuable enterprise, would take hold of him. And Frederick Lazarus would demand his own dues, as the vehicle for his assault.

Ricky warred within himself for some time. He was unsure how long. It might have been seconds, he might have stared at the screen in front of him for hours, fingers poised, frozen, above the keyboard.

He told himself that he would not be a coward.

The problem was, he thought, where did cowardice lie? In hiding. Or in acting?

A coldness swept over him as he made a decision. Who were you, Claire Tyson?

And where are your children today?

There are many kinds of freedom, Ricky thought. Rumplestiltskin had killed him to acquire one sort. Now he would find his own.

25

This is what Ricky knew: Twenty years earlier a woman died in New York City and her three children were turned over to the state for adoption. Because of that fact alone, he'd been forced to kill himself.

Ricky's first computer sorties, chasing Claire Tyson's name, had come up curiously empty. It was as if her death had erased her from the records he could access electronically as surely as it had erased her from the earth. Even with the copy of the twenty-year-old death certificate, he was initially stymied. The family tree programs that had displayed his own stack of relatives so rapidly, proved to be significantly less effective at tracing her. She seemed to stem from folks with far less status, and this lack of identity seemed to diminish her presence in the world. He was a bit surprised at the lack of information. The Find Your Missing Relatives! programs promised to be able to trace virtually anyone, and her apparent disappearance from any record rapidly obtained was unsettling.

But his first efforts weren't complete wastes. One of the things that he'd managed to learn in the months since his final vacation had begun, was to think considerably more tangentially. As a psychoanalyst, he'd learned the art of following symbols and tracing them into realities. Now, he was using similar skills, but in a far more concrete manner. When Claire Tyson's name didn't produce success, he began to search for other avenues. A computer sortie into Manhattan real estate records gained him the current ownership of the building where she had lived. Another inquiry led him to names and addresses in the city bureaucracy where she would have applied for welfare, food stamps, and aid to families with dependent children. The trick, Ricky thought, was to imagine Claire Tyson's life twenty years earlier, and then narrow that down, so that he could understand all the forces that were in play at that time. Somewhere in that portrait would be a link to the man who'd stalked him.

He also searched electronic telephone books for the north of Florida. That had been where she had come from, and Ricky suspected that if she had any living relatives — other than Rumplestiltskin — that would be where they were located. The death certificate listed an address for her next of kin, but when he cross-checked the address against the name, he determined someone different was living at that location. There were a number of Tysons in the area outside of Pensacola and it seemed a daunting task to try to ascertain who was who, until Ricky remembered his own scrawled notes from his few sessions with the woman. She was a high school graduate, he recalled, with two years of college before dropping out to follow a sailor stationed at the naval base, the father of her three children.

Ricky printed out the names of potential relatives and the addresses of every high school in the area.

It seemed to him, as he stared at the words on the sheets of computer paper, that what he was doing was what he should have done so many years before: try to come to know and understand a young woman.

He thought that the two worlds couldn't have been much different. Pensacola, Florida, is in the Bible Belt. Jesus-thumping, raised voices, praise the Lord and go to church on Sunday and any other day when His presence was needed. New York — well, Ricky thought, the city probably stood for pretty much everything anyone who grew up in Pensacola knew to be wrong and evil. It was an unsettling combination, he thought. But he was relatively certain of one thing: He was far more likely to find Rumplestiltskin in the city than in the countryside of North Florida. But he didn't think that the man had had no impact down South.

Ricky decided to start there.

Using the skills he'd already mastered, he ordered a fake Florida driver's license and retired military identification card from one of the novelty identification outlets on the Internet. The documents were to be sent to Frederick Lazarus's Mailboxes Etc. box number. But the name on the identification was Rick Tyson.

People were likely to want to help out a long-lost relative, he thought, who innocently appeared to be trying to trace his roots. As a further hedge, he made up a fictional cancer treatment center, and on invented stationery wrote a 'to whom it may concern' letter, explaining that Mr. Tyson's child was a Hodgkin's disease patient in need of a bone marrow match, and any assistance in tracing various family members, whose marrow DNA carried an increased chance of match success, would be appreciated and possibly even lifesaving.

This letter was wholly cynical, Ricky thought to himself.

But it would likely open some doors he needed to open.

He made himself an airplane reservation, made arrangements with his landladies and with his boss at the university maintenance department, switching around some workdays and hours to give himself a block of time, then he stopped in at the secondhand clothing store and purchased himself a simple, extremely cheap summer-weight black suit. More or less, he thought to himself, what a mortician would wear, which, he believed, was appropriate for his circumstances. Late in the evening of the day before he was to depart, wearing his janitor's shirt and work pants, he let himself into the theater department at the university. One of his passkeys opened the storage area where costumes for various college productions were kept. It did not take him long to find what he needed.

* * *

There was a heavy dampness hidden like a veiled threat in the heat of the Gulf Coast weather. His first breaths of air, as he walked from the air-conditioned chill of the airport lobby out to the rental car waiting area, seemed to hold an oily, oppressive, slick warmth far removed from even the hottest days up on Cape Cod, or even in New York City during an August heat spell. It was almost as if the air had substance, that it carried something invisible, yet questionable. Disease, he thought at first. But then, he guessed that was too harsh a thought.

His plan was simple: He was going to check into a cheap motel, then go to the address that was written on Claire Tyson's death certificate. He would knock on some doors, ask around, see if anyone currently at that location knew of her family's whereabouts. Then he would fan out to the high schools closest to the address. It wasn't much of a plan, he thought, but it had a journalistic sturdiness about it: knock on doors and see who had something to say.

Ricky found a Motel 6 located on a wide boulevard that seemed to be dedicated to little except strip mall after strip mall, fast-food restaurants of every imaginable chain, and discount shopping outlets. It was a street of sun-washed cement, glowing in the undeniable sun of the Gulf. An occasional palm or shrub-brush landscaping seemed washed up against the shore of cheap commerce like flotsam and jetsam after a storm. He could taste the ocean nearby, the scent was in the air, but the vista was one of development, almost endless, like a repeating decimal of two-story buildings and garish signs.

He checked in under the name Frederick Lazarus, and paid cash for a three-day stay. He told the clerk he was a salesman, not that the man was paying all that much attention. After surveying the modest room, Ricky left his bag and walked through the parking lot to a convenience store gas station. There, he was able to purchase a detailed street map for the entire Pensacola area.

* * *

The tract housing near the sprawling naval base had a certain uniformity to it that Ricky thought might be similar to one of the first circles of Hell. Rows of cinder-block framed houses with tiny splotches of green grass steaming beneath the sun and ubiquitous sprinklers dashing the color with water. It was a short-hair-and-page-boy-cut area; it seemed to Ricky, driving through, that each block had a quality to it that seemed to define the aspirations of the inhabitants; the blocks that were well mowed and modestly manicured, with houses freshly painted so that they glistened with an otherworldly bright white beneath the Gulf sun seemed to speak of hope and possibility. The cars that rested in the driveways were clean, polished, shining, and new. There were swing sets and plastic toys on some of the lawns, and despite the midmorning heat, some children were at play beneath the watchful gaze of parents. But the lines of demarcation were clear: A few blocks in a different direction and the houses gained a worn, more used appearance. Run-down, flaking paint, and rain gutters that were stained with use. Streaks of brown dirt, chain-link fences, a car or two up on cinder blocks, wheels removed, rusting. Fewer voices raised in play, trash cans filled past their brims with bottles. Blocks of limited dreams, he thought.

In the distance, he was aware that the Gulf, with its

expanse of vibrant blue waters, and the station, with great gray navy ships lined up, was the axis on which everything revolved. But as he moved farther from the ocean, deeper into disadvantage, the world he traveled in seemed limited, aimless, and as hopeless as an empty bottle.

He found the street where Claire Tyson's family lived, and shuddered. It was no better, no worse than any of the other blocks, but in that mediocrity, spoke volumes: a place to flee from.

Ricky was looking for number thirteen, which was in the middle of the block. He pulled up and parked outside.

The house itself was much the same as the others in the block. A single-story, small two- or three-bedroom home, with air conditioners hanging from a couple of windows. A slab of concrete served as front porch and a rusty black kettle grill was leaned up against the side. The house was painted a faded pink and had an incongruous thirteen in hand-lettered black near the door. The one was significantly larger than the three, which almost indicated that the person who'd put the address on the wall had changed his mind in midstroke. There was a basketball hoop nailed to the portal of an open-air carport that looked to his unpracticed eye to be six inches to a foot lower than regulation. Regardless, the rim was bent. There was no net. A weathered, faded orange ball rested against a stanchion post. The front yard had a neglected look to it, streaks of dirt sidled up against grass choked with weeds. A large yellow dog, chained to a wall, confined by a steel fence to the tiny, square backyard, started to bark furiously as he walked up the driveway. That morning's paper had been left near the street, and he picked it up and carried it to the front door. He touched the buzzer and heard the bell sound inside. A baby was crying inside, but quieted almost instantly as a voice responded, 'I'm coming, I'm coming . . . '

The door opened and a young black woman, toddler on her hip stood before him. She did not open the screen door.

'What you want?' she demanded, furious and barely constrained. 'You here for the TV? The washer? Maybe the furniture? Maybe the baby's bottle? What you gonna take this time?' She looked past him, out to the street, her eyes searching for a truck and a crew.

'I'm not here to take anything,' he said.

'You with the electric company?'

'No. I'm not a bill collector and I'm not a repossession man, either.'

'Who you be, then?' she asked. Her voice was still aggressive. Defiant.

'I'm a man with a couple of questions,' he said. Ricky smiled. 'And if you have some answers, maybe some money.'

The woman continued to eye him suspiciously, but now with some curiosity as well. 'What sort of questions?' she asked.

'Questions about someone who lived here once. A while ago.'

'Don't know much,' the woman said.

'Family named Tyson,' Ricky said.

The woman nodded. 'He be the man got evicted before we move in.'

Ricky took out his wallet and removed a twenty-dollar bill. He held it up and the woman opened the screen door. 'You a cop?' she asked. 'Some sort of detective?'

'I'm not a policeman,' Ricky said. 'But I might be some sort of detective.' He stepped inside the house.

He blinked for a moment, his eyes taking a few seconds to adjust to the darkness. It was stifling in the small entranceway and he followed the woman and the child into the living room. The windows were open in this space, but the built-up heat still made the narrow room seem like a prison cell. There was a chair, a couch, a television, and a red-and-blue playpen, which is where the child was deposited. The walls were empty, save for a picture of the baby, and a single stiffly posed wedding photo of the woman and a young black man in a naval uniform. He would have guessed the ages of the couple as nineteen. Twenty at most. He stole a look at the young woman and thought to himself: nineteen, but aging fast. Ricky looked back at the picture and asked the obvious question: 'Is that your husband? Where's he now?'

'He shipped out,' the woman said. With the anger removed from her voice, it had a lilting sweetness to it. Her accent was unmistakably Southern black, and Ricky guessed deep South. Alabama or Georgia, perhaps Mississippi. Enlisting, he suspected, had been the route out of some rural world, and she'd tagged along, not knowing that she was merely going to replace one sort of harsh poverty for another. 'He's in the Gulf of some Arabia somewhere, on the USS *Essex*. That's a destroyer. Got another two months 'fore he gets home.'

'What's your name?'

'Charlene,' she replied. 'Now what's those questions that's gonna make me some extra money?'

'Things are tight?'

She laughed, as if this was a joke. 'You'd best believe it. Navy pay don't go too far until your rating get up a bit. We already lost the car and be two months slow on the rent. The furniture, we owe on, too. That be the story for just about everyone in this part of town.'

'Landlord threatening you?' Ricky asked. The woman surprisingly shook her head.

'Landlord be some good guy, I don't know. When I got the money, I send it to a bank account. But a man at the bank, or maybe a lawyer, he called up and told me not to worry, to pay when I could, said he understood things were hard on military sometimes. My man,

Reggie, he just an enlisted sailor. Got to work his way up before he make any real money. But landlord be cool, nobody else be. Electric say they gonna shut off, that's why can't run the air conditioners or nothing.'

Ricky moved over and sat on the single chair, and Charlene took up a spot on the couch. 'Tell me what you know about the Tyson family. They lived here before you moved in?'

'That's right,' she said. 'I don't know all that much about those folks. All I knows about is the old fella. He was here all alone. Why you interested in that old man?'

Ricky removed his wallet and showed the young woman the fake driver's license with the name Rick Tyson on it. 'He's a distant relative and he may have come into a small amount of money in a will,' Ricky lied. 'I was sent by the family to try to locate him.'

'I don't know he gonna need any money where he be,' Charlene said.

'Where's that?'

'Over at the VA nursing home on Midway Road. If he's still breathing.'

'And his wife?'

'She dead. More'n a couple of years. She had a weak heart, or so's I heard.'

'Did you ever meet him?'

Charlene shook her head. 'Only story I knows is what I was told by the neighbors.'

'Then tell me that story.'

'Old man and old woman live here by themselves . . . '

'I was told they had a daughter . . . '

'I heard that, too, but I heard she died, long time ago.'

'Right. Go on.'

'Living on Social Security checks. Maybe some pension money, I don't know. But not much. Old woman, she got sick with her heart. Got no insurance, just the Medicare. They suddenly got bills. Old woman, she up and dies, leaving the old man with more bills. No insurance. He just an old, nasty man, got no neighbors like him none too much, no friends, no family anyone knows about. What he got same as me, just bills. People who wants their money. Up one day, comes late with the mortgage on the house, finds out that it ain't the bank he thinks that owns the note anymore, it be someone who bought the note from the bank. He misses that payment, maybe one more, the sheriff's deputies come with an eviction notice. They put the old guy out onna street. Next I hear, he's in the VA. I'm not guessing he's ever gonna get out of there, neither, except maybe feetfirst.'

Ricky considered what he'd just heard, then asked: 'You came in after the eviction?'

'That's right.' Charlene sighed and shook her head. 'This whole block be a whole lot nicer just two years back. Not so much trash and drinking, people fighting. I thought this be a good place to get started, but now ain't got no place and no money to move. Anyway, I heard the old man's story from folks across the street. They gone now. Probably all the folks knew that old man be gone now. But it didn't seem like he had too many friends. Old man had a pit bull, chained up in back where we got our dog now. Our dog, he just bark, make a commotion, like when you come walking up. I let him loose, he likely to kiss your face more than he be like to bite you. Tyson's pit bull, not like that none. When he was younger, he likes to fight that dog, you know, in those gambling fights. Those places, they got lots of sweaty white men betting money they don't have, drinking and swearing. That be the part of Florida that ain't for tourists or the navy folks. It be like Alabama or Mississippi. Redneck Florida. Rednecks and pit bulls.'

'Not a popular choice,' Ricky said.

'There's plenty kids in the neighborhood. Dog like that a threat to maybe hurt one of them. Maybe some other reasons folks ’round here don’t like him much.’

‘What other reasons?’

‘I heard stories.’

‘What sort of stories?’

‘Evil stories, mister. Mean, nasty evil, be all wrong and bad stories. I don’t know they’s the truth, so my mother, my father, they tells me not to go repeating things I don’t know for certain, but maybe you ask around somebody not as God-fearing as me likely to talk to you some. But I don’t know who. No folks left from that time.’

Ricky thought another moment, then asked, ‘Do you have the name, maybe the address of the guy you pay rent to now?’

Charlene looked a bit surprised, but nodded. ‘Sure. I make the check out to a lawyer downtown, send it to another guy at the bank. When I got the money.’ She took a piece of crayon from the floor, and wrote down a name and address on the back of an envelope from a furniture rental outlet. The envelope was stamped in red with the phrase: SECOND NOTICE. ‘I hope this helps you out some.’

Ricky pulled two more twenty-dollar bills from his wallet and handed them to the woman. She nodded her thanks. He hesitated, then pulled a third out. ‘For the baby,’ he said.

‘That’s nice of you, mister.’

He shielded his eyes from the sun as he walked back out onto the street. The sky above was a wide determined expanse of blue, and the heat had increased. For a moment he was reminded of the high summer days in New York, and how he’d fled to the cooler climate of the Cape. That was over, he thought. He looked toward where his rental car was parked by the curb and he tried to imagine an old man sitting amid his meager possessions by the side of the street. Friendless and evicted from the house where he’d lived a hard life, but at least his own life, for so many years. Cast out quickly and without a second thought. Abandoned to age, illness, and loneliness. Ricky stuffed the paper with the lawyer's name and address into his pocket. He knew who had evicted the old man. He wondered, however, if the old man sat in the heat and despair of that moment and understood that the man who had cast him out on the street was the child of his child who so many years earlier he'd turned his back upon.

* * *

There was a large, sprawling high school less than seven blocks away from the house that Claire Tyson had fled from. Ricky pulled into the parking area and stared up at the building, trying to imagine how any child could find individuality, much less education, within the walls. It was a huge, sand-colored cement building, with a football field and a circular track stuck on the side behind a ten-foot-high link fence. It seemed to Ricky that whoever had designed the structure had merely drawn an immense rectangle, then added a second rectangle to create a blocklike *T*, and then stopped, his architecture completed. There was a large mural outline of an ancient Greek helmet painted on the brick of the building, and the slogan HOME OF THE SOUTH SIDE SPARTANS! beside it in flowing, faded red script. The entire place baked like a pound cake in a pan beneath the cloudless sky and fierce sun.

There was a security checkpoint just inside the main entrance, where a school guard, wearing a blue shirt, black patent leather belt and shoes, and black pants, giving him if not the same status as a policeman, at least the same appearance, manned a metal detector. The guard gave Ricky directions toward the administrative offices, then had him walk between the twin posts of the machine, before pointing him on his way. His shoes clicked against the polished linoleum floor of the school hallway. He was between classes, so he maneuvered more or less alone between rows of gray-colored lockers. Only an occasional student hurried past him.

There was a secretary at a desk inside the door marked ADMINISTRATION. She steered him to the principal's office after he explained his reason for visiting the school. He waited outside while the secretary had a brief conversation, then appeared in the doorway to usher him in. He stepped inside and saw a late-middle-aged woman, wearing a white shirt that was buttoned to her chin, look up from where she worked at a computer screen, peering over glasses, giving an almost scolding, school-marmish look in his direction. She seemed mildly discomfited by his intrusion, and gestured toward a chair, while she swung around and sat behind a desk cluttered with papers. He sat heavily, thinking that he was taking a seat that had probably mostly known squirming students, caught in some malfeasance, or distraught parents, being informed of much the same thing.

'How precisely is it that I can help you?' the principal asked briskly.

Ricky nodded. 'I'm searching for information,' he said. 'I need to inquire about a young woman who attended school here in the late Sixties. Her name was Claire Tyson — '

'School records are confidential,' the principal interrupted. 'But I remember the young woman.'

'You've been here a while . . . '

'My whole career,' the woman said. 'But short of letting you see the class of 1967 yearbook, I don't know if I can be of much help. As I said, records are confidential.'

'Well, I don't really need her school records,' Ricky said, removing his phony cancer treatment center letter from his pocket and handing it to the lady. 'I'm really searching for anyone who might know of a relative . . . '

The woman read the letter swiftly. Her face softened. 'Oh,' she said apologetically. 'I'm so sorry. I didn't realize . . . '

'That's okay,' Ricky said. 'This is kind of a long shot. But, then, you have a niece who's this sick, you're willing to take any long shot there is.'

'Of course,' the woman said rapidly. 'Of course you would. But I don't think there's any Tysons related to Claire left around here. At least not that I recall, and I remember just about everyone who passes through these doors.'

'I'm surprised you remember Claire . . . ,' Ricky said.

'She made an impression. In more ways than one. Back then I was her guidance counselor. I've come up in the world.'

'Clearly,' Ricky said. 'But your recollection, especially after all these years . . . '

The woman gestured slightly, as if to cut off his question. She rose and went to a bookcase against a rear wall, and returned in a moment with an old, faux leather — bound yearbook from the class of 1967. She passed it across to Ricky.

It was the most typical of yearbooks. Page after page of candid shots of students in various activities or games, buttressed by some overly enthusiastic prose. The bulk of the yearbook was the formal portraits of the senior class. These were posed shots of young people trying to look older and more serious than they were. Ricky flipped through the lineup, until he came to Claire Tyson. He had a little trouble reconciling the woman he'd seen a decade later with the fresh-faced, well-scrubbed almost adult in the yearbook. Her hair was longer, and tossed in a wave over her shoulder. She had a slight grin on her lips, a little less stiff than most of her classmates, the sort of look that someone who knows a secret might adopt. He read the entry adjacent to her portrait. It listed her clubs — French, science, Future Homemakers, and the drama society — and her sports, which were varsity softball and volleyball. It also listed her academic honors, which included eight semesters on the honor roll and a National Merit Scholarship commendation. There was a quote, played for humor, but which to Ricky had a slightly ominous tone, 'Do unto others, before they have a chance to do unto you . . . ' A prediction: 'Wants to live in the fast lane . . . ' and a look into the teenage crystal ball: 'In ten years she will be: On Broadway or under it . . . '

The principal was looking over his shoulder. 'She had no chance,' she said.

'I'm sorry?' Ricky replied, the words forming a question.

'She was the only child of a, uh, difficult couple. Living on the edge of poverty. The father was a tyrant. Perhaps worse . . . '

'You mean . . . '

'She displayed many of the classic signs of sexual abuse. I spoke with her often when she would have these uncontrollable fits of depression. Crying. Hysterical. Then calm, cold, almost removed, as if she were somewhere else, even though she was sitting in the room with me. I would have called the police if I'd had even the slightest bit of concrete evidence, but she would never acknowledge quite enough abuse for me to take that step. One has to be cautious in my position. And we didn't know as much about these things then as we do now.'

'Of course.'

'And, then, I knew she would flee, first chance. That boy . . . '

'Boyfriend?'

'Yes. I'm quite certain she was pregnant and well along at that, when she graduated that spring.'

'His name? I wonder if any child might still be . . . It would be critical, you know, with the gene pool and all, I don't understand this stuff the doctors tell me, but . . . '

'There was a baby. But I don't know what happened. They didn't put down roots here, that's for sure. The boy was heading to the navy, although I don't know for certain that he got there, and she went off to the local community college. I don't think they actually ever married. I saw her once, on the street. She stopped to say hello, but that was it. It was as if she couldn't talk about anything. Claire went from being ashamed about one thing right to the next. The problem was that she was bright. Wonderful on the stage. She could play any part, from Shakespeare to *Guys and Dolls*, and do it wondrously. Real talent for acting. It was reality that was a problem for her.'

'I see . . . '

'She was one of these people you'd like to help, but can't. She was always searching for someone who could take care of her, but she always found the wrong people. Without fail.'

'The boy?'

'Daniel Collins?' The principal took the yearbook and flipped back a few pages and then handed it to Ricky. 'Good-looking, huh? A ladies' man. Football and baseball, but never a star. Smart enough, but didn't apply himself in the classroom. The sort of kid who always knew where the party was, where to get the booze, or the pot or whatever, and he was the one who never got caught. One of those kids who was merely slipsliding through life. Had all the girls he wanted, but especially Claire, on a string. It was one of those relationships you are powerless to do anything about, and know will bring nothing but sorrow.'

'You didn't like him much?'

'What was there to like? He was a bit of a predator.

More than a bit, actually. And certainly only really interested in himself and what made him feel good.'

'Do you have his family's local address?'

The principal rose, went over to a computer, and typed in a name. Then she took a pencil and copied down a number onto a scrap piece of paper, which she handed over to Ricky. He nodded a response.

'So you think he left her . . . '

'Sure. After he'd used her up. That was what he was good at: using people then discarding them. Whether that took one year or ten, I don't know. You stick in my line of work, you get pretty good at predicting what will happen to all these kids. Some might surprise you, one way or the other. But not all that many.' She gestured at the yearbook prediction. On Broadway or under it. Ricky knew which of those two alternatives had come true. 'The kids always make a joke along with a guess. But life's rarely that amusing, is it?'

* * *

Before heading to the VA Hospital, Ricky stopped at his motel and changed into the black suit. He also took with him the item that he'd borrowed from the property room of the theater department back at the university in New Hampshire, fitted it around his neck and admired himself in the mirror.

The hospital building had the same soulless appearance as the high school. It was two stories, whitewashed brick seemingly plopped down in an open space between, by Ricky's count, at least six different churches. Pentecostal, Baptist, Catholic, Congregational, Unitarian, AME, all with the hopeful message boards on their front lawns proclaiming unfettered delight in the imminent arrival of Jesus, or at least, comfort in the words of the Bible, spoken fervently in daily sessions and twice on Sundays. Ricky, who had gained a healthy disrespect for religion in his psychoanalytic practice, rather enjoyed the juxtaposition of the VA Hospital and the churches: It was as if the harsh reality of the abandoned, represented by hospital, did some measure of balancing with all the optimism racing about unchecked at the churches. He wondered if Claire Tyson had been a regular church visitor. He suspected as much, given the world she grew up in. Everyone went to church. The trouble was, it still didn't stop folks from beating their wives or abusing their children the remaining days of the week, Ricky thought, which he was relatively certain that Jesus disapproved of, if He had an opinion at all.

The VA Hospital had two flagstaffs, displaying the Stars and Stripes and the flag of the State of Florida side by side, both of which hung limply in the unseasonable late spring heat. There were a few desultory green bushes planted by the entranceway, and Ricky could see a few old men in tattered gowns and wheelchairs on a small side porch sitting about unattended beneath the afternoon sun. The men weren't in a group or even in pairs. They each seemed to be functioning in an orbit defined by age and disease that existed solely for themselves. He walked on, through the entranceway. The interior was dark, almost gaping like an open mouth. He shuddered as he walked in. The hospitals where he'd taken his wife before she died were bright, modern, designed to reflect all the advancements in medicine, places that seemed filled with the energy of determination to survive. Or, as was her case, the need to battle against the inevitable. To steal days from the disease, like a football player struggling to gain every yard, no matter how many defenders clung to him. This hospital was the exact opposite. It was a building on the low end of the medical scale, where the treatment plans were as bland

and uncreative as the daily menu. Death as regular and simple as plain, white rice. Ricky felt cold, walking inside, thinking that it was a sad place where old men went to die.

He saw a receptionist behind a desk, and he approached her.

'Good morning, father,' she said brightly. 'How can I help you?'

'Good morning, my child,' Ricky replied, fingering the clerical collar that he'd borrowed from the university property room. 'A hot day to be wearing the Lord's chosen outfit,' he said, making a joke. 'Sometimes I wonder why the Lord didn't choose, oh, those nice Hawaiian shirts with all the bright colors, instead of the collar,' Ricky said. 'Be much more comfortable on a day like this.'

The receptionist laughed out loud. 'What could He have been thinking?' she said, joining him in the humor of the moment.

'So, I am here to see a man who is a patient. His name would be Tyson.'

'Are you a relative, father?'

'No, alas, no, my child. But I was asked by his daughter to look him up when I came down here on some other church-related business.'

This answer seemed to pass muster, which is what Ricky had expected. He didn't think anyone in the panhandle of Florida would ever turn away a man of the cloth. The woman checked through some computer records. She grimaced slightly, as the name came up on her screen. 'That's unusual,' she said. 'His records show no living relatives. No next of kin at all. You're sure it was his daughter?'

'They have been deeply estranged, and she turned her back on him some time ago. Now, perhaps, with my assistance, and the blessing of the Lord, the chance of a reconciliation in his old age . . . '

'That would be nice, father. I hope so. Still, she should be listed.'

'I will tell her that,' he said.

'He probably needs her . . . '

'Bless you, child,' Ricky said. He was actually enjoying the hypocrisy of his words and his tale, in the same way that a performer enjoys those moments onstage. Moments filled with a little tension, some doubt, but energized by the audience. After so many years spent behind the couch keeping quiet about most things, Ricky actually found himself eager to be out in the world and lying.

'It doesn't appear that there is much time for a reconciliation, father. I'm afraid Mr. Tyson is in the hospice section,' she said. 'I'm sorry, father.'

'He is . . . '

'Terminal.'

'Then perhaps my timing is better than I hoped. Perhaps I can give him some comfort in his final days . . . '

The receptionist nodded. She pointed to a schematic drawing of the hospital. 'This is where you want to go. The nurse on duty there will help you out.'

⋆ ⋆ ⋆

Ricky made his way through the warren of corridors, seeming to descend into worlds that were increasingly cold and bland. It was as if, to his eyes, everything in the hospital was slightly frayed. It reminded him of the distinctions between the button-down, expensive clothing stores of Manhattan, that he knew from his days as a psychoanalyst, and the second-hand, Salvation Army world that he knew as the janitor in New Hampshire. In the VA Hospital, nothing was new, nothing was modern, nothing looked as if it worked quite the way it was supposed to, everything looked as if it had been used several times before. Even the white paint on the cinder-block walls was faded and yellowed. It was a curious thing, he thought, to be moving through the midst of a place that should have been dedicated to cleanliness and science, and get the sensation that he would need to shower. The underclass of medicine, he thought. And, as he passed the cardiac care units and the pulmonary care units and past a locked door that was labeled psychiatry, things seemed to grow increasingly decrepit and worn, until he reached the final stage, a set of double doors, with the words HOSPICE UNIT stenciled on them. The person who had done the lettering had placed the words slightly askew, one on each door, so that they failed to line up properly.

The clerical collar and suit did their job impeccably, Ricky noted. No one asked him for identification, no one seemed to think he was out of place in the slightest. As he entered the unit, he spotted a nursing station, and he approached the desk. The nurse on duty, a large, black woman, looked up and said, 'Ah, father, they called me and told me you were coming down. Room 300 for Mr. Tyson. First bed by the door . . . '

'Thank you,' Ricky said. 'I wonder if you could tell me what he's suffering from . . . '

The nurse dutifully handed Ricky a medical chart. Lung cancer. Not much time and most of it painful. He felt little sympathy.

Under the guise of being helpful, Ricky thought, hospitals do much to degrade. That was certainly the case for Calvin Tyson, who was hooked up to a number of machines, and rested uncomfortably on the bed, propped up, staring at an old television set hung between his bed and his neighbor's. The set was tuned to a soap opera, but the sound was off. The picture was fuzzy, as well.

Tyson was emaciated, almost skeletal. He wore an

oxygen mask that hung from his neck, occasionally lifting it to help him breathe. His nose was tinged with the unmistakable blue of emphysema, and his scrawny, naked legs stretched out on the bed like sticks and branches knocked from a tree by a storm, littering the roadway. The man in the bed next to him was much the same, and the two men wheezed in a duet of agony. Tyson turned as Ricky entered, just shifting his head.

'I don't want to talk to no priest,' he choked out.

Ricky smiled. Not pleasantly. 'But this priest wants to speak to you.'

'I want to be left alone,' Tyson said.

Ricky surveyed the man lying on the bed. 'From the looks of things,' he said briskly, 'you're going to be all alone for eternity in not too long.'

Tyson struggled to shake his head. 'Don't need no religion, not anymore.'

'And I'm not going to try any,' Ricky replied. 'At least not like what you think.'

Ricky paused, making certain that the door was shut behind him. He saw that there was a set of earphones dangling over the bed corner, for listening to the television. He walked around the end of the bed, and stared at Tyson's roommate. The man seemed just as badly off, but looked at Ricky with a detached expectancy. Ricky pointed at the headphones by his bed. 'You want to put those on, so I can speak with your neighbor privately?' he asked, but in reality demanded. The man shrugged, and slipped them onto his ears with some difficulty.

'Good,' Ricky said, turning back to Tyson. 'You know who sent me?' he asked.

'Got no idea,' Tyson croaked. 'Ain't nobody left that cares about me.'

'You're wrong about that,' Ricky answered back. 'Dead wrong.'

Ricky moved in close, bending over the dying man, and whispered coldly, 'So, old man, tell me the truth: How many times did you fuck your daughter before she ran away for good?'

26

The old man's eyes widened in surprise and he shifted about in his bed. He put up a bony hand, waving it in the small space between Ricky and his sunken chest, as if he could thrust the question away, but was far too weak to do so. He coughed and choked and swallowed hard, before responding, 'What sort of priest are you?'

'A priest of memory,' Ricky answered.

'What you mean by that?' The man's words were rushed and panicked. His eyes darted about the room, as if searching for someone to help him.

Ricky paused, before he answered. He looked down at Calvin Tyson, squirming in his bed, suddenly terrified, and tried to guess whether Tyson was scared of Ricky, or of the history that Ricky seemed to know about. He suspected that the man had spent years alone with the knowledge of what he'd done, and even if it had been suspected by school authorities, neighbors, and his wife, still he'd probably deluded himself into imagining it was a secret only he and his dead daughter shared.

Ricky, with his provocative question, must have seemed to him to be some sort of deathly apparition. He saw the man's hand start to reach for a button on a wire hanging over the headboard, and he knew that was the nurse call button. He bent over Tyson and pushed the device out of his grasp. 'We're not going to need that,' he said. 'This is going to be a private conversation.' The old man's hand dropped to the bed and he grasped at the oxygen mask, sucking in deep draughts of enriched air, his eyes still wide in fear. The mask was old-fashioned, green, and covered the nose and mouth with an opaque plastic. In a more modern facility, Tyson would have been given a smaller unit that clipped beneath his nostrils. But the VA hospital was the sort of place where old equipment was sent to be used up before being discarded, more or less like many of the men occupying the beds. Ricky pulled the oxygen mask away from Tyson's face.

'Who you be?' the man demanded, fearful. He had a voice filled with the locutions of the South. Ricky thought there was something childlike in the terror that filled his eyes.

'I'm a man with some questions,' Ricky said. 'I'm a man searching for some answers. Now, this can go hard or easy, depending on you, old man.'

To his surprise, he found threatening a decrepit, aged man who had molested his only daughter and then turned his back upon her orphaned children, came easy.

'You ain't no preacher,' the man said. 'You don't work with God.'

'You're mistaken there,' Ricky said. 'And considering as how you're going to be facing Him any day now, maybe you'd best err on the side of belief.'

This argument seemed to make some sense to the old man, who shifted about, then nodded.

'Your daughter,' Ricky started, only to be cut off.

'My daughter's dead. She was no good. Never was.'

'You think you maybe had something to do with that?'

Calvin Tyson shook his head. 'You don't know nothing. Nobody know nothing. Whatever happened be history. Ancient history.'

Ricky paused, staring into the man's eyes. He saw them hardening, like concrete setting up quick in the harsh sun. He calculated quickly, a measurement of psychology. Tyson was a remorseless pedophile, Ricky thought. Unrepentant and incapable of understanding the evil that he'd loosed in his child. And he was lying in his death bed and probably more scared of what awaited him, than what had gone past. He thought he would try that chord, see where it took him.

'I can give you forgiveness . . .,' Ricky said.

The old man snorted and sneered. 'Ain't no preacher that powerful. I'm just gonna take my chances.'

Ricky paused, then said, 'Your daughter Claire had three children . . . '

'She was a whore, ran away with that wildcatter boy, then run on up to New York City. That's what killed her. Not me.'

'When she died,' Ricky continued, 'you were contacted. You were her closest living relative. Someone in New York City called you up and wanted to know if you would take the children . . . '

'What did I want with those bastards? She never married. I didn't want them.'

Ricky stared at Calvin Tyson and thought this must have been a difficult decision for him. On the one hand, he didn't want the financial burden of raising his daughter's three orphans. But, on the other, it would have provided him with several new sources for his perverted sexual urges. Ricky thought that would have been a compelling, almost overwhelming seduction. A pedophile in the grips of desire is a potent unstoppable force. What made him turn down a new and ready source of pleasure? Ricky continued to eye the old man, and then, in an instant, he knew. Calvin Tyson had other outlets. The neighbors' children? Down the street? Around the corner? In a playground? Ricky didn't know, but he did understand that the answer was close by.

'So you signed some papers, giving them up for adoption, right?'

'Yes. Why you want to know this?'

'Because I need to find them.'

'Why?'

Ricky looked around. He made a small gesture at the

hospital room. 'Do you know who put you on the street? Do you know who foreclosed on your house and tossed you out so that you ended up here, dying all by yourself?'

Tyson shook his head. 'Somebody bought the note on the house from the mortgage company. Didn't give me no chance to make good when I was short one month. Just bang! Out I went.'

'What happened to you then?'

The man's eyes grew rheumy, suddenly filling with tears. Pathetic, Ricky thought. He curbed any nascent sensation of pity, though. What Calvin Tyson got was less than he deserved.

'I was out on the street. Got sick. Got beat. Now I'm fixing to die, just like you said.'

'Well,' Ricky said, 'the man who put you in this bed all alone is your daughter's child.'

Calvin Tyson's eyes widened and he shook his head. 'How that be?'

'He bought the note. He evicted you. He probably arranged to have you beaten as well. Were you raped?'

Tyson shook his head. Ricky thought: There's something Rumplestiltskin didn't know about. Claire Tyson must have kept that secret from her children. Lucky for the old man that Rumplestiltskin never bothered to speak with the neighbors or anyone at the high school.

'He did all that to me? Why?'

'Because you turned your back on him and on his mother. So, he repaid you in kind.'

The man sobbed once. 'All the bad that happened to me . . . '

Ricky finished for him, ' . . . comes from one man. That's the man I'm trying to find. So, I'll ask you again: You signed some papers to give the children up for adoption, right?'

Tyson nodded.

'Did you get some money, too?'

Again the old man nodded. 'Couple thousand.'

'What was the name of the people who adopted the three children?'

'I got a paper.'

'Where?'

'In a box, with my things, in the closet.' He pointed at a scarred gray metal locker.

Ricky opened the door and saw some threadbare clothes hanging from hooks. On the floor was a cheap lockbox. The clasp had been broken. Ricky opened it and rapidly shuffled through some old papers until he found several folded together, with a rubber band around them. He saw a seal from the state of New York. He thrust the papers into his jacket pocket.

'You won't need them,' he told the old man. He looked down at the man stretched across the dingy white sheets of the hospital bed, his gown barely covering his nakedness. Tyson sucked at some more oxygen and looked pale. 'You know what,' Ricky said slowly, his cruelty astonishing him, 'old man, now you can just go about the business of dying. I think you'd be wise to get it over with sooner rather than later, because I think there's more pain waiting for you. Much more pain. As much pain as you delivered on this earth multiplied a hundred times. So just go ahead and die.'

'What you going to do?' Tyson asked. His voice was a shocked whisper, filled with gasps and wheezes and constricted by the disease eating away at his chest.

'Find those children.'

'Why you want to do that?'

'Because one of them killed me, too,' Ricky said, as he turned to leave.

* * *

It was just before the dinner hour, when Ricky knocked on the door of a trim two-bedroom ranch house on a quiet street lined with palms. He was still wearing his priest's regalia, which gave him an extra bit of confidence, as if the addition of the collar around his neck provided him with an invisibility that would defy anyone who might ask questions. He waited while he heard shuffling inside, and then the door cracked open and he saw an elderly woman peering around the edge. The door opened a little wider when she saw the clerical garb, but she remained behind a screen.

'Yes?' she asked.

'Hello,' Ricky replied cheerily. 'I wonder if you might help me. I'm trying to trace the whereabouts of a young man named Daniel Collins . . .'

The woman gasped, and lifted a hand to her mouth to cover her surprise. Ricky remained silent as he watched the woman struggle to recapture her composure. He tried to read the changes her face underwent, from shock, narrowing to a harshness that seemed to him to be filled with a chill that reached right through the screen door. Her face finally set stiffly, and her voice, when she was able to use it, seemed to employ words carved from winter.

'He is lost to us,' she said. There were some tears that battled at the corners of her eyes, contradicting the iron in her voice.

'I'm sorry,' Ricky said, still maintaining a cheeriness that helped mask his sudden curiosity. 'I don't understand what you mean by 'lost'?'

The woman shook her head, not replying directly. She measured his priest's outfit, then asked, 'Father, why are you looking for my son now?'

He pulled out the phony cancer letter, guessing that the woman wouldn't read it carefully enough to find questions in it.

As she started to eye the document, he started to

speak, figuring that she wouldn't really be able to concentrate on what was written while he spoke. Distracting her from asking questions of him didn't seem like a difficult chore. 'You see, Mrs . . . Collins, correct? The parish is really trying to reach out to anyone who might be a marrow donor for this youngster who is related to you distantly. You see the problem? I'd ask you to take the blood screening test, but I suspect you're beyond the age where marrow can be donated. You're over sixty, correct?'

Ricky had no idea whether bone marrow ceased being viable at any age. So he made up a phony question where the answer was obvious. The woman lifted her eyes from the letter to respond, and Ricky reached out and took it from her hands, well before she'd had the opportunity to digest all of it. He said, as he did so, 'This has a lot of medical stuff in it. I can explain, if you'd prefer. Perhaps we could sit down?'

The woman nodded reluctantly and held the door open for him. He stepped into a house that seemed as fragile as the old woman who lived there. It was filled with small china objects and figurines, empty vases and knickknacks, and had a musty aged smell that overcame the stale air of the air conditioner pumping away with a banging sound that made him think some part was loose inside. The carpets had plastic runners and the couch, as well, had a plastic cover, as if the woman were afraid of any dirt that might be left behind. He had the impression that everything had a proper position in the house, and that the woman who lived there would be able to sense instantly any item that had shifted position even a fraction of an inch.

The sofa made a squeak as he sat.

'Your son, is he available? You see, he might be a match . . . ,' Ricky launched ahead, lying easily.

'He's dead,' the woman said coldly.

'Dead? But how?'

Mrs. Collins shook her head. 'Dead to all of us. Dead to me, now. Dead and worthless, nothing but pain, father. I'm sorry.'

'How did he . . . ?'

She shook her head. 'Not yet. But soon enough, I'm thinking.'

Ricky leaned back, making the same squeaking sound. 'I'm afraid I don't precisely understand,' he said.

The woman reached down and removed a scrapbook from a shelf beneath a coffee table. She opened it, flipped through several pages. Ricky could see newspaper stories about sports games, and he remembered that Daniel Collins was a high school athlete. There was a graduation picture and then a blank page. She stopped there, and handed it across to him. 'Turn the page,' she said bitterly.

Centered on a single sheet of the scrapbook was a single story from the *Tampa Tribune*. The headline was: MAN ARRESTED AFTER BARROOM DEATH. There were few details, other than Daniel Collins had been arrested slightly over a year earlier, and charged with homicide following a fight in a barroom. On the adjacent page, another headline: STATE TO SEEK DEATH IN BAR FIGHT SLAYING. This story, clipped and glued to the middle of another page, had a photograph accompanying it, of a middle-aged Daniel Collins being led handcuffed into a courtroom. Ricky scanned the newspaper clipping. The facts of the case seemed simple enough. There had been a fight between two drunken men. One of them had gone outside and waited for the other to emerge. Knife in hand, according to the state prosecutors. The killer, Daniel Collins, had been arrested at the scene, unconscious, drunk, bloody knife near his hand, victim spread-eagled a few feet away. The victim had been eviscerated in a particularly cruel fashion, the newspaper hinted, before being robbed. It appeared that after Collins had murdered the man and taken his money, he'd paused to swig another bottle of some cheap liquor, become disorientated, and passed out before fleeing the scene. Open and shut.

He read meager stories about a trial and a conviction. Collins had claimed that he was unaware of the killing, so addled with drink that night. It wasn't much of an explanation and it didn't work well with the jury. They were out deliberating for only ninety minutes. It took them an additional couple of hours to recommend the death penalty — the same explanation being offered up in mitigation that was ignored. Official death, cut and dried, wrapped up and packaged with a minimum of messiness.

Ricky looked up. The old woman was shaking her head.

'My lovely boy,' she said. 'Lost him first to that bitch girl, then to drink, now to death row.'

'Have they set a date?' Ricky asked.

'No,' the woman replied. 'His lawyer says they've got appeals. Going to try this court, that court. I don't really understand too well. All I knows is that my boy says he didn't do it, but it didn't make no difference.' She stared hard at the clerical collar snug around Ricky's neck. 'In this state, we all love Jesus, and most folks worship on Sundays. But when the Good Book says 'Thou Shall Not Kill,' it don't seem to apply to our courtrooms none. Us and Georgia and Texas. Bad places to do a crime where someone dies, father. I wish my boy'd thought of that before he took up that knife and got into that fight.'

'He says he's innocent?'

'That's right. Says he's got no memory of the fight at all. Says he woke up all covered in blood when the policeman shoved him with their sticks and with that knife by his side. I guess having no recollection isn't much of a defense.'

Ricky turned the page, but the scrapbook was blank.

'Got to save a page, I guess,' the woman said. 'For one last story. I hope I pass before that day arrives, for I do not want to see it come.'

She shook her head. 'You know something, father?'

'What's that?'

'It always made me angry. You know, when he scored that touchdown against South Side High, in the city championship, why, they put his picture right on the front page. But all these stories, over there in Tampa where nobody much knew about my boy at all, why, they were little stories, stuck way inside the paper, where hardly anyone ever saw them. It seems to me that if you're going to go about taking some man's life away from him in a court of law, why you ought to make a big deal of it. It ought to be special and right up there on the front page. But it isn't. It's just another little story that gets stuck back next to the broken sewer main and the gardening column. It's like life isn't all that important anymore.'

She rose and Ricky rose with her.

'Talking about this makes my heart feel filled with sickness, father. And there ain't no comfort in any words, not even the Good Book, to take the hurt away.'

'I think, my child, that you should open your heart to the goodness that you remember, and that way you will be comforted.' Ricky thought trying to sound like a priest made his words trite and ineffectual, which was more or less how he wanted them. The old woman had raised a boy who was to all outward appearances a proper son of a bitch, he thought, who started out his sorry excuse for life by seducing a classmate, dragging her alongside of him for a few years, then abandoning her and her children when they became inconvenient; and he ended up by killing another man over probably no reason at all, other than one created by too much liquor. If there was anything redeeming about Daniel Collins's silly, useless existence, he had yet to see it.

This cynicism, boiling around inside of him, was more or less confirmed by the words the old woman spoke next.

'The goodness stopped with that girl. When she got pregnant that first time, why, any chance my boy had, just went right away then. She lured him in, used all that woman cunning, trapped him, and then used him to get out of here and away. All the trouble he had, becoming someone, making his way in the world, why, I blame it all on her.'

The woman's voice left no room for any compromise. It was cold, clipped, and utterly committed to the idea that her darling boy had nothing to do with creating any of the trouble that befell him. And Ricky, the onetime psychoanalyst, knew there was little chance that she would see her own complicity. We create, he thought, and then, when that creation goes so wrong, we want to blame others, when it is usually ourselves to blame.

'But you think he's innocent?' Ricky asked. He knew the answer. And he did not say *of the crime*, because the old woman believed her son was innocent of everything he'd done wrong.

'Why, of course. If he said it, I believe it.' She reached into the scrap-book and found an attorney's card, which she handed to Ricky. A public defender in Tampa. He noted the name and number and let her show him out the door.

'Do you know what happened to the three children? Your grandchildren?' Ricky asked, gesturing with the phony medical letter.

The woman shook her head. 'They was give up, I heard. Danny signed some paper when he was in jail in Texas. He got caught doing a burglary, but I didn't believe it none. Did a couple of years in prison. We never heard from them no time again. I guess they's all grown up now, but I never seen any of 'em, not one time, so it's not like I think of them. Danny, he did the right thing by giving them up after that woman passed, because he couldn't raise three children he didn't know all by hisself. And I couldn't help him none, either, all alone here and being sick and all. So they became someone else's problem and someone else's children. Like I said, we never heard from them.'

Ricky knew this last statement was untrue.

'Did you even know their names?' he asked.

The woman shook her head. The cruelty in that gesture almost struck him like a fist, and he understood where the young Daniel Collins had found his own selfishness.

When the last of the day's heat and sunshine hit his head, he stood dizzily on the sidewalk for just a moment, wondering whether Rumplestiltskin's reach was so far, that it had put Daniel Collins on death row. He guessed that it was. He just wasn't precisely certain how.

27

Ricky returned to New Hampshire and back to life as Richard Lively. Everything that he'd learned on his trip to Florida troubled him.

Two people had entered Claire Tyson's life at critical moments. One had left her and her children adrift, and now occupied a cell on death row, claiming innocence in a state notorious for turning a deaf ear on such protests. The other had turned his back on the daughter he'd abused and the grandchildren who'd needed help, and years later he'd been turned out on the street equally cruelly, and now was condemned to wheeze away his final days on a different, but similarly unforgiving death row.

Ricky added to the equation beginning to form in his head: The boyfriend who beat Claire Tyson in New York was then beaten to death in his own turn, with a bloody *R* carved into his chest. The lazy Dr. Starks, who because of his own indecisiveness at one time failed to help the distraught Claire Tyson when she came pleading to him, was subsequently driven to suicide after every avenue where he might find help for himself was systematically destroyed.

There had to be others. This realization chilled his heart.

It seemed that Rumplestiltskin had designed a number of acts of revenge according to a simple principle: to each according to who they were. Crimes of omission were being judged and sentences being dealt out, years later. The boyfriend, who was nothing more than a thug and criminal, had been treated one way. The grandfather who'd denied his offspring's entreaties had been punished differently. It was, Ricky thought, a unique method of delivering evil. His own game had been designed with Ricky's personality and education in mind. Others had been dealt with more brutally, because they came from worlds where brutality was more refined. One other thing seemed clear cut: In Rumplestiltskin's imagination, there was no statute of limitations.

The end results, though, he took note, seemed to be the same. A consistent path of death or ruin. And anyone who might stand in the way, like the unfortunate Mr. Zimmerman or Detective Riggins were seen as impediments that were summarily erased with the same amount of compassion one would reserve for a horsefly that landed on one's forearm.

Ricky shuddered as he assessed how patient, dedicated, and cold-blooded Rumplestiltskin truly was.

He started to make a modest list of people who also might have failed to help Claire Tyson and her three young children when they were in need: Was there a landlord in New York who demanded rent from the destitute woman? If so, they were probably on the street somewhere, wondering what happened to their building. A social worker who failed to get her into an assistance program? Had they been ruined financially, and now forced to apply for the same program? A priest who had listened to her entreaties and suggested that prayer might fill an empty stomach? They were probably praying for themselves, now. He could only guess how far Rumplestiltskin's revenge reached: What happened to the city power worker who had turned off the electricity at her house when she failed to pay a bill on time? He didn't know the answers to these questions, nor did he know precisely where Rumplestiltskin had drawn his dividing line, separating the people he'd judged guilty, from however many others there might be. Still, Ricky knew one thing: A number of people had once upon a time come up far short and were now paying a price.

Or, more likely, had paid their debt. All the people who had neglected to help Claire Tyson, so that her only choice was to take her own life in despair.

It was the most frightening concept of justice that Ricky had ever imagined. Murders of both the body and the soul. It seemed to Ricky that he had often been scared since Rumplestiltskin had entered his life. He had been a man of routine and insight. Now, nothing was solid, everything was unsettled. The fear that ricocheted within him now was something different. Something he had difficulty categorizing, but he knew it left his mouth dry and a bitter taste on his tongue. As an analyst, he had lived in his well-to-do patients' worlds of convoluted anxieties and debilitating frustrations, but these seemed now to be uniformly petty and pathetically self-indulgent.

The scope of Rumplestiltskin's fury astounded him. And, at the same time, made perfect sense.

Psychoanalysis teaches one thing, he thought: Nothing ever happens in a vacuum. A single bad act can have all sorts of repercussions. He was reminded of the desktop perpetual motion machines that some of his colleagues had, where a group of ball bearings were hung in a row, and if one was lifted slightly, so that it swung against the others, the force would cause the last in the line to swing out and then bounce back, making a clicking sound and starting an engine of momentum that would only stop when someone injected their hand into the works. Rumplestiltskin's revenge, of which he'd been only a single part, was like that machine.

There were others dead. Others destroyed. He alone, in all likelihood, saw the entirety of what had taken place. Perpetual motion.

Ricky felt shafts of cold drip through his body.

These were all crimes that existed in a plane defined by immunity. What detective, what police authority, would ever be able to link them all together, because the only thing the victims had in common was a relationship with a woman dead for twenty years.

Serial crimes, Ricky thought, with a thread so invisible that it defied imagination. Like the policeman who had blithely told him about the *R* carved in Rafael Johnson's chest, there was always someone far more likely to wear guilt than the vaporous Mr. R. The reasons behind his own death were blatantly obvious. Career in tatters, home destroyed, wife dead, finances in ruins, relatively friendless and introspective, why wouldn't he kill himself?

And one other thing was abundantly clear to him: If Rumplestiltskin learned that he'd escaped, if he even suspected that Ricky still breathed air on this planet, he would be on Ricky's trail instantly with evil intentions. Ricky doubted that he would have the opportunity to play any game the second time around. It also occurred to him how easy it would be to dispatch his new identity: Richard Lively was a nonentity in the world. His very anonymity made his own quick and brutal death a relative certainty. Richard Lively could be executed in broad daylight, and no policeman anywhere would be able to make the necessary connections leading him back to Ricky Starks and some man called Rumplestiltskin. What they would find out was that Richard Lively wasn't Richard Lively and he would instantly become a John Doe, planted with little ceremony without a headstone in some potter's field. Perhaps a detective would wonder idly who he truly once was, but, inundated with other cases, the death of Richard Lively would simply be shunted aside. Forever.

What made Ricky so safe, also made him utterly vulnerable.

So, upon his return to New Hampshire, he greeted taking up the simple routines of his life in Durham with unbridled enthusiasm. It was as if he hoped he could lose himself readily in the steadiness of getting up each morning and going to work with the rest of the janitorial force at the university, of swabbing floors, cleaning bathrooms, polishing hallways, and changing lightbulbs, exchanging a joke or two with coworkers, speculating about the Red Sox's prospects for the upcoming season. He functioned in a world so insistently normal and mundane that it cried out to be painted in institutional pale blues and light greens. Once, when operating a steam cleaner across the carpet of the faculty lounge, he discovered that the sensation of the machine humming, vibrating in his hands, and the swath of clean rug that it created was almost hypnotically pleasant. It was as if he could disappear from who he once had been in the new simplicity of this world. It was a strangely satisfying situation; alone, a job that shouted out routine and regularity, the occasional night spent manning the telephone bank at the suicide prevention line, where he recalled his skills as a therapist, dispensing advice and throwing lifelines in a modest, controlled fashion. He discovered he didn't much miss the daily deposit of angst, frustration, and anger that characterized his life as an analyst. He wondered, some, whether the people he'd known, or even his late wife, would recognize him. In a curious way, Ricky thought that Richard Lively was closer to the person that he had wanted to be, closer to the person who'd found himself in summers on the Cape, than Dr. Starks had ever realized treating the rich and powerful and neurotic.

Anonymity, he thought, is seductive.

But elusive. For every second that he forced himself to grow comfortable with who he was, the revenge persona of Federick Lazarus shouted contradictory commands. He renewed his physical fitness training, and spent his free hours perfecting marksmanship skills on the pistol practice range. As the weather continued to improve, bringing warmth and bursting with color, he decided he needed to add outdoor skills to his repertoire, so he signed up for an orienteering class operated by a hiking and camping company under the name of Frederick Lazarus.

In a way, he'd been triangulated, in much the same way one finds his location when lost in the woods. Three pillars: who he was, who he'd become, who he needed to be.

He asked himself, late at night, sitting alone in the near-darkness of his rented room, a single desk lamp barely denting the shadows, whether he could turn his back on everything that had happened. Simply abandon any emotional connection to his past and what had befallen him, and become a man of complete simplicity. Live paycheck to paycheck. Take pleasure in basic routine. Redefine himself. Take up fishing or hunting or even just reading. Connect with as few people as possible. Live life with monk-like style and a hermit's solitude. Turn his back on fifty-three years of life, and say that it all started anew from the day he'd set fire to his home on the Cape and gone forward from there. It was almost Zenlike and tantalizing. Ricky could evaporate from the world like a puddle of water on a hot, sunny day, rising into the atmosphere.

This ability was almost as frightening as the alternative.

It seemed to him that he had reached the moment where he had to make a choice. Like Odysseus, his screen name, the route lay between Scylla and Charybdis. There were costs and risks with each selection.

Late at night, in his modest rented room in New Hampshire, he spread out on his bed all the notes and connections he had to the man who had forced him to erase himself from his life. Bits and pieces of information, clues and directions that he could follow.

Or not. Either he was going to pursue the man who'd done this to him, risking exposure. Or he was going to toss it all and make what life he could out of what he'd already established. He felt a little like some fifteenth-century Spanish explorer, standing unsteadily on the pitching deck of a tiny sailing ship, staring out at the wide expanse of deep green ocean and perhaps a new and uncertain world just beyond the horizon.

In the center of the pile of material were the documents that he'd taken from the old man Tyson on his death bed at the VA Hospital in Pensacola. In the papers were the names of the adoptive parents who had taken the three children in twenty years ago. That, he knew, was his next step.

The decision was: take it — or not.

A part of him insisted he could be happy as Richard Lively, maintenance man. Durham was a pleasant town. His landladies were nice enough folks.

But another part of him saw things differently.

Dr. Frederick Starks did not deserve to die. Not for what he'd done, even if wrong, at a time of his own indecision and doubt. There was no denying that he could have done better for Claire Tyson. He could have reached out and perhaps been the hand that helped her find a life worth living. He couldn't debate that he'd had that chance and that he had missed it. Rumplestiltskin was right about that. But his punishment far exceeded his complicity.

And this thought infuriated Ricky.

'I didn't kill her,' he said out loud, but whispering the words.

The room around him was as much a coffin as it was a life raft, he believed.

He wondered if he could ever take a breath of air, without it tasting of doubt. What sort of safety was there in hiding forever? Of always suspecting the person behind every window of being the man who had driven him to anonymity. It was an awful thought, he understood: Rumplestiltskin's game would never end for him, even if it had ended for the elusive Mr. R. Ricky would not know, never be certain, never really have a moment's peace, free from questions.

He needed to find an answer.

Alone in his room, Ricky reached for the papers on the bed. He rolled the rubber band that held the adoption documents together off the sheaf so quickly that it snapped.

'All right,' he said quietly, speaking to himself and to any ghosts who might have been listening in, 'the game starts up again.'

* * *

What Ricky learned swiftly was that social services in New York City had placed the three children into a succession of foster homes for the first six months after their mother died, until they were adopted by a couple who lived in New Jersey. There was a single social worker's report stating that the children had been difficult placements; that except for their last and unidentified foster home, they had proven to be disruptive, angry, and abusive in each group setting. The social worker had recommended therapy, especially for the oldest. The report was written in plain, bureaucratic cover-your-butt English, without the sort of detail that might have told Ricky something about the child who was to grow into the man who had tormented him. He did learn that the adoption was handled by the Episcopal Diocese of New York, under their charity wing. There was no record of money changing hands, but Ricky suspected some had. There were copies of legal documents relinquishing any claims on the children signed by old man Tyson. There was another document, from Daniel

Collins, signed while he was in jail in Texas. Ricky noted the symmetry of that element: Daniel Collins had rejected the three children while in prison. Years later, he is returned to prison under the rough guidance of Rumplestiltskin. Ricky thought that however the man who was once a rejected child managed this feat, it must have given him terrific satisfaction.

The couple who took in the three abandoned children was Howard and Martha Jackson. An address in West Windsor, a semisuburb, semifarmland locale a few miles away from Princeton, was given, but no other detailed information about the parents. They had taken all three children, which interested Ricky. There were questions in how they'd managed to stay together that were as potent as why they weren't separated. The children were listed, as male child Luke, twelve years; male child Matthew, eleven years; and female child Joanna, nine years. Biblical names, Ricky thought. He doubted that these names had remained connected to the children.

He made several computer sorties, but drew blanks. This surprised him. It seemed to him that there should have been some information available floating around in the Internet. He checked the electronic white pages, found many Jacksons in central New Jersey, but no name that dovetailed with those he had on the meager sheaf of papers.

What he did have was an old address. Which meant that there was a door he could knock on. It seemed his only alternative.

Ricky considered using the priest's garb and fake leukemia letter, but decided they had served their purpose once, and were best saved for another occasion. He ceased shaving instead, rapidly growing a spotty beard, and ordered a mock identification card from a nonexistent private detective agency over the Internet.

Another late-night inspection of the drama department's wardrobe room provided him with a fake stomach, a pillow-type device that he could strap beneath a T-shirt and which made him appear to be perhaps forty or fifty pounds heavier than his lean figure actually was. To his relief, he also found a brown suit that accommodated the extra girth. In the makeup cases, he also uncovered an extra bit of help. He slipped all the necessary items into a green garbage bag and took it home with him. When he got to his room, he added his semiautomatic pistol and two fully loaded clips to the bag.

He rented a four-year-old car that had seen better days from the local Rent-A-Wreck, which generally provided for students, and seemed more than willing to take his cash with few questions, the clerk dutifully taking down the information from the phony California driver's license that he provided, and the following Friday evening, when he'd finished his shift in the maintenance department, started driving south toward New Jersey. He let the night surround him, allowed the miles to hum beneath the tires on the rental car, and drove rapidly but steadily, a constant five miles per hour above the posted speed limit. Once he rolled down the window, feeling a breath of warm air slide into the car, and he thought that it was quickly approaching summer once again. If he'd been in the city, he would have begun trying to steer his patients toward some recognition that they could hold on to when his inevitable August vacation rolled around. Sometimes he could manage this, sometimes not. He remembered walking in the city in the late spring and early summer and how the flowers in the park and the burst of greenery coming forth seemed to defeat the canyons of brick and concrete that were Manhattan. It was the best of times, there, he thought, but elusive, replaced quickly by oppressive heat and humidity. It lasted just long enough to be persuasive.

It was well past midnight when he skirted the city, stealing a glance back over his shoulder as he cruised across the George Washington Bridge. Even in the dead of night, the city seemed to glow. The Upper West Side stretched away from him, and he knew that just out of his sight was Columbia Presbyterian Hospital and the clinic where he'd worked so briefly so many years earlier, oblivious to the impact of what he was doing. A curious blend of emotions slapped him, as he swept past the tolls, and arrived in New Jersey. It was as if he was caught in a dream, one of those unsettling, tense series of images and events that occupied the unconscious, that bordered on nightmare, just stepping back from that edge. The city seemed to him to be all about who he was, the car that rattled as he steered it over the highway represented what he'd become, and the darkness ahead, what he might be.

A vacancy sign at an Econo Lodge on Route One beckoned him and he stopped. The night desk was manned by a sad-eyed man from India or Pakistan, who wore a nametag that identified him as Omar, and who seemed a little put out that his half-sleep reverie was interrupted by Ricky's arrival. He did provide Ricky with a street map of the area, before returning to his chair, some chemistry books, and a thermos of some warm liquid that he cradled in his lap.

* * *

In the morning, Ricky spent some time with the actor's makeup kit in the bathroom of the motel room, giving himself a fake contusion and scar just to the side of his left eye. He gave the addition a purplish-red coloring that was bound to draw the attention of anyone he spoke with. This was fairly elemental psychology, he thought. Just as in Pensacola, what folks would remember there was not who he was, but what he was, here their eyes would be drawn to the facial blemish inexorably, not registering the actual details of his face. The scraggly beard helped conceal his features as well. The fake stomach hung beneath his T-shirt added to the portrait. He'd wished that he'd also gotten some lifts for his shoes, but thought he might try that sometime in the future. After dressing in a cheap suit, he stuck his pistol in one pocket, along with the backup clip of bullets.

The address he was heading to, he believed, was a significant step closer to the man who'd wanted him dead. At least, he hoped it was.

The area he drove through seemed to him to be curiously conflicted. It was mainly flat, green, countryside, crisscrossed with roads that probably had once been rural, quiet, and neglected, but now seemed to carry the burden of upscale development. He passed numerous housing complexes, ranging from the decidedly middle-class, two- and three-bedroom ranch houses, to far more luxurious, mock mansions, with porticoes and columns, bedecked with swimming pools and three-car garages for the inevitable BMW, Range Rover, and Mercedes. Executive housing, he thought. Soulless places for men and women making money and spending money as rapidly as possible and thinking that this was somehow meaningful. The blend of the old and new was disconcerting; it was as if this part of the state couldn't make up its mind as to what it was and what it wanted to be. He suspected that neither the older farm owners, nor the modern business and brokerage types got along very well.

Sunlight filled his windshield and he rolled down the window. It was, he thought, a perfectly nice day — warm, filled with springtime promise. He could feel the weight of the pistol in his jacket pocket and he thought that he would fill himself with winter thoughts, instead.

He found a mailbox by the side of a back road in the midst of some remaining farmland that corresponded to the address he had. He hesitated, not at all sure as to what to expect. There was a single sign by the driveway: SAFETY FIRST KENNELS: BOARDING, GROOMING, TRAINING. BREEDERS OF 'ALL NATURAL' SECURITY SYSTEMS. Next to this statement was a picture of a Rottweiler, and Ricky saw a little sense of humor in that. He drove down the driveway, beneath some trees that formed a canopy above him.

When he came out from under the trees, he pulled up a circular drive to a 1950s-styled ranch house, a single story, with a brick facade in the front. The house had been added onto, in several phases, with white clapboard construction that connected to a warren of chain-link enclosures. As soon as he stopped and exited his car, he was immediately greeted by a cacophony of barking dogs. The musty odor of waste matter was everywhere, gaining purchase in the late morning heat and sun. As he stepped forward, the racket grew. He saw a sign on the addition that said OFFICE. A second sign, much the same as the one by the driveway entrance, adorned the wall. In the kennel closest to him, a large black Rottweiler, barrel-chested and weighing over a hundred pounds, rose up on its hind legs, mouth open, baring teeth. Of all the dogs in the kennel, and Ricky could see dozens twisting about, racing, measuring the extent of their confinement, this one seemed the only one that was quiet. The dog eyed him carefully, almost as if it was sizing him up, which, he supposed, it was.

He stepped inside the office and saw a middle-aged man sitting behind an old steel desk. The air was stale with the scent of urine. The man was lean, bald, rangy, with thick forearms, which Ricky figured were muscled by handling large animals.

'Be with you in a sec,' the man said. He was punching

numbers onto a calculator.

'Take your time,' Ricky replied. He watched a few more keystrokes, then saw the man grimace at the total. The man rose and came toward him.

'How can I help you,' he said. 'Jeez, fella, looks like you were in some kind of fight.'

Ricky nodded. 'I'm supposed to say, 'You ought to see the other guy . . . ' '

The dog breeder laughed. 'And I'm supposed to believe it. So, what can I do for you? But, I would point out, that if you'd had Brutus at your side, there wouldn't have been a fight. No way.'

'Brutus is the dog in the pen by the door?'

'You guessed it. He discourages debate through loyalty. And he's sired some pups that will be ready for training in another couple of weeks.'

'Thanks, but no thanks.'

The dog breeder looked confused.

Ricky pulled out the fake private investigator's identification card that he'd acquired from the novelty outlet over the Internet. The man stared at it for a minute, then said, 'So, Mr. Lazarus, I guess you're not here looking for a puppy?'

'No.'

'Well, what can I help you with?'

'Some years ago a couple lived here. A Howard and Martha Jackson . . . '

When he spoke the names, the man stiffened. The welcoming appearance disappeared instantly, replaced by an abrupt suspiciousness, that was underscored by the step back the man took, almost as if the names being spoken out loud had pushed him in the chest. His voice took on a flat, wary tone.

'What makes you interested in them?'

'Were they related to you?'

'I bought the place from their estate. This is a long time ago.'

'Their estate?'

'They died.'

'Died?'

'That's right. Why are you interested in them?'

'I'm interested in their three children . . . '

Again the man hesitated, as if considering what Ricky had asked.

'They didn't have no children. Died childless. Just a brother lived some ways away. He's the one sold me the place. I fixed it up real good. Made their business into something. But no kids. Never.'

'No, you're mistaken,' Ricky said. 'They did. They adopted three orphans from New York City through the Episcopal Diocese of New York . . . '

'Mister, I don't know where you got your information, but you're wrong. Dead wrong,' the breeder said, voice abruptly filling with barely concealed anger. 'The Jacksons didn't have no immediate family 'cept that brother who sold me this place. It was just the old couple and they passed away together. I don't know what you're talking about, and I think maybe you don't know what you're talking about.'

'Together? How?'

'That wasn't any of my business. And I don't know that it's any of your business, either.'

'But you know the answer, right?'

'Everyone lived around here knew the answer. You can check the newspaper. Or maybe go to the cemetery. They're buried right up the road.'

'But you're not going to help me?'

'You got that right. What sort of private detective are you?'

'I told you,' Ricky responded swiftly. 'One that's interested in the three children that the Jacksons together adopted in May of 1980.'

'And I told you, there weren't any children. Adopted or otherwise. So what's your real interest?'

'I have a client. He's got some questions. The rest is confidential,' Ricky said.

The man's eyes had narrowed, and his shoulders straightened, as if his initial shock had worn off, replaced by an aggressiveness that spoke loudly. 'A client? Somebody paying you to come around here and ask questions? Well, you got a card? A number where I can reach you, if maybe I remember something . . . '

'I'm from out of town,' Ricky lied quickly.

The breeder continued to eye Ricky. 'Telephone lines go state to state, fella. How can I reach you? Where do I get hold of you, if I need to?'

Now it was Ricky's turn to step back. 'What is it that you think you can remember later that you can't remember now?' he demanded.

The man's voice had finally cooled completely. Now he was measuring, assessing, as if trying to imprint every detail of Ricky's face and physique. 'Let me see that identification again,' he said. 'You got a badge?'

Everything about the man's sudden change screamed warnings to Ricky. He realized in that second that he was suddenly close to something dangerous, like walking in the dark and abruptly realizing he was at the edge of some steep embankment.

Ricky took a step back toward the door. 'Tell you what, I'll give you a couple of hours to think this over, then I'll call you back. You want to talk, you remember something, we can get together then.'

Ricky quickly maneuvered out of the office and took several strides toward the rental car. The breeder was a few steps behind him, but turned to the side, and within a second had reached the kennel containing Brutus. The man unlatched the gate and the dog, mouth agape, but still silent, sprang immediately to his side. The breeder gave a small, open palm signal, and the dog instantly froze, eyes locked directly on Ricky, waiting for the next command.

Ricky turned around to face the dog and owner, and took the last few steps to the car door backing up slowly. He reached into his pants pocket and removed the car keys. The dog finally emitted a single, low growl, just as menacing as the coiled muscles in its shoulders and the ears perked, awaiting the release from the breeder.

'I don't think I'm going to see you again, mister,' the breeder said. 'And I don't think coming around here and asking any more questions is a real good idea.'

Ricky moved the keys to his left hand and opened his door. At the same time, his right hand crept into the suit coat pocket, gripping the semiautomatic pistol. He kept his eyes on the dog, and he concentrated hard on what he might have to do. Flick off the safety latch. Pull the pistol free. Chamber a round. Assume a firing position and take aim. When he did this on the range, he was never rushed, never hurried, and it still took several seconds. He had no idea whether he could get a shot off in time, and whether he could hit the dog. It occurred to him, as well, that it might take several rounds to stop the animal.

The Rottweiler would probably cross the space between them in two, three seconds at most. It crept forward, eager, inching a little closer to Ricky. No, Ricky thought, less than that. A single second.

The breeder looked at Ricky, and saw his hand creeping toward the pocket. He smiled. 'Mister private detective, even if that is a weapon you have in your pocket, trust me, it isn't going to do the trick. Not with this dog, right here. No chance.'

Ricky closed his hand around the grip of the pistol, sliding his index finger onto the trigger. His own eyes were narrow and he barely recognized the even tones of his own voice. 'Maybe,' he said very slowly and carefully, 'just maybe I know that. And I won't even bother to try to put a round into your dog there.

Instead, I'll just nail one right in the center of your chest. You're a nice big target, and trust me, I won't have any trouble hitting you. And you'll be dead before you hit the ground, and you won't even have the satisfaction of seeing your mutt there chew me up.'

This reply made the breeder hesitate. He put his hand on the dog's collar, restraining it. 'New Hampshire plates,' he said after a moment. 'With the motto Live Free or Die. Very memorable. Now get out of here.'

Ricky did not hesitate to slip into the car and slam the door shut. He removed the pistol from his jacket and then started the car up. Within seconds he was pulling away, but he saw the breeder in his rearview mirror, the dog still at his side, watching him depart.

He was breathing heavily. It was as if the heat outdoors had overcome the car's air-conditioning system, and as he bumped off the driveway up onto the black macadam road surface, he rolled down his window and took a gulp of the wind created by the car's motion. It was hot to the taste.

* * *

He pulled over to the side of the road to regain his composure, and as he did, he saw the entrance to the cemetery. Ricky steadied his nerves and tried to assess what had happened at the breeder's house. Clearly the mention of the three orphans had triggered a response. He guessed it was one from deep within, almost a subliminal message. The man had not thought about those three children in years, until Ricky arrived with a single question, and that had stirred up a response recalled from deep within him.

There had been something dangerous about the meeting that went far beyond the dog at the man's side. Ricky thought it was almost as if the man had been waiting years for Ricky, or someone like Ricky, to show up with some questions, and once his initial surprise that the moment he'd been awaiting for years had finally arrived, he knew precisely what to do.

Ricky felt a little queasy in his stomach as this thought churned about.

Just inside the cemetery entrance there was a small, white clapboard building, tucked off a little ways away from the roadway that sliced between the rows of graves. Ricky suspected it was something slightly more than a storage shed, and he pulled in front of it. As he did, a gray-haired man, wearing a matching blue set of work clothes not all that dissimilar to what Ricky wore at the university maintenance department, came out from the building, taking a step or two toward a riding mower parked to the side, but stopping when he saw Ricky emerge from the rental car.

'Help you with something?' the man asked.

'I'm looking for a pair of graves,' Ricky said.

'Got lots of folks planted here, who in particular you looking for?'

'A couple named Jackson.'

The old man smiled. 'Ain't nobody been up to visit them in a long time. People probably think it's bad luck. Me, I think anybody taking up residence here has experienced all the luck, good and bad, they're ever gonna have, so I don't care much. Jacksons' graves in back, last row, way over to the right. Take the road to the end, get out and head that way. You'll find it soon enough.'

'Did you know them?'

'Nope. What, you a relative?'

'No,' Ricky said. 'I'm a detective. Interested in their adopted kids.'

'They didn't have no family to speak of. Don't know nothing about no adopted kids. That would have been in the papers back when they passed, but I don't remember nothing about that, and the Jacksons, they were front page for a day or so.'

'How'd they die?'

The man looked a little surprised. 'Figured you know, coming up to see the graves and all . . . '

'How?'

'Why, it was what the cops call a murder-suicide. The old man shot his wife after one of their fights, then turned the gun on hisself. Bodies stewed for a couple of days in the house before the mailman realized nobody's picked up the mail, gets suspicious and calls the local cops. Apparently the dogs got at the bodies, as well, so there weren't much left, except some mighty unpleasant remains. Lot of anger in that house, you'd best believe.'

'The guy that bought it . . . '

'I don't know him, but they say he's a piece of work. Just as nasty as the dogs. Took over the breeding business, too, that the Jacksons had going there, but at least he killed all the animals that had eaten the former owners. But I'm thinking he's likely to end up that way, hisself. Maybe that's what wears on his mind. Makes him the nasty folk he is.'

The old man gave a grisly laugh and pointed up the incline. 'Up there,' he said. 'Actually, a pretty nice spot to rest for eternity.'

Ricky thought for a moment, then asked, 'You wouldn't know who bought the plot, do you? And who pays for maintenance?'

The man shrugged. 'Checks just come in, I don't know.'

Ricky found the grave site without any difficulty. He stood for a second amid the silence of the bright midday sun wondering for a moment whether anyone had given thought to a headstone for him after his suicide. He doubted it. He'd been as isolated as the Jacksons. He wondered, as well, why he'd never put up some sort of memorial to his dead wife. He had helped establish a book fund in her name at her law school, and he'd annually made a contribution to the Nature Conservancy in her name, and he'd told himself that these acts were better than some cold piece of stone standing sentinel over a narrow slice of earth. But standing there, he was less certain. He found himself caught in a reverie of death, thinking about the permanence and the impact on those left behind. He thought, we learn more about the living when someone dies, than we do the person who passed away.

He was uncertain how long he remained there, in front of the graves, before finally examining them. It was a joint headstone, and it merely said the names, the dates of their birth, and the date of their death.

Something bothered him, and he stared at this small bit of information, trying to discern what it was. It took several seconds before he made a connection.

The date of the murder-suicide was the same month that the adoption papers were signed.

Ricky took a step back. And then he saw something else.

The Jacksons were both born in the 1920s. They would have both been in their mid-sixties when they died.

He felt hot again, and he loosened the tie around his neck. The fake stomach seemed to pull at him, weighing him down, and the fake contusion and scar suddenly began to itch on his face.

No one can adopt a child, much less three children, at that age, he thought. The guidelines for adoption agencies would rule out a childless couple that age almost immediately, in favor of a younger, far more vigorous couple.

Ricky stood by the graves thinking he was looking at a lie. Not a lie about their death. That was true enough. But a lie somewhere in their life.

* * *

Everything is wrong, he thought. Everything is different from what it should be. Ricky was almost overcome with the sense that he was treading on the edge of something larger than what he'd expected. Revenge that was boundless.

He told himself that what he needed to do was to get back to the safety of New Hampshire and sort his way through what he'd learned, make some sort of rational, intelligent next step. He halted the rental car outside the office of the Econo Lodge, and stepped inside, spotting a different clerk. Omar had been replaced by James, who wore a clip-on tie that still managed to be skewed around his neck.

'I'm going to check out,' Ricky said. 'Mr. Lazarus. In room 232.'

The clerk pulled up a bill on the computer screen, and said, 'You're all set. Except there were a couple of phone messages for you.'

Ricky hesitated, then asked, 'Phone messages?'

James the clerk nodded. 'Guy from some dog kennel called, asking if you were staying here. Wanted to leave a message on your room phone. Then, just before you came in, there was another message.'

'Same guy?'

'I don't know. I just push the buttons. Never talked to the person. It just sticks a number up here on my call sheet. Room 232. Two messages. You want, just pick up the phone over there and punch in your room number. You can hear the messages that way.'

Ricky did as instructed. The first message was from the kennel owner.

'I thought you'd be staying someplace cheap and close. Wasn't too hard to figure out where. I been thinking about your questions. Call me. I think maybe I've got some information that might help you out. But you better get out your checkbook. Gonna cost you.'

Ricky pushed the numeral three to erase the message. The next message was played automatically. The voice was clipped and cool and astonishing, almost like finding a piece of ice on a hot sidewalk during a summer day.

'Mister Lazarus, I have just been informed of your curiosity concerning the late mister and missus Jackson, and believe I might have some information in that regard that might assist you in your inquiries. Please telephone me at 212-555-1717 at your earliest possible convenience, and we can arrange a meeting.'

The caller did not provide a name. That was unnecessary. Ricky recognized the voice.

It was Virgil.

Part Three

EVEN BAD POETS LOVE DEATH

28

Ricky fled.

Bag hurriedly packed, tires squealing, accelerating down the highway, he raced away from the motel in New Jersey and the familiar voice on the phone. He barely took the time to wash the fake scar from his cheek. In the space of one morning, by asking a few questions in the wrong places, he had managed to compress time, turning it from his ally into his enemy. He had thought he would slowly scrape away at Rumplestiltskin's identity, and then, when he'd managed to discover everything he needed, he would take a slow and sturdy approach to designing his own revenge. Make certain that everything was in place, traps set, and then emerge on an equal footing. Now, he understood, that luxury had disappeared.

He did not know what the connection was between the man at the kennel and Rumplestiltskin, but it surely existed, for following his departure, while Ricky was idly inspecting the grave site of a dead couple, the kennel owner had been making telephone calls. The ease with which the man had found the motel where Ricky had been staying was daunting. He told himself that he needed to be far more careful covering his tracks.

He drove hard and fast, heading back to New Hampshire, trying to assess how compromised his existence truly was. Random fears and contentious thoughts reverberated throughout him.

But one idea was paramount. Ricky could not return to the passivity of the psychoanalyst. That was a world where one waited for something to happen, and then, before acting again, tried to interpret and understand all the forces within. It was a world of reaction, of delay. Of calm and reason.

If he fell into its trap, it would cost him his life. He knew that he had to act.

If nothing else, he had to create the illusion that he was as dangerous as Rumplestiltskin.

He had just passed the WELCOME TO MASSACHUSETTS sign on the roadway, when an idea came to him. He saw an exit up ahead, and just beyond that the common American landscape marker: a shopping mall. He steered the rental car off the thruway, and into the mall's parking lot. Within a few minutes, he was shoulder to shoulder with all the other people, heading in to the array of stores, all selling more or less the same things for more or less the same prices, but packaged in different manners, giving shoppers the sensation they were finding something unique amid all the similarity. Ricky, seeing some dark humor in it, thought it a wildly appropriate spot for what he was about to do.

It did not take him long to find a gathering of telephones, near the food court. He remembered the first number easily. Behind him, there was a low buzz of people at tables eating and speaking, and he half covered the receiver with his hand as he dialed the number.

'*New York Times* classified.'

'Yes,' Ricky said, pleasantly. 'I'd like to purchase one of those small one-column ads for the front page.'

In rapid order, he read off a credit card number. The clerk took the information and then asked, 'Okay, Mr. Lazarus, what's the message?'

Ricky hesitated then said:

Mr. R. game on. A new Voice.

The clerk read it back. 'That's it?' he asked.

'That's it,' Ricky said. 'Make sure you uppercase the word *Voice*, okay?'

The clerk acknowledged the request and Ricky disconnected the line. He then walked over to a fast-food outlet, purchased himself a cup of coffee, and grabbed a handful of napkins. He found a table a little ways apart from most of the crowds, and settled in, with a pen in his hand, sipping at the hot liquid. He shut out the noise and the activity and concentrated on what he was about to write, tapping the pen occasionally against his teeth, then taking a drink, all the time calming himself, planning. He used the napkins as scratch paper, and finally, after a few fits and starts, came up with the following:

You know who I was, not who I am.
That is why you're in a jam.
Ricky's gone, he's very dead.
I am here, in his stead.
Lazarus rose, and so have I,
And now it's time for someone else to die.
A new game, in an old place,
Will eventually bring us face-to-face.
Then we'll see who draws the last breath,
Because, Mr. R., even bad poets love death.

Ricky admired his work for a moment, then returned to the bank of telephones. Within a few moments, he'd connected with the classified department at the *Village Voice*. 'I'd like to place an ad in the personals section,' he said.

'No problem-o. I can take that information,' this new clerk said. Ricky was mildly amused that the person in classified at the *Voice* seemed significantly less stuffy than their counterparts at the *Times*, which, when he considered it, was more or less as expected. 'What sort of heading do you want on the message?'

'Heading?' Ricky asked.

'Ah,' said the clerk. 'A first-timer. You know, the abbreviations like WM for white male, SM for sadomasochism . . . '

'I see what you mean,' Ricky replied. He thought a moment, then said, 'The top should read: WM, 50s, seeks Mr. Right for special fun and games . . . '

The clerk repeated this to Ricky. 'Okay,' he said, 'something else?'

'Oh, yes, indeed,' Ricky said. He then read off the poem to the clerk, making the man repeat the message twice, to be certain that he had it correctly. When he'd finished reading, the clerk paused.

'Well,' he said, 'that's different. Way different. This will probably bring them all out of the woodwork. The curious, at least. And maybe a few of the crazies. Now, do you want to pay for a box reply? We give you a box number, and you can access the replies by phone. The way it works, while you're paying for the box, only you can get the answers.'

'Please,' Ricky said. He heard the clerk clicking on a computer keyboard. 'All right,' he said. 'You're box number 1313. Hope you're not superstitious.'

'Not in the slightest,' Ricky said. He wrote down the number for accessing the answers on his napkin and hung up the phone.

For a moment, he considered calling the number that he had for Virgil. But he resisted this temptation. He had a few more things to arrange first.

* * *

In *The Art of War*, Sun-Tzu discusses the importance of the general choosing his battleground. Occupying a position of mystery, seizing a location of superiority. Taking the high ground. Being able to conceal one's strength. Creating advantages out of topographical familiarity. Ricky thought these lessons applied to him, as well. The poem in the *Village Voice* was like a shot across the bows of his adversary, an opening salvo designed to get his attention.

Ricky realized it would not take long for someone to arrive in Durham searching for him. The license plate number noticed by the dog kennel owner fairly guaranteed that. He didn't think it would be particularly difficult to discover that the plate belonged to Rent-A-Wreck, and soon enough, someone would show up, asking for the name of the man who'd rented that car. The issue he faced, he thought, was complex, but wrapped up in the single question: where did he want to fight the next battle? He had to choose his arena.

He returned the rental car, stopped briefly at his room, and then went directly in to his night job at the crisis hot line distracted by these questions, thinking that he did not know how much time he had purchased for himself with the ads in the *Times* and the *Voice*, but a little. The *Times* would run the following morning, the *Voice* at the end of the week. There was a reasonable likelihood that Rumplestiltskin would not act until he'd seen both. All the man knew, so far, was that an overweight and physically scarred private investigator had arrived at a dog kennel in New Jersey asking disjointed questions about the couple that records showed had adopted him and his siblings years earlier. A man hunting a lie. Ricky did not delude himself that Rumplestiltskin wouldn't see the links, find other signs of Ricky's existence rapidly. Frederick Lazarus, priest, would show up in inquiries in Florida. Frederick Lazarus, private investigator, arrived in New Jersey. The advantage Ricky had, he thought, was that there would be no clear-cut link between Frederick Lazarus and either Dr. Frederick Starks or Richard

Lively. One was presumed dead. The other still clung to anonymity. As he took his seat at a desk in the darkened office, behind a multiline telephone, he was glad that the semester was wrapping up at the university. He expected callers with the usual stressed out, final exams despair, which he was comfortable dealing with. He did not think that anyone would kill themselves over a chemistry final, although he had heard of sillier things. And, in the deep of night, he found that he was able to concentrate clearly.

He asked himself: What do I want to achieve?

Did he want to kill the man who had driven him to fake his own death? Who threatened his distant family and destroyed everything that had made him who he was? Ricky thought that in some of the mystery novels and thrillers that he'd devoured over the past months, the answer would have been a simple yes. Someone caused him great harm, so he should turn the tables on that someone. Kill him. An eye for an eye, the essence of all revenges.

Ricky pursed his lips and told himself: There are many ways to kill someone. Indeed, he'd experienced one. There had to be others, ranging from the assassin's bullet to the ravages of a disease.

Finding the right murder was critical. And, to do that, he needed to know his adversary. Not merely know who he was, but what he was.

And he had to emerge from this death with his own life intact. He wasn't some sort of kamikaze pilot, drinking a ritual cup of sake, then going to his own death with nary a care in the world. Ricky wanted to survive.

Ricky held no illusion that he would ever be able to return to Dr. Frederick Starks. No comfortable practice listening to the whinings of the rich and discomfited on a daily basis, for an easy forty-eight weeks of the year. That was gone, and he knew it.

He looked around himself, at the small office where the crisis hot line was located. It was in a room off the main corridor of the student health services building. It was a narrow spot, not particularly comfortable, with a single desk, three telephones, and a few posters celebrating the schedules of the football, lacrosse, and soccer teams, with pictures of athletes. There was also a large campus map and a typed list of emergency services and security numbers. In slightly larger print, there was a protocol to be followed in the case where the person manning the suicide prevention line became convinced that someone had actually attempted to kill themselves. The protocol explained the steps to take, to call police, and have the 911 operator run a line check, which would trace a call back to a location. This was to be used only in the direst of emergencies, when a life was at stake, and rescue services needed to be dispatched. Ricky had never availed himself of this capacity. In the weeks he'd worked the graveyard shift, he'd always been able to talk, if not common sense, at least delay, into even the most frantic of callers. He had wondered whether any of the young people he'd helped would have been astonished to know that the calm voice speaking reason to them belonged to a janitor in the chemistry department.

Ricky told himself: *This is worth protecting*.

A conclusion, he recognized, brought him to a decision. He would have to lead Rumplestiltskin away from Durham. If he was to survive the upcoming confrontation, Richard Lively needed to be safe and remain anonymous.

He whispered to himself: 'Back to New York.'

As he was reaching this realization, the phone on the desktop rang. He punched the proper line and picked up the receiver.

'Crisis,' he said. 'How can I help you?'

There was a momentary pause, and then he heard a muffled sob. This was followed by a string of disconnected words, that separately meant little, but taken together, said much. 'I can't, I just can't, it's all too much, I don't want, oh, I just don't know . . . '

A young woman, Ricky thought. He heard no slurring beyond the sobs of emotion, so he didn't think there were any drugs or alcohol involved in the call. Just middle-of-the-night loneliness and low-rent despair. 'Can you slow down,' he said gently, 'and try to fill me in on what is going on? You don't have to give me the big picture. Just right now, right this moment. Where are you?'

A pause, then a response: 'In my dormitory room.'

'Okay,' Ricky said, gently, starting to probe. 'Are you alone?'

'Yes.'

'No roommate? Friends?'

'No. All alone.'

'Is that the way you are all the time? Or does it just feel that way?'

This question seemed to cause the young woman to think hard. 'Well, my boyfriend and I broke up and my classes are all terrible and when I get home, my folks are going to kill me because I've dropped off the honors list. In fact, I might not pass my comp lit course and it all seems to have come to a head and . . . '

'And so something made you call this line, right?'

'I wanted to talk. I didn't want to do something to myself . . . '

'That makes eminently good sense. It sounds like this hasn't been the best of semesters.'

The young woman laughed, a little bitterly. 'You could say that.'

'But there are other semesters to come, right?'

'Well, yes.'

'And the boyfriend, why did he say he left you?'

'He said he didn't like being tied down right now . . . '

'And this reply made you, what? Depressed?'

'Yes. It was like a slap in the face. I felt like he'd just been using me, you know, for sex, and then with summer coming, well, he figured I wasn't worth it anymore. It was just like I was some sort of candy bar. Taste me and throw me away . . . '

'That's well put,' Ricky said. 'An insult, then. A blow to your sense of who you are.'

Again the young woman paused. 'I guess, but I hadn't really seen it that way.'

'So,' Ricky continued, still speaking in a solid, soft voice, 'really instead of being depressed and thinking that there's something wrong with you, you should be angry with the son of a bitch, because clearly the problem is with him. And the problem is selfishness, right?'

He could hear the young woman nodding in agreement. This was the most typical of telephone calls, he thought. She called in a state of boyfriend- and school-related despair, but really wasn't anywhere close to that state, when examined a little more closely.

'I think that's a fair statement,' she said. 'The bastard.'

'So, maybe you're better off without him. It's not like there aren't other fish in that sea,' Ricky said.

'I thought I loved him,' the young woman said.

'And so it hurts a bit, doesn't it? But the hurt isn't because you actually have had your heart broken. It's more because you feel that you engaged in a lie. And now you've had your sense of trust staggered.'

'You make sense,' she said. Ricky could sense the tears drying up on the other end of the line. After a minute, she added, 'You must get a lot of calls like this one. It all seemed so important and so awful a minute or two ago. I was crying and sobbing and now . . . '

'There's still the grades. What will happen when you get home?'

'They'll be pissed. My dad will say, 'I'm not spending my hard-earned dollars on a bunch of C's . . . ' '

The young lady did a passable harrumph and deepened her voice, capturing her father pretty effectively. Ricky laughed, and she joined him.

'He'll get over it,' he said. 'Just be honest. Tell him about your stresses, and about the boyfriend, and that you'll try to do better. He'll come around.'

'You're right.'

'So,' Ricky said, 'here's the prescription for this evening. Get a good night's sleep. Put the books away. Get up in the morning and go buy yourself one of those really sweet frothy coffees, one with all the calories in it. Take the coffee outside to one of the quads, sit on a bench, sip the drink slowly and admire the weather. And, if you happen to see the boy in question, well, ignore him. And if he wants to talk, walk away. Find a new bench. Think a little bit about what the summer holds. There's always some hope that things will get better. You just have to find it.'

'All right,' she said. 'Thanks for talking with me.'

'If you're still feeling stressed, like to the point where you don't think you can handle things, then you should make an appointment with a counselor at health services. They'll help you through problems.'

'You know a lot about depression,' she said.

'Oh, yes,' Ricky replied, 'I do. Usually it is transitory. Sometimes it isn't. The first is an ordinary condition of life. The second is a true and terrible disease. You sound like you've just got the first.'

'I feel better,' she said. 'Maybe I'll get a sweet roll with that cup of coffee. Calories be damned.'

'That's the attitude,' Ricky said. He was about to

hang up, but stopped. 'Hey,' he said, 'help me out with something . . . '

The young woman sounded a bit surprised, but replied, 'Huh? What? You need help?'

'This is the crisis hot line,' Ricky said, allowing humor to seep into his voice. 'What makes you think that the folks on this end don't have their own crises?'

The young woman paused, as if digesting the obviousness of this statement. 'Okay,' she said, 'how can I help?'

'When you were little,' Ricky said, 'what games did you play?'

'Games? Like board games, you know, Chutes and Ladders, Candyland . . . '

'No. Outdoor, playground-type games.'

'Like Ring Around the Rosie or Freeze Tag?'

'Yes. But what if you wanted to play a game with other kids, a game where one person has to hunt the other, while at the same time being hunted, what would that be?'

'Not exactly hide-and-seek, right? Sounds a little bit nastier.'

'Yes. Exactly.'

The young woman hesitated, then started thinking more or less out loud, 'Well, there was Red Rover, Red Rover, but that had more of a physical challenge. There were scavenger hunts, but that was a pursuit of objects. Tag and Mother May I and Simon Says . . . '

'No. I'm looking for something a little more challenging . . . '

'The best I can think of is Foxes and Hounds,' she said abruptly. 'That was the hardest to win.'

'How did you play it?' Ricky asked.

'In the summer, out in the countryside. There were two teams, Foxes and Hounds, obviously. The foxes took off, fifteen-minute head start. They carried paper bags filled with ripped-up newspaper. Every ten yards, they had to put a handful down. The hounds followed the trail. The key thing was to leave false trails, double back, put the hounds into the swamp, whatever. The foxes won if they made it back to the starting point after a designated time, like two or three hours later. The hounds won if they caught up with the foxes. If they spotted the foxes across a field, they could act like dogs, and take off after them. And the foxes had to hide. So, sometimes the foxes made certain that they knew where the hounds were, you know, spying on them . . . '

'That's the game I'm looking for,' Ricky said quietly. 'Which side usually won?'

'That was the beauty of it,' the young woman said. 'It depended on the ingenuity of the foxes and the determination of the hounds. So either side could win at any given time.'

'Thank you,' Ricky said. His mind was churning with ideas.

'Good luck,' the young woman said, as she hung up the phone.

Ricky thought that was precisely what he was going to need: some good luck.

* * *

He began making arrangements the following morning. He paid his rent for the following month, but told his landladies that he was likely to be out of town on some family business. He had put a plant in his room, and he made certain they agreed to water it regularly. It was, he thought, the simplest way of playing on the psychology of the women; no man who wants his plant watered was likely to run out on them. He spoke to his supervisor at the janitorial staff at the university, and received permission to take some accumulated overtime and sick days. His boss was equally understanding, and aided by the end of the semester slowdown, willing to cut him loose without jeopardizing his job.

At the local bank where Frederick Lazarus had his account, Ricky made a wire transfer to an account he opened electronically at a Manhattan bank.

He also made a series of hotel reservations around the city, for successive days. These were at less than desirable hotels, the sorts of places that didn't show up on anyone's tourist guide to New York City. He guaranteed each reservation with Frederick Lazarus's credit cards, except for the last hotel he selected. The final two of the hotels he'd selected were located on West 22nd Street, more or less directly across from each other. At one, he simply reserved a two-night stay for Frederick Lazarus. The other had the advantage of offering efficiency apartments by the week. He reserved a two-week block. But for this second hotel, he used Richard Lively's Visa card.

He closed Frederick Lazarus's Mailboxes Etc. mail drop, leaving a forwarding address of the second-to-last hotel.

The final thing he did was pack his weapon and extra ammunition and several changes of clothing into a bag, and return to Rent-A-Wreck. As before, he rented a modest, dated car. But on this occasion, he was careful to leave more of a trail.

'That has unlimited mileage, right?' he asked the clerk. 'Because I need to drive to New York City, and I don't want to get stuck with some ten cent per mile charge . . . '

The clerk was a college-aged kid, obviously starting up a summer job, and already, with only a few days in the office, bored out of his head. 'Right. Unlimited mileage. As far as we're concerned, you can drive to California and back.'

'No, business in Manhattan,' Ricky repeated deliberately. 'I'm going to put my business address in the city down on the rental agreement.' Ricky wrote the name and telephone number of the first of the hotels where he'd made a reservation for Frederick Lazarus.

The clerk eyed Ricky's jeans and sport shirt. 'Sure. Business. Whatever.'

'And if I have to extend my stay . . . '

'There's a number on the rental agreement. Just call. We'll charge your credit card for extra, but we need to have a record, otherwise after forty-eight hours, we call the cops and report the car stolen.'

'Don't want that.'

'Who would?' replied the clerk.

'There's just one other thing,' Ricky said, slowly, choosing his words with some caution.

'What's that?' the clerk answered.

'I left a message with my friend to rent a car here, as well. You know — good rates, good, solid vehicles, no hassle like with the big rental companies . . . '

'Sure,' said the kid, as if he was surprised anyone would waste their time having any opinions whatsoever about rental vehicles.

'But I'm not totally sure he got the message right . . . '

'Who?'

'My friend. He does a lot of business traveling, like I do, so he's always on the lookout for a good deal.'

'So?'

'So,' said Ricky carefully, 'if he should happen to come in here in the next couple of days, checking to see whether this is the place where I rented my car, you be sure to steer him right, and give him a good deal, okay?'

The clerk nodded. 'If I'm on duty . . . '

'You're here during the day, right?'

The clerk nodded again, making a motion that seemed to indicate being stuck behind a counter during the first warm days of summer was something akin to being in prison, which, Ricky thought, it probably was.

'So, chances are, you're going to be the guy he'll see.'

'Chances are.'

'So, if he asks about me, you just tell him I took off on business. In New York City. He'll know my schedule.'

The clerk shrugged. 'No problem, if he asks. Otherwise . . . '

'Sure. Just if someone comes in asking, you'll know it's my friend.'

'Does he have a name?' the clerk asked.

Ricky smiled. 'Sure. R. S. Skin. Easy to remember. Mr. R. Skin.'

* * *

On the drive down Route 95 toward New York City, Ricky stopped at three separate shopping malls, all located right off the highway. One was just below Boston, the other two in Connecticut near Bridgeport and New Haven. At each of the malls, he wandered idly down the central corridors amid the rows of clothing stores and chocolate cookie outlets until he found a location selling cellular telephones. By the time he'd finished shopping, Ricky had acquired five different cell phones, all in the name of Frederick Lazarus, all promising hundreds of free minutes and cheap long distance rates. The phones were with four different companies, and although each salesman filling out the year-long purchase and use agreement asked Ricky whether he had any other cell accounts, none bothered to double-check after he told them he didn't. Ricky took all the extras on each phone, with caller ID and call waiting and as many services as he could collect, which made the salesmen eager to complete the orders.

He also stopped at a strip mall, where, after a little searching, he was able to find a large office warehouse outlet. There he purchased himself a relatively cheap laptop computer and the necessary hardware to accompany it. He also bought a bag to place it in.

It was early evening, when he arrived at the first of the hotels. He left his rental car at an outdoor lot over by the Hudson River, in the West '50s, then took a subway to the hotel, located in Chinatown. He checked in with a desk clerk named Ralph who had suffered from runaway acne as a child, and wore the pockmarked scars on his cheeks, giving him a sunken, nasty appearance. Ralph had little to say, other than to look mildly surprised when the credit card in Frederick Lazarus's name actually worked. The word *reservation* also surprised him. Ricky thought it wasn't the sort of place that got many reservations. A prostitute working the room down the hall from Ricky smiled at him, suggesting and inviting in the same glance, but he shook his head and opened up the door to his room. It was as desultory a spot as Ricky guessed it would be. It was also the type of place where the mere fact that Ricky walked in with no bags, and then walked out again, fifteen minutes later, wouldn't gather much attention.

He took another subway over to the last of the hotels on his list, where he had his efficiency apartment rented. Here, he became Richard Lively, although he was quiet and monosyllabic with the man behind that desk. He drew as little attention to himself as possible, as he headed up to the room.

He went out once that night to a deli for some sandwich makings and a couple of sodas. The rest of the night he spent in quiet, planning, except for a single sortie out at midnight.

A passing shower had left the street glistening. Yellow streetlamps threw arcs of wan light across the black macadam. There was a little heat in the nighttime air, a thickness that spoke of the summer to come. He stared down the sidewalk, and thought that he'd never really been aware how many shadows there were at midnight in Manhattan. Then he guessed that he was one, as well.

He crossed town, walking blocks rapidly, until he found an isolated pay telephone. It was time, he thought, to check his messages.

29

A siren creased the nighttime air perhaps a block away from the pay phone where Ricky stood. He couldn't tell whether it was the police or an ambulance. Fire trucks, he knew, had a deeper, blaring sound, unmistakable in raucous energy. But police and ambulances sounded much the same. For a moment, he thought that there were few noises on the earth that spelled out the promise of trouble quite as much as siren sounds. Something unsettling and fierce, as if compromise and hope were being reduced by the harshness of the sound. He waited until the racket faded into the darkness, and the Manhattan standard quiet returned: just the steady noise of cars and buses working their way on the streets and the occasional rumble below the surface of a subway careening through the subterranean tunnels that crisscrossed the city.

He dialed the number at the *Village Voice* and accessed the replies to his personal ad at box 1313. There were nearly three dozen.

The majority were come-ons and promises of sexual adventure. Most of the respondents mentioned Ricky's ' . . . special fun and games' from his ad, which seemed to speak, as he suspected it would, in a particular direction. A number of people had concocted rhyming couplets to accompany his own, but, again, these promised sex and energy. He could hear unbridled eagerness in their voices.

The thirtieth, as he'd expected, was far different. The voice was cold, almost flat, filled with menace. It also had a metallic, tinny sound to it, making it seem nearly mechanical. Ricky guessed that the speaker was using an electronic masking device. But there was no concealing the psychological thrust of the reply.

Ricky's clever, Ricky's smart . . .
But here's a rhyme he should take to heart:
He thinks he's safe, he wants to play,
But where he hid, is where he should stay.
He escaped once, impressive, no doubt.
But this success, he shouldn't flout.
A second chance, another game,
Will likely just end up the same.
Only this time the debt owed me,
Will be paid in full, this I guarantee.

Ricky listened to the response three times, until it was well printed on his memory. There was something additional about the sound of the voice that unsettled him, as if the words spoken weren't enough, even the tones were filled with hatred. But, beyond that, it seemed to him that there was something recognizable in the voice, almost familiar, that seeped past the hollowness of the masking device. This thought pierced him, especially when he realized that this was the first time that he'd actually heard Rumplestiltskin speak. Every other bit of contact had been a step removed, on paper, or repeated by Merlin or Virgil. Hearing the man's voice created nightmarish visions within him, and Ricky shuddered slightly. He told himself not to underestimate the depth of the challenge he'd created for himself.

He played the other message responses in the mailbox, knowing that there would eventually be another, far more familiar voice. He was not surprised to hear her speak. Immediately following the silence that accompanied the brief poem, Ricky heard Virgil's voice on the recording. He listened carefully for the nuances that might tell him something.

'Ricky, Ricky, Ricky, how nice to hear from you. How truly special. And genuinely surprising, too, I might add . . . '

'Sure,' Ricky mumbled to himself. 'I'll bet it was.' He continued to listen, as the young woman went on. The tones she employed were the same as before, tough one instant, cajoling, teasing, then harsh and uncompromising. Virgil, Ricky thought, played this game just as hard as did her employer. Her danger lay in the chameleon colors she adopted; one minute trying to be helpful, the next, angry and direct. If Rumplestiltskin was singleness of purpose, cold and focused, Virgil was mercurial. And Merlin, whom he'd yet to hear from, was like an accountant, passionless, with all the iron danger that implied.

' . . . How you escaped, well, that certainly has some people in important circles reviewing their approach to things, I must say. A head to toe reexamination of what was thought to be the case. Shows just how elusive the truth can be, doesn't it, Ricky? I warned them, you know. I really did. I told them, 'Ricky's a very clever sort. Intuitive and fast-thinking . . . ' but they didn't want to believe me. They thought you would be as stupid and careless as all the others. And now look where it has landed us. Why, you are the very alpha and omega of loose ends, Ricky. The pièce de résistance. Very dangerous for all connected, I would suspect . . . '

She sighed, deeply, as if her own words told her something. Then she continued:

'Well, personally, I can't imagine why you want to go another round or two with Mr. R. I would have thought watching your deeply beloved summer home go up in flames — that was a genuinely nice touch, Ricky, a really smooth and wonderfully smart move. Burning up all that happiness along with all those memories, I mean, what other message could there have been for us? From a psychoanalyst, no less. Didn't see that one coming, not in the slightest — but, I would have guessed that experience alone would have taught you that Mr. R. is a very difficult man to best in any contest, especially contests that he designs himself. You should have stayed where you were, Ricky, under whatever rock you found to hide yourself. Or perhaps you should run now. Run and hide forever. Start digging a hole someplace distant and far away and cold and dark and then keep on digging. Because my suspicion is that Mr. R. will need better proof of victory this time around. Very conclusive proof . . . He's a very thorough individual. Or so I'm told . . .'

Virgil's voice disappeared, as if she'd hung up her telephone abruptly. He listened to an electronic hissing noise, then accessed the subsequent telephone message. It was Virgil for a second time.

'So, Ricky, I'd hate to see you have to repeat the outcome of the first game, but if that's what it's going to take, well, the choice is yours. What is the 'new game' you speak of, and what are the rules? I'll be reading my *Village Voice* with greater care now. And my employer is — well, *eager* doesn't exactly seem like the right word, Ricky. *Champing at the bit*, like some race-horse, perhaps. So, Ricky, we await the opening move.'

Ricky hung up the telephone and said out loud, 'It's already happened.'

Foxes and hounds, he thought. Think like the fox. Need to leave a trail so you know where they are, but stay just far enough ahead so to avoid capture and detection. And then, he thought, lead them directly into the briar patch.

* * *

In the morning, Ricky took the subway uptown to the first of the hotels where he'd checked in, but not stayed. He returned the room key to a disinterested clerk reading a pornographic magazine called *Large Ladies of Love* behind the counter. The man had an undeniable seediness to him, with ill-fitting clothes, a pockmarked face, and a lip marred by a scar. Ricky thought that you couldn't have found a better choice for the room clerk at that particular hotel in central casting. The man took the key with hardly a word, more or less engrossed by the bulk displayed in vibrant and explicit color on the pages in front of him.

'Hey,' Ricky said, getting the barest bit of attention response from the clerk. 'Hey, there's a chance a man might come looking for me with a package.'

The clerk nodded, but still not particularly focused, preferring, obviously, the cavorting creatures of the magazine.

'Package means something,' Ricky persisted.

'Sure,' said the clerk. A reply only the barest step beyond ignoring everything Ricky was saying.

Ricky smiled. He couldn't have defined a conversation better suited for what he intended. He glanced around, determining that they were alone in the drab and threadbare lobby, then he reached into his jacket pocket, and keeping his hands below the counter front, removed his semi-automatic pistol and chambered a round, making a distinctive sound.

The clerk abruptly looked up, his eyes widening slightly.

Ricky grinned nastily in his direction. 'You know that sound, don't you, asshole?'

The clerk left his hands out in front of him, flat on the table. 'Perhaps I have your attention, now?' Ricky asked.

'I'm listening,' the man replied.

Ricky thought he seemed practiced at the art of being robbed or threatened.

'So, let me try again,' Ricky said. 'A man with a package. For me. He comes asking, you're gonna give him this number. Take hold of that pencil and write this down: 212-555-2798. That's where he can reach me. Got it?'

'I've got it.'

'Make him give you a fifty,' Ricky said. 'Maybe a hundred. It's worth it.'

The man looked sullen, but nodded. 'What if I ain't here?' he asked. 'Suppose the night guy is here?'

'You want the hundred, you be here,' Ricky answered. He paused, then added, 'Now, here's the tricky part. Anyone else comes asking. I mean anyone, right. Anyone who doesn't have a package — well, you make sure to tell that person that you don't know where I went, or who I am or anything. Not one word. No help at all. Got it?'

'Man with the package only. Right. What's in the package?'

'You don't want to know. And you sure as hell don't really expect me to tell you.'

This answer seemed to speak volumes.

'Suppose I don't see no package. How'm I supposed to know it's the right guy?'

Ricky nodded. 'You got a point, buddy,' he said. 'Tell you what. You ask him how he knows Mr. Lazarus, and he'll reply something like, 'Everyone knows that Lazarus rose on the third day.' Then you can give out the number, like I said. You do this right, probably more than a hundred in it.'

'The third day. Lazarus rose. Sounds like some kind of Bible stuff.'

'Maybe.'

'Okay. I got it.'

'Good,' Ricky said, returning the weapon to his pocket, after lowering the hammer down to rest with a clicking noise as distinctive as the chambering sound which lifted it. 'I'm glad we had this little conversation. I feel much better about my stay here, now.' Ricky smiled at the clerk and pointed at the pornographic magazine. 'Don't let me keep you from advancing your education any longer,' he said, as he turned to leave.

There was, of course, no man with any package looking for Ricky. Someone different would arrive at the hotel soon, he thought. And, in all likelihood, the clerk would give all the relevant information to the person who came looking for him, especially when presented with the polar suggestions created by cash or bodily harm, which Ricky was certain Mr. R. or Merlin or Virgil, or whoever was sent, would employ in relatively short order. And then after the clerk had relayed the replies that Ricky had planted, Rumplestiltskin would have something to think about. A package that doesn't exist. Containing some information that was equally nonexistent. Delivered to a person who never was. Ricky liked that. Give him something to worry about that was utter fiction.

He headed across town to check in at the next of his hotels.

In decor, this hotel was much the same as the first, which reassured him. An inattentive and desultory clerk seated behind a large, scarred, wooden desk. A room that was singularly simple, depressing, and threadbare. He had passed two women, short skirts, glossy makeup, spiked heels and black net stockings, unmistakable in their profession, hanging in the hallway, who had eyed him with financial eagerness as he cruised past. He had shaken his head in their direction when one of them had offered an inviting glance his way. He heard one of them remark, 'Cop . . . ' and then they left, which surprised him. He thought he was doing a good job of at least visually accommodating the world he'd descended into. But perhaps, Ricky thought to himself, it is harder to shed where one has been in his life than he thought. You wear who you are both inwardly and outwardly.

He plopped down on the bed, feeling the springs sag

beneath him. The walls were thin, and he could hear the results of one of the women's coworkers' success filtering through the plasterboard, a series of moans and bangs, as the bed was used to advantage. Had he not been so directed, he would have been singularly depressed by the sounds and smells — a faint odor of urine seeping through the air passages. But the milieu was precisely what Ricky wanted. He needed Rumplestiltskin to think that Ricky had somehow become familiar with the netherworld, just as Mr. R. was.

There was a telephone beside the bed, and Ricky pulled it toward him.

The first call he made was to the broker who had handled his modest investment accounts when he was still alive. He reached the man's secretary.

'Can I help you?' she asked.

'Yes,' Ricky said. 'My name is Diogenes . . . ' He spelled the Greek out for the woman slowly, said, 'Write that down,' then continued, 'and I represent Mister Frederick Lazarus, who is the executor of the estate of the late Doctor Frederick Starks. Please be advised that the substantial irregularities concerning his financial situation prior to his unfortunate death are now under our investigation.'

'I believe our security people looked into that situation . . . '

'Not to our satisfaction. I wanted you to know we would be sending someone around to inspect those records and eventually find those missing funds so that they may be distributed to their rightful owners. People are very upset with the way this was handled, I might add.'

'I see, but who . . . ' The secretary was momentarily flustered, put off by the clipped, authoritarian tones that Ricky employed.

'Diogenes is the name. Please keep that in mind. I'll be in touch in the next day or so. Please inform your employer to collect all relevant records of all transactions, especially the wire and electronic transfers, so that we won't be wasting time at our appointment. I will not be accompanied by the SEC detectives on this initial examination, but that might become necessary in the future. It's a matter of cooperation, you see.'

Ricky guessed that the initials so cavalierly used as a threat would have an immediate and significant impact. No broker likes hearing about SEC investigators.

'I think you'd better speak with — '

He interrupted the secretary. 'Certainly. When I call back in the next day or so. I have an appointment, and another series of calls to make on this matter, so I will say goodbye. Thank you.'

And with that, he hung up, an evil sense of satisfaction creeping into his heart. He did not think that his onetime broker, a boring man intrigued only by money and making it or losing it, would recognize the name of the character who wandered the ancient world fruitlessly searching for an honest man. But Ricky did know someone who would instantly understand it.

His next call was to the head of the New York Psychoanalytic Society.

He had met the doctor only once or twice in the past at the sort of medical establishment gatherings that he'd tried so hard to avoid, and had thought him then to be a priggish and wildly conceited Freudian, given to speaking even to his colleagues in long silences, and vacant pauses. The man was a veteran New York psychoanalyst, and had treated many famous people with the techniques of couch and quiet, and somehow had added all those prominent treatments into an exaggerated sense of self-importance, as if having an Oscar-winning actor or Pulitzer Prize-winning author or multimillionaire financier on the couch actually made him into a better therapist or a better human being. Ricky, who had lived and practiced in so much isolation and loneliness right up to his suicide, did not think that there was the remotest chance that the man would recognize his voice, and so he did not even attempt to alter it.

He waited until it was nine minutes before the hour. He knew that the best likelihood of the doctor picking up his own telephone was right at the break between patients.

The phone was answered on the second ring. A flat, gruff, no-nonsense voice that dropped even a greeting from the reply: 'This is Doctor Roth . . . '

'Doctor,' Ricky said slowly, 'I'm delighted to have reached you. This is Mr. Diogenes. I represent Mr. Frederick Lazarus, who is the executor for the estate of the late Doctor Frederick Starks.'

'How may I help you?' Roth interrupted. Ricky paused, a bit of silence that would make the doctor uncomfortable, more or less the same technique the man was accustomed to using himself.

'We are interested in knowing precisely how the complaints against the late Doctor Starks were resolved,' Ricky said with an aggressiveness that surprised himself.

'The complaints?'

'Yes. The complaints. As you are completely aware, shortly before his death, there were some charges made against him concerning sexual impropriety with a female patient. We are interested in learning how that investigation of those allegations was resolved.'

'I don't know that there was any official resolution,' Roth said briskly. 'Certainly none on the part of the Psychoanalytic Society. When Doctor Starks killed himself, it rendered further inquiry pointless.'

'Really?' Ricky said. 'Did it occur to you, or anyone else in the society you head up, that perhaps his suicide was prompted by the unfairness and the falseness of those allegations, instead of his suicide being some sort of verification by self-murder?'

Roth paused. 'We, of course, considered that likelihood,' he answered.

Sure you did, Ricky thought. Liar.

'Would it surprise you, doctor, to learn that the young woman who made the allegations has subsequently disappeared?'

'I beg your pardon . . . '

'She never returned for follow-up therapy with the physician in Boston whom she made the initial charges to.'

'That is curious . . . '

'And that his efforts to locate her turned up the unsettling fact that her identity — who she claimed to be, doctor — was fake.'

'A fake?'

'And it was further learned that her charges were part of a hoax. Did you know this, doctor?'

'But no, no, I didn't . . . as I said, we didn't follow up, after the suicide . . . '

'In other words, you washed your hands of the entire matter.'

'It was turned over to the proper authorities . . . '

'But that suicide certainly saved you and your profession a great deal of negative and embarrassing publicity, did it not?'

'I don't know — well, of course, but . . . '

'Did it occur to you that perhaps the heirs of Doctor Starks would want his reputation restored? That exoneration, even after death, might be important to them?'

'I did not consider that.'

'Do you know you could be considered liable for that death?'

This statement drew a predictable, blustery response. 'Not in the slightest! We didn't — '

Ricky interrupted. 'There are more sorts of liability in

this world than legal, are there not, doctor?'

He liked this question. It went to the core of what a psychoanalyst is all about. He could envision the man on the other end of the telephone line shifting about uncomfortably in his chair. Perhaps a little sweat formed on his forehead or dripped down beneath his armpits.

'Of course, but . . . '

'But no one in the society really wanted to know the truth, did they? It was better if it just disappeared into the ocean with Doctor Starks, correct?'

'I don't think I should answer any more questions, Mr. uh . . . '

'Of course not. Not at this moment. Perhaps at a later time. But it is curious, isn't it, doctor?'

'What?'

'That truth is far stronger than death.'

With that statement, Ricky hung up the phone.

He lay back on the bed, staring up at the white ceiling and a bare lightbulb. He could feel some of his own sweat beneath his arms, as if he'd exerted himself in that conversation, but it wasn't a nervous dampness, rather a wet and satisfactory righteousness. In the next room, the couple had started up again, and for a moment he listened to the unmistakable rhythms of sex, finding it amusing and not altogether unpleasurable. More than one person having a little workday amusement, he thought. After a moment, he rose and searched around until he found a small pad of paper in the bedside table desk drawer and a cheap ballpoint pen.

On the paper, he wrote the names and numbers of the two men he had just called. Beneath those, he wrote the words: *Money. Reputation*. He placed check marks by these words, then wrote, the name of the third seedy hotel where he had a reservation. Beneath that, he scribbled the word: *Home*.

Then he crumpled the paper up and threw it into a metal wastebasket. He doubted that the room was cleaned all that regularly and thought there was a better than even chance that whoever came searching for him there would find it. Regardless, they would undoubtedly be clever enough to check the telephone records for that room, which would turn up the numbers he had just dialed. Connecting numbers to conversations wasn't all that difficult.

The best game to play, he thought, is the game you don't realize you are playing.

30

Ricky found an army-navy surplus store on his walk across the city, where he purchased a few items that he thought he might need for the next stage of the game he had in mind. These included a small crowbar, an inexpensive bicycle lock, some surgical gloves, a miniflashlight, a roll of gray-colored duct tape, and the cheapest pair of binoculars that they had. As an afterthought, he also bought a modest squeeze spray container of Ben's Bug Juice, with one hundred percent DEET, which, he thought ruefully, was about as close to poison as he'd ever considered putting on his body. It was an odd collection of items, he realized, but he wasn't certain precisely what the task he had in mind would require, and so he obtained a variety to compensate for his uncertainty.

Early that afternoon, he returned to his room and packed these, along with his pistol and two of his newly acquired cell phones, into a small backpack. He used the third cell phone to call the next hotel on his list, the one he had not checked into yet. There he left an urgent message for Frederick Lazarus to return the call as soon as he checked in. He gave the cell phone number to a clerk, then thrust that phone into an outside pocket of the knapsack, after carefully marking it with a pen. When he reached his rental car, he took out the phone and gruffly called the hotel a second time, leaving yet another urgent message for himself. He did this three more times as he drove out of the city, heading toward New Jersey, each time growing more strident and more insistent that Mr. Lazarus get back to him instantly, as he had important information to pass on.

After the third message on that cell phone, he pulled

into the Joyce Kilmer rest stop on the Jersey turnpike. He went into the men's room, washed his hands, and left the telephone on the edge of the sink. He noted that several teenagers passed him on his way out, heading to the bathroom. He thought there was the likelihood that they would grab the phone and start using it pretty quickly, which was what he wanted.

It was on the edge of evening when he arrived in West Windsor. The traffic had been crowded the entire length of the turnpike, cars lined up a length or two apart, traveling at excessive rates of speed, until everything slowed to a horn-honking, raised-voices, overheated crawl past an accident near Exit 11. Rubbernecking further limited the pace, as cars maneuvered past two ambulances, a half-dozen state police cars, and the twisted, impact-shredded shells of two compact cars. He could see a man in a white shirt and tie sitting in a half crouch by the breakdown lane, his head in his hands, obscuring his face. As Ricky crept past, the first of the ambulances took off, its siren starting up insistently, and Ricky saw a state trooper with a measuring wheel start to walk a skid mark on the highway. Another was poised by flares stuck in the black macadam surface, waving people on, wearing a solid, stern, and disapproving look, as if curiosity, that most human of emotions, was somehow out of place, or inappropriate at this moment, when, in actuality, it was merely inconvenient for him. Ricky thought that an analyst's sort of insight, as telling about who he'd once been, was like the current glare on the trooper's face.

He found a diner along Route One not far from Princeton where he stopped and killed some time eating a cheeseburger and fries that were actually cooked by a person and not by machines and timers. The day was stretched long with June light, and when he emerged there was still some time before darkness settled in. He drove over to the grave site where he'd been two weeks earlier. The old caretaker was gone, which he'd counted on. He was fortunate that the entrance to the cemetery wasn't locked or barred, so he pulled the rental car over behind the small white clapboard storage shack, and left it there, more or less concealed from the roadway and certainly appearing innocuous enough to anyone who might spot it.

Before slinging the backpack over his shoulder, Ricky took the time to slather himself in the Ben's Bug Juice and don the surgical gloves. These wouldn't conceal his scent, he knew, but at least they would help keep off the deer ticks. The daylight was beginning to fade, turning the New Jersey sky a sickly gray-brown, as if the edges of the world had been burned by the heat from the afternoon. Ricky threw the backpack over his shoulder, and with a single glance down the deserted rural road, started jogging toward the kennel where he knew the information he needed was waiting. There was still plenty of warmth rising above the black macadam, and it crept into his lungs rapidly. He was breathing hard, but he knew it wasn't from the exertion of running.

He turned off the roadway and ducked beneath the canopy of trees, sliding past the kennel sign and the picture of the barrel-chested Rottweiler. Then he stepped off the driveway, into the shrub brush and greenery that hid the kennel from the highway, and carefully picked his way closer to the home and the pens. Still hidden by the foliage, staying back in the first dark shadows of the approaching night, Ricky removed the binoculars from the backpack and used them to survey the exterior, taking a better look at the layout than he had during his first, truncated visit there.

His eyes went first to the pen beside the main entrance, where he spotted Brutus on his feet and pacing back and forth nervously. He smells the DEET, Ricky thought. And behind that, my scent. But he doesn't know what to make of it yet. For the dog, it was still simply in the category of out of the ordinary. He hadn't yet approached close enough to be considered a threat. For a moment, he envied the dog's simpler world, defined by smells and instincts and uncluttered by the vagaries of emotions.

Sweeping the glasses in an arc, Ricky saw a light click on inside the main house. He watched steadily for a minute or two, then saw the unmistakable wan glow of a television set fill a room near the front. The kennel office a little ways to his left remained dark, and, he guessed, locked. He made a final visual survey and saw a large rectangular spotlight near the roofline of the house. He guessed that it was motion-activated and that the field of range was directly in front of the house. Ricky replaced the glasses in his bag, and maneuvered parallel to the home, staying on the fringe of the underbrush, until he reached the edge of the property. A quick sprint would get him to the front of the kennel office, and perhaps would keep him away from triggering the exterior lights.

Not only Brutus was aroused by his presence. Some of the other dogs in their pens were moving around, sniffing the air. A few had barked nervously once or twice. Unsettled and unsure by a scent that was new.

Ricky knew precisely what he wanted to do, and thought that as a plan, it had virtues. Whether he could pull it off or not, he didn't know. He was aware of one thing, which was that up to this point he'd only skirted illegality. This was a step of a different sort. Ricky was aware of another detail: For a man who liked to play games, Rumplestiltskin had no rules. At least none that were constrained by any morality that he was familiar with. Ricky knew that even if Mr. R. didn't yet realize it, he was about to enter a little deeper into that arena.

He took a deep breath. The old Ricky would never have imagined being in this position, he thought. The new Ricky felt a single-minded, and coldhearted purpose. He whispered to himself: 'What I was, isn't what I am. And what I am, isn't yet what I can be.' He wondered whether he had ever been anything that he was, or anything he was about to become. A complicated question, he told himself. He smiled inwardly. A question that once upon a time you might have spent hours, days, on the couch, examining. No more. He shunted it away deep within him.

Lifting his eyes to the sky, he saw that the day's last light had finally slid away, and darkness was only moments from descending. It is the most unsettled time of day, he thought, and perfect for what he was about to deliver.

With that in mind, Ricky removed the small crowbar and the bicycle lock, and placed them in his right hand, gripping them tightly. Then he returned the backpack to his back, took a deep breath, and burst from the bushes, sprinting hard for the front of the building.

A bedlam of aroused dogs instantly creased the growing shadows. Yelps, howls, barks, and growls of all sorts and sizes pierced the air, obscuring the scrabbling sound his running shoes made against the gravel driveway. He was peripherally aware that all the animals were racing about in their small pen enclosures, twisting and turning with sudden dog excitement. A world of spastic marionettes, strings pulled by confusion.

Within a few seconds, he'd reached the front of Brutus's kennel. The huge dog seemed to be the only animal at the kennel with any sort of composure and his was filled with menace. He was pacing back and forth across the cement floor, but stopped when Ricky reached the gate. For a second, Brutus eyed Ricky, his mouth open in a growl, his teeth bared. Then, with shocking speed, the dog leaped across the area, throwing all hundred-plus pounds against the chain-link fencing that kept him contained. The force of the attack nearly knocked Ricky over. Brutus fell back, now frothing with rage, then again thrust at the steel chains, his teeth clacking against the metal.

Ricky moved quickly, rapidly threading the bicycle lock around the twin posts of the kennel door, snatching his hands back before the animal had time to seize one, then securing it, spinning the lock combination and dropping it. Brutus immediately tore at the black rubber-encased steel of the chain. 'Screw you,' Ricky whispered in a mocking tough guy accent. 'At least you ain't going nowhere.' Then he rose up and jumped over to the front of the kennel office. He thought he had only a few seconds left before the owner finally responded to the growing racket and din of arousal. Ricky assumed the man would be armed, but wasn't sure of this. Perhaps his confidence in Brutus at his side would minimize his own need for weapons.

He thrust the crowbar into the doorjamb and snapped out the lock with a creaking, splintering noise as the wood broke. It was old, and showed some warping with age and broke easily. Ricky guessed that the kennel owner didn't keep much of value in the office anyway, and didn't really envision a burglar testing Brutus. The door swung open, and Ricky stepped inside. He swung the backpack around to his front, stuffed the crowbar inside and removed his pistol, quickly chambering a round.

Inside was an opera of dog anxiety. The racket filled the air, making it hard to think, but giving Ricky an idea. Clicking on his flashlight, he raced down the musty, foul-smelling corridor where all the dogs were penned, stopping to open each cage as he ran past.

Within seconds, Ricky was surrounded by a leaping, barking tangle of breeds. Some were terrified, some were overjoyed. Smelling, yelping, confused but all aware they were free. Some three dozen dogs, of all different shapes and sizes, unsure what was happening, but more or less determined to be a part of it nonetheless. Ricky was counting on that basic dog-think that doesn't really understand all that much, but wants to be included in whatever is happening nevertheless. The sniffing and snuffling that flowed around and between his legs made him smile right through the nervousness of what he was doing. Surrounded by the pack of leaping, bouncing animals, Ricky returned to the kennel office. He was waving his arms, shooing the animals along, like some wildly impatient Moses at the edge of the Red Sea.

He saw the floodlight click on outdoors and heard a door slamming.

The kennel owner, he thought, finally roused by the racket, wondering what the hell has gotten into all the animals and not yet fully understanding that there might be a threat involved. Ricky counted to ten. Enough time for the man to approach Brutus's pen. He heard a second noise, above the roused dogs: The man was trying to open the Rottweiler's cage. A rattle of chain metal links and then a curse, as the man slowly grasped that the cage wasn't about to open.

It was at that moment that Ricky threw open the front door to the kennel office.

'Okay, guys, you're free,' he said, waving his arms. Nearly three dozen dogs bolted through the door, heading toward the warm New Jersey night, their voices raised in a confused song of joyous freedom.

He heard the kennel owner swearing wildly, and then Ricky stepped out into the darkness himself, remaining in a shadow at the edge of the spotlight's arc.

The man had been bowled over by the rush of animals, knocked back and down to one knee by the wave of dogs. He scrambled up, partially regaining his feet, searching for his balance. He was trying to catch them at the same time that they were jumping all over him, knocking him about. A welter of mixed beastly emotions — some dogs afraid, some joyous, some confused, all uncertain what was going on, knowing only that it was far out of the ordinary routine of kennel life, and eager to take advantage of it, whatever it was. Ricky smiled wickedly. It was, Ricky surmised, a pretty effective distraction.

When the kennel owner looked up, what he saw just behind the leaping, snuffling, tangled mass of animals was Ricky's pistol leveled at his face. He gasped, rocking backward in surprise, as if the hole at the end of the barrel was as forceful as the flood of dogs.

'Are you alone?' Ricky asked just loud enough to reach past the dogs' barking.

'Huh?'

'Are you alone? Is there anyone else in the house?'

The man caught on. He shook his head.

'Is Brutus's buddy in the house? His brother or mother or father?'

'No. Just me.'

Ricky thrust the pistol closer to the man, close enough so that the pungent odor of steel and oil and maybe death could fill his nostrils, without needing to own a dog's sensitive nose to understand what the potential was. 'Persuading me that you're telling the truth is important to staying alive,' Ricky said. He was a little surprised at how easy it was to threaten someone, but he had no illusion that he would be able to call his own bluff.

Behind the steel fencing, Brutus was in a paroxysm of fury. He continued to thrust himself at the metal, his teeth pressed up against the barrier. Foam streaked his jowls and his growl singed the air. Ricky eyed the dog warily. A hard thing, he thought, to be bred and raised for one single purpose, and then, when that moment came where all that training was supposed to coalesce, to be restrained by the frustration of a gate locked by a child's bicycle chain. The dog seemed to be almost overwhelmed by impotence, and Ricky thought that it was a little bit of a microcosm for the lives of some of his ex-patients.

'It's just me. Nobody else.'

'Good. Now we can have a conversation.'

'Who are you?' the man asked. It took a second for Ricky to remember that he'd been wearing a disguise on his first visit to the kennel. He rubbed his hand across his cheek.

I'm someone you're going to wish you'd been more pleasant to on our first meeting, Ricky thought, but what he said was: 'I'm someone you would probably rather not know,' simultaneously gesturing at the man's face with his weapon.

It took a few seconds for Ricky to get the kennel owner where he wanted him, which was seated on the ground, with his back up against the gate to Brutus's pen, hands out on his knees where Ricky could see them. The other dogs were wary of getting too close to the furious Rottweiler. By now, some had disappeared into the darkness and the countryside, others had collected near the owner's feet, and still others were jumping about, playing with one another, on the gravel driveway.

'I still don't know who you are,' the man said. He was squinting up at Ricky, trying to place him. The combination of the shadows, and the change in appearance worked to Ricky's advantage. 'What's all this about? I don't keep any cash here, and . . . '

'This isn't a robbery, unless you think of taking information as a theft, which I used to imagine was in some ways the same,' Ricky answered cryptically.

The man shook his head. 'I don't get it,' he said flatly. 'What do you want?'

'A while ago, a private detective came to see you with a few questions.'

'Yeah. So what?'

'I would like the same questions answered.'

'Who are you?' the man asked again.

'I told you. But right now, all you really need to know is that I'm a man with a gun, and you're not. And the sole means you have of defending yourself is locked behind a fence and feeling pretty damn bad about it, too, from the looks of him.'

The kennel owner nodded, but seemed, in those few moments, to gain a wary confidence and a good deal of composure. 'You don't sound much like the type who will use that thing. So maybe I won't say a damn thing about whatever it is you're so damn interested in. Screw you, whoever you are.'

'I want to know about the couple that died and are buried down the road there. And how you acquired this place. And especially the three kids that they adopted, that you said they didn't. And I would like to know about the phone call that you made after my friend Lazarus came to visit you the other day. Who did you call?'

The man shook his head. 'I'll tell you this: I got paid to make that call. And it was also worth my business to try to keep that guy here, whoever the hell he was. Too bad he split. I woulda had a bonus.'

'From who?'

The man shook his head. 'My business, mister tough guy. Like I said, screw you.'

Ricky leveled the pistol at the man's face. The kennel owner grinned. 'I've seen guys who will use that thing, and fella, I'm betting you ain't one of 'em.' There was a little bit of the nervous gambler in his voice. Ricky knew the man wasn't completely certain one way or the other.

The gun remained steady in Ricky's hand. He sighted down to a spot between the kennel owner's eyes. The longer he held his position, the more uncomfortable the man seemed, which, Ricky thought, wasn't unreasonable. He could see sweat on the man's forehead. But, in the same respect, Ricky thought, every second he delayed buttressed the man's reading of him. He thought to himself that he might yet need to become a killer, but didn't know if he could kill someone other than the primary target. Someone merely extraneous and ancillary, even if obnoxious. Ricky considered this for a second, then smiled coldly at the kennel owner. There's a noticeable difference, Ricky thought, between shooting the man who ruined your life, and shooting some cog in that machine.

'You know,' he said slowly, 'you're one hundred percent right. I haven't really been in this position all that much. It's pretty clear, to you, is it, that I don't have a great deal of experience in this area?'

'Yeah,' the man said. 'It's damn clear.' He shifted his position slightly, as if he was relaxing.

'Maybe,' Ricky said with a singularly flat voice, 'I should practice some.'

'What?'

'I said I should practice. I mean, how do I really know I will be able to use this thing on you, until I give it a bit of a workout on something a little less meaningful. Maybe significantly less meaningful.'

'I still don't follow,' the kennel owner said.

'Sure you do,' Ricky answered. 'You're just not concentrating. What I'm telling you is that I'm not an animal lover.'

As he said this, he lifted the pistol slightly, and keeping all the hours on the practice range up in New Hampshire in mind, Ricky slowly took in a deep breath, calmed himself utterly, and squeezed the trigger a single time.

The gun bucked harshly in his hand. A single report scoured the air. It whined into the darkness.

Ricky guessed that the bullet struck a bit of the fencing and split apart. He could not tell if the Rottweiler was hit or not. The kennel owner looked astonished, almost as if he'd been slapped, and he covered one ear with a hand, checking to see whether the bullet had sliced him as it raced past.

Dog bedlam returned to the yard, a siren of combined howling, barking, racing about. Brutus, the only animal confined, understood the threat he faced, and once again threw himself savagely at the chain links barring his path.

'Musta missed,' Ricky said nonchalantly. 'Damn. And to think I'm such a good shot.'

He sighted down the pistol at the frantic, furious dog.

'Jesus Christ!' the kennel owner finally spat out.

Ricky smiled again. 'Not here. Not now. Why, I daresay, this has nothing to do with religion. The more important issue is: Do you love your dog, there?'

'Christ! Hang on!' The kennel owner was nearly as frantic as the other animals tearing around the driveway. He held up his hand, as if to make Ricky pause.

Ricky eyed him with the same curiosity one might have if an insect started begging for its life before being subjected to a slap from the palm of one's hand. Interested, but insignificant.

'Just hang on for a second!' the man insisted.

'You have something to say?' Ricky asked.

'Yes, damn it! Just hang on.'

'I'm waiting.'

'That dog is worth thousands,' the kennel owner said. 'He's the alpha male, and I've spent hours, Christ, half my fucking life training him. He's a goddamn champion and you're gonna shoot him?'

'Don't see that you give me much alternative. I could shoot you, but then, I wouldn't find out what I need to know, and if, by some immense accident of police work, the cops ever managed to find me, why, I'd be facing significant charges — although you, of course, would find little satisfaction in that, being dead. On the other hand, well, as I told you, I'm not much of an animal lover. And Brutus there, well, to you he might be a paycheck, and maybe more, he might represent hours of time, and maybe even you might have some affection for him — but to me, why he's just an angry, slobbering mutt eager to chew my throat out, and the world will be far better off without him. So, given the choice, I'm thinking that maybe it's time for Brutus to head to that great old kennel in the sky.'

Ricky's voice was filled with mocking amusement. He wanted the man to think he was as cruel as he sounded, which wasn't hard.

'Just hold it for a second,' the kennel owner said.

'You see,' Ricky replied, 'now you've got something to think about. Is withholding information worth the dog's life? Your call, asshole. But make your mind up right away, because I'm losing my patience. I mean, ask yourself the question: Where are my loyalties? To the dog, who has been my companion and my meal ticket for so many years . . . or to some strangers who pay me for silence? Make a choice.'

'I don't know who they are . . . ,' the man started, causing Ricky to take aim at the dog. This time he held up both hands. 'Okay . . . I'll tell you what I know.'

'That would be wise. And Brutus will probably repay your generosity with devotion and by siring many litters of equally dumb and wondrously savage beasts.'

'I don't know much . . . ,' the kennel owner said.

'Bad start,' Ricky said. 'Making an excuse before you've even said anything.'

He immediately fired a second shot in the direction of the furious beast. This shot cracked into the dog's wooden hut in the rear of the pen. Brutus howled in insult and rage.

'Damn it! Stop! I'll tell you.'

'Then begin, please. This session has gone on long enough.'

The man paused, considering. 'It goes back a ways,' he began.

'I'm aware of that.'

'You're right about the old couple that owned this place. I don't know exactly how the scam was run, but they adopted those three kids on paper only. The kids were never here. I don't know exactly who they fronted for, because I came in after the couple was killed. Both of them in a car accident. I'd tried to buy this place from them a year before they died, and after they smashed up that car, I got a call from a man who said he was the executor of their estate, asking me if I wanted the place and the business. The price, too, was unbelievable . . . '

'Low or high.'

'I'm here, ain't I? Low. It was bargain basement, especially with all the property thrown in. A helluva good deal. We signed papers right quick.'

'Who did you deal with? Some lawyer?'

'Yeah. As soon as I said yes, a local guy took over. An idiot. Just does real estate closings and traffic offenses. And he was plenty miffed, too, because all he could say was I was getting a steal. But he kept his mouth shut, because I figure he was being overpaid, too.'

'Do you know who sold the property?'

'I saw the name only once. I think I recall the lawyer saying it was the old couple's next of kin. A cousin. Pretty distant. I don't remember the name, except that it was a doctor something or another.'

'A doctor?'

'That's right. And I was told one thing, absolutely clear, too.'

'What was that?'

'If anyone ever, anytime that day or years ahead, ever came asking about the deal or the old couple or the three children that nobody ever saw, I was supposed to call a number.'

'Did they give you a name?'

'No, just a number in Manhattan. And then about

six, seven years later, a man calls me one day, out of the blue, and tells me that the number has changed. Gives me another New York City number. Then, maybe a few years after that, same guy, calls up, gives me another number, only this time it's in upstate New York. He asks me if anyone has ever come visiting. I tell him no. He says great. Reminds me of the arrangement, and says there will be a bonus if anyone ever does. But it never happens until the other day when this guy Lazarus shows up. Asks his questions, and I run him out. Then I call the number. Man picks up the phone. Old man, now, you can hear it in his voice. Real old. Says thank you for the information. Maybe two minutes later, I get another call. This time it's some young woman. She says she's sending me some cash, like a grand, and that if I can find Lazarus and keep him there, there's another grand. I tell her he's probably staying at one of maybe three or four motels. And that's it, until you show up. And I still don't know who the hell you are, mister.'

'Lazarus is my brother,' Ricky said quietly.

He hesitated, thinking, adding years to an equation that reverberated deep within him. Finally he asked, 'The number you called, what is it?'

The man rattled off all ten numbers rapidly.

'Thank you,' Ricky said coldly. He didn't need to write it down. It was a number he knew.

He gestured with the pistol for the man to roll over.

'Place your hands behind your back,' Ricky instructed.

'Oh, come on, man. I told you everything. Whatever this is all about, hell, I ain't important.'

'That's for certain.'

'So, just let me go.'

'I just need to restrict your activity for a few minutes. Like long enough to depart, before you can get up, find some bolt cutters, and let Brutus there loose. I'm thinking that perhaps he'd like to have a moment or two alone with me in the dark.'

This made the kennel owner grin. 'He's the only dog I ever known that carries a grudge. Okay. Do what you got to.'

Ricky secured the man's hands with duct tape. Then he stood up.

'You'll call them, won't you?'

The man nodded. 'If I said I wouldn't you'd just get pissed because you'd know I was lying.'

Ricky smiled. 'A bit of insight. Quite correct.'

He paused, considering precisely what he wanted the kennel owner to say. Rhymes leaped into his imagination. 'All right, here's what you need to tell them:

Lazarus rises, he's closer still.
No longer pushing up the hill.
He's here. He's there.
He could be anywhere.
The game's afoot, and closing in.
Lazarus believes he's going to win.
It may no longer be your choice,
But better check this week's Voice.'

'That sounds like a poem,' the man said, as he lay on his stomach on the gravel, trying to turn his head to see Ricky.

'A kind of poem. Now we're going to have a lesson. Repeat it for me.'

It took several efforts for the kennel owner to get it more or less straight.

'I don't get it,' the man said, after mastering the poem. 'What's going on?'

'Do you play chess?' Ricky asked.

The man nodded. 'Not too good, though.'

'Well,' Ricky said, 'be thankful that you are just a pawn. And you don't need to know any more than a pawn needs to know. Because what's the object of chess?'

'Capture the queen and kill the king.'

Ricky smiled. 'Close enough. Nice speaking to you and Brutus there. Can I give you one piece of advice?'

'What's that?'

'Make the call. Recite the poem. Go out and try to collect all the dogs that have run away. That should take you some time. Then tomorrow wake up and forget any of this ever happened. Go back to the life you have for yourself, and don't think about all this ever again.'

The kennel owner shifted about uncomfortably, making a scrabbling sound in the gravel driveway. 'That might be hard.'

'Perhaps,' Ricky said. 'But it might be wise to make the effort.'

He stood up, leaving the man on the ground. Some of the other dogs had stretched out, and they stirred when he moved. Replacing the weapon in the backpack, Ricky kept the flashlight in his hand, and started to jog down the driveway. When he disappeared from any of the light that flooded the front area of the kennel, he picked up his pace, turning onto the darkened roadway, and heading fast toward the cemetery where he'd parked his car. His feet made slapping sounds against the black pavement beneath him, and he switched off the flashlight, so that he ran in the pitch-dark country. It was a little like swimming in a storm-tossed sea, he thought, cutting through waves that tugged at him from every direction. Despite the night that swallowed him, he felt illuminated by a single, glowing piece of information. The telephone number. It was, to Ricky in that second, as if everything from the first letter delivered to his office, right through that instant, was suddenly part of the same great, sweeping current. And then, he realized, perhaps it went much further. Months and years into his past, where something was catching him up and sweeping him along, but he had been unaware of it. The knowledge should have exhausted him, he thought, but instead, he felt an odd energy, and an equally odd release. He thought the understanding that he'd been surrounded by lies, and suddenly had seen some truth, was like a fuel, pushing him ahead.

He had miles to travel that night, he thought. Highway miles and heart miles. Both leading into his past, and pointing the way to his future. He hurried, like a marathon racer who senses the finish line ahead, beyond his sight, but measured in the pain in his feet and legs, the exhaustion creeping into his every breath.

31

It was a little after midnight when Ricky reached the tollbooth on the western side of the Hudson River, just to the north of Kingston, New York. He had driven quickly, pushing right to the limit of where he thought he could, but not be pulled over by some irritated New York state trooper. It was, he imagined, a bit of a microcosm for much of his past life. He wanted to speed, but wasn't quite willing to take the chance of truly flying. He thought the created persona of Frederick Lazarus would have pumped the rental car up to a hundred miles per hour, but he couldn't bring himself to that. It was as if both men, Richard Lively, who hid, and Frederick Lazarus, who was willing to fight, were on this particular drive. He realized that since he'd constructed his own death, he'd balanced between the uncertainty of taking risks, and the security of hiding. But he knew that he was probably no longer as invisible as he once believed he was. He guessed that the man searching for him was close behind, that all the crumbs and threads of clues and indications had been found, from New Hampshire straight back down the highway to New York City, and then over to New Jersey.

But he knew he was close, too.

It was the most deadly of races. A ghost pursuing a dead man. A dead man hunting a ghost.

He paid his toll, the only car crossing the bridge at that late hour. The tollbooth collector was in the midst of a copy of *Playboy* magazine, staring not reading, and barely looked in his direction. The bridge itself is a curiosity of architecture, rising hundreds of feet above the ribbon of black water that is the Hudson, illuminated by a string of green-yellow sodium vapor lights, descending to meet the earth on the Rhinebeck side in a rural, darkened bit of farmland, so that from the distance it appears like a glowing necklace suspended above an ebony throat, swallowed up by the pitch black of the shore. It was an unsettling ride, Ricky thought, as he steered toward the road that seemed to disappear into a pit. His headlights carved out weak cones of wan light against the surrounding night.

He found a place to pull over and removed one of his two remaining cell phones. He then dialed the front desk number at the last hotel where Frederick Lazarus was scheduled to be staying. It was a desultory, shabby, and cheap place, the sort of hotel that is only a single, fragile step above those that cater to prostitutes and their dates on an hourly basis. He guessed that the night deskman would have little to do, assuming no one had been shot or beaten that night on the premises, which, Ricky knew was a large assumption.

'Excelsior Hotel, how can I help you?'

'My name is Frederick Lazarus,' Ricky said. 'I had a reservation for tonight. But I won't make it there until tomorrow.'

'No problem,' the man said, laughing a little at the thought of a reservation. 'There will be as much room then as there is now. We're not exactly overbooked this tourist season.'

'Can you check to see if anyone left any messages for me?'

'Hang on . . . ,' the man said. Ricky could hear the telephone being placed on the counter. The man came on in a moment or two. 'Christ yes,' he said. 'You must be a popular guy. There's at least three or four . . . '

'Read them to me,' Ricky said. 'And I'll take care of you when I get there.'

The man read off the messages. They were the bunch that Ricky had left for himself, but no others. This made him pause.

'Has anyone been there, looking for me? I was supposed to have a meeting . . . '

The night clerk hesitated again, and in that hesitation Ricky learned what he needed. Before the clerk could lie by saying no, Ricky told him, 'She's gorgeous, isn't she? The type that gets what they want, when they want it, no questions asked, right? A lot more high-class than you usually get coming through the front door there, right?'

The clerk coughed.

'Is she there now?' Ricky demanded.

After a second or two, the clerk whispered, 'No. She left. A little less than an hour ago, right after she got a call on her cell phone. Took off real quick. And so did the guy she was with. They've been in and out of here all evening asking for you.'

'The guy she's with?' Ricky asked. 'Kinda round and pasty, looks a little bit like the kid you used to beat up on in junior high school?'

'You got it,' the clerk said. He laughed. 'That's the guy. Perfect description.'

Hello, Merlin, Ricky thought.

'They leave a number or an address?'

'No. Just said they'd come back. And didn't want me to let on that they'd been here. What's this all about?'

'Just a business arrangement. Tell you what, if they show, you give them this number . . . ' Ricky read off the last of his remaining cell phone exchanges. 'But make them slip you some cash in return. They're loaded.'

'Okay. Should I tell them you're going to be here tomorrow?'

'Yes. Might as well. And tell them that I called for my messages. That's it. Did they look at the messages?'

The man hesitated again. 'No,' he lied. 'Those are private. I wouldn't share them with strangers without your authorization.'

Sure, Ricky thought. Not for a penny less than fifty bucks. He was pleased that the man at the hotel had done precisely what he expected him to do. He disconnected the call, and sat back in the seat. They won't be certain, he thought. They won't know exactly who else is looking for Frederick Lazarus, or why, or what connection he has to what is going on. It will worry them and make their next step a little uncertain. Which is what he wanted. He looked down at his watch. He was sure that the kennel owner had finally gotten free from the duct tape handcuffs and after placating Brutus and rounding up as many of the other dogs as he could, had finally made his call, so Ricky expected at least one light to be on at the house where he was headed.

⋆ ⋆ ⋆

As he had earlier that night, Ricky left the rental car parked off a side road, out of sight from anyone who might have passed by. He was a good mile from his destination, but he thought he could use the time on foot to consider what his plan was. He could feel some excitement within him, as if he'd closed in finally on some answers to some questions. But it was coupled with a sense of outrage that might have been fury were he not struggling to restrain it. Betrayal, he thought to himself, has the potential to become far stronger than love. He felt a little queasy in his stomach, and recognized it for disappointment mingling freely with unbridled anger.

Ricky, once upon a time a man of introspection, checked the weapon he carried to make certain it was fully loaded, thinking that he had no real plan other than confrontation, which is an approach that defines itself, and realizing that he was closing in quickly on one of those moments where thoughts and actions coalesce.

He jogged forward through the surrounding blackness, his running shoes slapping at the macadam, joining with the ordinary sounds of a country night: the opossum scrabbling through the underbrush, the cicadas buzzing in a nearby field. He wanted to be a part of the air.

As he ran, he asked himself: Are you going to kill someone this night?

He did not know the answer.

Then he asked: Are you willing to kill someone tonight?

The answer to that question seemed much easier. He realized that a large part of him was ready to. It was the part that he'd constructed out of bits and pieces of identity in the months after his life had been ruined. The part that had studied all the methods of murder and mayhem available in the local library, and developed an expertise on the firing range. The invented part.

He pulled up short when he reached the drive to the house. Inside was the telephone with the number that he'd recognized. For a moment he recalled coming there almost a year earlier, expectant and almost panicked, hoping for any kind of help, desperate for any sort of answers. They were here, waiting for me, Ricky thought, obscured by lies. I just couldn't see them. It never occurred to me that the man who he believed had been the greatest help in his life turned out to be the man trying to kill him.

From the drive, he saw, as he'd expected, a single light in the study.

He knows I'm coming, Ricky thought. And Virgil and Merlin, who might have helped him, are still in New York. Even if they'd driven hard after he'd called, racing out of the city, they were still probably a good hour away. He took a step forward, hearing the sound of his feet against the loose stones of the gravel drive. Perhaps he even knows I'm here. Ricky searched around, trying to see a way of sneaking in. But he wasn't certain that the element of surprise was truly called for.

So, instead, he put the pistol in his right hand and chambered a round. He clicked the safety off and then walked nonchalantly up to the front door, like a friendly neighbor might in the midst of a summer afternoon. He didn't knock, he simply turned the handle. As he'd guessed, the door was open.

He walked in. A voice came from the study to his right.

'In here, Ricky.'

He took a single stride forward, raising the pistol in front of him, readying himself to fire. Then he stepped into the light that flowed through the doorway.

'Hello, Ricky. You are lucky to be alive.'

'Hello, Doctor Lewis,' Ricky replied. The old man was standing behind his desk, his hands flat on the surface, leaning expectantly forward. 'Shall I kill you now, or perhaps in a moment or two?' Ricky asked, voice flat with the hard restraints he'd looped around his rage.

The old psychoanalyst smiled. 'You would, I suspect, be justified in shooting in some courts. But there are questions you want answered, and I have waited up this long night to answer what I can. That is, after all, what we do, is it not, Ricky? Answer questions.'

'Maybe once I did,' Ricky replied. 'But no longer.'

He leveled the gun at the man who'd been his mentor. The man who'd trained him. Dr. Lewis seemed a little surprised. 'Did you really come all this way just to murder me?' he asked.

'Yes,' Ricky said, though this was a lie.

'Then go ahead.' The old doctor eyed him intensely.

'Rumplestiltskin,' Ricky said. 'All along it was you.'

Dr. Lewis shook his head. 'No, you are wrong. But I am the man who created him. At least in part.'

Ricky moved sideways, coming deeper into the office,

keeping his back to the wall. The same bookcases lined the walls. The same artwork. For a second, he could almost imagine that the year between visits hadn't actually taken place. It was a cold place, that seemed to speak of neutrality and opaque personality; nothing on the walls or the desk said anything about the man who occupied the office, which, Ricky thought darkly, probably said as much as anything. You don't need a diploma on the wall to certify being evil. He wondered how he had missed seeing it before. He gestured with his weapon for the old man to take a seat in the swiveling leather desk chair.

Dr. Lewis slumped down, sighing.

'I am getting old, and I do not have the energy I once had,' he said flatly.

'Please keep your hands where I can see them,' Ricky said.

The old man lifted his hands up. Then he pointed at his forehead, tapping it with an index finger. 'It is never what is in our hands that is truly dangerous, Ricky. You should know that. Ultimately, it is what is in our heads.'

'I might have agreed with you once, doctor, but now I have some doubts. And a clear-cut and enthusiastic reliance on this device, which, if you don't know, is a Ruger semiautomatic pistol. It fires a high velocity, hollow point, three-hundred-and-eighty-grain cartridge. There are fifteen shots in the clip, any one of which will remove a goodly portion of your skull, perhaps even the piece you just pointed to, killing you rapidly. And you know what's truly intriguing about this weapon, doctor?'

'What is that?'

'It is in the hands of a man who has already died once. Who no longer exists on this earth we share. Why don't you consider the implications of that existential event for a moment or two.'

Dr. Lewis paused, eyeing the gun. After a moment, he smiled.

'Ricky, what you say is interesting. But I know you. I know the inner you. You were on my couch four times a week for nearly four years. Every fear. Every doubt. Every hope. Every dream. Every aspiration. Every anxiety. I know you as well as you know yourself, and probably much better, and I know you are not a killer despite all your posturing. You are merely a deeply troubled man who made some extremely poor choices in his life. I doubt homicide will prove to be another.'

Ricky shook his head. 'The man you knew as Doctor Frederick Starks was on your couch. But he's dead and gone and you don't know me. Not the new me. Not in the slightest.'

Then he fired the pistol.

The single shot echoed in the small room, deafening him for a moment. The bullet tore through the air above Dr. Lewis's head, slapping into a bookcase directly behind him. Ricky saw a thick medical tome, spine out, suddenly shred, as it absorbed the shot. It was a work on abnormal psychology, a detail that almost brought Ricky to laughter.

Dr. Lewis paled, staggered, rocked momentarily side to side, then gasped out loud.

He steadied himself carefully. 'My God,' he blurted. Ricky could see something in the man's eyes that wasn't precisely fear, but more a sense of astonishment, as if something utterly unexpected had taken place. 'I did not think — ' he started.

Ricky cut him off with a small wave of the pistol. 'A dog taught me how to do that.'

Dr. Lewis rotated slightly in his seat and inspected the location where the bullet had landed. He burst out a half laugh, half gasp, then shook his head. 'Quite a shot, Ricky,' he said slowly. 'A remarkable shot. Closer to the truth than my head. You might want to keep what I said in mind over the next few moments.'

Ricky eyed the old physician. 'Stop being so obtuse,' he said briskly. 'We were going to talk about answers. Remarkable how a weapon like this helps focus one on the issues at hand. Think of all those hours with all those patients, myself included, doctor. All those lies and distractions and tangents and thick systems of delusions and detours. All that painstaking time spent in sorting out truths. Who would have thought that things could be uncomplicated so quickly by a device such as this. A little bit like Alexander and the Gordian knot, don't you think, doctor?'

Dr. Lewis seemed to have regained his composure. Rapidly his countenance changed, and he was now staring at Ricky with a narrow, angry gaze, as if he could still impose some control over the situation. Ricky ignored all the look implied, then, much as he had nearly a year earlier, he arranged an armchair in front of the old doctor.

'If not you,' Ricky asked coldly, 'then who is Rumplestiltskin?'

'You know, do you not?'

'Enlighten me.'

'The eldest child of your onetime patient. The woman you failed to help.'

'That I discovered on my own. Keep going.'

Dr. Lewis shrugged. 'My adopted child.'

'This I learned earlier tonight. And the two others?'

'His younger brother and sister. You know them as Merlin and Virgil. Of course they have other names.'

'Adopted, as well?'

'Yes. We took all three in. First as foster children, through the state of New York. Then I arranged for my cousins in New Jersey to front for us in an adoption. It was really pathetically simple outwitting the bureaucracy, which, I am sure you have already learned, did not really care all that much anyway what happened to the three children.'

'So, they carry your name? You discarded Tyson and gave them your own?'

'No.' The old man shook his head. 'Not so fortunate, Ricky. They are not in any phone book listing under Lewis. They were reinvented completely. Different names for each. Different identities. Different designs. Different schools. Different education and different treatment. But brothers and sister at heart, where it is important. That you know.'

'Why? Why the elaborate scheme to cover up their past? Why didn't you . . . '

'My wife was already ill, and we were beyond the age guidelines for the state. My cousins were convenient. And for a fee, willing to help. Help and forget.'

'Sure,' Ricky replied sarcastically. 'And their little accident? A domestic dispute?'

Dr. Lewis shook his head. 'A coincidence,' he said.

Ricky wasn't sure he believed that. He couldn't resist one small dig: 'Freud said there are no accidents.'

Dr. Lewis nodded. 'True. But there is a difference between wishing and acting.'

'Really? I think you're wrong there. But never mind. Why them? Why those three children?'

The old psychoanalyst shrugged again. 'Conceit. Arrogance. Egotism.'

'Those are just words, doctor.'

'Yes, but they explain much. Tell me Ricky: A killer . . . a truly remorseless, murderous psychopath . . . is this someone created by their environment? Or are they born to it, some infinitesimal little screwup in the gene pool? Which is it, Ricky?'

'Environment. That's what we're taught. Any analyst would say the same. The genetic guys might disagree, though. But we are a product of where we come from, psychologically.'

'And I would agree. So, I took in a child — and his two siblings — who was a laboratory rat for evil. Abandoned by birth father. Rejected by his other relatives. Never given any semblance of stability. Exposed to all sorts of sexual perversities. Beaten endlessly by any series of his mother's sociopathic boyfriends, who eventually saw his own mother kill herself in poverty and despair, helpless to save the only person he trusted in the world. A formula for evil, would you not agree?'

'Yes.'

'And I thought I could take that child and reverse all that weight of wrong. I helped set up the system where he would be cut off from his terrifying past. Then I thought I could turn him into a productive member of society. That was my arrogance, Ricky.'

'And you couldn't?'

'No. But I did engender loyalty, curiously enough. And perhaps an odd sort of affection. It is a terrible and yet truly fascinating thing, Ricky, to be loved and respected by a man devoted to death. And that is what you have in Rumplestiltskin. He is professional. A consummate killer. One equipped with as fine an education as I could provide. Exeter. Harvard. Columbia Law. Also a short stint in the military for a little extra training. You know what the curious aspect of all this is, Ricky?'

'Tell me.'

'His job is not that different from ours. People come to him with problems. They pay him well for solutions. The patient who arrives on our couch is desperate to rid himself of some burden. So are his clients. His means is just, well, more immediate than ours. But hardly less intimate.'

Ricky found himself breathing hard. Dr. Lewis shook his head.

'And, you know what else, Ricky, other than being

extremely wealthy, do you know what other quality he has?'

'What?'

'He is relentless.'

The old psychoanalyst sighed and added, 'But perhaps you have seen that already? How he waited years, preparing himself, and then singled out and pursued everyone who ever did his mother harm, and destroyed them, just as surely as they destroyed her. I suppose, in an odd way, you should find it touching. A son's love. A mother's legacy. Was he wrong to do that, Ricky? To punish all those people who systematically or ignorantly ruined her life? Who left her adrift with three small needy children in the harshest of worlds? I do not exactly think so, Ricky. Not at all. Why even the most irritating politicians opine endlessly how we live in a society that shirks responsibility. Is not revenge merely accepting one's debts and cloaking them in a different solution? The people he has singled out truly deserved punishment. They — like you — ignored someone who pleaded for help. That is what is wrong with our profession, Ricky. Sometimes we want to explain so much, when the real answer lies in one of those . . . ' The doctor gestured at the weapon in Ricky's hand.

'But why me?' Ricky blurted. 'I didn't . . . '

'Of course you did. She went to you desperate for help, and you were too wrapped up with the direction in which your own career was heading to pay enough attention and give her the assistance she needed. Surely, Ricky, a patient who kills herself when under your care — even if only for a few sessions — well, do you not feel some remorse of your own? Some sense of guilt? Do you not deserve to pay some price? Why would you think that gaining revenge is somehow less a responsibility than any other human act?'

Ricky did not answer. After a moment, he asked, 'When did you learn . . . '

'Of your connection to my adopted experiment? Near the end of your own analysis. I simply decided to see how it would play out over the years.'

Ricky could feel rage mingling with sweat within him. His mouth was dry.

'And when he came after me? You could have warned me.'

'Betray my adopted child in favor of my onetime patient? And not even my favorite patient, at that . . . '

These words stung Ricky. He could see the old man was every bit as evil as the child he'd adopted. Perhaps even worse.

' . . . I thought one might consider it justice.' The old analyst laughed out loud. 'But you do not know the half of it, Ricky.'

'What is the half I don't know?'

'I think that is something you will have to discover for yourself.'

'And the other two?'

'The man you know as Merlin is indeed an attorney, and a capable one at that. The woman you know as Virgil is an actress with quite a career ahead of her. Especially now that they have almost completed tying up all the loose ends of their lives. I think, Ricky, that perhaps you and I are the only loose ends remaining for the three of them. The other thing you should know, Ricky, is that they both believe it was their older brother, the man you know as Rumplestiltskin, who saved their lives. Not I, really, though I contributed to their salvation. No, it was he who kept them together, who kept them from straying, who insisted on their going to school and getting straight A's and then accomplishing much with their lives. So, if nothing else, Ricky, understand this: They are devoted. They are utterly loyal to the man who will kill you. Who did kill you once, and will do so again. Is that not intriguing, Ricky, from the psychiatric point of view? A man without scruples who engenders blind and total devotion. A psychopath who will kill you just as surely as you might step on a spider crossing your path. But who is loved, and in turn loves. But loves only those two. None other. Except, perhaps, me, a little bit, because I rescued him and helped him. So, perhaps I have gained a loyalist's love. Which is important for you to keep in mind, Ricky, because you have so little chance of surviving your connection to Rumplestiltskin.'

'Who is he?' Ricky demanded. Each word that the old analyst spoke seemed to blacken the world around him.

'You want his name? His address? His place of business?'

'Yes.' Ricky leveled the weapon at the old man.

Dr. Lewis shook his head. 'Just like in the fairy tale, right? The princess's messenger overhears the troll dancing about his fire, and blurting out his name. She doesn't really do anything clever or wise, or even sophisticated. She's just lucky, and so when he comes for his third question, she has the answer by dumb, blind luck, and thus survives, and retains her firstborn child, and lives happily ever after. You think this will be the same? The luck you have acquired which has you here, right now, waving a weapon in an old man's face will win you the game?'

'Give me his name,' Ricky said quietly, voice as cold and evil as he could make it. 'I want all their names.'

'What makes you think you don't know them already?'

'I am so tired of games,' Ricky said.

The old analyst shook his head. 'That is all life is. One game after another. And death is the greatest game of all.'

The two men stared across the room at each other.

'I wonder,' Dr. Lewis said cautiously, lifting his eyes

for a moment and examining a wall clock, then pausing with each word, 'how much time you have remaining?'

'Enough,' Ricky replied.

'Really?' the old analyst responded. 'Time is elastic, isn't it? Moments can last forever, or else evaporate instantly. Time is really a function of our own view of the world. Is that not something we learn in analysis?'

'Yes,' Ricky said. 'That's true.'

'And tonight, there are all sorts of questions about time, are there not? I mean, Ricky, here we are, alone in this house. But for how much longer? Knowing as I did that you were heading this way, do you not think I took the precaution of summoning help? How long before it arrives?'

'Long enough.'

'Ah, there is a wager I am not sure I would be so confident about.' The old analyst smiled again. 'But perhaps we should make it slightly more complicated.'

'How so?'

'Suppose I were to tell you that somewhere here in this room is the information you seek. Could you find it in time? Before help arrives to rescue me?'

'I told you, I'm tired of playing games.'

'It is in plain sight. And you have already come closer to it than even I guessed you might. There. Enough clues.'

'I won't play.'

'Well, I think you are wrong. I think you are going to have to play a bit longer Ricky, because this game has not concluded.' Dr. Lewis held both his hands up abruptly, and then said, 'Ricky, I need to remove something from the top drawer of this desk. It is something which will certainly change the manner that this game is being played. Something that you will want to see. May I do that?'

Ricky aimed the pistol at Dr. Lewis's forehead and nodded. 'Go ahead.'

The doctor smiled again, a nasty, cold smile that had nothing to do with humor. An executioner's grin. He removed an envelope from the drawer and placed it on the desktop in front of him.

'What's that?'

'Perhaps, Ricky, it is the information you came here seeking. Names. Addresses. Identities.'

'Hand it to me.'

Dr. Lewis shrugged. 'As you wish . . . ,' he said. He thrust the envelope across the desktop and Ricky eagerly grabbed at it. It was sealed and Ricky took his eyes off the old physician for an instant while he inspected the letter. This was a mistake, which he realized as soon as he'd done it.

He lifted his eyes and saw that the old man now had a grin on his face and a small, snub-nosed .38 caliber revolver in his right hand.

'Not quite as big as yours, is it, Ricky?' The doctor laughed out loud. 'But probably just as efficient. You see, you just made a mistake that none of the three people you are involved with would. And certainly not the man you know as Rumplestiltskin. He would never have taken his eyes off his target. Not for a second. No matter how well he knew the person he had targeted, he would never have trusted them enough to remove his eyes from them for even the briefest of times. Perhaps that should tell you how little chance you really have.' The two men were facing across the desktop, weapons aimed squarely at each other.

Ricky narrowed his gaze, feeling sweat gathering beneath his arms.

'This,' Dr. Lewis whispered, 'is an analytic fantasy, is it not? In the system of transference, do we not want to kill the analyst, just as we want to kill our mother or our father or everyone who has come to symbolize all that is wrong with our lives? And the analyst, in return, does he not have a murderous passion that he would like to exploit at much the same time?'

Ricky didn't reply at first. Finally, he muttered, 'The child may have been a laboratory rat for evil, like you say. But he could have been turned around. You could have done it, but you did not, right? It was more intriguing to see what would happen if you left him adrift emotionally, wasn't it? And it was far easier for you to blame all the evil in the world and ignore your own, wasn't it?'

Dr. Lewis paled slightly.

'You knew, didn't you?' Ricky continued, 'that you were as much the psychopath as he was? You wanted a killer, and so you found one, because that was what you always wanted to be: a killer.'

The old man scowled. 'You always were astute, Ricky. Think of what you could have made with your life had you been a bit more ambitious. A little more subtle.'

'Put the weapon down, doctor. You're not going to shoot me,' Ricky said.

Dr. Lewis kept the revolver trained on Ricky's face, but nodded. 'I do not really have to, do I?' he said. 'The man who killed you once will do it again. And this time he will not accept an obituary in the paper. I think he will actually need to see your death. Do you not?'

'Not if I have anything to say about it. And perhaps, once I find this great array of clues as to who he is that you say are here, perhaps I'll just disappear again. I succeeded once, and I suspect I can evaporate a second time. Perhaps Rumplestiltskin will simply have to settle for what he achieved the first time we played. Doctor Starks is dead and gone. He won that round. But I will go on and become whatever I want. I can win by running. I win by hiding. By staying alive and anonymous. Isn't that an oddity, doctor? We, who worked so hard to help ourselves and our patients confront the demons that pursue and torment them, can actually preserve ourselves by fleeing. We helped patients become something, but I can become nothing, and thus win. An irony, don't you think?'

Dr. Lewis nodded his head.

'I anticipated your response,' he said slowly. 'I imagined that you would see the answer that you have just provided me.'

'So,' Ricky said, 'I repeat: Put your weapon down, and I will take my leave. Assuming the information I need is in this envelope.'

'In a way, it is,' the old man said. He was whispering, with a nasty smile. 'But I have just a final question or two for you, Ricky . . . if you do not mind.'

Ricky nodded.

'I have told you of the man's past. And told you far more than you yet understand. And what did I tell you of his relationship with me?'

'You spoke of a kind of odd loyalty and love. A psychopath's love.'

'One killer's love for another. Most intriguing, do you not think?'

'Fascinating,' Ricky said briskly. 'And were I still a psychoanalyst, I would likely be intrigued and eager to investigate. But I am not. No longer.'

'Ah, but I think you are wrong.' Dr. Lewis shrugged his shoulders. 'I think one cannot walk away from being a physician of the heart quite as easily as you seem to think it can be done.' The old man shook his head in a negative. He still had not relaxed his grip on the revolver, nor had it wavered from Ricky's face. 'I think our time is up for the evening, Ricky. One last session. The fifty-minute hour. Perhaps now your own analysis is nearly complete. But the real question I have for you to take away from this is this, Ricky: If he was so devoted to seeing you kill yourself after you failed his mother, what will he want to happen to you when he believes you have killed me?'

'What do you mean?' Ricky asked.

But the old physician didn't reply. Instead, in a single sweeping gesture, he lifted the revolver up to his temple, grinned maniacally, and then fired a single shot.

32

Ricky half shouted, half screamed, in surprise and shock. His voice seemed to blend with the echo of the revolver's report.

He rocked back hard in the chair, almost as if the bullet that exploded into the old psychoanalyst's head had actually been diverted and struck him in the chest. By the time the reverberation from the gunshot had faded into the night air, Ricky was on his feet, standing at the edge of the desk, staring down at the man who once he'd trusted so implicitly. Dr. Lewis had slammed backward, twisted slightly by the force of death delivered to his temple. His eyes had remained open, and now they stared out with macabre intensity. A scarlet mist of blood and brain matter had painted the bookcase, and deep, maroon blood was seeping from the gaping wound down across the physician's face and chin, staining his shirt. The revolver that had delivered the fatal shot slipped from his fingers to the floor, its weight muffled by the fine Persian carpet beneath their feet. Ricky gasped out loud, as the old man's body twitched once with muscles coming into tune with death.

He breathed in harshly. It wasn't, he realized, the first time he'd seen death. When he'd been an intern, doing rotations in internal medicine and the emergency room, more than one person had died in his presence. But that was always surrounded by equipment, and teams of people trying to save life and fight off dying. Even when his wife had finally succumbed to cancer, that had still been part of a process that he was familiar with, and provided a context, even if awful, for what took place.

This was different. It was savage. It was murder,

specialized. He felt his own hands shake with an old man's palsy. He fought hard against the overwhelming instinct to panic and run.

Ricky tried to organize his thoughts. The room was silent, and he could hear his own labored breathing, like a man at the top of a high mountain, sucking in cold air without significant relief. It seemed that every sinew inside of him had tightened, knotted, and that only fleeing would loosen the tension. He gripped the edge of the desk, trying to steady himself.

'What have you done to me, old man?' he said out loud. His voice seemed out of place, like a cough in the midst of a solemn church service.

Then he realized the answer to his own question: He's tried to kill me. One bullet that can kill two people, because the old physician's death was likely to be taken hard by three people on this earth who had no restrictions on how they would respond. And they would blame Ricky, regardless of what evidence of suicide stared them in the face.

Only it was even more complicated than that. Dr. Lewis wanted to do more than simply murder him. He'd had the gun leveled at Ricky's face, and he could easily have pulled the trigger, even knowing that Ricky might return fire before dying. What the old man wanted was to endow all the people playing out the murderous game with a moral depravity that equaled his own. That was far more important than simply killing Ricky and himself. Ricky tried to breathe past the thoughts which flooded him. All along, he thought, this hasn't only been about death. It's been about the process. It's been about how death was reached.

An appropriate game for a psychoanalyst to invent.

Again he sucked at the thin air of the study. Rumplestiltskin may have been the agent of revenge and the instigator, as well, Ricky thought. But the design of the game came from the man dead before him. Of that he was certain.

Which meant that when he spoke of knowledge, he was likely telling the truth. Or at least some perverted, twisted version of the same.

It took Ricky a second or two to realize that he still clutched the envelope that his onetime mentor had handed him. It was difficult for him to strip his eyes away from the body of the old man. It was as if the suicide was hypnotic. But he finally did, tearing open the flap and pulling a single sheet of paper from the envelope. He read rapidly:

> *Ricky: The wages of evil are death. Think of this last moment as a tax I have paid on all I have done wrong. The information you seek is in front of you, but can you find it? Is not that what we do? Probe the mystery that is obvious? Find the clues that stare at us directly and shout out to us?*
>
> *I wonder if you have enough time and are clever enough to see what you need to see. I doubt it. I think it is far more likely that you will die tonight in more or less the same fashion that I have. Only your death is likely to be far more painful, because your guilt is far less than my own.*

The letter wasn't signed.

Ricky sucked in a new and seemingly unique panic with every breath.

He lifted his eyes and began to search around the office. A wall clock clicked quietly with each passing second, the sound suddenly penetrating Ricky's consciousness. He tried to do the travel math: When did the old man call and tell Merlin and Virgil and perhaps Rumplestiltskin that Ricky was on his way? From the city to the country home was two hours. Maybe a little less. Did he have seconds? Minutes? A quarter hour? He knew he had to get away, to distance himself from the death sitting in the seat before him, if only to gather his thoughts and try to determine what move he had left, if any. It was like being in a chess game with a grand master, he thought suddenly, moving pieces around a board haphazardly, all the time knowing that the opponent can see two, three, four, or more moves ahead.

His throat was dry and he felt flushed.

Right in front, he thought.

Sliding gingerly around the desk, trying to avoid even brushing up against the dead analyst's body, he started to reach for the top drawer, then stopped. What am I leaving behind, he thought? Hair fibers? Fingerprints? DNA? Have I even committed a crime?

Then he thought: There are two kinds of crimes. The first brings out the police and prosecutors and the weight of the state demanding justice. The second strikes at the hearts of individuals. Sometimes the two blend together, he knew. But so much of what had happened was predominantly the second, and it was the judge, jury, and executioner who were heading his way that truly concerned him.

There was no way around these questions. He told himself to have confidence in the single fact that the man whose prints and other substances were being left in the dead man's room was dead, too, and that might afford him some protection, if only from the police who would likely be there at some point that night. He put his hand on the drawer and pulled it open.

It was empty.

He moved swiftly to all the other drawers. They, too, were barren. Dr. Lewis had clearly taken the time to clean out anything that had been accumulated there. Ricky ran his fingers under the desk surface, thinking perhaps something was concealed there. He bent down and searched, but saw nothing. Then he turned his attention to the dead man. Breathing in sharply, he let his fingers travel inside the man's pockets. They, too, were clear. Nothing on the body. Nothing in the desk. It was as if the old analyst had taken pains to wipe his world clean. Ricky nodded in agreement. A psychoanalyst, better than anyone, he thought, knows what speaks about who one is. And it follows that seeking to wipe that identity slate clear, he would know better than most how to eradicate the telltale signs of personality.

Again, Ricky swept his eyes over the office. He wondered whether there was a safe. He spotted the clock, and that gave him an idea. Dr. Lewis had spoken about time. Perhaps, Ricky thought, that was the clue. He jumped to the wall and searched behind the clock.

Nothing.

He wanted to bellow in rage. It's here, he insisted.

Ricky took another deep breath. Perhaps it isn't, he thought, and all the old man wanted me to do was to be here when his murderous adopted offspring arrive. Was that the game? Perhaps he wanted this to be the end, tonight. Ricky seized his own weapon and spun back toward the door.

Then he shook his head. No, that would be a simple lie, and Dr. Lewis's lies were far more complex. There is something here.

Ricky turned to the bookcase. Rows of medical and psychiatric texts, collected writings of Freud and Jung, some modern studies and clinical trials in book form. Books on depression. Books on anxiety. Books on dreams. Dozens of books, filled with only a modest portion of the accumulated knowledge of man's emotions. Including the book that housed Ricky's bullet. He looked at the title, riding the spine: *The Encyclopedia of Abnormal Psychology*, only the *ology* of the last word had been shredded by his shot.

He stopped, staring forward.

Why did a psychoanalyst need a text on abnormal

psychology? Their profession dealt almost exclusively with the modestly displaced emotions. Not the truly dark and twisted ones. Of all the books lined up on the shelves, it was the only one slightly out of place, but this was a distinction only another analyst would notice.

The man had laughed. He'd turned and saw the place the bullet landed and laughed and said it was appropriate.

Ricky jumped to the bookcase and grasped the text from the shelf. It was heavy and thick, bound in black with vibrant gold writing on the jacket. He opened the book to the title page.

Written in thick red with a Flair pen right across the title were the words: *Good choice, Ricky. Now can you find the right entries?*

He looked up and heard the clock ticking. He did not think he had time to answer that question at that moment.

He took a step away from the bookcase, almost starting to run, and then stopped. He turned back and carefully took another text from a different shelf and placed it into the open space of the book he had removed, covering the textbook's absence.

Ricky took another quick look around, but saw nothing that spoke loudly to him. He took a final glance at the old analyst's body, which seemed to have grayed in the few moments that death had been there with him. He thought he should say or feel something, but no longer was sure what that could be, so instead, Ricky ran.

* * *

The deep onyx of night blanketed him as he slid from Dr. Lewis's country home. Within a few strides he was away from the front door, the light that seeped from the study, swallowed by the summer darkness. Standing in the black shadows, Ricky was able to look back quickly. The benign sounds of the rural area played the usual midnight music, no discordant tones to indicate that violent death was a part of the landscape. For a second he stopped and tried to assess how every piece of himself had been systematically erased over the past year. Identity is a quilt of experience, but it seemed to Ricky that so little existed of what he'd come to believe was himself. What he had left was his childhood. His adult life was in tatters. But both halves of his existence were cut away from him, with no apparent access. He thought this understanding left him part dizzy, part nauseous.

He turned and continued to flee.

Settling into a comfortable jog, footsteps mingling with the night sounds, Ricky headed back toward his car. He carried the abnormal psychology encyclopedia in one hand, his weapon in the other. He had traveled only half the distance, when he heard the unmistakable sound of a vehicle moving fast on a country road, heading in his direction. He looked up and saw the glow of headlights sweeping around a distant corner, mingling with the deep throaty sound of a large engine accelerating.

He did not hesitate. He knew immediately who was heading in that direction in such a hurry. Ricky pitched himself to the earth and scrambled behind a stand of trees. He ducked down, but lifted his head as a large, black Mercedes roared past. The tires sharpened the noise at the next corner.

When he raised himself up, he was already sprinting. This was flight in earnest, muscles complaining, lungs red-hot with exertion, moving as fast as he could through the night. Getting away was the only importance, the only concern. With an ear cocked behind him, listening for the telltale sound of the huge car, he raced forward. He told himself to find distance.

They will not stay long at the country house, he said to himself, urging his feet forward. A few moments only to measure the death in the study and to search for signs that he was still there. Or close by. They will know that only moments elapsed between the self-murder and their arrival, and they will want to close the gap.

Within minutes, he'd reached the rental car. He fumbled for the keys, dropping them once, but seizing them from the ground, gasping with tension. He threw himself behind the wheel and started the engine. Every instinct he had told him to accelerate. To escape. To run away. But he fought against these urges, trying hard to keep his wits about him.

Ricky made himself think. I cannot outrun them in this car. There are two routes back to New York City, the thruway on the western side of the Hudson and the Taconic Parkway on the eastern side. They will have a fifty-fifty chance of guessing right, and spotting me in the car. The out-of-state New Hampshire plate on the tail of the cheap rental car was a telltale sign indicating who was behind the wheel. They might have acquired a description of the vehicle and the license plate number from the rental agency in Durham. In fact, he thought this likely.

What he understood was in that moment he had to do something unexpected.

Something that defied what the three in the car would anticipate.

He thought his hands were shaking as he decided what to do. He wondered whether it was easier to gamble with his life now that he'd died once already.

He put the car in gear and slowly began to drive back in the direction of the old analyst's house. He scrunched himself down as low in the seat as he could get, without being obvious. He forced himself to maintain the speed limit, heading north on the old country road, when the relative safety of the city was to the south.

He was closing on the driveway to the place he'd just been, when he saw the headlights of the Mercedes sweeping down toward the roadway. He could hear the crunch of the big tires against the gravel. He slowed slightly — he did not want to pass directly in the big car's lights — giving them time to swing out onto the road, and head toward him, accelerating quickly. He had his high beams on, and as the Mercedes closed the space, he dimmed his lights, as one is supposed to, then just as they closed, blinked them on high again, like any motorist signaling with irritation at the approaching car. The effect was that both vehicles narrowly swept past each other with high beams on. Just as Ricky knew that he was blinded momentarily, so were they. He punched the accelerator as he passed, slinking rapidly around a corner. Too fast, he hoped, for someone in the other car to turn and make the license plate on the back.

He took the first side road he spotted, turning to his right, immediately switching off the car lights. He made a U-turn in the black, his way lit only by the moonlight. He reminded himself to keep his foot off the brake pedal, so that the red lights wouldn't light in the rear. Then he waited to see if he was followed.

The road remained empty. He made himself wait five, then ten minutes. Long enough for the occupants of the Mercedes to decide on one of the two alternative routes, and rachet the big car up to a hundred miles per hour, trying to catch up with him.

Ricky put the car back in gear, and continued to drive north almost aimlessly, on side roads and streets. Heading nowhere special. After nearly an hour, he finally turned the car around and changed direction again, finally steering back to the city. It was deep into the night and few other vehicles were around. Ricky drove steadily, thinking how close his world had become, and how dark, and trying to devise a way to restore light to it.

* * *

It was deep into the predawn morning when he reached the city. New York at that hour seems to be taken over by shifting shapes, as the electricity of the late-night crowds, whether they are the beautiful or the decrepit, seeking adventure, give way to the workday throngs. The fish market and trucking beasts looking to take over the day. The transition is unsettling, made on streets slicked by moisture and neon lights. It is, Ricky thought, a dangerous time of the night. A time when inhibitions and restraints seem lessened, and the world is willing to take chances.

He had returned to his rented room, fighting the urge to throw himself onto the bed and devour sleep. Answers, he told himself. He clutched answers in the book on abnormal psychology, he just needed to read them. The question was, where?

The encyclopedia contained 779 pages of text. It was organized alphabetically. He flipped through some pages, but initially could find nothing to indicate anything. Still, poring over the book like some monk in an ancient monastery, he knew somewhere within the pages was what he needed to know.

Ricky rocked back in his seat, taking a stray pencil and tapping it against his teeth. I am in the right location, he thought. But short of examining every page, he was unsure what to do. He told himself that he needed to think like the man who'd died earlier that night. A game. A challenge. A puzzle.

They are here, Ricky thought. Inside a text on abnormal psychology.

What did he tell me? Virgil is an actress. Merlin is an attorney. Rumplestiltskin is a professional assassin.

Three professions working together. As he flipped almost haphazardly through the pages, trying to think through the problem in front of him, he passed the few pages devoted to the letter *V*. Almost by luck, his eyes caught a mark on the initial page of the section, which started with 559. In the upper corner, written in the same pen that Dr. Lewis had used for his greeting on the title page was the fraction one and three. One-third.

That was all.

Ricky turned to the entries under *M*. In a similar location was another pair of numbers, but written differently. These were ¼, written one slash four. On the opening page of the letter *R*, he found a third signature, two-fifths. Two dash five.

There was no doubt in Ricky's mind that these were keys. Now he had to uncover the locks.

Ricky bent forward slightly in his seat, rocking back and forth gently, as if trying to accommodate a slight upset stomach, movements that were almost involuntary, as he concentrated on the problem in front of him. It was a conundrum of personality as complex as any he'd ever experienced in his years as an analyst. The man who had treated him to chart his own way through his own personality, who had been his guide into the profession, and who had provided the means of Ricky's own death, had delivered a final message. Ricky felt like some ancient Chinese mathematician, working on an abacus, the black stones making clicking noises as they were shunted speedily from one side to the other, calculations made and then discarded as the equation grew.

He asked himself: What do I really know?

A portrait began to form in his imagination, starting with Virgil. Dr. Lewis said she was an actress, which made sense, for she had constantly been performing. The child of poverty, the youngest of the three, who had gone from so little to so much with such dizzying speed.

How would that have affected her? Ricky demanded of himself. Lurking in her unconscious would be issues of identity, of who she truly was. Hence the decision to enter a profession that constantly called for redesigning one's self. A chameleon, where roles dominated truths. Ricky nodded. A streak of aggressiveness, as well, and an edginess that spoke of bitterness. He thought of all the factors that went into her becoming who she was, and how eager she'd been to be the point player in the drama that had swept him to his death.

Ricky shifted in his seat. Make a guess, he told himself. An educated guess.

Narcissistic personality disorder.

He turned to the encyclopedia entry for *N* and then to that particular diagnosis.

His pulse quickened. He saw that Dr. Lewis had touched several letters in the midst of words with a yellow highlighter pen. Ricky grabbed a sheet of paper and wrote down the letters. Then he sat back sharply, staring at gobbledygook. It made no sense. He went back to the encyclopedia definition, and recalled the one-third key. This time he wrote down letters three spaces away from the marked ones. Again, useless.

He considered the dilemma again. On this occasion, he looked at letters that were three words away. But before writing these down, he thought to himself one over three, so he went instead to letters three lines below.

By doing this, the first three dots produced a word: THE.

He continued rapidly, producing a second word: JONES.

There were six more dots. Using the same scheme, they translated to: AGENCY.

Ricky stood and walked to the bedside table, where, beneath the telephone there was a New York City telephone book. He looked up the section for theatrical talent, and found in the midst of a number of listings, a small advertisement and telephone exchange for 'The Jones Agency — A theatrical and talent agency catering to the up-and-coming stars of tomorrow . . . '

One down. Now, Merlin the attorney.

He pictured the man in his mind's eye: hair carefully combed; suits without wrinkles, tailored to the nuances of his body. Even his casual dress had been formal. Ricky considered the man's hands. The fingernails had been manicured. A middle child, who wanted everything to be in order, who couldn't tolerate the messiness of the disruptive life he'd come from. He must have hated his past, adored the safety of his adopted father, even as the old analyst had systematically twisted him. He was the arranger, the enabler, the man who had dealt with threats and money and savaged Ricky's life with ease.

This diagnosis came more easily: obsessive-compulsive disorder.

He turned rapidly to that section of the encyclopedia, and saw the same series of highlighted letters. Using the key provided, he swiftly came up with a word that surprised him: ARNESON. It wasn't exactly a jumble of letters, nor was it something that he recognized.

He paused, because this seemed to make no sense. Then he persisted, and found the next letter was *V*.

Ricky went back, checked the key again, knitted his brows, and then understood what he was being given. The remaining letters spelled out the word: FORTIER.

A court case.

He wasn't certain which court he would find Arneson v. Fortier in, but a trip to a clerk with a computer and access to current dockets would likely turn it up.

Turning back to the encyclopedia, Ricky thought of the man at the core of everything that had happened: Rumplestiltskin. He turned to the section under *P* which dealt with PSYCHOPATHS. There was a subsection, for HOMICIDAL.

And there were the series of dots that he'd come to expect.

Using the key already given him, Ricky quickly deciphered the letters, writing them down on a sheet of paper. When he finished, he sat up straight, sighing deeply. Then he clenched the paper in his hand, crumpling it into a ball, and angrily throwing it toward the wastebasket.

He let loose a string of epithets, which only masked what he'd half expected.

The message he'd come up with had been: NOT THIS ONE.

⋆ ⋆ ⋆

Ricky had not had much sleep, but adrenaline energized him. He showered, shaved, and dressed himself in a jacket and tie. A lunch-hour trip to a court clerk's office and some modest cajoling of one of the impatient assistants behind the counter had provided him with some information about Arneson v. Fortier. It was a civil dispute in superior court, scheduled for a pretrial hearing the following morning. As best as he could tell, the two parties were arguing over a real estate transaction that had gone bad. There were claims and counterclaims and substantial sums of money gone astray between a pair of well-heeled midtown Manhattan developers. The kind of case, Ricky imagined, where everyone was angry and wealthy and unwilling to compromise, which meant that everyone would end up losing, except for the lawyers representing each side, who would walk away with a considerable paycheck. It was so utterly mundane and ordinary, Ricky almost felt contemptuous. But with a black streak of nastiness coursing through him, Ricky knew that in the midst of all that posturing, pleading, and back and forth threats and posing between a handful of attorneys, he would find Merlin.

The court docket gave him the names of all the parties. None stood out. But one was the man he was seeking.

The hearing was not set until the following morning, but Ricky went to the courthouse that afternoon. For a few moments he stood outside the huge gray-stone building, looking up at the sweep of steps leading up to the columns that marked the entranceway. He thought that the building's architects dozens of years earlier had sought to endow justice with some sort of grandeur and stature, but after all that had happened to him, Ricky thought justice was really a much smaller and far less noble concept, the kind of concept that could fit into a small cardboard box.

He went inside, walking through the corridors, between courtrooms, fitting into the ebb and flow of people, noting elevator systems and emergency stairwells. It occurred to him that he could find the judge assigned to Arneson v. Fortier and probably discover who Merlin was merely by providing a description to the judge's secretary. But, he understood, that simple act would likely turn suspicious in quick order. Someone might remember later, after he'd achieved what he wanted.

Ricky — thinking all along like Frederick Lazarus — wanted what he had in mind to do to be utterly anonymous.

He saw one thing that he thought would help: There were many distinct types wandering through the courthouse building. The three-piece suits were clearly the attorneys with business within the walls. Then there were some less well heeled, but still presentable types. Ricky put these into a category that included the police, jurors, plaintiffs, accused, and courtroom personnel. All the folks that seemed to more or less have a reason for being there, and an understanding about what role they were to play. Then there was a third, fringe category, that intrigued Ricky: the buzzards. His wife had once described them to him, long before she was diagnosed, and long before her life had become nothing more than appointments and medications and pain and helplessness. They were the old pensioners and hangers-on, who found watching courtrooms and lawyers to be entertaining. They functioned a little like bird-watchers in the forest, moving from case to case, searching out dramatic testimony, intriguing conflict, perhaps staking out seats in courtrooms where high-profile, publicity-laden cases were taking place. In appearance, they were modest, sometimes only a cut above the folks who lived on the streets. They were a step away from a VA hospital or a retirement home, and wore polyester no matter how hot it was outdoors. An easy group, Ricky thought, to infiltrate for a few moments.

He left the courthouse with his plan already forming in his head. He took a cab first to Times Square, where he entered one of the many novelty stores where one can buy a fake edition of the *New York Times* with one's name in a headline. There he had the man with the printing machine make up a half-dozen phony business cards. Then he flagged another cab which bore him to a glass and steel office building on the East Side. There was a guard at the entranceway, who made him sign in, which he did with a flourish, signing Frederick Lazarus, and listing his occupation on the sheet as *Producer*. The guard issued him a small plastic clip-on badge with the number six on it, which designated the floor he was traveling to. The man didn't even glance at the sign-in sheet after Ricky handed it back to him. Security, Ricky thought, operates on perceptions. He looked the part and handled himself with a brusque confidence that defied being questioned by a man at the door. It was a small performance, he believed, but one that Virgil would likely appreciate.

An attractive receptionist greeted him when he entered the office of The Jones Agency.

'How can I help you?' she asked.

'I spoke with someone earlier,' Ricky lied. 'About a commercial shoot we've got coming up. We're looking for some fresh faces and checking out some of the new talent available. I was going to have a look through your portfolio . . . '

The receptionist looked slightly askance. 'Do you remember who you spoke with?'

'No, sorry. It was my assistant who made the call,' Ricky said. The receptionist nodded. 'But perhaps I could just flip through some headshots, and then you could steer me?'

The young woman smiled. 'No problem,' she said. She reached beneath the desk and came up with a large leather binder. 'These are the current clients,' she said. 'If you see anyone, then I can direct you to the agent who handles their bookings.' She gestured toward a leather couch, in the corner of the room. Ricky took the portfolio over and started flipping through it.

Virgil was the seventh photo in the book.

'Hello,' Ricky said under his voice, as he flipped the page and saw that her real name, address, phone number, and agent's name were listed on the back along with a list of off-Broadway theater performances and advertising credits. He wrote all this down on a pad of paper. Then he did precisely the same for two other actresses. He took the portfolio back to the receptionist, checking his wristwatch as he did so.

'I'm sorry,' he said, 'but I'm late for another appointment. There are a couple of people who seem to have the right look, but we're going to need to have a face-to-face before committing to anything.'

'Of course,' the young woman said.

Ricky continued to appear harried and hurried.

'Look, I'm in a terrible bind here, with time. Perhaps you could call these three and set up meetings for me? Let's see, this one at lunch tomorrow at noon at Vincent's over on East 82nd. Then the other two, say at two and four in the afternoon, same place? I would appreciate it. We're a little under the gun, here, if you know what I mean . . . '

The receptionist looked discomfited. 'Usually the agents have to set up every meeting,' she said reluctantly, 'mister . . . '

'I understand,' he said. 'But I'm only in town until tomorrow, then back to Los Angeles. Sorry to be so rushed on all this . . . '

'I'll see what I can do . . . . but your name?'

'It's Ulysses,' Ricky said. 'Mister Richard Ulysses. And I can be reached at this number . . . '

He pulled out one of the fake business cards. They were emblazoned with the title: PENELOPE'S SHROUD PRODUCTIONS. Acting as if this was the most natural thing in the world, he took a pen from the desk and crossed out a phony California exchange, and wrote in his last remaining cell number. He made certain that he obscured the fake number. He also doubted whether any of the agents had a classical education.

'See what you can do,' he said. 'If there's some problem, call me at that number. Come on, bigger breaks have occurred on less. Remember Lana Turner in the drugstore? Anyway, I have to run. More pictures to see, if you know what I mean. Lots of actresses out there. Hate to see someone miss a chance because they passed up a free meal.'

And with that, Ricky turned and exited. He wasn't sure whether his breezy, devil-may-care approach would work.

But he thought it might.

33

Before Ricky left for the courthouse the following morning, he confirmed with Virgil's agent the luncheon appointment, as well as the subsequent meetings with the two other actress-models that Ricky had no intention of attending. The man had asked a few questions about the commercials Ricky the producer was intending to shoot, and Ricky had answered breezily, lying elaborately about product placement in the Far East and Eastern Europe, and the new markets opening up in these areas, therefore the need for new faces to be established by the advertising industry. Ricky thought that he'd become adept at saying much that amounted to nothing, which he realized was one of the most effective sorts of lies one could tell. Any skepticism that the agent might have held dissipated rapidly in the fabric of Ricky's fictions. After all, the meeting might amount to something, for which he'd get ten percent, or it might amount to nothing, which left him no worse than he was already. Ricky knew that if Virgil had been a more established star, he might have had a problem. But she wasn't yet, which had helped her when it came time for her to help ruin his life, and he played on the necessity of her ambition easily and guiltlessly.

In his rented room, he reluctantly left behind his handgun. He knew he couldn't risk setting off a metal detector at the courthouse, but he had grown accustomed to the reassurance that the pistol gave him, although he still did not know whether he would be able to use it for its true purpose — a moment he believed was quickly closing in on him. Before leaving, though, he stared at himself in the mirror in the bathroom. He had dressed nicely, in blazer and tie, dress shirt and slacks. Well enough to slide easily into the crowds that would be sweeping in and out of the courthouse corridors, which, in an odd way, was the same kind of protection that the handgun offered, although less final in its actions. He knew what he had in mind to do, and he understood it was all a balancing act.

The edge, for him, he understood, between killing, dying, and being free was very narrow.

As he stared at himself in the mirror, he recalled one of the first lectures he'd ever heard on psychiatry, where the physician at the medical school had explained that no matter how much was known about behavior and emotions, and no matter how confident one was in diagnosis and in the course of action that neurosis and psychosis created, ultimately, one could never predict with total certainty how any one individual would react. There were predictors, the lecturer had explained, and more often than not, people would play out the scene that one expected. But sometimes they defied prediction, and this happened enough to make the entire profession often resemble guesswork.

He wondered whether he'd guessed right on this occasion.

If he did, he would be free. If not, he would be dead.

Ricky searched the corners of his image in the mirror. Who are you now? he asked himself. Someone or no one?

These thoughts made him grin. He felt a wondrous surge of almost hilarious release. Free or dead. Like the license plate on his New Hampshire rental car. Live Free or Die. It finally made some sense to him.

His thoughts crept over to the three people who had stalked him. The children of his failure. Raised to hate everyone who'd failed to help.

'I know you now,' he said out loud, picturing Virgil in his mind. 'And you, I'm about to know,' he continued, conjuring up a portrait of Merlin.

But Rumplestiltskin remained elusive, a shadow in his imagination.

This was the only fear he had left, he understood. But it was a substantial fear.

Ricky nodded to the image of himself in the mirror. Time to perform, he told himself.

There was a large drugstore on the corner, one of a chain, with rows of over-the-counter cold remedies, shampoo, and batteries. What he intended for Merlin that morning was something he remembered from a book he'd read about mobsters in South Philadelphia. He found what he needed in a section that contained cheap children's toys. Then the second element in a portion of the store that carried a modest selection of office supplies. He paid cash and after placing these items in his jacket pocket, Ricky walked back out on the street and hailed a cab.

* * *

He breezed into the courthouse building as he had the day before, appearing like a man with a purpose far different from that which he actually had in mind. He stopped in the second-floor bathroom and took out the items that he'd purchased, and prepared them in a few seconds. Then he killed some time before heading to the courtroom where the man he knew as Merlin was arguing a motion.

As he suspected, the room itself was only partially filled. Some other attorneys lounged about waiting for their cases to be called. A dozen or so of the courthouse buzzards occupied seats in the middle portion of the cavernous arena, some dozing, others listening intently. Ricky slipped quietly through the door, past the baliff who guarded it, and into a seat behind several of the old folks. He slid down, making himself as unobtrusive as possible.

There were a half-dozen lawyers and plaintiffs inside the bar, seated at sturdy oaken tables in front of the judge's bench. The area in front of both teams was filled with papers and boxes of pleadings. They were all men, and they were intent upon the reactions of the judge to what they had to say. There was no jury, in this preliminary stage, which meant that everything they spoke was directed forward. Nor was there any need to turn and play to the audience, because it would have had no discernible impact on the proceedings. Consequently, none of the men paid the slightest attention to the folks seated haphazardly about in the rows of seats behind them. Instead, they took notes, checked citations from legal texts, and busied themselves with the task at hand, which was trying to win some money for their client, but more critically, for themselves. It was, Ricky thought, a type of stylized theater, where no one cared anything about the audience, only the drama critic in front of them, wearing the black robes. Ricky shifted in his seat and remained hidden and anonymous, which was what he expected.

A surge of excitement raced through him, when Merlin stood.

'You have an objection, Mr. Thomas?' the judge demanded sharply.

'Indeed, I do,' Merlin replied smugly.

Ricky looked down at the list he'd made of all the lawyers involved in the case. Mark Thomas, Esquire, with offices downtown, was in the middle of the group.

'Then what is it?' the judge demanded.

Ricky listened for a few moments. The self-assured, self-satisfied tones of the attorney were the same that he'd remembered from their meetings. He spoke with a confidence that was the same, whether what he was saying had any basis in truth or the law or not. Merlin was the exact man who had come into Ricky's life so disastrously.

Only now he had a name. And an address.

And just as it had for Ricky, this would be like opening a door on who Merlin was.

He pictured the lawyer's hands again. Especially the manicured fingernails. Then Ricky smiled. Because in the same mental image, he noted the presence of a wedding ring. That meant a house. A wife. Perhaps children. All the trappings of the upwardly mobile, the young urban professional, heading aggressively for success.

Only Merlin the attorney had a few ghosts in his past. And he was brother to a ghost of the first degree. Ricky listened to the man speak, thinking what a complicated system of psychology was on display in front of him. Sorting through it all would have been an intriguing challenge for the psychoanalyst he once was. Sorting through it for the man he'd been forced to become was a significantly simpler issue. He reached into his pocket and fingered the children's toy he'd placed there.

On the bench, the judge was shaking his head, and beginning to suggest that the matters be continued over into the afternoon session. This was Ricky's cue to exit, which he did quietly.

He took up a position next to the emergency stairwell, waiting across from a bank of elevators. As soon as he spotted the group of lawyers exiting the courtroom, he ducked into the stairwell. He had lingered just long enough to see that Merlin was carrying two heavily stuffed briefcases, no doubt filled to overflowing with endless documents and court papers. Too heavy to carry beyond the closest elevator, Ricky knew.

He took the stairs two at a time, emerging on the second floor. There were several people waiting by the elevators for rides down the single flight. Ricky joined them, keeping his hand around the handle of the toy in his pocket. He stared up at the electronic device that shows the location of the car and saw that the elevator was stopped on the floor above. Then it began to descend. Ricky knew one thing: Merlin wasn't the type to move to the back and make room for anyone else.

The elevator stopped, and the doors swung open with a swooshing sound.

Ricky stepped up, behind the people getting on. Merlin was in the direct center.

The attorney lifted his eyes, and Ricky stared right into them.

There was a flash of recognition, and Ricky saw a momentary panic slide onto the attorney's face.

'Hello, Merlin,' Ricky said quietly. 'And now I know who you are.'

In the same instant, he lifted the child's toy from his pocket and brought it to bear on the attorney's chest. It was a water pistol, in the shape of a World War II German Luger. He squeezed the trigger and a stream of black ink shot out, striking Merlin in the chest.

Before anyone could react, the doors slid shut.

Ricky jumped back to the stairwell. He didn't run down, because he knew he couldn't outrace the elevator. Instead, he climbed up to the fifth floor, walked out and found the men's room. There he disposed of the water pistol in a wastebasket after wiping it clean of any fingerprints, just as he might have done with a real weapon, and washed his hands. He waited a few moments, then exited, walking through the corridors to the opposite end of the courthouse. As he had learned the day before, there were more elevators, more stairs, and another exit. Attaching himself surreptitiously to another group of attorneys exiting from other hearings, Ricky maneuvered down. As he expected, there was no sign of Merlin in the portion of the lobby he entered. Merlin wasn't in the position where he would want to do any explaining whatsoever about the real nature of the stains on his shirt and suit.

And, Ricky thought, he will come soon enough to understand that the ink Ricky had used was indelible. He hoped that he had ruined far more than a shirt, suit, and tie that morning.

* * *

The restaurant Ricky had chosen for luncheon with the ambitious actress had been a favorite of his late wife's though he doubted that Virgil had made that connection. He had selected it because it had one important feature: a large plate glass window that separated the sidewalk from the diners. Ricky remembered that the lighting in the restaurant made it difficult to see out, but not nearly as hard to see in. And the placement of the tables was such that one was more often being seen, than seeing. This was how he wanted it.

He waited until a group of tourists, perhaps a dozen German-speaking men and women wearing loud shirts and necklaces of cameras, sailed past the front of the restaurant. He simply tagged along with them, much as he'd done in the courthouse earlier. It is difficult, he thought, to pick one familiar face out of a group of strangers when not expecting it. As the gaggle of tourists cruised past, he quickly turned and saw Virgil sitting, as he'd expected, in a corner of the restaurant, waiting eagerly. And alone.

He stepped past the window and took a single deep breath.

The call will come any second now, Ricky thought. Merlin had delayed, just as he'd suspected he would. He'd have cleaned himself up, made his apologies to the other attorneys, all of whom had been shocked. What excuse had he come up with? Disgruntled opponent, bested in a lawsuit. The others could identify with that. He'd persuaded them all that calling the police was inappropriate, that he would contact the crazy man with the ink pistol's attorney — maybe seek a restraining order. But he would handle it all himself. The other men would have nodded in agreement and offered to testify at any moment, or even provide statements to the police, if requested. But this had taken some time, as had getting himself cleaned up, because he knew, no matter what, he still had to be back in court that afternoon. When Merlin finally made his first call, it would be to the older brother. This would have been a substantial conversation, not merely recounting what had happened, but trying to assess the implications. They would analyze their position and begin to consider their alternatives. Finally, still unsure precisely what they wanted to do, they would hang up. Then, next in line for a second phone call, would be Virgil, but Ricky had beaten that call.

He smiled, turned around sharply and headed straight through the restaurant's front door, moving swiftly. There was a hostess at the front, who looked up at him and began to ask the inevitable question, but he waved her off, saying, 'My date is already here . . . ' and striding quickly across the restaurant.

Virgil was turned away, then shifted when she sensed movement.

'Hello,' Ricky said. 'Remember me?'

Surprise struck her face.

'Because,' Ricky said, sliding into his seat, 'I remember you.'

Virgil said nothing, although she had rocked back in surprise. She had placed a portfolio of pictures and résumé on the table in anticipation of the meeting with the producer. Now, slowly, deliberately, she took it and slipped it to the floor. 'I guess I won't be needing that,' she said. He heard two things in her reply: tentativeness and a need to regain some composure. They teach that in acting class, Ricky thought, and right now she's reaching into that particular storage box, searching for it.

Before Ricky responded, a buzzing sound went off in her pocketbook. A cell phone. Ricky shook his head. 'That would be your middle brother the lawyer calling to warn you that I appeared in his life this morning already. And there will be another call, soon enough, from the older brother who kills for a living. Because, he, too, will want to protect you. Don't answer it.'

Her hand stopped.

'Or what?'

'Well, you should be asking yourself the question 'How desperate is Ricky?' and then the obvious follow-up: 'What might he do?' '

Virgil ignored the phone, which stopped buzzing.

'What might Ricky do?' she asked.

He smiled at her. 'Ricky died once. And now he might have nothing left to live for. Which would make dying a second time far less painful and perhaps even welcome, don't you think?'

He looked hard at Virgil, scouring her with his gaze.

'I might just do anything.'

Virgil shifted uncomfortably. Every tone Ricky used was harsh. Uncompromising. He reminded himself that the strength in his performance that day was to be a different man from the one so easily manipulated and terrified into suicide a year earlier. This, he realized, wasn't far from the truth.

'And so, unpredictability. Instability. A little manic streak, as well. Dangerous combination, no? A potentially volatile concoction.'

She nodded. 'Yes. True.' She was regaining some of her elusive composure as she spoke, which is what he'd expected would happen. Virgil, he knew, was a very centered young woman. 'But you're not going to shoot me here in this restaurant in front of all these other people. I don't think so.'

Ricky shrugged. 'Al Pacino does. In *The Godfather*. You've seen it, I'm sure. Anyone eager to act for a living has seen it. He comes out of the men's room with the revolver in his pocket and he shoots the other mobster and the corrupt police captain right in the forehead, then tosses the revolver aside and walks out. Remember?'

'Yes,' she said uneasily. 'I remember.'

'But I like this restaurant. Once when I used to be Ricky, I came here with someone I loved, but whose presence I never really appreciated. And why would I want to ruin the fine luncheon these other folks have planned? But mostly, I don't need to shoot you here, Virgil. I can shoot you any number of places. Because now I know who you are. I know your name. Your agency. Your address. But more important, I know who you want to become. I know your ambition. And from that, I can extrapolate your desires. Your needs. Do you think that now that I know who and what and where about you, that I cannot deduce whatever I need to know in the future? You could change your address. You could even change your name. But you cannot change who you are, nor who you want to become. And that's the rub, isn't it? You're as trapped as Ricky was. And so is brother Merlin, a detail that he learned this morning quite messily. You played the game with me, once, knowing every step I would take and why. And now, I will play a new game with you.'

'What is that?'

'It's a game called How Do I Stay Alive? It's a game about revenge. I think you already know some of the rules.'

Virgil had paled. She reached for a glass of ice water, took a long sip, staring at Ricky.

'He'll find you, Ricky,' she whispered. 'He'll find you

and kill you and protect me — because he always has.'

Ricky leaned forward, like a priest sharing a dark secret in a confessional. 'Like any older brother? Well, he can try. But, you see, now he knows next to nothing of who I have become. The three of you have been chasing around after Mr. Lazarus, and thinking that you had him cornered, what — once? Twice? Three times maybe? Did you think you missed him by seconds in the home of the one man who crossed both our paths the other night? But guess what? Poof! He's about to disappear. Any second now, because he's just about used up every little bit of usefulness in this life. But before he goes, perhaps he will tell whoever else it is I have lined up to become everything I will need to know about you and Merlin and now Mr. R. as well. And all that put together, well, Virgil, I think that makes me a very dangerous adversary.'

He paused, then added: 'Whoever I am today. Whoever I might be tomorrow.'

Ricky leaned back, slightly, watching the words he spoke register on Virgil's face. 'What did you tell me, once, Virgil? About your chosen name? 'Everyone needs a guide upon the road to Hell.' '

She took another long sip of water, nodding. 'That's what I said,' she replied softly.

Ricky smiled nastily. 'I think you chose your words well,' he answered.

Then he rose sharply, pushing the chair back quickly.

'Goodbye, Virgil,' he said, leaning toward the young woman. 'I think you will never want to see my face again, because then it might be the last thing you will ever see.'

Without waiting for her response, Ricky turned and walked briskly out of the restaurant. He did not need to see her hand shake, or her jaw quiver, though he knew these reactions were likely. Fear is an odd thing, he thought. It displays itself in so many external ways, but none is nearly as powerful as the blade it slices through the heart and stomach, or the current it puts into the imagination. He thought that for one reason or another much of his life had been spent being afraid of many things, a never-ending sequence of fears and doubts. But now he was delivering fear, and he wasn't sure he didn't like that sensation. Ricky let the noontime crowds absorb him, as he melted away from Virgil, leaving her behind, just as he had her one brother, trying to assess just what sort of danger they were truly in. Ricky cut swiftly through the throngs of people, dodging the bodies like a skater on a crowded rink, but his mind's eye was elsewhere. He was trying to picture the man who'd once stalked him to perfect death. How, Ricky wondered, will the psychopath react, when the only two people left on this earth he truly holds dear have been threatened to their core.

Ricky pushed forward rapidly on the sidewalk, and thought: He will want to move fast. He will want to resolve the matter immediately. He will not want to prepare or plan, as once he did. Now he will let cold rage utterly overcome all his instincts and all his training.

But most important: Now he will make a mistake.

34

Usually, once or twice each summer back in the years and vacations that seemed so distant to him, when his life was fit into normal, recognizable patterns, Ricky would make a reservation with one of the old and particularly accomplished fishing guides who worked the Cape waters hunting for big stripers and schools of bluefish. It was not that Ricky thought of himself as an expert fisherman, nor was he an outdoors type of any special note. But what he'd enjoyed was heading out in a small, open boat in the early morning, when mist still hung over the gray-black ocean, feeling a damp chill that defied the first streaks of bright morning light leaping across the horizon, and watching the guide pilot the skiff through channels, past shoals, to fishing grounds. And what he'd appreciated was the sensation that amid the acres of constantly changing waves, the guide would know which seascape held fish, even as they concealed themselves in the somber colors of the deep water. To slide a bait through so much cold space, taking so many variables of tide and current, temperature and light into the equation, and then to find the target, was an act that Ricky the psychoanalyst had admired, and constantly found fascinating.

Collecting his thoughts in his cheap New York room, he thought he had embarked on much the same process. The bait was in the water. Now he had to sharpen the hook. He did not think he would get more than a single opportunity with Rumplestiltskin.

It had occurred to him that after confronting the younger brother and sister, he could flee, but he knew instantly that would be useless. Then he would spend the entirety of his remaining life being startled by every unusual noise in the dark, nervous at any sound behind his back, afraid of every stranger who happened into his line of sight. An impossible life, spent running away from something and someone impossible to discern, always with him, ghosting every step Ricky ever took.

Ricky knew, as much as he'd ever known anything with certainty, that he had to best Rumplestiltskin in this final phase. It was the only way he'd really regain a grip on any semblance of life as he hoped to live it.

He thought he knew how to accomplish this. The first elements of his scheme had already been put in place. He could easily imagine the conversation between brothers and sister that was happening even as he sat in the cheap rented room. It wouldn't be a telephone conversation. They would have to meet, because they would have to see one another to reassure themselves that they were safe. Voices would be raised. There would be a few tears and considerable anger, perhaps even some insult and blame tossed about the room. Everything had gone smoothly for the three of them, wreaking murderous revenge on all the obvious targets of their past. Only one had come up a cropper, and that one was now the source of significant anxiety. He could hear the phrase 'You got us into this!' shouted across the room at the shadowy figure who had meant so much to them over so many years. Ricky thought, with some satisfaction, that there would be panic in that accusation, because he had managed to drive a small wedge into the bonds that linked the trio together. No matter how persuasive the need for revenge had been, no matter how cunning the plot was against Ricky and all the others, there was one element that Rumplestiltskin had not foreseen: Even with their compulsion to go along with him, the younger brother and younger sister still had aspirations of lives in the mainstream. Normal, in their own ways: A life onstage and a life in court, playing by certain rules, with recognizable strictures. Rumplestiltskin, alone of the three, was willing to live outside certain boundaries. But the two others were not, and that was how they became vulnerable.

It was that distinction that Ricky had found. And it was, he knew, their greatest weakness.

There would be harsh words between them, Ricky knew. As cruel as the game had been, and as murderous, the actual pushing, shooting, and killing had been left to only one of them. Ruining a reputation or savaging investment accounts were some nasty works. But none that actually saw blood. There had been a separation of evils, with the most suspect left in a single pair of hands.

Those jobs had fallen to Mr. R. Just as he had borne the brunt of beatings and cruelty as they grew up, so the actual violence had belonged to him. The others had merely helped him, reaping the psychological satisfaction that revenge provides. The difference between being an enabler and being the performer, Ricky thought. Only now, they understand, their complicity has come back to bite them.

They thought they were home free, Ricky thought. But they are not.

He smiled inwardly. There is nothing, Ricky decided, quite as devastating as realizing that now perhaps it is you who is being hunted, when you are so accustomed to being the hunter. And that, he hoped, was the trap he had set, because even the psychopath would leap for the opportunity to regain the position of superiority that was so natural for the predator. He would be pushed in that direction by the threat to Virgil and Merlin. What few threads of normalcy that Mr. R. retained were those that connected him to his brother and sister. If, deep in his psychopathological world, he had any remaining links to humanity, they came from his relationship with his siblings. He would be desperate to protect those. It is simple, really, Ricky insisted to himself. Make the hunter think he is hunting, closing in on his prey, when in reality, he is being drawn into an ambush.

An ambush, Ricky thought with some irony, that is defined by love.

Ricky found some scratch paper, and worked for a few moments on a rhyme. When he had it the way he wanted, he called the *Village Voice* classified section. Once again, as before, he found himself speaking with a clerk in Personals. He made some small talk, as he had on numerous occasions before. But this time he was careful to ask the clerk several key questions and deliver some critical information:

'Look, if I'm out of town, can I still call in and get the responses?'

'Sure,' said the clerk. 'Just dial the access code. You can call from anywhere.'

'Great,' Ricky replied. 'You see I have some business up on the Cape this weekend, so I have to head up there for a few days, and I still want to get the responses.'

'It won't be a problem,' the clerk said.

'I hope the weather is good. The forecast is for rain. You ever go up to Cape Cod?'

'Been to Provincetown,' the clerk said. 'It's pretty wild up there after the Fourth of July weekend.'

'No kidding,' Ricky said. 'My place is in Wellfleet. Or, at least it used to be. Had to sell it. A fire sale. Going up just to settle a few leftover matters, then back to the city and back to the grind.'

'I hear you,' the clerk said. 'I wish I had a place on the Cape.'

'The Cape is special,' Ricky spoke carefully, lingering over each word. 'You only really go in the summer, maybe a little in the fall or spring, but each season gets inside you in its own way. It becomes home. More than home, really. A place for starting and ending. When I die, that's where I want them to bury me.'

'I can only wish,' the clerk said, slightly envious.

'Maybe someday,' Ricky added. He cleared his throat to deliver the message for the classifieds. He had it run under the modest headline: SEEKING MR. R.

'Don't you mean 'Mr. Right'?' the clerk asked.

'No,' Ricky said. 'Mr. R. is fine.' Then he launched into what he hoped would be the last rhyme he would ever need to concoct:

Ricky's here. Ricky's there.
Ricky could be anywhere.
Ricky maybe likes to roam,
Ricky maybe has gone home.
Perhaps Ricky has gone to ground,
But Ricky likely can't be found.
Someplace old, someplace new,
Ricky will always elude you.
Mr. R. can search high and low,
Still he will never know,
When Ricky might return again,
As an adversary, not a friend,
Carrying evil, toting death,
Ready to steal someone's last breath.

'Intense,' the clerk said, with a long, slow whistle. 'You say this is a game?'

'Yes,' Ricky answered. 'But not one too many people should be eager to play.'

The ad was scheduled for the following Friday, which gave Ricky little time. He knew what would happen: The paper actually hit the newsstands the evening before, and that would be when all three of them would read the message. But this time, they wouldn't respond in the paper. It will be Merlin, Ricky thought, using his brusque and demanding lawyer's tones and obliquely threatening manner. Merlin will call the ad supervisor and work his way rapidly down through the paper's hierarchy until he finds the clerk who took the poem over the telephone. And he will question him closely about the man who called it in. And the clerk will quickly recall the conversation about the Cape. Maybe, Ricky wondered, the young man will even recall that Ricky said it was where he wanted someday to be buried, a small desire, in a way, but one that will trigger much in Merlin. After he acquires the information he will pass it to his brother. A modest act of insulation, to be sure, but a necessary one. Then the three of them will argue once again. The two younger ones have been frightened, probably more frightened than they have been since they were children and abandoned by self-murder by the mother they loved. They will say they want to join Mr. R. on his hunt, and they will say they feel responsible for the danger, and guilty, too, he thought, for making him take care of them once more. But they will not truly mean it, and the older brother will have none of it, anyway. This is a killing he will want to handle alone.

And so, Ricky thought, alone is how he will proceed.

Alone and wanting to finish once and for all what he had been led to believe had been completed. He will hurry toward another death.

* * *

He checked out of the cheap room, scouring it first for any signs of his existence. Then, before departing the city, he performed one other series of tasks. He closed out his domestic banking accounts at New York branches, then went into a midtown office for a bank located in the Caribbean. There he opened a simple checking and savings account for Richard Lively. When he'd completed the transaction, depositing a modest sum from his remaining cash, he exited the bank and walked two blocks up Madison Avenue to the Crédit

Suisse office that he had passed many times back in the days when he was merely another New Yorker.

A low-level bank official was more than willing to open a new account for Mr. Lively. This was merely a traditional savings account, but it had a single interesting feature. On one day, each year, the bank was to transfer ninety percent of the accumulated funds directly, by wire, to the account number that Ricky provided for the Caribbean bank. They were to deduct their fees from the remainder. The date he selected for this transfer was chosen with a rough sort of haphazard care: At first he'd thought to use his birthday, then he'd thought of his wife's birthday. Then, he'd considered the day that he'd faked his own death. He also considered using Richard Lively's birthday. But finally, he'd asked the executive opening the account, a rather pleasant young woman who had taken pains to reassure him of the complete secrecy and compelling sanctity of Swiss banking regulations, and asked her what her birthday was. As he'd hoped, it had no connection to any date that he could remember. A late March day. He liked that. March was the month that actually saw the end of winter and suggested the beginning of spring, but was filled with false promise and deceptive winds. An unsettled month. He thanked the young woman and told her that was the day he selected for any transfers.

After finishing his business, Ricky returned to the rental car. He did not look behind once, as he slid through the city streets, up onto the Henry Hudson Parkway heading north. He had much to do, he thought, and little time.

* * *

He returned the rental car and spent the day killing off Frederick Lazarus. Every membership, credit card, phone account — anything having to do with that particular persona was shut down, canceled, or closed out. He even swung around the gun shop where he'd learned to shoot, and purchasing a box of shells, spent a productive hour on the firing range squeezing off shots at a black silhouette target of a man that was easily configured in his imagination to be the man he knew who would close in on him swiftly enough. Afterward, he made a little small talk with the gun shop owners, dropping on them the news that he was expecting to move away from the area for several months. The man behind the counter shrugged, but, Ricky realized, still noted the departure.

And with that, Frederick Lazarus evaporated. At least on paper and in documents. He departed, too, from the few relationships that the character had. By the time he had finished, Ricky thought that all that remained of the persona he'd created was whatever murderous streaks he had absorbed within himself. At least, that was what he hoped still weighed within him.

Richard Lively was a little more difficult, because Richard Lively was a little more human. And it was Richard Lively who needed to live. But he also needed to fade away from his life in Durham, New Hampshire, with a minimum of fanfare and little notice. He had to leave it all behind, but not appear to be doing so, on the off chance that someone, someday, might come asking questions and connect the disappearance with that particular weekend.

Ricky considered this dilemma, and thought that the best way to disappear is to imply the opposite. Make people think your exit is only momentary. Richard Lively's bank account was left intact, with only a minimum deposit. He didn't cancel any credit cards or library memberships. He told his supervisor at the university maintenance department that family trouble on the West Coast was going to require his presence for a few weeks. The boss understood, reluctantly told

Ricky that he couldn't promise that his job would wait for him, but told him he would do everything he could to see that it was left open. He had a similar conversation with his landladies, explaining that he wasn't sure how long he would be absent. He paid an extra month's rent in advance. They had become accustomed to his comings and goings, and said little, although Ricky suspected the older woman knew he would never return, simply in the way she eyed him and the manner in which she absorbed what he said. Ricky admired this quality. A New Hampshire quality, he thought, one that accepts on the face what another person says, but harbors an understanding of the truth hidden within. Still, to underscore the illusion of return, even if not fully believed, Ricky left behind as many of his belongings as possible. Clothes, books, a bedside radio, the modest things he had collected while rebuilding his life. What he took with him was a couple of changes of clothing, and his weapon. He thought that what he needed to leave behind was evidence that he'd been there, and might return — but nothing that truly spoke about who he was or where he might actually have gone.

As he walked down the street, he felt a momentary pang of regret. If he lived through the weekend, he thought, which was really only a fifty-fifty proposition, he knew he would never return. He had developed an ease and a familiarity with the small world he'd participated in, and it saddened him to walk away. But he restructured the emotion within himself, trying to re-form it into a strength to carry him through what was about to happen.

He caught a midday Trailways bus to Boston, retracing a familiar route. He did not spend long in the Boston terminal, just long enough to wonder whether the real Richard Lively was still living, and half thinking that it might be interesting to head toward Charlestown

The spot he'd hoped to find was waiting for him, directly to the side of the center chimney that had graced the fireplace in the living room. A slab of ceiling and thick wooden beams had tumbled to the side, making a sort of decrepit lean-to, almost a cave. Ricky donned the poncho, seated the bug hat on his head, and removed the flashlight and semiautomatic pistol from his backpack. Then he crawled back into the darkness of the wreckage, concealed himself, and waited for night, the approaching thunderstorm, and a killer to arrive.

He saw some humor in it: What had he done? He had behaved like a psychoanalyst. He had provoked electric, runaway emotions in the person he wanted to see. Even the psychopath was vulnerable, Ricky thought, to his own desires. And now, just as he had for so many years of his own analytic practice, he was waiting for this last patient to come through the door, bearing with him all the anger, hatred, and fury, all directed at Ricky the therapist.

He fingered the trigger guard on his weapon and clicked off the safety. This session, however, wasn't intended to be quite so benign.

He leaned back and measured every sound, and memorized every shadow as they lengthened into darkness around him. Vision was going to be a problem that night. The moon would be obscured by clouds. The ambient light from other homes and distant Provincetown, would fade beneath the coming rain. What Ricky expected to rely upon was both certainty and uncertainty: The ground where he'd selected to wait was the most familiar tract in his life. This would be an advantage. And, more important, he was relying upon Rumplestiltskin's uncertainty. He won't know precisely where Ricky is. He is a man accustomed to controlling the environment in which he operates, and this, ultimately, Ricky hoped, was the least-controlled situation he could be placed in. A world the killer was unfamiliar with. A good place to wait for him that night.

Ricky was supremely confident that the killer would arrive, and soon enough, searching for him. As the man drove east from New York, he will understand that there were really only two potential locations for Ricky's presence. The beach where he'd faked drowning, and the home he'd burned down. He will come to these two spots, hunting, because despite what he might have learned from the clerk at the *Village Voice*, he will not really believe that there was any business other than the business of dying planned for the trip to the Cape. He will know that everything else was merely illusion, and that the real game was simply about one set of memories facing off against the other set.

35

The rain came in spurts throughout the first part of the night, falling heavily, with cracks of thunder and lightning strikes out over the ocean for the initial hours of his wait, before tapering off into a steady irritating drizzle. As the storm passed overhead, the temperature dropped a half-dozen or more degrees, giving the darkness a chill that seemed perversely out of place. There had been some wind with the line of thunderstorms, strong currents that tugged at the edges of his poncho, and made the rubble and charred remains around him creak, as if they, too, had unsettled business that night. Ricky remained hidden, like a hunter in a blind, waiting for the quarry to come into sight. He thought of all the hours he had spent silently seated behind the heads of patients on his couch, barely moving, rarely speaking, and thought it funny that all that time spent in contemplation had prepared him well for the wait that night.

He moved only occasionally, and then just to stretch and flex his muscles enough so that they wouldn't seize up with disuse but be available to him when needed. Mostly, he leaned back, the mosquito netting about his head, the poncho spread over his body, more a shapeless lump than human. From where he was concealed, he could still see across the open field that had welcomed visitors to his home, especially when the sky was streaked by bolts of electricity. He was situated in a position that allowed him to spot slices of headlights penetrating the stands of trees out by the main road, and he found that he could hear the car engines above the thick folds of black darkness.

He had only one fear: that Rumplestiltskin would find

more patience than he had.

Ricky doubted this, but wasn't completely certain. After all, the child had harbored so much hatred for years, and waited so long before springing his traps, it was possible that now, in this last stage, he might hesitate, and simply take up a position in the tree line and do more or less what Ricky was doing, which was waiting for some telltale motion before closing in. This was the gamble that Ricky was taking that night. But he thought his bet was well hedged. Everything he'd done was designed to provoke Mr. R. Anger, fear, and threats demand responses. A professional killer was a man of action. An analyst was not. Ricky believed that he had created a situation where his own strengths compensated for those of his adversary. His own training countered the killer's training. He will move first, Ricky insisted. Everything you know about behavior tells you this is true. In the game of memory and death that the two men were locked in, Ricky held the higher ground. He was fighting on land he knew.

It was, he thought, the best he could do.

By ten P.M. the world around him had funneled itself into a damp, musty arena of blackness. He found his senses heightened, his mind alert to all the nuances of the night. He hadn't heard a car, or spotted distant headlights in over an hour, and the rain seemed to have driven all the nocturnal beasts into their dens, so not even the scratching sound of an opossum or skunk searching for something to eat penetrated the air about him. It was, he thought, right at the moment when his heart and his determination should fail him, that doubt should creep into his imagination, trying to persuade him that he was waiting foolishly for someone who would not arrive. He mocked this sensation within him, insisting that the only thing he knew for certain was that Rumplestiltskin was close, and would be closer still, if only he persevered and waited. He wished that he'd had the sense to bring a bottle of water, or a thermos of coffee, but he hadn't. It is hard to plot murder, he thought, and remember the mundane at the same time.

He wiggled his fingers occasionally, and silently drummed his index finger along the side of the trigger guard. Once he was startled by a bat swooping through the air above him; another time a pair of deer emerged for a second or two from the woods. He could make out only the vaguest elements of their shapes, until they spooked and turned white tails and bounded away with unmistakable ballet leaps.

Ricky continued to wait. The assassin was likely a man accustomed to the night, and comfortable in it, Ricky thought. Daytime compromises much for a killer. It gives him vision, but makes him recognizable, as well. He thought: I know you, Mr. R. You will want to end all this in the dark. You will be here soon enough.

Some thirty minutes after the last car's headlights had swooped past in the distance, shrouded by the trees, a cone of light heading steadily away, Ricky spotted another car approach on the roadway. This one traveled a little slower, almost hesitant. Just the slightest element of indecision in the speed it traveled.

The glow paused near the dirt road entrance to his property, then sped up, and disappeared around a corner some ways away.

Ricky shrank back, burrowing deeper into the hole that concealed him.

Someone found what they were searching for, he thought, but did not want to display the discovery.

He continued to wait. Twenty more minutes passed in utter darkness, but Ricky now was curled like a snake, waiting. The glow of his wrist-watch helped him to measure what was happening just beyond what little sight he had. Five minutes, time enough to find a spot where he could leave the car unseen. Ten minutes, time to walk back to the entranceway to Ricky's property.

Another five minutes to slide along quietly, beneath the canopy of branches. Now, he's in the last line of trees, Ricky thought. Surveying the ruin of the house from a safe distance. He drew back into his lair, pulling his feet under the edge of the poncho.

Ricky looped tendrils of patience around his heart. He could feel adrenaline pumping wildly through his ears, and his pulse racing like an athlete's, but he calmed himself by silently reciting passages from literature to himself. Dickens: 'It was the best of times, it was the worst of times.' A line from Camus: 'Mother died today, or maybe it was yesterday.' This recollection made him smile through the terror that lurked within him. An appropriate passage, he thought. His eyes darted back and forth, searching the darkness. It was a little like opening one's eyes underwater. Shapes were in motion, but not recognizable. Still, he waited, because he knew that his only chance was to see before he was seen.

The drizzle had finally stopped, leaving the world slick and glistening. The chill that had first accompanied the thunderstorms fled, and Ricky could feel a thick, humid warmth seize hold of the world around him. He was breathing slowly, afraid that the asthmatic raspiness in every breath could be heard for miles. He glanced at the sky, and saw the outline of a cloud, showing up billowing gray against the black, scudding across the air, almost as if it was being rowed by some unseen oarsman. A little bit of moonlight slid into a hole carved by the cloud's passing, dropping like a shaft through the night. Ricky pulled his eyes from right to left, and saw a shape step away from the trees.

Ricky fixed on the figure, who stood outlined for just an instant by the wan light, more a shape of darkness that was colored a richer black than the night surrounding them. In that time, he saw the person lift something to his eyes, and then slowly pivot, like a lookout high on a boat's tower, searching for icebergs in the waters ahead.

Ricky shrank back farther, pressing himself back against the ruins. He bit down hard on his lip, for he knew immediately what he was facing: a man with night vision binoculars.

He froze in position, realizing that the outlandish costume of poncho and bug hat was his greatest defense. Amid the charred slabs of wood and piles of burned rubble, he would appear as just another shape of twisted wreckage. Like a chameleon who can change his color depending on the shade of leaf that it occupies, Ricky remained in position, hoping that there was nothing outward that presented even the smallest suggestion of humanity.

The shape moved subtly.

Ricky caught his breath. He did not know whether he'd been spotted.

It took every bit of mental energy he could collect to maintain his position. Panic lapped at the edges of his imagination screaming at him to run while he still had a chance. But he replied inwardly that his only chance lay in doing what he was doing. After so much that had happened, he had to bring the man moving through the darkness toward him within arm's reach. The dark shape moved obliquely across Ricky's field of vision. Moving cautiously, slowly, but not fearfully, slightly crouched over, presenting little profile, an experienced predator.

Ricky let out a long slow whistle of air. He did not see me.

The shape reached the onetime garden, and Ricky watched the man hesitate. He could see that he wore some cover over his head and face, matching his dark clothing. The shape seemed far more a part of the night than a person. Again something was lifted up, and again Ricky burned with tension as the night vision spyglasses swept over the wreckage of the place where he'd once enjoyed happiness. But again, the poncho hid his form, made him into a piece of debris, and the man hesitated, as if frustrated. He could see the hand holding the night vision glasses drop to his side, as if dismissing the surroundings.

The shape stepped forward more aggressively, standing now in what was once the doorway, searching the ruin. Then he stepped forward, stumbling slightly, and Ricky heard a muffled curse.

He knows I should be here, Ricky thought. But now he has doubts.

Ricky gritted his teeth together. He could feel a cold, murderous shaft within himself. He thought: Now you are unsure. It is not what you expected. And now you are doubting yourself. Doubt, frustration, and all the built-up anger you have for failing to kill me once when I made it so easy for you. This is a dangerous combination, because it is forcing you to do things you wouldn't ordinarily do. You are shedding precautions with every stride and uncertainty is in your every step, and now, suddenly, you are playing the game on my field. Because Dr. Starks knows you, now, and knows everything that is in your head, because everything you are feeling, all that indecision and confusion, is the currency of his life, not yours. You are a killer whose target isn't clear, and all because of the situation I've staged.

Ricky eyed the shape. Come closer, he said to himself.

The man stepped forward, stumbling slightly on a chunk of what was once a roof beam, trying to walk through a room that he did not know.

He stopped and kicked at the detritus.

'Doctor Starks,' the man whispered, like an actor on a stage, a secret meant to be shared. 'I know you're here.'

The voice seemed like dull razors scraped across the night.

'Come on out, doctor. It's time for an ending.'

Ricky did not move. Did not reply. He could feel every muscle he had tighten, pulled taut. But Ricky had not spent years behind the couch greeting the most provocative and demanding statements with silence to fall into the invitation that the shape urged.

'Where are you, doctor?' the man continued, turning back and forth. 'You weren't on the beach. So you should be here, because you are a man of your word. And this is where you said you would be.'

The man stepped forward, moving from shadow to shadow. He tripped again, banging a knee against what had once been a stairway riser. He cursed a second time, and straightened up. Ricky could see confusion and irritation, mingled with frustration, in the shrug of the man's shoulders.

The man turned right and left one more time, then sighed.

When he spoke, it was loudly, with resignation. 'If not here, doctor, then just where the hell are you?'

With a final shrug, the man finally turned his back to Ricky. And as the man turned, Ricky lifted his hand holding the semiautomatic pistol out from where it was concealed beneath the poncho, lifting it up as he'd been taught at the gun store in New Hampshire, holding it with both hands and bringing the barrel sight squarely in line with the middle of Rumplestiltskin's back.

'I'm behind you,' Ricky said quietly.

* * *

Now time seemed truly to lose its grip on the world around Ricky. Seconds that would ordinarily have collected themselves in an orderly progression into minutes seemed to scatter like flower petals caught in a strong breeze. He remained frozen in position, weapon bearing directly on the killer's back, his own breathing shallow and labored. He could feel surges of electricity racing through his veins and it took an immense amount of energy to keep himself calm.

The man in front of him stood immobile.

'I have a gun,' Ricky croaked, voice raw with tension. 'It is pointing at your back. It is a .380 caliber semiautomatic pistol, loaded with hollow-point bullets, and if you move even in the slightest, I will fire. I will get off two, maybe three shots before you can turn and bring your own weapon to bear. At least one of these will find the target and will likely kill you. But you know that, don't you, because you are familiar with the weapon, and the ammunition, and you know what they are capable of, so you have already made these calculations in your head, haven't you?'

'As soon as I heard your voice, doctor,' Rumplestiltskin replied. His tone was unruffled and even. If he had been surprised, it was not readily apparent. Then he laughed out loud, adding quickly, 'To think that I waltzed right into your aim. Ah, I suppose it was inevitable. You have played well, far better than I ever expected, and you have displayed resources I didn't think you possessed. But our little game is now down to its final moves, isn't it?' He paused, then said, 'I think, Doctor Starks, you would be wise to shoot me now. Right in the back. You currently have the advantage. But every few seconds that pass, your position weakens. As a professional having dealt with these sorts of situations before, I would strongly recommend that you not waste the opportunity that you've created. Shoot me now, doctor. While you still have the chance.'

Ricky did not reply.

The man laughed. 'Come on, doctor. Channel all that anger. Focus all your rage. You've got to bring these things together in your head, concentrate them into a single, centered entity, and then you can pull that trigger with nary a twitch of guilt. Do it now, doctor, because every second you let me live, is another second you may be taking off your own life.'

Ricky aimed straight ahead, but did not fire.

'Hold up your hands where I can see them,' he demanded instead.

Rumplestiltskin snorted another laugh. 'What? Did you see that on a television show? Or in the movies? Is doesn't work that way in real life.'

'Drop your weapon,' Ricky insisted.

The man shook his head slowly back and forth. 'No. I won't be doing that, either. It's a cliché, anyway. You see, if I drop my weapon to the ground, then I give up any options I might have. Examine the situation, doctor: In my professional judgment, you've already blown your chance. I know what is in your head. I know that if you could fire, you would have done so already. But it is a little more difficult to murder a man, even someone who has given you plenty of reasons for death, than even you thought. Doctor, your world is one of fantasy death. All those murderous impulses that you've listened to for all those years, and helped defuse. Because, to you, they exist in the realm of fantasy. But here, tonight, there is nothing but reality surrounding us. And right now, you're searching for the strength to kill. And, I'm wagering, not finding it rapidly. I, on the other hand, haven't quite the same journey to travel before finding the same strength. I wouldn't have worried even a bit about the moral ambiguity of shooting someone in the back. Or the front, for that matter. The proof, as they say, is in the pudding, doctor. As long as the target is dead, who cares? So, I won't be dropping my weapon to the ground, not now, not ever. Instead, it will stay in my right hand, cocked and ready. Will I spin around now? Take my best chance at this moment? Or shall I wait a bit?'

Ricky again remained silent, his mind churning.

'One thing you should know, doctor: If you want to be a successful killer, you need to not worry about your own sorry life.'

Ricky listened to the words that flitted through the darkness. A great unsettled sensation crept into his heart.

'I know you,' he said. 'I know your voice.'

'Yes, you do,' Rumplestiltskin replied, with a slight mocking tone. 'You've heard it often enough.'

Ricky felt suddenly as if he were standing on a sheet of slippery ice. Unsteadiness crept into his own voice. 'Turn around,' he said.

Rumplestiltskin hesitated, shaking his head negatively. 'You don't want to ask me to do that. Because once I turn around almost every advantage you have will be erased. I will see your precise position, and, trust me on this one, doctor, once I have you located, it will only be a short time before I kill you.'

'I know you,' Ricky repeated, whispering.

'Is it that hard? The voice is the same. The posture. All the inflections and tones, nuances and mannerisms. You should recognize them all,' Rumplestiltskin said. 'After all, we were in more or less the same physical relationship five times each week for nearly a year. And I wouldn't have turned around then. And the psychoanalytic process, isn't it more or less the same as this? The doctor with the knowledge, the power, dare I say it, the weapons, right behind the back of the poor patient, who can't see what is going on, but only has his paltry and pathetic memories to work with. Have things changed all that much for us, doctor?'

Ricky's throat was completely dry, but he still choked out the name.

'Zimmerman?'

Rumplestiltskin laughed again. 'Zimmerman is very dead.'

'But you're . . . '

'I'm the man you knew as Roger Zimmerman. With the invalided mother and the couldn't-care-less brother, and the job that went nowhere, and all that anger that never seemed to get resolved in the slightest despite all the yakkety-yak that filled up your office to no great advantage. That's the Zimmerman you knew, Doctor Starks. And that's the Zimmerman that died.'

Ricky felt dizzy. He was grasping inwardly at lies.

'But the subway . . . '

'That is indeed where Zimmerman — the real Zimmerman, who was indeed quite suicidal — died. Nudged to his demise. A timely death.'

'But I don't . . . '

Rumplestiltskin shrugged. 'Doctor, a man comes to your office and says he is Roger Zimmerman and he is suffering from this and that and presents as a proper patient for analysis and has the financial wherewithal to pay your bills. Did you ever check to be certain that the man who arrived at your door was in truth the man he said he was?'

Ricky was silent.

'I didn't think so. Because, had you done so, you would have found that the real Zimmerman was more or less as I presented him to you. The only difference was that he wasn't the person coming to see you. I was. And when it came time for him to die, he'd already provided what I needed. I simply borrowed his life and death. Because, doctor, I had to know you. I had to see you and study you. And I had to do that in the best way possible. It took some time. But I learned what I needed. Slowly, to be sure, but, as you've learned, I can be a patient man.'

'Who are you?' Ricky asked.

'You will never know,' the man replied. 'And, then again, you already know. You know of my past. You know of my upbringing. You know of my brother and sister. You know much about me, doctor. But you will never know who I truly am.'

'Why did you do this to me?' Ricky asked.

Rumplestiltskin shook his head, as if astonished at the simple audacity of the question. 'You already know the answers. Is it so unreasonable to think that a child would see so much evil delivered to someone he loved, see them beaten down and thrown into despair so profound that they eventually had to murder themselves to find salvation, and when this child reached a position where he could exact a measure of revenge from all the people who failed to help out — yourself included, doctor — that he wouldn't seize that chance?'

'Revenge solves nothing,' Ricky said.

'Spoken like a man who never indulged,' Rumplestiltskin snorted. 'You are, of course, mistaken, doctor. Like you have been so often. Revenge serves to cleanse the heart and soul. It has been around since the first caveman climbed down out of a tree and bashed his brother over the head for some slight of honor. But, knowing all that you know, about what happened to my mother and her three children, why is it that you think we are not owed something in return from all the people who neglected us? Children who were innocent of any wrongdoings, but summarily dismissed and abandoned and left to die by so many folks who should have known better, had they the slightest bit of compassion or empathy or even just a drop or two of the milk of human kindness within their hearts. Are we not, having come through those fires, owed something in return? Really, that is by far the more provocative question.'

He paused, listening to Ricky's silence in reply, then spoke coldly: 'You see, doctor, the true question before us this night isn't why would I pursue you to your death, it's why wouldn't I?'

Again, Ricky had no answer.

'Does it surprise you that I have become a killer?'

It did not, but Ricky didn't speak this out loud.

The silence slipped around the two men for a moment, and then, just as it would in the sanctity of his office, with a couch and quiet, one man broke the eerie stillness with another question.

'Let me ask you this? Why is it that you don't think you deserve to die?'

Ricky could sense the man's smile on his face. It would be a soul-dead, cold smile.

'Everyone deserves to die for something. No one is actually innocent, doctor. Not you. Not me. No one.'

Rumplestiltskin seemed to shake slightly, at that moment. Ricky imagined he could see the man's fingers curl around the grip of his weapon.

'I think, Doctor Starks,' the killer said, with a cold resolve that spoke of what was going through his imagination, 'as interesting as this last session has been, and even if you think there is still much more to be said, the time for talk has passed by. It is now time for someone to die. The odds are it is about to be you.'

Ricky sighted down the pistol, taking a deep breath. He was wedged against the rubble, unable to move either to the right or to the left, his route behind him blocked as well, the entirety of his life lived and life to live dismissed in so many moments, all for a single act of neglect when he was young and should indeed have known better, but did not. In a world of options, he had none remaining. He squeezed back on the pistol trigger, mustering strength and channeling will.

'You forget something,' he said slowly. Coldly. 'Doctor Starks has already died.'

Then he fired.

* * *

It was as if the man responded to the slightest change in the inflection in Ricky's voice, recognized at the first harsh tone of the first word, and training and understanding of the situation took over, so that his actions were incisive and immediate and taken without hesitation. As Ricky pulled the trigger, Rumplestiltskin dropped obliquely, spinning as he did, so that Ricky's first shot aimed at the direct center of his back, instead tore savagely through the killer's shoulder blade and Ricky's second shot sliced through the collected muscles of his right arm, making a ripping sound through the air, thudding as it hit flesh, and cracking as it pulverized bone.

Ricky fired a third time, but this time wildly, the bullet like a siren, disappearing into the darkness.

Rumplestiltskin twisted around, immediately gasping with pain, a surge of adrenaline overcoming the force of the blows that had struck him, trying to lift his own weapon with his instantly mangled arm. He grasped at the weapon with his left hand, trying to steady it as he staggered back, balance precarious. Ricky froze, watching the barrel of the automatic pistol rise, like a cobra's head, darting back and forth, its single eye seeking him out, the man holding it, tottering, as if on a steep cliff-side edge of loose stones.

The roar of the pistol was dreamlike, as if it were happening to someone else, someone far away and not connected to him. But the shriek of the bullet scoring the air above his head was real enough, and it catapulted Ricky back to action. A second shot cracked the air, and he could feel the hot wind of the bullet pass through the shapeless form of the poncho hanging from his shoulders. Ricky sucked in air, tasting the cordite and smoke, and again sighted down the barrel of his gun, fighting the electric sweep of combat shock that threatened to turn his hands palsied, and brought the barrel to bear on Rumplestiltskin's face as the killer crumpled to the earth in front of him.

The killer seemed to rock back, trying to hold himself upright, as if expecting the final, killing shot. His own weapon had slid toward the ground, hanging loosely by his side after his second effort, held only by twitching fingertips no longer responding to destroyed and bleeding muscles. He lifted his good hand to his face, as if hoping to deflect the coming blow.

Adrenaline, anger, hatred, fear, the sum of all that had happened to him came together right then, in that single instant, demanding, insisting, reaching within him and shouting commands, and Ricky thought wildly that finally at that precise moment he was about to win.

And then he stopped, because abruptly he realized he would not.

⋆ ⋆ ⋆

Rumplestiltskin had paled, face white as if moonlight was illuminating it. Blood that seemed like steaks of black ink was coursing down his arm and chest. He tried once more, feebly, to grasp his weapon and lift it up, but was unable. Shock was taking over rapidly, clouding his every motion and fogging his grip on events. It was as if the quiet that had settled on the two men, as the gunshot echoes faded, was palpable, blanketing every movement they made.

Ricky stared at the man whom he had once known and yet not known as a patient, and realized that Rumplestiltskin would bleed to death in relatively short order. Or succumb to shock. It's only in movies, Ricky thought, that a man can be shot with a high-powered round at close range and still be strong enough to dance a jig. Rumplestiltskin's chances could be measured in minutes, he guessed.

A part of him he had never heard before insisted he simply watch the man die.

He did not. He struggled to his feet and jumped forward. He kicked the pistol away from the killer's hand, then took his own and slipped it into his backpack. Then, as Rumplestiltskin mumbled something, as the man battled against the unconsciousness that would herald death, Ricky reached down and grasped his adversary around the chest. Struggling against the weight, Ricky lifted the killer up and with as great a burst as he could muster, threw him over his own shoulder, in a fireman's carry. He straightened slowly, adjusting himself against the weight, half struck by the ironies that seemed as dense as the humid air around him, and then he staggered forward, through the wreckage, carrying the man who wanted him dead out of the rubble of the farmhouse.

Sweat stung at his eyes, and he struggled with each stride. What he carried seemed far greater than anything Ricky ever remembered lifting before. He could feel Rumplestiltskin lose consciousness, and heard his breathing grow wheezy and labored, asthmatic with death lurking close by. Ricky sucked in great drafts of humid air himself, powering himself forward in sturdy, unimaginative steps, each harder than the previous one, each mountainous in challenge. He told himself that this was the only way to walk to freedom.

He stopped at the edge of the road. Night surrounded both men with anonymity. He dropped Rumplestiltskin to the ground, and ran his hands over the man's clothing. To his relief he found what he'd expected: a cell phone.

Rumplestiltskin's breath was coming in shallow, pained spurts. Ricky suspected that his first shot had fragmented as it struck the scapula, and that the burbling sound he could distinguish was from a torn lung. He stanched the man's wounds as best he could, then called the number long remembered for Wellfleet fire and rescue.

'Nine-one-one Cape Emergency,' came a clipped, efficient voice.

'Listen very carefully,' Ricky said slowly, deliberately, pausing between words, enunciating each with deliberate pace. 'I am only going to say this one time, so get it straight. There has been a shooting accident. The victim is located on Old Beach Road at the entrance to the late Doctor Stark's vacation home, the place that burned down last summer. He's right on the driveway. The victim has multiple gunshot wounds to the back shoulder and right upper arm extremity, and is in shock. He will die rapidly if you are not here within minutes. Do you understand what I've just told you?'

'Who is this?'

'Do you understand!'

'Yes. I'm dispatching rescue now. Old Beach Road. Who is this?'

'Are you familiar with the location I've given you?'

'Yes. But I need to know: Who is this?'

Ricky thought for a moment, then answered: 'No one who is anyone anymore.'

He disconnected the phone. He took his own weapon out and ejected the remaining bullets from the clip. These he tossed as far into the woods as he could. Then he dropped the pistol on the ground next to the wounded man. He also removed his flashlight from the backpack, switched it on and placed it on the unconscious killer's chest. Ricky lifted his head. He could hear a distant siren starting up. Fire rescue was located only a few miles away, on Route Six. It would not take them long to reach the location. He guessed that the trip to the hospital was another fifteen, maybe twenty minutes. He did not know whether the EMTs would be able to stabilize the wounded man or if the emergency room staff was capable of dealing with serious gunshot wounds. Nor did he know whether a suitable surgical team was on call. He looked down at the killer one more time, and could not tell whether the man would live through the next few hours. He might. He might not. For the first time, perhaps, in his entire life, Ricky enjoyed uncertainty.

The ambulance sound quickly grew closer, and Ricky turned and started to jog away, slowly for the first few steps, but then gathering pace rapidly until he was flat-out sprinting forward, feet pounding against the road surface with a steady rhythm, letting the nighttime darkness swallow his presence utterly, until he was completely hidden from sight.

Like a newly inspired ghost, Ricky disappeared.

36

OUTSIDE PORT-AU-PRINCE

It was about an hour past dawn and Ricky was watching a small lime green gecko dart about on the wall, defying gravity with every step. He watched the tiny animal move in spurts, occasionally pausing to extend its orange throat sac, before dashing forward a few strides, then stopping, pivoting its head to the right and then left, as it checked for danger. Ricky admired and envied the wondrous simplicity of the gecko's day-to-day world: find something to eat, and avoid being eaten.

Above him an old brown four-bladed paddle fan creaked slightly with each revolution, spinning the hot, dull air of the small room. As Ricky shifted his legs, swinging them out of bed, the mattress springs matched the paddle fan noise. He stretched wildly, yawning, running a hand through his thinning hair, grasping the pair of weathered khaki hiking shorts that hung from the bed stand and searching for his glasses. He rose and poured himself a small basin of water from a pitcher standing on a swaying wooden table. He splashed the water onto his face, letting some of the liquid run down his chest, then he took a threadbare washcloth and soaped it from a pungent bar that he kept on the table. He dipped the cloth into the water and washed himself as best he could.

The room Ricky occupied was nearly square, and more or less undecorated, with stucco walls once a flat vibrant white, but faded over the years into a color that seemed only one step away from the dust that hung above the street outside. He had few possessions: a radio which brought in spring training games on the

Armed Forces channels, some clothes. An up-to-date calendar sporting a bare-breasted young woman with an inviting look in her eyes had that day circled in black pen. It hung from a nail a few feet away from a hand-carved wooden crucifix that he suspected had belonged to the prior occupant, but which he had not removed, because it seemed to him that taking down a religious icon in a country where religion in so many weird and conflicting ways was so critical to so many people, invited bad luck, and, so far, he thought, his luck, on balance, had been quite good. He had built two shelves against one wall. These were crammed with a number of worn and well-used medical texts, as well as some brand-new ones. The titles of these ranged from the practical (*Tropical Diseases and Their Treatments*) to the more esoteric (*Case Studies in Mental Illness Patterns for Developing Nations*). He had a thick faux leather notebook and some pencils, as well, which he used for jotting down observations and treatment plans, which he kept on a small desk next to a lap-top computer and printer. Above the printer he kept a handwritten list of wholesale drug outlets in south Florida. He also had a small, black canvas duffel bag, big enough for a two- to three-day trip, which he had packed with some clothing. Ricky looked about the room, and thought that it wasn't much, but it suited his mood and his sense of himself, and though he suspected he could easily move into far nicer digs, he wasn't sure that he would do so, even after he ran the errands that would take up the remainder of the week.

He went to the window and stared out at the street. It was only a half block to the clinic, and already he could see people gathered outside. There was a small grocery across the street, and the proprietor and his wife, two incongruously large middle-aged folks, were setting out some wooden crates and barrels that contained fresh fruits and vegetables. They were brewing coffee, as well, and the smell reached up to him more or less the same time that the proprietor's wife turned and saw him standing in the window. She waved gaily, smiling, and gestured at the coffee simmering over an open fire, inviting Ricky to join them. He held up a couple of fingers, to indicate he would be along in a moment or two, and she returned to work. The street was already beginning to crowd with people, and Ricky suspected it would be a busy day at the clinic. The heat for early March was oddly potent, mingling with a distant flavor of bougainvillea, market fruits, and humanity, temperatures rising as quickly as the morning did.

He looked off at the hills, which alternated a lush and enthusiastic green with barren brown. They rose high above the city and he thought to himself that Haiti was truly one of the most intriguing countries on the planet. It was the poorest spot he'd ever seen, but in some ways the most dignified, as well. He knew that when he walked down the street toward the clinic, he would be the only white face for miles. This might have unsettled him once, in his past, but no longer. He reveled in being different, and knew there was an odd sort of mystery that accompanied his every step.

What he particularly enjoyed was that despite the mystery, the people on the street were willing to accept his odd presence without question. Or, at least, no questions to his face, which, when he considered it, seemed both a compliment and a compromise and one of each that he was willing to live with.

He descended from his room and joined the market proprietor and his wife in a cup of bitter, strong coffee, thick and sweetened with raw sugar. He ate a crust of bread that had been baked that morning, and took the opportunity to examine the abscessed boil on the proprietor's back that he had lanced and drained three days earlier. The wound seemed to be healing rapidly and he reminded the man in half-English, half-French, to keep it clean and to change the bandage again that day.

The proprietor nodded, grinned, spoke for a few moments about the local soccer team's erratic fortunes, and begged Ricky to attend their match the following week. The team was called the Soaring Eagles and carried much of the neighborhood's passions into each contest, with decidedly mixed and noticeably un-soaring results. The proprietor refused Ricky's offer to pay for his breakfast, meager as it had been. This was already a routine between the two men. Ricky would reach into his pocket, and the proprietor would wave anything that emerged away. As always, Ricky thanked him, promised to be at the soccer match wearing red and green Eagle colors, and stepped off briskly toward the clinic, the taste of the coffee still strong in his mouth.

The people crowded around the entranceway, obscuring the hand-written sign that read in large, black, uneven letters, with several mis-spellings: DOCTOR DUMONDAIS EXCELENT MEDICAL CLINIC. HOURS 7 TO 7 AND BY APPOINTMENT. CALL 067-8975. Ricky passed through the mob, which parted to let him through. More than one man tipped his cap in his direction. He recognized some faces from some of the more regular customers, and he smiled greetings in their directions. Faces flashed replies and he heard more than one whispered '*Bonjour, monsieur le docteur . . .*' He shook hands with one old man, the tailor named Dupont, who had made him a tan linen suit far more elegant than anything Ricky thought he might need after Ricky had obtained some Vioxx for the arthritis which afflicted his fingers. As he'd suspected, the drug had done wonders.

As he entered the clinic door, he saw Doctor Dumondais's nurse, an imposing woman who seemed to measure five feet two both vertically and horizontally, but who possessed undeniable strength in her large body, and a voluminous knowledge of folk remedies and voodoo cures applicable to any number of tropical diseases.

'*Bonjour*, Hélène,' Ricky said. '*Tout le monde est arrivé ce jour*.'

'Ah, yes, doctor, we will be busy all day . . . '

Ricky shook his head. He practiced his island French on her, and she, in return, practiced her English on him, preparing for the hope, he knew, that someday she would gather enough money in the strongbox she kept buried in her backyard to pay her cousin for a place on his old fishing boat, so that he would risk the treacherous Florida Straits and carry her to Miami and she could start over again there, where she had been reliably informed, the streets were cluttered with money.

'No, no, Hélène, *pas docteur. C'est monsieur* Lively. *Je ne suis plus un médecin . . .* '

'Yes, yes, *Mister* Lively. I know what you do say to me this so many times. I am sorry, for I am forgetting once again another time . . . '

She smiled widely, as if she didn't quite understand but still wanted to join in with the great joke that Ricky played, to bring so much medical knowledge to the clinic, and yet, not want to be called a doctor. Ricky believed that Hélène simply ascribed this behavior to the odd, and mysterious mannerisms of all white people, and, like the folks crowded at the clinic door, she could not care less what Ricky wanted to be called. She knew what she knew.

'*Le Docteur* Dumondais, *il est arrivé ce matin?*'

'Ah, yes, Monsieur Lively. In his, ah, *bureau*.'

'Office is the word . . . '

'Yes, yes, *j'oublie*. I forget. Office. Yes. He is there. *Il vous attend . . .* '

Ricky knocked on the wooden door and stepped

inside. Auguste Dumondais, a wispy, small man, who wore bifocals and had a shaved head, was inside, behind his battered wooden desk, across from the examination table. He was pulling on a white clinical coat, and he looked up and smiled as Ricky entered. 'Ah, Ricky, we shall be busy today, no?'

'*Oui*,' Ricky replied. '*Bien sûr*.'

'But, is not this day the day you are leaving us?'

'Only for a brief visit home. Less than a week.'

The gnomelike doctor nodded. Ricky could see lingering doubt in his eyes. Auguste Dumondais had not asked many questions when Ricky had arrived at the clinic door six months earlier, offering his services for the most modest salary. The clinic had thrived after Ricky was set up with an office much like the one he was standing in at that moment, nudging le Docteur Dumondais out of his own, self-imposed poverty, and allowing him to invest in more equipment and more medicines. Lately, the two men had discussed obtaining a secondhand X-ray machine from a clearing-house in the states that Ricky had discovered. Ricky could see that the doctor was afraid that the serendipity that had delivered Ricky to his door was going to steal him away.

'A week at the most. I promise to you.'

Auguste Dumondais shook his head. 'Do not promise me, Ricky. You must do whatever it is that you have to do, for whatever purpose that you have. When you return, we will continue our work.' He smiled, as if to display that he had so many questions that it was impossible for him to find one with which to start.

Ricky nodded. He removed his notebook from the bellows pocket of his shorts.

'There is a case . . . ,' he said slowly. 'The little boy I saw the other week.'

'Ah, yes,' the doctor said, smiling. 'Of course, I recall. I suspected this would interest you, no? He is what, five years old?'

'A little older,' Ricky said. 'Six. And indeed, Auguste, you are correct. It interests me greatly. The child has not yet spoken a single word, according to his mother.'

'That is what I, too, understood. Intriguing, I think, no?'

'Unusual. Yes, very true.'

'And your diagnosis?'

Ricky could picture a small child, wiry like so many of the islanders, and slightly undernourished, which was also a typical statement, but not tragically so. The boy had a furtive look in his eyes as he'd sat across from Ricky, scared even though he occupied his mother's lap. The mother had cried bitterly, tears streaking down dark cheeks, as Ricky had asked her questions, because the woman thought her boy to be the brightest of her seven children, quick to learn, quick to read, quick with numbers — but never speaking a word. A special child, she thought, in most every way. Ricky had been aware that the woman had a considerable reputation in the community for magical powers, and made some extra money on the side selling love potions and amulets that were said to ward off evil, and so, he understood, for her to bring the child to see the odd white man in the clinic must have been a truly hard-reached concession that spoke of her frustration over native medicines, and her love for the boy.

'I do not think his difficulty is organic,' Ricky said slowly.

Auguste Dumondais grimaced. 'His lack of speech is . . . ?' This became a question.

'A hysterical response.'

The small black doctor rubbed his chin, and then ran his hand across his glistening skull. 'I remember this, just a little bit, from my studies. Perhaps. Why do you think this?'

'The mother would only hint at some tragedy. When he was younger. There were seven children in the family, but now, only five. Do you know the family history?'

'Two children died. Yes. And the father, too. An accident, I recall, during a great storm. Yes, this child was there, that I remember, too. This could be the origin. But what treatment can we perform?'

'I will come up with a plan after some research. We will have to persuade the mother, of course. I don't know how easy that will be.'

'Will it be expensive for her?'

'No,' Ricky said. He realized that there was some design in Auguste Dumandais's request for him to examine the child at the same time that Ricky had a trip out of the country planned. It was a transparent design, but a good one, nonetheless. He suspected he might have done more or less the same. 'I think it will cost them nothing to bring him to see me after I return. But I must learn much more, first.'

Doctor Dumandais smiled and nodded. 'Excellent,' he said, as he hung a stethoscope around his neck, and then handed Ricky a white clinical jacket of his own to wear.

The day went by rapidly, busily, so much so that Ricky almost missed his CaribeAir flight to Miami. A middle-aged businessman named Richard Lively, traveling on a recently issued American passport with only a few modest stamps from various Caribbean nations, was waved through U.S. customs without much delay. He realized he didn't fit any of the obvious criminal profiles, which were invented primarily to identify drug smugglers. Ricky thought he was a most unique criminal, and one that defied categorization. He was booked on the eight A.M. plane north to La Guardia, so Ricky spent the night in the airport Holiday Inn. He took a lengthy, hot, soapy shower, which he enjoyed from both a sanitary and sensual point of view, and thought bordered on true luxury after the spartan accommodations he was accustomed to. The air-conditioning that defied the heat outside and cooled his room was a remembered treat. But he slept fitfully, in starts, tossing for an hour before his eyes closed, then waking twice, once in the midst of a dream about the fire at his vacation home, then again, when he dreamed of Haiti, and the boy who could not speak. He lay in the bed in the darkness, a little surprised that the sheets seemed too soft and the mattress too springy, listening to the hum of the ice machine down the hall, and an occasional footstep passing by in the hallway, muted by the carpet, but not completely so. In the quiet, he reconstructed the last call he'd made to Virgil, nearly nine months earlier.

⋆ ⋆ ⋆

It was midnight, when he'd finally covered the distance to the cheap room on the outskirts of Provincetown. He had felt an odd, contradictory sense of exhaustion and energy, tired from the long run, enthused by the thought that he had come through a night very much alive that should have seen his death. He had slumped down on the bed, and dialed the number of her apartment in Manhattan.

When Virgil picked up the call on the first ring, she said only, 'Yes?'

'This isn't the voice you expected,' he replied.

She fell instantly quiet.

'Your brother, the attorney is there, isn't he? Sitting across the room from you, waiting for the same phone call.'

'Yes.'

'Then have him pick up the extension and listen in.'

Within a few seconds, Merlin, too, was on the line. 'Look,' the lawyer started, blustery with false bravado, 'You have no idea — '

Ricky interrupted him. 'I have many ideas. Now be quiet and listen to me, because everyone's lives depend upon it.'

Merlin started to say something, but he could sense that Virgil had thrown a glance in his direction, shutting him up.

'First, your brother. He is currently in the Mid Cape Medical Center. Depending on their abilities, he will either remain there, or be airlifted to Boston for surgery. The police will have many questions for him, should he survive his wounds, but I think they will have difficulty understanding what crime, if any, was committed this night. They will have questions for you, as well, but I think that he will need both the support of the sister and brother he loves, as well as some legal advice before too long, assuming he makes it. So, I think the first task ahead of you is to deal with his situation.'

Both remained silent.

'Of course, that is for you to decide. Perhaps you will leave him to handle things by himself. Perhaps not. It is your choice, and you will have to live with your decision. But there are a few other matters that need to be dealt with.'

'What sort of matters?' Virgil asked, her voice flat, trying to not betray any emotion, which, Ricky noted, was just as revealing as any other tone might be.

'First, the truly mundane: The money you stole from my retirement and other investment accounts. You will replace that sum into Crédit Suisse account number 01-00976-2. Write that down. You will do this promptly . . . '

'Or?' Merlin asked.

Ricky smiled. 'I thought it was an old truism that no lawyer should ever ask a question they don't already know the answer to. So, I shall assume you know the answer already.'

This silenced the attorney.

'What else?' Virgil asked.

'We have a new game,' Ricky said. 'It's called the game of staying alive. It's designed for all of us to play. Simultaneously.'

Neither brother nor sister responded.

'The rules are simple,' Ricky said.

'What are they?' Virgil asked softly.

Ricky smiled to himself. 'At the time I took my last vacation, I was charging patients between $75 and $125 per hour for analysis. On average, I saw each patient four, sometimes five times each week, generally forty-eight weeks each year. You can do the math yourselves.'

'Yes,' she said. 'We're familiar with your professional life.'

'Great,' Ricky said briskly. 'So, this is the way the game of staying alive works: Everyone who wants to keep breathing enters therapy. With me. You pay, you live. The more people who enter the immediate sphere of your life, the more you pay, because that will buy their safety, as well.'

'What do you mean 'more people' . . . ?' Virgil asked.

'I'll leave that up to you to define,' Ricky said coldly.

'If we don't do as you say?' Merlin sharply demanded.

Ricky replied with a blank, level harshness. 'As soon as the money stops, I will assume that your brother has recovered from his wounds and is hunting me once again. And I will be forced to start hunting you.'

Ricky paused, then added, 'Or someone close to you. A wife. A child. A lover. A partner. Someone who helps your life be ordinary.'

Again, they were quiet.

'How much do you want to have a normal life?' Ricky asked.

They did not answer this question, though he already

knew what they would say.

'It is,' Ricky continued, 'more or less the same choice you once gave me. Only this time it is about balance. You can maintain the equilibrium between yourselves and me. And you can signal that equity with the easiest and really the most unimportant of things: the payment of some money. So, ask yourselves this: How much is the life I want to live worth?'

Ricky coughed, to give them a moment, then continued, 'This is, in some ways, the same question I would pose to anyone who sought me out for therapy.'

Then he had hung up.

* * *

It was clear above New York, and from his window seat he could make out the Statue of Liberty and Central Park and the World Trade Center, as the plane swept over the city and approached La Guardia. He had the odd sensation that he wasn't returning home as much as he was visiting some long forgotten dream space, more like seeing the wilderness camp where one had spent a single unhappy summer as a child, crying his way through some long parentally imposed vacation.

Ricky wanted to move swiftly. He was booked back to Miami on the last flight that night, and he didn't have much time. There was a line at the rental counter, and it took some time to extricate the car reserved for Mr. Lively. He used his New Hampshire license, which was due to expire in another half year and thought that perhaps it would be wise to relocate fictionally to Miami before returning to the islands.

It took about ninety minutes through modest traffic to get to Greenwich, Connecticut, but he discovered that the directions obtained over the Internet were accurate down to the last tenth of a mile. This amused him, because, he thought, life is never actually that precise.

He stopped in the center of town and purchased an expensive bottle of wine at a gourmet shop. Then he drove out to a home on a street that was, perhaps by the inflated standards of one of the nation's richest communities, fairly modest. The houses were simply ostentatious, not obscene. Those that fit this second category were located a few blocks over.

He parked at the bottom of the driveway outside a fake Tudor-style home. There was a swimming pool in back and a large oak tree in the front that had yet to bloom. The mid-March sun wasn't insistent enough, he thought, although it did have some weak promise as it filtered between branches that were still to blossom. An oddly unsettled time of year, he decided.

With the bottle of wine in hand, he rang the doorbell.

It did not take long for a young woman, no older than her early thirties, to answer. She wore jeans and a black turtleneck sweater, and had sandy hair that was swept back from her face, displaying eyes that were lined at the corners and some wrinkles, probably prompted by exhaustion, around the edges of her mouth. But her voice was soft and inviting, and she spoke, as she swung the door open, in a near-whisper. Before he could say anything, she said, 'Shhhh, please. I've just gotten the twins down for a nap . . . '

Ricky smiled back. 'They must be a handful,' he said pleasantly enough.

'You have no idea,' the young woman replied. She kept her voice very low. 'Now, how can I help you?'

Ricky held out the bottle of wine. 'You don't remember meeting me?' he asked. This was a lie, of course. They had never met. 'At that cocktail party with your husband's partners about six months back?'

The young woman looked carefully at him. He knew the answer should be no, she had no recollection, but she was brought up more properly than her husband had been, so she responded, 'Of course, ah, Mr . . . '

'It's doctor,' Ricky said. 'But you should call me Ricky.' He shook her hand, and then held out the bottle of wine. 'Your husband is owed this,' Ricky said. 'We had some business together a year or so ago, and I just wanted to thank him, and remind him of the successful outcome of the case.'

She took the bottle, a little nonplussed. 'Well, thank you, ah, doctor . . . '

'Ricky,' he said. 'He'll remember.'

Then he turned and with a little devil-may-care wave, walked back down the drive to his rental car. He had seen all he needed, learned all he'd needed. It was a nice life that Merlin had carved out for his family, one that held out much promise for being nicer still, in the days to come. But this evening, at least, Merlin would have a sleepless night, after uncorking the wine. Ricky knew it would taste bitter. Fear does that.

He thought of visiting Virgil as well, but instead merely had a florist deliver a dozen lilies to the film set where she had acquired a modest, but important role on a big-budget Hollywood production. It was a good part, he'd learned, one that, if handled well, might lead to much bigger and better roles in the future, although he had his doubts that she would ever play a character more interesting than Virgil. White lilies were perfect. One usually sent them to a funeral with a note expressing deep condolences. He suspected she would know that. He had the flowers wrapped with a black satin bow and enclosed a card, which read simply:

Still thinking of you.
s/Dr. S.

He had, he thought, become a man of far fewer words.

Other titles in the Charnwood Library Series:

EATERS OF THE DEAD

Michael Crichton

In A.D. 922 Ibn Fadlan, the representative of the ruler of Bagdad, City of Peace, crosses the Caspian Sea and journeys up the valley of the Volga on a mission to the King of Saqaliba. Before he arrives, he meets with Buliwyf, a powerful Viking chieftain who is summoned by his besieged relatives to the North. Buliwyf must return to Scandinavia and save his countrymen and family from the monsters of the mist . . .

THE SAVAGE SKY

Emma Drummond

1941: Rob Stallard, the unworldly son of a farmer, leaves war-torn London for a Florida airbase along with a group of RAF pilot cadets. He quickly develops a great passion and talent for flying, but is not so happy when he encounters US cadet James Theodore Benson III, son of a senator. Rob is instantly averse to a man who appears to regard flying as merely another string to his sporting bow. For his part, Jim sees Rob as a'cowpoke from Hicksville'. Personal dislike rapidly extends to professional rivalry, and a near-fatal flying incident creates bitter enmity between them that will last more than a decade.

THE UGLY SISTER

Winston Graham

The Napoleonic Wars have ended as Emma Spry tells her fascinating story . . . One side of her face marred at birth, Emma grows up without affection, her elegant mother on the stage, her father killed in a duel before she was born. Her beautiful sister, Tamsin, is four years the elder, and her mother's ambitions lie in Tamsin's future, and in her own success. A shadow over their childhood is the ominous butler, Slade. Then there is predatory Bram Fox, with his dazzling smile; Charles Lane, a young engineer; and Canon Robartes, relishing rebellion in the young Emma, her wit, her vulnerability, encouraging her natural gift for song.

NOW AND THEN

Joseph Heller

Here is the writer Joseph Heller's Coney Island childhood, down the block from the world's most famous amusement park. It was the height of the Depression, it was a fatherless family, yet little Joey Heller had a terrific time — on the boardwalk, in the ocean, even in school. Then, a series of jobs, from delivering telegrams to working in a Navy yard — until Pearl Harbor, the Air Force, Italy. And after the war, college, teaching, Madison Avenue, marriage, and — always — writing. And finally the spectacular success of CATCH-22, launching one of the great literary careers.

NIGHT PASSAGE

Robert B. Parker

When a busted marriage kicks his drinking problem into overdrive and the Los Angeles Police Department unceremoniously dumps him, Jesse Stone's future looks bleak. So he's shocked when a small Massachusetts town called Paradise recruits him as a police chief. Jesse doesn't have to look for trouble in Paradise: it comes to him. For what is on the surface a quiet New England community quickly proves to be a crucible of political and moral corruption replete with triple homicide, tight Boston mob ties, flamboyantly errant spouses, maddened militiamen, and a psychopath-about-town who has fixed his sights on the new lawman.